From the Depths of Evil

Book Ten of the Thulian Chronicles

Art Wiederhold & Charles Sutphen

Order this book online at www.trafford.com
or email orders@trafford.com

Most Trafford titles are also available at major online book retailers.

Printed in the United States of America.

ISBN: 978-1-4669-2254-9 (sc)
ISBN: 978-1-4669-2253-2 (e)

Trafford rev. 03/29/2012

www.trafford.com

North America & international
toll-free: 1 888 232 4444 (USA & Canada)
phone: 250 383 6864 • fax: 812 355 4082

Contents

From the Depths of Evil

In the 41st Year of the Reign of Arka-Dal

The Kalahari.

One of the most foreboding and hostile wastelands on the Earth. During the First Age, a race of short people known as the Bushmen dwelled here. In those days, one could actually survive the desert if one knew how. Once, long ago, there was water, plant and animal life. Then came the Great Disaster and all of that vanished along with the Bushmen.

Today a solitary figure walks among the dunes and scrubby vegetation. He passes a long dead river and tall, weather-eaten rocks. During his travels, he has heard no birds, not an insect. The Kalahari is silent save for his labored breathing and the crunching of the dry sand beneath his feet.

His journey took him from Thule to the kingdom of Kush and down into southwestern Africa. He has come here on a feeling, if you will. A feeling of dread. It forced him to come to the desert and search, even though he wasn't sure what he searches for. After many days of travel and walking many miles, he came at last to a flat, sandy valley secluded between three rocky cliffs. The valley is on the southern edge of the desert. Beyond this, a grassy plain stretches several miles to the south and east. Beyond the plain lies the Zulu Empire.

Merlin took a drink from his never-empty canteen and wiped his lips as he surveyed the valley floor. Like the rest of the Kalahari, it, too, was quiet.

Unnaturally so.

"What draws me to this place?" he wondered as he descended into the valley. "Why am I here?"

He saw nothing out of the ordinary, yet there was something about this place that made the end of his nerves tingle.

That's when he heard it . . .

The air became filled with a deep droning sound that brought to mind images of thousands of men chanting a single note. The sound caused the hair on his back of his neck to stand up. He sat down on a rock and watched in silent disbelief as the sand on the valley floor stirred in countless places. The movement became more pronounced with each passing second and made it appear as if the entire valley was liquefying in some manner.

Then it stopped.

Merlin was about to breathe a sigh of relief and leave the valley when he spotted something out of the corner of his eye. He turned and watched open-mouthed as one muscular, dark-skinned arm after another punched its way up through the sand. This strange sight continued until the entire valley floor looked as if it had been planted with some weird, terrifying crop.

Then, one-by-one, tall, lean and muscular warriors with long, braided locks, clawed their way to the surface. As each man escaped from the sand, he snapped to attention and faced north. Within an hour, every square foot of the valley was covered with them. They neither moved.

Nor breathed.

Or opened their eyes.

They just stood there at attention as if awaiting orders to march.

But from whom?

Whoever it was, was powerful enough to summon them from the Abyss of Hell and bind them to his will.

For what purpose?

There was nothing within hundreds of miles, save crumbling temples and abandoned ruins that had almost been reclaimed by nature. Why would anyone raise such and army in this miserable place?

He obviously wanted to keep his intentions secret and away from prying eyes until the right moment. Anyone who would dare to raise such and army surely had sinister plans in mind.

It was now up to Merlin to find out what those intentions were and who was behind this. He decided to return to Thule. To conserve energy, he walked back the way he'd come. As he trekked across the desert, he telepathically made contact with Gorinna. The Red Witch was, at that time, investigating a similar situation some 3,000 miles to the north in the region known as the Frozen Wastes.

"What did you see?" he asked.

"The same as you. There were thousands of them. They rose from beneath the frozen tundra and stood there without moving or breathing," Gorinna replied.

"Interesting," Merlin thought.

"Very," Gorinna agreed. "Any idea what they are or who is behind this?"

"Not yet. It's safe to say that whoever's behind this is not of peaceful intent. We must proceed with caution until we find out what's going on. Have you heard from Peace?"

"Not since he went into the Libyan Desert last week. Merlin, this worries me. Every fiber of my being is tingling. I fear that a great evil is behind this. There are enough Black Warriors to overrun every major empire on Earth," Gorinna warned.

"Indeed," Merlin said.

"We'd better warn Arka-Dal," Gorinna urged.

"I will leave that to you while I investigate this matter further. I'll see you in Thule when I know something more," Merlin replied.

"Be careful," Gorinna said.

"I shall. You do likewise," he said as he broke contact.

Arka-Dal looked up at Gorinna.

"Thousands you say?" he asked.

"Countless thousands. Both groups cover at least two square miles. One is gathered about 2,000 miles north and east of Iluk. The other is in the middle of the Kalahari," she replied.

"Both are far beyond our jurisdiction. Which of our allies is closest to Iluk?"Arka-Dal asked.

Leo thought for a moment, then sat back and folded his hands over his ever-widening belly.

"That falls within the territory of the Huns," he said. "The Vandals and Aryans are also nearby—but each is still nearly 1,000 miles from the ruins."

"The Frozen Wastes belong to no one. Those lands are said to be cursed. Only the most foolhardy dare dwell there," Gorinna reminded them.

"That makes it the perfect place to conceal an army," Arka-Dal said. "Who controls the Kalahari?"

"No one. There is no water in that region. It can't sustain life. Not even lizards live there," Leo replied. "The closest to it are the Kushites but even they hardly bother with that place."

"Again—a perfect place to hide an army," Arka-Dal said.

He rose and walked over to the large map on the wall. He picked up two red pins and stuck one in the Kalahari and the other in the Frozen Wastes. He then stepped back and studied the map.

"Both places are too far away for us to send scouts. For now, we'll have to rely on information that you and Merlin gather," he said as he turned back toward Gorinna. "As a precaution, I'll send letters to the Huns, Aryans and the Kushites to alert them to the possible threat these armies may pose."

He walked over to the bar and poured himself a glass of wine. He then picked up the bottle and two extra glasses and returned to the table. Leo and Gorinna helped themselves to the heady blue liquid.

"You don't seem all that worried about this," Gorinna observed.

"There's no sense in worrying about it until whoever's behind this tips his hand. For now, we watch—and wait," Arka-Dal said.

Four days later, Peace, the wandering grandson of Arka-Dal, arrived at the palace of Queen Hetshepsut in Memphis. Both the Queen and her son, Crown Prince Arkaneton, greeted him warmly and insisted that he join them for dinner. As they dined, he related some news that was both interesting and disturbing.

"I was in the Libyan Desert about 450 miles south and west of Carthage. I was exploring a most ancient ruin known as Harmarta to try and learn what went on there during the First Age. As I walked through the deserted streets, a loud droning sound caught my ear. I followed it to its source about 25 miles south of the ruins. There, on a flat, sandy plain, I saw something that both chilled and amazed me," he began.

"What did you see?" asked Arkaneton.

"The ground opened before my eyes. I watched as countless numbers of tall, dark skinned warriors rose from the earth. They stood there, row upon row upon row with their eyes closed. They neither moved nor breathed. It was as if they were *waiting* for something," Peace continued.

"Waiting? For what?" asked Hetshepsut.

"That I don't know," Peace replied. "From the looks of them, they were brought to this world for no good."

"Who would raise an army way out there?" asked Arkaneton's wife, Idut.

"Someone who does not wish to be seen," Arkaneton replied. "Hamarta is over 1,000 miles from here. That army poses more of a threat to Carthage than to Egypt. I'll send a letter to the king and warn him to be on the alert. Any idea who controls this army?"

"None. One thing I do know—those soldiers are neither alive nor dead. Someone summoned them forth from the dawn of Time—someone very powerful and of evil intent," Peace warned.

"This sounds bad. Early this morning, I received a radio message from Arka-Dal. He told me of two other such armies. One is in the Kalahari. The other is in the Frozen Wastes. From a purely military standpoint, I'd say it appears as if someone is preparing for a major strike against all of the great nations of the world. If these soldiers are as you say, how do you propose that we fight such an enemy?" Arkaneton asked.

"If they are indeed supernatural beings, they will fall before any weapons edged with silver," Peace said.

Arkaneton smiled.

"Good. We still have entire arsenals filled with the silver weapons we used against the demons from the Abyss[1] a few years ago. I'll have our arms masters issue them to our soldiers immediately," he said.

"Excellent. I'll go to Timbuktu. From there, I can keep watch on our friends. I'll contact you as soon as anything happens," Peace said.

"That's for later. Of course you're staying for the Feast of Isis?" Hetshepsut suggested in a tone that told Peace his aunt would not take "no" for an answer.

As they dined on roasted oxtails and various steamed vegetables and fresh baked bread, Hetshepsut told Peace of her ambitious plans to restore most of the great works, temples and monuments that were built by Egyptian kings of the First Age. They had already completed the restoration of the temple complex of Queen Hatshepsut and were halfway finished with Karnak. Once that was done, Hetshepsut said she planned to restore the Sphinx.

"We couldn't undertake such projects before. We simply didn't have the money for them. Egypt is wealthier than it has ever been before thanks to our great trade networks. That's why I decided to do this," she said.

"Isn't the labor cost quite high?" Peace asked.

"I borrowed an idea from great pharaohs of the past. I asked for volunteers to labor on the projects in exchange for food, housing and

---

1 Read THE DRIVEN

medical expenses for them and their families. Egyptians are always willing to donate their sweat and blood to our great building projects. Many believe it is their way to achieve a measure of immortality. As long as the monuments stand, their spirits will live on in the Afterlife," said the Queen.

"Our engineers and architects oversee the work crews. As of now, we have 10,000 laborers, stone cutters, carpenters, sculptors and painters working for the government—along with cooks, brewers, doctors, weavers and other support people," Arkaneton added.

"We're using old drawings and paintings of the ruined monuments as guides to help restore them. I want to make Egypt the jewel of Africa again," Hetshepsut said.

"That's quite a goal. Let's hope that whoever is in charge of those dark troops doesn't try to ruin it," Peace said.

In the middle of the night in a deserted region of southeastern Egypt, a solitary figure sits huddled near a fire. He is tall, gaunt in appearance and has dark hair and a beard flecked with gray. His steely blue eyes are piercing and his demeanor is world-weary and sinister.

Despite his dusty, ragged appearance, he was quite wealthy. He made his living as a scholar and dealer in antiquities, most of which he'd stolen from ancient tombs and ruined cities. He sold some to private collectors, most to dealers on the black market. He didn't care which, as long as they paid well.

As he watched the embers soar skyward, he drew his heavy cloak tighter to keep the bitter cold air from his body. Fate had brought him here.

Fate and a strange, almost crumbling map.

He had no idea how old the map was. He couldn't read the strange tongue it was written in and it had taken him years to fit the area depicted by the map into the modern world. Even then chance had aided him.

For the better part of his life, Balaam had been searching for the lost tomb of an ancient Egyptian wizard known as Armenopur. According to the legend, the wizard had stumbled upon one of the few existing copies of a certain tome. After many years, he had learned to read the strange text and he began to delve deep into its secrets. The deeper he delved, the more corrupt and twisted Armenopur became.

It was said that he learned the Spell of Summoning and used it to call up mighty armies from the bottom of the Abyss. But he could not command them until he was granted such power by the mythical sleeping god. To get that, he'd have to decipher the Spell of Awakening and bring him forth from his ancient crypt.

He never got the chance.

His plot was discovered. Armenopur was tried, convicted and sentenced to be buried alive. The book was interred with him and he was placed in an unmarked tomb. Then all references to him were expunged from the official records. It was as if he'd never existed.

Balaam knew that Armenopur existed. That's why he'd spent most of his life searching for his tomb. He wanted the book that was buried with him and the dark powers it might confer upon him.

It was to be the first step in his bid to take over the world.

Until a year ago, his search had been fruitless. He was getting old and tired. He was about to give up the search but a voice inside his head kept urging him to go to the library in Alexandria. After weeks of trying to ignore it, he finally gave in to the voice and made the long, arduous journey to Egypt.

He was in the Great Library of Alexandria going over maps in ancient, almost forgotten Atlases. He had been there for days. Had gone over thousands of maps. Still the region depicted on his map eluded him.

Frustrated, he was about to throw in the towel. He closed the cover on the last of the Atlases and stood up to leave. As he did, he ran straight into a tall, dark clothed man who happened to be passing behind him. The man was carrying several leather bound tomes, which he dropped when they collided. He recalled apologizing to the man for not looking where he was going. The man said it was "quite all right. No harm done."

He helped him gather up the books and carry them to a nearby table. The books, he recalled, were ancient—older even than the Atlases he had perused. The task done, the two shook hands.

That's when he felt it.

A sudden, sharp jolt that shot through his brain. He sat down to clear his head and shut his eyes. When he opened them again, the stranger was gone.

He shrugged and checked his map. To his astonishment, he discovered that the veil had been lifted from his inner mind. The series of meaningless symbols he had tried without success to decipher now made perfect sense to him. He was now able to read the strange tongue as easily as if he'd been born to it.

Elated, he sat back down to read.

That's when he also found the note.

It was written on a piece of parchment in the same language as that on the map. As he read it, his heart raced wildly. And it contained but a single word.

Armenopur.

At last he knew that the map would guide him to the long lost, legendary tomb of the Accursed One. His lifelong quest was about to come to fruition. He folded the note and put it into his pocket and returned to his research.

It still took him several more weeks to find a match. Even then, he wasn't sure. Not really. Over the millennia, names had changed. Landmarks had come and gone. Empires had risen and fallen. In the back of his mind, he wondered if the legend had any truth to it.

Was the Accursed One real?

Or was he a fairy tale intended to scare small children into being good?

The story dated to the dawn of the First Age, a time when myth and fact merged into legend.

It was yet another chance meeting that finally put him on the right trail . . .

It was a few months after his encounter in the library. After weeks of searching the high deserts of Libya, he grew disgusted with his quest and headed for the nearest town. One night, he was in a local tavern, his mind clouded by beer and hashish, when a tall, darkly dressed man walked up and sat beside him.

"How goes your quest, Mr. Balaam?" the stranger asked.

He turned to say something but the man's demeanor instantly disarmed him. But something about his charming appearance also seemed disturbing. Balaam felt there was more to this stranger than met the eye.

"Have we met before?" he asked cautiously.

"As a matter of fact, we have," the man replied with a smile.

"Where?" asked Balaam.

"Alexandria. In the library. You helped me pick up some books after we collided," the man said. "In return, I put you on the path toward that which you desire most."

"Oh. Are you a wizard?" Balaam asked.

"No. But I *do* use magic when the need arises," came the reply.

"What are you then?" asked Balaam as he took another sip of ale from his tankard.

"You will know the answer to that soon enough. I am he who makes wishes come true for those who summon me," the man said.

"I summoned no one," Balaam said. "I don't even know your name."

He was beginning to think the man was a con artist or crazy. The stranger smiled.

"It was not by name that you summoned me but by *intent*," he said. "I know what is in your heart. I know your deepest desires and ambitions. That which you want most is right at your fingertips, but you need to know how to look for it."

"You speak in riddles!" Balaam said in disgust.

"Life is a riddle. You seek the tomb of the Accursed One and that which is buried with him. Without my help, you would not find it even if you searched a thousand lifetimes," the man said. "So I have come to help you."

"Why would you do that? If you already know where it is, why don't you just go there yourself and use that book?" Balaam asked.

"I prefer to work through others, such as you. Think of me as a *puppeteer* of sorts," the man said smugly.

Balaam was growing irritated with him now.

"You want to use me as your damned *puppet?*" he asked.

"I prefer to think of you as my *assistant.* I can help you achieve the power and wealth you desire—but there is a *price.* My services do not come cheaply," the man said.

"And what do I have that you could possibly want?" asked Balaam.

"Nothing that you have not already forfeited. In fact, you'll hardly miss it at all, being the way you are," the man said.

"And just what are you referring to?" Balaam asked.

"Your immortal soul," the man said as he reached into his coat and took out a tri-folded parchment.

Balaam watched as he unfolded it before him and handed him a quill. He stared at the document in disbelief for a long time. After a while, he blinked and looked up at the stranger.

"You want my soul?" he asked.

"Yes," came the reply. "As I've said, you pretty much forfeited that the moment you summoned me. This contract is simply a formality to help us avoid any misunderstandings as to its disposition. You'll never miss it anyway. It's not like you've ever really used it."

Now Balaam understood exactly who and what this stranger was. He'd always believed him to be a myth but here he was, seated across the table from him, smiling as only he could.

He picked up the contract and read it. He found it to be cut and dry. He'd always been drawn to the occult and the dark power it represented. Until now, he never thought he'd get the chance to realize his grandest ambitions. Now those dreams were within his grasp. He looked at his companion.

"Only a fool makes a pact with the Devil," he said.

"And only a fool passes up the chance to attain his wildest dreams," the Devil said with a grin. "Would you abandon all your desires, your one chance to achieve the power and glory you crave for the sake of such a useless commodity as your soul?"

Balaam laughed.

"You have a point," he admitted. "You're offering me all I ever wanted for something that has no real value to me. I'd be a fool to turn this down."

"Then we have a bargain?" the Devil asked as he held out a quill.

Balaam nodded and took the quill from his hand. Then he chuckled as he signed his name to the contract.

"You'll help me become the ruler of all mankind and all I have to do is relinquish my soul? This sounds like I'm getting the better part of this bargain," he said as he handed him the contract.

The Devil smiled as he folded it and stuck it back into his pocket. Then they shook hands.

As they did, he felt a wave of deep revulsion pass through him. The Devil looked into Balaam's eyes and suppressed the urge to shudder. Balaam reeked of evil. Deep, nearly overwhelming evil.

"Now, where is this tomb?" asked Balaam.

"Not so fast. Because of the nature of my profession, I cannot reveal its location outright. But I am allowed to provide you with a series of clues and riddles that should eventually lead you to it. Once you locate it, you'll know exactly what to do," the Devil replied.

He stood to leave. As he did, he smiled down at Balaam.

"It is not often that I come across someone who is more foul and heartless than myself. You are quite a piece of work, Mr. Balaam. Our association should prove to be most interesting," he said as he vanished before his very eyes.

Pope Leo had been researching the legend of Armenopur ever since he found a reference to him in the crumbling pages of an ancient, worm-eaten book he had bought from an antiquities dealer in the Thulian market. The reference was sketchy and parts of the page it was on were missing. His curiosity piqued, he wrote to Queen Hetshepsut and asked what she knew about this ancient wizard.

She claimed she had never heard of Armenopur and that she could find no records of him in the Egyptian archives.

"I doubt he ever existed. He is most likely the creation of some ancient fantasy writer," she wrote back.

But Leo had a hunch she was wrong. He was aware of the ancient Egyptian censorship methods. They had a habit of expunging the names of their most detested criminals from all official records.

Could that be what happened to Armenopur?

If so, why?

Leo had an uneasy feeling about him. That's why he and Medusa decided to delve deeper into the archives to try and turn up more information. But when no further information was found, the portly pope began to think that Hetshepsut was right.

Gorinna had insisted on checking out the strange army in the Kalahari. Merlin didn't bother to dissuade her. Instead, the two journeyed into the wastelands and stood upon a hill overlooking the soldiers.

Gorinna studied them carefully.

Each stood nearly seven feet tall and was well proportioned and muscular. Their features were dark—nearly pitch black—and their faces were pointed. Each wore a loincloth secured at the waist by a wide golden belt, golden sandals and a gorget to protect his neck from edged weapons. Heavy bronze greaves protected their shins and each wore a strange, ornate bronze helmet with a face guard. Their weapons, mostly pole arms and wide-bladed swords, featured strange varieties of points, ax heads, blades and blunt ends. Gorinna scratched her head.

"I don't recognize the armor or weapons they carry," she said.

"As well you should not. These soldiers are from a time and place that predates the coming of Man. Their race has long since passed into oblivion," Merlin said. "Care to get closer?"

"Let's," she agreed.

They walked slowly down the hill toward the army.

"They look similar to the ones I saw in the Frozen Wastes but their weapons and armor are different. The ones up north are dressed more suitably for a cold climate," she said as they drew closer.

They walked slowly among the ranks of the silent army. Every once in a while, Gorinna placed her hand against a muscular chest to try to detect a heartbeat or listened carefully for the sounds of breath being drawn. But the soldiers remained as cold and lifeless as statues.

She also got the oddest sensations of being watched. Somehow, someway, the soldiers knew they were there. She heard Merlin come up behind her and turned.

"For now, they pose no threat to anyone. If I wanted to, I could easily destroy this entire host with a single spell—and you know it," she said.

Merlin grinned.

"You think so?" he teased.

"I *know* so," she insisted.

"Then try it," he challenged.

They returned to the top of the hill. Gorinna stretched out her arms and recited a spell. Merlin watched as ribbons of light leapt from her fingertips and ricocheted through the ranks of soldiers. Each time a ribbon struck a soldier, it fell to dust. Within minutes, the entire army was gone.

Gorinna smiled.

"See?" she asked.

"Watch," he advised.

To her dismay, the piles of dust quickly reformed themselves into row upon row of dark skinned troops. Within minutes, the entire army had reappeared. Gorinna emitted a long string of epithets.

Merlin laughed.

"How did you know this would happen?" she asked.

"I already attempted that spell—and several others—to no avail," Merlin replied.

"Why didn't you tell me?" she asked, more than little peeved at the wizard.

"You didn't ask," he said. "Whatever magic was used to summon these beings from the jaws of Hell also makes them impervious to any spells cast to destroy them. The only way to get rid of these soldiers is to find and destroy the person who summoned them."

"Are these Acherons?" she asked as they walked away from the field.

"No. Acherons are undead soldiers. These beings were never alive. They have been formed from the earth and air itself. They will not live until the final controlling spell is cast," Merlin explained.

"What book contains such a spell?" asked Gorinna.

"There is only one such book that I know of," he replied.

Gorinna nodded. She knew exactly what he was referring to and the thought made her uneasy.

"Ever since its inception, that book has caused nothing but trouble," she said.

"Indeed. Although it was meant only to be a source of information, it always seems to fall into hands of those who want to use the knowledge contained within it for their own evil purposes. I have spent a good portion of my years on Earth trying to find those books so I can keep them out of the wrong hands. Each time I think I've located the last, another one appears somewhere. It is almost as if the book is designed to reproduce itself," Merlin said.

They quickly returned to Thule. When they arrived, they found the Emperor and his usual lineup of friends seated at the long table in the dining room having supper. Gorinna slid into the vacant seat next to Kashi and helped herself to some of the food on the platters. Merlin went to the bar and poured himself a strong drink before he joined them. Arka-Dal took a swallow of wine.

"Did you find out anything?" he asked.

Gorinna told him what had happened in the Kalahari. When she finished, he emitted a low whistle.

"That's not good," he said as he sliced off a bit of the roast before him.

"Not good at all," Merlin agreed.

"Any idea what's going on?" Arka-Dal asked.

"I have a good guess, nothing more," Merlin answered. "But I think I'm on the right track. It has something to do with a very ancient legend. I found a reference to it in one of the more mysterious tomes in my library. It's very obscure and I doubt that anyone alive today has even heard of it."

"I'm listening," Arka-Dal said.

Merlin nodded. He took a deep drink from his glass and cleared his throat.

"Have you ever heard of the Accursed One?" he asked.

Arka-Dal shook his head.

"You mean the insane magician who attempted to take over Egypt?" Leo asked.

Merlin nodded.

"According to the legend, in 5,117 BCE of the First Age, a power mad royal magician of the Egyptian royal court named Armenopur, managed to get his hands on a very ancient book that had been concealed in a vault deep within the bowels of the Earth. After reading through several pages, he decided that the world needed to be refashioned in his image, beginning with Egypt itself. To do this, he needed to overthrow the ruling dynasty and make himself king.

Armenopur, hereafter known as the Accursed One, realized he needed help—big time help. He decided to summon forth the Elder Gods and try and convince them to aid him with his mad plan. He wanted to make a pact with them. He'd open a gate into our world and allow them to plunge the entire universe into darkness and chaos. In return, he would be given an army large enough to enable him to achieve his dream.

Fortunately, the pharaoh's police discovered his plot. They arrested Armenopur and dragged him before the pharaoh. After a brief trial, he was declared guilty of high treason and abuse of magical powers. The pharaoh ordered that his eyes be plucked out so that he couldn't see his way through the Underworld. He also had his tongue cut out so he couldn't utter the necessary spells to allow him to pass into the Afterlife.

Once this was done, the Accursed One was wrapped in unclean linen and placed into a crude sarcophagus with more than a thousand scarabs. The coffin was sealed and he was buried, along with the ancient tome, in an unmarked place. His name was then stricken from all records so that no one would ever find his grave or speak his name again.

But nothing remains hidden forever.

The sudden appearance of the black armies is proof that someone may be searching for or has already found the Accursed One's tomb and might be willing to broker a deal with the Elder Gods in exchange for personal power.

We must find this madman before he can fulfill the prophesy. If he finds the spell to summon the Sleeping God and awakens him, all Hell will break loose—*literally!*" Merlin explained.

Arka-Dal sipped his ale as he let this sink in.

"What is the name of this book you speak of?" he asked.

"The Necronomicon," Merlin said.

"Just how many of those books *are* there?" asked Leo.

"No one knows. In the beginning, there was only one. It was supposedly written by a High Priest of the Elder Gods. When he completed it, he went mad and committed suicide. All the other books are merely copies and translations of that original," Merlin said.

"The name, Necronomicon, was coined by a writer in the early 20th Century of the First Age. It's simply Greek for "Book of Dead Names". The original book had no title but it *was* translated into several now-dead languages. Of course, those translations often left a lot to be desired. Some things were twisted and their true meanings were lost. Others were accidentally—or purposely—omitted and with dire consequences," he added after a brief pause.

"Like all those who came before him, Armenopur didn't even suspect what would happen to him and everything else once he gated in the Elder Gods. One cannot summon nor control the Dark Ones. One can only become a conduit between their terrifying realm and ours," Gorinna said.

Merlin nodded.

"Once they are allowed into this universe, no power of man or god can force them back into their realm," he said.

Arka-Dal smirked and nodded.

"If Armenopur's grave is so well hidden, how will this fool find it?" he asked.

"I suspect he has help. Something supernatural must be guiding him every step of the way. Something dark and sinister. Without such help, he could never find it," Merlin said.

"You think he has the same help that the last of the Dragon Lords had?"[2] asked Kashi.

"Probably," Merlin replied.

Arka-Dal poured himself another ale as he allowed Merlin's comment to sink in.

"Why is that bastard fucking with *us*?" he asked.

"When you established Thule, you brought about an age of light and reason. You dispelled the very darkness and chaos he needs in which to thrive. Light and reason are his enemies. Since Thule represents both, he seeks to bring about its fall and bring an end to the Second Age," Merlin said.

---

2 Read THIRTEEN SKULLS & OTHER TALES

"So he's thrown down the gauntlet, has he? Well, he'll find us more than ready to accept his challenge," Arka-Dal said. "And where is this Tomb of the Sleeping God?"

"According to the legends, it is everywhere to be seen and nowhere to be found," Merlin replied.

"What in Hell does *that* mean?" asked Pandaar.

"It means we must wait until the location reveals itself to us. Once it does, we can act. If the time is right, we'll find it before our mysterious adversary does and awakens the Sleeping God," Merlin said.

"What happens if he gets there before we do? What happens if he awakens this god?" asked Gorinna.

"If the Sleeping God wakes, we can bend over and kiss our asses good-bye. No power on Earth can stop him from plunging this world into darkness and chaos. No power on Earth can prevent him from gating in more of the Elder Gods and restoring them to their awful power," Merlin said.

"What does our adversary get out of this?" asked Arka-Dal.

"He gets to command the Sleeping God's legions and serve at his right hand in his bid to trample all of the great empires of man into dust. In short, he gets power. Power enough to feed his already bloated ego and sense of self-importance," Merlin answered. "According to the prophesy, 'He who awakens the Sleeping God shall be rewarded with command over endless numbers of Dark Troops. In the names of the Elder Gods, he will trample all of the world's great empires beneath his sandals and the wealth of the world shall be laid at his feet.'"

"Does the Necronomicon offer any advice on how to prevent this?" asked Gorinna.

"It does, but it, too, is shrouded in riddles," Merlin said.

"As usual," Gorinna remarked.

"Indeed. According to the text, 'when that which burns brighter than the sun reveals itself, all will be as before'. This poses quite a conundrum. First, what burns brighter than the sun? And third—what is meant by the phrase 'all will be as before'?" Merlin said.

"Does the book say we have to put out this thing that burns brighter than the sun?" asked Kashi.

"No. It's quite vague," Merlin said. "Purposely so, I believe."

"Then we might have to put it out?" asked Gorinna.

"I don't know," Merlin replied honestly. "To put it out, we must first find it."

"But by putting out this light source—if it is indeed a light source—we might actually return the universe to the way it was when the Elder Gods ruled. It could also mean that we might force them to stay in limbo and keep things as they are," Gorinna mused.

"Now *that's* as clear as mud!" Pandaar remarked.

"Indeed," agreed Merlin. "Perhaps the true meaning of the phrase will be revealed to us when the time is right."

"Or perhaps not," Arka-Dal said. "If we decide right, the world will remain safe. If we decide wrong, the entire universe plunges into chaos. It's nearly impossible to figure out!"

"Sounds like fun. When do we start?" asked Pandaar.

Arka-Dal walked over to the large wall map and studied it carefully.

"If the hammer falls, it will fall hardest on Egypt and Kush since two of those armies are in Africa. Each is less than a week's march from their borders. The one to the north is in the middle of the Frozen Wastes—a full month's march from our frontier. Since they have no cavalry, they can't move very fast—not even on a dead run," he said as he pointed to each spot where the armies were located.

"Why not attack them *before* they move?" suggested Pandaar.

"In their current state, no Earthly weapons can harm them. Even if you chopped them to bits, they would simply reform within moments. A pre emptive strike would be futile at best," Merlin explained.

"Can we actually *kill* them?" Arka-Dal asked.

"All supernatural beings can be destroyed by silver edged or bluesilver weapons and magical swords. The problem lies in getting close enough to use them. That would also involve suffering large numbers of casualties," Merlin said.

"We could be facing a potential bloodbath," added Gorinna. "Any of their losses can easily be replaced. Ours cannot. In a war of attrition, they hold the upper hand."

"I'd rather not risk open warfare. I don't want a million widows and orphans wailing throughout Thule," Arka-Dal said. "We must find this madman before he locates Armenopur's tomb and uses the book to activate his armies. Any idea where that tomb might be?"

"Since Armenopur was Egyptian, his tomb is somewhere in Egypt, Libya or ancient Nubia. It would also be unmarked and heavily guarded with a variety of deadly curses and traps. Ancient Egyptians often buried their hated criminals in remote, almost inaccessible places to avoid contaminating sacred ground," Merlin advised.

"Do you think our madman knows where it is?" asked Kashi.

"Not yet. But I do believe that someone is guiding him to it indirectly so as not to make his quest seem too easy," Merlin replied. "That's the way *he* usually works things."

Balaam stirred the ashes with a stick as he thought about his strange deal. He hadn't seen his sponsor—if one could call him that—for several weeks. The map and riddle he was given led him to a small, narrow cave halfway up the face of the ancient peak called Jebelbarca which marked the border between Egypt and Kush. During the First Age, both Egyptian and Kushite kings believed Jebelbarca was sacred because of the odd promontory that once jutted upward from its base. The promontory resembled the asp on the front of a pharaoh's crown. It was gone now. Age and weather had reduced it to a pile of rocky rubble scattered on the desert floor.

Balaam had made the very difficult climb up to the cave. Inside, he found a single earthen jar which he kicked at with all of his might. When the jar shattered, he found a strip of papyrus amid the shards bearing the instructions to read it aloud from the top of Jebelbarca at the height of the full moon. He was to repeat this incantation three or four times, making certain to pronounce each and every word correctly. He realized the parchment was inscribed with a spell of summoning.

Once he was finished with the incantation, he was instructed to slash his left palm with a knife and allow the blood to fall onto the parchment. Then he was to burn it.

Balaam did all of this.

Then he rode out to the middle of the desert and waited.

He had no idea what he'd summoned or if the spell actually worked. After three days and nights of waiting, he was beginning to doubt everything. Then his "benefactor" appeared from nowhere, seated cross-legged on the other side of the fire.

"I sense doubt in you," he said.

"You should. I did as you instructed but other than the stinging in my left palm, I see nothing," Balaam said. "Just what, exactly, did that spell summon?"

"Tis best I show you. Look into the flames," the man said.

Balaam stared into the crackling fire and quickly became transfixed by the sight of countless rows of well-armed, dark-skinned soldiers arrayed in far and desolate places. He blinked and looked at his benefactor.

"What *are* they?" he asked.

"They are soldiers unlike any the Earth has ever seen before. *Your* soldiers," came the reply.

"Mine? How many?" asked Balaam as visions of conquest raced through his inner mind.

"One and a half million. They are poised to strike at the hearts of the world's greatest civilizations. They are yours to command," the man said with a grin.

Balaam ran his fingers through his tousled hair and took a deep breath.

"What if they aren't enough?" he asked.

The man laughed.

"You can summon more. As many as you need. They are as numerous as the grains of sand in the Sahara. Lead them well and all of the great empires will be trampled into the dust and their treasures will lay at your feet. All you need do is keep your part of the bargain," the man replied.

"I've already given you my soul—," Balaam began.

"That was just the price you paid for requesting my help. There are other things you must do before these soldiers are truly yours," the man said.

"Like what?" asked Balaam disgusted with himself for not reading the contract.

"All will be revealed at the proper time," the man said.

"Are they ready to march?" he inquired of his strange troops.

"Not yet. For now, they remain inanimate, lifeless hulks. They neither see nor move. In order to animate them, to get them to obey your commands, you must first find the lost tomb of Armenopur. Once you have done this, you must then locate the ancient book that was buried with him and recite three spells.

The first summons forth demon guardians to protect you from outside interference while you recite the other spells. The second sets your armies in motion, but in order to gain full command of them, you must recite the last and most powerful spell. That spell awakens the Sleeping God. Once awakened, you must vow to serve him forever. It is he who will give you the ability to command those armies," the man explained.

"That's it?" asked Balaam.

"Yes. But be careful to read each word of each spell *exactly* as it is written. Make not a single error in your pronunciation lest the consequences be dire," he warned.

"Where is this tomb?" Balaam asked impatiently.

"If you would find the tomb of the Accursed One, go to Meroe. Once there, go to the bazaar on the north end of the city and seek out one called Kaziri," he said as he slowly vanished from sight.

Balaam cursed.

Meroe was more than 250 miles away and the way was harsh and dangerous. He also had the sensation that he was being played for a fool. His benefactor had taken advantage of his lust for power and wealth and his deepest desires to rule the entire world. He had even provided him with enough soldiers to attain those goals—provided he was able to locate Armenopur's tomb and some sort of ancient book.

It seemed almost too easy.

Balaam felt there had to be catch—something he definitely wouldn't like. And just what was that second spell he mentioned?

He drew his cloak tightly around himself to ward off the night cold as he watched the flames.

He sighed.

He almost wanted to give the whole thing up. He also knew what would happen to him if he attempted to break his contract.

He had little choice but to see this game through to the end.

"Sometimes I think I'm getting too old for this shit," he said to himself.

He didn't realize that the spells he recited also released powerful energies. Powerful enough to attract the undivided attention of Merlin. It was this sudden release of magical energies that drew him to the Kalahari and caused him to contact Gorinna and Peace. The spells had opened portals that were little known and barely used. Portals into a dark, and terrifying world.

Although he knew the portals had been opened, he still had no idea who opened them or how he knew they existed. Try as he might, he simply could not pinpoint the source of power. That could men only one thing: the spell caster was *shielded* from him. It made tracking him virtually impossible.

He cursed under his breath as he paced the floor of the living room. Gorinna, Kashi, Pandaar and Arka-Dal were seated in the plush chairs around him, watching him pace. Arka-Dal barely paid Merlin any mind. He was too busy pondering possible courses of action he might take to find their adversary before those armies could be animated.

If they could find him before he activated his armies, all would be well. If he should find the tomb and cast the spell, they might still be able to foil his plans by solving the riddles.

"But what," he wondered, "do the riddles mean?"

When the Devil returned to his lair on the Lower Planes, his demon captain emerged from the shadows.

"It is done. His appetite has been whetted—just as I knew it would," the Devil remarked.

"Will he be able to locate the tomb?" the demon asked.

"He will—if he deciphers the clues I will give him. His lust for personal power runs deep. It was almost too easy this time," the Devil said.

"Do you not know where the tomb lies?" asked the demon.

"Of course I do," the Devil assured him.

"Then why use the human to find it?" the demon asked.

"All will become apparent in due time," the Devil replied.

He smiled to himself. Corrupting the power-hungry Balaam had been almost too easy. Now that the first part of his scheme had been set in motion, he decided it was time to begin the second—and most difficult—phase.

His intended target was none other than the famed Emperor of Thule himself. He knew it would be useless to personally appear before him and offer him even more wealth and power than he already possessed. Arka-Dal was above such things and the sudden appearance of the Lord of Hell might trigger more problems than he truly wanted.

Arka-Dal was larger than life. A living legend in the eyes of his subjects. He was heroic, level-headed, noble and considered to be incorruptible. He was just the type the Devil loved to bring down.

Hard.

He knew that Arka-Dal had a strong liking for beautiful, intelligent and unusual women. Under most circumstances, he'd send one of his legions of sexy seductresses to lure him over to the dark side. He had many beautiful young demons under his command. He called them his "Hell's Belles". As alluring as they were, he didn't think that any of them would be good enough for the job.

There was, he realized, only one real choice.

He summoned his daughter, Galya to his side. She was the Princess of the Lower Planes and her beauty was known to strike men speechless. She stood five feet, eight inches tall and had a slender, seductively perfect body, to go with her alluring and disarming smile and deep amber eyes that could make any man alive weak in the knees. Her skin was almost copper colored and looked warm and inviting. Her perfect face, with full moist lips, high cheekbones and penetrating eyes was crowned by long, wavy, jet-black hair that cascaded down her bare shoulders like an ebony waterfall. Two tiny horns protruded from her forehead and she had a long, pointed tail and leathery, bat-like wings. In short, she was temptation personified.

Irresistible.

Even her father felt attracted to her.

"You called?" she asked as she bowed before him.

"Yes. I have a task for you. One that will require all of your considerable talents. There is a human I want you to corrupt," he said.

"Another mere human? That's so ordinary, Father. Men are no longer challenges for me. Why not do this yourself?" she asked with a bored yawn.

"This man, I feel, is beyond my reach. But he *does* have a penchant for sexy women so *you* might have a better chance," the Devil replied. "Even so, he may prove to be quite the challenge."

"No mere mortal can resist the charms of Galya!" she boasted. "I have brought thousands to their knees."

"This one just might. His people consider him to be above reproach. Totally incorruptible. Hell, some even think he's a god! That's why I want *you* to find his weakness and use it to bring him down. I want his name to be dragged through the mud in such a manner that his people to lose all of their respect for him. In short, I want you to ruin him," he said.

"And just *who* is this incorruptible Human?" Galya asked.

"He is Arka-Dal, the Emperor of Thule," he replied. "Think you can handle him?"

She laughed.

"He will be as putty in my hands. I'll have him licking my feet in an hour. Every man has a price and no man has ever been able to say no to *me*!" she bragged.

"Don't be overly confident, my dear. Arka-Dal has dealt with demons and devils on several occasions. He has *always* prevailed. You must also be on guard against his powerful friends. Merlin and Gorinna should not be taken lightly," he warned.

"Merlin? The Sorcerer still lives?" she asked in wonder.

He nodded.

She frowned. She remembered when she had gone to Camelot to seduce the young Arthur. She was just about to nail him when Merlin intervened. After a long battle, she found herself cast back into the Lower Planes, where she had to remain for the next 100 years. She had wanted revenge against Merlin ever since.

"Who is this Gorinna you spoke of?" she asked.

"The Red Witch of Wesveria. She is almost as powerful as Merlin and knows several tricks that even *he* is unaware of. She can be quite merciless when it comes to protecting Arka-Dal and his family. Try not to cross either of them," he said. "And you might want to lose the horns and tail to appear less, er, devilish."

She smiled and left the room.

Her father's warning had made her curious. In order to make this less of a challenge, she decided to be at her sexy best. She bathed in light, scented water, brushed out her long raven hair and donned her skimpiest, sheerest dress. And she discarded her trademark horns and tail as the Devil had suggested.

As she looked herself over in the mirror, she smiled confidently.

"I don't care who he is! He'll not be able to resist me!" she boasted.

That evening, Arka-Dal was in the bedroom dressing after a long bath. The sound of flapping wings caught his attention. He turned and watched as the strangest—and one of the loveliest—young women he'd ever seen settled gently onto the balcony. Galya smiled seductively as she folded her wings behind her back and stepped into the room. She was wearing a sheer tunic of filmy white material secured at her slim waist by a narrow golden belt. Her garb left little to the imagination. It was even risqué by Thulian standards, which really caught his attention.

Arka-Dal was momentarily transfixed by her. She was without a doubt one of the most beautiful and alluring women he'd ever beheld. But he knew immediately who she was. The warm, dark copper skin and bat-like wings protruding from her shoulder blades gave her away. But it was her deep, dark magnetic eyes that attracted him most.

He'd expected to be overcome by a wave of intense, almost nauseating evil. Instead, he felt relaxed.

At ease with her presence.

It was as if he'd known her his entire life.

Galya sensed this, too.

It was a strange reaction indeed.

That's when he smiled and nodded, as if to greet her.

Arka-Dal's calm demeanor nearly disarmed her.

Unlike her other victims, this one neither flinched nor fled. He simply stood there admiring her.

She said nothing for a long time as she looked him over. He was tall, muscular, ruggedly handsome and carried himself with confidence. She quickly realized that he was a man who was used to being in control of every situation.

This one was no exception.

She circled him slowly, drawing closer with each orbit. All the while, she maintained eye contact. He showed no fear. No revulsion. In fact, he even smiled at her again.

"What manner of man is he?" she wondered as she touched his shoulder.

She stepped closer and looked him in the eyes. He met her gaze unflinchingly. She felt the strength in his body. She heard his heart beating. It was strong.

Steady and calm.

As was his demeanor.

She reached out and touched his shoulder. She felt the determination in his heart and mind and his iron will. She also felt his compassion.

And something else she couldn't fathom.

Something intangible.

"Nobility?" she wondered.

Arka-Dal studied her with equal fascination. He was especially drawn to her deep, amber eyes.

Her eyes sparkled.

With fire and intelligence.

Passion and curiosity.

And something else he sensed deep within her.

Something he *liked.*

Galya stopped circling and stepped back. She smiled seductively at him. He returned it and bowed his head respectfully. The gesture surprised her.

"Welcome to Thule," he said.

"I am Galya. I am the daughter of—" she began.

"I *know* who you are," he interrupted as he took in her charms.

"You *know* me?" she asked.

"Yes—and you are even lovelier than I had imagined—even with the wings," he said.

"You imagined me to be lovely?" she asked still trying to feel him out.

"Of course. You are the Devil's daughter and his chief seductress. How could one such as you be anything but beautiful. In fact, I think you are the most beautiful woman alive. I am honored by your visit," Arka-Dal replied honestly.

"Honored? Now *that's* one I've not heard before," she said sarcastically as she stretched her wings and folded them behind her.

"I'm surprised," he said.

"Are you really?" she asked.

"Yes. After all, not everyone gets a visit from such an important person. Your father must think I'm someone rather special to have sent you here. I feel sort of flattered," he said.

Galya was at a loss for words.

Their conversation had taken a most unexpected turn. In fact, *he* was leading it. She stopped to gather her thoughts, then decided to go for broke.

"You do not find me repugnant?" she asked as she walked closer.

"On the contrary, I think you're one of the most beautiful women I've ever seen. I feel privileged by your presence," he said.

His reply took her aback.

"That's another thing no one's ever said to me before," she said. "Don't you even *fear* me?"

"Not at all. What man could possibly fear one as beautiful as you?" he replied.

Again he flattered her. Yet she could tell he was quite sincere.

"Let's cut to the chase," she said. "My Father sent me here to make you an offer," she said.

"I guess that makes you his emissary. Before you begin, I must warn you that there is little I don't already possess and even less that I desire," Arka-Dal said graciously.

"We shall see," she said.

She then proceeded to try and tempt him with visions of more territory, more power and unimaginable wealth. When he politely declined all of this, she offered him immortality. To her surprise, he also refused this. Remembering her Father's words, she undid her garment and let it slide to the floor.

"Since you refused all of my other offers, I now offer you myself. I will be yours, now and forever, if you renounce all that you are and agree to do my Father's bidding," she said seductively.

"While your beauty is beyond mere words to describe and I would feel honored to be your lover, I respectfully decline your offer," he said without taking his eyes from the soft, dark triangle between her thighs.

She moved closer and opened her stance. He swallowed hard as she thrust her pelvis forward and used her fingers to pull open her soft labia to reveal the hot, moist channel behind them.

"Do you not find me the least bit attractive?" she asked as she rubbed the bulge that had appeared in his pants.

"I find you incredibly attractive," he said.

"Then take me!" she urged as she pressed her lips to his.

A sudden surge raced through her. She had never felt anything like it before. She was so surprised, she backed away and stared at him. That's when she saw that he had felt it, too.

"That was—"she began.

"Yes," he agreed. "It certainly was."

He reached down and picked up her tunic, smiled and handed it back to her. She nodded and slipped it back on. She decided that if she attempted to seduce him again, the results might be far different than she'd planned.

"Father is right. You *are* different," she said.

"And you are *enchanting*," he said softly.

Again with the compliments. Any other man would already be shaking at the knees and begging to be her slave. But *not* this one.

She was pondering her next move when the door opened and both Merlin and Gorinna entered.

The moment he saw Galya, Merlin stopped in his tracks and glared at her. She squinted at him and snarled as he prepared to cast a spell.

"We meet again, Sorcerer!" she said.

"Galya!" Merlin said, almost spitting her name.

At the same time, she noticed Gorinna circling to the right. Both were preparing to strike and she realized she had no way to save herself this time.

With no way out, she went into a fighting stance and emitted a nasty, serpent-like hiss. If she was to die, she was determined to take at least one of them down with her.

"This time, I'll finish you for good," Merlin vowed as he raised his hands.

To his astonishment—and Galya's—Arka-Dal stepped between them with his hands up.

"Stay your hands—both of you. Galya is here as an emissary and is a guest in this house. I forbid you to harm her or disrespect her in any way," he ordered.

While Arka-Dal shielded her, Merlin made eye contact with him. After a few seconds, he nodded.

"No. You are *not* bewitched. The words are truly yours," he said as he turned and bade Gorinna to lower her hands. She did so reluctantly but kept her eyes on Galya.

"She is the Devil's daughter," Merlin pointed out.

"I know. As an emissary from another ruler, no harm will befall her while she is in this house. Take no actions against her unless she acts first," Arka-Dal replied.

Galya sighed in relief and relaxed her guard.

She looked at Arka-Dal.

He had deliberately shielded her from their attack and had ordered them not to harm her in any way. He had called her an ambassador and said she was his guest. He had left her speechless.

Again.

"As long as you make no attempts to seduce or harm anyone in this house, you will remain under my protection. You are free to stay as long as you wish. You can come and go as you please. Feel welcome here. Feel safe here," he said softly.

She allowed herself to relax as she looked deep into his eyes. She saw no deceit in them. No fear nor feeling of repulsion.

"Father is right. You are *not* like the others," she said.

Merlin detected a note of confusion in her voice. The Devil's daughter didn't seem so sure of herself at the moment.

"I vow not to harm anyone for as long as I am here," she said.

"You *believe* her?" asked Merlin.

"I do. And I also *trust* her until she proves to me otherwise," Arka-Dal said.

They looked at each other.

Galya smiled at him.

"You have the run of the palace. Consider yourself at home here," Arka-Dal offered.

"Will I be under guard?" she asked.

"You're *not* a prisoner here. There's no need for guards," he replied.

Gorinna and Merlin were taken aback. This was a most unexpected turn of events.

Galya was also at a loss for words. Arka-Dal openly stated that he *trusted* her. No one had ever done *that* before.

"Why do you not fear me as other men do?" she asked.

"Why should I fear you? Are you some sort of monster?" Arka-Dal queried.

"Some say I am. They recoil from me in terror. Not you. You're different," she said.

"All I see before me is a very beautiful, intelligent woman. You're no more a monster than Medusa is," he said with a smile. "Anyone who calls you that doesn't really know you."

"And you *know* me?" she asked, quite puzzled by his statement.

"I think I do. I'd also like to get to know you better—if you'll let me," he said.

Arka-Dal's attitude completely disarmed Galya. She could sense that he wasn't lying. He meant everything he said. He wasn't playing any sort of game.

"You sound as if you actually *like* me," she said.

"I *do* like you. And I feel that I can *trust* you," Arka-Dal assured her.

"I've never heard *that* before," Galya remarked. "Why do you, of all people, trust me?"

"If I trust you, maybe you'll learn to trust me. You might even decide to stay here awhile," he replied.

"Stay? You really want me here?" she asked incredulously.

"Yes, I do," he replied softly.

Medusa, Chatha and Mayumi entered the room. All stopped in their tracks when they saw Galya. Arka-Dal calmly made the introductions. To Galya's surprise, Mayumi gave her a friendly hug and welcomed her. The other women shook her hand warily. None recoiled in horror or showed the slightest trace of fear. She found their reactions both unusual and somehow comforting.

"You look nothing like the old drawings in Leo's books," Medusa observed. "I see no horns nor tail."

"I decided to forego such accoutrements," Galya said with a smile. "Most people find them repelling anyway."

"Now that we all know each other, let's go downstairs. Of course, you'll join us for dinner," Arka-Dal said as he offered Mayumi his arm.

Galya hesitated but followed them downstairs. Pandaar, Zhijima, Kashi and Leo were already seated at the table when they entered. The Pope raised an eyebrow when Arka-Dal introduced Galya and offered her the seat between Merlin and Zhijima. She sat down and watched as the servants brought out platters of roasted meat, steamed vegetables, fruit, nuts and pitchers of wine and ale. She watched as the others helped themselves.

"We don't eat on the Lower Planes. In fact, I have never tasted food," she explained.

"You must try. Our chef is the finest in all of Thule and he might feel insulted if you didn't at least taste some of his dishes. I could explain what they are if you like," Arka-Dal offered.

"Thank you. I'd like that," she said much to her own surprise.

There were at least 20 dishes. At the urging of the others, Galya tried all of them. To her delight, she found herself enjoying the meal and paid close attention to Arka-Dal as he told her what condiments to try with each. He also suggested what wine or ale went with each dish. The meal lasted for hours, as did the conversation. Her dinner companions treated her like an honored guest and seemed genuinely interested in learning all about her and where she had come from. Naturally, the ever inquisitive Leo asked the most questions. She noticed that he was also making notes of her answers in a small pad. He seemed fascinated with Galya and was grateful for the opportunity to learn so much from her.

She also realized that Merlin and Gorinna had relaxed their guard—but only a little. They were keeping their eyes on her. Neither trusted her. Considering her long history, Galya decided that they had good reason not to trust her. It would take time to earn their trust.

The more she spoke with them, the more she liked them. She was especially fond of Arka-Dal and Mayumi.

The diverse nature of Arka-Dal's family also intrigued her. First and foremost in his life was the petite, beautiful raven-haired Empress Mayumi from far-off Nihon. Arka-Dal had rescued her from a shipwreck nearly four decades ago. They fell madly in love with each other and were married within a year. He loved and trusted her above all others and she absolutely adored him. [3]

---

[3] Read THE GATES OF DELIRIUM

Then there was Medusa.

The last of the Gorgons had fled to Thule to avoid being killed. Leo hired her to be his assistant. When her would-be killers tracked her down, Arka-Dal protected her. They became friends, then fell in love and married.[4]

"When most others looked upon me as a monster of the worst sort, Arka-Dal looked upon me as a woman in need of help and a place of refuge. We love each other very much. To the people of Thule, I am simply Arka-Dal's wife—and it matters not that I am a Gorgon," Medusa explained.

Chatha was also interesting. The young warrior princess from an alternate universe had been part of a wave of invaders who had overrun the isle of Crete. Arka-Dal had captured her during the battle to liberate the Minoans.

"We became friends, then lovers and eventually married," Chatha said.

The others also spoke of Arka-Dal's relationships with Hetshepsut, the Queen of Egypt and Elena, the Queen of Minos. Galya listened carefully to each of their stories and openly wondered how Arka-Dal's wives got along so well considering they had to share him.

It amazed her that all three wives and their children lived together in the palace and were closer than sisters. Galya detected no envy or competition between them. In fact, both Medusa and Chatha insisted that Arka-Dal's *real* wife was Mayumi.

She also realized that the women in the palace, including Gorinna and Zhijima, were more than just good friends. In fact, Gorinna admitted her affair with Zhijima openly and they even joked about it.

"Have you ever had sex with a woman?" Zhijima asked.

"Many times. I have often had to seduce women for my father's purposes," Galya admitted.

"Did you enjoy it?" asked Gorinna.

"That all depended on how well they could use their tongues!" Galya joked. "Do the rest of you have sex with each other?"

Medusa nodded.

"Sometimes I do it with Mayumi or Chatha," she confessed. "That only happens while Arka-Dal's away for a long time. We do it to relax."

---

4 Read THIRTEEN SKULLS AND OTHER TALES

"Do *you* ever have sex just for the fun of it?" asked Zhijima.

"Have you ever been in love?" asked Gorinna.

Galya confessed that she had no idea what love really was but she did say that she's had sex for the fun of it many times—when she could find a willing partner who wasn't scared witless by her.

"So far, the only man who has not feared me is Arka-Dal," she said.

For the entire meal, Galya barely took her eyes off Arka-Dal. She was especially attentive when he spoke. For some reason she couldn't yet fathom, she was fascinated by him. She took care to study every line on his face and the way his eyes seemed to flash and soften as he changed moods during a conversation. She laughed at his puns and jokes and enjoyed the way he and his friends poked fun at each other.

As the meal went on, she felt more relaxed, more at ease with herself and her new companions. She even exchanged jokes with her life-long foe, Merlin, about their past encounters.

"This is the first time I've actually sat down and broke bread with anyone. I have never experienced a more interesting evening. This has given me the chance to get to know and understand you better. I am grateful for this opportunity," she said at one point.

"And *we* are equally grateful that you've decided to stay and give us the same chance to get to know you better," Arka-Dal said as he raised his glass.

Galya and the others clinked theirs against it.

"Perhaps one day I'll get the chance to sit down and chat like this with your famous father. I'll bet *he* has some interesting tales to share," Arka-Dal said.

"He most certainly does," Galya assured him. "You are the only person I've ever met who has said that. Most people want to meet Father in order to conduct business with him. You're a most unusual man, Arka-Dal. I *like* you," Galya said with a smile.

Merlin raised an eyebrow at her statement. She saw his expression and laughed.

"Yes, Merlin. I truly *like* him. Galya, the Princess of Hell actually likes someone!" she said.

Merlin laughed heartily. He sensed that she actually meant it. He was also beginning to see a side of her he had been totally unaware of.

"I have heard that you can assume any form you wish. Is that true?" asked Leo.

"To a point," Galya replied. "Most of the forms I take on are merely very good illusions meant to strike awe or fear into a given person. This is the way I normally look. This is my true form, minus the horns, and pointed tail. I can shed my wings when I want to, too. Father tells me that I look almost exactly like my mother did before she was killed."

"If that's true, then your late mother must have been a breathtakingly beautiful woman," Arka-Dal complimented. "Did you say she was killed?"

Galya nodded.

"Father said it happened just days after I was born. She was killed during a sneak attack launched by his enemies. The attack came during a declared truce, so Father and his legions were caught by surprise. I've never met my mother," she said.

"I'm sorry," Arka-Dal said.

"There's no need to be. After all, you had nothing to do with it. But I appreciate your sympathy. So would Father," Galya said.

Merlin was surprised. He thought Galya was devoid of human emotions and had never thought of her as anything other than a monster. He wondered if this was all an act on her part.

She smiled at him.

"No, Merlin. This is not an act. My emotions and words are quite sincere," she assured him.

He blushed because he forgot she was capable of reading anyone's surface thoughts and because he also got caught. Galya laughed at his embarrassment. So did everyone else. Merlin also laughed at himself.

"I must say that you are most interesting and charming dinner guest. I hope we have a chance to chat like this again soon," he said.

"Nice recovery, Merlin!" Pandaar said as he held up his hand.

Galya laughed when Merlin high-fived him. Their conversations lasted well past midnight. Most of the others had already gone up to bed. Arka-Dal finished his ale and placed the cup on the table.

"Do you sleep?" he asked.

"Only on the Lower Planes and only during daylight hours," she replied.

"We have several guestrooms. Feel free to use one of you like. You can also wander around the palace if you want. We'll speak again tomorrow," he said as he stood and went upstairs with Mayumi.

"Thank you," she said.

That was the second time she had used that phrase. The generosity of her hosts had somehow compelled her to use it to acknowledge their kindness.

Not feeling the least bit tired, she elected to roam through the palace. Unlike most palaces, which were ostentatious displays of wealth and power, this felt more like a comfortable home. While it was well-decorated, it also conveyed the feeling that it was lived in. There were family portraits on the walls, cats lounging on the furniture, children's' toys strewn about in several places. It had just the right amount of clutter and chaos to make one feel at home.

There were three stories and 36 rooms in all. The central part was the largest. It had three stories. The east and west wings each had two stories and consisted mostly of the living quarters for Leo, Kashi and Gorinna, Pandaar and Zhijima and the household servants. Each wing had showers, full baths, balconies, large windows and plenty of closets. The west wing contained a large, well-equipped kitchen, butler's pantry, the chef's quarters and an ice locker where fresh meats, cheeses and other perishables were kept. The east wing had a large gymnasium and bath with a sunken tub, massage tables and other comforts.

The central portion contained the grand hall, throne room, justice center, parlor, war room, formal dining room and council room, on the first floor. The second floor held Arka-Dal's office, the ladies' sewing room/ lounge, private quarters for guests, bathrooms and a couple of small rooms.

The third floor was the Dal family's residence.

The basement contained the Royal Archives, Leo's office, library and research department.

Arka-Dal's favorite room was the large parlor just beyond the grand hall room, with its stone fireplace and comfortable leather couches. It had a well-appointed bar, a chess table, card table, dart boards, end tables, a long, low center table and various decorative pieces. Above the mantle hung a portrait of Mayumi and Arka-Dal's son, Armet at age three. Below it, Excalibur was mounted. Arka-Dal's famed teardrop steel shield with the black, two-headed eagle emblazoned upon it, hung on the wall next to the fireplace. The wooden floor was decorated with a beautiful, hand-woven carpet from Sundar.

It was here everyone gathered to relax, play games, drink and entertain guests. The children also played here and cats lounged lazily on the furniture.

A dozen maids kept the palace neat and clean, which was quite a feat considering they had to chase after the Dal children and several cats.

Galya liked what she saw.

The house reflected the personalities of Arka-Dal and his family. There was nothing ornate or imposing. Instead, it felt warm and inviting.

Her meanderings led her to the Royal Archives. Curious, she descended the stairs and pushed open the door. To her surprise, she saw Leo seated at his desk, transcribing the information she had given him into a large, heavy tome. She walked over and sat down in the chair across from him. Leo put down the pen and looked up at her.

"I want to thank you for all this information. I never would have been able to find out any of this on my own. You have filled a great void in our archives," Leo said.

She smiled.

"I am glad I was of some help to you. If you like, I could provide you with several volumes of more detailed information and histories on all 666 planes. There are books enough to fill all of the remaining space on your shelves," she offered.

"And what would *I* have to give to you in return?" Leo asked warily.

"Nothing at all. I am flattered by your curiosity and thirst for knowledge. Besides, my Father has millions of such books. He will never miss these," she said as she gestured toward the empty shelves across the room.

Leo watched in awe as hundreds of heavy, leather bound volumes materialized on the shelves one-by-one until all the empty spaces were filled. He noticed that each bore a number from one to 666. Delighted, he walked over and selected one of the books. He was surprised to discover that he could read it easily.

"I translated them into your language. I left nothing out," Galya assured him.

Leo stared at the books in disbelief. The Devil's daughter had provided him with reams of valuable information—an entire lifetime of arcana—and she had asked for nothing in return.

"I don't know how to thank you," he said after a while.

"You already have," she said as she left the archives.

She saw Merlin sitting in the parlor sipping brandy as he stared into the fireplace. She walked over and sat across from him. He glanced up at her but remained silent.

"You don't like me, do you, Sorcerer?" she asked.

"I don't *trust* you," he said. "I know why you've come."

"So does Arka-Dal, yet that doesn't seem to bother him," she said as she leaned back. "He is quite remarkable. I used all of my usual tricks on him. All of them failed. My Father was right about him."

Merlin chuckled.

"You find that amusing?" she asked.

"Yes. Don't you?" he asked.

"I nearly had Arthur until you showed up. I doubt that Arka-Dal *needed* your help," she mused.

"Arthur was weaker than I thought him to be. He *needed* my help. Arka-Dal is much stronger. What do you think of him now?" Merlin asked.

"He's charming, gallant and open minded. I find myself being drawn to him. When I kissed him, I felt things that I have never felt before," she said.

"You *kissed* him?" Merlin asked.

"Yes. I thought I had him then. But when our lips touched, I realized it was the other way around. I came here to reduce him to a babbling idiot or turn him into a power mad despot. I have never *failed* before. And I have never been *happier* that I did," she explained.

Merlin squinted at her.

"You're actually *happy* that you failed?" he asked. "Those are odd words coming from *you.* Yet, I sense that you truly *mean* them."

"I do," Galya assured him. "If not for him, I'd be dead now. I owe him my life. I will never harm or betray him. In time, you'll come to *believe* me."

"These are strange times, indeed," Merlin said. "I never imagined that the two of us would be seated here enjoying a pleasant conversation. I've always viewed you as evil incarnate, as a vile, heartless monster who took great delight in tormenting men."

"What do you think of me now?" she asked.

"I'm not sure what to think," Merlin answered. "I do know that I am beginning to like you."

"Well, that's a start, isn't it?" she said.

He nodded.

"But I still don't trust you," he said.

"That's only fair, considering my past history," Galya said. "Let me leave you with this thought: Arka-Dal *trusts* me. No man has ever given me that. I owe him my life and I will risk all that I have to see that no harm befalls him—ever!"

Merlin looked up at her.

"You actually mean that, don't you?" he observed.

"More than I have ever meant anything in my life before," she replied as she rose and walked away.

"Where are you going?" he called after her.

"I need to walk—and think," she said.

She walked out into the rose garden. The cool evening breeze felt pleasant on her bare skin. She walked amid the flowers and statuary and inhaled deeply. There was an abundance of aromas. She stopped to study several of the roses. She smiled as she ran her fingertips gently over the soft, moist petals. She had never really noticed flowers before. Never stopped to appreciate them. Now, she found herself surrounded by them.

And she enjoyed it.

After a while, she looked up at the balcony of Arka-Dal's bedroom. Curious, she spread her wings and flew up to it. As her bare feet touched the floor, she saw that the double doors were open. Arka-Dal, Mayumi, Medusa and Chatha were all asleep on the oversized bed. She sat down on the rail of the balcony and studied the sleeping Arka-Dal.

The Emperor fascinated her.

She had come to tempt him. To bring him down and ruin his life. To her surprise, he resisted all of her efforts. He knew who she was yet didn't recoil in fear or disgust. Instead, he treated her with dignity and respect.

Like an emissary.

Then he did what no other human had ever done before. He *protected* her from impending doom. He even invited her to join them for dinner, over which he spoke with her as an equal, a guest, or even a friend. Arka-Dal didn't feel the least bit threatened by her. In fact, she sensed that he was actually intrigued with her and had a burning desire to learn all he could about her and the place she had come from.

And the others treated her the same.

This experience was new to her. To Arka-Dal and his friends, she wasn't the hated Devil's daughter that so many others despised and feared. She was their guest and their curiosity was genuine.

The more she studied the slumbering Emperor, the more she wondered just what she'd gotten herself into. Before today, she had always felt supremely confident in her abilities to reduce any human male to a pile of quivering jelly. She had been just as confident she'd be able to do the same to Arka-Dal or at least seduce him and make him hers. Although he was clearly interested in her, his will remained unshakably strong.

"What manner of man *are* you?" she wondered.

He already had everything and anything he wanted, including three beautiful wives who would do anything for him. He desired nothing else. No power. No wealth. No new territories.

"What does one offer a man who has everything his heart desires? Father was right about him. He is no ordinary human. This one is a real challenge," she thought as she leaned against the railing.

She felt something warm on her back and turned slowly to see the sun rising in the east. As it rose, it turned the desert sky into a glorious light show of rose, pink and gold. She would normally have retreated into Hell at this time to conserve her powers. Sunlight sapped them and left her weakened. But something held her there. For the first time ever, she watched the sun rise and took great delight in the warmth of its rays on her skin.

And she didn't feel the least bit anxious.

Or weak.

Mayumi stirred next to Arka-Dal and sat up. She stretched and walked out onto the balcony. When she saw Galya, she greeted her cheerfully. Her open friendliness took Galya aback.

"I am glad you have decided to stay awhile. Please join us for breakfast. Aka-san will be very disappointed if you don't," Mayumi said pleasantly.

"Does my presence bother you at all?" Galya asked.

"Not really. I know that you have come to seduce Aka-san. If he decides to let you seduce him, there is little I can do to prevent that. I have learned not to be jealous. After all, he *does* have several wives. Perhaps one day, you will be another," Mayumi replied honestly. "If that happens, you will learn to share him with the rest of us."

Mayumi laughed to indicate she was joking. Galya laughed, too. This time, it was sincere and the sensation sort of relaxed her.

She turned back to watching the sun rise. Mayumi noticed her fascination and smiled.

"I guess you don't see many suns rise where you live," she said.

"This is my first. I never imagined that it could be so beautiful," Galya said. She sounded almost awed by it.

Arka-Dal, Medusa and Chatha soon awoke and joined them on the balcony. The Emperor seemed quite fascinated with Galya's description of her first sunrise and expressed his hope that it was the first of many she'd witness while in Thule. He then insisted she join them for breakfast.

When they entered the dining room, the usual crowd was already seated at the table. They all greeted each other cheerfully as Galya decided to sit next to Merlin. Like dinner the night before, Mayumi and the other women explained to Galya what each dish was and urged her to try them. This time, she eagerly helped herself to larger servings and seemed to take great pleasure in every morsel she put into her mouth.

"Normally, we of the Lower Planes don't eat. We get our nourishment from the energies of the planes or by ingesting manna. This is all so delicious. I can't believe what I've been missing all this time!" she said as she shoveled more eggs onto her plate.

Gorinna laughed.

"You're nothing like I expected you to be," she said. "I've always thought you to be seductively beautiful—and you are that—but also a vile, vindictive and heartless bitch. Instead, I find you to be just the opposite."

"I believe you have Arka-Dal to thank for that, Gorinna," Galya said. "For reasons I cannot yet fathom, he has brought out my better nature. Perhaps it's because that while most people loathe me, he makes me feel welcome and treats me like a true guest. No one has ever done this before."

"That is just the way Aka-san is," Mayumi said with a smile.

After breakfast, Arka-Dal invited Galya to walk with him in the rose garden. As they meandered down several winding paths past fountains, statues, floral designs and playgrounds, he noticed that Galya couldn't seem to keep her eyes off him. He asked her why she seemed to be so fascinated with him.

"It's because you are such an unusual man, Arka-Dal of Thule," she said.

"How so?" he queried.

"You act as if you actually trust me," she replied.

"Why shouldn't I? Don't you plan on keeping your word?" he asked.

"Of course I do. When the Crown Princess of the Lower Planes gives her word, she keeps it. What of your word to protect me?" Galya asked.

"If anyone attempts to harm you without provocation on your part, they will have to go through me first. I will defend you with every ounce of strength I have. You are our honored guest. No harm will befall you while you remain under this roof. I swear it," he assured her.

"What do you hope to gain by treating me so well?" she asked after a bit.

"Your trust," he said.

"My trust? Anything else?" she asked.

"Your friendship," he added.

"There must be something else," she said.

He simply smiled and said nothing. They continued their walk in silence for a few minutes, then Galya spoke.

"You are quite an enigma," she said.

"I'm only an enigma to my enemies. My friends understand me very well. You will, too, in time," he said.

"Most humans consider me to be their enemy. Why not you?" she asked. "After all, I was sent here to seduce you."

"You were sent here bearing an offer from your father. That makes you his emissary. An enemy would openly attack me. You tried to seduce me. I'd hardly call that an attack," he replied.

"Then you really didn't mind my attempt to seduce you?" she asked.

"Mind it? Hell, I'm flattered by it," he replied with a grin.

"I'm sort of glad that I failed," she said.

"I wouldn't exactly say that you've failed," he said as he took her hand and squeezed it.

"Now *you* flatter *me*!" she said. "The Empress also seems to like me but the other two do not."

"They'll get over it—once they come to know you," he said.

"What if they don't?" she asked.

"In that case, they'll just have to get used to you being around," Arka-Dal smiled.

"Every man desires something. What is that you desire most?" she asked.

"Peace, happiness and prosperity for myself and the people of Thule," he answered.

"What about immortality?" she suggested.

"I have no desire to live forever. I'm not a god. In fact, I don't even *believe* in gods. If they *do* exist, they've rarely done mankind any good," he said.

"Odd. That's what Father always says," Galya remarked. "The more time I stay with you, the more I like you."

"And the more I like *you*," he said as he put her arms around her waist and pulled her closer.

"This feels nice," she said as she leaned into him.

"Very nice," he agreed.

Galya squeezed his hand as they walked. It was at that instant she realized that she desired the same things he did. It was an epiphany of sorts. One she wasn't sure how to deal with.

Merlin and Gorinna watched their every move from a balcony overlooking the gardens.

"With each passing hour, they draw closer and closer to each other. I've always believed he could charm the pants off any woman but I never imagined he'd charm the likes of *her*," Gorinna observed. "She seems to be completely enamored with him."

"And he with her," Merlin said. "If their relationship blossoms to the point that it bears fruit, it will shake Hell to its very foundations."

"I wonder how her father will react to this once he finds out," Gorinna asked.

"I imagine it will throw him into a tailspin. After all, his only offspring has fallen for a mortal," Merlin said.

"Will they marry?" asked Gorinna.

"Perhaps. It is too soon to tell. If they do, theirs will be a long and happy union," Merlin replied.

"And where does Galya's father fit into all this?" asked Gorinna.

"That, my dear, remains to be seen," Merlin said.

Miles away in Memphis, Hetshepsut decided not to wait until the strange army began to move. She summoned Arkaneton to the throne room and ordered him to prepare the Western Army for the long march across the Libyan Desert.

"Shall I go with them, Mother?" he asked.

"Not unless the situation warrants it. In that case, I want you to take the rest of the army with you. Those strange soldiers must not reach the Nile Valley under any circumstances," she said. "Have Field Marshall Tutmose lead the first wave. General Horem Heb will be his second in command."

Arkaneton nodded.

He fully agreed with Hetshepsut.

"Not one soldier will reach any our cities, even if I have to sacrifice the entire army to prevent that," he assured her.

"Don't be so melodramatic. As in all such cases, use your best judgment. Retreat if you have to. I'll call out the reserves and lead the defense of the Valley personally if push comes to shove. Don't do anything foolish," she said.

Arkaneton agreed with her choice of commanders.

Although he was nearly 70 and walked with a slight limp, Tutmose was Egypt's most reliable and best field commander next to Arkaneton himself. His shaven head and nearly wrinkle free face belied his age as did his seemingly endless energy.

Horem Heb was five years older than Tutmose and was considered loyal, steadfast, courageous and inventive. Both had been personally promoted to their current rank by Hetshepsut for their roles in putting down the rebellion that nearly toppled her dynasty.[5] Along with Admiral Ramses, they were Arkaneton's most trusted field commanders. Like him, they were good at thinking outside the box and trusted their junior officers to make snap decisions to adapt to the ever-changing conditions on a battlefield.

While most of the senior Egyptian commanders shaved their heads in the traditional style, Arkaneton wore his hair shoulder length like his famous father, Arka-Dal. He also preferred to ride a horse during battles instead of the traditional chariots used by most Egyptian generals.

Because he was loved and respected by his soldiers, many of them adopted his more Thulian hairstyle. Many of the younger officers also elected to serve in the cavalry so they could move like lightning across miles of terrain and strike where needed most.

---

5 Read THE DRIVEN

Hetshepsut had created the Egyptian Light Cavalry regiments after observing how their Thulian counterparts performed in combat. She realized they'd be a good augmentation for the charioteers and infantry and gave her commanders more flexibility. Arkaneton then divided them into three distinct groups: lancers, horse archers and scouts. All had more than proven their mettle in battle several times.

He also modified the charioteers.

They now consisted of the heavy three-man chariots whose job it was to punch holes in enemy lines for the smaller, swifter light chariots with a driver and a skilled archer in each, to follow behind them and add to the enemy's confusion.

Horem Heb and Tutmose had also modified the infantry. The heavy infantry was trained in the Thulian style of fighting and could throw up a phalanx in seconds. The light infantry was there to exploit any holes in enemy lines made by the advancing phalanx or cavalry. The light infantry consisted of swordsmen, spearmen and axmen. They wore light chain and leather armor, steel helmets and carried smaller shields. Other infantry units consisted of archers, crossbowmen and peltists (men armed with slings and javelins).

Arkaneton then formed five armies. Each army consisted of two cavalry units, four infantry units, two chariot regiments and the usual support and medical people. In short, he modeled them after the Thulian armies—but on a smaller scale. Thulian armies consisted of 200,000 soldiers. Egyptian armies had only half as many troops at their disposal.

Tutmose and Horem Heb arrived at the palace sometime after midnight and were escorted to the War Room by one of the guards. Arkaneton greeted them warmly as they entered and helped themselves to flagons of chilled wine.

"The Western Army is ready to march," Tutmose reported. "You need only to give the order."

"Excellent. Leave at sunset. March all night and camp during the day to avoid the heat of the desert. Head west across the Libyan Desert and encamp at the oasis of Alquabara. That will be where we draw the line in the sand. Once there, send your scouts out to watch for any signs of an approaching army," Arkaneton said.

"Then you expect them to move soon?" Horem Heb asked.

"I'm not sure. There's no sense taking chances. Once that army moves, I want them stopped before they reach Egypt's population centers. They must not be allowed to reach the Nile," Arkaneton said.

"I understand. Anything else?" Tutmose asked.

"Yes. Take a radioman with you. I want to be notified the moment anything happens. As soon as you engage the enemy, I'll reinforce you with the Central and Eastern Armies," Arkaneton replied.

They finished their wine, rose and saluted. Arkaneton returned the salute and bade them farewell and good-luck. He watched them walk out of the room and shook his head. There were more than a half-million of those strange soldiers. Even with the entire Egyptian army blocking their route, they would be hard to stop. He also wondered if the silver edged weapons and arrows would actually work against them.

"What if Peace is wrong? What if silver doesn't kill them? Then what?" he thought.

The next morning, news reached Arka-Dal of the appearance of two more massive armies. One had suddenly appeared on the Salisbury Plane near Stonehenge. The other had popped up on the central plains of Mongolia. Arka-Dal advised all of the nearby rulers to put their armies on full alert but otherwise do nothing until the armies began to move.

After that, he gathered everyone in the War Room to show him where the armies were positioned. Merlin shook his head.

"That gives our enemy nearly four million soldiers. Each army is positioned where it can strike at the heart of a major nation or empire. Once they march, the world will become involved in a war the likes of which has not been seen since the First Age!" he said.

"We have to discover who is behind this and stop him before he can awaken the Sleeping God," Gorinna added.

"True. But where *is* the lost tomb and *who* is behind all of this? Anyone who thinks they can control one of the Elder Gods after allowing it back into our universe is beyond madness. He *must* be stopped!" Leo said.

"Calm down. We won't get anywhere sitting around arguing about it. I want you all to keep at that riddle. Somewhere in it are the clues we need to get to that tomb before this maniac," Arka-Dal said.

The appearance of two more armies surprised the Devil. He was annoyed that Balaam had summoned them. He also knew he'd keep doing so until he felt he had enough soldiers to overrun the entire world.

But the troops, no matter how numerous, did him no good without the ability to set them in motion and command them. To do that, Balaam had to locate the tomb, find the book and correctly read every spell.

Even the Devil's commanding generals were alarmed by Balaam's actions, but the Devil simply shrugged and told them to stay away—for now.

"If all goes as planned, those armies will never march," he said.

"And if all doesn't go as planned?" asked one of the generals.

"In that event, we either kiss our asses good-bye or got to war against Balaam and the Sleeping God," the Devil said.

"You mean we'd fight alongside the humans?" asked the general.

"I know that sounds like we'd be going against our own natures but you must admit, it beats the alternative," the Devil said.

Galya stood on the balcony watching the sun set and marveling at the rich bands of red, rust and gold that washed over the city. Chatha saw her standing there and walked out to join her. She leaned on the rail and looked her straight in the eyes. Galya sensed Chatha's strong dislike for her.

"Why are you still here?" Chatha asked.

"Arka-Dal invited me to stay as long as I wish and I decided to accept his invitation. There is much here that I like and much more to learn," Galya replied.

"I think you should leave," Chatha said.

"Why?" asked Galya.

"You're too beautiful. I don't trust you and I don't need the competition. Besides, Arka-Dal already has enough wives," Chatha said honestly.

Galya laughed.

"And are you afraid that I will become one of them? You're *jealous* of me?" she asked.

"Yes," Chatha admitted.

Galya liked her directness.

"You flatter me. I am no threat to you nor anyone else in this house. I am certainly not a threat to Arka-Dal!" she said.

"But you were sent to ruin him!" Chatha pointed out.

"That changed the moment I met him. He's different. He even protected me! No man has ever done that before," Galya said.

"Do you love him?" Chatha asked.

"I'm not sure how I feel about him. This is all so new to me. Right now, I'm more concerned with how he feels about me. It's strange. Such things meant little to me before," Galya replied.

"Are you sure you're the Devil's daughter?" Chatha joked.

"Last I looked I was," Galya said with a smile.

"What happened to your wings?" asked Chatha.

"I can shed them whenever I wish. Besides, I'm more comfortable without them now," Galya explained.

Chatha emitted a sigh.

"You're getting harder to dislike," she commented. "But I still don't trust you!"

Galya watched as Chatha left the room and walked down the hall. After the sun completely set, she went downstairs for a drink. She was developing a taste for Thulian brandy.

As she entered the parlor, she saw Mayumi seated on the sofa. She poured herself a brandy at the bar then walked over and sat next to her. As usual, the Empress greeted her with a warm smile.

"You don't seem to be as jealous of me as Chatha and Medusa are," Galya said.

"But I *am* jealous of you. Who *wouldn't* be? You are a most beautiful and alluring woman. I know why you've come, yet I am willing to give you the benefit of the doubt," Mayumi said honestly.

"Thank you. That's very generous of you," Galya said. "No wonder he loves you so much."

She looked at the cats lying about the room. One, a small black male, walked over and rubbed against her legs. She reached down and stroked his back. This made the cat purr contentedly.

Mayumi smiled.

"That is Fred," she said. "He is Aka-san's favorite cat and a good judge of character. Since Fred likes and trusts you, then I shall, too."

"I love cats. Father says they are the most perfect things on Earth—and the most intelligent," Galya said as she continued to pet Fred.

Mayumi giggled.

"Aka-san says the same thing!" she said.

While they talked, Merlin and Gorinna watched from the top of the landing. Gorinna scowled.

"They seem to be hitting it off," Merlin observed.

"Mayumi is like that with everyone. I don't know how she does it," Gorinna said.

"What do you think of our guest?" asked Merlin.

"I still don't trust her. What about you, Merlin? How do you feel about her?" Gorinna asked.

"I've had several run-ins with her over the centuries. She can be quite treacherous and formidable. I don't trust her, either, but we must bow to Arka-Dal's wishes and treat her as a guest," he replied.

"What do you suppose he's up to?" asked Gorinna. "Why is he treating her like this?"

"I believe he's fascinated by her—and curious about her. She seems equally fascinated with him. Whenever she failed in the past, she hurriedly fled the scene. This time, Arka-Dal invited her to stay and she did," Merlin said.

"No one's ever done *that* before. To top it all off, he actually protected her from harm. That had to rattle her," Gorinna said.

"Indeed," said Merlin.

At that very moment, Arka-Dal, Pandaar and Kashi were in the War Room going over plans for when the mysterious armies decided to move. Arka-Dal stood in front of the map while the others drank bottles of ale and went over reports from their scouts in the field.

"Anything new from those armies?" Arka-Dal asked.

"The three we know about still haven't moved. It's like they're waiting for a signal from someone," Kashi said.

"We got a report from Armet in Europe. He's received news of a fourth such army in the northern area known as Finnmark. He's asked the Faeries to check it out," Pandaar added.

"A fourth army? That gives our unknown enemy at least 2,000,000 troops so far. We have to find out who's raising this force and why," Arka-Dal said. "Any ideas?"

"None right now. If Merlin's right, it has something to do with Armenopur and that book he was buried with," Kashi said.

"Merlin *is* right," said Galya as she entered the room and sat down.

"Tell me what you know," Arka-Dal said.

"According to the ancient curse that was placed upon the tomb, only someone who is more evil and black hearted than Armenopur can safely open the sarcophagus. *That* will take some doing. I cannot imagine anyone more evil than Armenopur," Galya said.

"Not even the Devil himself?" asked Kashi.

Galya raised an eyebrow at his remark. Kashi smiled.

"Present company excepted," he said.

She laughed.

"I take no offense. Father must have found a real piece of work. He must be evil incarnate," she said. "Only one who is truly black of heart and soul will be able to command those armies or even enter the lost tomb."

"So your father's behind this?" asked Arka-Dal.

She nodded.

"What I don't understand is *why* Father wants him to find that tomb. I can't imagine what could be in it for him," she said.

"A soul?" asked Arka-Dal.

"No. There has to be something much *bigger* at stake," she said.

They watched as Galya suddenly touched her temples and closed her eyes as an unexpected telepathic message buzzed inside her mind. It was from her father. She'd been blocking him for days now.

"What do you want?" she demanded.

"I want to know how it's going," he said.

"Go away. I'm busy right now," she replied angrily.

"Doing what?" he asked impatiently.

"Living!" she said.

"What does that mean?" he insisted.

"I'll explain later. Maybe," she said as she cut him off.

She sat back and let out a deep breath. She saw the look of concern on Arka-Dal's face and smiled.

"That was Father," she said. "I told him not to bother me."

"How will he take that?" Arka-Dal asked.

"That remains to be seen," she replied.

The road to Meroe was rough and arid. Dust devils swirled up from time-to-time and made it difficult to breathe. By the third day, the dust devils merged into a full sandstorm. Balaam couldn't see and the fine dust plugged his nostrils and tore up his throat. Two days later, he staggered into the small village of Pakumara, which was little more than a dozen or so mud-brick houses clustered around an ancient well.

Balaam stopped at the first house and pounded on the door. After several minutes, the door creaked open and a frightened young boy peered up at him.

"Who are you?" the boy asked.

"I am lost and hungry. I desire food, drink and a place to rest," Balaam said.

The boy opened the door and let him in. Balaam saw a young couple seated near an adobe stove. A pot of gruel was boiling above the fire and a few loaves of crusty bread lay on a nearby table. The man stood up and offered his hand.

"I am Alifaq. I bid you welcome. We have little but I am bound by the laws of hospitality to share it with you," he said.

Balaam sat down near the fire. The man's wife filled a bowl with gruel and passed it to him while the man gave him some bread and a cup of warm water. Balaam ate slowly. The gruel burned his sand-parched throat, but he managed to get it all down. They ate in silence while the small boy clung to his mother and stared at the stranger.

When he finished, Balaam passed his empty bowl to the woman. He suppressed a surprisingly strong urge to rape and strangle her. The urge was so powerful, it took him several heartbeats to bring it under control.

"Thank you," he said hoarsely.

He rose and headed out the door. The family watched as he made his way through the lessening storm, pulling his horse behind him and wondered where the stranger had come from and why he was in such a hurry to leave.

The next afternoon, Gorinna found Arka-Dal seated behind his desk going over a stack of military reports from the various outposts. She walked over and plopped down in the chair next to him. He put down the papers and smiled at her.

"Just *what* are you up to?" she asked.

"Up to? With what?" he queried.

"Not with *what—who,*" she said. "Galya."

"I think you already know the answer to that," he replied.

"Be careful. She's *dangerous—and deceitful and treacherous, too*," she warned.

He beamed at her.

"*All* beautiful women are dangerous—especially *you*," he said. "As for the other things you say she is—I sense neither in Galya. She gave me her word and I believe her. So should you."

"I'll reserve judgment for now. I hope you prove me wrong," Gorinna said.

"I will. You'll see," Arka-Dal assured her. "When I declared her an ambassador from her father, I gave her a status she'd never held before. That status makes her our honored guest and places her under my protection. It also forces Galya to try to act according to the rules of international diplomacy and courtesy. Besides, I *like* Galya."

"So I've noticed," Gorinna pointed out. "I've also noticed that she truly likes *you*."

Arka-Dal laughed.

"Merlin told me that you've kissed her. What did you feel?" asked Gorinna.

"That's very difficult to explain. I felt excited. Warm. Tingly all over. Almost as if I'd been struck by lightning. I think she felt it, too," Arka-Dal said. "I've heard that Galya can bewitch and enslave a man with a single kiss."

"And rob him of his will and senses. But when I look into your eyes, I see that you have not changed. You have not fallen under Galya's spell. No man has ever done that before," Gorinna observed. "Merlin always said your will was strong."

"Oh, I've fallen under Galya's spell alright—just not in the way she expected," Arka-Dal said with a wink. "What will become of it is anyone's guess."

Gorinna laughed.

"From the way Galya's been hovering around you, I'd say that she's fallen under *your* spell, too," she remarked. "What does Mayumi think of all this?"

"She likes Galya. She sees a lot of good in her and thinks of her as a friend. And you know what a good judge of character she is," Arka-Dal replied.

"Mayumi is an excellent judge of character. If she sees much good in Galya, then there must be good in her. I'll keep an eye on her just the same—and another on *you*," Gorinna said as she rose and left the room.

When she turned a corner, she stopped and smiled.

Arka-Dal had called her "beautiful". He had never told her *that* before!

Since it was still quite early, she decided to round up Zhijima for their daily stroll in the rose garden.

Galya had also grown fond of the rose garden. She now took long, daily walks through it to lose herself in the sheer beauty of the roses, marble sculptures and man-made ponds and fountains. Now that she had become a day walker, she developed a deep appreciation and awareness of such things. It was on this afternoon that she became even more aware of the rather special relationship between Gorinna and Zhijima.

She was strolling down one of the narrow paths when the sound of soft moans caught her attention. Curious, she decided to investigate the source of the sound. The path ended at a small, grassy circle surrounding an elaborate fountain. In front of the fountain was a curved marble bench, upon which lay a very naked Zhijima. She was on her back with her legs straddling the bench. Her clothes were neatly piled a few feet away and her eyes were closed. Kneeling in front of her was Gorinna, also naked, with her face buried between Zhijima's thighs.

Galya watched as Zhijima writhed in ecstasy and realized she had arrived at the right moment. Seconds later, the diminutive Dihhuri queen climaxed. While she was still in the throes of her orgasm, Gorinna stood up. That's when Galya saw that she now sported a rather good-sized male member which she had given herself magically. Gorinna mounted Zhijima and proceeded to make wild, passionate love with her. She watched as Gorinna soon groaned loudly and began to move erratically on top of Zhijima, who was also groaning and gasping. Then both emitted loud sighs of relief as they came together.

When Gorinna withdrew, Galya saw that she no longer had the penis. She pulled Zhijima to her feet for a nice, long kiss while they stroked each other between the legs. That's when Galya stepped into the clearing. The two women smiled at her.

"We sometimes do this with the other women in the palace," Gorinna said. "Everyone knows about it. The men even make jokes about it. I seduced Zhijima a few years ago as sort of a joke. Somehow, we fell in love."

"You had a penis. I *saw* it," Galya pointed out.

"I transform myself with a spell. Sometimes, I'm the 'man'. Sometimes I let Zhijima be the 'man'. It enables us to experience the whole range of passionate emotions," Gorinna said.

"You're both very sexy. I wouldn't mind having a turn with either of you myself," Galya said as she ogled their naked bodies.

"Well, I'm always open to new experiences. Anytime you're in the mood, let me know," Gorinna said.

"The same goes for me," Zhijima assured her as she playfully lifted the hem of Galya's already revealing dress and stroked her vagina.

At that instant, Galya's underwear suddenly vanished to make it easier for Zhijima to play with her.

"I want you right now," Zhijima said as she stroked Galya's vagina.

"So do I," added Gorinna.

"Let's do it, then," Galya said as she pulled off her dress and tossed it on the grass.

Two hours later, the three tired, happy, sweaty women returned to the palace and took a nice, long, warm bath together. They joked and drank wine as they bathed. The barriers between them were gone now.

"Have either of ever had sex with Arka-Dal?" Galya asked.

"No!" they both replied in unison.

Gorinna giggled.

"I've always wanted to. But he and Kashi are the best of friends. Arka-Dal would never do anything that might hurt that friendship. Over the years, I've learned to look at him as sort of big brother. I keep my fantasies to myself," she said.

"What about you, Zhijima?" asked Galya.

"I'm in the same boat as Gorinna," she replied. "Besides, he already has four beautiful women he shares his affections with. I doubt he could handle another."

"Four?" asked Galya.

"Sure—counting *you*!" Zhijima explained. "We see the way you look at him. It's plain to see that you've fallen for him."

"I'm *that* transparent?" Galya asked.

They both nodded. She laughed.

"Have you ever been in love before?" Gorinna asked.

"No. Before I met him, men were simply things to be tormented or seduced, then tossed in a trash bin. I thought it would be the same with him, but I was wrong. So very wrong," Galya said.

"Welcome to the club!" said Gorinna and Zhijima as they clinked glasses with her and laughed.

Galya joined Arka-Dal on the balcony just after sunset. He poured her a cup of blue wine. She sipped it slowly to savor its fruity, almost tart flavor.

"Gorinna told me that you, her and Zhijima got to know each other better this afternoon," Arka-Dal teased.

She laughed.

"You could say that," she replied. "Do you realize that most of the people in this house still don't trust me?"

"Trust takes time—especially for someone with *your* history," he said.

"You trust me. Why?" she asked.

"I sense something *good* in you. Something I really like," he said. "You gave me your word and I know that you'll not break it."

She finished the wine and poured herself a refill.

"Careful or you'll get drunk," Arka-Dal cautioned.

"Devils can't become intoxicated, no matter how much we drink," she said.

"How would your father feel if he knew you decided to stay here?" Arka-Dal asked.

"He'd be pissed off—especially if he saw us sitting here like this," she replied.

"What if he orders you to return again?" he asked.

"I'll tell him to go fuck himself. I *like* it here. The longer I stay, the more I like it. I've never been treated so well before. No one has ever trusted me or protected me before. Thank you," she said.

"I'd always wondered what you really looked like," Arka-Dal remarked as he looked her over.

"Now that you've seen me, what do you think?" she asked.

"I think you're a most charming and alluring woman—even with your wings and horns. In fact, you're one of the loveliest women I've ever met," he said truthfully.

"You keep referring to me as woman, instead of a devil, which is what I truly am," she observed.

"You *are* a woman. Besides, there's a little bit of the devil in all of us," he said.

They laughed.

"Father always says that!" she said.

Mayumi walked out onto the balcony, dressed in a silk robe with an intricate floral pattern. She kissed Arka-Dal and greeted Galya with a warm hug.

"What are you talking about?" she asked as she helped herself to a cup of wine.

"We were talking about how my father would feel if he saw the way I was acting here,' Galya replied.

"And how does he expect you to act?" Mayumi asked.

"Like the bitch I've been my entire life," Galya said.

"I don't think you're a bitch," Mayumi said. "In fact, I think you are very nice."

"So do I," Arka-Dal added.

"I think that being here with you brings out a part of me I never knew existed," Galya said.

"Maybe it is the *real* you," Mayumi suggested. "The new you."

"I'm not sure that Father's going to like the new me," Galya said.

"Do you like the new you?" asked Mayumi.

"Yes. I like the new me very much," Galya replied.

"Then that's all that really matters," Mayumi said.

"You are a wise and kind woman," Galya remarked.

Mayumi smiled.

"I do not think of myself that way. I'm just practical. Aka-san says that I look at things with my heart instead of my eyes and that I can find something good in everyone," she said modestly.

"And I wouldn't have it any other way," he said. "That's why we're so perfect for each other."

"We have all anyone could ever wish for," Mayumi said happily.

"That's why I can't seduce you. You neither want nor need anything more as long as you have your love for each other," Galya opined. "I think I'm beginning to understand things a little bit better now."

Days passed.

The Devil hadn't been keeping contact with his daughter. Instead, he amused himself by driving Balaam to distraction with riddles and unnecessary side trips. When he finally decided to check on Galya, he was shocked to discover that she was walking side-by-side with her intended victim in the rose garden.

And they were holding hands!

He tuned in to their conversation. To his surprise, Galya was speaking quite openly with Arka-Dal. He heard her tell him about life on the 666th Plane and share her deepest thoughts with him.

She also seemed quite at ease with him.

Almost *happy*.

He pressed into her mind further and recoiled in shock at what he found. Instead of getting Arka-Dal to surrender his soul to her, his daughter had surrendered *her* soul (if one could call it that) to *him*!

Angry, he contacted her telepathically.

"Why are you still in Thule?" he demanded.

"I choose to remain here," she replied.

"Why?" he asked.

"I like it here. These people are kind to me," she said.

"Kind? Do they not know who you are?" he asked.

"They do but it matters not," she answered.

"You failed to do as I ordered. Kill him now and be done with it—or shall I do it for you?" he said.

"I will not harm him, Father. Nor will I allow you to harm him," she refused.

"And why is that?" he demanded as his patience began to grow thin.

"He protected me," she replied.

"Protected you?" he asked incredulously.

"Merlin and the Witch wanted to slay me the moment they saw me but he stood in front of me and ordered them not to. He also ordered them to treat me with respect and dignity as if I were an ambassador. No human has ever done this before," she said.

"Did he know why you'd come?" the Devil asked.

"Yes," she replied.

"And still he protected you? That's remarkable!" he said.

"He is remarkable, Father," Galya replied. "If you try to harm him or anyone else in this household in any way, shape or form, I will hunt you down and kill you. This I swear by all that is unholy."

He arched a pointed eyebrow at her defiant threat. Galya had never disobeyed him before. Never in all her years, had she threatened to turn on him to protect a human. He knew her well enough to know that her threat was not an idle one. He gave it one last try.

"Come home at once. I order you," he insisted.

"No. I am home. I'd tell you to go to Hell but you are already there," she said defiantly.

He laughed.

"Have it your way—for now," he said as he broke contact.

Galya's betrayal made his game more interesting. He realized that she would probably lead Arka-Dal and his friends to the lost tomb to prove her sincerity and he decided to run with this.

Back in the garden, Galya decided to tell Arka-Dal what had happened.

"Father just contacted me," she said.

"What did he have to say?" Arka-Dal asked.

"He ordered me to return but I refused," she said.

"I hope that doesn't bring you too much trouble," he said.

She laughed.

"I am the Devil's daughter. I am accustomed to trouble. It follows me everywhere. Only this time, I am on the receiving end," she said.

Merlin and Gorinna watched them from the balcony. Merlin shook his head.

"It appears that Galya has designs on Arka-Dal," Gorinna observed. "She hasn't left his side for days and he seems to really enjoy her company."

"This is a most remarkable turn of events indeed," Merlin said.

"Should we do anything about this?" asked Gorinna.

"No. Let nature take its course. If all goes as I hope, Galya will make a very powerful ally," Merlin said.

"Do you believe she's sincere in her affection for him?" Gorinna asked.

"As sincere as her kind can get. She willingly defied her father's wishes to remain with him. That speaks volumes," Merlin said.

"Looks like the Dal family tree is about to sprout a most unusual branch," Gorinna said. "Can she actually bear him children?"

"That remains to be seen," Merlin answered.

"Sometimes I wish that I could bear children," Gorinna said wistfully.

"If you did, you would forfeit your powers and shorten your life span by thousands of years. Such is the curse of being who we are. You know this, too," Merlin said.

"Yes, but I can still dream," she said with a forlorn sigh.

Balaam reached Meroe a week later. He was tired, dusty and thirsty. When he entered the city, he stopped some passersby and got directions to the bazaar. He rode up a wide street for several blocks until he finally came to a rectangular square filled with shops and stalls. The square was hemmed in by cafes, hotels, government buildings and kiosks. The air was thick with the aromas of cooking food and spices and exotic perfumes. The place was alive with shoppers and sellers.

He spotted a tavern at the far end and headed straight for it. As he quenched his considerable thirst and satisfied the rumblings in his belly, he asked the bartender where he could find Kaziri.

A small boy, about eight or so, overheard him and offered to take him to Kaziri as the way was too difficult to describe. He said Kaziri's shop was hard to find unless one knew exactly where it was. Balaam agreed. The boy led him up and down several streets and through some narrow alleys until they came to a dingy looking shop in the middle of a row of run-down houses.

"That is it. That is the shop of Kaziri," the boy said, pointing.

Balaam thanked him and gave him a gold coin. The boy beamed and stuffed it into his pocket, then ran away. Balaam walked up to the shop and rapped on the door. After several seconds, a raspy voice called out.

"Enter," he said.

Balaam pushed the door inward and saw a small, gray haired man with spectacles seated behind the counter. The shop was a tea shop and the man directed Balaam to a seat at the counter.

"What can I get for you?" he asked.

"Are you Kaziri?" Balaam asked.

"That is my name. Do you know me?" Kaziri asked.

"Only by name. An acquaintance of mine directed me to come here. He said that you would help me with my quest," Balaam said.

Kaziri squinted at him then nodded.

Balaam watched as he vanished behind a beaded curtain. He returned holding a large envelope which he placed on the counter before Balaam.

"This is what you seek," he assured him.

Balaam opened the envelope. Inside was a crude, hand-drawn map and a note. He unfolded the note and read it. He looked up at Kaziri.

"This tells me to go west, to a place called Timbuktu. Then I must follow this map north until I come to a mountain shaped like a falcon. That's *weeks* from here!" he complained in disgust.

Kaziri nodded.

"Once you find the mountain, you must recite the spell on the bottom of the map. Then all will be revealed to you," Balaam read aloud.

"Go well armed and provisioned," Kaziri said. "The way is difficult and quite dangerous."

Balaam folded the map and put it in his pouch as he muttered a series of curses under his breath. He thanked Kaziri and left. As the door shut behind him, the old man vanished amid sinister laughter.

"Fool! It's like shooting fish in a barrel!"

Timbuktu was indeed a ruin, a pale shadow that barely hinted at its glorious past. But it was far from deserted. Its deep wells were filled with clean, cool water and the handful of shops that still existed there made it an ideal stopping place for caravans and travelers. Less than 200 people actually lived there. Another hundred or so showed up only when caravans arrived. Then they faded into the desert when the caravans left. They came only to sell food and other needed items. Some were prostitutes and smugglers. After all, even those outside the law need to earn a living.

Peace arrived on the evening when the moon was at its fullest. He had come to Timbuktu to keep an eye on the strange army standing motionless several miles away. A caravan from central Africa had arrived the night before and the narrow streets were now crowded with people. There were guards, merchants, prostitutes, craftsmen, pickpockets and gamblers. A few women had even set up a makeshift brothel in one of the ancient structures. They beckoned to him as he passed by but he respectfully declined.

He saw people laughing, eating, drinking and gambling around campfires. The air was filled with the sound of flutes, stringed instruments and drums and the aroma of cooking food filled his nostrils. Few people bothered to look up when he passed. Those who did simply shrugged and went about their business.

Down a twisting back street, he found the house of Babayar, the scholar-historian of Timbuktu. Babayar had lived there his entire life, during which he spent most of his time gathering up every ancient book and scroll he could find and recopying each of them by hand. Babayar was a white-haired black man with a bushy beard and flashing hazel eyes. The two had known each other for ten years.

Peace opened the door and entered Babayar's house. As soon as Babayar saw him, he rushed to embrace him. After several minutes of pounding each other on the back and shaking hands, the two sat down near the fireplace. Babayar offered Peace a bowl of lentils and steamed rice and a piece of flat, spongy bread.

"It is good to see you again, my friend. You did not stay long the last time. In fact, you left in quite a hurry," Babayar said as he passed him a cup pf cool tea.

"I did so for good reason," Peace replied.

He then went into a long explanation. Babayar listened with great interest. He was aware of the legendary tomb of the Accursed One and had spent much time searching for it. Unlike Balaam, his was strictly a scholarly quest. He was simply seeking the truth.

When Peace finished, Babayar sipped his tea and shook his head.

"If the legends are indeed true, we must locate the tomb before your adversary does and destroy that book. The Necromonicon must not fall into the wrong hands lest tragedy unimaginable befalls us all," he said.

"How goes *your* search for the tomb? Any leads?" asked Peace.

"I found something about 50 miles to the south of Timbuktu. It may be a tomb. Most of it lies beneath the sand so I'm not sure what it is. We could check it out if you like," Babayar offered.

Peace thought about it and shrugged.

"We might as well, my friend. Even if it is not the tomb of Armenopur, it may still be a significant historical find. When can we leave?" he said.

"Tomorrow evening when the sun sets. It's much cooler and easier to travel at night," Babayar said. "For now, rest and make yourself at home. We'll have time enough to find that tomb—if it actually exists."

Peace nodded.

"You doubt it exists then?" he asked.

"Yes—and no. After years of searching and tracking down even the smallest clues, I have yet to come close to discovering its location. Yet the mere presence of those weird soldiers is enough to assure me that there is more than a little bit of truth to the legend," Babayar said.

He sipped his tea and continued.

"The person who summoned forth those armies obviously believes the tomb exists. According to the legends, the spell that will give him complete control over those soldiers is contained somewhere in the pages of that book and *it* is buried with Armenopur. Without that spell, those soldiers are useless."

Peace looked into his eyes.

Babayar was obviously excited by it all. The prospect of locating the tomb got the old man's juices going again.

They set out an hour past sunset the next evening. Besides their horses, they also brought along a pack mule laden with food, water and other gear suitable for excavating a tomb. Babayar was more enthusiastic than Peace could remember seeing him and he talked much of the time.

They followed an old caravan trail south for several miles to a small oasis that consisted of a pool of clear water, three date trees and a few scrubs. The oasis was deserted and Babayar set about pitching a tent.

"This is called Darshalam," he said.

"Place of Quiet," Peace translated. "The name seems appropriate enough. How much further to the ruins?"

"Another four days. We'd better load up on water. This is the last oasis we'll see for about three days," Babayar said.

They broke out cans of meat and sat down to eat. Babayar looked at the rising sun.

"In another hour, it will be far too hot to travel. The Sahara is a cruel mistress. This area is more desolate than most. Hardly anyone comes out this way. Fewer come back," he said.

His comment made Peace feel uneasy. He studied Babayar's face as he ate and wondered what there was about his old friend that seemed somehow different.

"Those soldiers must not be allowed to move. Once they begin their march, nothing—not even silver—can stop them," Babayar said. "If the one you seek finds that tomb and gets his hands on that book, he could very well bring about the end of humankind. If we come across him before we get there, we must kill him at once."

Peace nodded.

Babayar was blunt as usual. He was also right—as usual.

"If we get there before him, all we need do is burn the book so that neither he nor anyone else can make use of what's in it. That way, we won't have to kill anyone," Peace said.

Babayar shook his head.

"It's not that simple, my friend. There are *other* things in that tomb—evil things—that must also never come to light. We must kill him so he can never make use of them," he insisted.

"Are these things worse than the book?" Peace asked.

"*Nothing* is that bad. But there are some things that come fairly close to matching its inherent evil," Babayar said as he wiped the last bit of food from his beard and tossed away the empty can.

Balaam was also on his way to the ancient city. He traveled through the desert for days until, exhausted, he was forced to stop at a small town surrounding an oasis. He took a room at a small, run-down inn and crashed for the night.

The next morning, he staggered from his bed and over to the small wash basin in his room. As he splashed the luke-warm water over his face, he happened to glance at his reflection in the mirror above it. What he saw made him smile.

It was a crooked, evil grin.

His eyes had taken on a darker, more sinister cast. His face and beard were also darker and his lips seemed twisted at the corners. His quest for the ancient tome was having an unexpected—but strangely welcome—effect on the scholar.

He stepped back to study himself carefully.

Gone was the nondescript face of the elderly scholar who had spent most of his life combing through ruins and antique stores in search of the book. Gone was Balaam the wandering antiquarian.

The creature that stared back at him from the mirror was heartless and cruel. It reeked of evil and power.

Balaam smiled.

It was just the look he wanted now. This was the true Balaam. The Balaam who would soon topple the great empires of the world and bring about a new age of chaos and darkness.

"Look out, World! You are about to get a new master!" he said.

Galya saw Mayumi sitting on the balcony and walked out to join her. Mayumi smiled when she say down across from her.

"Your husband intrigues me like no other man I have ever met. When I first arrived, I offered him more power and wealth than any man on Earth could hope for. When he turned me down, I offered myself to him. Why can't I seduce him?" Galya asked.

Mayumi smiled her usual knowing smile. This, too, intrigued Galya.

"As you have discovered, Aka-san cannot be tempted by promises of wealth and power. He has never desired either and has more than he wants of both. Material things hold no interest for him," Mayumi said. "But I believe that you have *already* seduced him. He is very fascinated with you. You interest him on many levels."

"Then why hasn't he put the moves on me?" Galya asked.

"He *already has*. You just have not realized it yet," Mayumi said. "Aka-san *wants* you, Galya. He wants you very much. But you come with too many strings attached. Too many conditions. If you want him, you must *cut* those strings. Love must be unconditional or it is not love at all."

"Love?" asked Galya.

"Hai. I see it by the way you hang on his every word. I see by the way you follow him everywhere he goes and the way you hold his hand when you walk together. Mostly, I see it in your eyes when you look at him. You do not realize this yet, perhaps because you have never experienced it before. You *love* Aka-san," Mayumi said.

"Gorinna and Zhijima have said the same thing. Am I so easy to read?" Galya asked.

"Hai. Also, if you didn't love him, you would have left the moment you realized that you failed your assignment. Instead, you stayed, Galya. Now, I don't think you will ever leave Thule," Mayumi said.

Galya smiled at her.

"How did you grow so wise in but a single lifetime?" she asked.

"I am not wise. I just know how to read people, especially those I truly like," Mayumi replied.

To Galya's surprise, she discovered she enjoyed being in the company of Arka-Dal's children and they took a liking to her. She'd never really spent much time with children before and she took great pleasure in watching them at play or going through their daily lessons with Leo, Gorinna and their parents.

She found herself spending a lot of her time with them. They drew her into their games and made her feel as if she was one of the family. Like Arka-Dal, they showed no fear of her and seemed genuinely interested in learning about where she came from and her famous father.

She good-naturedly answered all of their questions and even amused them with simple illusions and magic tricks.

Arka-Dal was as good a father as any child could want. When he wasn't busy training to tending to affairs of state, he was playing with the children or teaching them things. He taught them to ride horses, swim, climb and how to make campfires, paddle boats and pitch tents. He taught them how to hunt and fish and to perform basic first aid on wounds, scrapes and cuts. He wrestled and rough-housed with them. Played baseball and taught them about life in general.

More important, he listened when they spoke, answered their questions and taught them how to figure things out for themselves. He encouraged them to learn new things, explore new places. Above all, he taught them how to be themselves.

Galya was amazed at the amount of time he dedicated to them and how much they enjoyed each others' company.

She was also surprised to learn that the Dal children had many playmates and friends outside the palace. Some of them were frequent guests in the house and often joined Arka-Dal's children for team sports on one of the many open fields near the palace and within the rose garden.

"Although my children are growing up in the palace, that doesn't make them better or superior to anyone else. The time will come when they must move beyond this house and make their own ways in the world. That's why I think it's very important they develop strong friendships with people outside the family. I did," Arka-Dal explained.

Galya also discovered that he was on a first-name basis with many of their parents. In fact, he knew most of them intimately. This familiarity surprised her and she told him so. He smiled.

"I am Emperor only because the people of Thule chose me to be so. Leo and the senate changed the Constitution to make the job a lifetime one in order to help stabilize and establish the Empire. They came up with the title not to set me above everyone else but because they couldn't think of anything else to call me," he said.

"There are no class distinctions, titles or castes in Thule. Here, everyone is equal. Everyone can rise as high and far as their talents and ambitions can take them. That's one of the things I insisted upon putting into the Constitution when Leo and I sat down to write it. Here, no one is above the laws of the land. Not even me," he added.

"You sound much like someone I knew many centuries ago. Perhaps you've heard of him? His name was Thomas Jefferson," Galya said.

"His writings are the very foundations of Thule," Arka-Dal said. "I even had a statue of him placed inside the Hall of Heroes, along with Washington, Franklin and Madison. Leo taught me about them when I was a young man. They became my inspirations."

"That's remarkable. No wonder I've sensed many of their traits in you. No wonder your people think you're a wonderful ruler. You're wonderful with your children, too" she said as they walked into the parlor.

"You're pretty good with them yourself. They really like being around you," Arka-Dal observed.

"I enjoy spending time with them. They're delightful to be with," Galya said.

"I think you'll make an excellent mother," he said.

"Me? A mother?" she piped, taken aback by his remark.

He nodded.

"Mayumi thinks you'll be a wonderful mother, too. Has such a thought ever occurred to you?" he asked.

"Not until this very moment. You really think I'd make a good mother?" she asked.

"From the way you interact with my children, you most certainly would. And if our future children look anything like you, they'll be exceptionally beautiful," he said.

Galya stared at him.

"Did you say *our children*? Did you just say what I think you said?" she asked.

Before he could answer, the children charged into the parlor and dragged their father off to the garden to play baseball. Galya plopped down on the sofa to think.

"He said 'our children'. I know I heard it. Was it just a slip of the tongue or did he mean it?" she wondered.

The more she thought about it, the more she smiled.

Mayumi was seated at the heavy wooden table in the kitchen chopping vegetables for the evening meal when Chatha and Medusa walked in. They sat down with her and began helping with the preparations. They chatted casually while they worked. Then Chatha steered their conversation to the subject of their visitor.

From the way they talked, Mayumi sensed they were both jealous and distrustful of Galya. Especially Chatha. It had taken her a long time to grow accustomed to sharing Arka-Dal with two other women and she didn't exactly relish the thought of sharing him with yet another. Mayumi listened to her rant and smiled. The smile annoyed Chatha.

"Aren't *you* bothered with Galya's presence?" Chatha asked.

"Not really. In fact, I like her," Mayumi replied honestly.

"Why?" asked Medusa.

"She loves Aka-san as much as we do. That is why I do not feel jealous of her or mistrust her," Mayumi answered.

"So you feel she is sincere?" asked Chatha.

Mayumi nodded.

"I see it in her eyes and the way she hangs on his every word. It is much the way we all look upon him, don't you think? Also, since she has been with him, she appears to be softer and gentler. She has shed her wings and is allowing a side of herself to emerge that she has long hidden. Love has changed Galya for the better," she said.

Medusa and Chatha nodded in agreement. Even they could see the difference in her. The changes made Galya seem more beautiful and seductively feminine than ever. This caused Chatha to feel even more insecure. She was afraid that Arka-Dal would pay less attention to her from now on. After all, Galya was drop-dead gorgeous.

Medusa was more at ease with herself and the situation. She was more than willing to share Arka-Dal with Chatha and Mayumi. After all, the three women were closer than sisters now. They would do anything for each other and Arka-Dal. If he did indeed marry Galya, she would treat her the same way.

But could the Devil's daughter change her stripes so easily?

Mayumi trusted Galya and she was a superb judge of character. Normally, this would be enough to quell any misgivings.

But Galya was different.

She had a very long history behind her. None of it was good.

Mayumi noticed the expression on Medusa's face and touched her hand.

"Do not worry. All will be well. You'll see," she said assuringly.

"But she's the Devil's daughter," Medusa pointed out.

"She may be the Devil's daughter, but she loves Aka-san. *Nothing* will ever change that!" Mayumi said.

Galya sat on the edge of Arka-Dal's desk with her legs slightly parted. His gaze traveled up her thighs to the dark triangle between them. Galya saw the front of his pants move and parted her legs even more. He smiled.

"You're a most interesting man," she said. "Other men would be falling all over themselves to have sex with me. Yet you keep resisting me. Why? Don't you want to have sex with me?"

"I would love to have sex with you," he replied.

"Why don't you?" she pressed.

"You were *sent* here to seduce me," he said.

"And I failed!" she said.

"No. You didn't fail. You've succeeded but not in the way you planned. I'd be lying if I said I wasn't attracted to you. You're the most alluringly beautiful woman I've ever known and I grow fonder of you with each passing day," he said.

To emphasize this, he took her in his arms and kissed her. It was a deep, lingering kiss that sent waves of excitement racing through them both. After a while, Galya broke off the kiss and smiled at him.

"I've never felt anything like *that* before," she said softly. "You really *do* want me!"

"Yes, I want you but only on your terms. When you truly want it and with no strings attached. In short, I want to make love with you," he said.

"Love?" she asked.

"Yes. We'll do it because you *want* to—not because you've been *told* to," he said as he placed his hand on her thigh.

He noticed that she felt much warmer than other women.

Almost hot.

"My body temperature is five degrees higher than a human's," she explained as she opened her legs as wide as she could. She watched his hand slide slowly upward and smiled. "And *that* part is hotter still!"

Deep on the Lower Planes, the Devil and some of his minions watched as Arka-Dal and Galya made love. He'd seen her do this many times. Yet this time, it was different. There was real passion to it. Real feelings. They seemed perfect for each other.

"You must feel pleased. Your daughter has seduced the Thulian Emperor," one of the demons said.

"That was more of a *mutual* seduction. Galya gave herself to him of her own free will. No deal was struck. No contract was signed," the Devil said sourly.

"Interesting. Now what happens?" asked the demon.

"I have no idea. Galya will likely do what she sees fit from now on," the Devil replied.

"You must teach her the consequences of her betrayal. You must show her that such things will not be tolerated," the demon stressed.

"Don't presume to tell me how to handle my own daughter!" the Devil said as he turned the demon into a large pile of variously colored mice.

The others watched the rodents scurry in all directions and melted back into the shadows. The Devil glared at them.

"Anyone else have a suggestion?" he demanded.

Silence.

He smiled.

"I thought not," he said.

He returned to eavesdropping on Arka-Dal and Galya. He heard her moan and call out.

"I love you!" she cried.

The words stung him like a slap in the face.

From his room at the inn, Balaam put the word out that he was seeking two men to guide him across the desert to Timbuktu and he offered a sizeable reward. Two days later, he was approached in a tavern by a tall, dark-skinned man with blue eyes and a goatee and his shorter, lighter companion. Both men wore typical Taureg garb and carried swords. The tall man introduced himself as Harvata and his companion as Ali. After a little bit of haggling, they agreed to guide Balaam to Timbuktu.

Balaam had agreed to pay each of them 100 pieces of silver for their services, but he had no intention of living up to his part of the bargain. After all, he reasoned, dead men had no need of cash.

Harvata and Ali had a similar fate in mind for Balaam. They planned to take him deep into the desert and kill him. Once he was dead, they would take everything of value he had and vanish to parts unknown.

They took the trail south for two days, then turned northwest. They skirted the southern border of Egypt for three more days and nights then entered the desolate Western Sahara. Balaam noticed that his guides seemed to be avoiding the better known caravan routes for some reason and figured that something was up. As they rode across the hot sand, he smiled to himself.

"I'm in good company," he thought. "We three deserve each other."

To avoid the scorching heat, they traveled by night and rested during the day. They saw no towns, no villages nor any other human beings during their trek and the only animals sounds came from hyenas screeching in the distance. Each afternoon, while his guides slept, Balaam went for walk to think about his situation. On the 14th day of travel, a large hyena approached him. He drew his dagger to ward off a possible attack. To his surprise, the animal spoke.

"Stay your hand, Balaam. It's only me," it said.

"And just *who* are you?" he demanded warily.

The hyena smiled and an image of an all-too-familiar face flashed through Balaam's mind. He sheathed his dagger and sat down on a dune. The hyena walked over and sat before him.

"Come to torment me with more riddles?" Balaam asked.

"I have come to tell you that your goal is in sight. Timbuktu lies 24 miles to the north. You know where to go from there," the animal said.

Balaam nodded.

"I know what you plan for your guides. A heartless bastard such as you would not plan otherwise. In this case, you're justified. Your guides plan to kill and rob you. This is common practice among their kind. Out here, there is no law. No one can touch them," the hyena said.

"I wonder why they haven't tried to kill me already? They've had many chances," Balaam mused.

"They want to make sure no one will ever find your corpse. In any case, they are now expendable. You no longer need them to find Timbuktu," the hyena said as it vanished into thin air.

Balaam smiled.

Two days later, he arrived in Timbuktu.

He was alone.

Galya spent much of her time getting to know the other women. She observed how they handled their collective children and began to wonder what it would be like to have one or two of her own.

Mayumi had already accepted and befriended her, mostly because she knew how she felt about Arka-Dal and the fact that he trusted her. She was sure that Galya would never betray that trust, even if it meant taking on her father in combat.

Chatha had been slow to warm up to her. She considered Galya a rival for Arka-Dal's affections. A *dangerous* one, at that. Despite her misgivings, she eventually grew to like her.

Medusa still wasn't convinced of Galya's intentions and told her so. She also threatened to turn her into a statue if she attempted to harm anyone in the palace.

Zhijima felt the same way Mayumi did. In fact, she was completely fascinated with the beautiful Devil and spent much of their time together asking her questions about her life on the Lower Planes.

Gorinna had also warmed up to her, especially after their interlude in the garden. But she still kept a close watch on her. The Red Witch didn't trust Galya and was very protective of her friends.

Galya understood this.

Trust took time. She had to *earn* it. Given her colorful past, she knew this wouldn't be easy.

Her relationship with Arka-Dal had already blossomed into an all-out love affair. For the first time ever, she willingly gave herself to someone with no strings attached. And he had given himself to her.

One morning as they walked hand-in-hand through the rose garden, she turned to him and spoke the words she never imagined she'd speak.

"I love you."

And she meant them. When Arka-Dal replied that he loved her, too, her heart took on wings. She laughed, cried tears of joy and almost sang all at the same time. She threw her arms around his neck and they kissed for a very long while.

That's when they felt the ground rumble beneath their feet. They looked up just as four, powerfully built, black and scaly demons with huge wings emerged from the earth and glared hatefully at them.

Both she and Arka-Dal went into defensive stances.

"Why are you here?" Galya demanded.

"Your father sent us to slay the human and bring you back to him," they replied in one deep voice.

"Leave now or I swear I'll make you suffer. You *know* what I can do!" she challenged.

"We have our instructions," the demons said as they swirled around them a few times and lunged.

To Galya's surprise, Arka-Dal stepped in front of her and punched the nearest demon square on the nose with all of his strength. The creature recoiled in surprise but moved in again. Before it could lay its hands on Arka-Dal, Galya struck it with a lightning bolt. The demon shrieked in pain and horror as it slowly melted into a steamy pool of bubbling ichor. The others lunged at Galya. Arka-Dal leapt at the nearest and seized it by the throat with both hands. Both he and the demon then tumbled to the ground and began exchanging blows and curses. The others went after Galya—much to their dismay.

She pointed a finger at each of them and uttered a spell. Almost instantly, they were changed into harmless swarms of colorful butterflies and moths. She turned in time to see the demon straddling

Arka-Dal's motionless body. Angered beyond words, she unleashed all of her fury at it. It imploded and fell to earth as a cloud of fine, black powder.

She raced over and cradled his head in her arms. She felt relieved when she saw he had only had the wind knocked out of him. He smiled up at her.

"Thank the Gods! You're all right!" he said as she helped him up. "You shouldn't have done that. Those demons would have killed you."

"I couldn't just stand there and let them threaten you, even at the risk of my life," he said. "Could they have killed you?"

"Working together they would have been too powerful for me to overcome. When you jumped in, you forced them to act individually. That weakened them enough so I could destroy them. But you didn't know that, did you?" Galya explained.

"No. I saw you were being threatened and I acted," he replied.

"You *saved* me!" she said.

"And you saved me," he pointed out.

"Is that was love is?" she asked as a thousand different emotions seemed to race through her mind and heart.

"Partly," he replied as they walked back to the palace.

The Devil had watched the turn of events from deep within his lair. Needless to say, he was more than a little surprised with the outcome. Instead of fleeing from the powerful demons like any normal man would, Arka-Dal fought with all of his might to protect Galya—and she had done the same for him.

"Most interesting. I may have to rethink my strategy," he mused.

That's when he heard Galya's angry voice inside his head.

"Father, you son of a bitch! If you do anything like this again, I'll kill you, even if I have to destroy all of the Lower Planes to do it!"

He had never seen her so angry before. From the tone of her voice, he knew that she meant every single word. His daughter did not make idle threats. He also realized that he could never force her to return.

He had sent his only daughter to seduce Arka-Dal. Instead, it had become a mutual seduction. He knew he'd have to deal with her at another time. For now, he had other fish to fry.

"It is time to put yet another twist in this plot," he said.

Later that evening, Galya sought out Merlin. She found him standing on the roof watching the sunset. He smiled at her.

He knew how she felt about Arka-Dal. He also knew that love was an alien emotion for a Devil, albeit a strong one.

"I saw what happened in the garden today. It was beautiful," he said. "In fact, we *all* saw it."

"Is love always like this?" she asked.

"Love is about sacrifice. It is about being willing to give up part or all of yourself for the benefit of the one you love. It is the strongest of emotions. It's what makes humans who they are," Merlin explained. "In time, you will understand."

They walked down to the parlor. Merlin poured them both drinks and they sat down on the couch together. They sipped in silence for a little while. Then Galya spoke.

"Arka-Dal is so different from any man I've ever met. He is *unique*," she mused. "He has none of the flaws that brought about the downfall of Arthur and your beloved Camelot."

"Jealousy brought Arthur to ruin and cost him his life. Arka-Dal is above all of that. His inner strength and character are remarkable. That is why I bestowed Excalibur upon him," Merlin said as he nodded at the shining sword above the mantle.

She stared at the sword.

"So *that* is the famous sword you once gave to Arthur! I've never seen it before," she said as she walked over to the mantle.

The sword seemed almost beautiful.

"So *he* is the "once and future king"?" she asked. "The one whose coming was foretold ages ago?"

Merlin nodded.

"If Thule is the new 'shining city on the hill', I vow that I will never let it go the way of Camelot," Galya pledged as she lightly ran her fingertips along the blade of Excalibur.

She felt the incredible power within the sword and knew that it could slay her with a single blow. Not even her magic could prevent that. She also knew that she need never fear it again.

Merlin heard her pledge and was totally floored by it. Galya and her father had gone through great pains to destroy Camelot. To hear her pledge to protect Thule from a similar fate left him speechless. Her pledge had also cast their relationship in an entirely new light. It had, in effect, made them *allies*.

Galya sat down on the couch. At the same moment, Fred jumped up and made himself comfortable in her lap. The cat purred loudly as she stroked him.

Merlin smiled.

Fred was never wrong.

Balaam's trek to Timbuktu had been an exceptionally bloody one. By the time he reached the ancient city, he had ruthlessly murdered a dozen unwary travelers, most of whom had made the mistake of inviting him into their camps. He slew men, women and children with uncommon delight. He even forced one of his victims to eat his own genitals. Another, he skinned alive and staked him out in the desert for jackals and vultures to feast upon.

Even the Devil winced at his behavior.

"Never in all my years have I encountered one whose heart and soul is so black, so devoid of compassion. This one makes Stalin look like a Catholic nun! His deeds make my blood run cold," he said. "This makes him the perfect man for the task I need completed."

"And when he completes that task? Then what?" asked a nearby demon.

"I will fulfill of the provisions in his contract to the letter as usual. He will get *exactly* what he desires. No more. No less," the Devil replied.

As Balaam walked through the now busy streets of Timbuktu, he was accosted by a pretty young woman. She beckoned him to join her for a night of pleasure in one of the small buildings nearby. He leered wickedly at her.

"How much?" he asked.

"Ten drachma," she replied.

"And what do I get for it?" he asked.

"Anything you like," she assured him.

He followed her inside. After nearly an hour and a half of rolling around on her makeshift bed, Balaam finally felt sated. He got up and dressed. She watched him and, as he turned to leave, she held out her hand.

"Ah, yes. Payment," he said.

He drew his dagger and plunged it right into the horrified girl's windpipe. As she struggled to breathe, he slit her throat from ear to ear and watched with glee as the life left her body in a waterfall of blood. He watched her crumple to the floor and laughed as he wiped the blade of his dagger off on her gown. Just before he left, he tossed ten drachma on her lifeless body.

"That felt good," he said as he went into the night.

In fact, he enjoyed that even more than the slaying of his two guides the evening before. He had slit their jugulars and took enormous pleasure in watching their lives gurgle out of them. He especially enjoyed the look of terror on their faces.

The Devil watched from his lair and laughed.

The first spell had done its work only too well. Once Balaam used it to summon forth his armies, his darker, evil side was released. In time, it obliterated all of his built-in controls.

The real Balaam was a totally evil and heartless monster. He had been held in check only by the fear of being caught and punished. That fear was gone now. Balaam didn't care. The personality that had held his evil side in check was now completely obliterated. He not only killed indiscriminately, he did it for the sheer pleasure it brought him.

"This one is a real piece of work. He's totally mine now. If anyone ever belonged on the Lower Planes, it is this one," the Devil mused.

Balaam left Timbuktu at sunrise, trailing a pack mule behind him laden with enough food and water to last for weeks. He had taken the supplies from three unwary merchants who had bargained with him in good faith, only to have the murderous madman slit their throats rather than pay for their goods.

Balaam found that he *loved* to kill.

It made him feel strong and powerful.

Godlike.

It was like a thirst he couldn't quench. The more he killed, the more he enjoyed it. It intoxicated him.

Soon, he thought, he would slaughter *millions.* Those who did not die in the coming battles would become his slaves. He would brutalize them and force them to labor on his monuments. He would have them erect huge statues of himself then force them to kneel down and worship him. If they didn't do as he said, he'd have them all killed.

Then he laughed.

"Perhaps I will kill them anyway," he said.

Peace and Babayar made their way ever southward. After three days and nights, they came upon a series of ancient foundations that had been all but buried beneath the shifting sands. The foundations once supported a large stone structure. Babayar said it was once a temple built to honor a long-forgotten goddess.

"There is a pile of small rocks in the middle of the place. If I'm right, they cover the entrance to some sort of tomb," he explained as he led Peace to the stones.

They studied them for a while.

"Do you think this is the tomb of Armenopur?" Peace asked.

"There is but one way to know for sure. Let us remove the rocks," Babayar said.

They labored away on the pile for several minutes. Babayar stopped to get a drink of water. He watched Peace work while he drank from the canteen, then capped it and drew his dirk. He crept up behind him, raised the dagger over his head and brought it down. Peace turned and seized his wrist. In the same instant, he drew his own dagger and plunged it into Babayar's heart. Babayar dropped his dirk and stared at Peace as he slowly fell to the ground.

"I was wondering when you'd reveal yourself," Peace said as he wiped the blood from his dagger and put it away. Just before he did, he held it up and smiled.

"Silver," he said.

Babayar shook his head.

"How did you know?" he gasped.

"The tone of your voice sounded different. Unfamiliar. You're a good copy but also an imperfect one," Peace replied.

The creature slowly assumed its true, demonic form before it died and turned to dust. Peace shook his head.

"It's safe to assume that you slew the real Babayar. Too bad. He was good friend and a wonderful scholar. I guess he came too close to the truth," he said. "You gave yourself away by knowing too much. Babayar searched for the tomb for decades without success and knew nothing about the book buried with Armenopur. That slip-up blew your cover, demon."

He looked around.

He was alone in the middle of a deserted ruin with no idea where the tomb was. His reason told him that since the demon was leading him south, the tomb most likely lied to the north.

But how far north?

And how would he know it if he found it?

He sat down on a pile of rubble to ponder his predicament.

A puff of smoke exploded next to him. He leapt to his feet and watched as a familiar—and sinister form—appeared. Peace took a swing at him only to have his fist pass harmlessly through him as if he weren't there.

The Devil wiggled his index finger at him.

"Now, now—let's not get nasty," he said. "I see you've survived. I don't know how you saw through his disguise. He was a good copy."

"Good—but not *perfect*," Peace said as he warily sat back down. "What do *you* want?"

"That's better. Now to business. I have come to help you," the Devil said.

"And just *why* would you do that?" asked Peace.

"Let us say that I have my reasons and leave it at that," the Devil replied.

"I don't *trust* you," Peace said.

"I'm not asking you to trust me. I have come to offer help. Do you want it or not?" the Devil asked.

"What kind of help?" asked Peace.

"You seek a certain tomb. So does another man whose intentions are darker than the night itself. The tomb lies seven days ride to the north and east of here. You will know its location when you come to the mountain shaped like a falcon's head," the Devil said.

"You're giving me directions to the tomb? Why? What's in it for you?" Peace asked.

"Everything, perhaps—and nothing," he said as he vanished.

Peace shook his head.

He mounted his horse and rode north, more certain than ever before that he was merely a playing piece in some bizarre game where the rules constantly changed.

The longer Galya spent with her new friends, the more she changed. She took on a softer, more feminine appearance and grew more and more relaxed. She enjoyed being in the company of Mayumi and the children and the pretty Empress had taken the time to show her how to cook Arka-Dal's favorite dishes and even how to sew. To Galya's delight, she discovered she had a knack for both.

Leo also loved having her around. She proved to be an endless and most reliable source of information on the workings of the Lower

Planes and her infamous father. She knew that this probably vexed her father but she didn't care.

"He'll get over it, Leo," she said. "He has no choice in the matter anyway."

She had even gone so far as to teach Gorinna and Merlin some of her more potent spells. This *really* annoyed her father. When he ordered her to stop, she told him to "fuck off". He grumbled but backed down. There was little he could do to stop her and she knew it. Galya was his equal in power and ferocity when angered.

And she *was* changing.

He wondered how far she'd actually go.

Was he about to lose her forever?

Was she really in love with Arka-Dal?

He put aside his thoughts and turned his attention to Balaam.

The man's evil knew no bounds.

Two days outside of Timbuktu, he came upon a wagon parked next to a campfire. Seated near the fire were a young couple and their six-year-old daughter. They were headed for Timbuktu for supplies and water as they were low on both. Still, they offered to share what they had with him.

He graciously accepted their offer. That night, he pounced on the man while he slept and bound him hand and foot to a wheel on the wagon. While he sat helpless, Balaam brutally raped and beat his wife while their little girl screamed in terror and tried to pull him off her. Balaam backhanded the girl. She fell to the ground unconscious. He laughed, turned her mother over and raped her again.

He then tied her to the wheel and forced them both to watch while he raped the poor, terrified child at least three times. He took particular delight in this. It made him feel powerful.

Almost like a god.

His evil lust thus sated, he drew his dagger and slit the girl's throat while her parents begged him for mercy. He then walked to the woman and did the same. As the light faded from her eyes, the last thing she saw was Balaam murdering her husband.

He took their food and water, tied it to his saddle and continued on his way, leaving the corpses of the murdered family to the vultures now circling overhead.

His black hearted brutality surprised the Devil. He'd rarely seen anyone who took such pleasure in killing helpless people. He knew that if Balaam got his way, he'd try to exterminate everyone on Earth.

But that wasn't what he had in mind.

Balaam was a pawn.

Nothing more.

He'd get what he bargained for. A contract was a contract and he always kept his word. But there was always a catch.

"As the Romans used to say: Caveat emptor. Let the buyer beware," he said with a smirk.

He decided to check in on Galya again.

She was seated on a marble bench in the rose garden staring into a pond while she contemplated her future. She was in love with Arka-Dal. And he also loved her. She knew this but wasn't quite sure how to handle it.

She also loved his friends.

They had all treated her with open affection.

She felt trusted.

Wanted.

Her thoughts were interrupted by her father.

"You seem troubled. I can sense it," he said.

"I am. More so than ever before. I have a huge decision to make," she replied.

"After what you did to my minions, I believe that you've already decided," he pointed out. "Do you understand the consequences?"

"Yes," she replied with certainty.

"In effect, you will become mortal. Are you prepared to make such a sacrifice?" he asked.

"Yes. I also meant what I said earlier. Try to harm him or anyone else in this house and I will hunt you down and kill you, even if I must destroy the entire universe to do so," she warned.

She heard him laugh.

"You find that amusing?" she queried.

"I find it amusing because I know that you mean every word of it. How does he feel about you?" the Devil asked.

"The same," she replied with a warm smile.

"Are you certain?" he asked.

"Yes. A woman knows such things. Words aren't necessary," she said. "Why are you showing such concern?"

"I don't want to see you get hurt," he said. "We will speak again soon."

Galya smiled.

This was the first time her father had shown any true concern for her well-being in eons. She also noticed that he had placed no demands on her.

Had he conceded defeat?

Or did he have something else up his sleeve?

At that moment, Arka-Dal and Mayumi were enjoying a nice lunch on the balcony overlooking the garden. From where they sat, they could easily see Galya walking along the trail with her hands behind her back.

"You love her, don't you?" Mayumi asked.

"Yes," he admitted.

As much as you do me?" she asked.

"I don't love anyone as much as I do you. You are my heart and soul. My very reason to exist," he said softly.

"It is good to hear you say that, even though I know it's true. I think you should marry her," Mayumi suggested.

"Why?" he asked.

"It would be best for both of you—and for everyone else. Her father would make a most interesting friend," she replied.

"Or become totally enraged. He's not real thrilled with the current situation. His daughter has fallen in love with a mere mortal. He feels betrayed," Arka-Dal said.

"You are no *mere mortal*," came a voice from the doorway.

They smiled as Galya walked onto the balcony and sat down across from them.

"That's quite a compliment. I hope I can live up to it," Arka-Dal said modestly.

Galya laughed.

Her laughter seemed lighter.

Happier.

"You have already exceeded it," she said.

"How long were you standing there?" he asked.

"Long enough to be assured that your feelings toward me are genuine and to hear what you said about Mayumi. Do you feel the same about your other wives?" she asked as she picked up an apple and bit into it.

"To a lesser degree I do. They understand and accept this. Besides, they are as close as sisters now. The best of friends, too," Arka-Dal assured her.

"Do I fit into that category now?" asked Galya.

"I think you're in a category all your own. You're rather special," he said.

Galya closed her eyes and wiped away some tears. As she did, she wondered how her father would react if he saw her cry—even tears of joy as these were. A princess of the Lower Planes simply didn't show such human weaknesses. Then again, no one had ever said that they love her, either.

When she opened her eyes, she was surprised to see Arka-Dal down on one knee before her. He took her hand in his looked deep into her eyes.

"Will you do me the honor of becoming my bride?" he asked.

Speechless, she looked at Mayumi. The Empress smiled and nodded approvingly. Galya threw her arms around his neck and kissed him with all of the passion she had inside of her.

"Yes!" she cried. "Yes! I will marry you!"

She brushed away her tears and beamed at him.

"I want children, too. Many children!" she said.

"As potent as Aka-san is, I am sure you will get your wish very soon," Mayumi said as she hugged them both warmly. "At the rate he's going, the world will soon be filled with Dals."

He laughed.

"Oh, by the way, I was concentrating on helping you find out who's behind all this trouble. The name Balaam came into my head. In a long-dead tongue, it means 'The Foul One'," Galya said when she regained her composure.

"Does he live up to it?" Arka-Dal asked.

"In *spades*! I sensed an evil so dark, so deep and so cold that it made me shiver with dread—and *that's* saying a lot!" she said.

"Where's he now?" asked Arka-Dal.

"I don't know. His whereabouts are being cloaked. It's probably Father's doing. Balaam must have made a contract with him," she replied.

"Good work," Arka-Dal said as he kissed her on the lips.

"Thank you. That's the first time anyone's ever called my work *good*. It sounds so odd," she joked.

Galya was now beside herself. Still stunned by Arka-Dal's proposal, she headed up to the roof to clear her mind. A series of emotions flooded into her. She wanted to sing, dance, laugh and weep for joy all at once.

Arka-Dal loved her.

No one had ever spoken those words to her before. What's more, he meant it. He really and truly loved her. Enough to ask her to marry him.

She hugged herself and did several pirouettes as she looked up at the sun.

"He loves me! He really loves me!"

She almost sang the words. She'd never felt like this before.

As she skipped and danced giddily on the roof, Merlin smiled at the wonder of it all. Galya, the hated daughter of the Devil, was in love with a mortal. It was enough to make one believe in miracles.

Galya spun around and opened her arms wide. That's when she saw Merlin. She lowered her arms and smiled.

"How long have you been standing there?" she asked.

"Long enough to watch you dance. You look truly happy," he observed.

"I *am* happy. In fact, I'm *beyond* happy. I have no words to describe exactly how I feel right now. It's as if a great weight has been lifted from me. Arka-Dal loves me!" she almost sang the last words.

Merlin shook his head.

Galya scowled at him.

"I see you still don't approve of me. Nor do you trust me. That matters not. All that really matters is that Arka-Dal loves me and I love him. We don't need yours or anyone else's approval," she said.

"And what of his wives? Don't you want their approval?" he asked.

"I have already befriended Mayumi. The others will come around once they get to know me better," she replied.

"What of your father? What will he say about this?" Merlin asked.

She shrugged.

"I don't care. Arka-Dal and I are to be wed and there's nothing he can do about it. Besides, I've already told him what I'd do to him if he interfered. He knows I mean it, too," she said.

Merlin smiled.

He saw she was sincere. There was no way to fake such happiness. She was madly in love with Arka-Dal and he with her. This was something even *he* didn't foresee. He left and went down to the parlor for a drink. As he walked to the bar, he spotted Gorinna leaning back on the sofa with a drink in her hand. He walked over and sat beside her.

"Is Galya still dancing on the roof?" she asked.

"Yes. I've never seen anything like it. She seems truly elated," Merlin replied as he sipped his ale.

"If Arka-Dal told *me* he loved me, I'd probably be dancing on the roof myself right now," she remarked. "Unfortunately, I'll never hear those words from him."

"You sound jealous of Galya," Merlin pointed out.

"I'm a little bit jealous of *all* his wives," she admitted. "They get to sleep with him. He barely notices me."

"Oh, he notices you alright," Merlin assured her. "It's just that you're married. To him, that makes you forbidden fruit. This is good. We don't need another Camelot."

She laughed.

"That still vexes you?" she asked.

"Indeed it does. I failed to see Arthur's character flaws until it was too late. I don't want that to happen here," he said.

"You worry needlessly, Merlin. Arka-Dal is above all the weaknesses that plagued Arthur. After all, who but *he* could charm the likes of Galya?" Gorinna said. "I wish them the best. I know they'll be happy together."

The Devil watched his daughter dance and spin and laugh. The sight fascinated him. He'd never seen her act this way and never imagined she would.

"You've lost your mind!" he transmitted via thought.

"Not my mind, Father. It's my heart that I've lost. He proposed to me! He actually asked me to marry him! Oh, happy day!" she almost sang.

Her elation was unmistakable.

"Love has caused you to lose your senses. Cease this nonsense and come home," the Devil urged, although not too hard.

"I am home, Father! I am with the man I love. Nothing else matters now," she replied as she pirouetted again.

She shut him out after that. He stopped watching and pursed his lips at this most unexpected turn of events. This did not go unobserved by Xxxzk, his demonic general-in-chief. He watched in silence as the Devil slumped back on his throne to allow the full impact of this to sink in.

"He *proposed* to her. He actually asked her to marry him. Well, I'll be *damned!*" the Devil said half in shock.

"Kind of puts an entirely new wrinkle on the situation, doesn't it?" asked Xxxzk.

"Yes, it does," the Devil said thoughtfully.

The demon squinted at him.

"Your daughter is happy now. You should rejoice. Instead, you look as if you've lost your only friend," the demon observed.

"This is a most disturbing and perplexing turn of events. If I interfere, all Hell will literally break loose. For the first time in eons, I'm not sure how to handle a situation. It's most unsettling," the Devil said.

"Long ago, one of my daughters took on human form and married a mortal. She willingly sacrificed all of her powers and immortality and she died happy, surrounded by her children and grandchildren. Her progeny still walk the Earth. All seem happy and well adjusted," Xxxzk said.

"How did *you* feel about it?" asked the Devil.

"I felt happy for her, as a father should feel. You should feel happy for Galya, too, and wish her well," the demon said.

"I suppose you're right, my old friend. It will just take me a while to get over the shock. Thank you," the Devil said.

Xxxzk bowed and vanished.

The Devil sighed as he allowed his thoughts to travel back to a time when he, too, was in love.

Galya's mother, Lilith, was a succubus and the loveliest of them all by far. She was also sweet and gentle and her smile was beyond compare. He fell madly in love with her. So madly, he forgot about his ongoing war with God and his minions. He also forgot about God's threat to make his life miserable in every way possible. He never thought he'd carry it out.

He could have commanded her to be his consort. Instead, he actually *courted* her. He showered her with gifts and attention and professed his undying love in every way he could think of. After months of courtship, they were wed. It was a grand ceremony, too. The finest ever seen on the Lower Planes. The celebration lasted for weeks.

The day of Galya's birth should have been a joyous one. Instead, God sent his avenging angels into Hell with orders to slay both mother and child. A wild, desperate battle ensued that left half the

Lower Planes in ruins and sent him fleeing into the deepest parts with his crying newborn daughter in his arms and tears in his eyes. The angels had slipped past his defenses and butchered his wife before he could save her. Somehow, he managed to slay them and take his baby to safety.

That triggered the War of Forever.

In the end, the Earth lay in ashes and ruins and those who had fought blindly in God's name were all but wiped out. The pitiful handful of survivors now cursed his name and returned to the old ways. Without his mindless worshippers, his power base was shattered. The small bands of Christians, Moslems and Jews who remained were not enough to sustain him and God faded into oblivion.

Even his angels, sick of the endless slaughter, had deserted him.

In short, God was dead.

Figuratively.

But the Devil's hatred for him and his minions had not abated. He ordered his demons to hunt down and kill every last angel until the entire ugly race was eradicated. Then he attacked God himself.

The battle lasted for centuries.

When it was over, God had been driven completely out of the cosmos and humankind was left to its own devices. By then, Elves and other Elder Races had returned to the world. And they brought the magic back with them. With them came other, nastier things who fed upon the souls of men.

The Devil now had competition.

More than he wanted.

The Second Age would have ended before it had begun if not for Arka-Dal and the other rulers who were allied to him.

Now Galya had fallen for the charismatic emperor—and she threatened to kill him if he attempted to interfere.

He sighed again.

Galya looked much like her mother. She also displayed many of her mannerisms and facial expressions. Now that she had found love, her softer, gentler and more feminine side was emerging. This reminded him of her mother even more.

Long ago, God and his minions had deprived him of the woman he loved and Galya of her mother. Now that Galya was in love, he decided he would do nothing to deprive her of it. Nor would he allow anyone else to do so.

"Is she truly in love?" he wondered.

He put aside those thoughts and returned to Balaam.

Galya was right about the man. The closer he came to realizing his dark ambitions, the blacker his heart grew. All traces of the wandering scholar were gone now. All that remained was a vile, sinister shell of a man bent on increasing his personal power, even if he had to destroy the world to get it.

He didn't mind forfeiting his soul. He had little use for it anyway. Once he came to power, *millions* would die. Those who survived the holocaust would become his slaves, forced to labor on monuments proclaiming his greatness.

Balaam's ego was amazingly large.

Even the Devil felt disturbed by him. While the man was a perfect foil, he wondered what would become of the Earth if he actually allowed him to fulfill his goals. Balaam, he knew, was evil personified.

The last time he encountered such evil were an Austrian dictator and a Russian autocrat of the First Age. Between them, they slew millions of helpless people and nearly destroyed human civilization. Neither had been his clients, but the Devil had to raise an even greater evil to defeat them both.

Would he have to do the same with Balaam?

His demon general reappeared and saw the look of consternation on his face.

"You seem vexed. Is this Balaam as bad as Hitler or Stalin?" the demon asked.

"If he ever comes to power, he will make both men look like Sisters of Mercy," the Devil replied.

"Will you uphold your contract with him?" the demon asked.

"Yes—and *exactly* as written. As always," the Devil said with a smirk.

"So, you've set him up?" asked the demon.

"As usual," the Devil replied.

When Arka-Dal and Galya told Leo and the others of their plans to wed, the Pope raised an eyebrow.

"I *can* see into the future but I must admit that I didn't see *this* coming," he said. "I guess the proverbial cold day has finally arrived in Hell. In fact, it must be snowing on the Lower Planes right this moment. I hope your father has a warm cloak."

She laughed.

"We'd best send him a few snow shovels," Kashi injected. "I must say that the Dal family tree is about to sprout a most interesting branch. I can hardly wait to see what your future children will look like."

"If they look anything like Galya, I'm sure they'll be quite beautiful," Mayumi said happily.

"I've told Father of our wedding plans," Galya said as she clung to Arka-Dal's arm.

"Oh? How'd he take it?" Arka-Dal asked.

"Better than I expected. He didn't even try to force me to return to Hell. Nor did he lose his temper. I was rather surprised," she said.

"What do you suppose he's up to?" asked Leo.

"That's hard to say with him. He *is* the Devil after all," Galya said.

"I guess congratulations are in order. When's the date?" asked Kashi.

"As soon as we stop whoever's behind those mystery armies," Arka-Dal promised.

Not everyone was happy about the pending union.

Neither Chatha nor Medusa was thrilled with the idea of having to share their husband with the beautiful devil. Neither of them fully trusted her yet but there was nothing they could do about it. Arka-Dal said he and Galya would soon wed and that was that. Galya knew how they felt but decided that they'd get over it in time—just like Mayumi did.

Chatha sort of liked Galya but was intensely jealous of her. Medusa was more suspicious of her. Before she learned to trust Galya, the devil would have to earn it somehow. Helping them defeat this Balaam character and her father along with him would do just that.

As the days passed, Galya tried to help Merlin, Leo, Gorinna and Arka-Dal solve the riddle. They approached it from every logical angle without success. After several days of this, Merlin was on the verge of pulling his hair out.

"What is everywhere to be found but nowhere to be seen? What on Earth does it mean?" he groaned.

"The other part is just as puzzling," Galya said in frustration. "I can think of nothing that burns brighter than the sun. Not even all of the fires of Hell combined are *that* bright."

"We'll never find that tomb before our adversary does," Arka-Dal concluded. "The best we can hope for is that he'll trigger some sort of power burst when he opens it. That should enable Merlin to pinpoint its location and track him down. But can we get there in time to keep him from waking the Elder Gods?"

"I can get us there in an eye blink," Galya offered. "That's much faster than either Merlin or Gorinna could get us there."

Merlin nodded.

"That would also bring your father onto the scene. Things could get ugly," Leo pointed out.

"I'll handle *him,*" Galya said.

"Then it's settled. But if he puts those armies in motion, we'll still have to find a way to stop them before they reach any population centers. If he uses that second spell, we're sunk unless we can figure out the meaning to the riddles," Arka-Dal said.

Far away in his lair, the Devil listened in on their conversation and chuckled to himself.

"It is just as I had hoped. Galya has cast her lot in with theirs. When she brings them to the lost tomb, I will meet her there and settle this matter once and forever," he said.

Balaam rode north for several days. When he was nearly out of water, he happened upon a young couple and two small children in a covered wagon who were following a little-used trail west. They offered him some of their water out of the kindness of their hearts. Balaam insisted on taking all of it. When the husband refused, he slit his throat with his dagger and laughed as he lay dying. His hysterical wife grabbed her children and tried to take cover in the back of the wagon. Balaam set it ablaze and waited for them to run out. He grabbed the wife and raped her while her terrified children watched. Then he raped her young daughter and slit her throat while the mother and son screamed and begged for mercy. While the woman kept screaming, he butchered the little boy, making sure she saw every gruesome detail of it. Then he finished off the woman by cutting her throat.

Exhilarated by his latest murderous rampage, he took their water and continued riding. On the second day, he spotted a row of three peaks in the distance and headed straight for them. Hoping to find one shaped like a falcon. The peaks were further away than he thought. It took him three days and nights to reach them. By then, he was completely out of water and nearly out of his mind from the oppressive heat. When he reached the nearest peak, he found a small, clear stream at the base of it and drank his fill. He also bathed and changed his clothes. Rejuvenated, he decided to make camp and eat.

While he dined, he studied the peaks.

To his dismay, none had the desired shape. At least he couldn't see it thanks to the glare of the sun. He decided to spend the night to see if the falcon would reveal itself with the rising moon.

As the moon rose from behind the mountains, they merged into one gigantic form. Balaam studied the massive shadow carefully. It took him several minutes but eventually he noticed that the top of the middle peak hooked to the left to form something resembling a bird's beak. The two flanking mountains, when viewed with it, formed the outstretched wings.

"That's it! That's the falcon!" he shouted gleefully.

The demon entered the lair and saw the Devil leaning over an ancient open book. As he approached, the Devil looked up.

"What news do you bring?" he asked.

"Your foil has located the falcon and is even now searching for the tomb," the demon said.

"Excellent. Let me know when he finds it. Anything else?" the Devil asked.

"Yes. The other has also reached the mountains," the demon reported.

"Just as I expected. Do nothing. I want to see how this plays out," the Devil instructed.

Peace reached the mountains a few minutes after Balaam began his climb. He saw the dark outline of the bird of prey and immediately realized where he was. He slid from his horse and walked toward the middle peak. Along the way, he found Balaam's camp, horse and pack mule.

"He's here and already climbing," he said as he looked around.

He searched the area. After several minutes, he located a narrow, sandy trail that led up the face of the mountain. Balaam's footprints were still fresh. Peace drew his sword and followed them.

Balaam was already halfway up. He was now bathed in sweat and breathing heavily as he anxiously searched for any sign of a tomb. He saw a rocky trail off to the left and followed it carefully. Each step sent handfuls of loose sand and rocks tumbling down the cliff and he had to cling to every handhold he could find to keep from falling. He was just about to give up when he came to an opening. It was barely big enough for him to enter on his belly but he managed.

He rolled headlong down a flight of crude steps and landed in front of a sand-encrusted rectangle. It was over four feet tall and at least eight feet long. His heart raced wildly as he hurriedly shoveled the sand off with his bare hands. Soon he found himself staring at a solid granite sarcophagus.

"This is it! This is the sarcophagus of Armenopur! I've found it!" he shouted.

His words echoed back at him as he reached into his leather pouch and pulled out a hammer and chisel and immediately set to work. He'd chiseled off half of the wax sealant when he stopped.

"I can't take the chance of being interrupted," he said.

He put down his tools and took out the parchment he had gotten in Meroe. He spread it open on the floor and slowly read the first spell. When he was finished, the sarcophagus lay open and he found himself surrounded by a horde of lithe, black, winged demons. Balaam laughed. The spell had not only enabled him to open the sarcophagus, it had also summoned forth a demon guard.

The demons came in various sizes, from that of a baboon to large bats. Their colors also varied, from dark red, to puke green, to mustard to pitch black and shades in between. All were winged and sported talons on their hands.

Balaam stopped and studied the horde, which just hovered around him in silence.

"Are you here to stop me?" he asked.

"We are here to protect you. Command us, Master, and we shall obey," the largest of them replied.

"Go outside and make sure no one has followed me. Do not allow anyone to interrupt me. Understand?" Balaam ordered.

"We understand," the demon said as he led his entire horde out of the cave.

Balaam looked inside the granite sarcophagus and saw a crude, unmarked wooden coffin. An ancient curse was carved into its lid, warning of nasty things that would befall anyone who dared disturb what lay inside.

He laughed.

"A pox on your curses! I'm too close to stop now!" he said as he began to hammer away at the coffin.

Peace had nearly reached the cave when the demons fell upon him. Their attack was sudden.

Furious.

And unexpected.

He fought back as best as he could under the circumstances. It proved to be too little too late. The demons quickly overwhelmed him and sent him tumbling heels-over-head down the path, pelting him with spells and stones along the way. By the time he hit the bottom, he was a mass of rags, dirt, dust, blood and bruises.

And he was out cold.

The demons then bound him with magic ropes and left him in Balaam's camp so the madman could decide his fate later.

Balaam remained in the tomb, diligently chipping away at the lid of the coffin, and tossing piece after piece to the floor behind him. After ten long, grueling hours of this, he stood back and eyed the contents.

The mummy—if one could call it such—was bound hand and foot with heavy iron chains. Its leathery face showed no eyes and its mouth, open wide as if caught in mid-scream, held no sign of a tongue. Dried, brittle scarabs lay all around him.

"This *has* to be Armenopur! He was obviously buried alive just like the legend said," Balaam said as he wiped the sweat from his brown and eyes with the back of his sleeve. "The book has to be here with him. But *where*? I don't see it."

He seized the mummy by the ribcage and pulled. It immediately fell apart amid a cloud of dust. The dust made him cough violently and he cursed as he picked Armenopur's broken body up piece-by-piece and tossed it away.

"The book! I've got to have that book!" he said as he frantically rummaged through the remains.

He soon had the entire coffin emptied. To his delight, he saw the faint outline of a door in the bottom. Using his dagger, he pried it open and tossed away the lid. He laughed. Inside was an ancient metal box, which he quickly retrieved and placed on the floor. He saw that it was locked and used his hammer and chisel to break it open. When he opened it, he just about shouted for joy as he reached inside and picked up the long-coveted book.

That's when the head demon entered.

"Strangers have arrived. They are almost upon us," he warned.

"Kill them all! No one must be allowed to disturb me now," Balaam growled as he gingerly opened the book.

The "strangers" were Arka-Dal, Pandaar, Kashi, Merlin, Gorinna and Galya. As soon as Balaam had read the first spell, Merlin was able to pinpoint his location by the amount of power emanating from it. True to her word, Galya then immediately transported the entire group to the lost tomb.

Before they began their climb, they happened upon the unconscious Peace. Merlin knelt to examine him and nodded that he was all right.

"A little worse for wear but otherwise unhurt," the wizard said.

Galya pointed up to the cave.

"The tomb is there," she announced. "And he is within. I feel *power* coming from within. *Great and evil power.*"

"Let's get going," Arka-Dal said.

"What about Peace?" asked Gorinna.

"I'll stay with him until he wakes," Pandaar offered.

"Suit yourself. Join us as soon as you can," Arka-Dal said as he hurried up the trail.

The others hurried after him.

They encountered the horde of demons halfway up the cliff. They hovered menacingly above them as both sides studied each other with great care.

"They are from one of the Upper Planes. They are very minor demons but dangerous just the same," Galya said.

"There must be a hundred of them," Kashi said as he brandished his sword.

The largest demon moved forward.

"You are not permitted here. Be gone or suffer the consequences," he shouted.

"Stand aside, minion, or feel my wrath!" Galya ordered.

"Who are you, woman, and why should I obey you?" the demon asked.

"I am Galya, Princess of the Lower Planes. Leave at once or pay the price for your stupidity. You *know* what I can do!" she challenged.

"We obey He Who is in the Tomb! He has ordered us to kill all intruders!" the demon said as it charged.

The rest followed his lead. Galya watched their descent and readied one of her more potent spells. Just before she could cast it, Arka-Dal drew Excalibur and charged straight into the onrushing horde. She watched in disbelief as he cut a path of death and destruction through their ranks. The demons recoiled in pain mixed with astonishment as they watched limbs, wings and heads fall to the ground with each swing of Arka-Dal's sword. A large group tried to circle around and attack him from the rear. That's when Galya released her spell.

And *what* a spell it was.

In less than an eye blink, the demons imploded and vaporized. Their surviving brethren saw this and beat a hasty retreat from the field. Arka-Dal watched them flee and laughed as he sheathed his sword. Galya ran over and hugged him.

Deep within his lair, the Devil watched and laughed.

"Balaam's minions flee in terror like the cowards they are," the large demon standing behind him said.

"They cannot withstand the combined might of Arka-Dal's blade and Galya's magic. I should have known that Merlin had given him Excalibur. Balaam has lost his guards. They will not attack Arka-Dal again," the Devil replied.

"When do *we* attack?" the demon asked.

"You don't. I'll personally handle this from here on," the Devil replied. "Return to the shadows. I will summon you if I need you."

Inside the tomb, Balaam was about to recite the next spell that would animate his armies. Before he could begin, what remained of his guards entered.

"Did you dispatch our unwanted visitors?" he asked.

"No. *We* have been dispatched instead. You're on your own, human. We will meet again in Hell," the demon said as he led his people from the tomb.

As soon as they left, he recited another spell. This time, a more powerful company of demons appeared.

"Command us, Evil One," the largest said.

"There are several people headed this way. Kill them," Balaam ordered.

The demons scurried off to do his bidding. As they emerged from the tomb, they spotted Arka-Dal's party and charged straight for them, screaming and yowling all the way.

Merlin made a throwing motion. Thousands of tiny sparkling bits hurtled toward the demons. They struck the ones in front and sent them screaming to the ground in flames where they exploded, raining bits of demonic flesh and ichor down on the party. The rest of the demons circled overhead several times and attacked again. Gorinna stepped forward and made a slashing motion with her right hand. Instantly, a dozen hideously malformed demonic heads became separated from their bodies and struck the ground. Their torsos followed a split second after.

More demons emerged from the tomb and joined the battle. This time, it was Galya who stemmed the tide by clapping her hands above her head three times as she screamed at the top of her lungs. The sound waves struck the demons with such force that it tore them limb-from-limb. Those who didn't get hit by the sonic waves fell upon Arka-Dal.

He disemboweled the first and severed the head, arm and right shoulder of another. He split a third in two at the hips and gutted three more while the rest of the demons fell before the combined powers of Merlin, Gorinna and Galya, while Kashi guarded the rear.

From deep within their lair, the Devil and several of his minions watched the battle unfold. While he laughed as demon after demon fell before the determined band, his minions recoiled in disgust at the sight of Galya fighting alongside the humans.

"You daughter fights with the humans!" said one.

"She betrays us!" cried another.

"Let us join the battle and teach her a lesson she won't soon forget!" said another to the cheers of the rest.

"If you join that battle, it is *you* who will receive that lesson. Galya is far too powerful for the pathetic likes of you or any other beings of the Lower Planes," the Devil said calmly.

"Let us attack her and see how powerful she truly is!" the demon insisted.

The Devil scowled.

The demon shrieked and turned to a pile of fine dust which blew away on the wind he conjured up. The rest of his horde fell silent.

"Attack my daughter and you will suffer the same fate!" he warned. "I will deal with her personally and in my own time. Understand?"

They nodded in unison.

"Good. Now let's relax and enjoy the show," he said as they returned to the battle.

Balaam knew his demons were getting butchered. He didn't care. They were merely pawns, sent to delay the intruders long enough for him to recite the last two spells. He slowly turned each ancient page as he searched for the Spell of Awakening. As long as he could do that, he didn't care how many demons died

After several minutes, his tired eyes settled on one of the spells he needed. He placed his finger on the page and slowly recited each precious syllable to the incantation that would set his dark armies in motion.

Tutmose was in his tent dining on a roast chicken. He had just pulled the last bit of white meat from the breastbone when a profusely perspiring Horem Heb barged in. Tutmose slid the meat into his mouth and eyed the elder general.

"That strange army has begun its march," Horem Heb reported. "They are headed this way at a nice, leisurely pace."

"Radio Arkaneton with the news and assemble the men. Make sure the chariots are fitted with silver edged blades," Tutmose ordered as he wiped the grease from his fingers on a napkin.

"You mean to attack?" asked Horem Heb as they walked out of the tent.

"It's better than waiting for them to reach us. I'll lead the chariots in the first wave. As soon as we've cut our way through them, follow up with the cavalry. Then we'll link up behind and attack from the opposite direction," Tutmose said.

"We've just two regiments to their half million. We cannot hope to defeat them," Horem Heb pointed out.

"We're not trying to. I want to throw the enemy into disarray and buy enough time for the Prince to assemble the rest of the army. Once we've scattered them, we'll return to Egypt and join the others," Tutmose explained.

"May the Gods go with you!" Horem Heb said.

"And with you," said Tutmose.

Twenty minutes later, all 400 chariots were arrayed in a long straight line atop a low hill. Tutmose was in the lead chariot. He waited until the enemy reached the bottom of a valley then ordered his men to charge. The Egyptians headed straight for the center of the enemy mass and slammed into them with the fury of a tsunami. The bold move appeared to work as the ground became littered with severed grinning heads, limbs and mangled torsos. Within minutes, the charioteers found themselves far to the rear of the enemy. Tutmose turned his chariot around and watched as Horem Heb's cavalry cut a similar swath of destruction through the enemy ranks. To his surprise, he realized that the strange soldiers barely reacted to the attack. A few bothered to hurl javelins at the passing riders and chariots, which killed a few horses and men, but for the most part, the enemy troops just kept marching east.

When Horem Heb's men reached Tutmose's chariots, a trumpeter sounded assembly. As soon as all of the Egyptian soldiers were arrayed, Tutmose ordered his men to charge again. This time, both chariots and cavalry charge together. The enemy didn't even bother to turn. They simply ignored the Egyptians.

"How rude! Let's teach them some manners!" shouted Horem Heb to his riders.

They expected this to be a repeat of the first charge. Instead, as soon as the front line of chariots drew close to the enemy, several thousand of them suddenly did and about-face and loosed their javelins straight into them. Dozens of horses and charioteers fell. As soon as a chariot came to a halt, dozens of enemy troops swarmed over them and butchered the drivers. Then the rest of the black troops drew their swords, turned and attacked.

The slaughter was on.

Somehow, the badly outnumbered Egyptians managed to fight their through the massive numbers of enemy troops and reach the top of the hill. This took an even more daring charge by the remainder of Tutmose's charioteers with Horem Heb's cavalry following right on their heels. As soon as Tutmose reached the crest of the hill, he had his trumpeter sound assembly. As the last of his battered soldiers gathered behind him. Tutmose sought out Horem Heb. When he found him, one of the surgeons was applying a bandage to a wound his thigh.

Horem Heb saluted.

"Those bastards trapped us. We barely escaped with our asses," he said.

"How bad did we get it?" asked Tutmose.

"We lost nearly half our men and a third of the chariots. We don't have enough left for another charge," Horem Heb reported.

Tutmose looked down at the advancing horde.

"Let us return to Egypt and join forces with the Prince," he decided.

Outside the tomb, wave after wave of demons appeared from thin air and attacked the group from all sides. Gorinna, Merlin and Galya dispatched most of them before they could get too close. Those who survived the spells were cut to ribbons by Arka-Dal who swung Excalibur as easily as if it had the weight of a feather. Kashi tried to join the fight but his silver-edged sword did little damage to these monsters from the Lower Planes.

Undeterred, Balaam continued scanning the pages of the ancient book in search of the one spell that would give him the unimaginable power he lusted after. He leafed through nearly five hundred pages before he found the necessary spell and began to recite it. He took great care to pronounce each and every syllable accurately lest the spell should go awry. Within seconds, he felt the floor of the tomb vibrate beneath him. The cave took on an eerie orange gleam. It sprang from the floor and slowly formed a transparent dome over him and the book. He smiled and continued reading.

Down below in the valley, Peace opened his eyes and winced. He blinked at the crackling flames as he struggled to a seated position. He realized that his hands and feet were now free from the ropes. He took a deep breath and exhaled to clear his mind. That's when he saw Pandaar seated on the other side of the fire and walked over to him.

The Panther looked up at him and grinned.

"Nice to see you up and about," he said as Peace sat next to him.

Pandaar handed him some food and a canteen. Peace unscrewed the cap and drank deeply.

"Those demons jumped me before I could defend myself. How'd you find me?" he asked.

"Galya brought us here," Pandaar replied.

"Who's Galya?" asked Peace.

"She's the Devil's daughter," Pandaar said.

Peace stared at him. Pandaar laughed at the expression on his face, then explained how it all came about.

"Grandfather has a talent for making the strangest friends, but this beats all," Peace said. "Where are they now?"

Pandaar nodded up the trail.

"They've gone up there to take out that crazy bastard who started this mess," he said.

"I don't know about you, but I didn't come all this way to sit this one out. I'm going after them," Peace said as he stood up.

Pandaar beamed at him.

"I *knew* you'd say that. Let's get going before we miss out on all the fun," he said.

They reached the others just in time to watch a second wave of demonic attackers flee from Merlin's withering light spell and Gorinna's pyrotechnics. Arka-Dal saw them coming and laughed as he pounded each of them on the back.

"It's good to see you conscious," he said to Peace.

Peace didn't reply. He was stunned to silence by the most exotically beautiful woman he'd ever seen. When he finally recovered his voice, all he managed to say was: "You don't look like a devil."

Galya giggled.

"But I *am*. In fact, I can be *very* devilish when I want to be," she assured him. "So you're the one who foiled Father's scheme in the Alps? Somehow I expected that you'd be a bit more *formidable*."

"I am quite formidable—when I *need* to be," Peace replied with a smirk.

She laughed.

"Did we miss anything?" asked Pandaar.

"Only the first two rounds," Kashi said. "The real fight is yet to begin."

"Then let's get to it. You know how much I love a good fight!" Pandaar said.

Balaam was oblivious to the fate of his minions. He was too engrossed in the ancient book to care about them. He leafed through the heavy tome one page at a time as he searched for the spell that would wake the Sleeping God.

In the back of his mind, he knew what consequences his action would bring, but he was too far gone, too blinded by his own ambitions to be concerned with that. The first of the spells had set his armies in motion. Soon, they would overrun all the great cities of Man and make him the sole ruler of all he surveyed, even though he knew that once the God was awakened, there would be nothing much left for him to rule.

"It's better to rule in Hell than to serve in Heaven!" he told himself.

As he turned another page, he smiled.

"It has to be here! The Spell of Awakening!" he shouted impatiently.

Arka-Dal and his party were almost at the entrance. They stopped to examine the narrow slit.

"We'll have to crawl in on our bellies," Kashi said. "Let me go first to check it out."

Merlin stopped and closed his eyes. When he opened them again, he looked at Arka-Dal.

"The strange armies have begun to march! He has recited spell of animation!" he said. "We must stop him before reads the spell of awakening or all will be lost."

"When I reach him, I'll put my fist down his throat and pluck out his vile heart!" Galya vowed as she watched Kashi crawl into the tomb.

"Me *first*!" said Arka-Dal.

The entrance to the crypt was guarded by two eight-foot-tall, muscular, blue-skinned demons with leathery wings and pointed tails. They stood with their arms folded across their chests and glared menacingly at the interlopers.

"None shall pass," one of them said.

"Stand aside or suffer the consequences," Arka-Dal warned as he brandished Excalibur.

The demon reached for him.

Arka-Dal swung and lopped his arm off at the elbow. The demon simply laughed as a new one instantly grew in its place. Before Arka-Dal could react, it seized him by the throat and lifted him off the floor.

"I'll crush you like a worm!" it threatened.

That's when its entire arm, up to the shoulder, suddenly turned to mist. As Arka-Dal hit the floor, the demons converged on Galya. This time, the arm did not regenerate, much to the demon's dismay.

"I am Galya, Princess of the Lower Planes and daughter of the Dark One. I command you to leave this place at once or go the way of your arm," she said defiantly.

"Forgive us, Our Lady. We did not know," the demons said as they respectfully bowed their heads and vanished.

She smiled at Arka-Dal.

"The way is clear now," she said.

They stopped just outside the entrance to the inner chamber. Galya held up her hand and shook her head.

"He's found it! He's reading the spell!" she warned.

"Let's move it! We have to interrupt him before he can finish reading it!" Arka-Dal shouted.

One at a time, they scrambled through the opening. When all were inside, they saw the orange glow and followed it to the burial chamber. There, through the orange haze that now surrounded him, they saw Balaam kneeling amid the rubble of the sarcophagus, preparing to recite the last spell.

Arka-Dal lunged toward him only to be hurled back by the strange shield. He scrambled back to his feet and touched it, only to pull his hand back to be rid of the painful sensation that rushed through him.

Merlin and Galya examined the shield.

"It's of no magic that *I've* ever encountered. I can't even determine what it's made of," Merlin said.

"I've never seen the likes of it before," Galya said. "It must be some magic of the Elder Races."

Balaam laughed at them.

"Nothing can penetrate that shield! You can't stop me. My armies are already on the march. Soon, they will trample all of the world's great nations beneath their sandals and I will rule over the remains like a god! All who live will be my slaves. To make this happen, I just need to recite one last spell," he boasted as he ran his fingers across the open pages of the book.

"Don't be stupid! If you read that spell, you'll unleash forces upon this world that no one—not even you—can control. You'll plunge the universe into chaos!" Merlin warned.

Balaam laughed again, then began to recite the spell of awakening.

Galya growled at him.

"Stand back! I'll burst that shield or die in the attempt!" she said as she raised her hands above her head.

Before she could utter a word, the orange glow suddenly dissipated. Balaam stared at them but continued reading. Or at least he *tried.*

To his alarm and dismay, he began to choke and wheeze. The harder he tried to speak, the more he coughed and his breathing grew more and more labored. He stopped reading and gripped his throat. He coughed harder. So hard that blood sprayed from his mouth and his eyes bulged noticeably.

They all watched as he fell to his hands and knees and gasped pitifully as the life slowly left his body. He fell down and rolled onto his back, spitting up blood all the time.

Merlin looked at Galya.

"I swear to you, Merlin, that this is *not* my doing," she said.

As Balaam drew his last breath, the chamber filled with sinister laughter. They turned and looked up to see the Devil hovering cross-legged ten feet above them.

"Father!" Galya gasped.

"Are you who I think you are?" Arka-Dal asked.

"Well, I'm *not* the Easter Bunny," the Devil replied.

Pandaar scowled.

"You're not what I expected," he observed.

"And what, pray tell, were you expecting?" the Devil asked.

"I thought you'd be wearing a blue dress. You know, like the song: Devil With the Blue Dress On," Pandaar said.

This elicited a collective groan from everyone in the room and earned him an elbow to the ribs from Kashi.

"Careful or I'll turn you into something *unspeakable*," the Devil warned.

"Something *worse* than he already is?" asked Kashi.

"Is *that* even possible?" asked Gorinna.

"I see your point. Is he always like that?" the Devil asked as he eyed Pandaar.

"Sometimes he's worse," said Kashi.

"In that case, I hope I never see you on the Lower Planes. It's bad enough down there without adding you to the mix," the Devil said to Pandaar.

"I always believed you to be a myth. You look nothing like the drawings in the old books," Kashi said.

"I am, as they used to say, the victim of a biased press. But I can take any form I wish for short periods of time. What you see before you now is my *natural* state," the Devil said as he floated to the floor and landed right in front of Arka-Dal.

To his surprise, the Emperor didn't even flinch.

"I sent my daughter to destroy you. Instead, she has fallen for you. This has never happened before," the Devil said.

"There's a first time for everything," Arka-Dal said.

"I expected her to bring you here and she did. You know, I came here with the intention to destroy you—"

He raised his hands as if to cast a spell. Galya immediately leapt in front of Arka-Dal.

"Father! Don't you *dare*!" she snarled protectively.

He lowered his hands and laughed.

"You killed *him* before he could recite the spell. Why?" asked Merlin. "Isn't *that* what you wanted?"

"No. The last thing I want is to bring back the Elder Gods. If they returned, they would wipe mankind from the face of the Earth. That would deprive me of eons of amusement. Without weak-minded humans, who would be left for me to toy with? My life would become unbearably dull," the Devil replied.

He squatted over the cold form of Balaam.

"There would be no more Balaams in the world. None left for me to tempt. No more souls to reap. In short, I'd have no reason to exist. I might even die in the truest sense of the word," he said.

He placed his hand on the book. It instantly turned to dust and blew away on an unseen wind until not a trace of it remained. The expressions on everyone's faces caused him to smile.

"Don't look so shocked. I hate that book as much as you do. Its very existence always leads men to try and bring back the Elder Gods or fool with things they never should. It threatens our very existence," he said as he stood up.

"Why didn't you do this before?" asked Arka-Dal.

"I couldn't. I had not the power to physically open this tomb. I simply am not *evil* enough. But *he* was. Balaam's darker side led me to him. I used him to help me locate the tomb. I offered him what he wanted most in order to get what I wanted. As for his soul—that was forfeited years ago when he committed his first foul deed as a young boy by murdering his grandmother while she slept. He was some piece of work!" the Devil said.

"What about the riddles? What do they mean?" asked Galya.

He saw the look in her eyes and smiled.

"*That* is the light that burns brighter than the sun. It is the one thing that is so strong, not even *I can* put it out. That light, my daughter, is *love.* In order to cancel out the spell of awakening, either Arka-Dal or you would have had to destroy that which you love most. The moment you fought to save each other, no matter the consequences, that light became inextinguishable," he said.

"Love is the answer to the riddle?" asked Merlin.

He nodded.

"What of the second part? What is everywhere to be seen yet nowhere to be found?" asked Arka-Dal.

"That which cannot be seen is the inherent evil that lurks deep within the hearts, minds and souls of most mortals," the Devil replied.

"And the *nowhere* part?" asked Merlin.

"You're standing in it. The ancient Egyptians buried Armenopur here then obliterated all mention of it from their records. To their way of thinking, this meant the tomb did not exist. Hence, it was *nowhere*," the Devil explained.

He smiled at Galya.

"You actually love him, don't you?" he asked. "The Crown Princess of the 666 Planes has actually fallen in love with a mere mortal."

"I mean no disrespect, Father, but he's no *mere mortal*," she corrected.

"You surprised me, Arka-Dal. I believed that you, like all men, had weaknesses I could easily exploit. That's why I sent Galya. To my dismay, you not only proved me wrong, you won her heart. I'm not exactly sure how to handle this," he said.

Arka-Dal pulled Galya close to him.

"You'll just have to learn," he said.

"I suppose I shall—in time," the Devil said. "You are an extraordinary man, Arka-Dal of Thule. You are far more formidable than any opponent I've faced before. You not only have the heart of my daughter, but my *respect* as well. I salute you."

"But what of your contract with Balaam?" asked Merlin.

"I promised him he would command great armies—and he did. Unfortunately, he did not specify how long a time period he would be allowed to command them. He wanted to find the lost tomb of Armenopur and the book that was buried with him. He wanted to be able to read the spells that would set his armies in motion and awaken the sleeping god.

I *gave* him the ability to read those spells but I never said that I would allow him to *cast* them.

I fulfilled the contract to the letter. It's not *my* fault Balaam failed to be more specific. Like they say, the Devil is in the details. When someone signs a contract with me, they get exactly what they want. No more. No less.

Balaam got *exactly* what he bargained for—and exactly what he *deserved,*" the Devil said smugly.

"You'd make a great lawyer!" Pandaar remarked.

The Devil scowled.

"There's no need to be insulting," he snapped. "You know, if it were not for the fact that I have an almost endless supply of twisted human beings to toy with, my existence would be almost unbearable. Being the ruler of Hell isn't exactly a bed of roses but *someone* has to keep the place in order. Can you even imagine what this world would be like if I didn't keep my minions under control? Yet no one gives me credit for preserving order. Instead, I am vilified by priests and everyone else."

Gorinna sighed.

"I almost feel sorry for you," she said.

"Sympathy for the Devil?" asked Pandaar.

"Why not? I could use a little once in a while, considering all I've done for mankind. I've given man the gift of curiosity, the thirst for knowledge, the desire to create and destroy and explore. If not for me, none of the great civilizations of man would have come to pass. Man would have no passion for life. No art. No science. No reason to even exist.

As for those fools who have bartered away their souls, I offered them nothing they didn't already desire. And, unlike certain gods who take great delight in tormenting their worshippers, I *always* keep my bargains," the Devil said.

He looked at Galya.

"If I ordered you to return to the Lower Planes, would you obey me?" he asked.

"No! I'm staying here!" she said adamantly.

"I see. Would you have really tried to kill me if I harmed one of your friends?" he asked.

"With every fiber of my being and with all I have at my disposal. I would have fought you to the bitter end," she said.

"I believe you would have," he said. "What of you, Arka-Dal? Would you have fought to keep Galya by your side, even if you knew it would cost you your life?"

"Without a doubt!" Arka-Dal replied.

"Amazing! Never in all the history of the world, has any man offered to risk his life for my daughter, especially after knowing who she is. This is a day that will live forever in my memory, for this is the day that love turned all of Hell upside down," the Devil said.

He turned to Galya and placed his hand on her shoulder.

"You have chosen well, my daughter. Live happy," he said.

"Just what is your name, exactly?" asked Arka-Dal.

"Over the millennia, I've had several. Which do you prefer?" he asked.

"I've just been calling you the Devil. I guess it'll do for now," Arka-Dal replied.

"Then the Devil it is. Perhaps, after we've grown more familiar with each other, I'll tell you my *real* name. That will come later, once you begin to feel more comfortable around me," he agreed.

"I imagine that, under the circumstances, we'll be seeing a lot of you around the palace," Arka-Dal said. "Now that you'll soon be a member of the family, our house is your house. You will always be welcome there."

"Now *that's* something I haven't heard in many millennia. No one ever welcomes me into their home unless they want something. In your case, I know that you don't, so your invitation is genuine. Thank you," the Devil said graciously.

"Now that's a phrase I've never heard you utter before, Father," said Galya.

"I expect you'll be hearing me utter many phrases you've never heard me utter before—given the circumstances. How do *you* feel about this, Merlin?" the Devil asked.

"While you are under Arka-Dal's roof, there will be no animosity between us. Beyond that is another matter," the wizard replied.

"And what of you, Peace?" the Devil asked.

"While you're under Grandfather's roof, you're family. Anywhere else and you're fair game," Peace said evenly.

Gorinna smiled at him.

"I don't care what you do so long as you don't do it in Thule or to anyone I know," she said.

"That's fair enough," the Devil said. He saw the way Galya clung to Arka-Dal and smiled. It was a fatherly type of smile. One she hadn't seen in ages.

"You look truly happy, my dear," he observed.

"I *am*, Father," she said softly.

"Good. Then I'm happy for you," he said as he touched her chin.

"You're nothing like I'd imagined. You're not quite the monster I expected," Arka-Dal said.

The Devil laughed.

"Like I said—I'm the victim of bad press," he said. "Now that you have my daughter's love and she has yours, I vow that from this day forward, I will help to protect all in your house and the Empire of Thule against all enemies and calamities, both natural and supernatural for as long as a single member of your line exists. Treat my daughter well, Arka-Dal."

"I will," the Emperor promised.

"I know," the Devil smiled. "I must leave you now to tend to more of my usual business."

"Where are you going this time?" asked Merlin.

"I think I'll go down to Georgia. I'm looking for a soul to steal," he said. "Just one more thing before I go—"

"And what is *that*?" asked Arka-Dal.

"Be sure to invite me to your wedding," he said as he slowly faded from sight.

"Did what I see happen really happen?" asked Pandaar.

"Indeed it did, my friend," Merlin assured him.

"Well I'll be damned!" Pandaar remarked.

"I used to believe that we *all* are damned. Now, I'm not so sure," Galya said as she looked into Arka-Dal's eyes.

"Merlin—what about those armies?" Arka-Dal asked.

The wizard closed his eyes, then opened them and smiled.

"They're gone. They've returned to the dust that spawned them," he said.

"Take us home, Galya," Arka-Dal said as he held her tight.

Before they left, they stopped to look at the broken remains in the rotted sarcophagus. The head was the only thing still intact and the mouth was wide open as if forever frozen in a last, terrified scream. Amid his remains were the dried shells of hundreds of large scarabs that had been placed inside with him before the sarcophagus was sealed.

"So *that's* what's left of Armenopur! Balaam's death was far kinder by comparison," Gorinna said.

"In the end, both got what they deserved," said Merlin.

"The demon who tried to trap me said there were other things buried with him. Things far worse than the book," Peace said. "Should we look for them?"

"No. Whatever is here must remain here. I'll seal the tomb after we leave so that no one will ever find it again. Armenopur has caused us more than enough trouble," Merlin said.

"Balaam almost succeeded, and would have if not for you, Galya," Arka-Dal said as he pulled her closer. "The world owes you—and your father—much."

"The world owes me nothing. I already have what I want," she said.

As they left the crypt, no one noticed the dust particles and crumbled bandages that had been the mummy of Armenopur were slowly reforming . . .

The Devil and several of his demon cohorts watched as Galya teleported everyone back to Thule.

"You're going to allow her to stay—just like *that*?" the nearest demon asked.

"Yes," the Devil replied.

"Without a fight? Why?" the demon pressed.

"It's what Galya truly wants. Besides, there is little I can do about it," the Devil answered.

"Then you have lost your daughter!" the demon said.

"I have not lost my daughter. Instead, I have gained a *son*," the Devil countered.

"You sound just like a *human*!" the demon sneered.

"There's no need to be insulting. Come. There is much work for us to do," the Devil said.

"In Thule?" the demon asked.

"No. I gave my word and I will honor it. There are a billion other souls we can harvest elsewhere. As long as human weaknesses exist, we shall not lack for work," the Devil assured them.

Later that night, while everyone else in the palace was asleep, Galya again found Merlin standing on the roof of the palace, lost in his thoughts as he watched the moon dance among the stars. He turned at her approach and smiled.

"Do you still have the gift of futuresight?" she asked.

"Yes. But so do *you*," he reminded her.

"I cannot see into *my own* future. There is much I wish to know and only you can help me," Galya said. "Will you?"

"I'll try. Ask your questions," Merlin said.

"Will I bear Arka-Dal a child?" she asked.

"Two in fact. One boy. One girl," he answered.

She beamed.

"What do you see for them?" she asked.

"They will grow up in the palace. Your son will become a great leader of men and will unrivaled in warfare. Your daughter will be known far and wide for her beauty, wit and wisdom," Merlin said assuringly.

"And Thule will live on?" she asked.

"Thule will live on," he assured her.

"What of Arka-Dal? Will he live long?" she asked.

He smiled.

"He will live a very long and fruitful life. In fact, he will live much longer than most men and so will those who are close to him," he said with a wink.

She laughed.

"I suspect that is of *your* doing, Merlin. Is he aware of this?" she asked.

"Not yet. But when he realizes that he has stopped aging, he will suspect that something is up. By then it will be far too late for him to do anything about it," Merlin said.

"Thank you," she said softly as she kissed him on the cheek.

He watched her walk away and smiled, feeling a little ashamed of himself for not telling her all that he had seen.

Isle of Wailing Souls

In The 41st Year in the Reign of Arka-Dal

The mist was everywhere.

Cold, thick and impenetrable, it clung to everything and everyone, both alive and dead, on the tiny island. The oppressive heat and humidity of the tropical climate worsened the effects of the mist, thus making breathing and movement difficult, even for the highly trained band of adventurers that were even now making their way through it.

The mist made it virtually impossible to see more than a dozen feet in any direction. This, too, made travel arduously slow.

Then there were the sounds. Bone-chilling cries and mournful wails, broken at odd intervals by demonic laughter or shouted epithets. They seemed to come from everywhere and nowhere at once. And they never ceased.

James Colla raised his hand to signal a stop. He opened his canteen and took a swallow as he tried to peer through the wall of mist which seemed to be closing in around them. He could plainly see the trees, reeds and other flora in his immediate area. Everything beyond them were shadows shrouded in misty gray.

He looked back at his companions.

Patrice Vertrez (Patty to her friends) was looking around nervously. The mist—and the things that moved within it—made her uneasy. She was always fearless in battle against things she could see or touch, things of substance. But she felt unsure of what lurked in the mist.

What were they?

Even James didn't know the answer to that.

That made Patty even more edgy.

Shazzar, the Jackal, appeared less nervous, but kept his eyes on the mist nonetheless. As usual, he refused to let their present situation get the better of him. Whatever was out there, could stay there. He decided that he'd deal with them only if he had to.

James smiled.

That was so typical of Shazzar.

And of Zorn Yaren.

The amber-eyed warrior feared nothing. At present, he leaned calmly against a tree while cradling his shotgun in his arm. Zorn seemed more concerned with the mental state of his younger brother, Rolf, than what lied in the mist.

And with good reason.

Rolf had been totally unhinged by the gruesome death of his beloved Jan[6] *and their unborn child. Although it had happened a few years earlier, Rolf had not yet fully recovered. He spoke very little these days. And when he did speak, he rarely made sense.*

James wondered how he'd react if they were caught up in a fight for their lives. Would Rolf be able to hold his own or would he fold like a French omelet?

He capped his canteen.

"Let's keep moving. The cove is just on the other side of these hills," he said.

The others followed him up the slightly steep, somewhat rocky hill. When they reached the top, they heard the waves crashing against the shore. The cove was less than a half-mile away. The ship that had brought them to this forsaken island was anchored less than a hundred yards off shore.

"What will we tell the captain about Dexter?" Patty asked.

"The truth," replied James.

As soon as their boots hit the sand at the base of the hill, they quickened their pace. Here in the cove, the mist was nearly nonexistent. They could see the edge of the beach and the dark blue water beyond. The sound of surf against rocks drowned out the wails and cries of the interior and gave the area a more normal feel.

But when they reached the edge of the water, their ship was nowhere in sight. Patty gripped James' arm.

"It's gone! We're marooned here!" she shouted above the crashing waves.

James reached into his cloak. He pulled a flare gun out of its holster, pointed it skyward and fired. They watched as the missile soared a few hundred feet above the island and exploded. As it slowly fell back to Earth, it bathed the entire beach with an eerie, flickering

---

[6] Read Realm of Blood

green light. They watched the waves and waited until the flare died out. After twenty minutes, the expected signal never came.

Shazzar cursed under his breath in several languages.

"Let's face it, James, the ship took off without us. We're stuck here," Zorn said.

James nodded but said nothing.

Zorn was right.

They'd been marooned on what was arguably the single most terrifying place on Earth with little hope of being rescued. If something had frightened their ship away, it was doubtful that the captain would return for them. Almost in disgust, he rammed the end of his staff into the sand and sat down beside it as his thoughts traveled back to the events that had gotten hem into this mess . . .

It all started one month earlier in the ancient port city of Shanghai. James and his friends had taken up residence in one of the Shaolin monasteries with the hope that the Zen masters there could do something to expel the inner demons from Rolf. After months of trying, even the monks had given up. The abbot there told James that Rolf was the only one who could help himself and it would probably take another, even more traumatic shock to bring him back to his right mind.

While this was going on, James immersed himself in the monastery's vast library. That's where he was, seated at a table, when the tall, dignified stranger found him. The man walked over and sat down across from him.

"Are you James Colla, the one called the Red Cleric?" he asked.

"I am. And you are?" replied James as he closed the large book he'd been reading.

"My name is Roman Dexter. I'm an antiquities dealer. I've been looking for you for some time now," the man said.

James looked him over.

Dexter—if that indeed was his name—stood over six feet tall. He was broad shouldered and sported a neatly trimmed goatee, short brown hair flecked with gray, and had steely blue eyes. He wore several ornate rings on his fingers, three of which bore ancient runes and rare gems. A large, ornate golden pendant hung from a gold chain around his neck and he was draped in a long black cloak made of silk and trimmed in gold.

From his dress, James could tell that he was a man of great wealth. His demeanor told him that Dexter was a man who was accustomed to having his own way.

"What do you want with me?" James asked.

"I have a proposal that should be of great interest to you and your companions. I have need of your unusual talents and I am willing to pay handsomely for those services," Dexter said.

"My friends and I don't usually hire ourselves out," James said.

He would have rejected him outright, but something about the man intrigued him. He thought he should at least listen to what he had to say. Besides that, he was growing bored with Shanghai.

"I realized that. I am well aware of your reputations. That's why I think you'll find what I have to say more than a little interesting. But this isn't the time or place to discuss such things. Meet me at the Golden Dragon restaurant around five this evening. Bring your friends. After you've heard my proposal, you can make your decision," Dexter said.

He rose and left the library.

James watched him leave.

They met Dexter at the appointed place and time. When they entered the Golden Dragon, they found him seated at a large round table that was covered with several dishes of the local cuisine. Bottles of wine and beer were next to each dish. Dexter smiled as they approached.

"Please dine with me while we talk," he said as he opened his arms in a gesture of welcome.

They feasted like royalty that evening. Each time a dish was or bottle was emptied, a pretty young waitress replaced with something more delicious. As they ate, Dexter told them what he wanted. James noted that he didn't go into too much detail. This told him that Dexter was hiding something from them. This made his proposal all the more intriguing—which, James realized is exactly what Dexter knew it would.

When he was finished, he sat back.

"What do you think?" he asked.

James looked him straight in the eyes. Dexter didn't flinch and this made James feel uneasy.

"Are you aware of the stories concerning the Isle of Wailing Mist?" James asked.

Dexter nodded.

"Then you are also aware that it lies inside the Forbidden Zone—and for very good reason," James said.

"I am quite aware of the stories. That's why I need your services to help me retrieve the artifact," Dexter said. "What I seek lies hidden in one of the underground bunkers built long ago by the First. Although I like to think of myself as being more than formidable, even I realize that I cannot hope to find the artifact without special help. That's why I came to you."

Shazzar visibly blanched.

Mourning Winds—as the Elves called it—had the most sinister reputation of any island in the Forbidden Zone. When the islands first bubbled up from beneath the ocean decades ago after a nasty quake, Thule and several other nations attempted to colonize them. They established a joint city on Vaalvik, the largest of the islands and sent ships out to explore the other islands in the chain.

The enterprise turned into a disastrous nightmare that led to the complete destruction of the colony and the largest of the islands.[7] A similar expedition, this one by the Wichtlein, was launched a decade later. This proved to be an even bigger disaster.[8] As a result, Thule and the other great nations in the region placed the islands off limits to would-be colonists and ships.

James had also read about those ill-fated expeditions. The islands had claimed over 500 lives and unleashed a nightmare that still plagued parts of the world. [9]

"No one in his right mind would dream of going to Mourning Winds," he said. "That's tantamount to committing suicide. Only a madman would even consider it."

"I assure you that I am not mad," Dexter said. "I am well aware of the risks and dangers that lurk there."

"Then why go?" asked Zorn.

"The artifact I seek is worth my life and the lives of hundreds of people. If I don't find it, then those lives are forfeit. If I do find it, much good will come from it—provided, of course, I am able to understand its true nature," Dexter replied.

"So this is some ancient medical device you seek?" asked Patty.

---

7 Read BAD LANDS

8 Read EVILUTION

9 Read THE YEAR OF THE BEAST

"In a manner of speaking. I will not know exactly what it does until I find it. Even if it doesn't do what I thin k it does, it will still be worth millions to either a museum or a collector," Dexter replied.

James thought it over. He still wasn't telling them everything.

"How will we find it?" he asked.

"I have a map of the island. I found it at an antique fair in Paris several years ago," Dexter said. "I'll show it to you once we're aboard the ship."

"What's it look like?" asked Zorn.

"That I'm not sure of," Dexter replied. "But trust me—we'll all know it when we find it."

After mulling it over for a few more minutes, James and his companions agreed to join Dexter's expedition. The sum of money he offered notwithstanding, they found this offer far too intriguing to turn down. James, for one, was anxious to see this artifact. He was also anxious to find out exactly what it did and what Dexter really wanted with it.

They met him on the main street leading toward the harbor at eight the following morning. He'd brought several porters along to carry their bags to the ship.

"Our ship is moored at number 17," Dexter said as they walked along the pier.

"Where'd you find a captain crazy enough to take you into the Forbidden Zone?" asked Patty.

"It took some persuasion—and four times the going rate—to convince him to take us there. The ship is called the Last Hope. It's owned by Captain Paulinus Varna and it sails out of Larsa," Dexter said.

"Larsa? So it's a Thulian ship," James remarked.

Dexter nodded.

"Varna is a merchant. I met him five days ago. He's headed west toward Calcutta. Normally, he'd follow the coastline from here. I convinced him that it was in his best financial interest to make slight detour into the Forbidden Zone. Every man has his price," Dexter said.

"Some will do anything for money," said Zorn.

"Even risk fates worse than death," Patty added.

"Indeed," said James.

A week later, the Last Hope found itself anchored in a sheltered cove about 100 yards from the southern shore of Mourning Winds.

Captain Varna ordered his men to lower a longboat into the water and bade James and the others "good fortune" as they climbed down the rope ladder one-by-one. He had refused to come ashore with them. He had also refused to allow any of his crewmen to go along. He did, however, promise to wait for them and to answer any distress flares they'd send up.

Ten minutes later, the wood bottom of their longboat scraped against the wet sand at the edge of the beach. As they stepped onto the shore, James glanced up at the line of dunes directly in front of them. The beach area was clear enough, but he could plainly see the mist rising above the hills.

Thick, ugly, gray mist.

Dexter touched his shoulder and nodded toward the hills.

"According to my map, there's a narrow trail on the other side of those dunes. We are to follow it into the mountains," he said.

"Then let's be on our way. The sooner we find your artifact, the sooner we can leave this place," James said.

They found the trail exactly where Dexter's map had indicated it was. Here, the mist was thick and clammy.

Almost suffocating.

On either side of the trail, which was barely wide enough for one man, was dense jungle. They followed the trail for a few yards when they began to hear the voices. At first, they were low and inaudible. The further they traveled inland, the louder the wails and moans became until they drowned out everything else.

And the mist grew thicker.

"This is more like a fog," Patty remarked.

"It's thick enough to cut with a knife," added Shazzar.

They soon began to see faint outlines of things, bodies and faces, hands, and other creatures moving in the mist. The things were all around them, watching—and waiting. The wails and moans remained steady.

All the while, they followed Dexter as he led them deeper and deeper into the jungle. At one point, the trail made a sharp right turn. That's where they lost sight of Dexter. Unable to see more than ten feet in front of them, the party stopped. James called out several times. Each time he did, the wails turned to laughter.

Maniacal, unearthly laughter.

"They're mocking us!" said Patty.

"Taunting us," James corrected.

That's when they heard the scream.

Loud and blood-chilling. It rose above the wails and laughter and reverberated through the jungle.

"That sounded like Dexter!" James said.

"It came from up ahead," said Shazzar as he plunged down the path.

The others followed. A moment later, they came to the base of tall tree. A leather pouch and one boot lay on the ground beneath it. James bent down and picked up the case.

"It's Dexter's. Split up and search the immediate area—but stay within earshot of each other," he said.

They searched for several minutes then met back at the tree. They were just about to give up when Patty felt something warm and wet dripping onto her shoulder. She ran her fingers through it and blanched.

"Blood!" she said.

Everyone looked up but the mist obscured everything. James raised his staff and sent a beam of light into the branches. There, more than twenty feet straight up, was the twisted and mangled body of their employer.

"Is that Dexter up there?" asked Shazzar.

"If it is, he doesn't look too good," said Patty.

"What on earth dragged him up there?" wondered Zorn.

"Whatever it was, it had to be incredibly strong. Dexter was no pantywaist," Shazzar said.

"I'll go up and see if he's still alive," said Patty.

They watched as she climbed the tree. Just as she reached Dexter's remains, something short and squat leaped at her from a nearby branch. Before she realized it, both her and her attacker were plummeting toward the ground. Somehow she managed to maneuver herself so that she was on top of her attacker when they landed with a loud thud. The fall knocked the wind out of the creature. Before it could recover, Patty drew her dagger and plunged it into its throat. As she stood up, James saw that she was shaken but unhurt.

"Dexter's dead," she announced.

"So's your friend," said Zorn. "That was quite a maneuver."

"Thanks. What *is* that thing?" asked Patty as they stooped to examine it.

The creature was humanoid in appearance but its facial features were hideously deformed and twisted. Its skin was cracked and peeling off in places like the paint of an old house that had been exposed to salt water. A golden earring dangled from its left lobe and its short fingers ended in hooked nails and it was dressed in dirty, ragged clothing.

"Those look like seafarer's trousers," James said.

"You mean this thing is a sailor?" asked Zorn.

"Perhaps he was—a long time ago. Or perhaps this creature slew a sailor and stole his clothing. We'll never truly know what this creature was," James said. "What concerns me now, is our immediate future. I'm all for leaving this place as quickly as possible lest we suffer Dexter's fate."

"You won't get an argument out of me. I'm with you," Zorn said.

"Count me in. I hate this place. The faster we leave it, the better," said Shazzar.

Patty nodded.

That's when they returned to the cove only to find that the Last Hope had left without them.

Mumbai.

Sindbad sat by the window of the tavern watching as sheets of heavy rain pounded the city. The rain was so bad, he could barely see his ship, the Saracen Moon, which was anchored at the end of the pier less than a hundred yards from the tavern. The normally crowded streets of this busy port city were deserted now. Most people with any sense were indoors waiting for the rain to stop.

It had been a long wait.

This was monsoon season.

He had hoped to avoid it but his fleet had been delayed in Nagoya when a lightning bolt shattered the main mast of the Black Diamond. It took them nearly three weeks to get it repaired. By then, the monsoon season had begun.

Oh well. At least we made it this far," he thought as he sipped his ale.

He could think of many worse places than Mumbai in which to wait out the monsoons.

With him at the table—which was cluttered with empty beer bottles—were his trusted crewmen, Kasim, Hassan and the surly Dwarf, Lum. Hassan was nearly asleep. Kasim was busy flirting with the plump barmaid, who became more attractive with each passing bottle of beer. Lum was the soberest of the three and that wasn't saying much.

Their cargo had to wait.

All five of their ships were laden with fine silks and ceramics from the Asian mainland, scented oils and rare woods from the Malay Peninsula, and other pieces of fine art. There was nothing in their holds that could spoil before they reached the markets of Thule.

"How much do you think we'll make this trip?" asked Lum.

"Around a half-million," Sindbad said. "Those repairs in Nagoya ate into our profits somewhat."

"We'll make it back on the next trip," Lum said. "That's our spice run."

Sindbad nodded.

Indian spices were in big demand in Thule and Egypt, as was Thulian olive oil in the Mongoblin Empire. Sindbad knew all the markets quite well. He'd been a merchant seaman since he had sailed with the crew of the White Squall at the age of twelve. By the time he reached 20, he was captain of the Saracen Moon. By 25, he'd added the other four ships to his fleet.

The Saracen Moon and her sister ships were the fastest, best-equipped merchant ships in the world. Each had started as a dhow and been modified several times as new technologies became available.

Unlike many other ships, Sindbad's had not been converted to steam. Boilers took up too much cargo space and were too unstable for his taste. He preferred sails and oars. Even so, his ships could still outrun most of the other ships that were afloat.

He sighed at the rain.

Lum signaled the barmaid for more beer, then lit his cigar.

"Where are we headed after Thule?" he asked.

"I think we'll take a month off to refit the ships. The men could use some shore time. As for our next destination—that will depend on what kind of deals I can make," Sindbad replied.

The barmaid waddled over with a tray full of bottles. As she put them on the table and picked up the empty ones, Hassan squeezed her behind. She giggled and left.

"You like 'em big, don't you, Hassan?" asked Lum.

"Yes—but not *too* big," Hassan said with a wink as he picked up one of the beers.

"We've been at this for a long time. Ever think of retiring?" asked Kasim.

"Not really. Do you?" Sindbad asked.

"Sometimes. But then I can't figure out what I'd like to retire to. The sea gets into a man's blood and doesn't let go," Kasim answered.

"I thought about retiring once," said Hassan.

"Oh? What happened?" asked Lum.

"I sobered up!" Hassan said with a laugh. "If I did retire, then what? Where would I go? What would I do? The sea is my home. I have yet to find any place that would make me want to drop anchor and stay."

"What about you, Lum? Ever think of retirement?" asked Sindbad.

Lum let out a loud belch, then answered.

"I'll retire the day you send my bones to Davy Jones' Locker."

Sindbad smiled.

Lum was a rarity. While most Dwarfs shunned the open sea, he actually embraced it. Other Dwarfs preferred to become miners, carpenters, smiths or stone masons. Lum preferred the life of a sailor.

And why not?

Ever since he joined Sindbad's crew, they'd sailed to more than 200 foreign ports. At each place, he sampled the exotic cuisine and drink and he'd slept with dozens of women. He'd also made more money than he'd ever dreamt of. Even though he'd almost been killed several times, he wouldn't dream of giving it up. Like Sindbad and the others at the table, Lum didn't have any particular place to call "home".

"How long have we been here now?" Lum asked.

"A week. Ten days at the most. Does it matter?" Sindbad asked.

"Not really. The food is good and hot and the women are hotter. What more could a man want?" Lum replied.

"How about dry underwear?" asked Kasim.

Everyone laughed.

At that point, a soaking wet officer of the local harbor patrol entered the tavern. As he shook the rain from his wide-brimmed hat, he looked around the room. When he spotted Sindbad, he walked over.

"Captain Sindbad?" he asked.

He nodded.

"I'm Hatra Murtri. The harbor master sent me to fetch you," the officer said. "Something has happened that may be of great interest to you."

Sindbad and the others rose and followed him into the rain. Murtri made no attempt to explain further as they walked along the almost deserted pier to the office at the far end. When they entered, Harbor Master Ramad Singh came out from behind his desk to greet them. Sindbad knew Singh quite well from his many stops in Mumbai. Singh showed them to chairs and sat back down.

"What's up?" asked Sindbad.

"We have a mystery on our hands—one that should interest you greatly," Singh replied.

"I'm listening," Sindbad said.

"Do you know a ship called the Last Hope?" Singh asked.

"Yes. She's a merchant ship that sails out of Thule. She's been sailing these waters for nearly 20 years. Varna owns her," Sindbad said.

"Two days ago, two of our patrol boats found her adrift about 35 miles from the harbor. When they signaled her, they got no response. The commander decided to pull alongside and board her to see why no one acknowledged his signals. The ship was deserted. There were no signs of anyone aboard. It looked as if it had been abandoned in a hurry," Singh explained.

"Abandoned? I know Varna. He'd never leave his ship unless it was floundering. That's not like him," Sindbad said. "Where's the Lost Hope now?"

"My tugs are bringing it in even as we speak. Since she's of Thulian registry and you are an agent of the government of Thule, I thought you'd like to come along with me to check it out," Singh offered.

"I sure would," Sindbad said.

Singh got up and put on his raincoat. Sindbad and his men followed him out into the rain to the edge of the pier. After a few minutes, two harbor patrol tugs appeared in the distance with the Last Hope in tow. They waited until she was secured to the side of the pier. Sindbad looked up.

"The sails and riggings are intact," he said. "That would account for how it got here. The wind blew her into Indian waters."

"Shall we go aboard?" asked Singh.

Sindbad nodded and followed him up the gangplank. The deck was littered with tools and bits of clothing.

"Looks like they left everything in place and jumped ship," Lum remarked.

"But why?" asked Singh. "As far as my men could tell, the ship hasn't been damaged. What would make sailors abandon a perfectly good vessel?"

Hassan accidentally kicked something metallic. He looked down and saw that it was a shortsword. He picked it up and brought it to Sindbad.

"This blade's chipped in several places as if it struck something hard," Sindbad said as he examined it. "Perhaps there was some sort of battle here."

"Perhaps. Let's search below," Singh suggested as he took the sword from Sindbad and handed it to one of his officers.

"The first place I want to search is Varna's cabin. I want to see his log and manifest," Sindbad said as they walked down the slippery wooden steps. "After that, we'll check out the crews' quarters and cargo hold. Keep your eyes open for signs of struggle. That could tell us if the ship was attacked by pirates."

"There are no pirates in these waters. There haven't been for years now thanks to our navy," Singh said.

"There are none that we know of," Sindbad corrected. "Every once in a while, a marauder manages to elude our patrols. This could be such a case."

Varna's cabin was right below the pilot house. When they opened the door, they found everything in order. The bed was made and an uneaten dinner was still on his desk. Kasim examined the food. It was dry and moldy.

"Looks like it's been here for weeks," he said. "It's so moldy, I can't even tell what it is."

"Something interrupted Varna's dinner," Sindbad mused as he walked over to the desk and opened the middle drawer. He smiled when he saw the two leather-bound books.

"Just what we need," he said as he lifted them out of the drawer. "We'll take these back to your office. Varna was a meticulous record keeper. With any luck, we'll find out what happened when we read them."

A thorough search of the rest of the ship turned up nothing. The cabins were in order and the hold was filled with crates of cargo that the Last Hope had taken on in Shanghai. Even the galley was in order, with plates of dried, uneaten food laid out on the long table-just as if the men had left everything in place and abandoned the ship in the middle of their meal.

Yet, there were no signs of struggle anywhere. No signs of a crew. No damage to the ship.

They left the ship and hour later.

Sindbad told his men he'd meet them in the tavern later and followed Singh back to his office.

James sat on a log and ate a banana as he contemplated their situation. Common sense told him to return to the beach and construct a small, sturdy boat that could take them off the island. That would be the safe and sand thing to do.

But James never liked to play things safe.

Curiosity about the strange island and the voices in the mist kept drawing him further and further inland. He wanted to know why Dexter had brought them there. What was the "artifact" that was valuable enough to risk his life for?

He looked at the others.

They'd been marooned on Mourning Winds for 13 days now. Food and water were no problem. The trees were filled with fruit and nuts and there were plenty of fresh water streams.

For the past two weeks, they'd been following Dexter's map. It was an imperfect guide at best and they'd been lost several times. Their forays off the beaten path—when they could find a path—had proven to be quite interesting. The deeper they went inland, the louder the wails and moans grew and more shapes appeared around them. Sometimes, hands reached for them out of the mist, only to be lopped off by Shazzar or Patty. When something got too close, Zorn blew it away with his shotgun.

At the moment, Zorn was seated with his back against a tree with his eyes shut. Rolf's amber eyes were wide open and seemed unusually bright. He kept looking into the mist as if he expected something to charge out of it. Patty was seated a few feet from Rolf, watching him as she peeled an orange. She was genuinely concerned for his mental health—perhaps more than she should be.

Shazzar walked around as he chewed on a strip of dried beef, his dark eyes watching the perimeter at all times.

They didn't like the place.

They didn't like the increasing noises.

They didn't like the dark shapes that danced just beyond their reach.

Or the faces that emerged suddenly from the mist only to fade back into it, always maddeningly out of reach.

But they didn't fear the place either.

They'd tried to explore their new "home", but the dense mists made that almost impossible. It was hard to pick up on landmarks or directions. Something in the mists played Hell with their compass and they couldn't tell if it was night or day. They could see no stars. No sun.

Nothing.

They often found themselves retracing their own steps or traveling in a circle.

They had discovered several massive concrete structures. Most had been partially buried by volcanic activities. Some had been reduced to piles of rubble. Each structure seemed bunker-like with thick walls, narrow slits for windows and heavy steel doors. They had even uncovered the wrecks of several ancient vehicles that had been reclaimed by the jungle.

When night fell, the ruins came alive with bloated worms that emitted an eerie green light and foot-long, black and slimy centipedes that fed on the worms. Malformed rats and other vermin skittered through the rubble. Some came to feast on the now-bloated centipedes. Others sought larger prey. These ground-dwelling creatures also fell prey to scores of large, hideous bats that swooped down and snapped them up with their long, dog-like muzzles. Here and there, amorphous blobs oozed across the ground, sucking up insects as they went.

James observed that these life forms did not dwell outside the ruins. The jungles belonged to the things in the mist.

To James, the ruins spoke volumes.

Mourning Winds had obviously been a military base of some sort. That meant that Dexter's "artifact" was probably some kind of ancient weapon. If Dexter knew about the weapon, most likely someone else did, too. Most likely, they would come looking for it, too.

Weapons designed by the First were usually highly dangerous and destructive. James decided that they had to find Dexter's "artifact" and destroy it before anyone else could use it against innocent people.

But what exactly *was* it?

And would he know it if he found it?

James shrugged and stretched.

"This is as good a place as any to spend the night," he announced. "We'll get some sleep and continue in the morning."

Sindbad entered the tavern a few hours later and found his men seated around the same table. Once again, beer bottles covered most of the tabletop. He walked over and sat down in the only empty chair.

"What was in the log?" asked Hassan. "Where was she bound?"

"According to Varna's log, she was bound for Calcutta but they took a slight detour," Sindbad replied.

"Detour? To where?" asked Lum.

"Mourning Winds," Sindbad said.

Lum visible blanched at the name.

"That's the Isle of Wailing Mist! That's in the Forbidden Zone!" he said.

"I know where it is. I've *been* there, same as you," Sindbad assured him. "In fact, I lost a handful of good men on that rock."

"That's insane!" said Kasim.

"I agree," said Sindbad.

"Are you sure they got there?" asked Lum.

"Yes. Varna wrote down every detail of their trip. They anchored in a small cove on the southern side of the island 14 days ago. Someone named Dexter and five others put shore and instructed Varna to wait for them. None of his crewmen went ashore," Sindbad said.

"How large a crew did the Last Hope have?" asked Lum.

"Besides Varna and the First Mate, there were 12 crewmen," Sindbad replied.

"Any more entries in that log that might tell us anything?" asked Hassan.

"No. The log ended on that date," Sindbad said.

"So to sum this up, the Last Hope left Shanghai with 20 people. One week later, it anchored off the Isle of Wailing Mist. Six people put ashore and the rest remained aboard to await their return. Now, two weeks later, the Last Hope is found drifting aimlessly in the harbor, with no one aboard and the cargo intact," Lum said.

"To make it even more interesting, Varna was a good captain with a good crew. People like that just don't go missing. Something happened on that island. Something terrible. Now it's up to us to find out what," Sindbad said.

"Why us?" asked Kasim.

"Since it's a Thulian ship, I radioed Arka-Dal and apprised him of the situation. Naturally, he ordered us to investigate. He wants us to go to Mourning Winds and check on those people who went ashore. He also advised me not to take any stupid chances. If things get too hairy, we're to pull out," Sindbad explained.

"That gives us an out," Lum said. "Any idea who the five people who went ashore with Dexter are?"

"No. The manifest just listed them as the "Dexter party," Sindbad said.

"Well, it's obvious to me that something took those men off that ship then set it adrift so they couldn't escape. The wind and tides then brought the Last Hope here. Want to bet that Varna and his crew are somewhere on that island?" said Kasim.

"If they are, they're probably all corpses by now. You know what happened to everyone else who tried to explore that place—and they were tough, seasoned fighters," Lum said.

"When we tried to establish colonies in the Forbidden Zone, they sent two ships and 44 men to the Isle of Wailing Mist. None of them were ever seen again," he added.

"The first time Thule tried to colonize the islands, and entire ship with 27 men was sent to check our Mourning Winds. When it didn't report back after two weeks, another was sent to search for it. It never returned, either. That's when the colony's leaders made the place off limits," Sindbad said.

"Then there was the incident with some of our own crewmen. We lost most of them, too," Hassan said.

"Don't remind me. They disobeyed a direct order by going ashore. In their case, curiosity killed the sailors," Sindbad said.

"What about this Dexter guy? Any more info on him?" asked Lum.

"In the manifest, he's listed as an antiquities dealer," Sindbad replied. "He also paid Varna three times the going rate to take him into the Forbidden Zone."

"What about the cargo? Anything unusual there?" asked Kasim.

"Not really. Just the usual trade goods. I don't like the idea of going back there any more than you men do. But we're under orders from Arka-Dal to investigate this and that's exactly what we'll have to do," Sindbad said.

"I never thought I'd see that place again. I still have nightmares," Lum said.

"So do I," Sindbad assured him. "How's our firepower?"

Hassan smiled.

"We still have 100 rifles and 10,000 rounds of ammo left from our last mission," he replied. "I think there's a case of grenades in the hold as well."

"Good. That should keep the boogey men at bay," Sindbad said.

"I pray to Allah that it will," said Hassan.

"When do we leave?" asked Kasim.

"At first light tomorrow," Sindbad replied.

Patty woke with a start. Her sudden movement caused the others to look up. She glanced over at James and saw the question in his eyes.

"I just had the most bizarre dream," she began. "In this dream, I was a knight. I had come home from a distant war with my squire at my side. When I arrived at my home town, I found that the entire country was being ravaged by the Black Death. Wagons loaded with bloated, blackened corpses rolled through the streets and there were warning signs painted on the door of nearly every house.

When we got to my castle, everyone inside was dead—except one solitary figure. He beckoned us closer. When we got close enough, I saw that it was Death himself. He was seated at a table with two chairs. On the table was a chess board and he motioned for me to sit in the empty chair. The next thing I know, we were playing chess. I knew that I had to win. If I lost, Death would claim me as surely as he had claimed most of the people in my homeland."

"Did you dream in color?" James asked.

"No. Everything was in black and white," Patty replied.

"Were you speaking Swedish?" he asked.

"Why, yes—we were," she replied.

"And were there English subtitles?" asked Shazzar.

"How did you know?" Patty asked.

"I think I saw that movie," James said with a smile.

"So did I. It was one of Bergman's best," Shazzar added.

"Who's Bergman? What are you talking about? What movie?" asked Patty.

"The movie was called "The Seventh Seal" and it was directed by Ingmar Bergman," James said in a tone that said she should have known that.

Frustrated, she picked up a rock and threw it at him. He ducked and laughed. So did the others. After a while, Patty did, too.

James stood and looked around at the mist shrouded vegetation. Tired of the darkness, he uttered a spell that caused the knob on the end of his staff to burst into a bright, white light. He looked down at the others who were still huddled around the campfire.

"It's time to move on," he announced.

They looked at each other and followed him into the mist. So far, they'd explored most of the southern part of the island. Outside of the things in the mist, they saw no other signs of life. But there were plenty of signs of death.

More often than not, their feet made crunching noises as they trod on human bones or rusted armor and weapons. James figured that these were the remains of those who dared to set foot on the island many years before. In the back of his mind, he wondered how many people had died in this place—and what was doing the killing.

The things in the mist were irritating but seemed harmless enough. So far, no real attacks had occurred. But the mournful wails and maniacal laughter were wearing at his companions' nerves.

So was the mist and oppressive humidity.

The light emanating from James' staff cut through the mist and enabled them to see a little bit better. At the same time, it both attracted and repelled the things in the mist.

The situation made Patty jumpy. She could see the malformed things moving around them in the mist. Their howls, moans and wails added to her nervousness. She'd never been afraid before and wasn't sure she was afraid now.

What was out there?

What was the source, the reason behind the incessant wailing?

What did they want?

She glanced back at the others.

Shazzar seemed edgy, too. He kept an eye on the mist and his sword drawn. James and Zorn remained stoic and wary while Rolf seemed not to mind the situation at all. In fact, he seemed to be somewhat detached from it all, like his mind was millions of miles away.

She sighed.

That was Rolf's *usual* state these days. Jan's loss had left him empty and almost robot-like. He rarely showed emotion anymore. Rarely laughed or smiled. He was simply on auto-pilot. Simply going through the motions of living without actually being alive. The real Rolf was gone, buried deep inside the empty shell that trailed her.

She'd cry for him—if she thought it would do any good.

The whole thing felt so bizarre to her. So surreal. She wondered if they'd been trapped in some nightmarish, alternate reality.

"Where's this trail taking us?" she called out.

"We'll find out when we reach the end," James called back.

"Fine! Be like that!" she snapped.

"At least we haven't come upon a deserted city or village," Shazzar remarked.

"The writers aren't through with us yet," James warned.

"Ten says they won't use that plot device this time," Shazzar challenged.

"Done!" accepted James.

They trudged on for hours. They passed more piles of rubble and came upon a narrow trail that looked as if it had been paved. James sipped water from his canteen as he studied the trail.

"What do you think?" he asked.

Shazzar shrugged.

"We might as well follow it. It's not like we have anything else to do," he said.

The trail twisted and turned through the jungle for a few miles. Eventually, they found themselves standing amid a complex of ruined concrete structures set around the base of a hill. A larger bunker, half-obscured with overgrowth, was in the side of the hill itself. It had no door.

James approached and shone his light inside of it. The bunker was empty save for bits of rubble and some weeds that had worked their way up through the cracks in the floor. He looked back at the others and saw they were exhausted.

"We'll set up here for the night," he said as he entered and dropped his pack.

The others did the same.

Except Rolf.

He elected to remain outside the bunker and watch the mist. Patty saw him standing there. She unpacked her knapsack and brought him a piece of dried beef. Rolf took it without saying anything. Patty tried to make him smile. When all of her efforts failed, she sighed and joined the others.

"Do you think he'll ever come out of it?" she asked.

James looked up from his meal.

"That's impossible to say," he said. "The Gods made him mad and only the Gods can cure his madness."

"I thought you didn't believe in gods," Zorn said.

"That's what you get for thinking," James joked. "This place isn't so bad. We might as well make this our base. It's out of the elements and the noise isn't so loud in here."

"I can still hear the wails, James. I can't get them out of my head. If we don't get off this rock soon, I'm afraid I'll end up like Rolf," Patty said.

"They're getting to me, too," Shazzar admitted.

"Me, too. Hell, the only one who doesn't seem to be bothered by this place is Rolf," Zorn added. "It's as if his madness somehow protects him from everything here."

"More likely, it serves to blunt the effects," James guessed.

They heard a sound at the door and watched as Rolf entered. He was holding the carcass of a small animal he had just slain. He walked over and placed it down in front of James.

"I killed us a rabbit," he said. "I got with my bow."

James studied the animal, which was the size of a small dog. It had long ears and strong hind legs like a rabbit, bit its face looked more canine and its mouth was full of nasty-looking, jagged teeth and fangs.

"Well, it's kind of a rabbit," he said.

"I don't care what it is as long as it's edible. I'm sick of fruit and beef jerky," Zorn said as he took out his knife.

In no time at all, he had the animal skinned and cleaned. Shazzar gathered wood from the jungle and started a fire just outside the bunker while Zorn tied the animal to a spit. Then they sat back and allowed Patty to work her culinary magic.

The monsoons had let up enough to allow Sindbad's small fleet to leave Mumbai the next afternoon. They sailed east along the Indian coast and turned directly south when they came around the horn. Sindbad estimated it would take them five days to reach the Forbidden Zone, provided the wind remained steady. Once they got there, they'd sail to Mourning Winds and anchor in the cove—just like the Last Hope had. Then they'd have to work up the courage to go ashore.

He wondered what they'd find there.

Would any of the crew of the Last Hope be alive? Was there actually anyone left to rescue?

He also thought about Dexter. Why would an antiquities dealer go to Mourning Winds? What was he after that was important enough to die for?

These were questions that Arka-Dal also wanted answers to. The Forbidden Zone had been used as a military base and weapons laboratory by the First. Arka-Dal feared that Dexter was after one of those weapons, either to sell to a wealthy client with deadly ambitions or to achieve his own ends. Arka-Dal ordered him to find that weapon and destroy it before anyone else got their hands on it.

But Mourning Winds had claimed the lives of at least a hundred good men. Would Sindbad's small force be able to survive long enough to complete their mission? Or would their souls be added to those already there?

These questions tortured Sindbad during the day and robbed him of his sleep at night. He realized that he wouldn't be able to rest at all until they got into and out of the Zone in one piece.

The next morning, James and his friends left the bunker. The mist seemed even thicker now. It fouled up their perception and sense of direction and cast the island in an eternal twilight from which there was no relief.

"I think that way is north," said James as he pointed. "If we keep heading that way, we should reach the volcano."

"Just what is this place, James?" asked Patty.

"During the First Age, it was some sort of experimental weapons lab and military complex. I think they were trying to create some kind of super weapon that would help them win the war," James replied as they began moving through the jungle.

"Do you think any of them would still work after all this time?" asked Patty.

"Yes. In fact, I'm sure that we've encountered one of those weapons a half a world away from here," James answered.

"What was that?" asked Zorn.

"The bugs," James said.

"The bugs were created as a weapon?" asked Patty. "How disgusting!"

"And they were one of their *lesser* weapons. Imagine, if you can, what else may be hidden here," James said.

"That boggles the mind!" said Zorn.

"Indeed," James said.

"So what are we looking for?" asked Zorn.

"Beats me. I think we'll know it when we see it. It probably won't be anything subtle and it's most likely guarded by all sorts of traps and weapons," James replied.

"So the nastier things get—" began Shazzar.

"—the closer we are to it," finished Zorn.

"Exactly!" said James.

"Well, at least there are plenty of fruit and nut trees on this island. Fresh water, too. We won't die of thirst or starvation," Patty said.

"Or old age," chimed in Rolf unexpectedly.

The comment caught everyone by surprise. James turned and studied him carefully. While the mist and wails dulled everyone's senses, Rolf's seemed to be heightened by them.

"I know something you don't," he half sung.

"Indeed," said James as he decided to keep a closer eye on the younger Yaren.

The mist didn't seem to bother Zorn all that much either. His amber eyes enhanced his vision. Although he couldn't see perfectly, he could see clearer than the others. He wasn't crazy about the wails, though. They were getting harder to block out. Even covering his ears didn't help.

"We keep stepping on bones and crushed armor wherever we go," he said. "Something here attacked and killed these men. Something real nasty. How come we haven't been attacked?"

"That's a good question, Zorn. At the moment, I have no answer for you," James said.

"The attack will come," Rolf said. "They're out there. There are dozens of them, too. Each bigger and nastier than the others. They're just waiting for the right moment to strike."

"How pleasant," Shazzar said. "How come you can see them and we can't?"

"I dunno. I just do," Rolf replied.

James stopped and scratched his head.

"Where to now?" asked Shazzar.

"I'm not sure. We need to find a high spot so we can see above this mist," James replied.

Zorn looked up.

"I could try to shinny up one of these trees," he suggested.

"I wouldn't," Rolf said.

"Why not?" asked Zorn.

"There are things in the branches. Ugly, nasty things," Rolf said.

"So much for that idea," said Zorn.

"Let's look for a high point, like a hill or something," James said as he started walking again.

They wandered through the jungle for another hour. After several twists and turns, they found themselves standing in front of a very familiar object.

"That tree looks like the one we passed an hour ago," Zorn pointed out.

"It should. That *is* the tree we passed an hour ago. We've gone in a complete circle," Shazzar said disgustedly.

"Just where in Hell are we?" asked Patty in frustration.

"Mourning Winds," said Rolf.

Patty squinted at him and suppressed an urge to strangle him.

Before she could utter another word, something large and dark charged out of the mist and landed a resounding blow to Shazzar's ribcage. The blow sent him tumbling into the mist until he vanished from sight. Patty raised her sword and swung. She felt the blade connect with something solid and pulled back to strike again. This time, her attacker seized her leg and tossed her into a nearby clump of ferns and thistle. She screamed in pain and anger as the thistle scratched her in several places.

Zorn aimed his shotgun right at the creature's blazing yellow eyes and pulled both triggers. As Patty freed herself from the thicket, she heard the roar of the shotgun. This was quickly followed by a loud shriek. She ran over to Zorn. He had a huge grin on his face as he reloaded his weapon.

"What *was* that thing?" she asked.

"I don't know—but it doesn't like the taste of shotgun shells," Zorn said. "I hit it point blank. I heard it scream, too, so I know I hurt it."

"You probably just pissed it off," Shazzar said as he picked himself up. "Good thing you shot it. It just about knocked my head off."

"Wasn't real," Rolf said.

"What do you mean?" asked James.

"It wasn't real," Rolf repeated.

"It seemed real enough to me," said Patty.

"Me too," said Shazzar as he massaged his aching side.

"Look!" Rolf said as he pointed to a nearby tree.

They all walked over and examined it. There was huge chunk of the bark missing from its trunk and wood splinters everywhere. Zorn reached over and plucked out the remains of his shells. He showed the fragments to James.

"Either my shells went clear through it—" he began.

"—or it was never really there in the first place," finished James.

"Told you it wasn't real," Rolf said.

"I'm beginning to understand," said James as he examined the shattered tree.

"Care to enlighten us?" asked Shazzar.

"There are *no* monsters in the mist. Instead, the monsters *are* the mist," James said.

"Huh?" came a chorus of voices as the others looked at him.

"The mist is some sort of defense system. Somehow or other, whatever controls it is able to tap into our subconscious minds and use our own fears and nightmares against us. For brief moments, the mist manifests itself into solid versions of those fears and attacks us. Although they seem quite real to us and anyone else who encounters them, they are only comprised of mist and smoke. That's why Zorn's shells passed through that thing," James explained.

"I told you it wasn't real," Rolf repeated.

"So you're saying that we'd better watch what we think?" asked Shazzar.

"Something like that," James replied. "But it's next to impossible to control your subconscious, so good luck with that."

"How come Rolf knew it wasn't real?" asked Patty.

James shrugged.

"I'm not sure—yet. It may have something to do with his trauma. But that thing *was* real. For a few seconds, it had enough mass and energy to do us actual harm," James answered.

"So Dexter and everyone else who set foot on this rock, were killed by monsters from their subconscious minds? Monsters from the id?" asked Shazzar.

James nodded.

"Ever feel like you're trapped inside an old science fiction movie?" asked Zorn.

"All the time," said Patty.

"How far are we from our bunker?" asked Zorn.

"About two miles. I think we should return to it. We've been wandering around in circles for seven hours now and I'm tired," James replied.

"I second that motion," Patty agreed.

Sindbad was seated behind his desk reading when Hassan and Lum entered his cabin. He looked up to acknowledge them.

"Just thought we'd tell you that we'll be entering the Zone the day after tomorrow," Hassan said.

"So soon?" asked Sindbad. He had not expected to be there for at least five more days.

"The winds held up and we made good time," Lum reported. "Still want only take 12 men ashore?"

Sindbad nodded.

"I don't want to risk any more men than we have to. The more we bring ashore, the more we expose to whatever's on that rock," he said. "I want the men well armed, too."

"Don't worry. We will be," Lum assured him.

"We?" Sindbad asked.

"Sure. You can't expect me to stay behind and let you have all the fun, now can you?" Lum replied.

"You have a strange idea of fun, my friend," Sindbad remarked.

"I know. But someone's gotta watch your back," the Dwarf said with a smirk. "Besides, I've always been kind of curious about that place."

"Curiosity killed the cat," Sindbad said.

"So what? I'm a *Dwarf*!" Lum joked. "Is it true that place is covered with bones?"

"That's what I've heard," Sindbad said. "Be careful lest your bones get added to them."

"Same to you," Lum shot back.

"What about me?" asked Hassan. "I'd like to go ashore with you, too."

"I need you to stay back with the fleet. But if you see our flares, put a rescue party together and come running."

"Aye-aye," Hassan said. "I'll pick the party right now."

The route back to the bunker proved to be treacherous. The mist obscured every landmark of the terrain, they found themselves lost more than once. Much to James' dismay, Rolf plunged ahead of the group. He moved at a fast pace, too. So fast, it was all they could to do to keep up with him.

Rolf paid them no mind. Off in own private world, he was chasing shadows in the mist. One, in particular, looked disturbingly familiar. He chased it for miles and miles. Then, when his legs were about to buckle from exhaustion, the shadow stopped and turned toward him. As he gasped for air, he watched it. The closer it got, the more familiar it looked.

"Jan!" he whispered as the shadow stopped ten feet in front of him.

"Come to me, my darling," it said as it held its arms out.

Mesmerized, he dropped his spear and stumbled toward it. The shade urged him onward until, after what seemed like an eternity, he melted into her embrace. She looked into his eyes and smiled.

That's when something clicked in his muddled mind.

Those eyes weren't Jan's eyes.

Nor was that smile.

Both seemed wicked and terrible.

Still entranced, he could not pull away. Instead, he opened his mouth to scream for help—only to feel her lips touch his and her long, snakelike tongue slither down his throat. Panic snapped him out of his trance and he struggled. The shade held on tightly and continued its deadly "kiss". Her tongue cut off his air and he began to choke. Just as he felt the life ebb from him, he summoned up all of his remaining strength and used it to hurl the creature from him.

Unable to breathe and hurting all over, Rolf fell to his knees. He watched helplessly as "Jan" vanished, only to be replaced by a horrid, twisted blob with many tentacles and a huge, gaping, bird-like mouth. He thought he heard mocking laughter as it moved in for the kill.

That's when he heard another, louder, sound.

Zorn's shotgun!

He smiled as the shells tore his attacker in half. The creature's body struck the ground and everyone watched in shock as each individual segment sprouted crab-like legs and skittered into the jungle.

"I don't fucking believe it!" Shazzar muttered as the things vanished in the mist.

James and Patty were already at Rolf's side. They helped him to his feet and somehow managed to find their way back to the bunker before he passed out.

He woke several hours later and started scratching and clawing at his arms and legs.

"What's wrong?" asked James as he watched his strange behavior.

"I don't know. I feel like there's things crawling around inside my body. I can feel them moving under my skin," Rolf said as he scratched even harder.

James placed his hand on Rolf's head.

"I sense something inside you. Some sort of presence," he said.

"Can you do something about it? It's driving me nuts!" Rolf asked.

"I can try," said James as he cast a healing spell over Rolf.

After a few minutes, the sensations ceased and Rolf was able to relax.

"Thanks. Did you kill them?" Rolf asked.

"I'm not sure," James said. "But at least you feel better."

Rolf went to the fire and sat down. A very concerned Patty handed him some food. He took it and started eating. Before he finished his meal, he dropped his plate and began writhing wildly. He flailed at his arms, chest and stomach.

"Make it go away! Make it stop!" he shouted.

Zorn and Shazzar held him down while James examined him. He watched in horror as several things writhed along Rolf's forearm. They were several inches long and just beneath his skin. The others gathered around as three wormlike things chewed their way through Rolf's flesh. James pulled each of them out. They were all bloated with blood—Rolf's blood. He tossed them outside the bunker.

"Blood worms!" he said in disgust.

Rolf screamed and grabbed his leg. James rolled up his pantleg just in time to see yet another, longer worm work its way to the surface. He pulled it out and tossed out into the jungle with the others. Now Rolf truly writhed in agony as at least a dozen more of the things burst through his skin. James pulled each one of them out and discarded them. Rolf kept screaming for him to make them stop.

"Do something, James! Help him!" Patty cried as tears rolled down her cheeks.

"We can do nothing but wait until all of them find their way out. Then I can heal his wounds. In the meantime, I can dull his senses so he doesn't feel the pain," James said.

As one large one burst forth from Rolf's chest, James grabbed it and tossed into the jungle as far as he could. By then, Rolf had stopped writhing.

"That's the last of them," James said as he applied his healing powers

Within seconds, his wounds were closed. Patty used the water from her canteen to wash the blood from his body. Zorn and Shazzar shook their heads in sympathy.

"That was close," Zorn said.

"Too close. Normally, blood worms enter the body via food or drink that's been contaminated with them. In this case, they formed a living colony and lured Rolf into a trap. Somehow or other, they—or whatever controls them—knew that Rolf would respond to an image of Jan. It's like they were able to read his thoughts," James mused.

"Will he be all right?" asked Patty.

"He should be, provided of course, there aren't any left inside him," James replied.

"Now there's a pleasant thought," Zorn remarked.

Patty was especially concerned about Rolf. As much as she hated to admit to herself, she had actually fallen for him. Jan's death had cleared the way for her. Normally, she would have taken advantage of such a situation, but her deep friendship for Jan had made her reluctant to do so.

Ever since Jan's death, Rolf had become distant and detached from the world in general. He'd never gotten over Jan. Judging by the way that creature was able to use her image to lure him into a trap, he wasn't ready to let go.

Not yet.

Zorn had bounced back from the loss of Mulan. Patty figured it was because he had only known her for two months. It was much harder for Rolf. He and Jan had grown up together and their love ran deep.

Maybe too deep.

Patty wondered if he'd ever let go.

The others knew of her dilemma. The Jackal sometimes teased her about it. James offered counsel whenever she asked for it. Other than that, they left her alone. It made her feel helpless.

For the first time in her life, she was actually in love with someone—and she had no idea how to deal with it.

She looked down at Rolf. Her instincts wanted to hold him close. Her common sense caused her to hold back.

There was also the *mental* aspect. Jans' death had unhinged Rolf. He suffered long bouts of deep depression where he'd go for days without eating or sleeping or even speaking to anyone. He'd also gone off by himself several times. He'd be gone for weeks. Each time he returned, he looked as if he'd gone through a threshing machine. He never told anyone where he'd gone or what had happened—and they never pressed him for answers.

Because of this, Patty feared that if she tried to push him into another relationship, it might unhinge him altogether. There was no telling how he'd react and that *really* worried her.

That's why she kept her feelings to herself and hoped for the best. The trouble was, it was eating her alive.

James stared into the crackling flames and pondered their predicament. Whatever dwelled within the mist seemed to be able to use their innermost thoughts and fears against them. From now on, they couldn't be sure what was real or illusion. He feared that their situation might soon become unbearable. The constant wails and moans and mind tricks just might be enough to eventually drive them insane. To him, that was a fate far worse than death itself.

His common sense told him to return to the beach and construct a raft. It was better to take their chances out at sea where they might be found by a passing ship. His curiosity told him to keep searching the island. He wanted to find out what Dexter was really after and what it did. He also wanted to locate the causes of all the wails and moans. But everything about the place seemed eager to kill them. He envisioned them fighting off one nasty monster after another in the vain hope of being rescued. No one knew where they were and only a true madman would dare set foot on the island to search for them.

He smiled.

Patty walked over to him. She sat down beside him, crossed her arms over her knees and rested her chin on them.

"How's Rolf?" James asked.

"Sleeping as if he hasn't got a care in the world," Patty answered. "Do you think he'll ever notice?"

"Notice what?" asked James.

"How I feel about him," she said softly.

"That, my dear, is a question that even *I* can't answer," James said. "His loss has made him mad. That madness has blinded him to all that is good in the world."

"You think he's nuts?" she asked.

James nodded.

"Ancient doctors would have diagnosed him as being manic depressive with suicidal tendencies. When he becomes depressed, he shuts out the world, then wanders off to try and get himself killed," he explained.

"Do you think he'll ever recover?" she asked.

"Perhaps—if given enough time. And he doesn't get himself killed first," James said.

Patty sighed.

It was the saddest sigh James had ever heard.

"I sure can pick 'em," she remarked.

"Indeed," said James.

Zorn came over and sat in front of them. He took some meat from the fire and gnawed it. He saw the forlorn look on Patty's face and put down the meat.

"I think Rolf's afraid," he said.

"Of what?" asked Patty.

"He's lost Jan. He's probably afraid that if he falls in love with you, he'll lose you as well. So he's put himself in some emotional shell to shut you out," Zorn replied.

"What about you, Zorn? You've lost Mulan, but you haven't shut out the rest of the world," Patty pointed out.

"I really miss her but life must go on. Mulan was a big part of my life for a brief moment but she's gone now. I have to deal with that. I hurt deep inside, but I refuse to curl up and die. There's too much to do and see yet," Zorn said after some thought.

"You are indeed made of stronger stuff, Zorn," Patty said.

"I didn't grow up with Mulan like Rolf did with Jan. Maybe that takes the edge off it somehow," Zorn added.

James took the map from his pocket and unfolded on the floor. The others gathered around as he studied the details.

"The highest point on this rock is this volcanic mountain here to the north. According to this map, we can reach it by following a twisting path through the jungle," he said after a bit.

"And just how do we find this path?" asked Shazzar.

James ran his finger along the bottom of the map.

"This stream goes right to it. From the looks of it, it's about five miles from where we are now. Just a short stretch of the legs," he said.

"A short stretch of the legs through Hell you mean," Zorn said. "It won't be easy to find that stream in all this mist. We can barely see ten feet in any direction. How will we know when we've found the stream?"

"When your shoes fill with water, you're there," James said with a smirk. "We'll head out as soon as Rolf recovers enough to travel."

Dawn.

Sindbad's fleet entered the Forbidden Zone. The two largest islands had been destroyed. Only Mourning Winds and two smaller islands remained. All three were practically unexplored.

They sailed past a series of red buoys warning them not to enter. By now, nearly everyone was standing on the deck of the Saracen Moon watching as the dreaded Isle of Wailing Mists came within view. Even from miles away, they could see that the entire island was shrouded with thick, gray mist.

Sindbad pointed to it.

"That's it. That's where that ship came from," he said.

Lum shivered and not from the cold.

"I don't like that place. We lost nearly 100 men on that rock. We never saw any of them again," he said.

"Any bugs there?" asked Hassan.

"I don't know what's on that island. No one ever came back to tell us about it," Lum replied.

"Some of my men did—but they never said anything about bugs," Sindbad said. "There's a sheltered cove on the south side. We'll anchor off there and take the longboats to the beach," Sindbad said.

"Still want to limit the party to a dozen men?" asked Hassan.

"Yes. Issue them rifles and enough ammunition to fight a small war. I want us to have a radio and flares, too. We'll send up a flare every two hours to let you know we're alive. If you don't see anything for six hours, weigh anchor and sail for Thule. Don't come after us. Understand?" Sindbad said.

"Aye-aye, Captain," Hassan said with a smile.

Sindbad smiled, too.

He knew Hassan too well. He knew that if the flares stopped going up, he'd lead a full-scale rescue mission and the risks be damned.

"The mist never goes away and those wails never stop. Even the sun can't penetrate the mist. It's kind of like a steambath," Lum said.

"That's what my men told us the last time we were here. I never thought we'd come back to this place or ever set foot on Mourning Winds," Sindbad said.

"The Gods work in mysterious ways," Lum said.

"Fuck the Gods! They hold no sway on that island," Sindbad said.

The closer they got to Mourning Winds, the louder the wails became. The eerie sounds chilled most of the crewmen to the marrow.

"Is that the wind?" one asked.

Sindbad turned and shook his head.

"There's no wind on Mourning Winds," he said.

"Then what is that sound?" asked another.

"No one's ever lived long enough to find out," Lum replied. "I hope we know what we're doing."

"Me, too," said Sindbad.

They sailed into the cove and dropped anchor some 1,000 yards from the beach. Sindbad watched as two longboats were lowered into the waves along with several boxes of ammunition, a dozen flares and a radio. He turned toward his shore party.

"All right, lads. Into the boats!" he ordered. "Who's my radio man?"

"I am, Captain," said a short, bearded man in a white turban.

"Good. Stay close to me, Habib," Sindbad said as he climbed down the cargo net and into one of the boats.

Hassan watched from the deck as they pulled away and made for the beach. Sindbad said they'd send up a flare every two hours. He checked his pocket watch and discovered that it had stopped. He attempted to wind it but the hands wouldn't budge. It was as if they had been frozen in place. He turned to a nearby crewman.

"What time do you have?" he asked.

"I can't tell. My watch stopped the minute we entered the Zone," the crewman said.

Hassan nodded.

"How in Hell am I going to keep track of the time now?" he wondered.

Rolf slept for three straight days. During that time, his wounds mysteriously vanished and he breathed easier. Patty hovered over him like a mother hen the entire time and took a lot of good-natured ribbing from Zorn and Shazzar. She didn't care anymore. They all knew how she felt. Only Rolf seemed oblivious to her feelings. As she watched him sleep, she wondered what life was like on that world of his and whether or not he was better off than the rest of them.

Rolf woke with a ravenous appetite. In fact, he ate everything Patty prepared for him and seemed a bit more relaxed somehow. He looked through the doorway at the mist and smiled.

"I like it here," he said suddenly. "It feels like home."

James raised an eyebrow.

Patty's jaw dropped.

"You *like* this place?" she asked.

Rolf nodded and smiled. It was a strange, almost surreal smile. Kind of like the one on the Mona Lisa. The smile made Patty shiver.

"Now that we're all rested, let's look for that stream," James said as he walked out of the bunker.

The others hurried after him.

They trudged through the mist and jungle for an hour in search of the stream on Dexter's map. Patty stopped and looked back at Rolf, who was bringing up the rear and keeping a close eye on the things milling around in the mist. He seemed calm. Almost too calm.

They soon came to a narrow, gravel-covered path that sloped gently upward. For a while, the going was easier.

"I wonder where this leads," said Shazzar.

"Keep following it and you'll find out," said James.

Patty covered her ears with her hands and screamed. The others turned and stared at her. He scream made Rolf laugh.

"Don't the voices bother you?" she asked.

"No. They drown out the voices inside my head. In fact, I find them most pleasant," Rolf replied.

"You hear voices inside your head?" she asked.

"Screams, actually. I keep hearing Jan's last scream over and over again. These voices drown it out," Rolf answered.

"I didn't know. I'm sorry," Patty said.

"Don't be. I feel much better now," Rolf said with that strange grin.

Patty shook her head as he walked past her. She glanced over at Zorn and James to se if they'd heard.

They had.

Was Rolf nuts? Had his mind snapped altogether? If so, what would happen next?

Zorn touched her shoulder to reassure her.

"I'll keep a real close watch on him," he promised. "And *you*, too."

The rescue party stepped out of the boats and walked across the beach. Before them loomed a series of high dunes, scrub-covered hills and the mist beyond. Lum walked over to him.

"This is a big rock," he said. "Do we split up?"

"No. There's strength in numbers. Stay together," Sindbad said as they marched inland.

"Fan out—but stay close enough to the man on either side of you to keep in sight. Search carefully. If you run into anything, shout!" he called out.

Sindbad called a halt about two miles inland. They were now on the other side of the hills and surrounded by the mist. The wails and moans were louder now. Several of the men seemed visibly nervous.

Lum stopped and checked his compass. He shook it several times then shrugged.

"What's wrong?" asked Kasim.

"Something here is making my compass go nuts. The needle just keeps spinning around. I can't tell which way is north," Lum said.

"Keep your eyes on that mountain and walk toward it. That's where we're headed," Sindbad called out.

"Then what?" asked Kasim.

"We climb it and try to get above the mist so we can get a better view," Sindbad said.

"The smell's getting worse," Kasim noticed.

"Any stronger and we'll have trouble breathing," said Lum as he lit his cigar.

Habib wrinkled his nose.

"Doesn't this place smell bad enough without you having to smoke that thing?" he said.

"It cancels out the smell. You should try one," Lum offered.

Habib shook his head and walked away. Kasim reached out and took the cigar from Lum's hand.

"I'll try one," he said. "Got a light?"

Lum struck a match and held it out. Kasim put the end of the cigar into the flame and puffed a few times. He coughed in the process, then took a deep draught and let it out. As he did, he sniffed the air.

"He's right. I can't smell the mist any more," Kasim said.

“Habib—bring me that radio,” Sindbad ordered.

Habib handed him the mike. Try as he might, Sindbad could not get the radio to work. All he heard was static. He handed the mike back to Habib.

“The radio’s as useless as the compass. Something on this island is screwing with out equipment,” Sindbad said. “We’ll have to stick with the flares.”

Lum fit one into a pistol and sent skyward. They watched it arc above the mist and burn brightly for a few minutes before it plunged back to Earth.

“I hope Hassan sees that,” Sindbad said as they continued inland.

Hassan *did.*

“That’s the first one. Keep watching the sky. There should be a flare every two hours,” he said to a nearby crewman. Try to keep track of the time as best as you can.”

“What if we don’t see another one?” the man asked.

“Then we’ll go ashore and find them!” Hassan replied.

After what seemed like an eternity of walking, James and company finally came to the stream. Shazzar stooped to refill his canteen. As the cool liquid bubbled into it, he noticed something in the water. When he leaned closer to see what it was, the sight of a ghastly, half-rotted face staring back him through empty eye sockets caused him to recoil.

The others looked into the stream and saw more faces. James shook his head as he recognized a few of them.

“These are crewmen of the Last Hope,” he said. “I know these faces well.”

Zorn nodded.

“You’re right. But there’s only four of them here. What about the others?” he asked.

“I have an ugly feeling that we’ll find the answer to that as we go along,” James replied.

They followed the stream until it abruptly ended at the base of a rocky cliff. The face of it ran straight up and looked far too smooth to climb. James looked to the right and left. The walls went on for several yards and vanished in the mist. He looked at Zorn and Shazzar, then pointed. They nodded and took off in opposite directions. James sat down on a nearby rock to await their return.

Zorn was the first to return with his shotgun resting on his shoulder.

“What did you find?” asked James.

“Nothing. These cliffs go on for miles without a break,” Zorn answered.

A few minutes later, Shazzar emerged from the mist. He walked up to James and pointed in the direction he’d come from.

“There’s a path about a half-mile south of here. It goes up into the cliff,” he said.

“Take us to it,” said James as he stood.

As the others walked off, Patty glanced at Rolf. He was simply standing and staring into the mist. She tapped his shoulder and he looked at her without really seeing her.

“You coming with us?” she asked.

He nodded and followed her.

The path—if one could it that—was very narrow and roughly cut into the side of the cliff. The going was hard and steep, with each step resulting in a small avalanche of stones and dust. This made their climb even slower, especially when combined with the mist and humidity. Two hours later, they finally reached the crest and found themselves looking down into a wide, shrouded vale.

Shazzar wiped the sweat from his eyes and peered into the mist. He soon spotted something and pointed.

‘There! About 20 feet down to the left,” he said.

The others looked where he pointed.

“Those look like steps,” said James.

“It sure as Hell doesn’t look like a natural rock formation. Someone *made* those steps,” Zorn said. “Anyway, it provides us with an easier way down.”

“Agreed. Let’s go but be as quiet as possible. The people who made those steps might still be around,” James said.

It took less than ten minutes to reach the bottom of the steps. In the vale, the mist was even thicker. Dark, barely discernable shapes loomed within it and the voices became whispers and eerie laughter.

“These sounds make my skin crawl,” Patty said.

“They’re starting to get to me, too,” admitted Zorn.

As they crossed the vale, they realized they were in a forest of tall poles. With each step they took the sound of bones crunching beneath their feet filled the air. Patty stopped by one of the poles to sip water from her canteen. As she drank, she let her eyes wander upward. When she saw the dark, mangled shape at the top of the pole, she emitted a loud shriek that caused the others to race over to her. When they reached her, she was speechless. She looked at James and pointed upward.

"Now I understand why those steps were made" he said.

At the top of the pole were the skeletal remains of a man in tattered clothing. James used his staff like a flashlight and aimed it at several other poles to reveal similar scenarios. There were hundreds of poles and each one of them ran through rotted human remains.

'This is a forest of impalement," he said.

Shazzar whistled as he looked around.

"There must be hundreds of them here. It looks like we're standing in the middle of some ancient execution ground," he said.

"We are," said James. "These are the remains of all those poor fools who dared set foot on this island. If we look carefully enough, we may yet find the rest of the crew who brought us here."

"Whoever runs this place doesn't like visitors," Zorn said. "From the looks of what's left of their clothing, most of these men were sailors. Some appear to be short and stocky, kind of like Dwarfs."

"I recall reading something about several parties of Dwarfs who attempted to explore this place. None ever returned," James said. "Some of these appear to be recent executions. That means whatever did this must still be around. I advise you to watch your backs."

"You can say that again," said Shazzar.

"That again," Zorn echoed.

This earned him a sharp elbow to ribs from Patty to show that this was no time for jokes.

They soon found several raised, wooden platforms. Each one was covered by layers of bleached, white bones and armor. Shazzar picked up a skull and hurled it at Zorn. He ducked and cursed.

"This island is nothing but one big tomb. Death is everywhere. It's in the land. I can even smell it in the air," Patty said.

"So that's what that smell is. I thought it was coming from Zorn," Shazzar quipped.

"I think you're smelling your own foul breath," Zorn shot back.

Sindbad raised his hand to signal a halt. He then closed his fist as a sign he wanted silence. He stood quietly and listened for a while. All he heard were the mournful wails in the mist around them.

"What are you listening for?" asked Kasim.

"I thought I heard loud snapping noises—like something was following us. You hear anything?" Sindbad asked.

"Just this damned wailing," Kasim replied.

"Hey you guys. I'm getting tired. How about taking a break?" said Habib.

"We might as well. Achmed—stand watch while we rest. I'll relieve you in 15 minutes," Sindbad decided.

Achmed was a tall, thin man who sported a bushy beard. He checked his rifle as he walked over to a nearby boulder and sat down. He then struck a match and lit his pipe as he watched the mist.

Lum lit another cigar and plopped down beside Sindbad and Kasim.

"I hate this place. It eats too many lives," he said.

"Let's hope we don't give it any more to feed on," Kasim said.

A loud scream suddenly brought everyone to their feet. Most held their rifles at the ready as they peered into the mist. Sindbad and four others ran over to where Achmed was last seen but the man was nowhere in sight.

"Search the area. He has to be here somewhere," Sindbad said.

They searched for a good hour. When they regrouped near the boulder, all they had found was Achmed's left boot and his rifle, which was twisted into a pretzel knot. Everyone stared at the weapon in disbelief.

"By Allah! What could have done *this*?" asked Habib.

"Anything powerful enough to do that to a rifle will have done much worse to Achmed," Sindbad reasoned.

"Maybe he managed to escape?" suggested Kasim.

"Let's keep moving. Maybe we'll run into him along the way," Sindbad said.

"Or maybe we'll run into whatever took him," said Lum.

"Now *that's* a pleasant thought," Kasim remarked as they followed Sindbad into the mist.

Gunnar Larsen was now at the point. He was trying to follow a narrow trail through the jungle. He stopped and squatted. The others caught up with him. He stood and faced them.

"I found tracks," he said. "There are several sets and they all appear to be headed inland," he said as he pointed north. "Whoever made these were probably aboard that abandoned ship."

"Do you think they're still alive?" asked Lum.

"I can't tell from the tracks," Gunnar said.

"Let's follow the tracks as far as we can. That's the only way we'll find out anything," Sindbad said.

Lum fired another flare and watched until it died out.

"That makes two. Think Hassan saw it?" he asked.

"If he didn't, he's probably rounding up a search party," Sindbad said as they followed the trail.

James pulled the cap from his canteen and sipped as he watched the flickering light fade away.

"What's up?" asked Zorn.

James pointed at the light.

"I'm giving whoever sent up that flare a chance to catch up with us," he said.

He took another swallow and put the cap back on the canteen. Shazzar grinned.

"It's good to know that someone's looking for us," he said. "They must have found our ship."

"Perhaps," said James.

They had finally climbed out of the vale and were making their way north across fairly rough terrain. James stopped several times to check the map and to give whoever else was on the island time to catch up with them. The further inland they traveled, the louder the wails and moans became. Now, mocking laughter was added to the mind-numbing sounds.

Several times, Patty clapped her hands over her ears in hopeless attempts to make the noise stop. Each time she either cursed or shouted at the things in the mist to make it stop. Each time, the laughter grew more mocking.

James saw that her nerves were frazzled. He'd never seen her like this. She had always been the calmest under stress. The most reliable. But she had never been in a place like this before. None of them had. The incessant wails were even getting to him.

Rolf didn't seem to be bothered by the sounds. In fact, he often mocked them. He even dared the things in the mist to attack and had threatened to go in after them if they didn't. His behavior was growing more erratic.

Hassan had not seen the flare.

He and the crewmen of all five ships were too busy fighting off the waves of sickeningly pink, slimy humanoids that had crawled up the sides of the ships and attacked them. Each of the creatures had webbed hands and feet and dorsal fins running down their backs. Their eyes and mouths were fish-like and they reeked of seawater. The creatures had emerged from deep beneath the sea and were aboard the ships before anyone realized it.

If their plan was to surprise the sailors, they succeeded.

But if they also planned to overpower them, they failed miserably.

Sindbad's men fought back with the ferocity of tigers and, after a long and bitter battle, finally drove them back into the sea. As the battle raged, the air resounded with gunshots and screams of pain and anger.

It was enough noise to wake the dead.

But no one on shore heard anything. The heavy mist acted like soundproofing materials. Sindbad had no idea that his fleet was under attack.

When the last of their attackers' bodies were tossed overboard, Hassan ordered the fleet to raise anchor and sail out to safer waters. They dropped anchor 2,000 yards further out to avoid another attack.

Hassan asked for a head count. To his great relief, only three men had been killed. Everyone else was accounted for.

"Now we know what happened to the crew of the Last Hope," he said as he recorded the events in the ship's log.

Lum stumbled over something and fell to his knees. He released a stream of expletives then used his hands to brush away the wet dirt from the object that caused him to trip. After a few seconds, he pulled a large, metal object from the ground and held it up.

"A Dwarf battle helmet," he said.

A few of the other men also searched the immediate area. They found several more helmets, breastplates, boots and assorted weapons half-hidden beneath years of jungle growth. A Dwarf skull was still inside one of the helmets. They also found arm bones, rib cages, thigh bones and other remains. All had been fractured, as if struck by something very heavy.

"This is a graveyard. There must be the remains of at least 20 Dwarfs here," Sindbad observed.

"Now I know what happened to one of our parties," Lum said as he gingerly placed the helmet on the ground. "Looks like these poor devils were torn to pieces."

"But by what?" asked Kasim as he glanced around nervously.

"I detest this rock. Does that infernal wailing never cease?" asked Habib as he attempted to cover his ears. "It's as if the entire place is crying!"

A loud roar of pain and terror echoed through the jungle. A few seconds later, a large, heavy object sailed past them and crashed into the trunk of a tree. They heard bones breaking when it hit, followed by a dull thud as it fell to the ground. They ran over and saw it was one of their crewmen. His head had been twisted so that he now faced backwards.

"It's Rashid! He was guarding our backs!" said Gunnar.

"Too bad for him that no one was guarding his," Sindbad said.

Lum heard something moving behind him. He turned with both pistols drawn to see what it was.

That's when he saw it.

He pointed both pistols at it and cocked them. The sound of the hammers clicking caught the thing's attention and it immediately charged the Dwarf. Lum fell backward to avoid being hit. At the same time, he fired both weapons. The roar of the flintlocks resounded through the jungle as the bullets struck the thing at point-blank range.

Lum rolled over and scrambled to his feet only to discover that the thing had vanished.

The others gathered around him as he peered into the mist. The wails were even louder now. More grating on the nerves.

"I can't believe you missed at that range," said Habib.

"I didn't. My shots went right through it," Lum said.

"You mean that was an illusion?" asked Gunnar.

Lum looked down at the remains of Rashid and shook his head.

"No illusion did *that!*" he said.

A few miles away, James signaled a halt. The others stopped and listened as a faint report of gunshots reached their ears.

"That came from the south," Shazzar said.

"Indeed," said James. "Let's slow down to give whoever they are a chance to catch up."

"What if they're not friendly?" asked Patty.

"In that case, they'll wish they hadn't," Zorn replied as he loaded his shotgun.

After they buried Rashid, Sindbad and his men sat down to rest and eat. They'd been on the island six hours now. Lum sent up the third flare a few minutes earlier to let Hassan know they were all right. Now, he was seated with his back to a tree, cleaning his pistols. Kasim sat next to him munching on a mango he'd plucked. Sindbad walked over and sat between them.

"How many men did we lose so far?" he asked.

"Two," said Lum. "Do you think we killed any of those things?"

Sindbad shrugged.

"It's hard to say. I'm not sure about anything at the moment," he said.

"Just where in Hell are we going anyway?" Lum asked.

Sindbad pointed at the cone in the distance.

"There. We'll head for that volcano and hope we find someone along the way," he said.

"And if we don't?" asked Kasim.

"We'll write them off as lost or dead and return to the ships. I don't want to spend any more time on this rock than we have to," Sindbad replied.

Lum chuckled.

"Both Vaalvik and Norvik were crawling with those bugs. Do you suppose there are any on this rock?" he asked.

"I hope not. The mist and shadows are bad enough. There might even be things here that are far worse than the bugs," Sindbad said.

"There are at least 100 Dwarfs who'd be able to tell us what's here—if they'd lived," Lum said.

"And a handful of stupid sailors," added Kasim.

Sindbad stood and got everyone on the move again. Before long, they found themselves wading through a shallow stream. A couple of the men tripped over things beneath the surface and nearly jumped out of their skins when they saw the decayed bodies staring up at them.

"These look like sailors," Lum remarked.

"They're probably crewmen from the Last Hope," Sindbad opined. "Keep moving. We'll be out of the water soon enough."

When they reached the other side, Sindbad decided they should follow it as the stream appeared to run north toward the volcano. He reasoned that it would keep them going in the right direction and they could always follow it back if things hit the fan.

Gunnar quickly found another set of tracks and signaled a halt. The others gathered around as he pointed.

"These tracks are fresh and they're headed north," he said.

"Let's follow them," Sindbad said. "How far ahead do you think they are?"

"A few hours. A day perhaps," Gunnar replied. "It's hard to tell in this muck."

James and his friends had seen the third flare. They slowed to a crawl to allow their "pursuers" time to catch up. They had left the vale far behind now and were on a wider gravel road. The mist was so dense, they had trouble staying on the path and would have gotten lost several times if not for the light from James' staff.

As they turned around a bend, something dark and massive suddenly loomed out of the mist. Startled, Zorn let loose with both barrels. The roar was nearly deafening. When the smoke cleared, they saw nothing.

"Just what in Hell did you shoot at?" asked Shazzar.

"I'm not sure. At least I scared it away," Zorn replied.

"You scared me, too. Those shots almost made me jump out of clothes," Patty complained.

"Maybe I'll fire my shotgun again," Zorn suggested with a dirty smirk.

Patty kicked him in the shin and stomped past him while he hopped up and down. Rolf laughed. It was the first time that anyone had heard him laugh for several months.

The gravel road meandered northward for several miles and ended at the base of the volcano. James lifted his staff and shone the light over two, eight-feet-tall concrete structures on either side of the road. Each was about six feet square and had a six foot door cut into it. Both structures were partially covered by vines and weeds.

They walked over to the one on the right and peered inside. There, on the floor, was a dust-covered mummified corpse in what was left of a uniform.

"This was a guard post long ago," James said.

"Now it's a tomb," added Zorn.

The mist swirled closer. They walked past the guard station and up a paved road until they came to a huge, metal double door that had been built into the volcano. Shazzar pulled out his dagger and scraped it against the door. To his surprise, millennia of rust and moss simply flaked off to reveal the shiny, silver surface of the door.

"It's no metal I'm familiar with," he said. "The rust just fell off of it when I touched it."

James ran his fingers over the metal.

"It's some sort of alloy. Probably titanium blended with several other metals. From the looks of this, it must have been a military installation. This was all built to protect something important," he said.

"Protect what?" asked Patty.

"The only way to answer that is to go inside," James said.

They stepped back and watched as James raised his staff and rapped the door three times. On the third rap, the doors slowly opened with a loud scrape-screeching sound. They stopped halfway. A gust of musty, cold air escaped from the opening and hit them head-on. Patty covered her nose and mouth.

"Smells like rotting fish," said Zorn.

"I wouldn't go in there if I were you," Rolf warned.

"Why not?" asked Shazzar.

"There are things in there. *Dangerous* things," he replied.

James ignored him and walked through the doorway. The others quickly followed. As soon as they stepped inside, banks of bright lights suddenly flickered to life. James doused the light on his staff and looked around.

They were now in a huge circular cavern. To the left, a set of metal steps led up to a catwalk that went halfway around the cavern and ended at a rectangular structure with a long, rectangular window. To their right was a line of heavy trucks, small light trucks and several other vehicles that dated back to First Age. Each one was painted dark green and had a white star painted on the hood. Some were covered with canvas or netting. All were covered by inches of dust and the tires were flat from centuries of neglect. Wooden crates of all shapes and sizes were stacked against the wall and there were at least a dozen more mummified corpses lying around.

They walked over to one of the trucks and pulled away the canvas. Patty started when she saw the uniformed mummies staring back at her with sardonic grins on their leathery faces. Each one wore a strange helmet and carried a rifle, as if they were preparing to go to war.

"This must have been the staging area. These poor devils were responding to some sort of security threat but never made it out of here," James guessed.

"What kind of threat?" asked Zorn.

"Only these men know that—and they are in no position to tell us," James said. "I'd be very wary here. I recall reading about similar places on the islands that once existed nearby. The colonists dug too deeply. They awakened some sort of horror that nearly wiped them out. The same thing happened to some Dwarfs ten years later."

"You mean the bugs?" asked Patty.

"Exactly. The bugs were created here. They were meant to be some sort of weapon but no one knew how to control them. There may be more of them in here—or something far worse," James replied.

He stopped and rechecked the map.

"I believe this is where Dexter was taking us. The artifact is somewhere in this complex," he said.

"Maybe it's in one of those crates?" suggested Shazzar.

"There's one way to find out," Zorn said as he walked over to one and drove his fist through the top.

The rotted, ancient wood splintered easily. The sound reverberated through the complex and disturbed a nest of bats. They spread their wings and flapped through the open door to feed on the mosquitoes.

James laughed.

The bats had startled Patty and Shazzar. Zorn and Rolf simply watched them fly away.

"Whatever Dexter was after isn't in that box," Zorn said.

As they walked down a corridor, Shazzar's foot hit a loose tile. This was followed by a loud whirring noise.

"Hit the deck!" he yelled as he dove to the floor.

The others followed his advice just in time to see a thing red light burn its way across the hall. The light melted the metal plates on the wall and left it smoldering. James examined it.

"What was *that*?" asked Zorn as he picked himself up.

"I'd believe it was some sort of particle beam weapon. It was triggered when Shazzar stepped on that loose plate," James replied.

Shazzar looked around sheepishly.

"I almost bought us the farm," he said.

"Indeed. Try to be a little more careful from now on. This place is probably loaded with protective devices." James said. "At least you realized what you did in time to warn us. The next time, you might not be so lucky."

They wandered around in search of more doors. They found a set of double ones on the opposite end of the chamber. Again Shazzar ram his knife over it. This time, it gave off sparks.

"This is steel," he said.

"How do we open it? I don't see a handle," Zorn wondered.

James spotted a keypad with ten numbers and four colored keys. He tapped Shazzar's shoulder. The Jackal nodded and looked around.

"There are two small vents just above us. My guess is that it's some sort of security device," he said.

"Do you think it still works?" asked Patty.

"Well, the last trap still worked," Zorn reminded her.

Shazzar studied the keypad. There were ten numbers on three lines. A yellow button at the bottom read 'ENTER'. He reasoned that the red button to the left would set off an alarm and decided to avoid that completely.

"Do you think you can find the right combination?" asked Patty.

"I can try. Stand back in case I trigger the trap," Shazzar said as he knelt before the keypad.

They watched as he tried several combinations without any luck. He stood and scratched his beard as he pondered the problem.

"I've tried just about everything I can think of. Any ideas?" he said.

Zorn raised his shotgun and fired directly at the keypad. Then everyone ran for cover as a cloud of light green gas erupted from the vents. The gas rose up to the ceiling, lingered there for several minutes, then dissipated.

Zorn came out of hiding and strode toward the open doors. As he reached them he called back to the others.

"Anybody coming with me?"

This chamber was also carved into the mountain and was more oblong than circular. The walls and floor were covered with steel and there large consoles everywhere. Bones, skulls, dust and cobwebs littered the floor. A mummified man was seated at one of the consoles, his outstretched hand resting on a series of buttons. James studied him for a while.

"This man was a scientist. I can tell by the long frock he wore," he said. "It looks like he died in the middle of something."

He pulled the man's hand away from the keys. It snapped off at the elbow and he tossed it to the floor. He then reached out and pressed one of the keys. To his surprise, the entire room lit up and several screens flickered to life. The others gathered around as he pressed more keys. Images of Earth appeared on the screen immediately in front of them. Aerial views of oceans, rivers, mountains and great deserts.

"These images are being taken from miles above the Earth," James said. "The ancients created many devices that could do this. They called them satellites."

"What amazing technology! It's hard to believe that they wiped themselves out. They were so advanced," Patty said as she watched the screen.

"It was a case of too much technology for their own good. Most of what they created was used for weapons. They had great skill but lacked the wisdom to use their skill for mankind's greater good," James said almost sadly.

Rolf walked over to another console and laughed. The others turned and asked what he was watching. He pointed to the screen.

"Look!" he said.

They gathered around and watched as a cartoon cat chased a small, brown mouse around a construction site.

"What is it, James?" Patty asked.

"The ancients called them cartoons. They were created to amuse people. Apparently, not everyone in this complex was conducting experiments," James replied.

They walked around examining the bodies. One, in particular, caught their attention. He was stretched out on the floor, his arms akimbo with a rusted pistol in his right hand. James examined the side of his skull and shook his head.

"This one shot himself," he said. "Something scared him so much, he decided to take his own life rather than face what was coming."

"I wonder what that was," said Shazzar.

"Let's hope that we never find out," said Zorn.

They found a small door on the other side of the room. This one had a knob. Shazzar turned it then screamed in pain as sparks flew everywhere.

"Damn! That hurt! I should have know it would be booby trapped," he said as he shook the numbness from his hand.

The others laughed.

Zorn walked over and kicked the door as hard as he could. To his delight, it jumped off its hinges and hit the floor with a loud metallic ring. Almost immediately, the lights flickered on inside.

"*That's* how we open doors," Zorn said smugly.

Shazzar chuckled.

"Maybe you should lead the way from now on," he suggested.

"No way, Jose!" Zorn said as they entered the room.

This was also lined with steel and was empty save for a set of spiral steps. One set went up to a catwalk that encircled the entire room. The other set went down into the floor.

"Dexter was after an artifact that was quite valuable. Where would *you* hide such a thing?" James asked.

"Most people would hide important objects deep inside a vault. I say we should go down," Patty said.

"Are you making me an offer?" asked Zorn in jest.

"*Pervert!* You know damned well what I meant," she snapped.

"I think she's right. I say we go down," Shazzar added.

"Is this was a military complex, the most important and powerful things would have been kept in a place that was impervious to attack. Someplace that was radiation proof as well. Their only logical choice would have been to place those objects as deep into the Earth as possible," James said as he studied the metal steps.

"What's powering this place, James? Since all the lights and consoles still work, there has to be some sort of inexhaustible power source," Zorn said.

"I've been wondering about that exact same thing," James said. "Even atomic energy would have died out after so many millennia."

"Well, this *is* a volcano. Maybe it's geothermal," Shazzar suggested.

"I doubt that. In order to tap into the power of the volcano, they would have had to sink lines miles into the Earth. They couldn't have used this volcano for that. It's far too hot and far too unstable. At best, it would make a most unreliable power source and it would have been next to impossible to compensate for heat surges caused by eruptions," James explained.

"What then?" asked Patty.

"Perhaps the answer lies at the bottom of those steps," James said.

The trek through the jungle became akin to running a gauntlet. Creatures of all shapes and sizes emerged from the mist to assail Sindbad and his men as they traveled inland. Some were human in shape. Others more dog-like. Some even had multiple arms and carried crude weapons. They attacked with fangs, claws and hooked beaks and their favorite victims were those in the rear.

Sindbad and his men responded to these attacks with equal ferocity and sprayed bullets everywhere. Whenever one of the creatures was hit, it turned to dust and vanished back into the mist. Once there, it regenerated and rejoined the attack. All the while, the wails and moans grew louder and louder.

Maddening.

"It's like running through a nightmare. A living, breathing nightmare," said Kasim as he fired his rifle directly into the face of a creature that had suddenly loomed before him.

It was then that heard it.

A blood curdling scream that nearly canceled out the wails and sounds of the battle. When the last echoes of the scream stopped, their attackers suddenly melted back into the mist.

Everyone stood with their weapons at the ready as they peered into the mist. When nothing happened after several minutes had lapsed, they relaxed. Some even sat down to rest.

Sindbad sipped water from his canteen as he watched the mist. They were down to seven men now. Five good men had been killed or taken by the mist monsters. He looked around and saw Kasim seated with his back against a rock.

"How's our ammo?" he asked.

"We have less than half of what we started with," Kasim replied.

"That's just enough for us to get our asses off this rock," Lum said as he sent up another flare.

It was the sixth one he'd sent up since they set foot on the island. That meant they'd been ashore for twelve hours now.

Sindbad looked up at the volcano. The bottom half was completely hidden by the mist, but he could see the cone clearly. There was no smoke rising from it. The volcano was asleep.

"Let's get moving," he said.

Gunnar was able to pick up the trail again on the other side of a hill. They followed them to a gravel road.

"That's as far as I can take it," Gunnar said. "Pick a direction."

"We were headed north toward that volcano. I say we keep heading north," Sindbad said.

They followed the road for more than an hour. When they came to the guard post, they stopped and stared at the mummified remains of the guard. The wails were now getting louder. Sometimes they became horribly shrill or mocking. They did their best to ignore the sounds as they continued up the road.

Fifty yards in front of the open doors, they were attacked by slimy, pink-skinned creatures in tattered rags. A short melee ensued that resulted in Sindbad's men gunning down every last one of the creatures.

The shots that rang out were loud.

Loud enough to be heard inside the complex.

"Listen!" said Rolf as he put a finger to his lips.

Unfortunately, he attempted to use Patty's finger. She pulled her and away and threatened to slap him silly.

"I hear gunfire," Rolf whispered.

The others stopped eating and stood up. They heard several more reports followed by a few single shots.

"Sounds like a battle," said Zorn.

"Indeed," said James. "Whoever it is, they are close at hand."

"Maybe it's a rescue party," suggested Shazzar. "Or what's left of our crew."

"Should we join them?" asked Patty.

James shook his head.

"No. Let's relax and wait for them here," he said. "Be ready in case they happen to be hostile."

Rolf suddenly started shaking all over. His face contorted and he tore at his hair.

"Make it stop! Make it stop!" he screamed at the top of his lungs.

Alarmed, Patty raced over. As soon as she touched his shoulder, his shaking and screaming stopped. That's when he looked at her and smiled mischievously.

"Just kidding," he said.

Patty snapped.

She called Rolf every name she could think of in several languages as she rained blow after blow on him. Zorn and the others laughed until their sides ached. When Patty finally stopped punching him, Rolf's body was covered with black and blue bruises.

Patty stood with her fists on her hips and glared at Rolf.

"What have got to say for yourself now, Mr. Yaren?" she demanded.

Rolf grabbed her and gave her big kiss on the lips. Patty shoved him away and began punching him again. Halfway through this, even she started to laugh. By the time she stopped, Rolf was on his knees trying to shield himself from her flying fists.

James rapped the floor with his staff. The others stopped laughing and turned in his direction.

"Someone's approaching," he announced.

"I hear them, too. There are seven of them," Rolf said.

Patty wondered how he knew that as she looked into his eyes.

"Zorn—" James began.

"I'm already on it," Zorn replied as he checked his shotgun to be sure it was loaded, then headed through the door.

He was halfway across the second chamber when he saw Sindbad and his men enter from the opposite direction. He turned around and went back to the others.

"What did you see?" asked James.

"Seven men are headed this way. They should be here any minute," Zorn replied as he aimed his shotgun at the entrance.

"Don't fire until we find out who they are and what they want," James instructed as he stood next to him.

A few minutes later, Sindbad and his crew entered the chamber. As soon as they saw Zorn and the others, Sindbad signaled a halt.

"Who are you?" Zorn called out.

"My name is Sindbad. I'm the captain of the Saracen Moon," Sindbad replied as he and James looked each other over. "Who are you?"

"My name is Colla. James Colla. And these are my friends," James answered.

"You're the Red Cleric?" asked Sindbad.

"The one and only," James replied.

"What on Earth are you doing here?" asked Sindbad.

"A man named Dexter hired us to help him locate an artifact. I believe it's somewhere in this complex, but I have no idea what to look for," James said.

"What happened to Dexter?" asked Lum.

"The things in the mist killed him almost as soon as we set foot on this rock," Shazzar said. "And it wasn't pretty."

"I've heard of you Captain. You have quite the reputation," James said. "Why are you here?"

"That ship you were on was of Thulian registry. It drifted into the bay near Mumbai. There was no one aboard and no signs of struggle. When I reported it to Arka-Dal, he ordered us to check into it. So here we are," Sindbad replied.

"How did you know the ship came from here?" asked Patty.

"I read the ship's log. Captain Varna kept detailed records of the journey. "Any idea what happened to the crew?"

"None. After Dexter was killed, we returned to the cove only to discover that the ship had sailed off without us. We saw a few of the crewmen lying dead in a stream. Other than that, it's anyone's guess what happened to them," James said.

"If Dexter's dead, why are you still searching for the artifact?" Sindbad asked.

"To make sure that no one else finds it. If that artifact is on this island, it is most likely some sort of weapon. This was a weapons development laboratory during the First Age and you know as well I how destructive and deadly their creations were," James said. "I think Dexter was seeking some sort of ancient weapon, either to sell to the highest bidder or to further his own ambitions. Since he knew about this place, most likely others must also know of it. We cannot allow anything that was left here to get loose. Those bugs were bad enough."

"Bugs? So you ran into them, too? Where?" asked Sindbad.

"In the Midwestern area of North America. They were raiding villages and forcing captive artisans to make weapons for them," James replied.

"Make weapons? Sounds like they're getting smarter," Sindbad said.

"Indeed they are. They had even learned battle tactics. I think each generation becomes more intelligent than the last. It probably has something to do with whatever brain matter they absorb from their hosts prior to hatching," James said.

"What happened to the bugs?" asked Lum.

"We located their nest and dynamited it to seal them inside. With any luck, they won't get out. That was ten years ago," James said. "Worry about the bugs some other time, Sindbad. What we find here could be far worse."

"That's a comforting thought," said Lum as he lit his cigar.

"Got another one of those?" asked Shazzar.

Lum pulled one from his pocket and passed it to him. Shazzar sniffed it then put it into his mouth while Lum lit it for him. He took a deep draught and let it out slowly.

"Not bad. Your own blend?" he asked.

"Uh-huh. I get the leaf from India and add a few spices to give it some bite," Lum replied with a sense of pride.

"I didn't know you smoked," Zorn remarked as he watched Shazzar puff away.

"I do—but only once in a great while. And only cigars or pipes," the Jackal replied.

"Would you care to join us in our search?" asked James.

"Wild horses couldn't keep us away now. Lead on, my friend," Sindbad replied.

They climbed down the spiral steps one-by-one. With each step they took, the wails grew louder and louder. Some of the men clapped their hands over their ears but it was to no avail. The sounds could not be shut out.

When they reached the bottom of the steps, they were in a smaller domed chamber. This, too, had walls and floors of steel. In the middle of the chamber stood a large cube. It had several gauges and dials on one side. A thick, black cable ran out of the other side and down into a deep hole some ten feet from the cube. Metal ducts, more cables and a bank of flickering lights completed the scenario. The cube stood nearly 20 feet tall and wide.

And the wails were louder here.

Deafening.

Maddening.

Patty clapped her hands over her ears and screamed to drown out the sounds as she followed James and the others to the cube.

"What is it?" asked Sindbad.

"From all my knowledge of the First, I'd say that it's part of weapon system of some sort. From the size of it, I'd say it's very powerful."

"It's still running, even after all these years," said Patty.

"I wonder what powers it," James said as he placed his hand on the side of the cube.

Almost immediately, visions of thousands of tormented souls flashed through his mind. With great difficulty, he pushed himself away. As he did, the gauges on the side went haywire.

"I can tell you this—it's not geothermal or solar," he said when the buzzing in his head stopped. "Nor is it atomic."

He walked around and checked the gauges. Each of the needles were in the red or danger zones. He realized that the power was building inside the cube.

"Is it a bomb? I've heard that they built some very powerful ones," Patty asked.

James shook his head.

"It's not a bomb, but it will act like one if it blows," he said. "I think this is some sort of defensive device, one that's designed to explode and destroy everything for miles around."

"A doomsday device?" asked Lum.

"Most likely. It appears to be running amok right now. If any of those needles reach the end of the danger zone, it will explode and take us with it. We have to figure out how to turn it off. But first, I must learn exactly what we're dealing with," James said.

"How?" asked Rolf.

"What *are* you? Some kind of Indian?" teased Shazzar.

"No. I mean how are you going to find out what it is without setting it off?" Rolf asked.

"By merging with it," James said. "I'll astrally project myself into the device. Once inside, I'll seek a way to shut it down safely."

As James stood before the device trying to decide what to do, Sindbad chatted with the others.

"When you pointed that shotgun at us, I wasn't sure what to think. As soon as James introduced himself, I knew exactly who you were—Zorn Yaren," he said.

"I guess I do have a reputation of sorts," Zorn said.

"I heard all about your exploits when we were in Nihon. That bit with the dragon was quite impressive," Sindbad said.

'Thanks," Zorn said modestly.

"And you must be his brother, Rolf. I'm pleased to meet you all," Sindbad said as he shook their hands.

He was keenly aware of the tragic deaths of their friends but thought it best not to mention it.

"Strange as it seems, we've heard quite a lot about your exploits," Patty said. "You're quite extraordinary—and you have balls."

"I almost lost them on several occasions," Sindbad said. "You have to be the mysterious and beautiful Patrice Vertrez. You are far more lovely than I've ever imagined."

"And you are indeed a *sailor*!" Patty remarked.

She looked over at Rolf to see if he's react to her flirtations with Sindbad. His amber eyes showed no emotion.

"You love him, don't you?" Sindbad observed.

"Yes. I've tried everything I could think of to get a rise out of him but I have nothing to show for it," she said.

"Well, you've already gotten a rise out of me," Sindbad assured her.

James walked all around the device several times. Every now and then, he placed his hand on it. When he did, the wails grew louder and sounded more anxious and pitiful. He stepped back and took a deep breath.

"I'm ready now," he said. "Stand back and don't try to go in after me no mater what happens. Understand?"

The others nodded.

James handed his staff to Patty. He took another deep breath and walked up to the cube. He then placed both hands on it and concentrated on willing himself into the inner workings of the apparatus. He needed to become one with it in order to find out what it was and what it was capable of doing. He felt his essence leave his body and willed it ever so slowly into the cube. At the same time, he had to keep his own wits about him to avoid being sucked into the heart of the cube where he ran the risk of being absorbed by it.

At the core, he found himself floating in a sea of swirling, tormented faces. They swam around him in erratic patters, their mouths open, Their pain and lamentations tore at his soul. There were countless thousands of them and all were crying for help. It was so pitiful, he wanted to escape from the cube. But he forced himself to listen.

What he heard, disturbed him like nothing else ever had before.

"Free us, Red Cleric! Please free us!"

"Set us free! We beseech you!"

"Help us pass into the light!"

It was then he realized what they were and what the terrible purpose of the machine was. Despite himself, he began to weep.

"Please save us, Red Cleric!"

"Help us!"

"Set us free!"

The voices grew louder and louder. More pitiful. More pleading. He looked into the very heart of the device and saw thousands of them. They powered the device with their essence. They gave it purpose.

They made it live!

"I will free you," he said. "I will help you pass into the light."

He willed himself out of the machine. When his essence returned to his body, he fell to his knees. The others watched as he dried the tears from his eyes and stood up. Patty passed him the staff.

"What's wrong, James? What did you see?" asked Patty.

"I saw souls. Thousands of them. Within this cube are the life forces or souls of countless helpless people. They have been captured against their will so their energies can feed the cube. The cube, in turn, uses that energy as a power source," he said.

"You mean that cube is a generator?" asked Sindbad.

"Yes. The essence from the souls provide power to this entire complex. Their lamentations are the source of the wails and moans. Their sorrow and anger create the mist. The machine prevents them from crossing over into the light. Theirs is a most terrible fate," James said sadly.

"How awful!" said Patty.

"Indeed. They cannot find peace. They cannot be released. Their sorrow and anger are overwhelming. It sucked the breath from me and nearly suffocated me. I also feel that all those who have died on this island since are also trapped within the cube. It eats souls. The cube has a voracious appetite," James said as he sat down on the metal floor.

"You make it sound as if it's alive," said Sindbad.

"In a very real sense, it is alive," James said. "An entity that feeds on souls may begin to seek them out. The more souls it devours, the more powerful it will become. It may even begin to think of itself as a god. It already thinks to a degree. If not shut down, it may become sentient. We cannot allow that to happen."

"Why use souls?" asked Patty.

"They are a cheap, eternal power source," James said. "A soul's energy never dies out. One soul by itself wouldn't be much use, but *thousands* would provide them with limitless power."

"What do you suppose it's powering?" asked Sindbad.

"My guess is that it's some sort of super weapons system," James replied. "Perhaps something powerful enough to take out the whole world."

"Then let's find the sucker and disconnect it," Zorn suggested.

"Therein lies the problem," James said. "Most weapons systems built by the First had what was known as a fail safe mechanism. Basically, it was switch that soldiers could trip if and when something went wrong. It usually involved typing a secret code into a computer. If someone attempted to shut the systems down and typed in the wrong code, the devices would run amok."

"Well, there's a keyboard on that panel," Shazzar pointed out. "But we don't know the correct code."

"We can't just punch numbers at random. The computer will believe we're the enemy and—" James said.

"BOOM!" Rolf finished with a wave of his hands.

Sindbad whistled.

"I'm certain that this was not the artifact Dexter had in mind. What he was after has to be portable," James surmised.

"Why not just free the souls in the cube and deprive the device of power?" asked Patty.

"The weapons built by the First were dangerous and tricky. If the artifact we seek is a weapon, depriving it of power may set it off," James said.

Patty looked at the cube.

The wails sounded so pitiful, she wanted to cry.

"If we disconnect the generator, would that free the souls trapped within it?" she asked.

"Yes. They will then be free to pass into the light," James assured her.

"Then the risk is worth it," she said.

"Not if we set off a weapon that destroys the entire world. I fear that the cube is wired directly into such a device. It may even be the fabled 'Doomsday Weapon' the First were rumored to have built," James said.

"Why would anyone sane build such a weapon?" asked Sindbad.

"Those were dark days, Captain. There was constant warfare that left vast stretches of the planet in ruins. I believe that each side in that war built such a device and planned to set it off if they felt they were losing. It may have been a 'Doomsday Weapon' that ended the First Age and brought about the Great Darkness," James said.

"That's insane!" said Kasim.

The others nodded.

At that moment, the wails and moans grew louder. Patty clapped her hands over her ears and wept as the combined sorrow of thousands of tormented souls washed over her.

"These poor souls have been trapped her for too long, James. We have to free them!" she said.

"If the souls of those who created this device are also trapped within it, then it's a fitting punishment. Yet, I can't just turn my back on the rest of them. I'll set them free but first we must find what Dexter was searching for," James promised.

"Lead on then. We're with you all the way," Sindbad volunteered.

The walls of the room looked seamless. James realized that the First would have had another way out, some sort of emergency exit. He walked around the room and tapped the wall with his staff. About halfway around, the sound was different. He smiled.

"This is it. There's a secret door in this wall," he said.

"I don't see any door," said Lum as he perused the wall.

"Of course you don't. The man said it was secret," Sindbad jabbed. "How are you going to open it?"

"Like this!" James replied as he spread his arms and uttered a spell.

To everyone's amazement (save James' usual crowd), the door blew open with a loud, ringing sound.

"Shall we?" asked Shazzar.

"You go first," said James.

They followed Shazzar down the corridor for several yards. Without warning, a blue light flickered on and off rapidly, giving off a sort of strobe effect. While they tried to grow accustomed to the lights, a soft whirring sound caught their attention. They stood in silence and watched as two robots, the size of small dogs, emerged from hidden panels in the walls on either side. The robots were on treads and acted like miniature tanks.

"Stand still. Perhaps they won't see us," James cautioned.

To his dismay, the robots stopped less than 20 feet in front of them and opened fire. Bullets now ricocheted off the metal walls and floor as a wild firefight erupted in the confined space. Sindbad shouted at his men to concentrate all their firepower on one robot at a time to try and overwhelm it. The tactic worked. Bits and pieces of first one then the other robot flew in all directions. When the smoke cleared, the hall was littered with smoldering debris.

But the strobes were still going strong.

Sindbad looked around and saw Habib and Lum kneeling next to one of his men, a pool of blood spreading out from beneath his still body.

"Poor Ishmael bought the farm," Lum said.

"Anybody else get hit?" Sindbad called out.

"I took one in the calf. I can't walk at the moment," Kasim said.

"Stay put. We'll pick you up on the way back," Sindbad said.

James looked around.

"This place is loaded with defensive traps. We might have to fight our way to the device," he said.

"I sure as Hell hope you're wrong!" said Shazzar.

"Amen!" added Patty.

Rolf simply smiled as if he knew what was coming. His smile irked Patty and she had to keep herself from punching him.

"Just be grateful those things weren't bullet proof," James said as they continued down the hallway. "If they had been, we'd be where Ishmael is now."

"How'd they know we were there?" asked Lum.

"They probably had heat sensors. They located us by our body heat," James replied.

"Clever!" said Patty.

"Yes, isn't it?" James asked.

"Just what in Hell *are* we looking for?" Sindbad asked.

"Something small enough for a man to carry. The First often put the triggering devices to the weapons in special brief cases. Look for something like that," James answered.

The hallway went on for another hundred feet then stopped in front of a blank wall. Shazzar stopped and scratched his beard as he studied the apparently smooth surface. James gripped his shoulder.

"If it's hidden, it's probably booby trapped," he warned.

"This is real good, James. I can't see anything that might give it away. This is going to take time," Shazzar said.

They watched and waited.

And waited.

And waited.

Shazzar tried everything he could think of but simply could not find a secret door in that wall. Perplexed, he leaned against the right side of the hall—and fell into a large square room. The sudden movement of him hitting the floor triggered the hidden light source and the room burst into life. As he picked himself up, the others entered.

All around them were desks with instrument panels and screens on them. Seated behind each panel was a desiccated corpse in the sad remnants of a uniform. Some were slumped over their panels. Others lay back in the chairs with their arms dangling to either side. Dust and webs were everywhere.

"I think we've found what used to be called the nerve center of this complex," James said. "What we seek should be in here. Look for a safe or something."

A quick search turned up a heavy stainless steel safe. It was bolted to the metal floor and featured a heavy handle and large combination knob.

Shazzar knelt and studied the safe.

"Maybe what we're looking for is inside," he said.

"Think you can open it?" asked Zorn.

Shazzar smiled.

"There hasn't been a safe made that *I* can't crack," he boasted. "Now be quiet so I can hear the tumblers click."

They watched as he pressed his ear to the door and turned the knob, first left, then right, then left again. He did this several times then sat back on his heels and looked back at them.

"It's unlocked. How much you wanna bet it's trapped?" he asked.

"That would be a fool's bet," said James. "I want you all to move to the right of the door—now!"

They did as he said and hugged the wall. Shazzar pulled a fishing line from his pocket and tied one end to the handle of the safe. He then slowly let it out as he joined the others.

"Now!" James said.

Shazzar tanked on the line and pulled the door open. To their surprise—and relief—nothing happened. They walked to the front of the safe and looked inside. There were two metal brief cases and a dusty old book inside. Shazzar took these out and placed them on a nearby table. James opened the book and leafed through it.

"This book is blank save for a single page in the middle and it contains a series of six numbers," he said as he showed it to the Jackal.

"Most likely, they're the combinations to these cases," he said.

Shazzar checked the numbers in the book then used the first set to open one of the cases. When he raised the lid he laughed. So did everyone else who saw it. Inside were three pairs of socks, a comic book, the almost petrified remnant of an old sandwich, and two large keys. One was red. The other was green.

"The only deadly thing in here is that sandwich," Shazzar joked. "These keys look important."

"Open the other case," instructed James.

Shazzar did so. Inside, was a control panel with two large slots for keys and another small booklet. James picked up the booklet and turned the cover. Inside it read: USAF and REMOTE DETONATION CONTROL DEVICE.

"Jackpot!" he said with a smile. "This device is the trigger for some sort of weapon system. Most likely, this is what Dexter was after. It fits the need of being light enough for a single man to carry."

"What about a married man?" asked Zorn.

Patty groaned and punched him on the arm. He laughed.

"If this is here, the weapon system it controls must also be somewhere in this complex," James said. "The word 'detonation' suggests that it must be some sort of bomb, maybe one that's powerful enough to take out most of the world. We must locate this bomb and disable it so that no one else can ever make use of it."

"There's another door on that far wall," Sindbad pointed out. "Let's try that way."

This door slid open automatically as they approached. James pointed. Shazzar nodded and went through first. They gave him a 30 second head start then followed. As the walked along the long, narrow hallway, banks of hidden lights flickered one every few feet. The hallway echoed with their footsteps. James reasoned that this is what the designers had in mind. Metal floors made it virtually impossible to sneak up on anyone. The hallway ended at the open door of a steel room with a high vaulted ceiling. In the middle of the floor was a dust and cobweb draped platform that contained another control panel. Atop the platform sat a huge. Metal, egg-shaped object about 20 feet tall. They gathered around and stared up at it.

"Is that the bomb?" asked Sindbad.

"I believe so," said James. "We'll have to destroy its detonation system. It's probably behind that control panel."

"Let's find out," said Shazzar as he walked over and blew the dust off. This done, he used his hand to pull away the cobwebs. That's when the lights of the control panel flickered on and started flashing.

There were nine banks of lights, beginning at the bottom with yellow and progressing to red at the top.

"Holy shit! It activated itself!" Shazzar said as he stepped back.

A metallic female voice from a hidden source then warned them it was TWO MINUTES TO DETONATION.

Shazzar used his knife to pry the face from the control panel. Inside were a tangled knot of different colored wires. As he studied the setup, the voice came back.

"SIXTY SECONDS TO DETONATION . . . 59 SECONDS . . . 58 SECONDS . . .

"How do I disable it?" asked Shazzar.

"Cut one of the wires. That should stop the countdown," James suggested. "If you cut the wrong wire . . . "

"I know—BOOM!" Shazzar said as he stared at the wires.

"Which one? There are several colors here," Shazzar shouted above the loud warning voice.

"FORTY-FIVE SECONDS TO DETONATION . . . 44 SECONDS . . ."

"Which one do I cut?" he shouted again.

"The black one," James replied.

"Are you sure?" asked Shazzar.

James nodded and stepped back. Shazzar took a deep breath and gently picked up the black wire. He was about to cut it but hesitated. What if James was wrong? What if cutting the black wire set off the bomb?

"THIRTY SECONDS TO DETONATION . . . 29 SECONDS.."

"Hurry man! Cut that wire!" James shouted.

Shazzar inhaled. He was sweating bullets now and his hands were shaking as he gently lifted the black wire and closed his eyes. As he applied pressure with his knife, he silently prayed to every god he could think of and even made up a few more of his own. He felt the wire snap. To his relief, nothing happened.

Instantly, the bomb and the voice went silent and the lights stopped flickering. Shazzar exhaled and sat back on his haunches. He looked up at James and smiled.

"That was good guess on your part, James," he said.

"I never guess," James replied. "I simply know."

"Look at the size of that bomb. How on Earth did Dexter plan to get it out of here?" asked Lum.

"He didn't. All he needed was the remote control device in that case. With that, he could have detonated the bomb from any point of the globe," James replied. "If he had attempted to move the bomb, it would have automatically gone into countdown mode—like it did when Shazzar just brushed the cobwebs from it. It was a very sensitive device."

"Now what?" asked Patty.

"Tear out the bomb's innards and destroy the control panel and the remote device. Smash them into pieces so that no one can possibly reassemble anything," he said.

He watched as Sindbad, Zorn and Shazzar reached inside the bomb and began pulling out handfuls of wiring, circuits and various other devices. Within minutes, the innards of the bomb were scattered all over the room. Zorn opened the brief case and fired both barrels of his shotgun straight into it. The case blew into a hundred pieces and he kicked them around the floor to mingle them with the rest of the debris.

"So much for this Doomsday Weapon," he said.

"Indeed," said James. "Now, let's free those poor souls in that cube."

A few minutes later, they were back in the chamber that contained the cube. James told everyone else to stand back as he approached the cube. The closer he got, the louder the wails and moans grew. He closed his eyes and placed his hand on the side of the cube. Again, he saw countless, tormented faces. Again, he heard them call his name as they pleaded with him to set them free. Their sorrow almost overwhelmed him. He fought back the urge to weep.

He uttered an incantation then stepped back and struck the side panel as hard as he could with his staff. The panel shattered amid a shower of sparks and a column of flame shot up from it.

He stepped back and watched. The cube was silent for a moment. Then it began to glow brighter and brighter. A pattern of a million different colors began to swirl in its center as it began to hum loudly. The glow increased in intensity with each passing second until they could barely see.

Then the cube erupted.

There was a loud explosion, the force of which threw everyone in the room to the floor. Then came the almost deafening sound of shattering glass. Then came the silence. The humming had gone and the room was dark.

James stood and lit the end of his staff. He looked around at the thousands of ebony shards that were once the prison to thousands of trapped souls. They used to glow with the energy of those souls. Now, they were dead and cold.

Everything was silent now.

Gone were the moans and wails.

Gone was the mocking laughter and taunting voices.

James smiled and breathed a sigh of relief. The came a voice from all around him. So soft, only he could hear it.

"Thank you, Red Cleric! Thank you!" it said as it faded away.

"I don't hear them anymore," said Sindbad. "They're gone."

"You did it, James. You helped them move into the light," Patty said softly, almost in awe.

"That was magnificent!" Shazzar whispered.

They left the chamber and walked through the now pitch black and silent complex. With no energy from the trapped souls to power it, the complex was now as dark and silent as a tomb. An hour later, they stepped out into the open air. To their surprise, the damp, all-clinging mist that had lent the island its name was gone. They looked up into a deep blue sky with wispy clouds and a bright, warm sun. Before them stretched miles of lush tropical jungle that led to a white, sandy beach.

"It looks like a tropical paradise now," Patty remarked.

"An it will remain a paradise now that the mist is gone," James said as they moved along the trail toward the cove.

Mourning Winds, the Isle of Wailing Mists was no more.

They found the Saracen Moon anchored only a few yards offshore. Hassan and a handful of the crewmen were barbecuing a wild pig they'd caught on the beach and bottles of beer and rum were everywhere. Sindbad shook Hassan's hand when he walked up.

"When the mist went away, we decided it was all right to come ashore. Armando here shot this pig, so I thought it best not to waste it," Hassan explained as he passed out bottles of beer and rum. As the part progressed, the other ships entered the cove and more sailors joined the fun. Some brought instruments. Since Patty was the only woman among them, she found herself dancing with one happy sailor after another. James even joined the fun.

"I never knew you could dance," Patty remarked as they twirled around.

"There is much you still don't know about me," James said with a sly smile.

As the party continued, James sat down next to Sindbad.

"Where are you bound, Captain?" he asked.

"My first stop id Mumbai to take on a load of spices. From there, we sail to Thule," Sindbad replied.

"Good. We'll part ways in Mumbai. I have business further north and west," James said.

"What sort of business?" asked Sindbad.

"I'm headed into the Indus Valley to check out rumors of supernatural activity," James said.

"The phantom riders?" Sindbad asked.

James nodded.

"I received a letter from Ariandel Singh. He's the magistrate for that region. He asked me for help," he said.

"If what I've heard about the phantoms is true, you're in for a most interesting trip. If I didn't have business elsewhere, I'd probably go with you," said Sindbad. "What about this place?"

"Now that the curse has been lifted, I think it would make a most pleasant resort. Has anyone ever explored the smaller islands to the south?" James asked.

"Not that I'm aware of. Now that we're here, would you like to check them out? Most of them are so small that they vanish when the tide comes in. There are three larger ones but even they are too small to be of much use," Sindbad offered.

"There's time enough for that later—after I find out what's behind these phantom riders," James said.

The party lasted well into the wee hours of the morning. Around noon the next day, Sindbad's fleet departed from the cove. James and the others stood on the deck of the Saracen Moon watching as the mountains of Mourning Winds faded in the distance. Without saying a word, Rolf sidled up to Patty and slipped his hand in hers. She didn't react. She just held it as tightly as she could . . .

The Liberator and the Lion

In the 41st year of the reign of Arka-Dal.

All is well in the Empire as the people of Thule celebrated the birth of the twins Lorco and Mara, the offspring of Arka-Dal and his fifth "wife", Chatha, the pretty warrior-queen. As the celebratory fireworks lit up the night sky, the wizard Merlin stood on the balcony of the palace with the royal family and watched. Yet his mind was not on the events transpiring before him. Instead, it was miles away, to the northeast, where a young warrior and his army of freed slaves and disenfranchised misfits were, at that very moment, carving out a new "empire" in what remained of the Turkish-dominated areas of Asia Minor.

What caught Merlin's attention was the way this young general piled up victory after victory against much larger, better equipped forces. He had even taken several small Turkish cities and forced thousands of frightened civilians to seek refuge in Scythia. And he did this by copying many of Arka-Dal's battle tactics. This told Merlin that the young general was most likely an admirer of the Emperor.

This was further underscored by the fact that wherever he went, he destroyed everyone and everything that trafficked in human cargo. To many of the slaves he freed, Joshua was a liberator and they flocked to his army by the thousands. Like Arka-Dal, Joshua ordered his soldiers not to harm civilians or loot private property and shops. He concentrated his efforts on military targets as much as possible and tried to keep collateral damages to a minimum. He had also talked many of his former foes into joining his army.

Something else he'd borrowed from Arka-Dal's playbook.

"Never leave an enemy to your rear."

As this "liberator" cut a bloody swath across Asia, little did he realize that he would soon have to pit his military skills against the very man he admired most.

Joshua rode across the battlefield and watched as his men looted the bodies of the slain Turks of money and useable weapons. The battle had been short and quite bloody. It had been especially bloody for the Turks.

This had been the last gasp for the Sultan's army. He had gambled everything he had left on one cast of the dice in a futile effort to stem the tide. The Sultan had been confident of victory.

Overly so.

Although his force outnumbered that of Joshua's four-to-one, they fell victim to one of the young general's carefully planned traps and were slaughtered. When the Sultan realized the battle was lost, he fled from the field in great haste along with most of his spoiled nobles and their wives who had come out to watch his "victory".

It was over in three short hours.

Violent, bloody hours that left the immediate landscape awash in red and shattered corpses. The sight made the young general sick to his stomach.

Again.

Joshua's skill as a battlefield commander he humbly attributed to his study of Arka-Dal's tactics. His instincts to assess and react swiftly changes, his ability to read and use terrain to his advantage and the way he always led from the front reminded many of his officers of the legendary Thulian Emperor.

But, he wondered, as his men gathered up the dead and wounded, did such sights also sicken Arka-Dal? Did visions of the dead haunt *his* dreams, too?

When he set out to destroy the Turks, he never imagined how truly horrific war could be. He lost close friends. He saw fields made barren and villages destroyed. And the sight of newly-widowed women and orphaned children weeping over the bodies of their slain husbands and fathers broke his heart.

Did Arka-Dal feel the same?

These terrible images became etched in his soul. Would they ever fade? Would he ever find peace?

Nearly 20,000 Turks and a third the number of his own men lay dead on the field. Many other Turks had surrendered. The rest fled to the west to join the Sultan and to fight again.

Joshua had won.

Again.

The victory gave him control of most of the region east of the Caspian Sea. During the last six months, he had conquered a territory spanning over 80,000 square miles. He had taken seven large cities and a dozen smaller towns. Many had surrendered without a fight after their garrisons had fled. He didn't bother to garrison his own men in those places. His war was not with the hapless civilians but with their sultan. He simply resupplied his soldiers at each city and continued the chase.

Joshua was also aware that his conquests were making the rulers of the vast Indian Empire nervous. Many of his soldiers feared that if they came too close to the Indian Frontier, Chandragupta might send his army out after them. To ease Chandragupta's concerns, he sent an emissary to the Royal Court to assure the Emperor that no Indian territories would be invaded. The emissary emphasized that Joshua's war was against the Turks and Trollegs, both of whom were notorious for trading in slaves.

India had no slaves.

Even if it did, Joshua was not foolish enough to think he could ever wage a successful campaign against an empire that boasted one of the largest, best trained and best led armies on Earth.

What he didn't yet realize was the fact that his campaign had also caught the attention of several Thulian military observers whose scouts were keeping a close watch on his relentless march westward. Before long, he would come to the shores of the Caspian Sea, which was a formidable barrier, especially to someone without a navy.

Would he stop there?

Would he stop after he'd destroyed the Turks? Or did he have other goals in mind?

Joshua was somewhat of an enigma.

He had come seemingly out of nowhere to lead a huge, well-trained army. He was young, tall and handsome. He liked to wear his dark brown hair long and loose and was clean shaven. He had steel gray eyes and a keen eye for terrain and tactics. He was equally adept at siege warfare as he was in open, pitched battles. Many of his tactics showed that he was a student of warfare—especially those tactics used with great success by Arka-Dal.

It was only logical for him to do this. Joshua admired Arka-Dal, both as a great ruler and a field commander. He had read everything he could find about the Thulian Emperor, especially his tactics and diplomatic skills. He studied the Thulian army system and modeled his own army after it. And he had trained his soldiers in the same way.

And just like Arka-Dal, he chose his commanders on merit and skill rather than family connections. This made perfect sense to

Joshua. After all, more than two thirds of his soldiers were former slaves and field laborers. They had no family connections. Hell, most of them had no families.

While Thulian scouts and spies learned all they could about Joshua's field tactics and the makeup of his ever-growing army, the answer to one great question still eluded them.

But who *was* Joshua, exactly?

While the world pondered that question, Joshua dismounted and walked toward a cluster of his officers. Many saluted as he approached. One, his closest friend and advisor, Cadmus, simply nodded.

"That was a brilliant plan, Joshua. The Turks never stood a chance," Cadmus said with a smile.

"How many of our men did we lose?" Joshua asked as he removed his helmet and tucked it under his left arm.

"A few hundred. The Turks, however, lost their asses. What do we do with our prisoners?" Cadmus replied.

"The same as always. Pardon them. Give each man a gold piece and send them on their way. We have no place to keep them," Joshua ordered.

"Aren't you worried that they might rejoin the Sultan and fight against us again?" asked another officer.

Joshua shrugged.

"If you show mercy to your enemy, you make him a friend. If some choose to fight beside the Sultan again, so be it. We will deal with them when the time comes," he said philosophically. "Where did the Sultan flee to?"

"He rode west like the Devil himself was chasing him," Cadmus said as he pointed.

Joshua laughed.

"The Devil *is* chasing him," he said. "See to our dead and wounded then regroup our forces. We ride west at dawn."

The war to the east also caught the attention of King Terraeus, the last of the decadent Magan Dynasty that had ruled Trollegia for nearly 400 years. Trollegia was on the western shore of the Caspian Sea. It was nestled between the sea and a range of crooked, rocky mountains that divided Trollegia from Thule to the south and west. Although Trollegia wanted to have economic ties with Thule, Arka-Dal desired to have little or no contact with them after their recent change of government.

The Trollegs were a warlike, decadent people. Their nation had little resources save for the regiments of mercenaries they hired out to whoever needed them. Trolleg soldiers were among the toughest, best-trained troops in the world and their unit commanders were fearless and daring. Many of them served as personal bodyguards to kings, dukes and other monarchs. Some served as far away as England.

They also traded in slaves—and that was the very thing that kept Thule from developing ties with Trollegia.

When Arka-Dal insisted that the Trollegs abandon the foul practice, Terraeus refused. After all, his nation made almost as much money selling slaves as it did hiring out mercenaries. Abandoning the slave trade was tantamount to committing economic suicide. It was also something they had always done. Each time their armies scored a victory, they gathered up the prisoners and sold them to Turkish slavers for a good profit. The better ones were forced to serve in the armies of various sultans and pashas. The rest were either resold in other countries or sent to labor in mines and quarries until they died. When the Trollegs took a city, they sold the women and children to the Turks as sex slaves or kept them for themselves. It was said that there were at least two slaves for every Trolleg citizen. Like the Spartans before them, the Trollegs also feared an uprising and kept tight reins on their slaves.

Disgusted, Arka-Dal cut off all but the most basic diplomatic channels to Trollegia. He also allowed their naval ships to make port calls, provided that no slaves were aboard.

But it wasn't always so. Decades earlier, Trollegia was ruled by a wise old king named Thessalus. During the Great War, he sent 60, 000 of his best soldiers under the command of his most able General Wodens to fight alongside Arka-Dal against the Barbarian Hordes. Thessalus desired closer ties with Thule and had eagerly agreed to abolish slavery in order to gain those ties.[10]

Ten years later, Thessalus died in his sleep. With no heirs to the throne, Wodens was declared king by the Senate. He ruled well for another four years and died under very mysterious circumstances. There were rumors that he'd been poisoned by the captain of his guard. His sudden death left a power vacuum. This led to a long, bloody civil war between the more enlightened Trollegs and hard line traditionalists who wanted to reestablish the old ways.

---

10 Read THE GRAND ILLUSION

The traditionalists won.

And they chose Terraeus, the last surviving member of a former ruling house, as their king. Within two years after he ascended the throne, the Trollegs reverted to their ancient ways and their old habits. In fact, Terraeus had his old enemies rounded up and either executed or sold into slavery. He then confiscated their estates for himself. Anyone who objected met a similar fate. It was by these brutal methods that he reduced the Senate to a group of fearful old men who simply rubber-stamped all of his edicts.

Trollegia returned to being a harsh martial society in which women had little or nothing to do with the workings of the government—which consisted of the king and six generals. Most of those who were too impaired by wounds or age to be part of a regiment scratched out meager livings from the soil as farmers or artisans. Trolleg craftsmen were renown the world over for their work with bronze and iron and it was said their women wove wondrous tapestries.

But their major trading partner had been Byzantium. That trade had dwindled to a mere trickle since the Hellenes became allies of Thule. In return for opening Thule's vast markets to Hellenic goods, Arka-Dal had insisted the Hellenes emancipate any slaves they still held and give up all ties to any other nations who traded in human cargo. The Hellenes quickly agreed to this. In the process, they severed most of their trading ties with Trollegia.

So did Egypt and India.

When the almost bankrupt council of merchants in Vesuvia tried to force Terraeus to abandon the slave trade in favor of free trade with Thule and its allies, the king steadfastly refused.

"We are who we are. We will not abandon our traditions that have served us so well in the past. We must never forget who we are," he said.

The merchants grumbled. Many of them abandoned their shops and migrated to Byzantium and Thule. Those who stayed saw their business dwindle to near-nothing. The few foreign goods that managed to enter Trollegian markets now cost far more than the average citizen could afford.

Terraeus seemed not to know or care about the economic plight of his subjects. In fact, there was very little he did know. But he knew who Joshua was.

He also knew that he'd turn his attention toward Trollegia once he was finished with the Turks. When he did, Terraeus planned to send his regiments out to destroy Joshua's army and bring his head back to the capital on a pike.

"After we crush this upstart commander, we'll go across the sea and claim the Turkish lands for ourselves. Joshua's invasion has left the Sultan's army too weak to defend his territories. We should have no trouble filling the power vacuum," Terraeus told his generals.

"Wouldn't such a move on our part provoke Thule to take action? The Emperor might view it as an attempt to seize the eastern provinces," General Adamis pointed out.

"Arka-Dal has no love for the Turks, not after Byzantium.[11] You don't see any Thulian armies mustering to move against Joshua, so they will not move against us when we move into the territory," Terraeus assured them. "To make sure there is no misunderstanding, I'll send a letter to Arka-Dal before we move in."

Terraeus looked at the map on the wall.

"Most likely, Joshua will lead his forces north and attempt to go around the sea. I want six regiments of our best soldiers waiting there for him. In the event you are overrun, retreat into Caradum. Let him besiege the city and waste his men trying to breach those walls. Keep him engaged long enough for me to send another four regiments up to hit him from the south. Once those regiments arrive, I want you to launch a counter attack from Caradum and drive Joshua's army into the sea!" he decided.

"And if that fails, Your Majesty?" asked Adamis.

"We'll meet them here on the plains of Lloigor. We will not allow them to reach the capital!" Terraeus said.

It was getting late and he was thirsty.

Leo put down the pen and stretched to get the kinks out of his neck and shoulders. Then he stood and walked up the stairs. He'd been working several hours now, trying to read and catalog all of the information Galya had given him about the things in the Abyss. Her people had fought the things many times over the millennia. And the battles always ended in a draw.

As he entered the parlor to get a drink, he was surprised to see Merlin and the Devil seated opposite each other and engaged in a spirited conversation. They smiled when he walked past them to the

---

11 Read THIRTEEN SKULLS & OTHER TALES

bar. Leo poured himself a glass of wine and sat down on the sofa next to Merlin.

"It's good of you to join us, Leo," the wizard said. "We were just discussing the merits of good and evil in helping to maintain the universal balance. What are your thoughts on that?"

Leo mulled it over while he sipped his wine.

"I say that nothing can exist without an exact opposite to act as a counterbalance. For example, light is nothing without darkness, order means nothing without chaos, and so on," he said. "It stands to reason that good cannot exist without evil and vice versa."

"That's exactly *my* argument," the Devil said. "Everything has to have an opposite or it is nothing at all."

"I agree to a point. I say that the opposites need not be extremes," Merlin added.

"Please! One cannot be a 'little bit good' any more than one can be a 'little bit evil'. I *do* agree that both need to be tempered with reason and sound judgments to avoid causing total chaos. My experiences over the ages prove that," the Devil said.

"Yes indeed. We do not need another Great Disaster," Merlin laughed.

"I will take *some* of the blame for that but not *all.* Anyone who thought they could win such a war was completely insane. We must make sure that it never happens again," the Devil said.

"Here's one for you," Merlin said. "Now that you have sworn to protect Thule, are you a little bit good or a little bit evil?"

The Devil laughed and slapped his knee.

"That's a good one, Merlin! I'm afraid that you have me there for I truly have no answer. I will say this—Galya's relationship with Arka-Dal has completely changed the way she acts and looks. I think she has found her true self here. Her *good* self. Although I have lost my star seductress, I am happy for them both," he said as he held up his glass.

Merlin and Leo clinked theirs against it and drank to the health of the lucky couple.

"How do your minions on the Lower Planes feel about all this?" asked Leo.

"It's business as usual. Those who dared question the situation have paid the ultimate price. The rest have more than enough of their normal duties to keep them busy," the Devil replied.

"So business is good?" asked Leo.

"It's so good, I can afford to throw my support behind the Empire without worrying about having enough souls to harvest. The people of Thule make up less than 10% of the Earth's population, so there are still plenty of souls to go around." The Devil said.

He finished his drink and went to the bar to get another.

"You know what's really strange? This is the first and only place in the entire universe where I actually feel welcome. This is the only place where I can come and be treated as a guest and a friend," he said.

"And the only place where we don't try to kill each other," Merlin pointed out.

They clinked glasses again and laughed.

Galya was in the library with Arka-Dal. While the Emperor went over some important paperwork, she studied the titles in his collection of favorite books. Most were reprints of Fist Age classics that Leo had given him in his youth. One, Sun Tzu's "The Art of War", was a gift from Ogadai, the Mongoblin Emperor.

The collection was interesting.

There was Plato's Republic, Machiavelli's The Prince, The Rise and Fall of the Roman Empire, and books about the greatest generals of the First Age, such as Alexander, Julius Caesar, Hannibal, Napoleon Bonaparte, Robert E. Lee, Ghengis Khan and a variety of books on naval tactics of various eras. The most curious was a collection of essays and letters written by Thomas Jefferson.

Galya smiled.

"Your personal favorites?" she asked.

He looked up and nodded.

"They've come in handy over the years," he said as he put down his pen. "Especially The Art of War."

"Which is your favorite?" she asked.

"Thomas Jefferson," he replied. "His writings have influenced me the most. Without them, Thule would be quite different than it is now."

"I knew him, you know," she smiled. "You chose wisely. Books tell a lot about a man's character."

"And what do those tell you about *mine?*" he asked.

She walked over, put her arms around his neck and kissed him.

"They tell me that I have chosen wisely," she said. "Father says the same thing. He likes you. What's more, he really *respects* you. And you both have much in common."

"So I keep finding out," Arka-Dal said with a chuckle. "Just recently I found out that he, too, detests slavery and those who keep or deal in them."

"That's true. Father has always been a strong believer in free will. He has never forced anyone to do business with him and he has always offered people choices. It's not his fault that most never bother to read the fine print in their contracts," Galya said.

Arka-Dal laughed.

"Caveat emptor!" he said.

"Exactly!" she agreed. "I've noticed that you enjoy playing chess with Leo—but you play a different strategy game with Mayumi and Master Koto. It is rare to see a non-Asian play Go."

"I'm still learning that one. It's almost the exact opposite of chess. When I play Go, I have to apply the principles of The Art of War in order win. It's a game of subtlety and deception. Chess is more like Western warfare. It's a game of attrition aimed at wiping out your opponent's army and capturing his king. Both come in handy on the battlefield in one way or another," he explained.

"I've heard that this Joshua also plays chess," Galya said.

"Yes—but I doubt he's even heard of Go," said Arka-Dal. "By the way, what's your favorite book?"

"Dante's Inferno, of course," she said with a smile.

Galya still prowled around at night. Although she now felt comfortable in broad daylight and loved to watch the sun rise each morning, old habits were hard to break. During the day, she spent as much time as she could with Arka-Dal or helping Leo and Medusa with their research of the Lower Planes. She had learned to play chess, too. In fact, she was now able to defeat Leo on a regular basis.

She also spent a lot of time with the other women and their children, who seemed delighted with her. She even enjoyed playing games with them. And she was learning how to help care for infants thanks to Chatha's twins.

The Thulians, she discovered, were a friendly people. Now that they were familiar with her, many waved or greeted her when she walked through the streets and markets. A few even stopped to converse with her—just as they did with everyone else who lived at the palace. There were no class barriers between Thulians. No titles. The people even treated Arka-Dal as if he were a member of their family. It was an attitude he openly encouraged, too.

Once their wedding was announced, the Thulian merchants wasted no time. The markets of the Empire quickly became flooded with commemorative plates, cups, trinkets, clothing items and various paintings of Galya, Arka-Dal and the rest of the royal household. Even the toy makers got into the spirit of the occasion by producing several different versions of Galya dolls. Some even included detachable wings and horns.

Galya found it all quite amusing—and somewhat embarrassing.

The other women told her that she'd get used to it eventually because the same thing happened when each of them married Arka-Dal. Medusa added that while most of the items bearing likenesses of her and Chatha had since vanished from the stores, the items bearing Mayumi's images remained very popular.

"That's because the people of Thule love Mayumi above all others. To them, she will always be their Empress and the one true love of Arka-Dal," Chatha explained. "The people *adore* Mayumi as much as they do Arka-Dal. That will never change."

Galya smiled at Mayumi.

It was easy to understand why the people felt that way about her. Galya adored her, too. After all, Mayumi was the first member of the family to accept and befriend her and the two had developed a strong bond.

Mayumi smiled back, then blushed.

Galya laughed at her modesty.

The longer Galya stayed in Thule, the more she loved it.

And the more she loved Arka-Dal.

"You seem to be doing well here, Galya," her father observed.

"I am. I love it here, Father. Thule is a wonderful place. Life is wonderful!" she almost gushed.

He smiled and touched her cheek.

"That is what love does for you," he said softly.

"Oh? And what do *you* know of love, Father?" she teased.

"I know much although I have not experienced it for longer than you can imagine. I am happy that you have gotten the chance," he said. "You've changed since you've been here. Your appearance is softer now and you seem more at ease. You look more feminine—and far less menacing. I like it."

"So does Arka-Dal," she beamed.

"You're sacrificing much for him," he pointed out.

"I know. He's worth it, Father. You'll see," she said.

"He's a good man. In all my existence, he is the only human I have ever respected," the Devil replied.

"Me, too," she said as she gripped his arm. "Will you be here for our wedding?"

"Nothing in this or any other universe can keep me from escorting you down that aisle on your day of days. I will be here. I promise," he assured her.

As Joshua and his army pursued the fleeing Turks, they came upon the fortress city of Baraclava. The city sat atop a high, flat-topped hill in the middle of a wide plain. Its walls were stone and ten feet thick and 20 feet high. The Turks boasted that it was impregnable. Even Cadmus thought so and advised Joshua to bypass it.

But he was unwilling to leave an intact enemy stronghold to his rear. After studying the situation carefully, Joshua decided to take Baraclava.

While his artisans constructed catapults, siege towers and heavy rams, he had the rest of his army chop down every tree in a nearby forest and erect a wooden wall around the entire city.

"This will prevent the Turks from escaping. They'll either be forced to waste their manpower trying to break through or slowly starve to death for lack of supplies. The wall will also provide our men with cover from Turkish arrows while we prepare the siege machines to batter down their walls," he explained.

Alarmed, the Turk commander inside the city ordered several attacks against Joshua's workers in an effort to stop construction. Each time, the attackers were forced back into the city after suffering heavy losses. After a week of this, the commander ordered a halt to the attacks and the people inside Baraclava watched anxiously as the wall slowly encircled the entire city. Once the wall was completed, the siege began in earnest.

For two straight weeks, Joshua's catapults lobbed heavy rocks and fireballs into Baraclava. The bombardment started at sunset and lasted until dawn. As soon as the catapults fell silent, Joshua launched attacks against weakened spots in the walls. The attacks weren't intended to capture the city. Indeed, his men retreated after only a few minutes. The attacks were intended to deprive the enemy of sleep and wear down their resistance. But the Turks were determined to hold out.

At the start of the third week, Joshua's scouts brought him news of a larger Turkish force moving toward Baraclava. Instead of quitting the siege, Joshua ordered his men to construct a second wall a half-mile beyond the first.

"While the first wall keeps the defenders trapped within the city, the second wall will keep the relief force from lifting the siege. They will be forced to waste their soldiers' lives in an effort to break through. When they are weakened enough, we'll ride out and attack them," he said to his commanders.

For good measure, he also ordered his men to dig a 15 foot deep trench around the outside of the second wall and line it with sharpened stakes. When the stakes were in place, he filled the trench with oil then had his men cover the whole thing with loose straw and dirt. Any attacking force would fall into the trench before they realized it was there and would become easy marks for his archers—if they survived the trap itself.

With this done, he ordered his men behind the wall to await the arrival of the relief column. He didn't have to wait long.

The new Turkish army arrived three days later and were astonished to find themselves staring at a strong wooden rampart. After looking the situation over, their commander ordered his men to attack. Joshua's men watched as the Turkish cavalry thundered toward the wall, waving swords and shouting at the tops of their lungs—and fell right into the trap. Before they could stop their charge, the first two rows of cavalry plunged headlong into the trench. As both men and horses became impaled on the wooden stakes, the air became filled with the screams and moans and curses of the Turks. Those behind them managed to stop themselves before they joined their brethren in the trench—but this placed them within killing range of Joshua's archers. Hundreds of Turks toppled from their saddles as the air grew thick with arrows. Some of the Turks tried to return fire but it was to no avail.

Disgusted with his losses, the commander had his trumpeters sound the retreat. The Turks rode off with their tails between their legs as Joshua's men jeered them.

As the sun set, Joshua continued the bombardment of Baraclava. The commander of the relief column figured that Joshua's attentions were turned elsewhere now and decided to renew the attack. This time, he had his men dismount and creep into the pit. There, they would await his signal to attack. They brought scaling ladders with them so they could climb out of the pit and assail the walls.

At first, the plan seemed to work.

The Turks easily reached the trench and carefully climbed into it to avoid joining their dead comrades on the stakes. That's when they found themselves standing knee-deep in a dark, unctuous liquid. By the time they realized what it was, it was too late. Joshua's men appeared on the ramparts and began tossing flaming torches into the trench. The oil ignited instantly. Within minutes, the entire trench was ablaze and the men trapped within it were quickly burnt beyond recognition.

With the screams of his terrified soldiers ringing in his ears, and the air stinking of burning flesh, the Turkish commander ordered his men to retreat. As soon as he saw the Turks turn away from the wall, Joshua ordered his cavalry to counterattack. The gates flew open, ramps were lowered and Joshua's horsemen poured out. They struck the Turks from the rear and turned their retreat into a total rout. Those who found themselves trapped by Joshua's men fought back with surprising ferocity. The rest fled with surprising speed.

The Turk commander inside the city decided to seize the moment to break through the wall. He ordered every last man he had left to attack while Joshua's men were occupied with the relief column. They easily reached the ramparts and battered down the gate—only to run right into the rest of Joshua's army that was waiting for them on the other side.

Joshua had anticipated such a move and had set yet another trap. The Turks were quickly surrounded and the slaughter began. Cut off from the safety of the city, the beleaguered Turks did all they could to fight their way back. But Joshua's men seemed to be everywhere now and they could find no avenue of escape. After a two hour long slugfest, most of the Turks lay dead on the field—along with their commander.

At sunrise the next day, Joshua and his men entered the defenseless city in triumph. The war-weary citizens were relieved when he issued orders to his troops to "not loot the shops or homes nor molest the citizens of Baraclava under penalty of death. We are not bandits. We are soldiers and I expect every one of you to act accordingly."

He did, however, empty the city's treasury and distribute the money to his troops. He also had his men confiscate half the cattle and goats so that his army could be fed. A house-to-house search turned up many weapons which he also issued to his soldiers along with those they had taken from the dead Turkish soldiers.

After spending a week in Baraclava tending to his wounded men, Joshua gathered up his army and continued his march south in pursuit of the Sultan.

His stunning victory at Baraclava disheartened the Turks. Many people abandoned their cities and villages and fled south while Turkish regiments torched everything they thought Joshua and his men might make use of. At the same, this encouraged most of the remaining slaves to leave their masters. Many enlisted in Joshua's army and were quickly trained by his more seasoned troops. Others slew their owners and left the area as fast as they could. They wanted no part of this war. All they wanted was freedom.

Joshua caught up with the fleeing remnant of the Sultan's army at a narrow pass called El Kahlida. The Sultan had hoped to reach the pass ahead of Joshua's army, but Joshua got there first with his cavalry and cut off their retreat. With nowhere to go, the Sultan threw every last horseman he had left at Joshua's line. As soon as both sides were locked in a deadly saber battle, the Sultan himself led his infantry into the fray.

It was the moment that Cadmus had been waiting for. He ordered his bugler to sound the charge and led his eager foot soldiers into the pass. They hit the Sultan's men from behind and scattered them like leaves on a wind. Twenty minutes later, the battle was over and Joshua had the Sultan's head on a pike.

But his victory was bittersweet.

Cadmus, his long-time friend and second in command had been killed by an arrow to the back of his neck. Joshua ordered him burned with honor along with the rest of his fallen soldiers.

The second spot now fell to Maltry, an able but careful cavalry commander. After the funeral, Maltry paraded the 2,000 captured Turks before Joshua. Magnanimous in victory, Joshua gave each of them a gold piece and sent them home after extracting vows that they would not bear arms against him from thereafter. Some of the Turks even volunteered to join his army.

Of course, he accepted their offer.

He needed all the troops he could gather as he turned his eyes toward his main target.

Trollegia.

The decaying nation was on the western shore of the Caspian Sea. It was a formidable barrier. One that forced him to delay his invasion plans long enough to build a fleet large enough to ferry his troops across and to destroy what was left of the Trollegian navy.

He decided to attack by land and sea. He would lead the bulk of his army north and around the edge of the sea and enter Trollegia through the mountain passes. A smaller force would be placed aboard transports and land several miles south of the Trolleg capital. He would also construct two dozen triremes and sic them on the Trolleg fleet to make sure they couldn't harass his transports.

All of this would take time.

Perhaps weeks.

While his carpenters built the ships, he decided to spend the down time recruiting more soldiers from among the Turkish slaves and other enemies of the Trollegs and consolidate his hold on his conquered territories. He also sent his best spies and scouts into Trollegia to study and map potential battlefields, passes, roads and inland waterways that could be used to transport large numbers of troops and wagons. It was another page he borrowed from Arka-Dal's playbook. To be successful, one had to know and understand one's enemies and learn as much about his country as possible. This way, you could anticipate your enemy's moves and force them to fight on terrain of *your* choosing.

Like Arka-Dal, Joshua realized that knowledge and tactics won wars—not huge numbers of soldiers. A good general won battles by outthinking and anticipating his enemy's moves.

Deception didn't hurt, either.

Both Joshua and Arka-Dal had a knack for making their enemies think they were somewhere else, thus forcing them to deploy their troops to cover the supposed targets. Once the enemy was on the move, the real attack would hit them either while en route or somewhere else they weren't expecting. This usually worked and it enabled a small force to defeat much larger armies by wearing them down.

Arka-Dal received the news of the destruction of the Turks with near indifference. He had no love for those people and viewed Joshua's conquest of them as a fitting punishment for what they had done to Byzantium a few years earlier.

He did, however, pay close attention to the tactics Joshua used to destroy them. It was almost as if Joshua was a mirror image of himself. He didn't know if he should be flattered or annoyed with Joshua for borrowing his tactics. He did like the fact that Joshua was also daring and somewhat innovative.

"The kid has balls—big ones," he said.

"Do you suppose he's read Sun Tsu?" asked Leo.

"I don't know, but he's clearly studied *my* campaigns. He's been winning some impressive victories while suffering minimal losses. He knows how to make use of the terrain. He seems to be able to read the minds of opposing generals well enough to counter most of their moves and he's a whiz at taking fortified cities without prolonged sieges. He also seems to be real good at dividing his forces and striking where least expected. He's good, Leo. Real good," Arka-Dal said with a smile.

"He's certainly made short work of the Turks," Pandaar added.

"No loss there. The Turks are slavers. They got what they deserved," Arka-Dal said.

"Do you think he'll stop with the Turks?" asked Pandaar.

"Given what we know about him, I doubt it. He has a score to settle with the Trollegs. A big one. The real question is: will he stop *there*?" Arka-Dal replied.

"What if he doesn't?" Pandaar asked.

"Then we'll have to cut those big balls of his off." Arka-Dal said.

Arka-Dal had made a point of learning all he could about Joshua. He's sent his best spies and scouts into the Turkish territories to gather information. They returned with a most interesting tale.

Joshua was the youngest son of a Kurdish pasha. Thirty years ago, the Trollegs invaded the western half of Kurdistan in search of gold and slaves. They found plenty of both. In the process, they burned several small towns and cities and slaughtered thousands of Kurds and Armenians. Among them were Joshua's parents.

In true Trolleg fashion, they slew all of the old people and carted off the children, young women, men and cattle. They took the gold and cattle back to Trollegia and sold the slaves in the Turkish markets. Joshua was one of those slaves.

For 15 years, he worked 16 hour shifts in various mines and fields for a brutal Turk businessman. Then he escaped.

He fled into the Kurdish highlands and began gathering up an army. Most of his soldiers were escaped slaves or those he had "liberated" from mines and work farms. Most had been sold to the Turks by the Trollegs. Some had been captured directly by the Turks. For five years, he trained and equipped his army. When his army numbered 20,000, he struck.

And with incredible suddenness and ferocity.

One-by-one, the Turkish strongholds fell before him. As his victories mounted, more and more freed slaves joined his ranks. Now, at the end of his Turkish campaign, his army numbered nearly 50,000—and it was still growing. Soon, he would have more than enough trained soldiers to exact revenge and wreak havoc on those he detested most.

The Trollegs.

Because of them, he had lost his family, lost his home and was forced to lead a miserable life as a slave of the Turks. He was deprived of his childhood, his mother's love and the chance to lead a normal, happy life. That's why he swore to destroy the Trollegs and anyone else who traded in human flesh.

Despite all of this, he wasn't a brutal man. He took great pains to ensure that his armies did no harm to ordinary civilians, especially women and children. He ordered his men to leave their homes and shops intact when possible—unless, of course, the owners used slaves to run them. In such instances, he had his men execute the owners, loot and burn their property and free the slaves.

On the field of battle, he was equally generous and pragmatic. After each battle, he freed his prisoners after extracting oaths from them not to take up arms against him again. Many of the defeated troops had opted to join his army, thus adding more crack soldiers to his regiments.

"By treating these people with dignity and respect, they will be more willing to cooperate with us. I don't want enemies at our backs, Maltry. I want *allies.* Never forget that we are soldiers. We do *not* harm civilians!" Joshua once explained.

"Not even *Trolleg* civilians?" Maltry asked.

"Not even them," Joshua said. Then with a grin he added, "in most cases, anyway."

When Leo learned of Joshua's background he smiled.

"He sounds much like Spartacus, the Greek slave who led a rebellion against his Roman masters during the First Age," the Pope observed.

"As I recall, Spartacus was defeated and crucified," Arka-Dal remarked.

"Do you plan to crucify Joshua?" Leo asked.

"I'll do much *worse* to him if he decides to cross into Thule," the Emperor replied. "For now, we'll sit and watch what he does to Trollegia."

"I think it will be most interesting to see what the Trollegs do when he invades their country," Leo said. "Although they are a highly skilled military society, they are quite decadent. Even their best mercenary units aren't what they used to be and most of their better commanders are dead. Their present king has never led troops into combat and their most experienced general has been retired for nearly 40 years."

"And who would that be?" asked Arka-Dal.

"I believe his name is Amrosius Pitar," Leo replied.

"What do you know about him?" Arka-Dal asked.

"Not very much," Leo said.

"Then find out all you can. I have a feeling that this Pitar will play a big part in the upcoming war and I want to know more about him," Arka-Dal said.

While he kept an interested eye on Joshua's campaigns, the women of the palace concerned themselves with other matters. They had taken Galya under their wings and had spent several weeks showing her around the Empire cruising up and down the Tigris-Euphrates Rivers in the royal yacht.

The Princess of Hell eagerly took everything in. She tried every type of food and beverage she saw, frequented the marketplaces and began to dress in the latest Thulian fashions, which mostly consisted of short, bright colored, light dresses tied at the waist and bare shouldered. Thule was mostly hot and dry and the dresses were practical. Thulian women also liked to show off their legs. So did Galya.

She had also shed her bat-like wings in order to appear less "devilish" and to fit in better with the people of Thule.

Now that Arka-Dal had officially proposed, Mayumi and the other women plunged into the planning of their nuptials as if it were the most important event on Earth. Galya could hardly believe this was happening or that Arka-Dal's other wives were helping her.

It also amazed her that, although the Thulians knew who and what she was, none of them seemed to mind that she was walking among them or that she was to be their Emperor's next wife. Whatever made Arka-Dal happy also made them happy.

Mayumi and Leo put it into perspective for her.

"Aka-san accepts you, so the people accept you. That is the way it is here. That is what Thule is really about," Mayumi said.

"Arka-Dal is Thule and Thule is him. The two are one and the same," Leo added. "Without Thule, there would be no Arka-Dal.

Without Arka-Dal, there would be no Thule, no shining city on the hill, to act as a welcoming beacon for all who desire freedom and the chance to make something of themselves. So the people feel what is good for him is also good for the Empire."

Galya realized that there was something special about Thule the moment she met the Gorgon, Medusa. That opinion was further enhanced when she met the Minotaur, Jun. Medusa was Arka-Dal's number two wife. Jun was now the field marshal of Thule's Northern Army. Both had come to Thule to avoid being persecuted by their countrymen. In Greece they were considered monsters and hunted to near extinction. In Thule, they were heroes.

She also learned that Arka-Dal and Merlin were once fierce enemies. Now, their bond of friendship was unbreakable. Merlin had even bestowed the fabled Excalibur on him because he decided that only Arka-Dal was worthy enough to wield the magical sword.

Her father had warned her that she might lose her special powers if she gave birth to a child. That act of love might even cause her to become *mortal*. Galya didn't care if she grew old and died as long as she and Arka-Dal were together.

Would he actually come to their wedding? If he did, would his presence cause a commotion? After all, most of Thule's important holy men would be there, even the arch bishop of the Christian church. All would be there to give them the traditional blessings. Would a Christian bless the union of the Emperor and the Devil's daughter?

She had also met Perseus.

He and two of his companions had come to Thule to find and slay Medusa. Instead, they had all enlisted in the Army of Thule. His two friends were now dead and Perseus held the rank of colonel in the Central Army and was among the Emperor's closest friends. When Medusa introduced him to Galya, the Greek was so taken with her beauty that he asked her if she had a sister he might marry one day.

"No. I am the only one," she said. "A handsome man such as you should have no trouble finding a bride. There are many beautiful women here in Thule."

"But none as beautiful as *you*. Arka-Dal is certainly a lucky devil to be marrying the likes of you," Perseus remarked.

She smiled.

"No. *I'm* the lucky devil," she said.

And she meant it.

The invasion of Trollegia began with an ill-fated pre-emptive strike. The bull-headed Terraeus, against the advice of General Adamis, decided to take the war to Joshua rather than wait for him to march on Trollegia. He sent Adamis and nearly every last soldier he had north around the Caspian Sea to "surprise the barbarians in their camp".

The reluctant Adamis obeyed his king.

On a cool December morning, they left Trollegia with 1,400 cavalry and 8,000 infantry and took the pass north into the mountains. Adamis hoped they could travel undetected until they emerged from the passes.

But it was a forlorn hope at best.

The passes were crawling with Joshua's scouts. They soon spotted Adamis' columns and alerted Joshua. To everyone's surprise, he decided against an ambush. Instead, he assembled his army at the mouth of the pass on a flat, narrow plain and awaited Adamis' arrival.

When the Trollegs exited from the pass, Adamis was stunned to see two large squares of infantry waiting on the plains. After studying the situation, he decided to attack immediately. He formed his cavalry into a large wedge and arrayed his infantry behind them in the traditional phalanx. He planned to use the cavalry to punch holes in the enemy formations then follow up with the infantry before they could regroup. When his men were ready, he ordered his buglers to sound the attack.

Joshua, who was on a knoll between the two squares, watched from astride his horse as the Trolleg cavalry slammed into his first square. The square broke into two wings and allowed them to pass while archers at the rear of the formation turned and let loose with a veritable rain of arrows. At that moment, the Trolleg phalanx also crashed into the first square.

Just as Joshua planned, the square broke and retreated behind the second square which was now engaged in a brutal battle with Adamis' cavalry. Naturally, the Trolleg phalanx followed them into the fray. To Adamis' surprise, the "fleeing" infantry suddenly turned and locked shields. This maneuver stopped the Trolleg advance in its tracks as their shields collided with a great clatter.

Now that both sides were inextricably engaged in combat, Joshua had his trumpeter sound the next signal. Within minutes, Maltry arrived with nearly 4,000 cavalry from two directions. They encircled the Trollegs and cut them to ribbons before Adamis could give orders to counter this tactic.

It was over within the hour.

Joshua allowed the few surviving Trollegs to retreat back into the pass without pursuit while his men gathered up the dead from both armies and burned them. Among the dead was General Adamis himself and most of his officers.

When the ragged remnants of Adamis' legions reached the capital, the news of their defeat threw the senate into a panic. Many packed their valuables and fled west into the mountains. Others boarded the first ships they saw.

Command now fell to Terraeus himself.

At his disposal were 4,000 personal guards, some 600 horsemen and the 1,300 men that had survived the first battle.

The city's walls were ancient but very thick and strong with defensive towers at 100 yard intervals. In all of Trollegia's long history, the capital of Vesuvia had never been taken.

A prudent commander would have waited for Joshua to bring the war to Vesuvia where a long siege would cost him dearly. But Terraeus was not such a commander.

He placed his remaining soldiers aboard transports and sailed across the Caspian Sea to attack Joshua's main camp. It was the last, desperate gamble of a madman.

To Terraeus' surprise, he landed his entire force on the beach unmolested. A long, high ridge separated Joshua's camp from the sea. Terraeus decided to camp on the beach that night and march on Joshua the next morning.

But the weather gods proved to be a fickle bunch.

At dawn, a heavy rain struck the region followed by a thick fog that shrouded the ridge. It was so dense that the soldiers could barely see the standard bearers and many units soon drifted off the main trail during the march. Fearing ambush, Terraeus sent out cavalry patrols to try and locate the enemy. These patrols soon ran straight into several units of Joshua's cavalry and a wild melee ensued along the ridge. After an hour-long battle, Joshua's cavalry turned and headed back to their camp. One of Terraus' scouts reported that Joshua's entire army was in retreat. Believing he had engaged the main force, Terraeus decided to seize the ridge and immediately led his troops into action. He then ordered his second in command, Nicanor, to follow with the rest of the army as soon as possible.

As the Trollegs crested the ridge, they encountered Joshua's main force already formed for battle. The wily commander had assembled his troops and raced up the ridge to beat the Trollegs to the top. Undaunted, Terraeus formed a phalanx and sent it headlong into Joshua's formation with the intention of shattering it completely. Instead, Joshua's men broke into small units and sidestepped the attack. As the Trollegs attempted to push through, Joshua's men fell on their flanks and cut them to ribbons.

When Nicanor's men reached the crest, they ran directly into Joshua's right wing under the command of Maltry. The Trollegs were quickly overwhelmed and Maltry's men killed everyone within reach. Nicanor's men broke and ran after he was slain, leaving Terraeus exposed on the left.

Maltry immediately took advantage of the opening. He ordered his men to stop pursuing the fleeing Trollegs and pivot to the left rear. They hit Terraeus' men from the rear and slaughtered most of them. Those who weren't killed fled back toward the ships as fast as they could.

Of the 40 ships that had left Vesuvia, only six returned. The rest were now in Joshua's hands and most of the Trolleg strike force lay dead on the beach south of his camp. Terraeus was not among them.

As soon as the tide of battle turned, so did the king. He fled from the field along with his entourage and left his hapless soldiers to their fate.

To make matters worse, when news of Joshua's stunning victory reached the fortified city of Caradum, the city fathers packed all their valuables, including the town treasury, and fled south. With only two companies of soldiers left to defend it, Caradum ceased to be of any importance to Joshua. He decided to bypass it and concentrate on taking out the capital.

He did, however, send a few companies of soldiers to blockade all of the roads leading into and out of Caradum.

Terraeus' gamble had given Joshua the transport ships he needed to ferry his soldiers across the Caspian Sea. To show his appreciation, he sent a messenger to Vesuvia with a letter thanking the "good people of Vesuvia for their generosity and the fine ships they provided". He also promised to be "equally generous" once he entered the city at the head of his army.

Panic quickly swept through the city.

The very wealthy fled along with the senate. So did Terraeus and his family. Vesuvia now lay in the hands of its poorest citizens and several companies of city guards. But they had no leader.

All of the military commanders had been killed in the two battles. After some deliberation, the desperate citizens turned to the only experienced general they had left—the long-retired Ambrosius Pitar.

Pitar was a short, balding man with a handlebar mustache and sparkling blue eyes. He was nearly eighty years old and walked with a decided limp, the result of a tumble he'd taken down a flight of stairs while drunk several years earlier. In his younger days, he'd been a good administrative officer and had a certain genius for logistics. Because of this, he rose through the ranks to the level of general.

As a field commander, he was a disaster.

Forty years earlier, while the Trollegs were battling Turks and Scythians for control of the region, he was given command of 20,000 troops and told to take a small, virtually undefended city overlooking a slow-moving river.

This was Pitar's first field command.

On a hot July morning, he marched his army to the river and managed to ford it without incident. His vanguard fell upon the city and, after a short and nearly bloodless skirmish, they managed to drive out the two companies of Turks that defended it. The Turks retreated to their fortified position on the heights overlooking the city. Pitar studied the heights carefully.

Defenders had a clear field of fire and could riddle attackers with arrows and grenades without fear of being driven out. Just below the heights was an ancient sunken road with a rail fence on one side. The road was just beyond bowshot from the heights. Much to the dismay of his sub commanders, Pitar ordered his entire force to march into the road and wait for further orders. The bemused Turks watched as the well-trained and disciplined Trollegs marched to the road and arrayed themselves in groups of 1,000. The heights were far too steep for cavalry, so Pitar left them to protect the city he'd just taken.

An hour later, Pitar ordered his men to assail the heights. The Turks waited until they came into easy range and let them have it. Pitar's front ranks fell like dominoes, but the Trolleg's kept advancing. They managed to get halfway up before the Turks rained grenades down on them. This proved to be too much. Pitar ordered the buglers to sound "retreat".

His battered army returned to the sunken road and regrouped. After a brief rest, Pitar ordered another attack . . . and another . . . and another. All with the same horrifying results. When the sun finally set, almost 4,000 Trollegs lay strewn all over the heights.

Pitar rested that night.

The next morning, at sunrise, he ordered yet another attack.

This time, some of the Trollegs did manage to reach Turkish positions but were driven off after a nasty sword battle that left most of them dead or wounded. The rest of Pitar's force retreated down the slope with hundreds of Turkish arrows speeding them on their way.

Pitar ordered a retreat after that.

He offered to resign when he returned to Vesuvia. Instead, the king gave him another army and ordered him to drive "an inferior force of Scythians" from the mountains to the north. Pitar had 12,000 men this time, 3,000 of which were cavalry.

To his horror, this "inferior force" turned out to be a crack Scythian army of skilled horse archers and light cavalry. To make things even worse, he managed to lead his men into a well-planned trap that got his vanguard of cavalry separated from the main body, surrounded and cut to pieces while the bulk of the Scythians attacked him from the rear. By sheer luck, Pitar managed to escape with about 2,000 men.

Again, he offered to resign when he returned to the capital.

Instead, he got command of yet another army and was told to attack the Turkish stronghold at Balaklava. With him were two other armies led by less experienced generals. The result was a bloody stalemate that left more than half the men on both sides lying dead on the field. Pitar's group suffered the heaviest losses. The five-day battle resulted in a truce between the two peoples.

Pitar was then given command of the city guards, which were a rag-tag bunch of grizzled veterans and misfits. This is where he excelled. Within six months, he ousted most of the misfits and replaced them with strong, honest young men and women who could not be bought. He also reorganized the entire police force and doubled up on night patrols.

As a result, crime in the capital dwindled to nothing.

A year later, Pitar retired to his estate five miles outside the walls of Vesuvia where he became known for producing a most excellent wine.

But he could not shake the reputation he had as the worst general in Trolleg history. He was glad to be out of the army and thankful that he could run his vineyards in peace. He never imagined that he'd be called upon again.

Then came the letter that summoned him to the senate.

When he arrived the next day, he was greeted at the door by two spearmen. They saluted him as if he were someone of importance and escorted him into the large, circular chamber that was the senate's main hall. There, he saw only seven elderly men dressed in white and gold robes. The rest of the seats were ominously empty.

Pitar bowed before the man in the high backed chair. The man nodded and bade him be seated.

"Are you General Ambrosius Pitar?" the senator asked.

"I was a general. I've been retired for nearly three decades," Pitar replied.

"We have summoned you here because your country once again has need of your services. The wolf is at our door. We need someone of your qualifications to keep that wolf at bay," the senator said.

"Me? I'm no soldier. I haven't commanded troops in any capacity for years. When I did, the results were often catastrophic!" Pitar said.

"We are well aware of your record, General Pitar, yet we have turned to you in this, our darkest hour," the senator said.

"Why me? Is there no one else?" Pitar asked.

"No. All of our other commanders have been slain in battle and our emperor has deserted us when we needed him most. A large enemy host will soon assail this city. We need you to defend it," the senator said. "Your past record shows that while you are an inept field commander at best, you did have a certain genius for logistics and defense. We now call upon you to recall those abilities. The fate of Vesuvia—indeed all of Trollegia— now lies in your hands. I know that you will not let your people down."

Pitar was speechless.

For three decades he had brooded over his military failures. He had a reputation for being the worst general in Trollegian history and he had always yearned to erase that reputation. Now he was being offered a chance to do just that and he wasn't sure he wanted the job.

"I'll do it under one condition," he said after some thought.

"Go on," the senator said.

"I must be the *supreme dictator* with all of the powers the title implies. I do not want my decisions questioned under any circumstances. That is the only way that I will accept your call to duty," Pitar said.

To his astonishment, the senate agreed to his demand. In fact, the chairman stepped down from his seat and handed Pitar the gold baton that was the symbol of authority. He silently accepted it.

"What are your orders, *Your Excellency?"* the senator asked.

"I need a complete inventory of all of our food supplies, medical supplies and other stores. By dusk, I want all of the actual fighting men we have left in the city, including the reserves, assembled in the main square. That includes every last man of the City Guard as well," Pitar said. "I also need all the information you have on our enemies."

The senators hustled out of the room to do as he asked.

That evening, a now uniformed Pitar stood before his soldiers—if you could call them such—and studied them carefully. Barely one in three were skilled fighting men. Another third were reserves who had not been activated for years. The rest were city guardsmen, more suited to running down thieves than warfare. Many were badly out of shape. Several dozen sported nasty war wounds from long ago. To their credit, not a single man shirked his duty. They all gathered up their weapons and assembled in ten neat squares in the large, open plaza in the middle of the city.

A junior officer walked beside him as they inspected the troops. His name was Wahai and he was one of the survivors of the last battle against Joshua's troops.

"How many do we have here?" Pitar asked.

"Six thousand, Sir," came the reply.

"So few? We need nearly twice that number to effectively defend the city walls," Pitar said with a raised eyebrow.

"There are none left in Vesuvia, Sir," Wahai said. "We have exhausted our supply of manpower."

"There is *another* source," Pitar said after a pause. "There are many slaves in Vesuvia, are there not?"

"Thousands," Wahai assured him.

"I'll issue a proclamation," Pitar said.

What he did next was unheard of in the history of Trollegia. He called for volunteers from among the slaves. Many were now masterless since their wealthy owners had fled to parts unknown to avoid the siege. They really had nowhere else to go and nothing at all to look forward to. To sweeten the deal, he offered freedom and full citizenship to any man or woman who enlisted.

"Anyone who is willing to fight for this nation is henceforth a free person and shall have all of the rights that come with that freedom," he said. "His family members will also be set free in honor of his willingness to serve."

Within three days, his defense force had nearly doubled in size. He now had enough soldiers to defend the city's walls, which were formidable under any circumstances.

Vesuvia sat on the edge of the Caspian Sea and had a large, deep natural harbor. The waterfront was like any other waterfront in any other country, with shops, warehouses, wooden piers, saloons, whorehouses and gambling dens. Beyond that stood the 30 foot tall eastern wall with its thick oaken gates and towers that rose an additional ten feet. The wall was a mile long with towers every 100 yards.

The north wall faced an open plain and a series of rugged mountains just beyond. It, too, was 30 feet tall. The north wall had two large gates and ten towers and was protected by a 100 foot wide moat that also ran around the base of the west and south walls.

They also had 40 defensive catapults and ballistae, large oil caldrons and plenty of ceramic grenades. The walls of Vesuvia were so strong that no one in their right minds would even think of assailing them.

No one, that is, except Joshua.

Water was no problem for the city. A swift underground river fed it. The river ran directly under the city and no one really knew where its source was. Pitar sent his soldiers out into the countryside to gather up all the grain and livestock they could find and bring it back to the city. He also ordered them to put the torch to everything they couldn't bring back so the enemy couldn't make use of it.

He then turned his attention to the waterfront.

There were hundreds of wooden structures along the pier, structures the enemy could make good use of. Pitar ordered his men to burn then entire area to the ground, despite the protests of the senators and shopkeepers.

At the end of the week, Pitar took inventory.

They had enough food and medicine to withstand a very protracted siege. Without help, he knew that Vesuvia would eventually fall. The food would run out and the usual battles and disease would exact a heavy toll of his men.

But where would such help come from?

Trollegia had few friends and virtually no diplomatic ties with anyone else in the region. Thule was its closest neighbor but they weren't exactly "friends". It was then he concocted a bold plan to draw Thule into the war.

He decided to send his entire fleet into Thulian waters. He hoped that Joshua's ships would pursue them and that a battle would erupt in one of Thule's many harbors. If the destruction spilled over into one of their cities, it might force Thule into entering the conflict to protect itself.

It was a gamble at best.

A desperate gamble.

It would all be for nothing is Joshua's fleet caught the Trolleg ships in neutral waters. His ships *had* to enter Thulian waters. The battle *had* to take place close enough to a Thulian city to make the people feel threatened.

And Thule *had* to enter the war on *his* side.

"Are you sure you really want to do this?" Wahai asked.

"We have no other choice," Pitar said. "Send the fleet away as soon as you spot the enemy's ships entering our harbor."

He also figured that the main enemy force would march through the narrow Ramallo Pass and enter Trollegia from the north. To slow their advance, he sent 500 of his most seasoned troops into the pass and ordered them to hold at all costs. Pitar knew that such a small force could hold that pass against a hundred times their number and believed that Joshua would waste many of his soldiers trying to break through.

Joshua received the news of Pitar's promotion calmly. He was very much aware of the old man's capabilities. He also knew that Pitar would avoid open battles at all costs and try to get him to waste his soldiers in futile attacks on Vesuvia's walls.

When his scouts reported that Pitar's men had taken up residence in the pass, he decided to take a more direct route to Vesuvia. He rounded up every ship he could find, loaded his men and supplies onto them and sailed across the Caspian Sea. Within four days, all of his soldiers, horses and supplies were standing on the beach a few miles south of the city. When everyone was assembled, Joshua marched them north.

The vanguard, under Maltry's command, soon happened upon a large force of Trolleg soldiers also headed to the capital. As soon as he spotted the vanguard, the Trolleg commander, a seasoned professional named Malo, organized his column into three groups with himself heading up the center. His right flank was commanded by his younger brother, Reyn. A captain named Ibelin commanded the left. With mostly open desert before them, Malo decided to head for a river 30 miles to the west to water his men and horses.

Maltry immediately led his vanguard to confront them. To his surprise, instead of fighting, the Trollegs turned away from the river and marched north without stopping to water their men or horses.

Maltry later described this as "contrary to their own best interests." From that moment on, he knew he had the Trollegs exactly where he wanted them.

As the brutal sun beat relentlessly down on the heavily armored Trollegs, they slowed to a virtual crawl. This enabled Maltry's skirmishers to harass them every step of the way with nasty hit-and-run attacks that left several Trollegs dead and wounded. This tactic further slowed their march and their casualties continued to mount.

Late that afternoon, Joshua arrived at the head of two cavalry regiments and immediately attacked the Trolleg rear. At the same time, he had Maltry send another regiment around their column to cut them off from the river and to block their retreat route. By nine a.m. the next day, the Trollegs found themselves surrounded and cut off from any water supply.

Malo stubbornly urged his men onward. Joshua's constant attacks broke down their compact formations and the rear column became almost hopelessly strung out. This allowed Joshua's men to happily slaughter Trolleg stragglers and prompted Ibelin to send a rider to Malo warning that he was in danger of being overrun. Malo then did the inexplicable.

He halted his march and had his men pitch camp in an attempt to concentrate his forces for a counter attack the next day. As the exhausted and thirsty Trollegs staggered into camp, Joshua laid his plans to crush them.

Under cover of darkness, he had his men bring up plenty of water and thousands of arrows to prepare for the upcoming battle. At the same time, he ordered his men to stack up dry brush upwind from the Trolleg camp. When the sun rose to the east, Joshua's men ignited the brush just as a fortuitous wind roared in from the north.

Within seconds, Malo's entire camp was obscured by a thick cloud of choking smoke which blinded them as Joshua's men closed in, loosing a storm of arrows as they advanced.

Keeping his cool, Malo gathered his cavalry around him and ordered Reyn to counter attack in an effort to bring the battle to them. At the same time, Maltry struck Malo's camp from the rear with 2,000 cavalry. They came screaming out of the smoke swinging swords and firing arrows at everything that moved in front of him. The attack was so fierce, the startled Trollegs scattered. In the confusion, Malo was killed.

Meanwhile, Reyn's charge met only open air as they galloped through the smoke. Realizing what had happened, he ordered his men to wheel about and return to the camp. His order came too late. His men rode straight into a curtain of arrows that unhorsed half of them within five minutes. Reyn then tried to lead his men west only to run right into another wing of Joshua's cavalry. The stubborn Trollegs were determined to go down swinging and met Joshua's men with the ferocity of a raging storm. The battle was short, nasty and bloody. Only a handful of Reyn's men made it back to the main camp. Reyn himself was never seen again.

The rear guard had caved in. Ibelin's men continued to fight on in small bands of five and six while Joshua's cavalry galloped around them loosing arrows and hacking at them with swords and axes. By now, the smoke had cleared. Ibelin found himself seated on his horse atop a small hill in the middle of the field. With him were some 250 heavy cavalry and half that number of infantry. He rallied the men under his standard and led a furious charge against Maltry's men who now stood facing him. Maltry counter attacked and drove the Trollegs back up the hill. Again, Ibelin regrouped his men and charged.

It proved to be his last.

Maltry's counter attack broke Ibelin's charge and somehow managed to surround what was left of his men. Hopelessly trapped by a far superior force, Ibelin did the only thing he could under the circumstances. He struck his colors. When Joshua saw this, he ordered his men to break off the attack and approached Ibelin under a white flag. Ibelin dismounted, drew his sword and, on one knee, presented it to Joshua. He symbolically accepted it then returned it to Ibelin, hilt first.

"I accept your surrender, good knight," Joshua said, "but you may keep the sword that has served you so well for all these years."

"What are your terms, my lord?" asked Ibelin.

"Tell your brave men to lay down their arms and return to their homes and families. Their war is over now. I bear them no grudge," Joshua replied.

A stunned Ibelin thanked him profusely for his generosity. When Joshua's terms were relayed to his men, the Trollegs cheered. They then saluted Joshua and, weaponless, they marched off the field with their wounded in tow.

Maltry shook his head.

"That's a lot of men you just set free. What if they gather up more arms and return to fight us?" he asked.

"I doubt they will. If they do, I'm sure we'll be able to handle them without too much trouble. Now gather up the men. We march to Vesuvia tomorrow," Joshua replied.

Pitar quickly realized that Joshua had made an end run and recalled his men from the pass. By the time they reached Vesuvia, Joshua's army had the city completely encircled.

Maltry wanted to attack the returning troops but Joshua ordered him to allow them safe passage.

"This way, we'll know exactly where all of their soldiers are. Once inside Vesuvia, they'll have no way out again unless we lift the siege," Joshua explained. "Now, let's take out their ships."

Pitar had anticipated this.

As soon as Joshua's biremes appeared on the horizon, he ordered his entire fleet to sail south and make for the nearest Thulian port. Joshua's fleet saw them fleeing the harbor and gave chase. Joshua watched this from the beach and realized what Pitar was up to. He attempted to recall his fleet but his headstrong captain, Cohelo, failed to heed his signals.

Joshua cursed vehemently for a few moments. He then turned to his other officers.

"I hope Cohelo catches them before they reach Thulian waters or all Hell will break loose," he said. "Any damage, however accidental, will bring Thule into the war. But we can't do anything about that. For now, we'll concentrate on taking the city."

From his vantage place on the city walls, Pitar watched helplessly as Joshua's men cut down every tree within miles and began constructing siege machines of every shape and size. They constructed ballistae, catapults, siege towers and trebuchets that could hurl massive rocks over great distances. Within a week, nearly 200 war machines stood ready for battle.

While this was being done, Joshua ordered several small unit attacks against various parts of the city's walls to probe for weaknesses. As expected, each attack was easily repelled and no weaknesses were found. Vesuvia's defenses were as formidable as they were reputed to be. This meant that the siege would take time.

Far to the north and west, Joshua's troops had run the last of the Turks out of Anatolia. The few Turks who did manage to escape attempted to enter Thule as refugees but were stopped at the border by units of Arka-Dal's Northern Army under the command of newly-promoted General Perseus. He had them rounded up and placed in a large holding camp while he radioed Thule for further instructions.

To Perseus' relief, Arka-Dal told him to escort the refugees to the nearest large city and allow the local police to deal with the situation. Leo raised an eyebrow when he overheard him give the order.

Arka-Dal had driven the Turks out of Asia Minor in retaliation for what they did to Byzantium. In the process, he destroyed several Turkish cities and villages and left them unable to defend themselves. The survivors fled east to join their brethren hundreds of miles away. Unfortunately, they arrived just months before Joshua began his campaign.

The ensuing bloodbath created a flood of frightened refugees. The Scythians and Huns allowed them safe passage but each had refused to help. In desperation, the Turks turned to the very Empire that had all-but obliterated their civilization.

Arka-Dal appreciated the irony in this. He also appreciated the fact that he could not, in good conscience, turn these people away. To do so would go against the very ideals that all Thulians held dear.

"You're allowing the Turks to enter Thule?" Leo asked, knowing that Arka-Dal had little love for these people.

"Perseus said that most of the refugees were women, children and old folks. They pose no threat to the Empire and have nowhere else to go, thanks to this Joshua. Never let it be said that we Thulians turned our backs on people in need," Arka-Dal replied. "All are welcome here, even those who were once our enemies."

Between Anatolia and Trollegia was the territory of the Scythians. Their king, Tamarlane, had taken a keen interest in the war raging on both sides of his territory. He had even sent several regiments of his feared light cavalry to protect his borders and to make certain the war didn't spill over into Scythia. To his north and east, Atilla, lord of the Huns, also mobilized his troops. Both kings also sent dispatch riders to Thule bearing letters advising Arka-Dal that they were ready to join him if Joshua and his army threatened Thule.

Meanwhile, more and more runaway slaves filtered into Joshua's ranks and swelled his numbers to more than 65,000. This even included several hundred runaways from Vesuvia itself.

At first glance, Joshua's soldiers were a motley bunch. They were clad in bits and pieces of whatever armor they were able to scrounge from the battlefields and looted armories, so they didn't resemble any sort of cohesive force. Their weapons ranged from well-made military ones to home-made maces, clubs, war hammers, axes and even farm implements. Despite their appearance, they were battle-hardened and well-disciplined.

And fiercely loyal to Joshua.

Pitar's men were well-equipped professional soldiers with bronze helmets, breastplates, grieves and heavy shields. They wielded fine weapons and were willing to fight to the last man.

The city's defenses were also quite strong and included cauldrons of boiling oil that could rain down from gargoyle-like spouts, trebuchets, machines that could fire hundreds of steel bolts at close range and makeshift hand grenades.

Joshua smiled.

"We are an irresistible force facing an immovable object," he said to Maltry. "This will test our soldiers like nothing else before."

"We've taken cities before," Maltry pointed out.

"But none as well appointed as this. This will be a siege even the Gods will remember," Joshua said.

"And who's side are the Gods on?" asked Maltry.

Joshua smiled.

"Whoever's cause is most just," he said.

That night, Joshua's siege began. The people of Vesuvia were subjected to a fierce bombardment of heavy rocks, rockets and intermittent balls of flaming straw that crashed onto the roofs of shops and homes and set them ablaze. Pitar's fire brigades reacted quickly and doused the fires before they could so any real damage while the local citizens took cover in cellars and saloons. At dawn, Joshua halted the bombardment and launched infantry attacks against the east and south walls. Pitar's troops easily repelled both attacks with arrows and grenades and the fighting broke off before noon. An hour of quiet was then broken as both sides slung rocks at each other with their war machines for several hours. When the sun set, Joshua resumed his bombardment.

This continued for several days with neither side doing much damage to the other. A frustrated Joshua studied the detailed map of the city and its immediate area his spies had provided. Vesuvia was supplied with fresh water by an underground river. If he could find the source of that river and dam it up, it would not only deprive the city of drinking water but might also provide his troops with an attack route.

But where did this river spring from?

Only the Trollegs knew and they weren't about to tell him.

To find it, he ordered his engineers to dig wells every 50 feet in a circle around Vesuvia. He reasoned that sooner or later, they would hit water. If they were real fortunate, it would be the river itself.

Meanwhile, he'd continue with the attacks.

Two days later, the events that Joshua feared the most came to pass. Cohelo's fleet pursued the fleeing Trolleg ships 300 miles south. When the Trollegs entered Thulian waters, they turned right and steered straight into the deep water port of Odensa, a trading center of nearly 40,000 people. Against the warnings of his subordinates to turn back, Cohelo chased the Trollegs into the harbor and attacked. To his delight, the Trolleg ships turned and came after him and a brief but bloody battle ensued.

As both fleets slugged it out in the harbor with fireballs and heavy ballista shots, the people of Odense climbed onto their rooftops to watch the show. After a half-hour of close combat that saw five Trolleg ships eddy to the bottom of the bay, the remaining Trollegs broke away from the battle and attempted to flee to the pier. Cohelo saw this and gave chase. He managed to ram one and shatter its hull and oar bank but the other was out of reach. Angry, he ordered his men to launch a fireball after it. To his dismay, the errant missile sailed harmlessly over the mast of the Trolleg ship and crashed into a row of wooden buildings. The buildings erupted with a great, loud roar and sent everyone who had been seated on the roofs scrambling for their lives.

As the fire spread, hundreds of Thulians joined the local fire brigade to try and save the rest of the dock while the ships continued to slug it out just a few hundred yards offshore.

Of course, the alarm went out to the local navy base down the road. Admiral Orem Bey responded by sending all twelve of his triremes out after the troublesome combatants. By the time they reached the harbor, all of the Trolleg ships lay at the bottom along with half of Cohelo's fleet. Bey ordered three of his ships to break away from the fleet and round up survivors while he continued in hot pursuit with the rest.

He caught up with Cohelo's ships some 25 miles later. Not wanting to be captured, Cohelo turned toward them determined to go down swinging. Bey ordered his gunners to take aim at the lead ship and fire. Seconds later, Cohelo's flagship and most of his crew were literally blown to pieces by the cannonade. The rest of his ships surrendered without a fight. Bey escorted them back to the base and wired Thule with news of the incident.

When Arka-Dal received the report, he radioed Perseus and ordered him to mobilize the entire Northern Army.

"We'll be there in six days," he said. "I'll take charge on arrival. It's time to teach this upstart a lesson."

The next morning, Galya, Merlin and Mayumi watched from the roof of the palace as Arka-Dal and his usual band of brothers rode off to war at the head of a company of cavalry. As they passed from sight, Galya turned to Merlin.

"Why do you not go to war with them? With your powers, you could destroy an enemy army with a simple wave of your hand. As I recall, you've done that many times before," she asked.

"Yes. I *could* make short work of Joshua's soldiers. Arka-Dal and I have an unspoken agreement. Gorinna and I only join him against *supernatural* foes. He much prefers to personally lead his men into battle. This is good for their morale because it shows that he is one of them. He travels as they do. He eats what they eat and shares the same dangers and hardships," Merlin replied with a grin.

"If he were riding out to face a powerful wizard or an army of demons, we would be at his side. Joshua is human as are his soldiers, so we stay behind," Gorinna added.

She saw the worried expression on Galya's face and squeezed her hand.

"You'll get used to it. We *all* had to," she assured her.

Galya nodded. It was then and there she decided that if a supernatural army ever threatened Thule, she would summon forth her 30 legions of Hell's best troops to defend it. At the same time, she suppressed a powerful urge to chase after Arka-Dal to be at his side when the battle begins.

"Love is hard, isn't it?" she asked.

"Sometimes," Gorinna replied. "That's why it's so strong."

Galya walked away and went back down into the palace. She spotted Mayumi seated on the balcony and realized she was watching the horizon. It was as if she could still see Arka-Dal, even though he had long since passed from her view.

She smiled.

Mayumi had watched her beloved husband ride off to war many times over the years. Each time, she probably stayed on that balcony long after he'd gone, hoping and praying that he'd return safely. The nights they spent apart must seem like eons. Yet, she bore it all so bravely. She put on such a good front for their people.

"How does she do *that*?" Galya wondered. "Will *I* be able to do that, too?"

There was still so much to learn about being human. So much to learn about love.

And faith.

She walked over and sat down with Mayumi. The pretty little Empress smiled and nodded as if to assure her all was well. A few moments later, Chatha, Medusa and Zhijima came out to join them. Zhijima brought a bottle of wine and several glasses with her, which she filled and passed out.

The five of them sat and drank until the bottle was empty . . .

Joshua received the news of the sea battle calmly. As the messenger left his tent, he paced the floor to think through the situation. Cohelo's error in judgment did exactly what Pitar hoped. By setting fire to the dock at Odense, he forced Arka-Dal to enter the war. His scouts already told him that Thule's entire Northern Army was being mobilized. That could only mean one thing—they were preparing to march into Trollegia.

It would take Arka-Dal at least a week to reach his Northern Army headquarters. It would take that army another week to reach the Trolleg border. That meant he had less than two weeks to take Vesuvia. If and when his engineers found the source of the river, he would put his all-or-nothing plan into play.

"Where is the source?" he wondered.

Once he found it, he'd have his men cut it off. The people of Vesuvia had food enough for several weeks but without water they'd die of thirst in less than a week. Or be forced to surrender. He'd rather they choose the second option. He wanted to avoid unnecessary bloodshed if possible and take the city intact. But he knew the Trollegs too well. They'd rather die fighting to the last man than give up their last stronghold. The coming battle would be a bloodbath. His soldiers would have to fight hard for every inch of the city. Thousands would die and Vesuvia would be destroyed in the process.

"So be it," he said.

The next morning, Maltry and two spearmen arrived at Joshua's command tent with a rather rotund and bearded man in tow. Joshua looked up from his maps and squinted at them.

"This man insists on seeing you, Joshua," Maltry said.

Joshua studied the man. He stood about six feet tall and was dressed in a bejeweled turban and fine silk robes. He sported a jeweled dagger in his cummerbund and wore several gold and diamond rings. He was, without a doubt, a man of considerable wealth and one who was accustomed to having his way.

"And who might you be?" Joshua asked.

"I am Ali-Beyhar Hassan, a merchant en route to Vesuvia from Samarkand. I come to you with a complaint," the man said haughtily.

"Go on," Joshua urged.

"A group of your soldiers waylaid me this morning and confiscated three wagon loads of my merchandise. I demand that you return said merchandise or pay me the market value of the goods," Hassan said with an air of arrogance that irritated the Hell out of Joshua and invoked a smirk from Maltry.

"And what is said merchandise?" asked Joshua.

"Thirty-seven beautiful young women," Hassan replied.

"Women? You mean slaves?" asked Joshua.

"Yes. They are worth a pretty drachma in most markets and I demand them back!" Hassan said rudely. "After all, they are *my* property!"

Maltry watched as Joshua's face slowly turned red and took a step back.

"No man has the right to own another! People are *not* merchandise, nor will they ever be as long as I live to defend their rights!" Joshua raged.

"But they *are* my property and I demand fair payment for them!" Hassan insisted.

Maltry rolled his eyes.

"Oh, you'll receive fair payment all right," Joshua said.

He turned to Maltry and the two soldiers standing behind Hassan.

"Flog this vermin out of my camp. If he returns, hang him from the nearest tree," he ordered.

"It'll be a pleasure!" Maltry said as he gripped Hassan's arm and dragged him from the tent.

Joshua watched until they were out of sight. Then he heard the unmistakable cracks of a leather whip against flesh and smiled as the merchant screamed like a terrified child. After each crack, he heard his soldiers laugh and cheer.

"Justice is served," he said to himself.

At the edge of the camp, Maltry gave Hassan a horse and told him to get lost. The angry merchant galloped south as fast as he could. Seven days later, he came upon the camp of the Thulians and managed to get an audience with Arka-Dal. The Emperor, Pandaar and Kashi listened to his story with more than a little amusement. Then, to Hassan's horror, Arka-Dal ordered his men to "whip this dog from their camp".

His body now covered with painful welts and open cuts, Hassan decided it would be best for his health and general well-being to find something other than slaves to trade in. Six months later, (or so it was reported) he opened a hot dog stand in the bustling market of Osumel and changed his name Al-Nathan.

"There's much I admire about this Joshua," Arka-Dal said. "We have much in common."

"Yes. You both detest slavers. That tells me he's a man of high character," Pandaar remarked. "Too bad you have to face each other in battle."

"True—but that doesn't mean that I have to *kill* him," Arka-Dal smiled.

Eight days after whipping Hassan out of his camp, Joshua got just the break he was hoping for. One of the wells his engineers dug struck water. *Running water.* Realizing they'd at last found the source of the river, they hurried to his tent with the news. Joshua immediately sent ten men into the well to track the river back as far as they could. After ten hours of searching through narrow tunnels and caverns, they finally located the source deep inside a bell-shaped cavern about 40 miles from Vesuvia's west wall.

After some discussion, the engineers decided to build a makeshift dam about 200 feet from the cavern. It took several days, but when they were finished, the raging river had been reduced to a mere trickle.

It was past midnight when a soldier brought the news to Pitar in his quarters. The old man dressed quickly and followed the soldier down to the lowest level of the palace. Sure enough, the massive hydraulic pumps that fed the river water into the city's pipes and wells were now silent.

"That bastard's cut off the water supply!" Pitar said. "He must have dammed it at the source."

"What are your orders?" asked a nearby officer.

"Take two squads down into the channel, locate the dam and get rid of it. I want our water supply restored by this afternoon," Pitar commanded.

He knew that if it remained dry, the enemy could use the channel as a way into the city. In that case, any attacks on the walls would be purely a diversion designed to keep his men pinned down long enough for the main attack force to enter Vesuvia. He *could* easily collapse the tunnel but that would deprive him of all hope of bringing water into the city. Without water, they'd be forced to surrender.

He decided to surround the palace with a full regiment of his best fighters and send another company into the lower levels to try and stop the enemy there. If Joshua's men did use the channel, he hoped to contain them within the palace.

"This is like playing chess on a large scale," he thought.

Joshua was thinking along those same lines. Yes, he would send 500 of his best troops into the channel and try to enter Vesuvia from below. But the all-out attack he had planned would *not* be a diversion. He thought that if he could apply constant pressure to each of the city's walls as well as threaten it from below, Pitar's men would be stretched too thin to effectively cover the entire city.

The two squads sent into the channel to locate the dam ran straight into Joshua's men who had entered from the opposite end. After a short, bloody melee, all of Pitar's men lay dead and Joshua's men continued their advance.

Joshua's attack had now begun in earnest. Battalions of determined troops, many armed with scaling ladders and hooks, assailed every wall of Vesuvia at the exact same time under the cover a ferocious barrage of fireballs, rockets, large stones and other nasty missiles. Their attack was answered with equal ferocity as the city's defenders hurled missiles and rained hundreds of arrows down upon their heads. As Joshua's men drew closer, the Trollegs tossed grenades among them and sent dozens flying in all directions. Eight massive siege towers were pushed up to the walls. Each was armed with a heavy battering ram and sheets of rockets, which they launched as soon as they got close to the walls.

Pitar watched helplessly as the rockets blew most of his defenders from the ramparts amid eruptions of fire, sparks and smoke. Dozens of charred corpses fell to the street while others rolled around frantically to out the flames that threatened to consume their bodies. Those that remained bravely clung to their positions and made ready to repel the invaders with swords, axes and spears. The few archers that were still alive continued to shower Joshua's men with arrows as fast as they could loose them.

While the men below used the rams to try and smash down the gates or drive holes through the massive walls, those on top lowered heavy wooden platforms. Six of the eight struck the top of the ramparts and embedded themselves into the stone with heavy iron spikes. One was struck by a shot from a trebuchet and shattered into a thousand pieces. The blow not only destroyed the tower, it killed almost all of the men inside.

Joshua winced as dozens of men fell helplessly to their deaths. Some landed on the heads of their comrades. Others became impaled on their upright spears. The defenders followed this up with a hail of flaming arrows which put a fiery end to what remained of the tower.

The last tower was hit dead-center by a fireball before it could be put into play. The flames ignited the rockets and the ensuing explosion sent wood, metal, battered and flaming bodies and rockets streaming all over the battlefield. Some exploded amid Joshua's own troops. A few actually struck the city walls and blew some of the startled defenders off. A few more spiraled harmlessly into the air and exploded in what looked like a holiday fireworks display.

Joshua watched from the crest of nearby hill as one siege tower after another reached the wall and his men streamed across the planks to come to grips with the stubborn defenders. True to their reputations, the Trollegs clung tenaciously to every inch of the walls and fought with the ferocity of a mother bear defending her cubs. Hundreds of men from both sides toppled from the walls, some still locked in hand-to-hand combat with their hands around each others' throats. Each time his men happened to clear off a section of a wall, Pitar sent more men in to plug the gap. This tactic only served to delay what the old general knew to be inevitable.

Without reinforcements, Vesuvia would fall.

Inside the city, a wild battle had erupted in and around the palace as hundreds of Joshua's shock troops poured out of the channel only to come nose-to-nose with Pitar's men. Within an hour, the gleaming, polished floors and steps of the palace were stained with blood and shattered organs. Neither side gave quarter. Everyone knew this was a fight to the finish and Trollegs never retreated. Any of Joshua's men who made it out of the palace were quickly cut down by waiting archers. If they managed to avoid the archers, they were hunted down by gangs of armed, angry civilians and beaten to death.

Pitar skillfully directed the defense of Vesuvia from his vantage point atop the north wall. Each time Joshua's men looked like they would break through, Pitar deftly shifted his men to block them.

After five long hours, Joshua realized the battle was becoming a bloody stalemate. In frustration, he decided on a dangerous tactic. He ordered his artillerymen to lob fireballs into the city as fast as they could.

"Aim over the ramparts. Strike the center of the city. I want Vesuvia to burn!" he ordered.

Pitar was soon astonished to see at least a dozen large, fiery missiles soaring high over the city. They hovered at the top of their arcs for a moment then plunged downward. A couple landed harmlessly in open plazas. The rest struck the wooden roofs of several buildings, including the palace, and set them ablaze. As flame and smoke rose upward from the inner city, several of the soldiers attempted to break away from the battle. Pitar stopped them in their tracks and ordered them back to the walls.

"This battle's not over yet! Back to your posts! No one leaves until this is over," he barked.

"But we have to put out the fires!" one man moaned.

"We have barely enough men to hold the walls. We can't spare anyone. Let the city burn!" Pitar shouted.

Civilians bearing buckets of water rushed around and attempted to put out the fires. But even more fireballs struck the city. As more and more blazes erupted, the frustrated firefighters began dropping from exhaustion. Others raced to take up their places but it was to no avail. Within an hour, the entire central section of Vesuvia was a raging inferno. Still Pitar refused to allow his men to leave the walls and the battle continued in all of its brutal glory as the Trollegs refused to surrender so much as an inch of ground.

Joshua looked to the west. The sun was setting now. That meant the battle had been raging for nearly ten full hours. He had committed every last soldier he had to the attack and still the Trollegs held. He felt they were too close to give up now, but his men were almost at the breaking point. They'd soon be too exhausted to fight and would probably retreat to their camps to recuperate. He had no reserves. No fresh troops to send into the battle.

There was only so much even the best of soldiers could endure before battle fatigue overtook them. He briefly contemplated ordering his buglers to sound the retreat.

It was at that point the sky opened and a torrential rain struck the coast. The soft, sandy ground around Vesuvia soon became a quagmire and the heavy rains began to douse the fires that had almost destroyed the city.

Pitar looked up at the rain and laughed.

The storm was a godsend. Soon the fires would be out and, if the rain continued, it might force an end to the battle.

But the Gods had *other* ideas.

With violent storms come thunder and lightning. The supercharged bolts lit up the sky and the rolling thunder drowned out the sounds of battle.

As Joshua watched, a stray bolt struck the city's western gates and blew them off their hinges amid a hail of dust, stone and splinters. This was the moment he'd been waiting for. As soon as the dust cleared, he leapt onto his horse, drew his sword, and led all of his cavalry straight toward the open gate.

"The gods have given us a gift! Let's make use of it! Follow me, men!" he shouted as he waved his sword above his head.

Pitar watched his dazed defenders as they tried to regain their senses. When he saw what remained of the mighty gates, he cursed at the top of his lungs. He then attempted to assemble enough men to plug the opening but they proved to be too little and too late. Joshua's cavalry thundered into the city and cut them to ribbons before they could put together an effective defense. Pitar mounted his horse and galloped through the narrow streets exhorting his men to fight to the last man as the battle spread from the walls and into the inner city.

"Give no quarter! Fight for your lives! Show them how Trollegs die!" he shouted at the top of his lungs wherever he went.

Some of his men even stopped to cheer as he rode past. Others were too busy fighting to even hear him. Despite the determination and courage of his troops, Vesuvia fell to Joshua's men a few minutes after midnight. During the battle, an arrow found its way into Pitar's windpipe and killed him instantly. As he toppled from his horse, his left foot became entangled in the stirrup and the frightened animal proceeded to gallop through the city's streets with Pitar's body in tow.

The sight angered the Trollegs. Instead of losing heart, they dug their heels in deeper and fought even harder. In several places, Joshua's infantry fell back and allowed the archers to finish off knots of stubborn defenders. In some places, groups of armed civilians attempted to bar their way but they proved to be no match for Joshua's trained troops. After taking a few casualties, most of the would-be soldiers melted back into their homes and dark alleys.

The rain continued all through the battle, leaving the streets awash with mud, blood and dead men. When the sun appeared in the eastern sky, the battle for Vesuvia was over. Not a single Trolleg soldier had surrendered. Not a single Trolleg soldier remained alive and more than half the civilian population lay dead on the streets among them.

Joshua walked through the silent streets and shook his head. The entire city was nothing more than piles of smoldering ruins. Every major building had been damaged and most of the homes and shops had been destroyed. Stunned women with their children in tow roamed the streets in search of missing loved ones. Some wept beside mangled bodies. A few just stood and glared at Joshua's men with hate in their eyes.

The destruction was far more than Joshua wanted it to be. Vesuvia was finished both as a major port and a livable city. He ordered his men to help the surviving civilians as much as possible. Right now, they were busy piling up the dead in every open space they could. There was no time to bury them. They would have to be burned.

Joshua was victorious, but neither he no his soldiers felt like celebrating. Besides, another, even larger problem now loomed on the horizon in the form of the Emperor of Thule.

Arka-Dal and the entire Northern Army were already en route to Trollegia. By the time Vesuvia fell, they had entered the pass that cut through the Scythian Range and were moving north at a steady pace.

Arka-Dal was in no hurry. He had no intention of coming to the aid of Vesuvia. Thule had little contact with Trollegia and he had no real love for anyone who traded in or kept slaves. His intentions were to make Joshua painfully aware of the fact that his war had spilled over into Thule and caused extensive damage to one of its cities. Such things were not tolerated by Arka-Dal or the Thulian citizens. He also wanted to test his mettle on the battlefield to find out if was as good a general as he was reputed to be.

"What if he apologizes?" asked Perseus.

"The time for apologies has passed. I've sent a messenger to his camp bearing a letter of challenge. If he is any kind of soldier, his honor won't allow him to refuse it," Arka-Dal said.

"What about the Trollegs?" asked Kashi.

"Damn the Trollegs. When all is said and done, they suffered a fate they truly deserved. What happened to their so-called king?" Arka-Dal asked.

"When last seen, he was headed due west. I think he's headed for Rome," Kashi said. "He stopped in Constantinople for a few days to hire a ship. I heard he had lots of gold with him. Most likely, he stole it from the treasury before he left."

"Joshua's men are probably searching for him right now," Pandaar added. "I heard he wants his head on a pike."

"I hope he gets it," Arka-Dal said.

Dawn.

Maltry found Joshua standing atop the north wall of the city looking out on across the plains. He walked over and saluted.

Joshua nodded.

"What have you to report?" he asked.

"We've taken about 3,500 captives, mostly women and children," Maltry said. "What do we do with them?"

"We have no place to keep them and can't spare anyone to guard them. They pose no threat to us. Give them food and water and let them go where they will. I care not what befalls them," Joshua replied.

He sighed.

His war was over. Trollegia was his now. But he had made no plans on what do with it. He also had thousands of soldiers to tend to.

He decided to share everything in the treasury with them, but what happens afterward? Where do they go?

"What now, Maltry? What now?" he asked as they stood looking at the remains of the once-opulent palace in the center of Vesuvia.

Maltry shook his head and ran his fingers through his hair. Before he could answer, a dusty soldier in a Thulian uniform galloped up to them. The soldier dismounted and saluted. Joshua returned it and ordered him to speak.

"I bring a message from Arka-Dal," the soldier said as he handed him an envelope.

Joshua opened the envelope, took out the letter and read it. As he did, he raised an eyebrow. When he was finished, he handed it to Maltry who almost choked when he read it.

"He's challenging us to meet him in open battle at the valley called Parayno. That's about 35 miles north of the Trolleg border. He has thrown his lot in with the Trollegs!" Maltry remarked.

"No. He does not come to save the Trollegs. He comes to punish us for damaging his seaport. He sees us as a threat to Thule. To him, we're a hostile, invading army," Joshua said. "And he intends to teach us a lesson."

"What will you do?" asked Maltry.

Joshua smiled.

He knew that Arka-Dal had chosen Parayno because its terrain suited him best. He also knew from his own scouts that there was only one way into or out of Parayno.

"The Lion's got us where he wants us, Maltry," Joshua mused. "I have a feeling that he's setting us up—but good. The only chance we have is to try and beat him to the valley. We must get there first to keep him from using the high ground to his advantage."

"And if we don't get there first?" Maltry asked.

Joshua laughed.

"I'll decide that once I see how he has arrayed his troops," he said.

"This is insane!" Maltry pointed out.

"War is insane. We will march to Parayno and meet the Thulians in open battle. The Lion has challenged us. As men of honor, we cannot refuse," Joshua decided.

He turned to the waiting messenger.

"Tell your Emperor that we will be at Parayno in six days," he said.

The messenger saluted and jumped back onto his horse. They watched as he sped away.

"Is that wise? The Lion of Thule has never been bested in battle. Wouldn't it be wiser to fold our tents and return to Anatolia?" Maltry asked.

"No. If we do that, Arka-Dal is sure to follow and the war will be carried into our own lands. Our homes would be devastated. Our people would be scattered to the four winds. It would take us decades to recover. It is far better to meet them at Parayno, on the field of battle like the soldiers we profess to be," Joshua said.

"And if we are defeated?" Maltry asked.

"We lay down our arms and ask for terms. The mark of a good general is to know when you are beaten. I will not see our men slaughtered for no good reason. We can try to withdraw and fight another day, but that would only delay the inevitable. Besides, we might beat *them.* Arka-Dal is not the only commander who is undefeated in battle," Joshua said with a smile. "Prepare the men. We march tomorrow."

The messenger returned to Arka-Dal's camp two days later with Joshua's reply. Arka-Dal laughed when he heard it. Kashi and Pandaar, who were dining with him in his tent, smiled.

"I told you he wouldn't be able to pass it up," Arka-Dal said. "The upstart's on his way to Parayno now."

"This should be interesting. From everything I've heard, this Joshua is a student of your tactics. It'll be sort of like fighting a younger version of yourself," Pandaar said.

"Maybe. While the tactics are mine, they are only as effective as those who carry them out. I rely on and trust each of our commanders to do the right thing at the right time. At Parayno we'll see how good his junior officers really are. That's what will decide the outcome," Arka-Dal said.

Arka-Dal's network of scouts and spies had brought him constant reports of the war in Trollegia. As a result, he knew all about Joshua's penchant for "borrowing" some of his own tactics for use on the battlefield. He also figured that "the young upstart" would try to use one of those tactics against him.

"I can almost read his mind," he said. "He's used the Thulian Bull and the phalanx in several battles with great success. I think he'll attempt to use them against us at Parayno."

"I know what that means," said Pandaar. "You have a plan in mind to counter the bull."

"Sort of. I think I'll let him use it. Once he's closed the horns around our troops, I'll have him exactly where I want him," Arka-Dal said. "He's about to get a hard lesson in the art of war."

"From the master himself!" beamed Kashi.

"I get a feeling that we're going to love this one," Pandaar said as he sipped his wine.

"You will—but Joshua *won't*!" Arka-Dal said.

The Thulian army arrived at Parayno a day ahead of Joshua's. While his men pitched their tents behind a series of rolling hills to the west, Arka-Dal rode onto the field and committed the terrain features to memory. Parayno was a wide, flat plain situated between a line of rocky mountains to the north and south and the hills to the west. It was about 15 miles wide and nearly twice that deep. There was only one way into Parayno—and one way out.

"What would I do if I were Joshua?" he thought. "What would I do if I came and saw an entire army arrayed in the center of the plain?"

He smiled.

He rode back to camp and summoned Pandaar, Perseus and Kashi to meet with him in his tent. When they arrived, he went over his battle plan. As always, it was simple, easy to execute—and deadly.

"If I were Joshua, I'd divide my forces into three groups and try to encircle our phalanx which will be arrayed in the center of the plain. I place it under your command, Perseus. I want you to hold your ground long enough to force Joshua to commit his entire army, then gradually fall back to the hills. Once you reach the hills, reform the phalanx and stand your ground," he explained.

"Pandaar—you'll be behind the hills with the other half of the infantry. As soon as Joshua's men come into range, riddle them with arrows and javelins then charge onto the field to reinforce the phalanx. As soon as you're engaged, Kashi and I will sweep in from each wing with the cavalry and encircle them."

"What if he doesn't use the bull?" asked Pandaar.

"In that case, we'll exchange arrows with each other until Tamarlane's men arrive," Arka-Dal said. "If all goes well, the Scythians will be here before dusk and strike Joshua's men from behind."

"The hammer and anvil?" Kashi asked.

Arka-Dal nodded.

"Joshua's no dope. He'll have scouts all over the place. He'll know when the Scythians are close," Kashi pointed out.

"He already does. Tamarlane's scouts have been harassing their rear guard for the past three nights. Most likely, Joshua and his men aren't getting much sleep," Arka-Dal said.

Perseus laughed.

"You thought of everything," he said.

"Not everything. I came up with the master plan. I leave the finer details up to you as usual. Keep in close contact with the telepathic headbands and change tactics as the need arises. Be prepared to exploit any hole or weakness in the enemy's lines and don't hesitate," Arka-Dal said.

"Are we taking prisoners?" asked Pandaar.

"Yes. Give quarter when it is asked for and don't slay their wounded," Arka-Dal ordered. "This is not a fight to the death."

When Joshua arrived the next morning, he found the Thulian army already on the field. He rode to the top of a nearby slope and studied the formation. As he had predicted, they had assumed their famous phalanx position: an impenetrable wall of shields and spears that could withstand any frontal attack when stationary and could steamroller through any standing army when on the march.

Joshua saw only infantry.

It was only the "head" of the bull.

"Where are the horns?" he asked himself. "And why has Arka-Dal brought so few troops? Where is his cavalry?"

Joshua smiled.

Had Arka-Dal thrown down the gauntlet? Was he daring him to attack? Daring him to try and break the phalanx?

"I'll accept that challenge!" he decided.

He gathered Maltry and his other officers around him and outlined his plan of attack by drawing it in the dirt.

The plan was simple and very direct. The infantry would form a huge wedge and drive straight into the center of the phalanx. As soon as they punched a hole through the Thulian line, he and Maltry would exploit it with the cavalry. He thought it was a battle plan worthy of Arka-Dal himself.

But timing was everything. Would his exhausted soldiers be able to react quickly enough to make the plan work? Thanks to the Scythians, they had very little sleep for the last four nights. Even their meals had been rudely interrupted by their sudden cavalry attacks.

In fact, the constant threat of the Scythians had forced Joshua to keep his scouts to the rear to warn of an attack. He never had time to scout out the valley. If he had, he would have spotted Arka-Dal's hidden troops.

His men were tired and hungry. When the fighting started, he knew they—like all soldiers—would feel that initial rush of adrenalin. Would it be enough?

By contrast, the Thulians were well-rested and well-fed.

He looked at his weary commanders and took a deep breath. Then, in his best commander's voice, he issued the fateful orders.

"They say the Thulian line has never been broken. We shall be the first to break it! To your regiments! We attack in one hour!"

His officers cheered and hurried to their units. Joshua leapt upon his horse and rode to the crest of a low hill as they formed ranks.

Arka-Dal watched as Joshua's troops moved into position. When he saw them form a wedge, he smiled. He had positioned Perseus' infantry in the center of the field as the bait and Joshua had taken it just as he had expected.

"Now we'll see just how good a field general you really are, Joshua!" he said as he lowered his visor.

Joshua ordered his trumpeter to sound the attack. As the trumpet signal blared over the field and echoed in the mountains, the soldiers cheered and attacked the center of Arka-Dal's phalanx.

Perseus' men stood their ground and waited until the "point" of the wedge slammed into their wall of shields and spears. While the men in the front row of the phalanx held the attackers at bay, those in the lines behind them stabbed at them with their pikes. Despite this thorny obstacle, Joshua's men pushed ahead with incredible determination and ferocity. Perseus waited a few minutes to make it seem real, then gave the pre-arranged signal. To Joshua's delight, the phalanx began to "buckle" at the center. To his dismay, they formed a horseshoe and attempted to encircle his wedge. But this left their flanks exposed.

It was just the opening he'd been hoping for.

"Now!" he shouted as he led his cavalry into the fray.

Perseus saw them approaching and ordered his men to fall back to the base of the hills. Before Joshua's cavalry reached the Thulian lines, they were already in retreat. He laughed to himself.

"We have them now! The day is mine!"

Perseus and his men reached the base of the hill then turned and reformed the phalanx. This sudden and well-executed maneuver caught their pursuers off guard and dozens of them died when they collided with the wall of shields and spears before they could stop themselves. Joshua's men then backed off to reform their lines for another attack in coordination with the cavalry who had now caught up with them.

Once the lines were formed, Joshua ordered them to attack.

That's when Pandaar's infantry emerged from behind the hills and let loose with their javelins. These javelins were modeled after the ones used by the soldiers of Imperial Rome and were devastatingly deadly at close range. Their heavy steel shafts and points punched through the shields and armor of Joshua's front ranks as if they weren't there and just about broke the back of his charge. Pandaar's archers followed up with a rain of arrows that forced Joshua's men to kneel and cover themselves with their shields. Those who didn't cover up became human pin cushions within seconds.

When Joshua's attack stalled, Pandaar raised his sword and led his men into the battle. They charged around the phalanx and hit Joshua's men from two sides. Undaunted, Joshua committed the rest of his cavalry to counter the trap.

It was exactly what Arka-Dal was waiting for.

To Joshua's horror, two large groups of Thulian cavalry charged in from the north and south. He ordered every man he had close at hand to break off and intercept them but it was too late. Within minutes, the Thulians had completely encircled Joshua's army and were systematically herding them toward the center of the field, where they'd be packed too close together to effective swing their weapons.

Joshua knew he was overmatched.

The Lion of Thule had done it again. Arka-Dal had anticipated and countered his every move and had made him look like a fool.

He looked around the field. Chaos reigned everywhere as men on horseback and foot battled each other to the bitter end. His men were tough and battle-tested. They stood their ground tenaciously. Yet, they were no match for the well-oiled Thulian war machine. No matter how hard they fought, they still lost ground. Within minutes, hundreds, perhaps thousands, of good, brave men would lay dead or wounded on the battlefield.

Joshua also knew that a large force of Scythian cavalry was headed his way. If they reached the field before he could retreat, it would be over. He was about to have his trumpeter signal a retreat when he spotted Arka-Dal galloping across the field. There was no mistaking the Lion of Thule's teardrop shield with the black, double-headed eagle painted on it. He watched as several of his men sought to intercept him, but Arka-Dal dispatched each of them with incredible ease, either by shattering their shield and weapons or unhorsing them. Most of the soldiers were left bruised but otherwise unhurt. They just knelt or sat on the ground and watched as Arka-Dal rode on.

Joshua was also in the thick of the battle, fending off one Thulian soldier after another in a fashion similar to Arka-Dal's. As he fought, he kept scanning the immediate for any sign of the Emperor and for any slight opening in the Thulian lines he might be able to exploit.

He soon realized that no such gap would appear.

The Thulian war machine was too disciplined and too efficient. It's commanders reacted quickly to plug any hole that happened to appear in their lines. Joshua realized he was trapped.

Arka-Dal soon reached an open area of the field. That's when Joshua saw him. He shouted, reared up on his horse then rode toward him. When Arka-Dal saw him, he raised the visor of his helmet and waited until Joshua drew nearer.

When he was in range, Joshua raised his visor to get a better view of his idol and opponent. Arka-Dal was more muscular than he'd expected. Astride his snow white steed, he looked almost god-like. Joshua put aside his admiration and hailed him.

"My name is Joshua. Are you the Lion of Thule?" he asked.

"I've never heard myself referred to in that way. Yes, I am Arka-Dal. Your ships destroyed one of my ports. I've come to teach you some manners," the Emperor replied.

"I have no quarrel with you. The destruction was an accident and I'm sorry if any of your people were hurt. Why *else* have you come?" Joshua demanded.

Arka-Dal smiled.

"To see if you're as good as I've heard," he said.

Joshua laughed.

"I was hoping you'd say that!" he said.

The two men sized each other up for a few moments, then raised their swords in salute. Arka-Dal lowered his visor and charged. Joshua did the same.

Both men met in the middle of the clearing and exchanged blows as they passed. Both stopped, turned and charged again. Again, both men's swords clanged harmlessly against their shields as they galloped past. Again they turned and charged.

This time, Arka-Dal ducked under Joshua's blade and deftly cut his saddle strap. The surprised Joshua tumbled from his steed and hit the ground hard. Arka-Dal dismounted and waited for him to regain his senses.

Joshua rose slowly to his feet, shook the cobwebs from his head and charged right at him. Arka-Dal sidestepped and tripped him. As he hurtled forward, the Emperor turned and slammed the hilt of his sword into the back of Joshua's helmet. The blow sent him to the ground face-first and caused him to see stars.

He expected Arka-Dal to move in and finish him off. Instead, he waited until Joshua regained his senses again. Joshua picked up his sword and saluted. Arka-Dal returned it.

"Let's see what you're made of," he said.

Joshua unstrapped his helmet and tossed it to the ground. Arka-Dal did likewise. For a few moments, both men circled each other warily, then Joshua sensed an opening and attacked with his sword raised. To his astonishment, Arka-Dal cut his sword blade in two. Joshua lunged at him with the remaining half only to have Arka-Dal cut that in two as he sidestepped him.

Joshua held up his broken sword and stared at it. There were barely four inches remaining above the hilt now. He dropped the now-useless weapon to the ground and let go of his shield. Arka-Dal watched as he fell to one knee and raised his right hand in surrender.

"I yield!" he shouted.

Arka-Dal lowered Excalibur and walked over to him.

"This battle is ended. Call off your men," he said.

Joshua stood and looked for his trumpeter. He found him seated atop his horse not 100 yards away.

"Sound the surrender!" he ordered.

The man raised the trumpet to his lips and sounded the call. It took several tries before everyone heard it above the din of battle. The last of Joshua's men ceased fighting just as Tamarlane and his Scythian horsemen appeared on the horizon.

An hour later, Joshua, Kashi, Pandaar, Tamarlane and Jun were inside the command tent drinking wine and discussing the terms of the surrender with Arka-Dal. Joshua explained why he had attacked Trollegia and destroyed what was left of the Turks. He also apologized for what happened to the Thulian port and agreed to pay for all of the repairs with the money he took from the Turks and slave traders.

Arka-Dal accepted his proposal and both men agreed that the nation of Trollegia no longer existed as all of its cities had been destroyed and what remained of its people were now scattered throughout the region.

As for what to do with it:

Joshua said he had no desire to claim it for his own. He had simply set out to punish them for trading in slaves and for what they did to his family.

"I don't care what you do with Trollegia or its people. All I want is their cowardly king and his advisors. I want them to pay for what they did and I will never cease searching for them," Joshua said.

"That's fine with me. I have no love for that vermin or his people. I hope you do find them and give them what they deserve," Arka-Dal agreed. "As for the Turks, well, everyone knows how I feel about *them*, especially after what happened in Byzantium. I leave their fate in your hands."

He got up and looked at the map on the table.

"Vesuvia was an excellent deep water port in its heyday. It shall be so again. Between the both of us, we have more than enough resources to rebuild it and make it better, but the question then becomes who shall administer it?" he said.

"Maybe we can turn it back over to the Trollegs?" suggested Kashi. "They ran it before."

"Maybe—but they no longer have a working government—thanks to Joshua and his men," Arka-Dal said. "It'll take months to repair it and even longer to set up a workable body to oversee its operations."

"Then you should appoint one of your engineers to govern it," Joshua said.

Arka-Dal smiled.

"Why ours? Why not one of yours?" he asked.

"I only have one and he's more skilled at *destroying* cities than building them," Joshua replied. "Although he might appreciate the irony in helping to rebuild Vesuvia, I'm not sure he has the proper skills."

"Then he can work *with* my engineers," Arka-Dal offered.

Joshua laughed.

"Consider it done," he said as he extended his hand.

Arka-Dal shook it.

"Now, what do we do with the rest of Trollegia?" asked Tamarlane.

"After Vesuvia is rebuilt and the people have returned, we'll let *them* decide," Arka-Dal said. "They can remain independent and under Thule's protection—provided they outlaw slavery—or they can annex themselves to either Joshua's empire or Thule."

"Empire? I don't have an empire," Joshua said. "I released all of the Turkish prisoners weeks ago after they pledged to stop trading in human beings. I released all of the Trolleg prisoners before we left Vesuvia. I desire no territories. I'm *not* a conqueror!"

"Ah, but you are," Arka-Dal pointed out. "You overran thousands of square miles of Turkish land and destroyed several sultanates in the process. Those people you left behind need someone to govern them now, someone to help them get their lives back together and rebuild their cities. Like it or not, *you* are that someone."

"Responsibility comes with any conquest," Tamarlane added. "Those people you disenfranchised will now look upon you as their sovereign. You must prepare yourself to act the part."

"Long live the king!" shouted Pandaar with a sarcastic grin.

"I never thought of it like that," Joshua said. "I'm a soldier! I know nothing about running a country. I don't even know how to set up a government."

"Neither did I when I was elected emperor of Thule. Luckily, I was surrounded by good people who helped me every step of the way. If you like, I'll have Leo give you some pointers," Arka-Dal said.

"*Pope* Leo? Your chief advisor?" asked Joshua.

Arka-Dal nodded.

"I'm flattered. But why are you offering to help me?" Joshua asked.

"I think it's because you remind me of myself. I've kept an eye on your campaigns for the last two months and I liked what I saw. You're a fine general and I think you'll make a fine king, too. I also want to help you because I'd rather have you as a friend than an enemy," Arka-Dal answered. "I also don't want to have come back up here to teach you another lesson."

"Under such circumstances, I cannot refuse! I accept your generous offer. From this moment forward, we shall be friends and allies. Let nothing stand between us ever again," Joshua said as they shook hands.

News of the victory resulted in the usual wild celebration all throughout the Empire. When Arka-Dal told the others about the nickname Joshua had given him, they all laughed.

"The Lion of Thule? That's a new one!" said Leo.

"How do *you* feel about it, Aka-san?" asked Mayumi.

"I guess I have many nicknames. It seems that each time I win a battle, I get another. The Turks call me the "Hammer of God" and "the Punisher." I guess such things go with the territory," Arka-Dal said as he sipped his brandy.

"In the Abyss, you're called the 'Demonslayer'. In the Lower Planes, you're known as the 'Devil's Nightmare'. Other creatures of darkness refer to you as the 'Bringer of Light that Kills'. But I really like this last one," Galya said.

"Add another one to that," Chatha said. "We Atlanteans call him a savior."

"Lion of Thule fits much better," Medusa commented.

"Which name do *you* prefer, my darling?" asked Galya.

"Arka-Dal," he said. "Nicknames force one to try and live up to them, to try and meet other peoples' expectations. When you try to do that, things can go terribly wrong. I am Arka-Dal. Nothing more and nothing less."

"What became of Terraeus and his escorts?" asked Leo.

"They were last seen to the north and west of Byzantium. They're probably headed into the Balkans. Joshua's agents are in hot pursuit. I imagine they'll soon catch up with them and finish Terraeus once and for all," Arka-Dal said.

"If anyone deserves to die, it's Terraeus. He's caused a lot of misery. I've heard rumors that he thinks he's a god," Leo said.

Arka-Dal laughed.

"Absolute power corrupts absolutely," Galya said.

"Indeed," agreed Leo. "The sultan and his entourage simply dropped off the face of the Earth. No one's seen any of them since Joshua destroyed their kingdom."

"Joshua's agents are looking for them, too. I'm sure they'll turn up one day," Arka-Dal said. "I have my men searching for him as well. Since Thule now has many Turkish citizens, I don't want him to come back and try to foment a revolt or something worse. He's worse than Terraeus."

"I doubt we'll have any trouble from the Turks. They've all taken the oath to become Thulian citizens and many of the men have opted to enlist in our armies. From what I've seen and heard, they had no love for their sultan either," Leo said.

"Are the Turks finished as a people?" asked Medusa.

Arka-Dal shook his head.

"No. Their culture, customs and language remain intact. Things like that can never be taken from someone. Over time, they'll adopt Thulian customs and we'll adopt some of theirs. Eventually, the lines between our cultures will be erased. It's already happened with the Janissaries and Atlanteans," he said.

"It was the way with *our* ancestors. They were a brutish, almost barbaric lot when they invaded the Valley. Eventually, they took on the trappings and customs of those around them. Each generation takes us further away from those dark days," Leo said.

"That's why it's so difficult to define exactly who Thulians are. The people here are a cross section of all mankind because everyone wants to come here. When they do, they bring part of their culture and history with them and it blends in with the rest. Thule is much like ancient Rome in that way," Medusa said.

"It is a true melting pot," Leo added.

"To me, a Thulian is simply a person who lives in Thule, obeys the laws and is willing to serve the Empire in times of need. I can think of no better definition than that," Arka-Dal said.

"I can't either," Leo admitted.

One month after Arka-Dal's triumph in Trollegia, he and Galya were wed in a simple, elegant and traditional ceremony in the grand hall of the palace. All of the governors, cabinet members, Barbarian kings and assorted foreign dignitaries were in attendance, as well as the highest ranking priest or cleric from every major religious sect in the Empire.

Mayumi and the other women planned the entire wedding which included decorating both the palace and the adjacent rose garden for the event. It was there that the rest of the citizenry would celebrate with free food, drinks, bands, dances, games and even fireworks.

"Thulians love parties. They especially love parties that are thrown by Arka-Dal because everything is free of charge and because they love their Emperor," Leo explained to Galya. "Just wait until you see them celebrate the births of your children!"

It was during this period that Galya met Arkaneton and his wife, Idut. She was surprised to learn that Idut was a wraith. She was spawned in a shadowy realm that lies somewhere between the world of the living and the land of the dead and had all of the usual wraith characteristics, such as the pale, almost snow-white skin which remained perpetually cool to the touch. She also had long, jet-black hair and sparkling dark eyes that starkly contrasted with her skin color.

Galya soon discovered that Idut's quiet outward demeanor masked a ready, quick wit and a subtle, somewhat sarcastic, sense of humor.

Her daughter, Mut, was also pale skinned. Unlike her mother, she was gregarious, vivacious and bossy and she usually took charge of the other children when she was visiting her grandfather, Arka-Dal.

Galya and Idut immediately hit it off.

Arkaneton was also quite warm and he welcomed her into the family with the same sincerity as his father. Galya also noticed how very much like Arka-Dal he looked, both in facial features, size and in the confident way he carried himself.

"The Dal family has many interesting lines," she observed over dinner.

"We sure do," Medusa beamed. "We're probably the most diverse family in the entire history of the world."

"And it's about to become even *more* diverse," added Chatha as she smiled at Galya.

"I must say that I admire Arka-Dal's taste in women. Every one of his wives is a real beauty and each brings something special to the royal line," Leo said as he winked at Galya.

She laughed.

"Only *he* could have gotten *you* to fall in love with him," Mayumi pointed out. "He's a most special man."

"Yes, he is *very* special," Galya agreed happily.

At long last, the day of the big event arrived. Good to his word, Arka-Dal invited Galya's father to the wedding. The Devil arrived three hours early and looked resplendent in his long, black satin cape with the gold trim, scarlet lining and jeweled clasp. The rest of his outfit was, of course, black and he carried a bejeweled walking stick.

Everyone knew who he was. After all, there was no mistaking the horns or the sinister, yet inviting, smile.

When he saw Galya emerge from a side chamber wearing her wedding gown, he had to summon all of his willpower to keep from weeping. He smiled broadly as he offered her his arm.

"In all of my long existence, I never once imagined such a day would arrive. I have never seen a more lovely bride. You fill my heart with a joy which I have not felt since the day you were born," he said softly.

She smiled and took his arm.

"I'm really surprised with you, Father. When I told you I was going to marry Arka-Dal, I expected you to throw a royal tantrum and do everything within your power to prevent it. Instead, you have been strangely supportive. Why?" asked Galya.

"Long ago, I was robbed of happiness. That heinous act turned my life to ashes and my heart to stone. I have felt empty inside ever since. Now that I see how truly happy you are, I have decided to give you my blessings. I have decided that no one, especially not me, has the right to interfere. Arka-Dal is a most amazing man. You could not have chosen a better one. I think you two are a perfect match," he said.

That's when Galya noticed a tear roll down his cheek. She wiped it away and smiled.

"I've never seen you weep before," she remarked.

"I haven't since the day you were born—and the day your mother was killed. This day brings me such joy that I have difficulty containing it. You shouldn't be surprised. When all is said and done, I am no different than any father who is about to give his daughter away in marriage," he replied.

At that point, the trumpets blared.

"There's our signal. It's time," Galya said.

As Arka-Dal waited at the foot of the throne platform with Leo, the Devil gleefully walked his daughter—who looked magnificent in her simple, dark red silk gown—down the aisle and officially "gave" her away.

Then Leo performed the legal, binding ceremony and stepped back to allow the other priests to come forward. One by one, they stepped up to the happy couple and gave them their official blessings. All but Pastor Dyne Romani of the Christian Church.

When it was his turn to give the blessing, he obviously balked. Arka-Dal noticed the lack of color in his cheeks as he stared at Galya and her father.

"Why do you hesitate?" asked Leo. "Go on with the ceremony."

"Alas, I cannot do so in good conscience," Romani said nervously.

The Devil squinted at him which made his knees shake even harder.

"Might I ask *why*?" he demanded.

"You're both *devils.* To recognize or bless such a union flies in the face of all that I believe in," Romani replied honestly.

The Devil was infuriated.

"How *dare* you insult my daughter on this day of days?" he growled.

Before he could say anything more, Galya held up her hand to quiet him. He stood back and fumed as she approached Romani.

"I understand how you feel, pastor. Given our long and checkered histories, you have no reason to feel otherwise, nor do I have a right to expect a blessing from a representative of your church. Besides, I do not *need* nor *desire* one," she said softly.

She turned and smiled up at Arka-Dal.

"With or without anyone's blessing, we are as one, forever united by our love and respect for each other. *That* is *all* the blessing *I* need," she added.

The Devil beamed.

"Well spoken, my daughter!" he said proudly.

As Galya and Arka-Dal kissed, Gorinna gave the signal to set off the fireworks above Thule to signify to all of the people that the union was completed. In keeping with a very ancient tradition, Galya and her father danced the first dance while everyone else watched. Arka-Dal saw Romani in a corner and walked up to him and patted his shoulder. Romani looked down.

"I am sorry, Sire," he said humbly.

"Don't be. The blessings are a custom— not a mandate," Arka-Dal said.

"You could have *ordered* me to do it," Romani said.

"True. That would have forced you to set aside your beliefs to satisfy my ego. That would be coercion. I would *never* order you to do that. Relax. This is a celebration. Enjoy the party," Arka-Dal said as he walked to the danced floor and tapped the Devil on the shoulder. He smiled and backed away to allow Arka-Dal to finish the dance with Galya.

To his surprise, Romani walked over and engaged him in polite conversation. Intrigued, he answered all of Romani's questions about the underworld and other supernatural doings.

"This is incredible," Romani said after a while. "Never in my wildest dreams did I think I would get an opportunity like this. Imagine the likes of me having a fine chat with *you*."

"And now that you've actually met me, what do you think?" the Devil asked.

"I don't know. You don't appear to be as foul or evil as I've been led to believe. I may have to rethink many things after this day," Romani admitted.

The Devil laughed.

"You're not half the jackass I took you for, either," he said as he clapped him on the back. "You do realize that if Galya had not stepped in to save you, I would have turned you into something truly nasty?"

"I'm beginning to realize that," Romani replied.

The Devil smiled at the happy couple.

"My daughter means the world to me. This is the proudest moment of my existence. I never thought she'd find the right man or be this happy. See how she smiles?" he boasted.

"She *is* quite lovely," Romani admitted.

"Over time, you'll get to know Galya. Hell, you might even grow to *like* her," the Devil said. "See the look in Arka-Dal's eyes? That's *love!* No one has ever *loved* Galya before. Other men have always feared or recoiled from her. Not him. He loves her and most of all, he *trusts* her—and so do the others. Hell, I even think he trusts *me!*"

"The Emperor *trusts* you?" Romani asked almost in astonishment.

"And why shouldn't he? After all, I am a man of principle. I always *keep* my bargains. What other being can say *that*?" the Devil explained.

He saw the look on Romani's face and chuckled.

"Think of this way—when in all of my history have you known me to break a contract or renege on a promise?" he challenged.

Romani thought for a while then shook his head.

"I cannot recall any such incident," he admitted.

"Exactly. Even your so-called god couldn't boast of that. He failed to keep his word time and again. He even tormented people just to amuse himself. Think of what he supposedly did to poor Job and how many times he's demanded human sacrifices! I never did that!" the Devil pointed out.

"Did you not have the power to prevent this union?" Romani asked.

"No. Once Galya makes up her mind, no power in the universe can make her change it. When I saw how they looked at each other, I decided not to interfere. I've always wanted her to be happy," he replied.

"Leo told me that you swore an oath?" Romani asked.

"That I did. I swore to help protect Arka-Dal and Thule from all future enemies, both human and supernatural, forevermore. As long as a single one of his line still lives, this land will flourish—and I keep my vows," the Devil assured him.

"I am humbled, Sir. It appears that I have much yet to learn," Romani said.

"Indeed you do," the Devil said.

When the music ended, he and Romani walked over to the happy couple. The pastor watched as the Devil kissed and embraced his daughter then shook hands with Arka-Dal. Romani walked up to them and placed his hands on their foreheads and recited his official blessing.

"Thank you," Galya said.

"Thank your father, my dear. He opened my eyes this night and I have eaten much crow," Romani replied. "If you'll excuse me, I must find some strong ale to wash the taste of that bird from my mouth."

Arka-Dal and the Devil laughed while everyone else in the room cheered. The Devil wished them well. He shook Arka-Dal's hand and kissed Galya on the forehead. Then, he bowed and took his leave by vanishing into thin air.

Arka-Dal held up his goblet in salute.

"Your father certainly has a lot of style," he commented.

"He said the same thing about you," Galya said as she hugged him tight. "Where will we honeymoon?"

"How about on my yacht? We can take a nice, leisurely trip downriver to the winter palace and spend some time on the beach," he suggested.

"I like the idea of going to your winter palace—but we won't have time to go to any beach," she said with a playful wink.

"Funny—I was just thinking the exact same thing!" he said as they hugged again.

Merlin and Gorinna grinned while they drank wine.

The Dal family tree had sprouted another—and most curious—branch.

Note:

Six months later, the port of Vesuvia was up and running under joint Thulian and Trolleg control. The city was renamed Arkadia in honor of the Emperor. A month later, what remained of the Trollegian people voted to petition Arka-Dal to be admitted into the Empire of Thule. Two weeks after he met with the Trolleg delegation, he signed the pact admitting the former nation of Trollegia into the Empire.

As for Joshua, he devoted his time and energy establishing and solidifying his hold on Anatolia. He also managed to repay Thule for the damage his fleet caused to Odense and compensated the shopkeepers and families for their financial losses. True to his word, he abolished slavery in all its ugly forms and modeled his nation after Thule. In the process, he established strong commercial, cultural and military ties with Thule and its allies and promised to promote peace in the region.

Terraeus and his party were ambushed and killed by bandits at a pass leading into Transylvania. Joshua's agents found and identified their remains three weeks later and brought Terraeus' rotting head back to Vesuvia as proof.

The sultan and his men were never seen again.

The Legacy

In the 41st year of the reign of Arka-Dal

It was the Year of the Games.

In the autumn of every sixth year, the finest athletes from around the world gathered at the Great Arena and Field five miles to the south of Thule to compete in the World Games.

Besides the athletes, the games attracted thousands upon thousands of onlookers and fans. Hotels and inns were filled to capacity for fifty miles in all directions and the area around the arena was packed with concession stands, souvenir stalls, musicians, magicians, entertainers, circus acts and other types of "entertainment" such as bookies and prostitutes. The area was well-patrolled by Thulian police as such large crowds also tended to attract pickpockets and other petty criminals.

The Games lasted three weeks and were open to both men and women from every race and nation. The winners of each competition received a bronze laurel wreath crowning him or her "champion" and half his weight in gold. The runners up received a silver medal and one fourth his weight in gold while those who finished third earned 20 pounds of gold and a bronze medal.

The athletes competed in chariot races, horse races, boat races, swimming, foot races, archery, boxing, wrestling, weight lifting, javelin and discus throwing and jousting. Each match was judged by a past champion who's decision was final.

Arka-Dal and Mayumi presided over both the opening and closing ceremonies. Each took turns awarding the prizes to the winners.

In years past, Arka-Dal competed in the jousts. On two occasions, he was crowned champion and he donated his prize money to charity. Now, he participated only in a ceremonial capacity.

His son, Arkaneton, competed in this year's chariot races. He won the wreath by finishing first in three of four matches and second in another. His young wife, Chatha, won the archery competition when she miraculously split her opponent's arrow in two after he had scored a bull's eye. The modest Chatha attributed this to "sheer dumb luck". Of course, she had also hit the bull's eye with each of her previous 23 shots. The man who's arrow she split, had matched her shot-for-shot, thus sparking a furious round of betting with the local bookies.

Perseus tried his hand in three competitions.

In wrestling, he was eliminated when his opponent unceremoniously dumped him on his head after a brief match. He came in fourth in the foot races and seventh in the discus throw. Perseus took this all with good humor.

"It's not about winning," he said. "I just love to compete."

Far way from the noise of the arenas and on a back street of the eastern quarter, stood the only Christian church in the Empire. Monsignor Bartolomy was in his study going over several months worth of church documents. Many concerned the church's long war against the Devil and his minions. As he closed one of the heavy books, he sat back and sighed.

Did the Devil really exist?

If so, what would he ask him if he had the chance?

A knock on the door broke his reverie.

"Please enter!" he called.

The heavy door creaked open. Bartolomy beamed as Leo entered.

"It's good to see you again, my friend. To what do I owe the pleasure of your visit?" he said warmly as the two shook hands.

"I've brought along someone I'd like you to meet," Leo said as he opened the door wide.

Bartolomy's jaw dropped when he saw who it was. The Devil nodded graciously and extended his right hand. Bartolmy clasped it numbly and offered him a seat. Leo sat in the empty chair next to him. Both watched as Bartolomy rushed out of the room and returned a moment later bearing a platter of wine, fruit and cheese which he placed on the desk before them.

"Are you who I think you are?" he asked.

"I am," the Devil assured him.

Sensing the Monsignor's nervousness, he smiled as if to assure him all was well. Bartolomy relaxed as the tension left his body.

"This is amazing! I can hardly believe my eyes. Until this very moment, I wasn't sure that you actually existed," he gushed.

The Devil laughed.

"I get that a lot," he said.

"I don't understand. This is a church. I didn't think you could safely enter such places," Bartolomy observed.

"I can when invited in. I am here at Leo's request. He said that you might have some questions for me," the Devil replied.

"I do! I do! But first, tell me how you've come to know Leo," Bartolomy said.

Leo explained all of the happenings over the past several months. When he finished, Bartolomy looked stunned.

"I was unaware of all this. As you know, I've been abroad this past year. I just returned two days ago," he said.

"I'll give you this—you don't seem to be as rattled by me as Romano was. It took him most of the night to warm up to me. You seem more open-minded," the Devil said.

"I am in most maters. Can I ask you something?" Bartolomly hedged.

"As away," the Devil said.

"Did you know Jesus?" he asked.

The Devil nodded.

"I knew him quite well. In fact, I'm the one who made him what he is today," he said.

"Would you mind explaining that?" Bartolomy asked.

"Gladly. To begin with, his real name was Abu Ben Josef. He was a tall, muscular and hot-tempered carpenter of little noteworthy skills. He was also an itinerant rabbi as was the custom in those days. He traveled. He preached. And he built things. But no one listened when he spoke and *that* really pissed him off. Above all, Jesus wanted to be famous. He wanted people to listen to him. He needed mindless followers to worship him and hang on his every word. He even craved immortality.

That's where I came in.

For the usual price, I agreed to make him everything he desired. All he had to do was speak the words I gave him and allow me to work certain 'miracles' through him to wow the masses. Eager to be adored, he willingly signed the contract and our work began. Through him, I changed water into wine and fed thousands of people from a single fish and loaf of bread. I gave new legs to the lame and crippled. I gave sight to the blind. The Lazarus resurrection was my masterpiece if I do say so myself.

Before long, he was famous. He even had an entourage of disciples. He was so easy to lead. In the end, he got everything he desired and I got his soul," the Devil said.

"But he was crucified!" Bartolomy pointed out.

"Yes. His painful death made him famous. His phony "resurrection' which *I* staged, spread that fame far and wide and spawned the Christian religion. Thousands of years have passed and people like you still worship him as if he's some sort of god," the Devil replied.

"So he wasn't our savior?" asked Bartolomy.

"Not hardly. Some savior! He couldn't even save himself from a very painful death. But it *did* make him a *martyr*. Without that little detail, his name would have faded into the dust of history," the Devil answered.

"If this is true, then our entire religion is nothing but a sham!" Bartolomy said.

"All religions are shams," the Devil said.

The Monsignor stared at the Devil.

"So you are the true founder of Christianity?" he asked.

"Indirectly. And you and your followers have been persecuting me for it ever since," the Devil said.

"How ironic!" Bartolomy said.

The Devil laughed.

"Actually, I find it rather amusing. I think you will, too, once it sinks in.," he said.

They had a long, pleasant and, for Bartolomy, enlightening discussion.

"I know this sounds strange coming from someone like me, but feel free to drop in and chat with me anytime," Bartolomy offered when they were finished.

"You're right. That does sound strange. We'll get together again when I have more time. As they say, the Devil's work is never done," the Devil replied as he and Leo walked to the door with Bartolomy.

"Neither is the *Lord's*!" Bartolomy said with a wry smile.

It was during this carnival-like time that Sindbad and his crew sailed into Thule's harbor to make some needed repairs to their five ships and to deliver more goods to the local markets.

As was their usual custom, they took rooms at the Black Boar Inn. Sindbad gave his sailors two weeks shore leave after paying them their share of the profits. Then he, Lum, Kasim and Hassan sat down at their favorite table in the tavern and began downing flagons of ale and wine.

On the afternoon of their third day in port, they were at the table eating dinner and drinking when Hassan noticed a short, pudgy-looking man with wire framed glasses enter the inn. He had a leather briefcase tucked beneath one arm and he seemed to be looking for someone.

Hassan pointed at him.

"I wonder who that guy is?" he asked.

"I don't know—nor do I care," Lum said between belches as he wiped the ale from his lips with his sleeve. "He's not looking for me, that's for sure."

Much to their surprise, the man fixed his gaze on them as if trying to determine who they were. After several seconds, he nodded.

"Are you sure? He's headed this way," Sindbad said.

The man approached the table and stopped in front of Lum. He looked up and sneezed, then wiped his nose on his shirt sleeve.

"Are you Lum Pentassal?" the man asked.

"Yeah. What's it to you?" Lum replied grumpily.

"My name is Michael Bernhardt. I'm an attorney. I have a letter for you," the man said as he opened his briefcase and pulled out a large brown envelope.

Lum took it and squinted at the name on the upper left hand corner.

"Is this some kind of joke?" he asked.

"Not at all. Your cousin, the late Hercemes Pentassal, left this envelope with me before he went on his last voyage. He left implicit instructions to deliver it to you two years after his death. My firm tried to deliver this months ago but you were out at sea. So when I heard that Sindbad's fleet had arrived, I made a few inquiries and found out that you were here. Now that I've fulfilled my obligation, I bid you farewell," Bernhardt said as he turned and walked out of the inn.

Lum stared at the envelope.

"Don't keep us waiting! Open the damned thing!" Sindbad said.

"Can't stand the suspense, huh?" Lum chided as he slowly tore open the flap and removed the contents.

Inside were two folded parchments and a heavy iron key. Lum put the key in his vest pocket and unfolded each of the parchments. He spread tem out on the table as the others watched.

"Maps?" asked Sindbad. "Maps of what?"

"This one here is a map of the mountains that are the home to us Wichtlein. The line stretching from the center and off the page seems to be some sort of road into the southern part of the Teutonic Empire. That's where our ancestors were once enslaved and forced to work the mines," Lum said as he passed the map around the table.

"The second one I'm not real sure of. It looks like a map of one of the mines. Why would Herc leave me this? What am I supposed to do with this?" he wondered aloud.

"Could be that he left something down in that mine he wanted you to find," Sindbad suggested.

"You're probably right. Looks like I need to make a trip back home. I'll need at least three months leave," Lum decided.

"No problem. Want us to go with you?" Sindbad asked.

"No. This is something I have to do myself. Thanks for the offer anyway," Lum said as he refolded the maps.

"Three months from now, we'll be in Constantinople. We'll meet you at the docks. May Allah go with you!" Sindbad said as they shook hands.

"And with you. I'd better get back to the ship and pack my things. I'll be seeing you!" Lum said as he rose and left the inn.

While Lum traveled back to his homeland at a leisurely pace, rumors of his inheritance galloped ahead of him. Before long, nearly everyone in the Dwarf kingdom knew that the last member of the Pentassal family—in fact, the last living member of the *ruling* family—was en route.

It took him two months to get there. When he finally crossed the Alps ands reached the land of the Wichtlein, the chiefs of every Dwarf clan turned out to greet him. After exchanging introductions and hearty handshakes, they followed him to the Great Hall of the Clan Wolfen for a traditional and lengthy, no-holds-barred feast.

For days on end, he regaled them with tales of his adventures with Sindbad and told them in detail how Zalena and Herc had met their ends. Between the stories were courses of meat, songs, dancing and heavy drinking. By the time it ended, the Great Hall stank of beer and ale and resounded with the heavy snoring of passed-out Dwarfs lying amid empty bottles, bones, broken flagons, dishes and other party detritus.

Lum snapped out of his alcohol induced coma three days later and found himself lying in a large, comfortable bed with heavy covers. As his vision slowly returned, he realized he was in a room with a vaulted ceiling.

It was Herc's old room.

Since he was the last of the Pentassals, it was *his* room now.

His house.

His clan.

He rose, stretched and stumbled to the adjoining bathroom to shower. Feeling better, he dressed and went back down to the Great Hall. It was already clean. In fact, no signs of the wild party could be seen. One of the servants spotted him and ushered him to a long table for a breakfast of fat beef sausages, eggs, dark bread and strong coffee. He asked her to sit with him and talk while he ate.

Through her, he learned that Herc's refusal to wear the crown or become president had thrown the Great Council into chaos for several years. Eventually, they ironed out their problems and held another general election. An old, wizened Dwarf from the Brown Bear Clan named Kraus Hamnel managed to get himself elected president. But his term was nearly up and he had publicly wondered if Lum had come to claim the throne.

"I guess I should pay him a visit to allay his fears. I have no interest in ruling anybody," Lum told her. "Besides, only the one who can unite the two halves of the crown can become king—and no one's seen *that* for decades!"

He arrived at the President's House late that afternoon. Old Hamnel greeted him warmly and escorted him to the parlor. A servant brought in a tray of snacks and bottles of ale. Hamnel smiled when Lum assured him he wasn't interested in becoming president or king.

"I'm a sailor. I've just come here to see what Herc left me," he said. "I didn't think I would cause such a stir."

"Of course your visit caused a stir," Hamnel said. "For years, everyone believed that Hercemes had possession of the Iron Crown, which he took from Zalena after she fell in battle. Most now believe that he willed the crown to you."

"I don't know what he left me. His lawyer gave me a letter from him, a map and this damned key," Lum said as he unfolded the map and placed it before Hamnel.

"There's the problem. Almost everyone her thinks this map shows where he his the crown and that the key opens the box that contains it," Hamnel said.

"Do you think Herc left me the crown? Why in Hell would he do that? I don't want it!" Lum said.

Hamnel shrugged.

"That's something only Herc knew—and he took that to the grave with him," he said.

Lum stared at the map.

"I'm not familiar with this region. Can you help with this?" he asked.

Hamnel studied the map for a few moments then pointed out several landmarks he needed to watch for and easy roads to take. He noted that the trail ended at the entrance to a narrow valley.

"I have no idea what to tell you about that. No one ever enters that valley. It's supposed to be cursed or something," he said.

"How long do you think this will take?" Lum asked.

"If the weather holds up, about three or four days. If it rains, that road will turn to mud in minutes and slow you down to a crawl," Hamnel replied.

"Anything else I should know?" asked Lum as he folded the map and stuck it back into his pocket.

"I advise you to travel well-armed. There are still some people who covet that crown. If they believe this map will lead you to its location, they might try to take it from you," Hamnel warned.

"They can *try*," Lum said with a grin. "Thank you, Mr. President. You've been a big help.

They shook hands and Hamnel escorted him to the front door. Just before Lum left, Hamnel what he planned to do if Herc had indeed left him the crown.

Lum shrugged.

"Beats me. I guess I'll decide that when—and if—I find it," he said as he walked away.

Three shadowy figures watched Lum leave the President's House from their shelter amid a grove of pine trees. They had taken a keen interest in everything he did.

Too keen.

One was portly, even for a Dwarf and well-attired in silken robes. He sported several heavy rings on his stubby fingers and his beard was neatly trimmed and combed. The others were rather rough, but ordinary looking, but had sinister casts to them.

"Do we jump him now, Boss?" one asked.

"No," said the well-dressed Dwarf. "Follow him. Let him lead us to the crown. Once he finds it, we'll kill him and take it from him. That way, no one will be able to connect us to his murder."

As Herc walked up the narrow, winding street to his Hall, a tiny, winged female fluttered down from a nearby tree and alit on his shoulder. He stopped and smiled when he saw it was one of Faeries.

"Hello, there. Who are you and why have you come to me?" he asked.

"I am called Lunae. I have come to warn you," she said.

She related all she'd heard when she eavesdropped on the trio in the pine grove. Lum smiled and thanked her. She fluttered off and he continued toward the Hall. Just before he entered, he cast a quick glance over his right shoulder. He spotted three Dwarfs lurking in the shadows across the street. They darted into a doorway when he looked at them to avoid being seen.

"Too late," Lum said to himself as he entered the Hall.

Now that he knew exactly where was going, Lum packed his knapsack and left the Hall early the next morning. He traveled south on foot and acted as if he hadn't a care in the world. He knew he was being followed and decided to let his new "friends" make the first move. He also wondered why the had taken such an interest in his inheritance.

"Just what did you leave me, Herc?" he asked aloud.

He followed the road out of town until it forked. He stopped to check his map, put it back into his pocket, and took the left fork. His three shadows became five at this point and kept following him at what they thought to be a safe distance.

As he followed the meandering road deeper into the mountains, Lum thought about his situation. It was reasonable to assume that Herc's map was leading him to where he supposedly hid the Iron Crown. After all, he was the last of their people to have it. Since he had no use for it, he probably buried it somewhere and then drew the map to show where it was.

"But why leave it to me?" Lum wondered. "I sure as Hell don't want it. I don't want to be the king anymore than Herc did. What am I supposed to do with it?"

As for the group shadowing him, he decided they'd best keep their distance if they knew what was good for them. Even if he didn't want the crown, he damned well wasn't going to hand it over to those greedy bastards.

"Damn you, Herc! Look what you've gotten me into!" he thought.

Lum continued to walk for two more days. His shadows stayed behind him, trying their best to stay "unnoticed".

The long trek was wearing on the rich one's henchmen. They were staring to become anxious. They wanted to get this over with so they could collect their fees. Their leader sensed their frustration and cautioned against taking any action.

"Just keep following him. He'll lead us to the crown eventually," he said.

"How do you know he's looking for it?" asked one his men.

"I have inside information that he knows where it is. Once he finds, we'll take it from him then I'll become the king of the Wichtlein," the rich one said confidently.

"What if you can't unite the halves? What will you do with it then?" asked another.

"I'll auction it off to the highest bidder. There are more than enough greedy lords among us Dwarfs who'd be willing to pay plenty to have it," the boss replied.

"What if Lum won't give it up?" asked another.

"In that case, we'll just have to *reason* with him," said another henchman.

"That could pose a problem. That Lum's a tough bastard and he packs firearms. We'll have to get the drop on him somehow," another said.

"Just who is this inside source you mentioned anyway?" asked the largest of the henchmen.

"A powerful man. A man of wealth and taste," the boss replied. "We struck a bargain. I get the crown and he gets something I have little use for."

The next day, the main trail ended at the entrance to the valley. Lum puffed on his cigar as he looked around. The entrance was very narrow, barely large enough to a rider and horse to wiggle through. The cliffs on either side were of granite and rose almost straight up, casting the entrance in darkness.

He took another, final puff of the cigar and tossed the butt away. There was a chill in the air now. He tightened his serape and strode into the entrance.

The trail sloped upward for several hundred yards then tilted to the right. The ground was loose and gravelly.

Rough going.

Here and there, he saw small furry animals scurry about or heard hawks crying overhead. Other than that, the path was quiet. After several hours, it widened into a large, bell-shaped valley surrounded by jagged cliffs. Lum stopped to sip from his canteen and consult the map.

He was about to curse vehemently when he realized the map ended at the entrance to the valley when he happened to glance down. To his surprise, there was a large arrow pointing straight ahead. It had been etched into the hard ground. Beside it was the letter "H".

Lum smiled and looked to where it indicated. It pointed to the base of the cliffs across the way. He folded the map, stuck it into his hat, and followed the arrow.

Lum soon found himself standing at the mouth of a large cavern. He pulled a cigar from his vest pocket, stuck it in his mouth and lit it. He took a deep puff and exhaled as he listened quietly for signs of life. Hearing nothing, he entered the cavern. As he walked down the rocky slope, he checked his revolvers to make certain they were loaded then stuck them back into his holsters.

About a hundred feet past the entrance, a flight of small bats fluttered past him. Their sudden movement caused Lum to flinch. He laughed at his own reaction and kept walking. The cavern soon grew pitch black. Unperturbed, he kept walking. Unlike Humans, Dwarfs could see very well in dark places, their vision being the product of countless generations spent beneath the Earth in various mines and Dwarf cities. When he reached a "T", he stopped and rechecked his map.

To his dismay, the map showed the "T" but didn't indicate which way to go. He refolded the map and stuck it back into his hat as he looked around for anything that would tell where to go.

That's when he found a large "H" etched into the ground in front of the right fork. Lum followed it. The deeper he went, the narrower the tunnel became. In several places, he had to sidle his way through as it was barely wide enough to let him through.

"Where is this taking me?" he wondered. "What did Herc hide down here?"

The tunnel emptied into a high, vaulted cavern of stalagmites and stalactites. In the center was a large pool of liquid that exuded sulfur. On the other side of the pool were three openings. Lum again checked the map. This time, it indicated he should use the opening straight ahead. He shrugged, tossed away what was left of his cigar, lit another one and kept going.

As soon as he entered, he felt and heard something crunching beneath his feet. He looked down and saw that the floor was covered with bones of every shape and size imaginable. Most appeared to be animal bones. Some he couldn't identify.

"Something lives down here," he said to himself. "Something that *hunts!"*

He drew one of his revolvers and kept going.

His feet splashed through a pool of shallow water and sent echoes along the passageway. He briefly wondered at the source of the water, then put the thought from his mind.

"What if the thing that hunts down here heard that? Will it then hunt *me?*" he wondered.

He stopped and listened.

Nothing.

He took a deep breath, exhaled and kept walking. He had a feeling he was being followed. A feeling he just couldn't ignore.

He came to another place where the passage split off in two directions. He took the map from his hat and studied it again. Satisfied, he put it away and took the left passage. As he did, his foot struck something metallic. He looked down and saw that it was an old, battered and rusty war helmet of Dwarf design. He also spotted more bits of broken armor and a bent sword further up the passage.

"At least you went down swinging," he said to the helmet. "I wonder who you were and what you were doing down here. I guess I'll never know."

He was about to move one when he heard a faint splish-splosh sound. He smiled.

"Looks like I'm not alone," he said. "May the Gods help whoever they are when they find me."

He had an idea who his followers might be. At his welcoming party, the leader of the High Council, Menoris, had shown more than a casual interest in where he was going. If it was him, he most likely brought his goons along to help.

"Like *that* will make any difference!" he laughed.

He stopped and lit another cigar.

"Just what in Hell *did* you hide down here, Herc?" he thought as he blew a puff of smoke and continued on his way.

A few minutes later, his shadows happened upon the remains of the slain warrior. One of them visibly balked at the sight of the battered armor.

"Whatever's here hates Dwarfs," he remarked.

"I think it hates everything. I hope it's no longer around," another said nervously.

"These remains are *decades* old. Whatever did this must be dead by now," said the biggest of the goons.

"We're wasting time. Let's keep after Lum," the boss ordered.

They walked down the passage as quietly as they could. After a while, they, too, heard the splish-splosh sounds and stopped. The sounds seemed to be coming from all around them.

Growing impatient with their hesitating, the boss ordered them to move on.

"We'll deal with whatever made that sound later," he said sternly.

Meanwhile, Lum had entered a large, circular cavern with a vaulted roof. A few bats flit past his head as he entered and the floor was partially covered with guano. Lum lit another cigar and looked around.

The place seemed empty save for a pile of small rocks in the center. Lum rechecked his map. He smiled when he saw that Herc had placed an X right in the middle of the very same room.

"Damn, Herc. You sure went out of your way to hide this," he remarked as he put away the map and walked toward the pile of rocks. He set his knapsack down and began removing the rocks one and two at a time. It took his several minutes to reveal the heavy, iron-bound chest beneath them. The chest was padlocked. Lum reached into his pocket. He took out the rusted key and applied it to the lock. It worked perfectly. Lum sat back and smiled.

"I guess it's time to check out my inheritance," he said.

When he raised the lid, he sat back and whistled. There, on the bottom of the box, were the two halves of the missing Iron Crown of the Wichtlein. He picked up one of the halves and examined it.

"So this is what you wanted me to find. I'd always wondered where you'd hid it," he said as he thought of his late cousin. "But what am *I* supposed to do with it?"

He put it back into the box and turned the key in the lock. His thoughts went back to the time the High Council tried to get Herc to unite the crown. They wanted him to be the new king after Zalena died. Zalena was Herc's younger sister. She was the last Wichtlein to unite the two halves of the crown. She was the first—and last—queen the Dwarfs had ever had. When she was killed, the crown split in two. According to the legend, only the one destined to be the true king could unite the pieces and wear the crown. Herc had refused to even attempt to put it together.

Instead, he forced the High Council to adopt a Thulian-style constitution and hold an election to select their new king. When the people elected Herc, he adamantly refused the job and insisted they try again. After holding three more elections and getting the same results, the High Council threw up their hands. They chose a Triumvirate to head up Wichtlein affairs until a proper solution could be found. That was *years* ago.

In the course of the elections, Herc snatched the crown and hid it.

"Why leave it to me? I don't want to be king!" Lum said aloud.

"But *I* do!" came a deep voice from behind him. "Hand over that box! It belongs to me!"

Lum turned to see Menoris, and four of his henchmen standing in the doorway. He sneered at them.

"How do you figure that?" he asked.

"Herc stole the contents from us. What's inside should have been mine but he took it and hid it down here. If not for him, I'd be the king of the Wichtlein right now. He deprived me of my god-given right to rule our people!" Menoris said.

Lum laughed.

"Nobody would want a king like *you!* You're nuts!" he said.

"The decision is mine to make—not yours. Now hand it over," Menoris demanded.

"Try and take it—if you've got the balls!" Lum said as he drew his revolvers.

Menoris pointed.

"Kill him!" he ordered.

Before his henchmen could move, two shots echoed through the mine. When the smoke cleared, one sat with his back against the wall holding his guts in and another lay face-down in a pool of his own blood.

Lum looked at the other two.

"If you don't want to get shot, I suggest you leave now," he said.

They both turned and fled from the chamber, leaving their boss alone to face Lum. Menoris drew his dagger and hurled it at Lum. The dagger struck his hat and pinned it to the wall. Menoris ended up on the floor after being shot in both kneecaps. Lum retrieved his hat and picked up the box. Before he left the chamber, he shot Menoris once in each elbow, rendering his limbs useless.

"You can find your own way out of here," he said as he left Menoris moaning on the floor.

Lum moved quickly now. He figured that the shots would attract the thing that hunts and he didn't want to stick around to find out what it was. Menoris, of course, had no choice. He could only lay there quaking with fear as the heavy, shuffling footsteps grew louder and louder. By the time Lum reached the sulfur pool, he heard Menoris' terrified screams echo through the caverns . . .

He didn't return the crown to the High Council. Instead, he carried it to Venice and reboarded the Saracen Moon in the harbor just as it was about to set sail on another long trading expedition.

He found Sindbad in the pilot house. The two embraced and pounded each other on the back.

"Welcome aboard, Lum! I was afraid you might miss this trip," Sindbad said.

"I'm glad I didn't. I hate being on land. The sea's the only place for me now," Lum said.

"How was your trip? What did Herc leave you?" Sindbad asked.

Over dinner that night, Lum told him all that had happened. Sindbad and the others listened, then laughed when he told them how he'd left Menoris. After dinner, Lum and Sindbad went up on deck. Lum had the wooden box with him.

As they stood on the deck watching the waves, Lum picked up the box and tossed it into the sea. He and Sindbad watched it sink.

"Why'd you do that?" asked Sindbad.

"I did it to make sure no one ever finds it again," Lum replied.

"What's in it?" Sindbad queried.

"Trouble. Nothing but trouble," Lum replied as he walked away from the rail.

When they reached Thule several days later, the entire nation was celebrating the births of the latest additions to the Dal line. Fireworks lit up the sky and the streets were crowded with revelers.

Their Emperor's fourth wife had given birth to twins.

The girl was fair skinned with dark brown hair and earned the name Melody because of her almost musical sounding cry. The boy looked much like Galya and his cries, which sounded much like the cries of a bird of prey, earned him the name Hawk.

Galya's infamous father was on hand for the event and she beamed up at him as he proudly cradled the twins in his arms. That's when she saw him do something she had not seen him do since her wedding day.

He wept.

And they were tears of joy.

"This day will be joyously celebrated on every single one of the Lower Planes! This is one of the happiest day of my life and I have you and Arka-Dal to thank for it! You have made me a grandfather—of *twins*! They are the most beautiful infants I have ever beheld," he gushed as he snuggled with each of them.

Galya and Arka-Dal laughed.

Merlin, Leo and Gorinna were also amazed by his behavior. It was more than a little bit strange to see their long-time adversary acting just like any new grandfather would.

The Devil had also brought them gifts. Twin rings, one ruby and one emerald, which were to be given to the twins when they were old enough to understand what they were. The rings would enable them to locate each other over any distance, even beyond dimensional borders. They would also be able to use them to reunite with each other upon uttering a certain phrase. He created the rings especially for the twins. As such, they would be useless to anyone else.

He hugged them close awhile then placed them gently back in Galya's arms. He then leaned over and kissed her on the cheek. While the others fawned over the newborns, Merlin stood back and pondered how much of Galya's power each had inherited and whether they' d be able to keep their darker natures under control. The Devil noticed the expression on his face and walked over.

"This is a time for rejoicing! Why do you look so glum? You look as if someone has just walked over your grave," he said.

"I was pondering which parent the twins would favor most," Merlin replied as he sipped his wine.

The Devil smiled.

"In a perfect world, they would take equal parts from both. But, alas, there is no such thing as a perfect world. What do you see in their future?" he asked.

"Too much—and perhaps, not enough. Their future is shrouded for now," Merlin answered.

"And this worries you, of course," the Devil said.

Merlin nodded.

"You don't seem very concerned," he observed.

"I'm much too elated right now. Galya has not only married better than I could have hoped for but she has made me the proud grandfather of twins. I am beside myself with happiness. I hope you'll forgive me, but such emotional displays are quite rare for me," the Devil said as he slapped Merlin on the back.

"Lighten up, my friend! We will be here to ensure they choose the right path," he said.

Merlin laughed.

"I never thought I'd ever hear you call me *friend*, especially not after all of our run-ins!" he said as he slapped him in return.

"That's all water under the bridge right now. Things have changed of late," the Devil said as they clinked glasses.

"They have indeed," Merlin agreed.

The Devil stayed long enough to join everyone in another toast, then bade them farewell. He said that he had to tend to his "usual business" and vanished into thin air, leaving both Arka-Dal and Merlin secretly relieved that his "business" didn't include either of them.

The Devil *was* elated.

His new grandchildren ensured that his connection to the human world would continue, although on a different level. He also wondered if the ancient legends were true. Now that Galya had given birth to half-human children, would she *really* lose her magical powers? Was she now *mortal*?

Only time would tell and he had an overabundance of that.

Galya didn't care about old legends. As she sat in her bed cradling her newborn children, her heart virtually sang. She had experienced something wonderful. Something magical. She was the wife of Arka-Dal and the mother of their children. Nothing in either Heaven or Hell could top that!

The Old Man and His Cat

In the 42nd Year of the Reign of Arka-Dal

Storms in the Valley are quite rare. When they do come, they can be long and violet, with heavy rain, loud thunder claps, startling lightning flashes and high winds.

This storm was no exception.

It is also said that strange things sometimes emerge from the storms. Some believe that monsters dwell within them and come out between lightning flashes. Some say that the storms open "gates" into other worlds and allow the creatures and demons from the other side to enter our world.

But that is merely superstition.

Or is it?

The Red Boar in was one of the largest and most popular waterside taverns in all of Thule. It was so popular that even such a violent storm as the one currently pounding the Valley couldn't keep customers away. On this night, the inn was filled with customers. A dozen sailors from a nearby ship were inside drinking and throwing their hard-earned money at the equal number of street girls who were eagerly trying to separate them from it. Almost everyone inside was drunk, or nearly so.

No one paid any mind to the thin, hunched-over, hooded figure who came in from the storm. The lone barkeep watched as he slowly limped across the wooden floor, dragging his bum right leg behind him with each painful step until he reached a small table in the far corner of the room. The stranger pulled the chair from beneath the table and sat down with his head bowed.

The barkeep noticed that the man was drenched to the skin, yet he didn't bother to remove his cloak or pull back the hood that covered his face in shadow. As the barkeep approached the table, the man reached into the folds of his cloak and took out a small black cat, which he placed on his lap. Although the man was soaked, the cat appeared to be quite dry.

The barkeep reached the table.

"How can I help you, sir?" he asked.

The man never bothered to look up. The cat, however, trained its bright yellow eyes on him.

"I seek someone," the man said.

His voice had an odd echo to it, as if was coming from someplace other than him. He glanced down at the cat. Was the stranger speaking through his cat or was the cat speaking through him? The barkeep shook his head to clear it of the weird thought.

"And just who is it you're looking for?" the he asked.

"I seek the Red Witch," the man replied.

"Gorinna? And just *why* would she want to speak with the likes of you, if you don't mind my asking?" the barkeep queried.

The man reached back into his cloak and took out a bronze coin. He handed this to the barkeep.

"She will wish to speak with me when she sees this," the man said as he placed a most unusual-looking coin his palm. "Take this to her. I'm certain it will whet her curiosity. I will await her here."

The coin was so unusual that the barkeep realized it might be very important. Besides, who was he to question a customer's request? He tucked the coin into his pocket and walked over to a hook on the wall where his rain cloak hung and slipped it on. The stranger didn't even look up when the barkeep hurried out into the storm to deliver his message.

Gorinna was in the Royal Archives going over a few of the things in the books Galya had given them with Leo when the barkeeper arrived at the palace door. Although the man was in awe of being anywhere near the palace, he was nearly dumbfounded when the guard not only admitted him but escorted him to the waiting room. The barkeeper sat down in one of the plush chairs and watched as his escort vanished down a corridor. Several minutes later, the beautiful Gorinna entered. He stood and bowed respectfully.

"Relax," she said. "The guard told me that you had a message for me."

"Indeed, my lady," the barkeep said as he fumbled through his vest pocket for the strange coin. When he found it, he placed it in her open hand.

"He said he wanted to meet with you as quickly as possible. He also told me to give you that coin. He said you'd know what it was," the barkeep explained.

Gorinna turned the coin over and over as she examined it. It was ancient. So ancient, she had never seen its like before. It was also made of a metal she couldn't identify—and it *vibrated.*

Magic?

She looked at the barkeep.

"Describe this man," she said.

The man did as she asked. When he'd finished, she shook her head.

"You say the cat speaks for him?" she asked.

"Yes, my lady. Or he speaks through the cat. I can't be sure which," the man replied.

"Thank you," she said. "Help yourself to something from the bar of you like, then return to your establishment and inform your visitor that I'll meet him there in two hours."

The barkeep bowed and shuffled out of the room.

Gorinna stared at the coin. One side was completely blank. The other was engraved with the image of a large-headed, multi-tentacled deity.

"Cthulhu!" she thought as she suppressed a shudder.

She showed the coin to Leo. The Pope raised an eyebrow as he turned it over in his hand several times. When he was finished, he tossed it back to her.

"It's electrum," he said. "It's a blend of gold and silver with some other element I an unfamiliar with. It's also incredibly old."

"Any idea where it came from?" she asked.

"I haven't a clue. It might be connected to some long-dead civilization that predated the First Age. It might even be from another dimension. Of course, I'm only guessing. What are going to do?" Leo asked.

"I'm going to meet with this stranger and find out why he wants to see me. Once I learn that, I'll decide what else to do," she replied.

It was late afternoon when she arrived at the inn. As she walked through the swinging doors, she spotted a hooded figure seated at a far table. There was a black cat on his lap which turned its gaze toward her as she approached.

"Welcome, Gorinna. I knew you'd come," the cat said.

As she pondered who was talking for who, she sat down across from them. The cat yawned.

"How do you know me?" she asked.

"Everyone knows you. You're quite famous," came the response.

"I see. What do want of me?" she asked.

"I need you help to obtain a rather special artifact from a faraway temple," he said. "This temple sits in the center of a long-forgotten city where ancient kings committed unspeakable acts in the names of their twisted gods. The city stands empty now and half-obscured by the jungle that tries to reclaim it."

As he spoke, Gorinna got the odd sensation that he was using magic to cloak his true identity. She also realized that he actually was "speaking" through his cat, hence the weird disembodied vocal effects.

The man intrigued—and disturbed her.

"Why do you need me? Why not just enter this temple yourself?" she asked.

"Alas, no man can enter that sacred place. The spirits and entities who guard it allow only women inside. Yet, or so the legends go, those women who have entered it have never been seen again. I believe that only a woman of very special talents such as yourself can hope to enter that place and come out alive. That is why I've traveled all this way. You have a reputation for braving the unknown and your powers are almost legendary," he said.

"That coin you sent to me—" she began.

"Yes. It *did* come from that city," he said.

This intrigued her. The coin wasn't made of any Earthly alloy that she was aware of and it literally vibrated with hidden power. Was it used as part of a ritual at the temple? And where was this place? She searched his face for hidden answers but saw nothing but shadows. She looked down at the cat who simply yawned at her.

"I have several questions," she said.

"I will reveal all but only *after* you've agreed to help me," the cat said. "What say you?"

"You've piqued my curiosity," she said. "But you know the old saying: curiosity killed the cat but satisfaction brought him back."

The cat squinted at her.

"No offense," she said.

"None taken," the cat assured her. "Does that mean you'll help me?"

"There's no way I could pass up such a challenge. When do we start?" she replied.

"Meet me here at eight o'clock tomorrow morning," the man said.

"Done!" she agreed.

When Gorinna mentioned her decision at the palace, both Chatha and Medusa insisted on going with her. The young warrior queen of Atlantis claimed she was becoming bored "just hanging around the palace".

"I need adventure in my life. I grew up with a sword in my hand and was trained to fight like a warrior. If I don't do something soon, I'm afraid that my fighting skills will deteriorate and fail me when I need them most," Chatha explained.

"I, too, need this adventure. After all, I am a historian and this temple sounds like an ideal place to explore. Besides, I can handle a sword as well as any man I know and I have my special 'talent' to fall back on in an emergency," Medusa chimed in.

Gorinna then went to Arka-Dal and told him of her meeting with the strange man. As she described him in detail, the Emperor gave her a weird look which she picked up on immediately.

"What's wrong? Do you know this man?" she asked.

"In a manner. Many years ago, Merlin told me about an old acquaintance of his. The man you described sounds a lot like him, especially the part about talking through his cat," Arka-Dal said.

"What did Merlin say about him?" Gorinna asked.

"He said he was very old and very powerful. He also lived by his own set of rules and implied that he couldn't be completely trusted," Arka-Dal said.

"I got that same feeling when we made eye contact. I like his cat, though," Gorinna joked. "Do you think we should go with him?"

"Why not? I'm curious to know what he's after and why. Besides, the three of you can take care of yourselves better than most men I know. Go with him but be careful. Your first impression is probably correct in his case," Arka-Dal said.

He put his hand on her shoulder.

"Knowing you as well as I do, you've already made up your mind to go and there's nothing I can do to stop you," he said.

She giggled.

"You always *could* read me," she said.

"I've known you too long and too well," he said. "Do you feel this sorcerer is evil?"

Gorinna shrugged.

"Not in a pure sense. I feel he's more *amoral*. I think his own interests come above all others and he doesn't care what he has to do to get what he wants," she said.

"Take the headbands with you. They have a thousand mile range and I want you to keep in constant contact with me in case anything goes wrong. I want to know where he leads you and what he's after," Arka-Dal decided. "And *that's* an order!"

"Have you seen Merlin lately? There's much I'd like to ask him about this man," Gorinna asked.

Arka-Dal shook his head.

"Merlin comes and goes as he pleases. I haven't seen him in weeks," he said. "Another thing I remember from my conversation with him is that he said this wizard practiced a most *unusual* form of magic. Merlin didn't elaborate, but he left me with the impression that this guy is dangerous."

"I'll remember that. Thanks," Gorinna said as she left the room.

She met Medusa and Chatha in the hallway and told them what Arka-Dal said.

"I'm not worried," Medusa said. "If he pisses me off, I'll just turn him into a statue!"

They all laughed and went into the parlor to get some wine from the bar.

Later that evening, Mayumi watched Chatha pack for her trip and smiled at her choice of weapons. Chatha glanced up at her and wrinkled her nose.

"Why are you smiling?" she asked.

"Since when do you prefer Nihonjin weapons to your own sword?" Mayumi asked.

"When I started training with Koto-san, I realized the katana was far superior to my sword. It's much lighter and can cut through almost anything. It's also better suited to the Atlantean two-handed style of fighting. I like the yumi because it has longer range and greater knock-down power, although it *is* somewhat difficult to draw," Chatha explained.

Koto Masaichi was Arka-Dal's personal trainer. He had been hand-picked by Emperor Jimu Tenno for the position. When not teaching Arka-Dal and his friends the arts of the samurai, Koto acted as a diplomat to the Thulian royal court.

He was 44, tall and wiry.

And every inch a samurai.

Arka-Dal considered him one of the finest swordsmen on Earth—and a personal friend.

Pandaar, Kashi and Chatha also trained under his watchful and demanding eyes. Koto took great pride in his work and was a perfectionist. Each time one of his charges made a mistake, he took great pains to show them how easily they might have been killed. He then corrected their mistakes and taught them several ways to look for and take advantage of their opponents' weaknesses.

Koto instructed them in the use of the sword, spear and bow as well as unarmed combat techniques. It was his way of insuring they'd stay alive under even the worst of battlefield conditions.

When he wasn't training, he wrote haiku and painted nature scenes and sent letters and gifts to his family in Nihon. Unlike his predecessor, he no longer had any desire to prove himself in battle. He'd gotten enough of that during the Shigimatsu rebellion.[12]

"Are you good with the yumi?" asked Mayumi.

Chatha shrugged.

"Koto-san says I need work. I'm bringing it with me—just in case," Chatha said.

"Sounds like Koto-san has turned you into a samurai," Mayumi joked.

"Hell, I'll never be *that* good no matter how much I practice. Do you ever train with Koto-san?" Chatha asked.

"Once or twice a month. Mostly, he teaches me jiu-jitsu and karate. I can use a katana if I have to but I'm not very good," Mayumi said modestly.

Chatha laughed.

"You're better than you admit. I've watched you practice. Leo told me that you also study military tactics and strategy. Is that true?" she asked.

"Hai. It was Aka-san's idea. He said that if anything happened to him, I would become the commander-in-chief of our armies. I may even have to defend Thule one day. So I try to learn to be prepared but I also pray that I will never have to do it," Mayumi said.

Chatha nodded.

She knew exactly how Mayumi felt. Being the daughter of an Atlantean king, she also had to be prepared to take over should her father die in battle. When Arka-Dal captured her, he relieved her of that possibility.

"Will you mind the twins while I'm gone?" she asked.

---

12 Read REALM OF BLOOD

"Of course I will. You need not have asked," Mayumi replied with a smile. "I will treat them as I have always done so—as if they were my own children."

"I know. It's just that I've never left them before," Chatha said apologetically.

"There is no need to explain. I, too, am a mother," Mayumi assured her.

Chatha smiled and nodded.

There were several young children running around the palace of late and all of the women in Arka-Dal's life treated them as if they were their own. Even the son of the late Hercemes Pentassal fit right in with the rest of the family. The children brought new life to the palace, whose wide halls always seemed to echo with the sounds of their playing.

"There! It's done!" Chatha said as she tightened the strap of the bedroll.

"When do you depart?" asked Mayumi.

"Tomorrow morning. I have no idea where we're going or when we'll return. It's all so mysterious," Chatha said as she put the bedroll in a corner of the room. "I guess that's what appeals to me and impels me to go."

"Be careful," Mayumi cautioned said as she sat down on the edge of the bed.

"Don't worry. I trust that old man as far as I can throw a mammoth. Besides, the three of us make quite a formidable team, don't you think?" Chatha said.

Mayumi laughed.

A warrior queen, a witch and a Gorgon *did* make quite a team. All were accustomed to combat and hardship. All seemed nearly absolutely fearless. Mayumi wondered if the old man really understood what he had gotten himself into. If he didn't now, he certainly would soon enough.

It might have been even *more* formidable.

Galya *wanted* to join them but the changes occurring in her body due to her pregnancy were taking an almost agonizing toll on her. As her pelvis expanded to make room for the twins now growing inside her womb, her pain increased.

Mayumi advised her to remain in the palace to avoid jeopardizing her unborn children. Although disappointed, Galya bowed to her wisdom and agreed it would be best to stay at home.

"I had no idea this would be so damned painful!" Galya moaned.

"If you think this is painful, just wait until you give birth!" Mayumi teased.

Galya emitted a groan and stumbled back to her room to rest. Mayumi watched her and chuckled to herself.

At the appointed time, the three women rode up to the front door of the Red Boar and reined their horses to the front rail. When they entered the almost deserted inn, they found the strange wizard seated at the exact same table where he was the day before. It was as if he had never moved. They walked over.

"I'm here, just as I agreed. I brought a couple of friends along, too," Gorinna said as she slid a chair out and sat down.

The cat squinted slightly as Chatha also slid a chair out and straddled it.

"I knew you would bring help," the man said through the cat. "And formidable help at that."

Chatha smiled.

The cat yawned as she introduced herself. Chatha thought that was kind of rude but typical for a cat. Medusa walked around the table and introduced herself. She expected him to at least nod or look in her direction to acknowledge her presence but the wizard never moved. Instead, it was the cat who looked up.

"You're the Gorgon," he said. "We may have need of your unusual talents before this day is done."

Medusa frowned. She had hoped to conceal that fact from the wizard and was surprised at his comments.

"Very little remains hidden from me for long—and *your* fame has also spread beyond the borders of Thule," the cat said.

Medusa laughed as she sat down. Her true nature was certainly no secret in Thule. Until the wizard pointed it out, it never occurred to her that she was known outside the Empire.

"Our horses are outside. We've brought enough provisions to last six days. Will they be enough?" Gorinna asked.

The cat seemed to smile.

"Where we are bound, we will have no need of horses nor provisions. All we will need are our weapons and our wits," he said.

The women looked at each other and shrugged.

"You mean we'll be traveling light?" asked Chatha.

"Ah, yes. *Light* is exactly the right word," he said smugly.

The wizard stood and snapped his fingers. Suddenly, the entire room was awash in bright, almost blinding light. When it dissipated, they found themselves standing in the middle of a wide, rectangular plaza of an ancient, ruined city.

Gorinna blinked.

The city was surrounded by a dense tropical rainforest and it was incredibly humid.

"Where *are* we?" she asked.

"On the other side of the world," said the cat.

"But it took only a second—"she began.

"Less," the cat interrupted.

"You moved us thousands of miles in an eye blink? How?" asked Gorinna as the shock began to wear off.

"*We* did not move. I did not bring us here. Instead, I brought our destination to us," the cat explained.

The women stared at him incredulously.

"Incredible. We traveled a great distance without actually moving. What sort of magic is that?" asked Gorinna. "It defies all of the laws of science and magic."

"The magic I wield is very ancient and not of this world," the cat said. "It obeys no laws save that of my own will. But it, too, has its limits."

"Are those limits the reason you brought us here?" asked Medusa.

"Partly," came the reply.

Gorinna again peered at him. Try as she might, she simply couldn't get a good look at his face, which seemed to eternally shrouded in the shadows of his cowl. Was he purposely concealing his features? Why?

The cat seemed to smirk at her as if were reading her thoughts.

"Just who are you, old man?" she asked.

"My identity will reveal itself to you in due time," the cat said. "For now, I suggest you concentrate on the task at hand."

"Fair enough," said Chatha. "Where is this temple you told us about?"

He pointed a long, bony finger northward.

"It is there, on the far end of this plaza. Lovely, is it not?" he said.

The temple was one of many stone structures in a vast complex of pyramids and long, rectangular buildings. It rose more than 200 feet above the dark, green canopy of the jungle and was partially obscured by vines, weeds and other growth. What could still be seen was nearly breathtakingly beautiful—and ominous.

The temple sat atop a platform of huge, perfectly cut rectangular stones about 160 feet high. It could be reached by a flight of 200 stone steps that went straight up the center of the eastern wall. At the base of the steps were two huge serpent heads with open mouths. Their stone bodies undulated upward on either side of the steps until they reached the upper platform. There stood a rectangular building with one large opening, flanked by life-sized statues of sick, twisted gods.

Evil gods.

Gods who demanded absolute obedience.

Gods who demanded blood.

Human blood.

The statues seemed to glare down at them malevolently. Gorinna stared up at them and suppressed the urge to shudder. The old man seemed to sense her misgivings and smiled.

"I see that you recognize some of the gods depicted here," he said.

"Unfortunately, yes," she said as she continued to study the structure.

It's beauty and construction were almost mesmerizing. Those who constructed it were obviously master builders and stone cutters. The blocks were fitted together so precisely they needed no mortar to hold them in place.

The steps themselves were festooned with ornate glyphs that told of heroic deeds, great battles, great kings and important events.

And tragedy.

She sensed several mass graves beneath the earth. Each contained thousands of victims.

The base of the temple stretched for a quarter mile in both directions from the steps and was also decorated with these glyphs—and stylized human skulls.

Gorinna stared at the heads of the serpents.

Their mouths were wide open. There was hole in each of their tongues and their mouths were stained dark red.

She shuddered.

She knew what those stains were.

"How many were sacrificed here?" she wondered.

"Too many!" came the answer from the thousands of tortured souls who still haunted the place. "Too many."

She forced the voices from her inner mind and turned to the old man.

"What is this place called?" she asked.

"No one living today knows. Its name died along with the ones who dwelled here many ages ago," he said though his cat. "Be most careful. The local natives fear this place above all others. Over the centuries, many of their young women have vanished. They believe that the evil spirits who still dwell here took them and sacrificed them to the gods."

"I sense death here," Gorinna said. "Terrible and painful death. There is much pain here. It is embedded in these very stones and strange glyphs."

"No wonder the natives fear this place," Chatha said. "It gives me the creeps."

"Just what in Hell are we looking for?" asked Medusa as she studied the imposing structure.

"You will know when you find it," the old man replied.

"If you're so powerful, why don't *you* find it?" asked Chatha.

"Many ages ago, one of my ilk did indeed attempt to enter the temple. Too late did he realize that the magic that created it also neutralized his powers. He was discovered by the guardians. Unable to defend himself, he was quickly subdued and sacrificed to one of their foul gods.

Or so the story goes.

No man, no matter how powerful, can enter this place and expect to live. Those who built it do not suffer any man to enter. Only women may do so and many of those who have were never seen again," the man replied.

"And *that's* why you need us!" Medusa smiled.

"*Exactly!*" he said.

Gorinna studied the structure carefully. She could sense a strange, almost omnipotent energy emanating from it. It was quite alien, too. She'd never felt anything like it before and it made her skin crawl. As for the object of their search, she decided that whatever it was had to be extremely powerful or important, otherwise he would not have sought their help. She knew this man was powerful, too. Yet even with his powers, he feared to enter the temple.

"What's in there?" she wondered. "Why can't he enter?"

She took a deep breath, exhaled, and walked toward the temple. Medusa and Chatha followed close behind. The old man and his cat watched intently as they shuffled through the knee-high grass to the bottom of the steps.

"This looks like a Maya or Aztec city. Leo taught me their alphabets. Yet the glyphs are *different* in subtle ways. I've never seen anything like these before," Medusa said as she stopped to study the ones carved into the base of the first few steps.

She looked at the platform some 200 feet above. The steps were stained dark red—as were the gaping mouths of the serpents on either side of the steps.

"They sacrificed people on the altar above. Their blood ran down into channels and came out of the serpents' mouths. It was probably captured in pots or urns by priests as it poured out," she assumed.

"How do you explain the stains on the steps?" asked Chatha.

"They probably sacrificed so many people that their blood overflowed from the channels and ran down the steps," Gorinna said almost in disgust. "If this temple is dedicated to a goddess, she must have been a real bloodthirsty bitch!"

They slowly ascended the steps to the top of the platform. At the very top of the steps was a curved sacrificial stone. Two narrow channels ran from each side and beneath the stone floor, which was littered with broken human bones and ceremonial objects. Behind the altar stood a badly weathered obsidian statue of a rather voluptuous woman. In her left hand, she held a wide-bladed knife. In her right, a human skull. Her face was too badly worn to make her features.

"There's our goddess," Gorinna remarked.

"I wonder who she was?" mused Chatha as she looked up at the statue.

"Whoever she was, she sure as Hell wasn't nice," Gorinna said. "Let's go inside."

Behind the statue was a set of heavy bronze doors decorated with lurid scenes of war and mayhem. Rape seemed to be the most prominent theme and some of the depictions made Medusa blanch with horror. To their surprise, they door easily swung inward when Gorinna pushed it.

Just beyond the door was a scene of nightmarish proportions. They found themselves standing at the top of a flight of wide marble steps leading down several feet into a high-vaulted, rectangular great room. Despite the passage of time, the ancient décor was still visibly opulent, even ornate. Yet they weren't looking at the décor. Instead, they found themselves staring at the remains of an ancient battle.

Everywhere they looked, they saw corpses in various degrees of advanced decay and mummification. Directly in front of them lay two corpses. One lay on its back, a rusted sword still in his left hand and his arms akimbo. On top of him lay the skeleton of a woman with both hands clutching the dagger imbedded in the man's chest. She still had long, blond locks sprouting from her mummified skull and a long spear buried in the middle of her back. They saw other corpses as well. Most were still locked in mortal combat as if they had died fighting over something. The floor was littered with bodies, body parts and battered armor and shields.

Gorinna knelt and looked the place over.

"Must have been one Hell of a fight," she said. "Notice anything strange?"

Medusa and Chatha scanned the room.

"Half the bodies are those of women," Chatha observed.

"Exactly. Most likely, they were the guardians of this temple. They died trying to protect it from these men," Gorinna said.

"I wonder how far the men got?" asked Medusa.

"Do you suppose the object of our search is still here?" Chatha asked.

"There's only one way to find out," Gorinna said as she stood and walked down the steps.

The others followed.

"From the looks of the dust covering everything, I'd say this battle happened centuries ago," Medusa said.

Gorinna nodded.

They walked across the great room and through a pointed arch. As soon as they entered the inner chamber, the light dimmed considerably. Gorinna held up her right hand. A bright, white ball of light formed above her open palm.

"That's better," she said. "Now we can see."

This room was also cluttered with decayed corpses and rusted weapons. With Gorinna in the lead, they walked quickly past the bodies toward a large, rectangular opening flanked by two ornate columns depicting more scenes of human sacrifice and mayhem. The scenes were quite vivid.

"These look like traditional Maya glyphs," Medusa said as they stopped to study the columns.

"What do they mean?" asked Chatha.

"All who enter must give themselves and their blood to the goddess of death," Medusa translated. "This is a place of human sacrifice. The Maya were notorious for that. Most of their bizarre deities demanded human blood and hearts."

"This place reeks of death and terror. The walls and floors almost ring with the screams of their victims," Gorinna said softly.

"Didn't the Maya die out during the First Age?" asked Chatha.

"Yes. They are long gone," Medusa assured her.

"Then who are *they*?" asked Chatha as a tall, strikingly beautiful woman wearing an ornate gold and feather headdress and a dozen scantily clad spear-wielding female warriors emerged from a side door.

The tall woman looked at them and smiled. Then she spoke. To their surprise, they understood every word.

"I am Shizimora, daughter of King Akahuatl and high priestess of the Cult of the Virgins. I bid you welcome to our temple," she said. "Long have I awaited your coming. At long last, the ancient prophesy can be fulfilled. I can go to my eternal rest knowing that this temple and the treasures within are in your capable hands."

"You know why we've come here?" asked Gorinna as she sized the priestess up. She could sense power emanating from her.

Magical power.

The priestess nodded.

"That which you seek is in the next room. But none of you will be allowed to leave this place. The goddess has sent you to take my place. You will be its guardians now," the priestess said haughtily.

"I hate to burst your bubble, but if you're looking for new priestesses, we aren't them. And as for what's in that room—well, it's leaving with us," Gorinna said defiantly.

"Then you are thieves! In that case, you must die!" the priestess said. "Kill them!"

As her temple guards rushed out with spears held high, Medusa calmly lowered her hood. Her action caused the attacking women to look in her direction. Their mistake proved to be their undoing.

The priestess watched in horror as, one-by-one, her guards turned to statues. Angered, she waved her hand. An invisible force struck Medusa and pinned her against the opposite wall. At the same time, the guards slowly returned to their flesh and blood selves.

"Finish them!" the priestess commanded.

Chatha intercepted their charge with one of her own. The startled guards fell back as she deftly sawed off the heads of their spears and skewered the nearest one through her stomach. Before they could rally again, Gorinna let loose with a spell that unleashed a hail of nasty barbed darts. The spell slew half of them. The rest fled from the scene as quickly as their feet could carry them and vanished through the side doors.

The priestess hurled a spear at Gorinna. Chatha knocked it down with her sword in mid-flight. Before the priestess could turn and face her, she threw her sword as hard as she could. It struck the priestess in the chest and sent her tumbling backwards into the next room. Chatha hurried up after her. All she found was a pile of dried, ancient bones and tattered cloth surrounding her katana.

"What happened?" she asked as the others joined her.

"The priestess wasn't alive. She died centuries ago but her spirit remained bound to this temple until she could get someone to release her. She's free now, thanks to you," Gorinna said as she examined the bones.

"And the guards?" asked Medusa.

"They're real. The spirit of the priestess bound them here. They, too, are now free," Gorinna explained. "Free to return to the homes and families."

"At least we've accomplished some good here," Chatha said. "Now where do we go?"

"She said that what we seek is inside that room," Medusa pointed out. "Maybe that's what our friend outside wants, too."

"Let's check it out," Chatha said.

The room was round with a high, vaulted ceiling. The walls were decorated with paintings of strange gods and ritualistic killings and the floor was smooth and white. In the middle of the room stood a simple altar made of white stone.

They looked at each other then slowly walked toward it. Three steps from the altar, the entire room began to vibrate. They felt it all through their bodies. The sensation was sort of relaxing.

Pleasant.

Sensual.

Then the room suddenly went pitch black.

They stopped in their tracks and waited.

A brilliant yellow light emanated from the ceiling and fell upon the altar. The light was so bright, they were forced to shield their eyes from it lest they be stricken blind.

When it finally dimmed, a large, leather-bound tome materialized on the altar. Medusa scowled.

"A book? He sent us after a damned book?" she asked.

They moved closer. Gorinna reached out and gingerly picked the book up. She then ran her fingers over the strange gold printing on the cover.

"This isn't just *any* book," she said.

"Is it the Necronomicon?" asked Medusa.

"No—but it could be just as dangerous in the wrong hands," Gorinna answered. "We must make certain it *doesn't* fall into them."

Chatha and Medusa watched as Gorinna magically created a duplicate. At the same time, the original vanished into thin air. She picked up the copy and smiled.

"I see you don't trust that guy any more than we do," Chatha said with a knowing grin. "Where's the original?"

"In a very safe place. Now let's get out of here and give this copy to our, er, employer," Gorinna said.

They hurried out of the temple as fast as they could. The old man and his cat watched as they descended the steps and raced to where he stood. He saw the heavy leather tome in Gorinna's hands and smiled crookedly.

"Is this what you want?" she asked as she held it up before him.

He nodded.

"Let me have it!" the cat said as his human host reached for the book.

Gorinna tucked it in the crook of her arm.

"I will—but only *after* you've taken us back to Thule," she said. "Until then, I'll keep it."

"Think so?" the man challenged.

Before Gorinna could react, the book vanished from beneath her arm and materialized in his wrinkled hands. He grinned evilly at her. Gorinna stepped toward him but ran right into an invisible barrier. Undaunted, she stepped back and clapped her hands. The barrier dissolved and she moved forward.

Her second spell knocked the book from his grasp. He quickly recaptured it while deftly blocking her third spell. He then made a fist and thrust it at her several times. She had no time to protect herself. Each thrust felt like she was being kicked by a mule. She tumbled back several feet and tried desperately to maintain her balance. The old man moved his fist in an uppercut motion. The unseen blow struck Gorinna under her chin and knocked her off her feet. Before she hit the ground, she aimed another spell at him which opened a pit beneath his feet. To her dismay, he simply hovered above it as if he were still on solid ground.

"This is getting tiresome. I grow bored with your childish antics. Be gone, witch!" he said with a wave of his hand.

The next instant, all three women found themselves standing in the rose garden in front of the royal palace of Thule.

Medusa blinked to be sure it was real. Chatha looked around and shrugged.

"We're back! He sent us home," she said.

"But he's gone with the book and we've no way to track him," Medusa said sadly.

"He's gone alright—but all he has is a copy. Remember?" Gorinna said as she triumphantly held up the original book.

"That's good. But he'll soon realize he has a fake. Then he'll come looking for the real one," Chatha said.

"I *expect* him to," Gorinna said as they walked up the steps and into the palace.

They found Arka-Dal and Leo playing chess in the parlor. Gorinna walked over and handed the book to Leo.

"I brought you something," she announced.

Leo looked at the cover.

"Secrets and Spells of Things Dark and Unholy," he read. "Why give this to me?"

"Open it and read the author's name," Gorinna instructed.

He did. When he saw the name, he whistled. He then showed it to Arka-Dal.

"Alzari?" he asked. "Where'd you get this?"

Gorinna told him about their adventure. Halfway through her story, Merlin, Mayumi and Galya entered the room. Arka-Dal passed the book to them. Merlin seemed amused. Galya laughed outright.

"Any truth to it?" Arka-Dal asked.

"Knowing the reputation of the author, I'd say very little," Merlin replied. "Most of Alzari's writings were mindless ramblings."

"Still that old acquaintance of yours seems to be very interested in it," Gorinna said. "There must be more to this book than we think."

"What do you plan to do with it?" asked Galya.

"We could use it to prop up a crooked table or to hold a door open," Medusa suggested. "Beyond that, it's merely a curiosity."

"Or you could burn it as you did the others," Merlin suggested.

Arka-Dal passed it back to Gorinna.

"Do what you think best," he said as he turned back to the chess match. "Whose move is it?"

"Mine," said Leo as he moved his bishop. "Checkmate!" he announced.

While Arka-Dal laughed and challenged Leo to another match, Gorinna walked to the fireplace and tossed the book into the crackling flames.

Galya nodded approvingly and handed her a goblet of brandy.

"Was Alzari one of your father's clients?" Gorinna asked.

"Yes. He made a contract with Father in order to learn all of the secrets of those who served the Elder Gods. Father enabled him to attain this knowledge. In the end, it drove Alzari mad. The poor fool lived his last three decades tormented by visions he insisted on seeing. His sleep was plagued with nightmares and his waking moments were filled with hallucinations and psychological pain. When death finally took him, Alzari was actually grateful," Galya said.

"Those books are accursed," Leo added as he moved his bishop to take Arka-Dal's rook.

Arka-Dal responded by capturing his queen with a knight.

"Since they're nothing but trouble, why did *you* try to seek them out, Merlin?" Galya asked.

Merlin shrugged.

"I was so afraid they would fall into the hands of a madman that I became obsessed with finding them. That obsession nearly drove *me* mad and almost caused me to destroy mankind's best hope," he said. "I'm glad I failed."

"It wasn't for lack of trying!" Arka-Dal called out.

"I wasn't trying to kill you, my boy. I was testing you, to find out what you were really made of," Merlin said with a wink toward Galya.

"Some test! Couldn't you just have made it some sort of written quiz and make it easy for all of us?" Arka-Dal joked. "Checkmate!"

Leo laughed as he studied the board.

"Why so it is! Another match?" he asked.

"Why not!" Arka-Dal said as they reset their pieces.

Far, far away, the old wizard re-materialized in his secret lair. Triumphant, he walked over to his work table and placed the heavy tome upon it. As the cat perched on his right shoulder, he reached down and slowly opened the cover. To his surprise, the first page was completely blank. He turned the pages faster and faster, only to discover that all were equally blank save for the final page. He looked down at the bright yellow smiley face and slammed his fist into it as hard as he could.

He then flew into an uncontrollable rage that lasted several minutes. The cat watched as he tore the pages from the ersatz book and strew them around the room. After several minutes, he regained his composure and sat down in his tall-backed chair. The cat moved to his lap and smiled as he stroked it.

"You got me this time, witch. You got me good, too. But you haven't seen the last of me!" he said.

The Guardian

In the 42nd year of the reign of Arka-Dal

It was a quiet morning. Arka-Dal, Kashi and Pandaar had just finished their daily workout and were in the study drinking ale and catching up with the local news. Leo, the portly religious advisor, rushed into the room. Arka-Dal glanced up from his newspaper as Leo poured himself a large brandy and sat down at the table with him.

"You look excited. What's up?" Arka-Dal asked.

"I think an important discovery may have been made," Leo said.

"Where?" Arka-Dal asked as he closed the paper.

"In the downtown mall," Leo said. "A group of city workers were trying to trace a leak in one of the city's underground drainage systems. They thought they located it at one of main intersections and started digging a trench. That's when they found something unusual. The local antiquities minister, Kalo Hyrrah, rushed to site. When he saw what they'd uncovered, he radioed me here."

"Oh? Just *what* did they find?" asked Arka-Dal.

"A heavy metal, rectangular slab. It measures eight feet long by four feet wide. Hyrrah believes it's made of some sort of bronze alloy and could be thousands of years old. It may even date back to when the first city of Sumer was erected on that same site," Leo said.

"First city? Just how many cities were here?" asked Kashi.

"At least eight according to our records. The first was built around 6,000 BCE of the First Age. The city was destroyed several times by various natural disasters and invaders. The survivors simply rebuilt new cities on top of the ruins," Leo explained. "Several civilizations have come and gone on this site. Thule is simply the latest."

"Was there anything *before* the first city was built?" asked Kashi.

Leo shook his head.

"No one really knows. Hyrrah said there was an inscription on the slab. He made a copy and sent it over by messenger last night. Here—" he said as he handed Arka-Dal the paper.

Arka-Dal studied it for a long time then shook his head.

"What sort of writing is this?" he asked.

"I have no idea. I've never seen anything like it. Neither has Medusa and she's an expert on ancient languages. I tried to match it against the oldest alphabet we have on file but it's not even close. Those symbols are unlike anything we've found anywhere else. The slab itself may be some sort of door. At least it's the right size for a door but Hyrrah said there are no knobs, locks or apparent hinges anywhere. What's more interesting, he said it's warm to the touch, rather than cool like most metal objects," Leo said.

He was almost gushing with excitement.

"That *is* interesting. Have Hyrrah rope off the entire area to keep souvenir hunters and looters away. If that *is* a door, we need to learn what it's a door *to*," Arka-Dal said.

"Should I tell him to keep excavating?" asked Leo.

"By all means. Make sure he keeps us informed of anything he finds that may offer a clue as to what that door means. I have a strange feeling that there's something on the other side that's waiting to bite us in the ass," Arka-Dal said.

"I was afraid you'd say that. Whenever you get that feeling, all Hell breaks loose around here," Pandaar said.

That same afternoon, Leo and Medusa traveled to the site and watched as Hyrrah's men cleared layers of earth and mud away from the door. They worked deliberately. The men in the pit shoved soil into wicker baskets and passed them up to other men who emptied them onto a nearby pile. The pit itself was ten feet deep by seven feet wide and twelve feet long.

"It's taken us all night to clear this," Hyrrah said as they climbed down the wooden ladder into the pit to study the strange metal door.

Leo knelt and ran his hand over it. It felt strangely warm and vibrant. Almost as if it were alive. He shook the thought from his head and used a brush to uncover the rest of the door. What he saw sent a chill down his back.

Before him was the raised image of a being so bizarre that it strained the imagination. Yet, it seemed eerily familiar.

It seemed to be a hideous combination of several beings—human, animal and even a squid. The torso was muscular and humanoid. The head was large and bulbous with deep set eyes and a beak for a mouth. Instead of arms, six squid-like tentacles radiated from its shoulders.

Above and below it were several strange runes in a language Leo didn't recognize. Medusa copied the symbols into her notepad as she stared at the image.

Leo stood and brushed the dirt from his robes.

"Have you ever seen anything like this before?" he asked Medusa.

She shook her head.

"Have you?" she asked.

"I'm not sure," Leo replied as he looked at Hyrrah.

The doctor also shook his head.

"What do you think?" Hyrrah asked as they climbed back to the surface.

"I don't know what to think at this point," Leo said as he glanced back at the door. "We'll take the inscription back to the archives and see if it matches any of the ancient languages we have on file. As for the image—that thing gives me the creeps!"

"Me too," Medusa echoed.

"Any instructions?" asked Hyrrah.

"Yes. Keep at it and notify me when you're ready to open the door. I want to be here for that," Leo said.

Later that day, they showed the runes to Gorinna. She studied them for several minutes then shrugged.

"They seem to be a combination of several dead languages," she said. "Some of the symbols look like Sanskrit. This one here resembles an ancient Hebrew glyph and the rest are unfathomable."

"That's the way I feel, too," Leo said. "It seems to be a language in its earliest stage of development."

Medusa showed the sketch she had made of the image on the door. The moment she saw it, the color left Gorinna's cheeks. She stared at Medusa.

"Are you *sure* this is what it looks like?" she asked.

"I'm positive. Why? Do you know what it is?" Medusa asked.

"I pray that I'm wrong, but I believe this is the supreme ruler of the Elder Gods," Gorinna replied.

Leo blanched noticeably.

"I just got the sensation of someone walking over my grave," he said after the color returned to his face.

"Tell Hyrrah to be very careful, Leo. That image was placed on that door as a warning. I'm *sure* of it!" Gorinna cautioned.

"We'd better tell Arka-Dal. We don't want whatever's down there to bite him in the ass," Leo said.

Five days later, Arka-Dal and his usual group were at the dig site watching Hyrrah's workers fit a heavy block and tackle to all four corners of the heavy door. One of the men looked up at Hyrrah and gave him the "thumbs up" signal. Hyrrah signaled to the other workers to get out of the pit. Once everyone was safely out of the way, two other men worked the wooden crank and began to raise the strange door.

The door groaned and the pulleys creaked noisily for several minutes. This was followed by a loud cracking sound which Arka-Dal understood was being made by the hinges being pulled apart. Once the door came loose from its frame, two workers jumped into the pit and pushed it out of the way. Hyrrah then ordered the pulley operators to set the door down in the back of nearby wagon so it could be transported to the history museum for further study.

This done, Hyrrah lit an oil lamp and smiled at Arka-Dal.

"Shall we see what lies beneath?" he asked.

"Lead the way, Dr. Hyrrah," Arka-Dal said as he gestured with his hand.

One-by-one, they climbed down the wooden ladder into the pit. To their surprise, they found a flight of concrete stairs leading further down into the structure. Hyrrah went in first. As soon as he reached the bottom, everyone heard him cry out.

"Holy shit!"

They charged in after him. He was standing in the middle of a large rectangular chamber, holding the lamp over his head as he examined what appeared to be a statue lying atop a raised metal slab.

"Leo! What do you make of this?" Hyrrah asked as they gathered around the figure.

They stared at the strange statue. It was nearly 15 feet long with a muscular, humanoid body. The arms were longer than a man's and its powerful legs ended in feet that looked more like rectangular blocks. Its hands consisted of two long, taloned fingers and opposable thumbs. It had no sex organs and its face was flat and noseless with large, seep-set eyes and a long slit for a mouth. It had holes for ears and no hair of any sort.

Leo studied it for quite some time before he ventured an opinion.

"I have no idea what this is supposed to be. It's either an idol dedicated to some bizarre god or it may contain a mummy of some sort. It resembles a sarcophagus, although it's not of any culture that *I'm* aware of," he said.

Medusa tapped it with her knuckle.

"It appears to be made of clay," she said.

"Then it may, indeed, be a sarcophagus." Leo said.

"Are you saying this could be a tomb?" Arka-Dal asked.

Leo shrugged.

Hyrrah's assistant tapped him on the shoulder and pointed to another opening in the south wall. The doctor followed him into the room while the others stayed behind to study the statue. After a few minutes, Hyrrah and his assistant emerged from the next chamber.

"If it's a tomb, it doesn't belong to any ancient king. This place contains no gold, statues nor other treasure that one would expect to find in royal tombs. And there are no signs of forced entry, so this hasn't been looted. But it *does* contain some rather unexpected artifacts," he announced.

"Like what?" asked Leo.

"Come into the next chamber and see for yourself," Hyrrah said.

The chamber contained three small wooden tables, a chair and several long shelves that were cluttered with books, bottles, vials and beakers and an assortment of apothecary bottles. An astrological chart was painted on the ceiling. All were covered by several layers of dust.

"Interesting," said Medusa as she walked around the room.

"Indeed. This appears to be the lair of an alchemist," Leo said.

"You mean one of those guys who tried to turn base metals into gold?" asked Pandaar as he picked up one of the bottles and blew the dust from it.

"Among other things. They were also healers, astrologers, pharmacists and surgeons. Some even dabbled in magic," Leo explained. "Much of their research led to cures that are still used today."

"So our friend out there was an alchemist?" asked Gorinna.

Leo shrugged.

"If he was, he was really big and really ugly," he said as they walked into the antechamber.

They stopped to study the odd looking statue again.

"This is from no culture that I'm aware of," said Hyrrah.

"Maybe this has nothing to do with *culture*," Gorinna said as she ran her hand over the statue. "This thing gives me an uneasy feeling. I don't like it."

"You sense some sort of magic in it?" asked Arka-Dal.

She nodded.

"A dark, sinister magic. I feel that this was created to fulfill a specific task," she replied.

Arka-Dal raised an eyebrow. He turned to Leo, Medusa and Hyrrah.

"I want you to keep digging into this. Find out everything you can about this place. If possible, find out who built it and what our friend here is supposed to be. If you uncover any information that this thing might cause us some real trouble, seal the crypt immediately. Then backfill it so no one else can find it," he said.

"As you wish. We'll work in shifts. My assistant and I will work the first one," Hyrrah offered.

"Good. Medusa and I will return to the archives to see if we can uncover any references to this. We'll return tomorrow afternoon to relieve you," Leo agreed.

"One more thing—this is a relic from the First Age. My experiences with such things have rarely been good. Be careful. This thing could be another one of their nasty weapons," Arka-Dal warned.

As they climbed out of the crypt, Medusa seized Gorinna's arm and whispered in her ear.

"Did you really sense something evil down there?"

"Yes," Gorinna said.

"How evil?" asked Medusa.

"Evil enough to make me sick," Gorinna answered.

Work on the crypt went smoothly for the next few days. The teams managed to catalog all of the artifacts in the second chamber and even located a third, smaller chamber beneath it. This was apparently the living quarters as it contained several trunks filled with musty old clothes, a table with a face bowl and ewer and a large wooden bed, the headboard of which contained the same eerie image that was on the door. The bed was still neatly made to suggest that whoever lived here had walked out and never returned. Everything was layered with inches of heavy dust and cobwebs clung to every corner like hideous shrouds.

"Interesting," observed Medusa. "I see nothing anywhere in this place that could have been used as a light source. There are no candles, lamps or lanterns of any kind."

"This suggests that this entire structure was originally above ground, probably at street level. After all, several cities have since been built over it so that's a logical guess," Leo said.

A shout from Hyrrah caused them to hurry back out into the main chamber. The doctor was running his hands up and down an apparently blank stone wall. He turned and asked Leo to come over.

"Run your hands along this area and tell me what you feel," he instructed.

Leo did as he was told and stepped back.

"There's a seam of some kind. I can feel it just beneath the stucco. Another door?" he asked.

Hyrrah nodded.

"There must be another chamber behind this wall. But why was it hidden? What secrets does it contain?" he wondered.

"Don't open it until I make my report to Arka-Dal. This entry was covered for a reason and we may not like what's behind it," Leo said.

That evening, Leo and Medusa made a preliminary report to Arka-Dal. He listened carefully to their findings, then asked questions of his own.

"Have you deciphered the strange alphabet?" he asked.

"No. But we have narrowed it down to what's known as the pre-biblical era. That would place somewhere between 7,500-6,500 BCE of the First Age," Medusa said. "As far as that goes, we not even sure what civilizations existed at that time."

"The symbols seem to be a cross between cuneiform and very ancient Hebrew. I believe it might have been one of the first written languages," Leo added. "But we're only guessing at this point."

"And the statue?" Arka-Dal asked.

"He's *still* a mystery. We've conducted a few tests and discovered that it's hollow. Other than that, we have nothing to report," Leo said.

"So the place was built by some sort of alchemist or wizard of the First Age. We don't yet know if this was his place of business or his crypt. And we still have no idea what the symbols mean," Arka-Dal summed up.

"That's about it," Medusa said.

"Keep at it. Perhaps when you enter that third chamber, you'll find some answers," Arka-Dal said.

"There's no stopping now, my lad. I feel we're getting close to solving this mystery once and for all," Leo agreed.

The next night, the full moon was at its brightest. While Hyrrah worked in the alchemist's chamber, his assistant snoozed on a chair near door. Around midnight, a beam of moonlight found its way into the antechamber. It shone directly upon the face of the strange statue. After a while, its large, deep eyes took on an eerie orange glow. Slowly, almost imperceptibly, it stirred as if the moonlight had infused it with life. After countless millennia of lying dormant, the statue sat up. Its blank eyes scanned the crypt and saw the light of Hyrrah's oil lamp flickering in the next room. After several more minutes passed, it stood up and walked toward it . . .

When Leo and Medusa arrived at the site early the next afternoon, they found the place to be strangely quiet.

"They must still be asleep," Medusa said. "They must have a long night."

As they walked toward the opening, she noticed several large, rectangular indentations in the dust nearby. They seemed to be moving away from the opening. She glanced at Leo.

"Footprints?" she asked.

He shrugged.

"If they are, they're unlike any I've seen before," he said.

"You'd better shout so they know we're coming down. I wouldn't want to take them by surprise," Medusa suggested.

"Hyrrah!" Leo shouted.

When no answer came, he looked at Medusa and nodded toward the opening. Just before they stepped down into it, Leo called out again.

Nothing.

Just his voice echoing through the silent complex.

When they reached the antechamber, they stopped dead in their tracks. The huge platform where the strange idol had lain was now empty.

"Where did it go?" Medusa wondered as they walked around the platform.

"I can't imagine. It was far too heavy to be moved," Leo said.

"Not without a pulley system and I see no trace of that here," Medusa said as she studied the floor. "All I see are footprints—large, deep ones."

Leo knelt down and checked the depth with his finger. He looked up at her and shook his head.

"I don't like this," he said. "Let's keep searching."

"Dr. Hyrrah has to be around here somewhere," Medusa agreed as they moved deeper into the tomb.

The next room was where Hyrrah and his assistant had set up their office. To their shock, the makeshift desks, chairs and bottles of testing agents were shattered and strewn about the room. Amid the debris, they found the mangled, headless corpse of Hyrrah's assistant lying in a pool of his own blood. Blood was splattered on the walls and ceiling as well.

"Is that?" asked Medusa.

"I believe so," Leo replied.

"Where's his head?" Medusa wondered aloud.

Leo looked at the ceiling and pointed. Medusa looked up and almost gagged. The man's head was embedded in the ceiling, as if pushed into it with great force. In fact, it was barely recognizable.

"Where's Hyrrah?" asked Medusa as she regained her composure.

They walked into the next room. Their eyes immediately went to a large dark mass that seemed to be oozing from a small hole in the wall. Curious, they walked over to examine it. Medusa turned her head to look away. The hole was packed with a mass of broken bones, flesh and clothing. A long line of dark red blood was still cascading down the wall and puddling on the flood.

Leo shook his head sadly.

"Looks like we've found the good doctor—or rather, what's left of him," he said.

"What could have done such a thing? What sort of monster murders men like this?" asked Medusa as she fought to keep her cool.

"And just *where* did that statue go? Has it been stolen? If so, who stole it and why did they take it?" wondered Leo as they walked out of the tomb.

On the way out, Leo stopped to study the strange footprints again. A sudden chill ran down his spine. He looked up at Medusa.

"Are you thinking what I'm thinking?" he asked.

"Yes. But I pray to the gods that I'm wrong! We'd better tell Arka-Dal what happened here," she replied.

"I agree. But first we must inform the local police so they can seal this place off from curiosity seekers."

Arka-Dal took the news with his usual calm. When Leo finished his report, he simply shook his head.

"And you think the statue might be responsible for this?" he asked.

"I'm almost certain. For one, it was far too big and heavy to be carried off by thieves. For another, there were several large, rectangular prints leading away from the entrance. And only something that possesses superhuman power could kill men like Hyrrah and his assistant were killed," Leo said in summary.

"It was the most gruesome thing I'd ever seen," added Medusa.

"So where *is* it? Something that big must have been seen by somebody," Arka-Dal said as he paced the floor.

"So you would think. Yet there have been no reports of any sightings. It's as if the statue just disappeared," Leo said. "This entire episode is more than a little strange."

"There's also evidence of another hidden chamber beneath the first one," Medusa pointed out. "Unfortunately, Hyrrah and his assistant were murdered before they could open it. Perhaps the answers to our questions are down there."

"It's time we took a long, hard look at that site," Arka-Dal said.

An hour later, Arka-Dal, Leo, Medusa, Gorinna, Pandaar and Kashi arrived at the dig site. A squad of city police had roped off the area to keep out curiosity seekers and the rest of Hyrrah's work crew while a team of medics carted out two large, burlap sacks containing the pitiful remains of the doctor and his assistant. Arka-Dal waited as they loaded the sacks into the back of an ambulance wagon, then walked over to the police sergeant who seemed to be in charge of the operation. The officer saluted at his approach.

"What's the situation?" the Emperor asked.

"Pretty bad, Sir. The inner chamber is a total wreck and there's blood stains everywhere. My men found evidence of two more hidden rooms. One is just off the inner chamber. The other is below the first room. It appears that neither have been unsealed," the sergeant reported.

Arka-Dal thanked him and walked through the barrier to the entrance of the site. He knelt down and studied the large, rectangular prints. There were several of them. They seemed to be headed west. He stood up and walked back to the others.

"Whatever made those tracks is big and heavy and was moving toward Andaar Plaza. If we want to find out what did this, we should follow the tracks as far as we can," he said.

Pandaar looked down at the nearest set of prints.

"Are you sure we *want* to find it?" he asked. "Anything that big could be very dangerous."

"That's all the more reason we *must* find it," Arka-Dal said. "Leo—you and Medusa go into the site and try to salvage what you can. Look for anything that might shed some light on this situation. Then return to the palace and try to decipher those weird runes."

Leo nodded.

He watched as Arka-Dal and the others followed the tracks across the street and disappeared behind some buildings, then he and Medusa climbed down the stairs into the site. The immediately went into the inner chamber. The place was in worse shape than they previously thought. Just about everything was completely destroyed. Broken bottles, jars and vials lay strewn across the floor amid debris from broken tables, chairs, shelves and piles of white dust that were once books and scrolls. Leo knelt, picked up a handful of dust and let it sift through his fingers. He sighed.

"All that ancient knowledge—gone forever! What a shame," he lamented as he stood and brushed the remainder from his hand.

"Maybe it's for the best," Medusa said as she walked around the room. "This looks as if it was done deliberately. There's not one single thing still intact."

"Indeed," said Leo. "But why? What is it hiding?"

They followed the prints until they vanished on the paved streets. Kashi and Pandaar searched high and low but could turn up no other prints. Frustrated, they were about to turn back when the sounds of people running and screaming caught their ears.

"It's coming from the plaza!" Arka-Dal shouted as they raced toward the commotion.

When they reached the plaza, they saw people fleeing in all directions as stalls and carts were being violently overturned. A few people were even swept off their as if being struck by gigantic brooms. But try as they might, they could not see the cause of the trouble.

Arka-Dal drew his sword and looked back at the others. Kashi and Pandaar followed his lead then all four cautiously approached what seemed to the center of a small, invisible storm moving down the street. They saw three more terrified people get swept aside. The force seemed to be moving slowly toward them. Then all suddenly fell quiet. Kashi walked out into the middle of the street and looked around. After a few seconds, he turned to Arka-Dal and shrugged.

That's when all Hell broke loose again.

They watched in disbelief as some unseen force seized Kashi's shirt, lifted him off the ground and hurled him into the wall of a nearby building. He bounced off and landed face down in the street. An old man with a walking stick and a young woman carrying an armload of groceries suffered similar fates. The old man was literally pile-driven head first into the sidewalk where his skull shattered like a melon. The young woman was simply brushed aside as if she were a pile of leaves.

"Whatever's doing this is invisible!" Pandaar shouted.

"As usual, you have a knack for stating the obvious," Gorinna said.

"Gorinna—make it visible so we can see what we're fighting!" Arka-Dal yelled above the noise of the panicking crowd that was now running in all directions.

Gorinna raised her hands and gestured. A second later, the sparkling outline of a tall, thick, muscular humanoid appeared in the square. To her surprise, it charged straight at her. She quickly switched spells and tied the creature up in a web of glimmering energy. It stopped, examined the trap, then stretched its arms over its head.

To her—and everyone else's astonishment, both the creature and the magical trap vanished into thin air.

"Where'd it go? There's no trace of it!" she gasped.

"That's the damnedest thing I ever saw. How could something that size simply disappear like that?" Pandaar asked as he ran toward Kashi.

"Just how did you *expect* it to disappear?" asked Arka-Dal as he and Gorinna ran with him.

Pandaar reached Kashi first and rolled him over.

"How is he?" Gorinna asked.

"That thing rang his bell pretty good, but he'll be okay," Pandaar said as he helped Kashi up.

By now two squads of well-armed police were on the scene helping with the injured and clearing up some of the debris. Kashi shook his head and winced in pain. Gorinna smiled at him.

"You'll be fine after I've hit you with a healing spell—but you'll have to rest for two of three days to regain your full strength," she told him.

"Make sure he does," Arka-Dal said. "Any idea what that thing was?"

"From the outline, I'd say it looks like the missing statue. But that's only a guess," Gorinna said.

"Think you can kill it?" he asked.

"I don't know," she replied. "It slipped through my holding spell with incredible ease. It may be magic proof."

"This sounds worse by the minute," Pandaar remarked.

Arka-Dal walked over to the captain in charge of the police squads. The officer came to attention when he drew close.

"We were lucky," the captain said. "Whatever it was only killed two people. It could have been much worse—and would have—if you hadn't shown up."

"I'm afraid you're giving us too much credit. That thing made fools of us. After your men clean up this area, I want you to put the entire force on full alert. Have your men keep watch and report anything unusual as soon as it happens. Unless they've no other option, tell them not to engage that thing. I don't want anyone else killed," Arka-Dal said.

The officer saluted and walked off to see to his men.

"We have a huge problem," Gorinna said. "We have to find something that's invisible and can vanish at will. We need more help."

"Merlin's at the palace this afternoon. Let's enlist him," Arka-Dal said.

When they arrived at the palace, they found Merlin in the parlor with Mayumi, Galya and Chatha, sipping wine and looking comfortable as usual. He looked up when they entered and raised his goblet as a greeting. Arka-Dal and Leo sat down on couch and filled Merlin in on recent events. The wizard listened intently while he continued to imbibe.

"And it vanished without a trace?" he asked.

"It didn't even leave a footprint," Arka-Dal said. "Any idea what we might be dealing with?"

"It could be one of several things, given your description. The fact that it might be an animated statue is most intriguing," Merlin said. "Legends abound of guardian statues that come to life when someone disturbs what they've been set to guard. The stories go back to the pre-dawn of man and stretch from India to Greece."

"No Greek made that statue," Medusa avowed. "It was far too crude."

"I see. I think the best place to start is in the archives. I also want to see the image you copied from the door and the strange inscriptions. Perhaps they will provide us with a clue," Merlin suggested.

"When do you wish to start?" asked Leo.

"There's no time like the present," Merlin replied as he rose and refilled his goblet. He smiled at them and winked. "Sometimes it is best to try and look at things while slightly inebriated. Besides, you wouldn't want me to get thirsty, would you?"

Arka-Dal laughed as he watched him, Leo and Medusa leave. Hours passed. When he didn't see any of them at dinner that evening, he decided to check on their progress.

He went down to the archives and found Leo, Medusa, Gorinna and Merlin seated around a large table. Several stacks of books lay atop it and Medusa was groaning and pulling at her hair. They looked up when he sat down with them.

"What are we dealing with people?" Arka-Dal asked.

"A 14-foot tall, quarter ton humanoid who can become invisible and vanish at will. He also seems to be impervious to magic spells," Leo said.

"Is it alive or dead?" Arka-Dal asked.

"Both—and neither," Leo replied.

"Care to explain?" Arka-Dal asked.

"Our adversary fits the Cabbalah's description of a golem. The nearest I can make out from the information we have on hand, golems were created from clay and infused with life by magic," Leo said.

"Any idea what it wants?" asked Arka-Dal.

"Not a clue," Medusa said. "We have very little information about golems in the archives. It's very ancient and almost obscure Hebrew folklore."

"Perhaps the rabbi, Saul, might be able to go into more detail," Arka-Dal suggested.

"I was thinking along those very same lines," Leo said with a smile.

"Any idea how old that site is?" asked Arka-Dal.

"I used my magic to get a reading. It dates back to 5400 BCE of the First Age—the very dawn of the coming of the Jews," Gorinna said. "In those days, they were more mystical than spiritual. They dabbled in all sorts of magic and charms and even worshipped dozens of different deities."

"Interesting," Arka-Dal mused. "And the image on the door?"

"We still believe it may depict one of their Elder Gods, or even a demon," Medusa said.

"It's not any Elder God that I'm aware of," Merlin said with certainty.

"Nor is it a demon," said Galya as she entered the room. "I've studied it for hours. I know every demon on all of the Planes and that image fits none of them. I asked Father's opinion and it stumped him, too."

"What of the inscription?" the Emperor asked.

"It appears to be an early form of *several* alphabets, such as Hebrew, Sumerian and even Indus Valley script. But it's so different from any of them that we haven't been able to decipher anything," Merlin said. "It's nothing that I've ever seen before."

"So we still have no real idea what it means?" Arka-Dal asked.

"Not at this point," Merlin said. "Gorinna's guess is as good as any right now. Alchemists were known to carve or paint wards and images on the doors of their shops to both protect themselves from evil and to identify the fields of knowledge they specialized in. Perhaps the one who built this specialized in demonology?"

"The golem and that image are connected somehow. I can *feel* it," said Gorinna.

"So far, that thing's killed four people and damaged several buildings. We have to stop it before it does anything else," Arka-Dal said.

"First, we must *find* it, my boy," Leo pointed out. "With its abilities, that won't be easy."

"Get on it," Arka-Dal said as he rose and left the room with Galya.

Gorinna noticed that Medusa watched Galya's every move but her expression remained unchanged.

"You don't seem to be irritated by Galya's presence like you used to," she observed.

Medusa smiled.

"Neither do you," she said. "I really like her now and her children are adorable. There is no jealousy between us."

And there wasn't.

The four wives were as close as sisters now and their family ties were stronger than steel. Once everyone got to know the *true* Galya, she became real easy to like—and trust.

Gorinna liked her, too.

So did Merlin.

What's more, they trusted her completely.

To make matters even more interesting, Merlin and Gorinna had grown to like Galya's infamous father.

"Things get stranger around every week," Medusa continued. "I wonder who Arka-Dal will marry next?"

Gorinna and Leo laughed.

"It's time to visit the rabbi," Leo announced.

Saul was the senior rabbi of Thule's small community of Jews. He was also a good friend of Leos' and had once served in the Thulian Army out of respect for Arka-Dal and Thulian Law. He now spent most of his days studying the Talmud and performing rituals for his followers.

Saul was in his seventies and sported the neatly-trimmed beard that was the mark of his station. His hair and beard were flecked with white, silver and gray, which gave him the look of a man who possessed great wisdom. Saul, in his own humble way, would be the first to deny this. He simply thought of himself as a servant of his god and his people.

He kept a small residence behind the temple, which also included a library with an extensive collection of ancient texts and a small museum of Hebrew artifacts. Leo and Gorinna found Saul seated at his desk in the library. He was going over the Torah with a magnifying glass when they entered. He smiled and raced over to greet them each with a warm embrace. He offered them some black tea and sweets as he showed them to seats near his desk.

"What brings you here, my friends?" Saul asked as they sat down.

"We have a slight problem. If it's what I think it is, it's right up your alley," Leo said.

"I'm all ears," Saul said.

Leo explained all that had happened since Hyrrah discovered the site. He went into great detail with Gorinna filling in anything he was a little fuzzy on.

Saul leaned back in the chair and looked at them.

"You say this thing is a golem?" he asked.

"I'm not really certain. I was hoping that you would shed some light on this. To be honest, I have very little idea as to what a golem is," Leo admitted.

Saul nodded.

"In our folklore, a golem is an image or idol that has been brought to life by means of a shem or magical charm," he said. "This myth has been handed down since the beginning of the First Age."

"What is a shem?" asked Gorinna.

"A shem is a combination of letters in the Hebrew alphabet that form a sacred word. Usually, it's one of the names of God. It's written on papyrus and either placed in the golem's mouth or tacked to its forehead," Saul explained.

"The golem itself takes many forms. At first, it was a perfect servant but it had a bad flaw of following directions too *literally.* They were also created as guardians of certain places, people or objects. During the First Age, Rabbi Judak Low created a golem to wreak havoc and revenge upon his enemies—with calamitous results. The one you described seems to fall into this latter category," he added.

"How does one stop a golem?" asked Leo.

"By removing the shem," Saul replied. "Without that, the golem is merely an ornamental statue."

"Removing the shem sounds next to impossible! How does one get close enough to do that without being killed?" Medusa asked.

"You must find a way to knock it down and pry its mouth open. That's the way it was supposedly done according to the legends. But, there are, however, a few things about your golem that trouble me. It has rather unique magical abilities. No golem that I've ever read about can do what you said this one did," Saul said.

"Any idea why it's moving around?" asked Leo.

"It appears to be *searching* for something. That also means it was created to complete a specific task. This is also quite unique," Saul answered.

"By the way, what happened to Rabbi Low?" asked Medusa.

Saul smiled and shrugged.

"No one really knows. Some chronicles say that the golem killed him. Others that the people of the town burned him at the stake for witchcraft. Either way you look at it, he came to a very bad end," Saul said.

"What might this golem be searching for?" asked Leo.

"Could be anything. An ancient treasure or perhaps a sacred object. Only the golem knows the answer to that," Saul guessed.

They thanked him and left.

At dinner that evening, they told the others what Saul had said. Merlin shook his head.

"It's a golem alright—but no self-respecting rabbi created it. Whoever brought this to life also endowed it with magical abilities.

That means it was created by a sorcerer. As to its purpose, that's anybody's guess," he said.

"Discover its purpose and we might be able to defeat it," Arka-Dal said matter-of-factly. "We know that the vault it was in dates back to the Biblical Era of the First Age. Hence, whatever it's seeking must be a relic from that same era. Saul said it could be looking for a sacred object. What sacred objects existed at that time?"

"There were several," Medusa said.

"Which are specifically associated with the Jews?" Arka-Dal asked.

"The Ark of the Covenant is the first that comes to mind," said Leo. "It's never been located.

"Yes it has," Galya said smugly.

"Then *where* is it?" asked Merlin.

"On the 664th Plane of Hell," she replied. "It's in Father's private collection."

"The Ark is in Hell?" asked Leo with more than a little surprise. "How deliciously ironic! The Ark was supposedly given to the Jews by God himself. It's their most sacred object."

"How did your father come by it?" asked Merlin.

"He snatched it from Solomon's Temple moments before the Babylonians sacked it. He just couldn't bear to see it destroyed. After all, it is one of his finest pieces of work," Galya said.

"*His* work? You mean to say that the Devil created the Ark?" asked Leo.

Galya nodded.

"He created it to hold the sacred tablets he gave to the Jewish high priests. I believe they were later called the Ten Commandments—but they are nothing like they are described in the Old Testament," she said. "For one, there were over 600 of them originally. It was a well thought out code of law and justice. When Yaweh's minions got hold of them, they discarded most of them and came up with ten that suited their purposes. But the originals are still in the Ark."

"What else is in that Ark?" asked Leo.

"The One True Name of God—one they were to invoke to protect themselves from his wrath. But when they did try to invoke him, he screwed them over royally and scattered them across the Earth. The god of the Hebrews and Christians was a mean-spirited, vengeful and vindictive deity. He always took great delight in tormenting the Jews, so Father decided to help them," Galya explained.

"And just how did their god take this?" asked Merlin.

"He sicced the Babylonians on the Jews and told them to wipe them off the face of the Earth. Lucky for them, they are a very resilient people. They have a knack for overcoming the worst of times. I think that's why Father likes them so much," Galya said.

Merlin laughed so hard he shed tears.

"If that golem's seeking the Ark, it has a very long way to go," Galya remarked.

"Indeed it does," said Merlin. "You know, the more I learn about your father, the more I actually like him. He's quite a fellow."

"Father would be very pleased to hear you say that. He's always liked *you* despite your differences," Galya said.

Leo was still in shock.

The idea that the Devil actually created the Ark of the Covenant to help protect the Jews from god's wrath went counter to all he'd ever read. He wondered how Saul and the Monsignor would take such news. After some consideration, he decided against telling them. After all, there was no sense in turning two such minor religions inside-out. He glanced over at Kashi.

He'd been raised in a mosque by five Ayatollahs to be a devout Muslim. Instead, Kashi had decided it was all so much bullshit. He kicked Islam to the gutter and decided to form his own relationship with Allah and whatever other gods were out there.

Leo himself was more than a little open minded. He didn't follow any particular group of gods or religion, mostly because he could not prove nor disprove that gods existed. Instead, he studied every religion inside and out. He kept the things that made good sense for himself and discarded most of the ritualistic crap. Along the way, he became the world's leading expert on gods, religions, religious laws and mythology. It was this knowledge that led Arka-Dal into naming him the Pope of Thule—which simply meant that Leo was his chief advisor on religious affairs.

Arka-Dal—like most of his close friends—followed no particular religion or gods. Like Leo, he was reserving his judgment until someone could prove that gods existed—or didn't. This attitude was also shared by most of the Thulian people, who had little or no use at all for gods but didn't mind if other people worshipped.

Arka-Dal poured himself another glass of wine and sipped it as he mulled over what was said.

"I guess we can rule out the Ark. What *other* artifacts could it be after?" he asked.

"If that golem dates to a time before the Jews became an established people, there's no telling what it's after. Very little information still exists from that era and the script on the door is indecipherable. In fact, our alchemist may not have been Jewish at all—and that makes this situation even more problematic," Leo said.

"Indeed," echoed Merlin. "The earliest known records of the Hebrews date to 5,800 BCE of the First Age. Our "tomb" is at least 500 years older. Supposedly, the Hebrews didn't yet exist."

"I see. Any guesses?" Arka-Dal asked.

They all shook their heads. He finished his wine and poured himself another.

"I want you to return to that dig and open those other rooms. The answers might still be down there somewhere," he decided.

The sun was at its highest.

Leo and Medusa stood back and watched as the workmen labored in the midday heat. Sweat streamed from every pore of their muscular bodies as they took sledge hammers and picks to the inner wall of the so-called tomb. After what felt like an eternity had passed, a large opening appeared before them.

"Step back," said Leo as he moved forward and stuck his head through the opening.

The room smelled musty, which was only natural since it had been sealed for several millennia. Seeing nothing through the settling curtain of dust and debris, Leo turned to the foreman.

"Have your men cart away the rubble. When they're finished, there might be other rooms we'll need access to," he said.

"You got it, Boss," the foreman said.

Leo and Medusa lit a lantern and stepped into the room while the men carried out baskets of dirt and broken rock. The room was large, almost perfectly square and quite empty. As they walked across the floor, Leo nearly tripped over something beneath the layers of heavy dust. His curiosity aroused, he bend over and brushed the dust away with his hands.

"Well I'll be—," he muttered.

There, chiseled into the middle of the stone floor was an exact copy of the strange figure that was on the entrance of the tomb. This time, it was nearly twice as large.

"It's him again!" Medusa said almost in disgust. "I'd love to find out who or what it is."

"Perhaps we shall before this is over. Let's just hope we don't live to regret it," Leo said.

"There might be another chamber beneath this," Medusa suggested.

"Let's find out. I'll call the workers in and have them break though it," Leo said as he walked back through the opening.

He spotted the foreman talking to two of his men and walked over.

"I have another task for you," Leo said.

As the foreman received his instructions from Leo, they heard hurried footsteps on the stairs. Arka-Dal turned to see a sweaty guard appear in the doorway.

"Sire! That thing's come back!" he shouted.

"Where?" asked the Emperor.

"Shallow Harbor Road," the guard answered.

"That's only eight blocks from here," Kashi said.

"You and Gorinna get on it. Don't take any unnecessary risks but try to find some way to contain out friend," Arka-Dal ordered.

They both nodded and bounded up the stairs. Arka-Dal turned his attention to Leo and Medusa again.

"Let's try to decipher these odd runes before we pry open this hatch. For all we know, they may be a warning," he said.

By the time Kashi and Gorinna reached Shallow harbor Road, the golem was on a rampage. They arrived just in time to see it pick up a passing fruit wagon and toss it across the street. The wagon slammed into a wall with a loud noise and sent splintered wood, fruit, wheels and other debris flying in all directions. Luckily, the driver had abandoned the wagon just as the golem seized it. His horse, however, was a broken wreck amid the debris.

People ran for their lives as the thing plodded up the street. Hapless city guards pelted it with spears and stones and anything else they could lay their hands on but it was all to no avail. All of their missiles glanced harmlessly off the thing and it kept plodding relentlessly up the street.

"I have an idea," Gorinna said as she raised her hands above her head.

"What are you going to do?" asked Kashi.

"Arka-Dal told me to contain it, so I guess I'll do just that," she said as she uttered an incantation and let her spell fly.

In an eye blink, the golem found itself completely encased by a gigantic, inverted and clear bell which stopped it in its tracks. It reached out with one hand to examine its new prison the stepped back. Everyone watched as it raised both fists and pounded the bell several times.

It held.

"You did it! You trapped it!" Kashi shouted as he hugged Gorinna.

"I doubt he'll escape this time," she said smugly.

Her expression changed to one of astonishment and dismay as the golem began to rotate faster and faster like a top. The gyrations kicked up a great cloud of dust and rock that obscured it within the bell. The sound was also deafening and caused everyone nearby to clap their hands over their ears. When the sound stopped, the bell stood empty save for a mound of earth in the center. Gorinna eliminated the bell and raced over to the spot the golem had stood. When Kashi caught up with her, she was standing there cursing in several languages.

"That thing bored its way out and filled in the escape tunnel with dirt behind itself," she said as she clenched her fists and let out another long string of epithets. Kashi let her vent for awhile. When she'd finished, she took a deep breath and knelt to examine the mound of earth.

"How on Earth did it manage to do that?" asked Kashi.

"What he did should have been impossible. I even made sure that I sealed the trap beneath his feet. No one, not even Merlin, could have escaped that!" Gorinna said.

"I beg to differ," came a voice from beside her.

She stood up and smiled as Merlin appeared from thin air.

"You saw?" she asked.

"Yes. It was quite fascinating," he replied as they walked back down the street together.

"What are we dealing with, Merlin?" she asked.

"I'm not sure. I've never seen its likes before," the wizard said. "One thing is certain—that is no golem. No golem created by man can do what that thing just did. Golems are *relentless.* They are created to fulfill a single purpose and they keep going until that purpose is fulfilled. They do not run away. They cannot vanish into thin air. If that's a golem, it was created by a means that I am unaware of."

"That's what Saul said," Kashi pointed out.

"Saul should know. After all, golems are part of Hebrew folklore," Merlin said.

They returned to the site and reported what happened to Arka-Dal and the others. The Emperor emitted a deep breath in frustration while Merlin knelt to examine the image on the floor. As he reached out to touch it, sparks leapt out of it and forced him to recoil.

"That's odd. It didn't do that when I touched it," Gorinna said.

"I didn't?" Merlin asked, surprised at her comment.

"No. See?" she said as she ran her hand over it.

Nothing happened.

Merlin attempted to touch it once again. Again, sparks crackled from it.

"Interesting. If I didn't know better, I'd say it was designed specifically to keep *you* out," Leo observed.

"Perhaps it was," Merlin said as he rubbed the numbness from his hand.

"If that's the case, then whoever made this must have *known* you. But this place is thousands of years old—" Medusa said.

"And *still* young by *my* standards," Merlin smiled. "If this was built by an acquaintance of mine, I can't imagine who that was. The image is unfamiliar to me, yet the source of the magic is somehow familiar. This was placed here as a protective ward."

"That means the answer to our golem problem lies beneath it. Can you break it?" Arka-Dal asked.

"I think so," Merlin replied. "But doing so might bring the golem down on us and I'm not certain I can deal with him."

"Do it," Arka-Dal decided.

Merlin pushed everyone back a few steps and raised his hand. He then went into a deep state of concentration as he silently mouthed the words to one of his spells. They watched as the slab became engulfed by a soft, blue glow and a low hum filled the chamber. A second later, the door caved inward and a gust of stale, putrid air rushed into the chamber. The smell was so potent, it forced everyone to dash for the surface where they coughed and spat for several minutes.

"What was that? Some sort of trap?" asked Pandaar as he recovered.

"No. That was the stench of time," Merlin said cryptically.

Kashi climbed down and sniffed.

"It's safe now," he shouted.

They found another flight of stone steps that lead down into another rectangular chamber. Gorinna used her light spell to illuminate the room, which was furnished only with a small, round wooden table. Atop the table was a small, coffin-shaped box. They approached it cautiously. The closer they got to the table, the more nauseas Gorinna felt. Merlin noticed her uneasiness and touched her arm.

"I feel it, too," he said.

"Whatever's in that box reeks of evil," she said. "It's weighing on me like a wet blanket."

Merlin stretched out his arms to either side.

"Stand back while I check this out," he said.

They stood and watched as Merlin placed his hand on the box—then quickly recoiled as sparks engulfed it. He waved his hand over it. The box sizzled ominously, popped a few times, and then became silent. Satisfied, he reached out and opened the lid. The others gathered around as he took out a small clay statue and stood it upright on the table.

Merlin studied it with great care. He picked it up and turned it several times. He even pressed it to ear and listened before passing it to Gorinna.

"Tell me what you hear," he said.

She held it to her ear awhile then stared at him.

"It sounds like the beating of a human heart," she said. "But why?"

"A golem needs a source of power to give it movement and purpose. Without one, it's nothing more than a lifeless statue. Hebrew legends say a spell written on a piece of paper and placed inside the golem's mouth powered it. But this magic is far more ancient than that. Instead of a shem, whoever created this creature used an outside power source—and this statue could be that source," Merlin explained.

Gorinna put down the statue and backed away. They stared at her as he obviously fought down the urge to vomit.

"What did you hear?" asked Merlin.

"There's a heart inside the statue—a living, beating human heart!" she forced out.

Arka-Dal looked at it and shook his head.

"Are you saying that someone was sacrificed to power that thing?" he asked.

Merlin nodded.

"Most likely the victim was one of the mage's slaves or assistants. I doubt he gave up his heart willingly," he said.

"If this is the power source, then logically, if we destroy it, we'll shut down the golem," Arka-Dal said.

"It sounds reasonable," Leo said.

"I'll have to test it to be sure," Merlin decided.

"How?" asked Arka-Dal.

"I'll decide that when our friend reappears," Merlin replied.

Arka-Dal ordered a squad of city guards to secure the site then he and everyone else walked back to the palace. Their dinner conversation was lively, to say the least as they talked about the golem and who might have created it.

"The magic involved here is quite different than I'm used to dealing with, yet is seems familiar somehow," Merlin said.

"Anyone who'd kill a human being in order to use his heart to power that thing is one nasty son-of-a-bitch," Gorinna added. "I've never seen such a spell before and hope I never do again."

"You said it seems familiar. Could this be the work of your friend with the cat?" asked Arka-Dal.

Merlin nodded.

"But that site is *thousands* of years old. It dates to the earlier part of the First Age!" Leo pointed out.

"And still young by *my* standards," Merlin said. "If this was indeed created by my old acquaintance then there must be a very sinister purpose behind it."

Arka-Dal thought about the last two appearances the golem made and went over its most logical route in his mind.

"It appears to be headed in a northeasterly direction. If it continues on its current path, the next stop would be the Hall of Heroes. What was there before?" he asked.

Leo shrugged.

"There's no way of knowing without doing some serious excavation work. That could take years. Like I've said, there were at least a half dozen major cities and civilizations on this exact spot over the millennia. What our friend is seeking lies buried beneath tons of debris now," he said.

"Even if we did excavate, we still might not find anything. Most likely, the thing it's looking for is long gone. But the golem has no way of knowing that. It's just a mindless machine following a preprogrammed directive," Merlin added.

"If it was created by our friend with the cat, you can bet the object it's searching for will be of no benefit to mankind," Gorinna said. "There's something puzzling me about your friend, Merlin."

"And what is it that puzzles you, my dear?" Merlin asked.

"Many mages and witches have animal familiars. Many are black cats or white hares or even owls. In the case of your friend, is he the magic user and the cat his familiar or is the other way around?" Gorinna queried.

Merlin smiled and shook his head.

"I've never been able to discern that. I know that he speaks through the cat but I have never understood why. It is a most *unusual* arrangement," he said.

"All this is moot. We must find a way to stop that golem before anyone else gets hurt," Arka-Dal said.

Merlin ran his hand over the odd statuette on the table between them.

"I think this little fellow is the solution to that problem. When the golem reappears, let *me* handle it," he said.

"If you stop that thing, you'll piss off whoever made it," Pandaar warned.

"That's exactly what I hope to do. I want to smoke him out and force a long overdue confrontation," Merlin said.

"Can you handle him?" asked Arka-Dal.

"That remains to be seen," Merlin said. "In any event, it will make for a most interesting encounter."

"Maybe we should sell tickets," Pandaar joked.

"That's fine—but I insist on half the gate," Merlin joked back.

Pandaar laughed.

"Is the man with the cat one of your father's clients?" asked Medusa.

Galya shook her head.

"Oh, no. I'd have heard about this one. I have no idea who this magician is of from where he derives his unusual powers. From what you've said about him, I'd say he's no joke," she said.

"He's not the type to seek out the Devil's nor anyone else's help. The man is mentally unbalanced and more than a little paranoid. He's too suspicious to ask help of anyone he considers to be a threat," Merlin said.

"He asked *me* for help," Gorinna pointed out.

"Yes—and he told you *why.* At the time, he figured you were no threat to him. I'm sure *that's* changed now," Merlin said. "You beat him at his own game and made off with the book. He'll not forgive that."

"Does this guy have a name?" asked Kashi.

"He has had several over ages. I don't know which one he goes by now," Merlin replied. "I do know that his quest for forbidden knowledge and power has driven him insane and *that* makes him even more dangerous."

Later that evening, Merlin and Gorinna sat in the parlor and drank wine while Arka-Dal and Mayumi played a game of Go. Medusa was in the archives with Leo trying to decipher the strange runes they found in the vault. Chatha and Galya tended to the children. The other women in the Dal household understood the bond between the Emperor and Empress and usually gave them a lot of "alone time". Merlin observed as he usually did and marveled at how well Arka-Dal's wives got along with each other. Their friendships ran deep and strong. If there was any real jealousy between them, they kept it well hidden.

"You've been spending more time here than usual lately. Any particular reason?" asked Gorinna.

"I like it here. It feels more like a home than my own abode. I enjoy the harmony of this house and its people," he replied.

"Do you think our friend with the cat is really behind this?" she asked.

"One never knows with the likes of him. This does have his stamp all over it. It feels like something he would do. Since he created the golem so very long ago, I tend to wonder if he even remembers doing it," Merlin said.

"That thing is long past its 'use by' date, that's for sure," Gorinna said. "I'd love to know what it's after. Wouldn't you?"

"Not really," Merlin said. "Anything missing this long can stay missing."

Arka-Dal rose and went to the bar. He poured himself a brandy and a wine for Mayumi. He stopped in front of Merlin.

"You're up late, old friend," he commented.

"I rarely sleep this early," Merlin said. "Besides, everyone's awake now. Even your children."

Arka-Dal nodded.

"I keep thinking about the golem. Where do you suppose he goes when he vanishes?" he asked.

"I'd say he drops into another dimension somehow," Gorinna suggested. "He certainly leaves no trace behind."

"I agree," Merlin said.

The next day passed without incident. Leo, Medusa and a crew of workmen returned to the vault—as they now called it—and searched anew for more hidden rooms. Halfway through the day, one of the men called out that he had found something. Leo immediately contacted Arka-Dal who, along with Merlin and Gorinna, raced to the site. They arrived just as the workmen broke through the north wall.

"We found another chamber," Leo said as they watched the workers clear away the debris. "This was sealed on purpose."

"To keep us out or something in?" asked Merlin as he picked up a lantern and walked through the opening.

Gorinna and the others were right behind him. What they saw made their blood run cold.

"Oh my!" said Merlin as he shone the light upon piles of human bones skulls that littered the stone floor. The bones were heaped around a stone altar. On either side stood large stone vats built to catch the blood that ran down the channels.

"This is a sacrificial chamber," he said. "And it was apparently put to good use by whoever built this place."

Gorinna stooped down and picked up one of the skulls and turned it over and over. She lay it down gently and picked up another. They watched as tears rolled down her cheeks.

"They were all *children*," she said. "All of them less than five years old. What sort of monster could do this to innocent children?"

"The kind who worships an even more monstrous god," Merlin said as he studied the altar. "There must be *hundreds* of them down here. That meant that hundreds of families were robbed of the joy of seeing their children grow up. What a tragedy."

"There's that strange god again," Leo said as he pointed to an image chiseled into the ceiling right above the altar. "Didn't the Elder Gods demand human blood as a sacrifice?"

"Those horrific beings demanded all sorts of foul things," Merlin said as he studied the image. "I'm still not sure just who this one is."

"It seems to be a combination of several beings, none of which make sense," Medusa said. "It is certainly not human. Nor does it look like any animals that I'm aware of."

"I'll have the workers gather up these bones and try to give them a proper burial. It's the least they deserve," Leo said sadly.

Arka-Dal nodded.

"Does your old acquaintance believe in human sacrifice?" he asked.

"I can't imagine *what* he believes in," Merlin replied.

They head heavy footsteps behind them and turned just as one of the city guards entered. He saluted Arka-Dal.

"Sir! That golem has returned," he said.

"Where?" asked Arka-Dal.

"One block to the west of the Hall of Heroes," the guard reported.

"This is where I come in," Merlin said as he suddenly vanished.

He reappeared not a hundred feet from the golem and watched as it lumbered toward the Hall. Merlin spread his arms then clapped his hands. A fireball appeared and launched itself at the golem. It struck it dead center and showered the area with sparks and embers. The golem stopped and turned toward Merlin.

"Now that I've got your attention," the wizard said as he pulled the statuette from the folds of his cloak. He raised it high then slammed it to the ground as hard as he could. At the same instant, the golem fell to its back with a great crash as if something very powerful had knocked its feet out from under it. Merlin smiled as the golem scrambled to its feet and plodded toward him. Just before it reached him, Merlin pulled out his dagger and plunged it into the chest of the statuette. Just as he expected, blood gushed from the statuette and dripped to the ground. At the same time, the golem clutched its chest as if were having a heart attack, reeled back several feel, spun around and fell face-first to the street.

Merlin tossed the statuette to the ground and walked over to the golem just as a squad of soldiers, Arka-Dal and the others ran up. The golem remained completely still.

"Is it dead?" asked Gorinna.

"Yes," Merlin said. "It will bother us no more."

"What do we do with our friend here?" asked Arka-Dal.

Leo beamed.

"I've an idea. Since the golem is now completely harmless, why not put him and his little brother on display in one of our museums?" he suggested.

"Why not turn the entire vault into a museum? Your historians and craftsmen could recreate the smashed furnishings and other equipment. You can place the golem back on its table and place the statuette in a glass case nearby along with information on what they are and how they were used. I'm sure it would be quite popular," Medusa said.

"That's a great idea! What do you think?" asked Leo.

Arka-Dal nodded.

"First, I want to have a good long look at the vault to make sure there aren't any more surprises. We also need to learn more about the time period this came from and who built that vault. Do you think that's possible, Merlin?" he asked.

"Anything is possible if one perseveres," Merlin said as they walked back to the vault.

At the exact instant Merlin plunged his dagger into the small figure, two young men riding with their friends thousands of miles away suddenly clutched at their chests and emitted painful groans. The younger brother, Rolf, toppled from his horse and hit the ground hard while Zorn struggled to remain in the saddle. The leader of the group, James Colla, watched as Patrice Vertrez leaped off her horse and rushed to Rolf's aid.

"Are you alright?" she asked as she helped him to his feet.

"I'm okay now," he said as he rubbed his chest. "I just got this sudden pain. It was like someone stabbed me in the chest."

"Me, too," said Zorn. "I thought I was having a heart attack or something. But the pain's gone now."

James dismounted and examined each of them. Finding nothing, he shrugged and mounted his horse.

"Both of you appear to be alright. Whatever it was did no apparent harm," he said.

"That's what you say! I bruised my ass when I hit the ground," Rolf complained. "What do you think it was?"

"I have no idea right now. There's a village just beyond that next hill. We'll stop there for the night and I'll check you both again to make sure no harm's been done," James said.

As he watched the others ride on ahead of him he wondered if the saga of the Brothers Yaren was about to take yet another bizarre twist.

Earthfall

In the 42nd year of the reign of Arka-Dal

The Devil sat on the jagged, broken edge of a tall, ruined tower perched atop a high black mesa. The tower overlooked miles of charred, crumbling buildings, twisted steel girders, fallen bridges and broken roads that were the remains of a once-great city. Long ago, eight million people thrived here. Now it belonged to wolves, hyenas, rats and other scavengers that roamed its rubble strewn streets.

This was the result of some of *his* work—*indirectly*. He had attempted to bring down a handful of already-corrupt politicians and military leaders and cause some chaos within the country. Instead, millions had died.

Needlessly.

The chaos spread beyond the borders of the city-state and led to the nightmarish wars that led to the Great Disaster and the Dark Age that followed. It also flooded Hell with billions of unwanted souls—most of whom did *not* belong there. It took his people millennia to sort the mess out and left him with more than a little egg on his face.

Ever since, he'd been picking his marks carefully in order to avoid another such disaster.

Those he could not sway he assigned to Galya. She had *never* failed. Then she met Arka-Dal and fell madly in love with him. They had even married and she had borne him twins. Because of this, he swore an oath to protect Thule for as long as a descendant of Arka-Dal and Galya walked the Earth. And he *always* kept his vows.

The man he'd wanted to bring down more than any other was now his *son-in-law.*

To make maters even stranger, Merlin, his sworn enemy, was now his ally because, he, too, protected Arka-Dal. The sorcerer had even given him the fabled Excalibur.

It was enough to beat the Devil.

And it did.

Life just didn't get any stranger than that!

"Oh well," he said to himself. "There are plenty of easy marks out there for me to sway. Too bad that none will prove to be as challenging as Arka-Dal."

The desert sky provides a clear, unobstructed view of the heavens for the people of Thule. Shooting stars are among the most common sights. That's why hardly anyone in the Empire paid much attention when one streaked across the night sky. Even the astronomers paid it little mind. Had they bothered to observe it, they would have realized that this one was quite different.

It didn't burn up in Earth's atmosphere like most meteorites. It plummeted toward the Great Gray Wall mountain range to the north and west of Thule. Unlike most meteorites, this didn't fall in a straight path. About 1,000 feet above the ground, it suddenly leveled off, then zigzagged several times before crashing into the mountains with a loud boom and a huge flash of orange light.

Arka-Dal and his usual companions were dining on the balcony of the royal palace, as was their habit on most warm nights, when the strange meteorite caught their attention. They stared in disbelief at the unusual path it took and how it lit up the entire valley when it struck the earth.

Arka-Dal looked at Leo who was seated across from him.

"What do you make of *that*?" he asked.

"That was *no* meteorite. I'd bet the state treasury on it," Leo replied.

"Then what was it?" asked Medusa.

Leo scratched his head.

"I don't know, my dear. I've never seen anything behave like that before. From the odd pattern it flew, I'd guess it was some sort of flying machine," he said after a while.

"A flying machine? You mean like the ones the First used to have?" asked Arka-Dal.

Leo shrugged.

Arka-Dal scowled.

Kashi turned away from the rail of the balcony and returned to his seat.

"I'd say it crashed about 400 miles northwest of here. That's an eight day ride, even under the best conditions," he said. "Of course, we'll have to leave right away."

Arka-Dal laughed.

Kashi could read him like an open book. He knew he'd never be able to resist checking this out. From the looks on everyone else's faces, he knew they all felt the same.

"Would you like to join us on this one, Leo?" he asked.

Leo beamed and nodded.

"I wouldn't pass this up for the world," he said.

"Outpost 17 is in that immediate area. I'll radio the post commander and tell him to seal off the site until we can investigate it. There's no sense taking chances until we're sure the area's safe," Pandaar said.

"Get on it. I want everyone ready to ride by sunup tomorrow," Arka-Dal decided.

The Great Gray Wall was the series of tall granite peaks that separated the lush Valley States from the almost waterless Western Desert. There are 14 passes through the mountains. All are different in size, appearance and general makeup. Even climate and weather conditions vary wildly from pass to pass.

Three of the passes are well-traveled caravan routes that connect the Valley to the coastal nations. Rivers and streams dissect each of these passes, making them ideal places for horses, men and camels. Most of the others passes are used by herdsmen, nomadic tribes and outlaws.

Each pass is protected by two small stone forts—one on the desert side and one on the Valley side. The forts are called "outposts" and the size of the fort and the number of soldiers stationed at each reflects the importance of the passes they protect.

Outpost 17 was a four acre stone fort on the eastern side of the Great Gray Wall. Its 400-man garrison guarded the central pass that led through the mountains and into the Western Desert. Nearby were two small villages that served as the recreational outlets for the soldiers at the fort. Outside of the usual bars, gambling dens and whore houses, there was little to do around Outpost 17.

The area to the east of the fort was the open grasslands known as the Yboe. The only things there were herds of cattle and a score of scattered ranches. Outpost 17 was where one was stationed when his career was nearly at an end.

Such was the case of Captain Bern Haikum. He had enlisted in the army at the age of 16 and had served with honor for 35 years. He was a tall, baldheaded man with a bushy gray mustache. He was a pragmatic, mostly unimaginative man who reacted well during emergencies.

As soon as the object made contact with the side of the mountain, Haikum sent 40 men under the command of Sergeant Haim Faez out to secure the area and to make sure that no one had been injured. As soon as Faez left the fort, the radioman came running into Haikum's office with the orders from Pandaar-Vli.

Haikum laughed.

"Please inform Pandaar-Vli that I have already taken care of the situation. Tell him that I shall meet them at the crash site," he said.

He chuckled as the radioman left the office. He walked over to the large map of the region on his wall and studied it carefully. If the object landed where he believed, it was at least 30 miles away from inhabited areas. But shepherds and cattlemen often grazed their herds in the mountain passes. He wanted to be sure that it didn't strike any of them.

Like Arka-Dal, he figured it couldn't have been a meteor. He, too, had wondered at the bizarre path it traveled. He had read that the First had launched many large objects into space before the Great Disaster. Could one of them have returned to Earth after all those millennia? If not, then *what* was it and *where* did it come from?

He decided to join his men at the site and leave the real investigation up to the Emperor and his friends when they arrived.

The object would provide a pleasant break from the boring routine of the fort. It was something unusual that would tide him over until his scheduled retirement in six weeks. As the sun rose in the sky, Haikum mounted his old gray mare (who, like him, wasn't what she used to be) and headed to the crash site ten miles away.

When he arrived early that evening, he saw that his troops had roped off the area and stationed guards to ward off the curious. As he approached the check point, Sgt. Faez ran out to greet him.

Faez was a large, barrel-chested man with several battle scars. Like Haikum, he was pragmatic and more than a little bit skeptical.

"Where's the site?" asked Haikum as he slid down from his horse and handed the reins to a nearby soldier.

"Up ahead about 1,000 yards. You're not going to believe this!" Faez said as they walked through the pass together.

They walked through a trail of rubble that had been kicked up when the object hit the ground and skidded like a discus into the pass. The rut it created was several inches deep in spots, indicating that whatever struck the ground was heavy and probably smooth. Had it been a meteorite, it simply would have created a crater on impact. Haikum saw no sign of that. The ruts intrigued him.

They came to a massive mound of rocks and earth and shattered trees and stopped. Faez pointed although the gesture wasn't needed.

"By the Gods!" was all Haikum could utter as he beheld the cylindrical metal object protruding from the mound.

When the Emperor and his company arrived later that week, they found Haikum's soldiers hard at work in the pass. Half of the men were digging around the object with shovels. The rest were either on guard or carting away the earth away and dumping it on the other side of the pass. Haikum saluted when he saw Arka-Dal. The Emperor returned the salute as he surveyed the situation.

"What do we have here?" he asked.

"As far as I can tell, it's some sort of heavy metal object. My engineer estimates that more than half is still beneath the ground. The impact was so great, it kicked up mounds of soil and rocks and left this deep rut in the ground," Haikum reported.

"Any idea what it is?" asked Leo as they walked toward the object.

"Not a clue. It's cylindrical and made of some sort of alloy that appears to be very tough. In fact, despite the impact, there's not even so much as a scratch on it," Haikum said.

"Interesting," said Leo as he examined it closer.

"It's just as you said, Leo. It's not a meteorite. Now we just have to figure out what it is and where it came from," Arka-Dal said as he touched the side of the object.

"Did your engineer have time to write a report?" Leo asked.

"He wrote a preliminary report. I have it in my office back at the outpost," Haikum replied.

"I'd like to read it," Leo said.

Arka-Dal nodded in agreement.

"As you wish. The outpost is a half hour ride from here," Haikum suggested.

"Let's get going then," Arka-Dal said. "Have your men keep digging. We may have to move that thing to Thule for a closer examination."

"*That*, my boy, will be an engineering feat in itself," Leo said.

When they reached the outpost, Haikum led them to his office. Arka-Dal, Leo and the others sat down around his desk while he opened his file cabinet, took out a folder and passed it to Leo. He scanned it quickly and passed it to Arka-Dal. After a few minutes, he handed the folder to Gorinna.

"My compliments to your engineer. He was more thorough than I thought he'd be, given the unusual circumstances. I'll radio Thule and have our civil engineers come out and give that thing a good going over," he said.

"I was hoping you'd say that, Sir," said Haikum. "We'd appreciate all the help you can send. I, for one, am anxious to find out what that thing is."

"Aren't we all," Arka-Dal commented. "Meanwhile, have your men excavate as much of the object as possible—but be careful. We don't know what it is. It may prove to be dangerous."

"I understand. We'll take all the usual precautions," Haikum said as Gorinna handed him the file. "When can I expect the engineers?"

"I'll have them out here within the week," Arka-Dal promised. "Meanwhile, I want you keep alert. If anything unusual happens with that thing, I want you to notify me at once. Don't take any unnecessary chances with it."

Arka-Dal and his party left the outpost early the next morning. Before they did, the Emperor went to the radio room and contacted Jun at Northern Army Headquarters. He ordered him to send his chief engineers to the pass to examine the object and write a report. Jun promised to have them out there within three days.

It was nearly two weeks before their report arrived at the palace. As soon as the messenger brought it to the Emperor, he handed it to Leo and told him to go over it.

"Read it carefully then tell me what you think," he said as he plopped down in the chair in front of Leo's desk.

Medusa was also in the archives, doing some research on a strange inscription that was copied from a recently discovered ruin far to the north. Leo told her to stop what she was doing and come and have a look at the report.

As Leo read the engineers' report and shook his head. The thing in the pass didn't resemble any of the ancient spaceships that had been built by the First.

"A craft of any sort would have some sort of propulsion system and a port for viewing where it was going. This doesn't," he said as he passed the report to Arka-Dal.

The Emperor leafed through it and sighed.

"According to this, the object has no doors, windows, visible engines or seams. It simply appears to be a 42 foot long metal cylinder. Something like that couldn't possibly fly," he said.

"Exactly. What's in that pass goes against all of the known laws of physics and aerodynamics that I am aware of. To make matters even more interesting, there isn't a dent or scratch anywhere on it. Considering the force of the impact, it should have shattered. Right now, our men should be out there hauling away chunks of wreckage. Instead, the object is in perfect condition and far too heavy to move in one piece," Leo added.

"What's it made of?" asked Arka-Dal.

"I have no clue—yet," Leo replied. "It's an alloy no one's ever seen before. I'm guessing that it's titanium based because that's what the First made their craft out of. I may be wrong."

Arka-Dal nodded.

"Is it from somewhere on Earth?" he asked.

Leo shrugged.

"No nation that I know of currently has the technology to fashion anything like this. I'm convinced that it can't be from here," he replied.

Arka-Dal raised an eyebrow.

"Then you think it's from *another* world?" he asked.

"I'd say that would be a safe bet," Leo said. "Oh—one more thing. It seems to be hollow."

"Hollow? Then there might be *passengers* aboard. If so, they might need medical attention—if they're alive," Arka-Dal said.

"Opening that cylinder could prove to be very risky. It could contain alien bacteria or viruses that might be fatal to humans. I recommend that we proceed with extreme caution," Leo explained.

"I agree. Have the engineers take all the necessary precautions. I don't want to trigger any sort of plague," Arka-Dal said as he left the archives.

Medusa looked up at Leo.

"What we have is a puzzle wrapped inside an enigma," she commented. "What if it's some sort of weird weapon?"

Leo shook his head.

"In that case, we'd better bend over and kiss our asses good-bye," he said with a smile.

Upstairs, Galya and Mayumi were in the bedroom. They had just finished bathing. Both were naked. Galya studied Mayumi's figure. She was perfectly proportioned and her skin was almost flawless.

Almost like fine porcelain.

They had been discussion their mutual love for Arka-Dal and how they would gladly do anything for him. Mayumi finished drying herself off and sat down on the bed next to Galya.

"I think you are the most beautiful woman I ever saw," Mayumi said. "No wonder Aka-san fell in love with you."

"I love him, too. But there's someone I love just as much," Galya said as she leaned close.

"And who is *that*?" Mayumi asked, although she already knew the answer.

"I love you," Galya said as she placed her hand on Mayumi's thigh.

The Empress smiled and parted her knees as Galya's hand moved slowly upward. She didn't normally have sex with women but she found Galya irresistible. Her kisses were electrifying. Her touches thrilled her and her tongue drove her wild with desire. After that first time, she gladly parted her knees for Galya every time she wanted her to. And Galya gladly did the same for her.

"Mmmm. That's good. Give me more!" Mayumi cooed as Galya's tongue danced between her legs.

Things in the valley were quiet. The object ceased to attract much attention from the locals and most likely didn't pose a threat. Nonetheless, the ever-cautious Haikum decided to maintain an around-the-clock guard on the strange object. He assigned two men to each four hour watch and checked on the site daily. For days, nothing unusual happened.

Then came that fateful night.

The two guards sat atop a pile of rubble smoking their pipes and joking as they normally did. Most of the men at the Outpost considered the watches a piece of cake. Since it relieved them of other, more unpleasant duties, Haikum had no trouble getting his soldiers to volunteer.

As the two soldiers talked, they heard an eerie low humming sound. They dropped their pipes and looked around. The humming grew louder and louder.

"I think it's coming from the cylinder," one man said.

"It has to be coming from it. There's nothing else out here but that thing and us," the other said as they walked toward the object.

As they approached, the object began to emit a light green glow, which grew more intense with each passing second. The humming also grew louder and louder and soon reached a point where the guards couldn't hear anything above it. They approached the cylinder with their spears at the ready and with great caution.

They never saw what hit them.

The next watch arrived three hours later to find their comrades sprawled face-down on the ground. They rushed over to see what was wrong—and recoiled in disgust at the sight of their dry, leathery skin and sunken faces.

An hour later, Haikum and the company doctor and a squad of well-armed soldiers arrived. The captain watched and waited while the doctor examined the dead soldiers. After a few minutes, he stood and shook his head.

"I've never seen anything like it. There's not a drop of bodily fluids in either of them. They almost look as if they've been *mummified*," he said.

"What did this?" Haikum asked.

"Be damned if I know. There are no signs of a struggle or any tracks nearby. You'd better inform the Emperor," the doctor suggested.

Haikum did just that.

While they waited for Arka-Dal to arrive, he also doubled the guards. Arka-Dal, Leo, Gorinna, Pandaar and Kashi arrived in Gorinna's magic bubble two hours later. They landed in the pass. Haikum saw them and rushed over. He saluted. Arka-Dal returned it.

"Report, Captain Haikum," he said.

Haikum told him all he knew. When he was finished, the Emperor turned to Gorinna and pointed to the cylinder.

"Use your magic to check that thing out. I want to know what's inside," he said.

She walked to the side of the cylinder and placed both her hands on it. The metal felt unusually cool, despite the fact it had been sitting in the desert sun for several weeks. She walked slowly around it, making sure to keep one hand pressed against it the entire time. When she returned to her starting point, she pressed the other palm against it. After several minutes passed, she placed her ear to the object.

Nothing.

Frustrated, she stepped back and folded her arms across her chest. She then raised her hands and concentrated on "seeing" through the hull. She tried for a long time. When her temples began to throb painfully, she lowered her hands and rubbed the sides of her head. Then she walked back to the others.

"Anything?" asked Arka-Dal.

"Eyes. I saw eyes," she replied.

"Eyes? You mean there's someone in there?" asked Leo.

"I didn't say that. I said I saw eyes. Two large, dark green eyes," Gorinna corrected.

"Human eyes?" asked Kashi.

"I don't know. I've never seen their like before. They just made contact with mine then my head began to ache and I had to stop," she replied.

"Anything else?" asked Arka-Dal.

"I sensed emotions," she said.

"Which ones?" asked Leo.

"Fear and *hunger*," she answered. "Whatever's inside that thing is hungry. It desperately needs to feed but it's also afraid. *Very afraid.*"

"That might explain what happened to those guards. They became food for whatever's in the cylinder. It probably lives on body fluids, such as blood. It attacked them and sucked them dry then fled back to its lair to avoid detection," Leo surmised.

"You make it sound like a *vampire*!" Pandaar said.

"Perhaps it *is*," Leo said.

"We need to lure it out and kill it before it can suck the blood out of anyone else. I'll have Haikum bring up a couple of small cows and tether them nearby. Then we'll wait and see if that thing takes the bait," Arka-Dal decided.

"And if it does?" asked Kashi.

"We'll try to kill it before it can flee back into the cylinder," Arka-Dal replied.

For two days and nights, nothing happened. The cows which were chained to stakes embedded in the ground lazily grazed on the sweet grass near the cylinder. Guards watched from the top of a nearby cliff and waited.

On the afternoon of the third day, Faez, who was on watch, radioed back to the Outpost that the cylinder was glowing. Arka-Dal, Haikum, the others and a squad of horsemen hurried to the scene and arrived just in time to see an indistinct gray blur emerge from the side of the cylinder and move toward the oblivious cows. The rapid-moving figure briefly obscured the animals then sped back into the cylinder at a speed they couldn't even guess at. By the time they reached the cows, they were lying on their sides and looked as dry as old leather.

Arka-Dal dismounted to examine one of the cows.

"So much for that idea. Anyone get a good look at it?" he asked.

"All I saw was a blur!" said Gorinna.

"Same here," said Kashi.

"It left no tracks of any sort. That means it doesn't travel through the same physical space and time we do," Leo observed.

"Care to explain that?" asked Arka-Dal.

"Anything, even objects that move at high velocity, have mass. Such things always leave tracks or prints. Anything that doesn't move in the same time or space as we do, *won't* leave tracks because it doesn't exist in our dimension," Leo said.

"So that's why it appears to be moving so fast?" asked Gorinna.

"Most probably. We see it in a time other than the present. It probably moves in the future, so it can't leave tracks because it hasn't been here yet," Leo replied.

"That's as clear as a barrel full of slime," said Pandaar.

Arka-Dal wrinkled his nose.

"So we're dealing with something that transcends our space and time? And that's how it can move into and out of an object that has no visible doors?" he asked.

"Something like that," Leo replied.

"Do you suppose it's intelligent? Can it be reasoned with?" Kashi asked.

"That is not known at this point," Leo answered.

Arka-Dal studied the cylinder.

"How on Earth do we get in there to deal with this thing?" he asked.

"I could try to get us inside," Gorinna offered. "But since we don't know what we're dealing with, we could end up like those cows."

"I hope not. I've never looked good in leather," Leo joked.

"Me neither," said Pandaar.

"*You* never look good in *anything*," Kashi jabbed.

Pandaar replied by extending his middle finger.

Faed ran down from his post and pointed at the cylinder. It was glowing again. Before anyone could react, something emerged from it and made a bee-line straight for Arka-Dal. A split second before it reached him, he dropped to one knee. In the same instant, he drew his sword and slashed at his attacker, using the draw/killing stroke he had learned from his trainers.

The creature emitted a high-pitched, agonizing wail that echoed through the valley. A thick, foul-smelling liquid gushed out of it and splattered Arka-Dal just as it fell motionless to the ground before him. He bent over to examine his kill as the others ran over to him.

The creature was lean and sinewy with long, muscular arms, boney fingers and a pressed-in face. Its hideous mouth sported a long, ugly beak that tapered to the width of needle and it was sparsely covered by coarse, gray hair.

"What the fuck is *that*?" asked Pandaar.

"It appears to be some sort of alien primate," Leo said.

"Is it an animal or a person?" asked Arka-Dal.

"Perhaps it is a bit of both," Leo suggested. "I won't know until I've had the chance to dissect it."

They looked at the cylinder then back at the creature.

"I can't believe that this thing has the intelligence to build and navigate such a ship," Gorinna remarked.

"Perhaps it did neither," Leo said.

"Explain," said Arka-Dal.

"This appears to be a most primitive life form, barely on the level with one of our gorillas or chimpanzees. Such a creature could not have built this ship," Leo said with a measure of certainty.

"Are you sure? If it can come and go as it pleases—" Gorinna began.

"I see where you're going with this," Leo said. "Even a chimp can learn to master certain skills if given enough time. If this ship came from a distant world, this creature had *years* to learn how to master some of the technology. When you think about it rationally, that's not so big a stretch."

"We *have* to get inside that thing. We need to know if there are more of these things aboard and if it has a crew in need of help," Arka-Dal decided as he looked at Gorinna.

She nodded.

"Gather close to me," she said as she raised her arms.

They moved next to her and waited as a bright white light shimmered around them. This was suddenly followed by complete darkness. When they were able to see once again, they found themselves standing in the middle of a large open cargo bay filled with cages of various sizes.

"This is incredible," Arka-Dal said. "The inside seems vastly larger than the outside would indicate."

"This is all due to the fact that this ship occupies a completely different time and space than we do," Leo explained.

"This looks like some sort of zoo," Kashi pointed out. "We're surrounded by cages."

"Let's look around—but be careful," Arka-Dal said as he drew his sword.

They walked through the cargo bay and peered into each cage. All contained various animals—or what remained of them.

"These animals appear to be long-dead. They look as if they've been mummified," Pandaar said.

"Every one of them contains some sort of animal," Arka-Dal added as he studied the dried carcasses.

"Not all of them. This one's *empty*," said Kashi as he stood in front of a long, rectangular cage. "These bars have been pushed *outward.*"

"Looks like whatever was in it escaped. Most likely, it was our furry friends," Arka-Dal said.

"They must have broken out and feasted on the other animals," Leo observed. "When they finished with them, they probably went after the crew."

"Do you suppose any of the crew are still alive?" asked Pandaar.

"I *sense* something," Gorinna warned. "We're being *watched.*"

"Draw you weapons and be alert. Watch each others' backs and kill anything that jumps out at you!" Arka-Dal ordered.

"You don't have to tell me *twice!*" Pandaar said.

"How many do you think there are?" asked Leo, referring to the creatures.

"That cage looks like it could hold at least four of them," Gorinna said.

"Let's hope that's all there are," Arka-Dal said as they headed toward the open door on the opposite wall.

They walked down a long, wide corridor for several minutes. The entire ship was dimly lit by hidden light sources, so there was no need for Gorinna's magic. They soon came to another open door, this one human sized. Arka-Dal poked his head through the opening and looked around.

"There's some stairs to the right. They go up," he said.

"Let's check them out," said Pandaar as he took the lead.

They walked up to a landing. The stairs turned sharply left and went up again then led to another deck with cabins on either side.

All the doors stood open. One looked as if it had been battered in. They explored each cabin they passed. There were eight in all. Six contained the dried remains of crewmen in metallic jumpsuits of various colors. Two clutched strange pistols in their dead hands. One man was sprawled across a desk. Another lay on his back in bed.

"These people were taken by surprise. Those things moved so fast, they never had a chance to defend themselves," Arka-Dal said.

"They never expected them to break out of that cage. They probably didn't know they were capable of doing that," Gorinna said.

"Are we still being watched?" asked Leo.

She nodded.

"How close is it?" asked Kashi.

"Very close," she replied.

They heard heavy breathing behind them. Before they could react, something large and hairy charged out of the shadows and barreled into Arka-Dal. The Emperor rolled with the blow and immediately sprang back to his feet and took a fighting stance. The creature glared menacingly at him then charged again. He braced for a blow that never came. Gorinna intercepted the creature with one of her more deadly spells. When it struck, all that collided with Arka-Dal was a cloud of fine dust.

He sneezed.

"Thanks," he said.

"Glad to be of service," she said with a bow.

"Do you sense any other life forms here?" he asked.

"Yes. And they are watching us," she warned.

"Are they more of these creatures?" asked Pandaar.

"Definitely—and they're pissed off. I think I just killed one their mates," she replied.

"That's too fucking bad! With any luck, the rest of them will soon join it," Pandaar scoffed.

"Perhaps we should try to capture one of them for study. After all, these are strange, new animals," Leo suggested.

"No, Leo. These things are dangerous. We can't allow them to thrive. There's no telling what diseases or germs they may have brought with them. Such things could destroy all the life on this planet if allowed to spread. We have to hunt them down and kill them.—just to be on the safe side," Arka-Dal countered.

"You're right, of course," Leo agreed. "But I still think it's a shame we have to kill them all."

"Maybe we'll save one for you—as a pet!" Kashi joked.

"No thanks. I'd much rather have a cat!" Leo said.

They walked to the end of the corridor and found another set of steps. They climbed them up to a large, open area that contained three long tables and what appeared to be a kitchen/serving area against the left side.

"Must be the galley," Pandaar said.

"You have a knack for stating the obvious," Kashi quipped.

"Yeah—and your fly is open," Pandaar said.

Kashi stopped to check.

"No it isn't!" he said.

"Made you look, didn't I?" Pandaar said smugly.

"May you wake up next to an ugly camel," Kashi cursed.

"Oh, your mother's in town?" quipped Pandaar.

As they walked through the galley, they found five more crew members lying on the floor. Two clutched weapons. One of which appeared to be a rifle of some sort. All were as dry as leather. The room itself was a wreck with chairs, utensils, broken glass and other debris scattered about.

"Everything here points to a nasty battle," Kashi said.

"The crew must have run in here to make their stand," Pandaar said.

"Yes—a *last* stand," Leo observed.

"Are we still being watched?" Arka-Dal asked.

"Every step of the way," Gorinna replied.

"How many?" he asked.

"I can't tell. It keeps changing," she said.

They left the galley and continued down the hall. They soon came to another flight of stairs that led upward to a closed metal door. There were two strange symbols on it.

"I wonder where that goes?" pondered Leo.

"Let's find out," Arka-Dal said.

As they approached the door, it slid open automatically and the lights came on inside. They entered and saw a large screen that covered almost the entire front wall. Below it was a long console with hundreds of brightly colored keys. There were four chairs in front of it. Two were still occupied.

Behind this were two smaller consoles. The chairs lay on their sides. There were bits of debris scattered over the floor and seven bodies. Six were emaciated humanoids in bright blue metallic jumpsuits. The seventh was one of the creatures. Two of the crewmen had the strange-looking pistols in their mummified hands. All were as dry as dust—including the corpse of the creature.

"Interesting," Leo remarked. "It appears that this creature has also been drained of all its body fluids. Those things must also feed on each other."

"Now *that's* comforting!" Pandaar said as he looked around the room.

"This must be the bridge," Kashi said. "This was the command and control center of the ship."

Arka-Dal sat down in one of the empty seats and stared at the strange symbols on the keyboard. Try as he might, he could not make heads or tails of them. Leo and Gorinna walked over and peered over his shoulder. He glanced up at them.

"What do *you* make of these?" he asked.

Leo shrugged.

"I have never seen their like before. This is no Earthly language that I'm aware of," he said.

"I don't know it, either," Gorinna added. "This ship most likely came from another planet. It may have taken *years* to get here."

"The science involved in this is amazing. These people must be millennia ahead of us. Think of what we might accomplish with such a ship!" Leo said.

"Once we've hunted down the last of these creatures, I'll have our men reverse engineer this to see what makes it tick. Once we learn all there is to learn about this and the people who built it, we may build one of our own," Arka-Dal said as he stood up.

"Do you intend to explore the stars?" asked Leo.

Arka-Dal laughed.

"No. But I am interested in new technologies we can safely adapt for the betterment of our people. The stars can wait," he said.

Gorinna smiled.

That was exactly what she'd expected him to say.

"There may be other ships up there, searching for this one. Once they find it, they'll also find *us*. I'm not too sure I'd like that," Arka-Dal said as they left the bridge.

"They may not have peaceful intentions. They might even try to stick us in cages like the creatures on this ship," Leo warned.

"That's why we need to learn all we can about this ship. We need to have a fighting chance—just in case," Arka-Dal said.

"Technology is one thing, but we have *magic*," Gorinna said rather smugly.

"But what if they have magic?" Leo posed.

"You're just full of pleasant thoughts, aren't you?" Pandaar said.

As they walked along the corridor, Gorinna raised her hand. The others stopped.

"What's wrong?" asked Kashi.

"Something's nearby. It's watching us. I can sense it," she said.

"Why doesn't it attack?" asked Arka-Dal.

"It's curious about us. It's trying to figure us out before it does anything," she replied.

"That suggests *intelligence*. It's animal, but intelligence nonetheless," Leo said.

"Like a chimp," Arka-Dal added.

"Indeed—only it doesn't eat bananas," Leo said with a smirk.

As Kashi turned the next corner, something large and hairy charged out of the wall to his left. It moved so swiftly that it barreled into him before he realized what was happening. The impact knocked him against the opposite wall. As he bounced off, he drew his pistol and fired two shots just as it charged again. Its momentum carried it forward. This time, Kashi managed to sidestep it. The creature smashed into the wall and screamed in pain. Before Kashi could get off another shot, it whizzed past him and vanished through the wall.

The others reached his side just as he regained his feet.

"What happened?" asked Arka-Dal.

"One of those things attacked me. I managed to shoot it before it could finish me off," Kashi said.

"Where is it then?" asked Pandaar.

"It went right through that wall over there," Kashi said with a nod.

"You mean you only *wounded* it?" Pandaar asked.

Kashi nodded.

"Great! Now it's pissed off. Good fucking work!" Pandaar said with disgust. "Now we *have* to track it down."

"Can we?" Arka-Dal asked as he looked at Gorinna.

"I can't sense it anymore. It's gone," she said.

"Gone? Where?" he asked.

"I don't know. I can tell you this: it's *not* on this ship," she replied.

"Shit! That means it's outside somewhere. It'll cause all sorts of Hell before we can track it down. Anything else aboard?" Arka-Dal asked.

"Yes—and it's watching us," she said.

Haikum and Faed waited outside the cylinder with a company of their soldiers. Most of the men just sat on the nearby rocks and talked while their officers paced nervously and watched the strange ship. A few of the men napped in the shadows of the cliffs or gambled with dice and cards.

"They've been in there for an hour now," Faed said. "What's happening?"

Haikum shook his head.

"I wouldn't worry about them. That bunch can handle anything that comes their way," he said.

That's when he happened to glance skyward. A bright speck way off in the distance caught his attention. He watched for awhile, thinking it might be a shooting star. When it suddenly changed course and leveled off, he realized it wasn't. He tapped Faed on the shoulder and pointed.

"What do you make of *that*?" he asked.

Faed shielded his eyes as he watched the object change course again.

"Beats me. I've never seen anything like it," he said.

By now, most of the soldiers were also looking skyward, pointing and making guesses as to what the object could be. The object circled the area several times then suddenly stopped and hovered above the valley. Haikum used his mathematical skills to estimate its size in relation to the distance and size of the nearest mountain.

"That thing's almost a mile long," he said.

"How can anything that big fly?" wondered Faed.

"It must be searching for the cylinder. There can't be any other reason," Haikum surmised.

Faed nodded.

If Leo was right and the cylinder was a ship from another world, then logically, the object above them now was also such a ship.

"What do we do?" asked Faed.

"We watch—and wait," Haikum replied.

Arka-Dal and his group continued to search every inch of the alien ship. They walked through open bays filled with metal crates and cabinets. They trekked down long passageways and up narrow metal stairs. They explored the engine room and marveled at the propulsion system then finally made their way back to the area that contained the cages. All the while, Gorinna sensed they were being watched. Whatever it was remained in the shadows. It was studying them. Trying to learn their weaknesses and waiting for the right moment to attack.

She sensed there were two of them.

One always remained to their right. The other stayed to the rear.

"They're sizing us up," she said. "And they're *afraid.*"

"Good. Maybe their fear will cause them to make a mistake," Arka-Dal said hopefully.

At that point, the creature in the rear emerged from the wall and charged at Pandaar. The warrior turned and lashed out with his sword. His movement was swift.

Like greased lightning.

The creature never had a chance.

Its head went spinning off to Pandaar's left. The headless torso flew past him and crashed into a pile of empty cages with enough noise to wake the dead. Pandaar smiled and sheathed his sword.

"Too bad for him I was ready for his charge," he said.

"That makes four down—counting the one the crew killed," Leo counted. "Do you sense any others?"

"I did sense one to our right. It's gone now," Gorinna said.

"You mean its left the ship?" asked Arka-Dal.

"Yes," she replied.

"Damn! That makes two that we have to hunt down," Kashi said.

"We won't find them hanging around here. Take us out, Gorinna," Arka-Dal decided.

When they were safely outside, they realized that all of the soldiers were shading their eyes and looking skyward. A few were pointing. Haikum saw them and ran over. At the same time, he pointed at the sky.

"It just appeared from thin air. I don't know what it is," he said.

Arka-Dal and the others looked up at the large, silvery ship hovering above the mountains. After a few seconds, two silvery, elliptical objects emerged from the side of the ship and slowly circled overhead. They each appeared to be over 100 feet long and half that as wide. They made no noise whatsoever as they stopped suddenly and hovered.

Everyone stood and watched as the strange objects settled gently to the ground without so much as kicking up a speck of dust. Arka-Dal waved at Haikum.

"Have your men form up in three squads behind us. Keep your weapons at the ready, but do nothing until I give the order," he said.

Haikum saluted and carried out his orders as a large, circular opening appeared in the side of each object. Arka-Dal watched as two long, metal ramps slid forward and touched the ground. Seconds later, a lithe female figure in a metallic blue jumpsuit appeared in one of the openings. She had a rectangular panel in her hands and was obviously pressing the keys. When she seemed satisfied with the data, she put aside the keyboard and removed her helmet. Long, dark green locks cascaded from beneath it and draped over her shoulders. She took a deep breath and walked slowly down the ramp. As she drew nearer, Arka-Dal saw that her skin was pale blue. Her eyes were slightly larger than normal and almond shaped with large, very dark, pupils. Her lips were full and almost sensuous and slightly darker than the rest of her skin.

Two other figures appeared in the opening of her ship and followed her down the ramp. A short while later, three others emerged from the second ship. All had green hair and the same large, dark eyes. One other was also a female who stood a few inches shorter than the first. The men were tall and stocky

As the first woman approached Arka-Dal, she raised her open right hand to signal both a greeting and to show that she was unarmed. It was a universal gesture which Arka-Dal quickly returned. She nodded and smiled.

Arka-Dal wondered if he'd be able to communicate with these strange beings. When she was just a couple of feet away, he greeted her in Thulian. She stopped and gave him a puzzled look, then quickly adjusted a small instrument attached to her left shoulder. Then, to his surprise (and relief) she returned his greeting in his own language. She saw the expression on his face and smiled.

"This device is a universal translator," she said again touching the gadget on her shoulder. "It enables us to become instantly fluent in any language after hearing only a few words spoken. I am called Ketayla. I am the commander of this search and rescue party. We were able to locate this ship by following its distress signal. We come in peace."

"I am Arka-Dal, Emperor of Thule. I bid you welcome. Where do you come from?" he asked.

"Our world is called Mallendi. It is in a galaxy over one million light years from here. We have never ventured this far before. I did not know that another advanced civilization existed in this solar system," she replied.

"Is this one of your ships?" he asked as he pointed to the cylinder.

"Yes. It is an explorer ship. Its crew are scientists and zoologists. They were gathering up specimens of plant and animal life from the outlying worlds. We were on routine patrol when we picked up their distress signal," Ketayla said. "Have you been aboard?"

"Yes. We spent several hours aboard hunting down some rather dangerous creatures," Arka-Dal said.

Ketayla listened as he explained what had happened. When he finished, she nodded.

"Those creatures are called veyas. They survive by draining the liquids from other living creatures. When they broke free from their cage, the ship's captain must have activated the signal. Were there any survivors?"

"None that we could find. Those veyas killed the entire crew. Any idea how many were aboard?" Arka-Dal asked.

She hit a button on her keyboard.

"According to the ship's manifest, there were six specimens aboard. How many did you kill?" she asked.

"We killed three," Arka-Dal replied. "Your crewmen killed another."

"Unfortunately this means that two have escaped. The veyas are cunning predators. They can adapt well to any environment and have the ability to mimic any other life form that has the same body mass. They also have voracious appetites and must feed twice within one of your months," Ketayla explained.

Arka-Dal escorted Ketayla and her crew to the cylinder and waited outside while they went aboard. They reappeared a half-hour later. Ketayla looked distressed.

"It is as you have said. All are dead. The veyas even killed the other specimens," she said. "Such a sad end for so many good people."

"What will you do with the bodies?" Arka-Dal asked.

"On our world, we bury them in the ground and place markers on their graves," one of the men said.

"We do the same here," Arka-Dal said. "I'll have my soldiers help with the burials if you like."

"That is most kind of you. You have our thanks," another man said graciously.

"What is your world called?" asked Ketayla.

"We call it Earth," Arka-Dal said as they walked back to the others. "What will you do with the ship?"

"It is too heavy to transport back to our world and it has sustained much damage. I leave it in your hands to do with as you will," Ketayla said.

He turned and looked at the cylinder. The fact it was being left behind stunned him. If his men could somehow reverse engineer it, Thulian science and technology would undergo unimaginable changes. Ketayla saw the expression in his face and smiled.

"Do not worry, Arka-Dal. Nothing aboard that ship can be converted for use as a weapon. It is simply for carrying cargo and transportation. Even the handguns you saw aboard are only able to stun their targets. We are a *peaceful* people and have not known war for more than a million of your years," she assured him.

"In the beginning, we were much like other races. We had frequent wars. In fact, we nearly obliterated our entire civilization three times. Each time, we had to start all over. The last time it happened, those who survived decided to abolish war from our world. Our scientists, teachers and philosophers banded together to form a government. After new laws were in place, they created a police force which rounded up and destroyed all the weapons they could find. Those who resisted were eliminated. It took another 200 of your years to rebuild our cities. This time, we made them better, cleaner and safer. We have been at peace since. Now, we pursue only knowledge and we explore the universe," the second woman added.

She then introduced herself as Qyana and said she was a biologist.

"What if you're attacked from outside? How will you defend yourselves?" Arka-Dal asked.

"We have taken measures to assure that will never happen," Ketayla replied without offering to explain further.

When they reached the others, they exchanged greetings and introductions. When she learned that Leo was the keeper of the Archives, Ketayla became interested in learning more about them.

She instructed her crewmembers to return to the cylinder and remove the bodies while she continued to engage Arka-Dal, Leo and Gorinna in a lively conversation about life on Earth and how it compared to their world.

As they talked, Arka-Dal studied Ketayla with great interest. He wondered if everyone on her world looked so similar and if that similarity made things a little bit boring. She smiled at him.

"Yes we do—and it does," she said as if she could read his thoughts. "Especially when it comes to mating."

He laughed.

"As for our blue skin and larger eyes—our world is further from our sun than yours. Our eyes are larger to enable us to see better in our eternal twilight. Our skin is pale because the rays of our sun are much weaker and our world is colder. It will take us awhile to adapt to your climate. We feel quite hot here. So hot, it may be more comfortable for us to wear your type of clothing," she explained as she eyed Gorinna's short red dress.

"I can help you obtain some," Gorinna offered.

"I would appreciate that greatly," Ketayla said.

"What else can you tell us about the veyas?" asked Leo.

"Very little. They are a rare species that we found on a nearly dead star called Rigelis-Varga. They are secretive and elusive. We know that they feed off any living things that cross their paths and that they hibernate for weeks between feedings," Oyana said.

"Your world is an ideal environment for them. It contains unlimited food sources and many places in which to hide. If a mated pair escaped, they might even be able to *breed,*" added one of the men.

"How many offspring can they produce in a single lifetime?" asked Gorinna.

"That is still not known," Oyana replied.

"So what we have are two highly intelligent, adaptable and dangerous life forms with the potential to reproduce running loose on our world. That's not good," Arka-Dal said.

"One more thing—they tend to remain in a hunting area until their food sources run out," Ketayla said. "One of your cities would be perfect for them. We aren't 100% certain, but there is some evidence that they are able to change their appearance to mimic local life forms."

"That makes them even more dangerous," Arka-Dal said. "I'll put the word to all of our local army posts and police forces to be on the lookout for anything out of the ordinary. If any one gets killed and it happens to resemble the work of a vampire, we'll investigate ourselves."

"Would you mind if we stayed here for a few weeks? Your world is fascinating and I'd love to take some time to learn more about it," Ketayla asked.

"You're welcome to stay as long as you like. In fact, you can be our guests at the palace," Arka-Dal offered.

"Thank you. That is most generous," Ketayla said graciously. "While we are there, can I have access to your archives, museums and zoos?"

"Most certainly. In fact, I'll be happy to escort you," Leo offered.

"We would like that," Oyana said.

"Where is your capital city?" asked Ketayla.

"It's about a three day ride from here," Arka-Dal said.

"If we take our ship, we can be there in less than one of your hours. Is there a place nearby that is large enough for us to land?" asked Oyana.

"There's a large open field just to the west of the city. You can land there," Arka-Dal said.

"Excellent. When we get aboard you are welcome to join us on the bridge. You can help us navigate," Oyala said.

Arka-Dal ordered Haikum to have his men bury the alien dead. He and the others then followed Ketayla and her crew up the ramp into her ship. Haikum and the other soldiers watched as the ship lifted off and soared upward to rejoin the mother ship. When the mother ship zipped off toward the south, the two officers, their soldiers and the alien crewmen from the second ship turned to the grim task of removing the bodies from the cylinder and digging graves for them.

After all of the crewmen were buried, Haikum and his men bade farewell to the aliens as they boarded their ship and flew south to join their brethren. He then marched his dirty, tired soldiers back to the outpost. No one noticed the two figures lurking in the shadows, watching as they filed past.

When the huge craft appeared in the sky above Thule, it naturally caused quite a sensation. Nearly everyone stopped what they were doing to watch as it slowly circled the city twice before gently settling down on the open prairie just beyond the western wall. Thousands of curiosity seekers rushed out of the city to get a better look at it. They gathered around and waited for it to do something.

"Interesting. Your people didn't panic at the sight of our ship," one of the pilots observed. "Have they seen starships before?"

"Not that I know of. We Thulians are a nosy sort. Rather than flee from the unknown, we usually try to understand it," Leo explained. "Besides, most of our people are well-educated and not prone to such fears."

The people watched as a door opened on the side of the ship and a long metal ramp slid to the ground. They moved closer to see who would emerge. When they saw it was Arka-Dal and his friends, they cheered and clapped. As soon as the Emperor's party reached the ground, Ketayla and her crew exited the ship. A group of people from the local newspapers rushed forward and started asking questions. Ketayla and her officers answered as best as they could. They seemed genuinely surprised by the attention. Then, in a show of friendship, they invited the onlookers to go aboard and tour the ships.

As the aliens followed Arka-Dal and his party to the palace—with half the people trailing them—they allowed themselves to take in the smells, sights and sounds of the city. Ketayla found it all nearly intoxicating.

"What is your world like, Ketayla?" asked Arka-Dal.

"Mallendi is about a third larger than your world and we have two moons. The atmosphere and vegetation are similar to yours but our sun is much dimmer. Also, we have only one race of people back home. I see people of many different races around us. Are all Earth cities like this?" she replied.

"I like to think that Thule is rather unique," Leo said.

"How many people live on your world?" asked Arka-Dal.

"Less than a million at last count," Oyana replied.

"Why so few?" asked Leo.

"Unfortunately, ours is a dying race. There are very few children produced anymore. In fact, our birth rate is nearly zero. There are so few of us that most of our planet has reverted to wilderness. We all live in five small cities—one on each continent," said Ketayla.

"Are your people sterile?" asked Leo.

"Most of our men are. The few offspring we produce are sickly and weak. They survive thanks to our advanced medical knowledge, but that doesn't help our race in the long run. Mallendi will be void of people in another generation or so," Oyana said with a note of sadness.

"You people are vibrant and energetic. We were like that once," Ketayla said as she looked around.

"What happened?" asked Arka-Dal.

"We stopped fighting," said one of the men. "When we abolished war, I think we also abolished our zest for life with it. Scientific pursuits are interesting but they rarely produce excitement. We have become *tired*."

"Do you have wars here?" asked Oyana.

"All the time," Arka-Dal replied. "Too many, I think."

"When a person has something he values enough to fight for, it keeps him alert and alive. It gives life meaning," Ketayla said.

"Don't your lives have meaning?" asked Arka-Dal.

"We *used* to," said Oyana. "Our ancestors used to have something worth fighting for. Our eternal peace took that away from us. We're stagnant now. Listless."

"That's why we are dying," said the man.

"That's a pity. Is there anything we can do to help?" asked Arka-Dal.

Ketayla smiled at him.

"Perhaps there is," she said.

Once they reached the rose garden, the aliens reveled in the brightly colored flowers, ornate statuary and elaborate fountains and ponds. Several of the locals waved or greeted Arka-Dal by name. He waved back and even stopped to joke with some of them, as did his friends. Ketayla found this strange until Leo explained how Arka-Dal preferred to run the country.

But it was the short, colorful and rather revealing fashions of the women that fascinated her most. Gorinna noticed this.

"Don't women wear dresses on your world?" she asked.

"No. Everyone of both sexes wears a jumpsuit. Only the colors differ to show someone's rank or occupation. Here, the women and men dress as they please. It's very refreshing," Ketayla said.

Once inside the palace, they were greeted by Mayumi, Medusa, Galya, Chatha and Zhijima and a horde of happy, raucous children. Arka-Dal made the introductions and noticed that both Galya and Chatha were eyeing Ketalya carefully. But she and the other women in her party seemed more interested in observing the children as they romped through the palace.

"Your children seem quite healthy and robust. Are all Earth children like this?" asked Ketayla.

"Most of them are. When our ancestors survived the Great Disaster, their children grew immune to most diseases and radiation. A sickly child is rare now," Leo explained.

"How long do your people live?" she asked.

"An average of 125 years," Leo said.

"That's amazing. Our life spans are a few years less," Ketayla said as she watched two of the children go at each other with toy swords. "Are all these children yours?"

Arka-Dal nodded proudly.

"He has two others in other countries," Mayumi pointed out.

"Most Thulian families have two or three children. A few have more," Leo said. "When people are happy and prosperous, they tend to have more children."

"Not us," Ketayla said sadly. "Each generation produces less and less and we are prosperous."

"But are you *happy?*" asked Mayumi.

"No," she said honestly.

"If your people ever decide to leave Mallendi, you are more than welcome to live here," Arka-Dal offered. "We have more than enough room."

"It is worth considering. Such a move may save us from extinction," Ketayla mused. "But I doubt that our governing council would go for it. Mallendi is a beautiful place. We are very proud of it. It would be very difficult for most of us to leave it."

"I understand. We feel much the same about Thule," Leo said.

Arka-Dal took the aliens on a tour of the palace, then invited them to dine with everyone else.

Dinner proved to be an adventure. The newcomers quickly learned how to use the simple Earth utensils and were more than happy to sample each of the dishes that were placed before them. As they ate, Mayumi explained what each dish was and how it was made. Ketayla seemed especially interested in this and said that on her world, she was considered to be a very good cook. Both women agreed to show each other how to prepare their traditional meals.

When dinner ended, most of the alien crewmembers decided to explore the city. Arka-Dal offered to provide them with guides to help explain the various sights and customs. They accepted his offer eagerly.

The women showed Ketayla, Oyana and the six other women to guest quarters and their private baths. After years of deep space travel, they decided that the clean, scented warm water felt good on their skin.

Real good.

While they bathed, servants brought them fresh towels and new dresses. Ketayla donned the bright green one and accented it with a narrow gold belt. The dress was very short, too. It barely reached mid-thigh. Oyana put on the dark red dress and silver belt and studied her reflection in a nearby mirror. Both decided to let their hair hang loose like the Thulian women.

When they were finished dressing, they liked what they saw.

"I could get used to this style," Oyana said as she studied her reflection. "It's very light and comfortable."

"I agree. I may never wear a jumpsuit again. I've always hated them anyway. I think we should take back several of these dresses—enough to last the rest of our lives," Ketayla said.

"Maybe we'll start a trend. Maybe when the other women see us, they, too, will shed their drawn jumpsuits. At least it might produce some excitement," Oyana remarked.

"I hope so. Mallendi needs some excitement. It needs anything to break the monotony," Ketayla said. "These dresses might be just the spark we need."

"We need more than a spark, Ketayla. Mallendi needs a *conflagration*!" Oyana said.

Arka-Dal and the other men in the palace really sat up and took notice when the women came down in their new dresses. Arka-Dal even whistled at Ketayla and commented on her sexy legs and figure. She beamed at his remarks.

"I've never been told anything like that before. Thank you. Your words make me feel like a woman again," she said modestly. "I do have one question about these dresses,"

"And what is that?" asked Mayumi.

"What do you wear under them?" she asked.

"Uh—what exactly *are* you wearing under it?" asked Medusa.

"Nothing," Ketayla replied.

"Oh. In that case, we'd best provide you with some underwear to avoid any embarrassing moments," Mayumi suggested. "Please follow me and I will see that you get the proper clothing."

The men grinned as they women followed Mayumi back upstairs. Ketayla turned to Arka-Dal and winked.

"Looks like you've got yet another woman after you," Pandaar joked as he poked him with his elbow. "Don't you ever get tired of being a sex object?"

"No—and jealousy will get you nowhere," Arka-Dal joked back.

The aliens stayed for two full months. During that time, their scientists copied almost every book in the archives with machines they called data collectors. They each had one and they used them to take pictures of things that fascinated them while touring the Empire.

Also during that time, Ketayla became more than a little interested in Arka-Dal. She seemed to follow him everywhere. She even toured the nearby military bases with him and went for a sail upriver on the royal yacht.

When no one was around one evening, Ketayla smiled at him and slowly parted her knees. Naturally, he looked. Ketayla's vagina had no hair and looked exactly like any other woman's. The sight gave him an erection—which she noticed immediately.

"I see that you are interested in my body," she said.

"What man *wouldn't* be? You're incredibly sexy," he said without taking his eyes from her crotch.

"I want to have sex with you. I want to feel what sex is like with a *real* man," she said as she knelt before him and undid his pants.

They made love several times that night. Ketayla was almost insatiable and her vagina was exquisitely tight. She also knew how to use it—as well as the other orifices of her body.

Unknown to them both, Mayumi and Galya were watching them from their vantage point on the second floor landing. They laughed and joked about it.

"I figured she wanted him," Galya said.

"*Every* woman wants him!" Mayumi said. "When I realized how pretty she was, I knew he would not be able to resist her."

"Shit, I can hardly resist her myself," Galya admitted. "I wonder what her pussy tastes like?"

"There is only way to find out," Mayumi teased.

"Do you want to find out, too?" Galya asked.

Mayumi shook her head and kissed her on the lips. At the same time, she slid her hand between Galya's thighs.

"There is only one pussy I want to taste," she whispered.

Galya did get her wish. Somehow, she managed to get her hand up Ketayla's skirt. While she played with her vagina, she got the woman so excited that she easily convinced her to have sex with her. When they emerged from Ketayla's room late the following evening holding hands, both were nearly spent. They found Mayumi on the balcony watching the stars and sat down with her. She smiled at Ketayla.

"How was it?" she asked.

"Incredible! I've never experienced sex with a woman before. Now, I want to try *all* of you," Ketayla replied.

And she did.

Before she left Earth, she had sex with every woman in the palace several times. She even bedded a couple of the servants and Oyana. She also had sex with Arka-Dal several more times.

"I am determined to have your child. I want a son who will be strong and brave. Tough and intelligent. I want him to be exactly like you instead of the poor specimens who try to pass for men on my world," she told him. "Besides, most of them are sterile or disinterested in sex."

"Can you actually bear a human child?" he asked.

"Yes. I've already done a DNA test. We nearly match. Most likely, both of our peoples sprang from the same mother race eons ago. By the way, now that we have had sex many times, according to the customs of my world, we are married," she said.

Mayumi, who was seated nearby, emitted a laugh. Ketayla gave her a quizzical look.

"That makes six wives now!" Mayumi joked.

"Seven if you count Oyana," Ketayla said.

Mayumi raised an eyebrow at this. She wasn't aware that Oyana had also nailed him—and more than once.

"Does she also want to bear a child?" Mayumi asked.

"She most certainly does," said Ketayla. "Our race is almost extinct. Without fresh DNA and energy, we'll die out in another millennia or two. We *need* you, Arka-Dal. We need you because you are the best candidate to help our race survive. You offered to help in any way you could. This way is best."

"I'll do what I can," he said modestly.

"Good. There are eight of us altogether. Do you think you can impregnate us all?" Ketayla asked.

Arka-Dal looked at Mayumi, who was still laughing, mostly because she knew that Ketayla was serious. She actually wanted him to impregnate all the female members of her crew.

"Well, will you do it?" Ketayla asked again.

"How do the other women feel about this?" he asked.

"They are all quite eager and excited, especially since I've told them how good you are," Ketayla said.

"What if I said no?" he hedged.

"They would feel very insulted and hurt by your refusal. They would feel that you think they are too ugly to mate with. They would feel unworthy," Ketayla explained.

Mayumi laughed harder.

"If you refuse, Aka-san, you might cause a serious diplomatic incident," she joked.

"I'll do it," he decided.

"I knew you'd want to rise to the occasion," Mayumi said, tongue-in-cheek.

He laughed.

"Good. I already told them you would anyway," Ketayla said with a laugh. "I will introduce the first one to you tomorrow. You'd better get some sleep. She has a reputation for being like a wild animal in bed."

When the visitors bade farewell to Thule six weeks later, Ketayla, Oyana and all six of the other women were carrying Arka-Dal's seed.

"Eight more Dals! Can the universe stand that many?" asked Kashi.

"It will just *have* to," Pandaar said. "I hope those women know what they've gotten themselves into. Eight Dal offspring could just about ruin their entire race!"

"I doubt it. I rather think they've gotten exactly what they asked for—and needed. In another generation or two, the Mallendans might be just like us," Leo said.

"Now *that's* depressing!" Pandaar joked.

"Imagine how bad it would have been if they were carrying *your* seed!" Kashi sniped.

"Yes. It's a good thing they selected Arka-Dal. There's no telling what monsters they'd give birth to if you had impregnated them!" Gorinna added.

Pandaar emitted a string epithets. This made them both laugh.

Just about everyone in Thule gathered on the prairie and waved as the giant ship lifted off. Arka-Dal and his friends stayed and watched until it finally passed from their sight.

"I wonder what our children will look like and if I'll ever meet any of them," Arka-Dal said as they walked back into the city. "What did you think of Ketayla, my love?"

"She is very pretty, very friendly and she has a delicious pussy," Mayumi said.

"I'll say she has!" Galya echoed.

"You can say that again!" added Medusa.

"She really knows how to use her tongue, too," added Gorinna.

"Umm-humm," said Zhijima and Chatha.

"You didn't seem to be jealous of her like you were of me, Chatha," Galya pointed out.

"I didn't need to. I knew they would be leaving soon—unlike a certain beautiful devil we all know and love," Chatha replied as she squeezed Galya's hand.

Then everyone laughed until it hurt.

As she stood on the bridge watching the pretty blue marble called Earth vanish in the distance, Ketayla wiped tears from her almond eyes. Oyana saw this and gently touched her arm. They were both still wearing Thulian dresses—as were the rest of the women of the crew.

"You actually love him, don't you?" Oyana asked.

"Yes. I never told him that. Do you think he knows?" Ketayla asked.

"I'm sure of it," Oyana replied. "Will we return one day?"

"Perhaps. I would love to see him again. I also want our future son to meet him. I want him to know who his father is," Ketayla said. "What about you?"

"I would like to return with you," Oyana replied. "I want him to get to know his child."

"At least we will get to speak with him. I left one of our intergalactic communicators behind and showed him how to use it. I don't want him to forget me—ever," Ketayla said.

"I don't think he ever will," Oyana assured her.

Far down on the planet below, two apelike creatures made their way slowly up the cliff overlooking a large metal cylinder. Halfway up, they stopped and watched the scores of engineers and laborers as they attempted to learn the secrets of the alien craft. After several minutes, the creatures turned away from the valley below and continued their climb. They stopped at the mouth of a small cave to look around, then went inside.

The floor of the cave was littered with the bones and dry carcasses of sheep and goats. The creatures had feasted well since their arrival. They would soon feast again.

But that would come later. For now, they had to sleep . . .

The Curse of the Cat

In the 43rd year of the reign of Arka-Dal

Arka-Dal opened his eyes and blinked a few times. He saw nothing but darkness. As his mind cleared, he became aware of the fact that he was lying on a cold, stone floor. After several more minutes, he forced himself to sit up.

His head throbbed slightly, sort of like the way he felt after he drank too much.

"How the fuck did I get *here?* And where *is* here?" he thought as he stood.

He noticed that he was still wearing his usual chain mail hauberk and tunic. His helmet was gone. So, too, were his shield and sword.

"I know I had them when I left Assur," he thought.

His vision gradually adjusted to the inky blackness. He was standing in the middle of large square room, surrounded by four stone walls. In one wall was a tall wooden door. The other walls were featureless save for their crudely-worked masonry.

"A dungeon? Or an underground lair? What *is* this place?" he said to himself. "And where are the others?"

He had ridden out of Assur early in the morning. Pandaar, Kashi, Perseus and Gorinna were with him. He recalled heading north to the Lizard People's city, Garchem, for his annual visit.

And that's all he could remember.

"The only way to find out where I am is to leave this room. Let's see what waits beyond that door," he thought as he walked over and gave it a hard shove with both hands.

To his surprise, it swung easily inward with a loud, rusty creak. When he stepped inside, a bright beam of light from a hidden source suddenly shone down upon a tall, wooden stand. Arka-Dal pursed his lips. The stand held his missing shield and Excalibur, which was still in its scabbard. He looked around warily.

"This is too easy," he thought as he approached the stand.

He reached out and picked up Excalibur. When nothing happened, he strapped it to his waist and grabbed the shield. The light gradually faded away. Just before the room went dark, he spotted two more doors in the wall directly behind the stand.

"I don't get it. Why disarm me then give my weapons back to me without a fight? Someone's playing games with me. Well, I guess I'll go along with this until I discover who's behind this," he thought as he walked around the stand and stared at the doors.

"Now, which one do I go through?" he wondered.

He pressed his ear to the one on the left and heard the sound of water gurgling over rocks. He stepped back and listened at the other door.

Nothing.

He tried to push it but it held fast. He returned to the other door and pushed hard. It gave a little. Encouraged, he pushed harder. The door suddenly came off its hinges and fell to the floor with a loud clatter and splash as it struck the pool of water inside. Arka-Dal stepped inside and studied his surroundings.

The room was smaller but also square. The stone floor was covered with a few inches of dark, putrid water that seemed to bubble up from the middle. The bubbling motion gave him the impression of something breathing just beneath the surface and the gurgling was louder. He looked across the pool and saw large black letters painted on the wall. The writing was Thulian—but of a very ancient variety.

And the message they conveyed was simple, direct—and ominous.

"ENTER MY SON AND BE DAMNED—ALZARI."

He stared at the words.

Alzari, the Poet, who's own writing drove him mad, was cursed by his own immortality. That very immortality had driven him insane.[13]

"Did you *really* write this warning, Mad Poet? If so, what were you trying to warn about?" Arka-Dal said to himself.

He thought back to the years that he and Merlin fought two long, bloody wars over possession of the fabled Books of Alzari.[14] As far as he knew, all of those Books had been destroyed. The idea that this warning could have been left behind by Alzari intrigued him.

It also repelled him.

---

13 Read THE GRAND ILLUSION

14 Read THE AVENGER OF THULE

"Haven't you caused us enough trouble with your damned Books? What more do you want of us?" he asked aloud.

He heard a harsh gurgling sound behind and turned just in time to ward off the blow from a huge, watery fist with his shield. The force of the blow sent vibrations up his arm to his shoulder and splashed water all over him. Before he could react, two more heavy blows struck his shield. The second sent him flying against the wall. He bounced off but retained his balance.

A huge, serpent-like form, made completely of water took shape in front of him. The creature was thick and tall and it glared at him with baleful eyes.

"A water elemental!" he said almost in awe.

The elemental lunged. Arka-Dal sidestepped it and lashed out with Excalibur. The sword's blade passed harmlessly through the elemental and struck the stone floor. The creature laughed and lunged again. This time, Arka-Dal charged at it shield first. The impact splattered the elemental and almost drowned Arka-Dal. As he struggled back to his feet, he heard that gurgling noise again.

He rose to one knee with his shield above him and watched as the water swirled into a thick column which again took on a serpent form. The elemental reared back with its mouth open wide then lunged for him.

The room suddenly became filled with a weird tinkling sound that reminded Arka-Dal of hundreds of wind chimes going off at once. When he lowered his shield he was surprised—and relieved—to see that the elemental had been changed into a sculpture of solid ice.

"That'll teach him some manners," said a voice from behind him.

He stood and smiled at the figure in the doorway.

"Gorinna! Am I ever glad to see you!" he said as she entered the room.

"I was walking down the hall when I heard the commotion. Lucky for you I got here when I did," she said. "We'd better get going. That freeze spell won't hold that demon for too much longer."

That's when she noticed the writing on the wall.

"Alzari? I'd hoped we heard the last of that fool," she said almost in disgust. "But what does *he* have to do with this place?"

"That's a good question. You said you were walking down a hall when you heard the noise—where is it?" Arka-Dal asked as they left the room and shut the door behind them.

Gorinna pointed at another open door.

"Let's go," Arka-Dal said.

They pushed it open all the way and found themselves staring down a long hallway with four lit torches in iron sconces.

"Your doing?" he asked.

She shook her head.

"They were lit when I got here," she said.

"Just where *did* you come from?" he asked.

"I came through a door that's just around that corner," she replied pointing. "I woke up in a small room with one door which led out into this hallway. As I walked along the hall, the torches lit themselves one-by-one. That's when I found you."

"Sounds like you were led to me. Someone wanted you to find me, which is odd considering how much trouble they went through to separate us in the first place," Arka-Dal said.

"In that case, we'll probably stumble over the others pretty soon," Gorinna said.

"Then what?" asked Arka-Dal.

"We find out where we are and get our asses out of here," Gorinna answered.

As they wandered down one long corridor after another, following torches that suddenly sparked to life, the heavy humidity of the underground complex began to take its toll. After more than an hour of this, Arka-Dal decided to rest. He sat down and leaned against a wall. Gorinna plopped down next to him.

"Just where *are* we?" she asked. "This place goes on forever."

"We'll find our way out eventually," Arka-Dal assured her. "We always do."

She laughed.

"We've been in worse fixes over the years. A few nearly killed us. But we always came out of them. I think it's because we believe in each other so much," she said.

"You sound as if you've given it a lot of thought lately," he said.

"I have," she said. She yawned. "I'm tired. I guess it's this stagnant air. It saps my strength."

To his surprise, she rested her head on his shoulder. To her surprise, he put his arm around her to make her more comfortable. It was the closest contact they'd ever had and she liked the way it felt.

"We've known each other for a very long time. How do you feel about me—I mean really, deep down inside?" she asked out of the blue.

"What do you mean?" he hedged.

"Do you like me? Love me? Find me attractive or sexy? How do you *really* feel about me?" she clarified.

"All of the above," he said. "You're one of my best friends and I love you deeply. And I've always found you alluring. So much so, in fact, that it sort of scares me."

She laughed.

"I sometimes have fantasies about you," she admitted. "Sexual fantasies. I often wonder what it would feel like to make love with you. Do you have such fantasies about me?"

"Yes, I do," he said.

"How often?" she pressed.

"Too often," he said honestly. "Sometimes I think it's too bad you're married to Kashi. If you weren't, we'd be screwing like jackrabbits every chance we'd get. You might even be my wife."

She smiled and snuggled closer.

"I hoped you'd say that," she said. "Thank you."

"For what? Having sexual fantasies about you?" he joked.

"Among other things," she said. "Do you think we'll ever get to fulfill our fantasies about each other?"

He laughed.

"Well, this is a nice way to start," he joked as he stroked her hair. "But there's a time and a place for everything. This is neither."

"I know. I'm glad we had this talk. I want you to know that I feel the same way about you. If the time and place ever do feel right, I will gladly spread my thighs for you and the consequences be damned!" she said softly.

Her words surprised him. He realized that if Gorinna ever did spread her thighs, he would find her impossible to resist. Just holding her close made his heart beat faster. That's why he'd kept physical contact with her to a minimum over the years. He looked into her eyes and suppressed an urge to kiss her.

"I won't do anything to hurt Kashi," he said.

"Neither will I—but it's nice to dream," she said.

He smiled. This subject had come up among him, Kashi and Pandaar several times. They were all aware of her crush on him and they often teased him about it. They also knew how he felt about her.

Kashi had even suggested that he "give her a try" once in a while. Of course he knew that he never would.

Or did he?

They'd never been this close. They'd never really touched before. This felt good.

Too good.

He took a deep breath and stood up. She looked at him and smiled.

"We'd better keep moving," he said.

He held out his hand. She took it and pulled herself up.

"Why the hurry? Afraid of starting something?" she asked coyly.

"More than you know," he confessed.

"You really think I'm sexy?" she asked.

"Hell, Gorinna. You're one of the sexiest women I know. It's all I can do to keep my hands off you," he admitted. "That's why I'm rarely alone with you. I don't trust myself."

She laughed and squeezed his hand tighter.

"We're alone *now*," she hinted.

"No we're not. Whoever's behind this is probably watching our every move," he said.

"Maybe we should put on a show for him?" she suggested.

"Like I said: there's a time and place for everything. This is neither," he repeated. "But I warn you, any more talk like this and all bets are off!"

Gorinna snuggled closer.

"What do you think is my sexiest feature?" she asked.

"Your mind," he replied without hesitation. "Followed very closely by your body."

She smiled because she knew he really meant it. Her magic kept her perpetually young-looking. In fact, she still looked the same as she did when they first met. But her body was stronger, leaner and more athletic-looking thanks to her years of training. Arka-Dal always told her that she looked better each day.

"One day . . ." she began.

"We'll see," he said as if he could read her mind.

They walked along the corridor hand-in-hand for a few moments. Along the way, torches sparkled to life to guide them.

To what?

Gorinna leaned closer and smiled. Holding his hand felt more exciting to her than such things should be. She wondered if he felt anything similar? Wondered if he could feel her heart racing?

"This is nice," she said softly.

"Better keep your mind on our surroundings or we'll end up in coffins," he cautioned. "But you're right. This *is* nice."

Worlds away, the enigmatic Ned the Knower stood on the highest tower of his keep and rechecked the alignment of the stars and planets in the night sky. After careful study, he concluded that all was where it should be. Despite this, he had a strange feeling that all was not right with the universe. Something seemed off.

But what?

Try as he might, he could not rid himself of his uneasiness. Something was wrong somewhere. He could feel it in his bones.

But what?

He recalculated the information he had in his mind. When he finished, he checked it again and again.

Nothing seemed amiss.

The universe was in order. All was at peace. Even the Underworld was quiet. Almost unusually so, save for the brutal war of attrition going on at the edge of the Abyss. That, he knew, would eventually have some bearing on the world of men. He would deal with it then.

Ned tried to relax but couldn't. Something was about to happen. Something *big.* Whatever it was gnawed at him like a cancer and deprived him of sleep. Everything he felt went against what he saw or read in the stars. For the first time in history, the Knower was stumped.

It was enough to shake the very pillars of the universe. Ned actually didn't know what was about to happen. He didn't know the cause of his unease. He just knew that something was very wrong somewhere.

But what?

He retreated to his inner sanctum to consult his most ancient scrolls and oracles in an effort to find out. Perhaps there he would find the answers.

Pandaar roamed aimlessly down one dark passageway after another, following the series of torches that seemed to spark to life as he approached. The flickering torches broke through the heavy blanket of pitch darkness and seemed to be showing which way to go. Next to each torch stood a heavy wooden door. Each time, he pushed the door open only to find himself standing in yet another passageway.

He felt as if he'd been walking for hours.

He saw nothing save the torches and was growing frustrated.

"Where the fuck am I?" he asked aloud.

The last thing he remembered was bedding down for the night next to a campfire. The next thing he knew, he was here.

But where, exactly, *was* here?

His head throbbed slightly, too. It almost felt like a hangover. He wondered where the others were, too, as he massaged his temples and kept walking.

He came to what appeared to be a sharp turn. As another torch came to life, he found himself staring at a message painted in almost fluorescent letters on the wall in front of him.

"Thy greatest fear lies around this corner."—Alzari.

The name made the hair on his neck tingle ominously. As he pondered the meaning of the words, a loud shriek caught his ear. The shriek was followed by cries for help. The voice was distinctly female. What's more, it sounded eerily *familiar.*

Having nothing better to do, he sought out the source of the screams and cautiously crept around the corner. What he saw next caused his heart to leap to his throat.

There was his beloved wife, Zhijima, her wrists chained to a stone pillar atop a flight of steps, screaming in terror as six, large, lizard-like beasts with glowing yellow eyes, long forked tongues and sharp teeth circled her hungrily.

She looked straight at him then.

"Help me, Pandaar! Help me!" she shouted.

Without another thought, he drew his weapons and charged right at the beasts, bellowing with rage all the while. The creatures turned and flicked their tongues at him menacingly as he lunged recklessly toward them—only to crash hard into a blank stone wall.

The impact jarred his swords from his grip as he bounced off the wall and landed on his behind. Stunned, he shook his head to clear it and looked around.

The room was empty.

"A fucking illusion?" he asked as he stood and retrieved his weapons.

He still had no idea where he was of how he got there. He spotted another door on the opposite wall and eased it open. As he did, he heard voices coming down the corridor. Determined to make a fight of it, he drew his weapons again and plunged through the opening—and crashed right into Arka-Dal and Gorinna.

They collided amid loud yelps of pain and tumbled to the floor. When Arka-Dal saw who it was who ran into them, he let loose a barrage of epithets that questioned Pandaar's birthright. Pandaar replied in kind as they helped each other up.

"Now we are three," Gorinna said. "I wonder who else is here with us?"

"Just where on Earth *are* we?" asked Pandaar.

Arka-Dal told them what they'd seen and Pandaar told them about the illusion. When he was finished, Gorinna whistled.

"That illusion depicted your greatest fear. That means whoever's behind this is able to read our deepest thoughts and use them against us," she said. "From here on, we'd best guard out thoughts carefully."

"The longer I'm here, the less I like this place," Arka-Dal said.

"I got a question for you—what does *Alzari* have to do with this?" asked Pandaar.

"That, my friend, is the 64,000 Dal question," Arka-Dal replied.

When Arka-Dal didn't arrive at Ft. Odin, the Northern Army Headquarters, for his meeting with Field Marshall Jun, the Minotaur decided to wait a while longer. He figured that something must have delayed his friends and that they'd probably show up before midnight. When they didn't, Jun went to the Communications Center and radioed the Royal Palace. After several tries, he finally roused the sleeping operator and sent him to wake up Empress Mayumi.

Jun paced the floor while he waited. A few minutes later, he heard a female voice crackle over the receiver.

"Ohayo gozaimasu, Jun-san. Why are you calling at this hour?" she asked.

"I hate to worry you, Mayumi, but Arka-Dal and the others haven't arrived yet. They're ten hours overdue. Have you heard from any of them since they left Nineveh?" Jun replied.

"No. I last heard from Aka-san five days ago when they were in Assur. I can't imagine what has delayed them," Mayumi said.

"Neither can I. The roads are safe and the weather is fine. I'm thinking of sending out a search party," Jun said.

Just then, a sleepy and yawning Chatha walked into the radio room to see what the commotion was about. Mayumi glanced up at her with a worried expression.

"Aka-san is missing," she said. "Jun is thinking of sending out a search party for them."

Chatha was suddenly wide awake now. She took the sender from Mayumi and sat down at the console while the Empress made room for her.

"This is Chatha, Jun. What's the nearest city to your base?" she asked.

"That would be Nineveh. It's about 75 miles south of here," Jun replied. "I know they left there about three days ago. That's the last time I heard from them. Should I send out a search party?" Jun asked.

"No. Wait until we arrive. Medusa and I will go with you," Chatha decided. "We'll leave here at once."

Mayumi glanced at the young warrior queen. Chatha was now in her take-charge military commander mode and she decided to let her have her way. The young Atlantean was fiercely loyal to Arka-Dal and Mayumi knew it would be useless to try and stop her from looking for him.

"Very well," Jun agreed. "Meanwhile, I'll round up my best scouts."

"Don't bother. We're bringing something *better* than your scouts," Chatha assured him.

"Oh? And what would *that* be?" Jun asked.

"Merlin!" Chatha said.

Jun laughed and signed off. Chatha put down the sender and hurried upstairs to wake Merlin and Medusa. Along the way, she stopped to tell Zhijima what was happening. She vowed that they'd find Arka-Dal and the others even if they had to turn over every rock in the Empire.

Merlin was already wide awake. The wizard had come to Thule to consult with Leo on a rather obscure bit of arcana. Mayumi insisted that he stay the night and he had eagerly agreed. Though he tried to sleep, his slumber was broken by an urgent metal communiqué from a very perplexed Ned the Knower. After a long "chat", they both realized that something in the universe was definitely out of whack. Whatever was causing it was quite intangible, yet it could affect the workings of time and space itself. Like Ned, Merlin had no idea what it could be.

He suggested that Ned contact the Devil to see if he had a clue. The Knower replied that he would do so but only as a last resort. He didn't like nor trust the Devil and would rather keep him out of this.

Merlin laughed and told Ned to try and put aside his differences with the Devil, as he had done. Ned found the wizard's change in attitude amusing—and somewhat troubling.

"The Devil is what he is. He can no more change his evil ways than a leopard can change its spots," Ned warned.

"There was a time when *I* was not trusted nor liked by those who now consider me a close friend," Merlin reminded him. "Times change and people must change with them or all will be for nothing in the long run. Galya's deep love for Arka-Dal has altered her father's attitude greatly and has sworn to protect this land for as long as a member of Arka-Dal's line exists. And even *you* must admit that the Devil *always* keeps his word."

"With a few nasty twists," Ned added. "There is always a catch."

"Not *this* time," Merlin countered.

"We shall see, my friend. Right now, we have a small problem to solve," Ned reminded him.

After they broke contact, a single—and very disturbing name—kept popping into Merlin's mind.

Alzari.

But what, he wondered, could the Mad Poet of the Dark Times have to do with all this? He knew that Alzari had written four books and in the process, he had gone insane. All four volumes had been destroyed. No known copies of any of them existed.

So it couldn't have anything to do with any of his books.

Or could it?

After all, Gorinna *did* bring one back from that strange temple. Was it actually written by Alzari? Or was it written by some shady copier of antiquities looking to make some fast money? Since that, too, had been destroyed, there was no way of knowing.

He rose from the bed and walked to the door. He waited a second and opened it just as Chatha raised her fist to knock. She lowered her hand and smiled.

"You're needed," she said.

"I know," he responded as he followed her down the hall.

Many miles to the north, a most unusual band of travelers rode through the desert. At the head was a powerfully built man of undeterminable age and dressed in red robes. Beside him rode a well-tanned man with a neat beard dressed mostly in black who looked more than a little bit dangerous. Two amber-eyed men, one armed with a shotgun; and a beautiful, athletically built woman with long dark hair, followed behind them.

They had ridden out of Osumel days earlier and crossed the Tigris-Euphrates Rivers near Thule. After stopping for supplies, they rode north from Thule. Their pace was steady and unhurried.

When they reached the top of a sandy hill, they looked out upon a vast wasteland of arid brown soil and stunted, scraggly brush. To the distant south, they could barely make out a series of crumbling minarets and pale white structures.

James pointed.

"That's Darad Zur," he announced.

"Those are the cursed ruins?" asked Patty. "They don't look like much from here."

"Most ruins aren't much to look at. Darad Zur, however, is *special,*" James said.

"What's so special about it?" asked Shazzar.

"Darad Zur is a place of mystery and horrific legends. Over 100 explorers have vanished within those walls," James answered.

"And *that's* why we're come here, of course," said Zorn with a grin.

James nodded.

He and Zorn were cut from the same cloth. Neither could resist a mystery, especially one that involved death and legendary hauntings. James was there to solve the mystery of the disappearances. He also wanted to learn what those adventurers were after and why they thought it was worth risking their lives for.

"Let's go. I ain't afraid of no ghosts," Zorn said as he rode down the hill.

The others followed after him.

"What if the things there are *worse* than ghosts?" asked Shazzar.

"I'm not afraid of *anything!*" Zorn bragged.

"Just don't do anything foolhardy that might get us all killed," warned Shazzar.

"Now *when* have I ever done anything foolhardy?" Zorn asked indignantly.

"Well, there were those lycanthropes in Makhrek," said Patty.

"And those bugs," added Shazzar.

"Don't forget that dragon," James chimed in.

"All right! I get the message!" Zorn said as he held up his hand. "I'll admit the dragon thing was my way of showing off for Mulan, but those other incidents were unavoidable."

"How come you never show off for *me*?" asked Patty.

"You already know what I can do," Zorn said.

Rolf laughed.

"You didn't need to show off for Mulan, either," he said. "She fell in love with you at first sight."

"But you have to admit it was a nice touch," Zorn said smugly.

"What if that shotgun hadn't have brought the dragon down?" asked James.

"In that case, we most likely wouldn't be having this conversation right now," Zorn replied.

Kashi rolled over and opened his eyes. As he forced himself to grow accustomed to the darkness, his eyes focused on a luminous image of a great bird with outspread wings that was painted on the ceiling above him. He sat up and looked closer. The image had an eerie, almost ghost-like glow to it.

As he stood, his temples throbbed painfully. He rubbed tem until the pain subsided and checked his belt. He smiled when he realized that both his sword and pistol were still there. He leaned over and checked his boot.

"My dagger's still there, too," he said to himself. "Where on Earth *am* I?"

As if in answer, he heard a rusty squeak behind him. He turned and watched as a heavy wooden door swung slowly inward. As soon as it opened all the way, a torch on a wall in the passageway beyond flickered to life.

"Well, I'd be a poor guest indeed if I refused such an obvious invitation," he said as he stepped through the door.

As he walked slowly down the long corridor, he got the strangest sensation that he was being watched. Although he couldn't see anyone, he knew someone was nearby, waiting to spring whatever trap lay ahead. He drew his pistol and checked it to be sure it was loaded.

As he turned the next corner, he was nearly blinded by a sudden flash of bright white light. He cursed as he tried to shield his eyes. He cursed even louder when something large and heavy struck him on the side of his face and sent him tumbling into the nearest wall. Before he hit the floor, he fired his pistol. The shot echoed through the hallway and ricocheted off a wall. Kashi staggered to his feet and looked around. The hall was pitch black now.

He reached out with his left hand and touched the wall. Using it for a guide, he sidled along the corridor. A few minutes later, the rough-carved stones gave way to something wooden.

"A door?" he wondered.

He stopped and pushed inward. To his surprise, it swung inward. Before he could react, something grabbed his arm and pulled him inside. He struggled until he heard a familiar voice.

"Relax, my love. It's just us," Gorinna said.

He let his eyes grow accustomed to the torchlight inside the room and smiled when he saw his friends.

"Am I glad to see *you!* Just where on Earth *are* we?" he asked as Gorinna hugged him tightly.

"Be damned if I know," said Arka-Dal. "It looks like some sort of dungeon or underground maze. How we got here is anyone's guess."

"You're bruised!" Gorinna commented as she touched his face.

"Yes. Whatever hit me had the kick of a mule," Kashi said. "It still stings but I'm alright. Where's Perseus?"

"My guess is that we'll soon find out. Whoever's brought us here seems to be herding us toward each other for some reason," Pandaar said.

"And he's playing with out minds. It's hard to tell what's real down here. Be doubly careful," Arka-Dal warned.

The loud creaking of rusted hinges caught their attention. They turned and watched as a heavy door swung open just to their right. As it did, a torch flickered to life in the corridor beyond.

"Let's do this," Arka-Dal said.

"I'll take the lead," Kashi volunteered. "We don't need to fall into any more traps than we have to."

"I'll drink to that!" said Pandaar.

"You'll drink to anything!" Kashi joked.

It was nearly two a.m. when Galya walked in on the others as they were preparing to leave. She was dressed in a dark green cloak and a short red dress tied at the waist by a thick leather strap which supported a shortsword in a scabbard. The other women smiled at her.

"I'm going with you," Galya announced. "I may not have my powers but I can use a sword better than anyone I know. I will not sit idle when our husband may be in trouble."

Merlin nodded.

"If you're ready, we'll leave," he said.

The women gathered close to him. He raised his arms and encased them in a large, golden bubble. Seconds later, they were high in the air and zipping northward at great speed.

As they sailed over the country, Galya's thoughts traveled back in time a few days to a most unexpected turn of events.

She was in the nursery sewing. Little Hawk was in his crib crying. She heard his cries, but chose to ignore them. She was in the midst of attempting some intricate stitching and didn't want to break her concentration. Besides, all the child wanted was his rattle and that, she thought, could wait.

His wails grew louder.

"Be patient, Hawk! I'll be there in a moment," she called out just as she finished the last bit of work.

She put it down and turned just in time to see Hawk's rattle float slowly across the room and into his tiny, outstretched hand.

"By all that is unholy! The boy's inherited my powers!" she gasped as she walked to the crib.

Hawk beamed up at her. He tried to shove the rattle into his mouth. When he realized it was too big, he simply shook it happily and laughed. Galya laughed, too. She reached into the crib and picked him up.

"Most interesting," came a voice from the door.

"Merlin! You saw?" she asked.

"Indeed I did," he replied. "How long has the boy been doing that?"

"I just noticed it this very moment," Galya answered. "The little scamp's full of surprises."

"Most children are. If he does have your powers, you must train him in the proper uses of them. You must train him well, too," Merlin said.

"I shall. Will you help me?" Galya asked.

He nodded.

"I am certain that Gorinna will also help," he said. "Have you seen anything similar from Melody/"

"Not yet," Galya replied.

"What have *you* retained?" Merlin asked.

"I can use simple telekinesis. I can still contact Father telepathically and I can see very well at night—even through the deepest shadows," Galya summarized.

"But those are merely your *natural* abilities. They have nothing at all to do with magic," Merlin mused. "Hawk may have inherited those abilities. Still, we must keep watch over him to see if he shows signs of being able to cast spells."

She nodded.

"Did you foresee this?" she asked.

"I saw *something*. The vision was clouded as if I were trying to peer through heavy gauze. I wasn't sure what it was," he said.

It was half-truth.

And she knew it.

The look of concern in his eyes spoke volumes. He saw something in her son's future. Something that disturbed him. She decided not to press him further.

He smiled and touched her shoulder.

"It's all right," he assured her. "Everything will be just fine."

"Should we tell the others about this?" she asked.

"Of course. They, too, will have a hand in shaping your son's future. A *big* hand," he said.

Arka-Dal and the others took the news in stride.

"I always knew Hawk would be someone special—just like *you*," Arka-Dal said as he kissed Galya on the forehead.

She snapped out of her reverie and looked at Merlin. He was busy watching the terrain zip by beneath them. She sighed. Medusa heard her and clutched her arm as if to tell her all would be well. Chatha simply smiled.

Perseus woke to the sensation of rough, cold stone scraping his chin. He pushed himself up and turned over. His shield and helmet were lying next to him and his sword was still strapped to his back. He grabbed his helmet and placed it over his head as he stood and surveyed his strange surroundings.

The place was dark.

And cold.

"A dungeon?" he wondered as he picked up his shield.

As his eyes grew accustomed to the darkness, he spotted a tall wooden door in the wall in front of him. As there were no other doors in the room, he decided to use this one to get out. To his surprise, it swung open easily with a low "creak". Cautiously, he drew his sword and stepped through the door.

As soon as his feet hit the hallway, a torch flickered on not ten feet from where he stood. Perseus felt the hair at the back of his neck tingle. He looked around and saw nothing. He took a deep breath and walked down the hall. As he neared the torch, it went out. Another sparked to life ten feet further away.

"I'm being led," he thought. "But by who?"

He walked down the hall and saw a large wooden door. A light shone through a crack in the ancient boards. He felt the hairs on the back of his neck tingle as he approached. The door creaked inward just as he reached it.

He entered cautiously.

In the center of the room was a blazing fire pit. Just beyond it was stone pillar with a battered, half-naked man chained to it by the wrists.

The man looked familiar.

Eerily so.

As Perseus approached, the man looked up.

"Horatio!" he gasped.

The eyes stared vacantly back at him as if trying to focus. Perseus studied the man. His body was covered with open wounds and pus-filled sores. In short, he looked as if he'd been through a thresher.

"Perseus. Is it really you?" the man asked after a long interval.

"It's me, my friend," Perseus assured him as he rushed forward.

Only inches from his target, Horatio suddenly broke free of his chains and pounced on him with the energy of a hungry animal. Perseus fended him off with his shield and stared as his "friend" morphed into a long-armed, fanged and hairy beast bent on killing him. It growled and attacked again with even more ferocity. It grabbed his shield and tried to fling it aside. Since it was strapped to Perseus' arm, he sailed across the room with it and hit the floor hard.

As he cleared the cobwebs from his mind, he saw the creature beat its chest, bellow angrily, and charge again. This time, Perseus rolled with the blow. At the same time, he drove his sword upward as hard as he could. The blade sawed through the creature's breastbone and came out the other side. It hissed nastily at him as the life slowly faded from its pupil-less eyes. Disgusted, he pushed it off of him and regained his feet. As he pulled his sword free of the carcass, he looked around the room. The fire was now out.

As he cleaned the foul smelling blood from the blade, he vowed not be so easily tricked again. He walked back into the hall and smiled as another torch flickered to life several yards away.

"Lead on, Mac Duff!" he said.

Jun was waiting on the parade ground when the large golden ball appeared in the sky above the fort. He watched as it slowly settled to the ground and vanished. Jun grinned when he saw the three well-armed women and Merlin standing in its place. He acted surprised to see that Galya was with them.

"I've been expecting you," Jun said as they shook hands.

"It's good to see you again, Jun," said Chatha. "We'll need horses."

"Saddled and waiting at the stables even as we speak," Jun assured them as they walked toward a series of low wooden structures. "Is Perseus with them?"

"Yes," Medusa replied.

"Good. That makes them even more formidable. That Greek is a good fighter, especially when he has his back to the wall," Jun said.

"I take it that you still haven't heard from them?" asked Merlin.

"Not a peep," Jun answered.

"I don't like the sound of that," Medusa said.

Ten minutes later, they rode through the gates of the fort and took the main road south to Nineveh. With any luck, they hoped to be able to pick up their trail outside the city and follow it to wherever they had gone.

Merlin, however, believed they didn't need to travel to Nineveh.

"If we could locate their last campsite, I can use it to try and find them by picking up their aura," he said. "It's a little bit tricky, but I know I can do it."

"I'm all for that. It would save us days of searching," Jun agreed. "But there may be hundreds of old campsites along the way. How will you know which one is theirs?"

"Don't worry about that. I'll know which is theirs," Merlin assured him.

Perseus wandered the labyrinthine passages for what seemed like hours, following one flickering torch after another.

He knew he was being led.

But by who?

He figured he'd find out soon enough. As he turned down another corridor, he saw a half-open door several feet away. He took a deep breath and walked toward it. He could see a bright light from within.

Another trap?

There was one sure way to find out.

He barged in shield first and laughed when he saw Arka-Dal and the others standing in the middle of the room staring at a strange message that was painted on the wall.

"This is thine own personal Hell. May you find it as pleasant as I have found mine."—Alzari. Em

The Emperor turned and smiled.

"Perseus! It's about time you showed up," he joked as they shook hands.

"Where are we?" asked the Greek.

"We haven't a single clue yet," Gorinna replied as she and Kashi sat down against the far wall to rest.

Pandaar and Arka-Dal joined them.

"Take the load off awhile and help us figure this mess out," Kashi called.

Perseus sat down next to Arka-Dal. He removed his helmet and ran his fingers through his hair to massage his scalp. As he did, he studied the strange message on the wall before them.

"Who is this Alzari who has left his name all over this place?" he asked.

"No one's really sure. Little is actually known about him. He was a writer and a poet who lived sometime during the Great Darkness. He supposedly delved into the occult and arcane secrets of the First. When he attempted to compile all of this forbidden knowledge into a series of books, he went insane in the process. Legends say he has written four books. I found three of them just before I became

Emperor. I had no idea what was in them and I didn't want to know. Merlin and I were enemies then. He also wanted the books. To keep them out of his hands, I burned them. [15]

A rumored fourth book proved to be a myth. In Iluk, I met a man who claimed to be Alzari. If he really was the Mad Poet, he would have been thousands of years old,"[16] Arka-Dal said. "I doubt that he really was Alzari but he most certainly was mad."

Perseus shook his head.

"All this trouble over books?" he asked.

Arka-Dal nodded. Perseus looked up at the message again.

"Do you believe Alzari *wrote* that?" he asked.

"I don't know what to believe," Arka-Dal replied.

"What happened to Alzari?" Perseus asked.

"That's a good question," said Gorinna. "According to some sources, he wandered aimlessly through the deserts and ruins and eventually died. No one knows where he died or the location of his tomb. Even Merlin doesn't know his fate."

"I can tell you what *ours* will be if we don't find our way out of here," Pandaar interjected. "This place is filled with all sorts of traps. To make things worse, we've no food or water."

"I agree with Pandaar. Our situation doesn't look too good," Kashi added.

"Neither do *you* but that's beside the point," Pandaar jabbed.

It was well past midnight when they located the campsite. Merlin slid from his horse and walked over to the pile of charcoal in the middle of the clearing and crouched before it. After several long minutes of peering into the pile of charred wood and rocks, images of the missing royal party entered his inner mind. He saw Arka-Dal and the others seated around the fire, eating and laughing. Their horses were grazing a few yards away and all seemed right.

The images were in real time. He concentrated harder and fast-forwarded several hours. Now, everyone was asleep in their bedrolls around the fire. No one was on watch as no watch was needed. He saw a great, black shadow suddenly cover the entire camp. When the shadow moved on, everyone was gone. Only their empty bedrolls remained. Even their horses were gone.

---

15 Read THE AVENGER OF THULE

16 Read THE GRAND ILLUSION

"What was *that?*" he wondered.

He decided to try another spell. He stood and closed his eyes awhile. When he opened them again, he was surrounded by three-dimensional images of the royal party asleep in the bedrolls. He stepped back and watched as the shadow returned. It was huge and deep black. It soon covered the entire camp. Merlin felt it turn numbingly cold around him and fought off the chill. The shadow lingered several minutes then slowly melted away, taking everyone with it.

Including their horses.

But this time, it left a small bit of itself behind. It was enough to enable Merlin to track it to its point of origin.

"Now I know where you've taken them," he said with a grin as he returned to the others a mounted his horse.

"Well?" demanded the Minotaur.

"I know where they are. It's a ruin called Darad Zur about 150 miles north from here," Merlin replied.

"Never heard of it," said Jun as they rode away from the campsite.

"I'm not surprised. Few people know it exists. Those who do, shun it. They say the ruins are *cursed* and all sorts of evil things dwell there. The brave few who have ventured into Darad Zur were never seen again," Merlin explained.

"Why'd they go there?" asked Chatha.

"They didn't *go* there. Someone *took* them there," Merlin corrected.

"Who?" asked Medusa.

"That, my dear, is something we may soon find out," Merlin said. "Let us make haste to Darad Zur. I fear that out friends are in grave danger."

"If anything's happened to Arka-Dal, I'll find the bastard behind this even if I have to tear the place apart brick-by-brick!" Galya vowed.

The others nodded.

"What do you know about Darad Zur?" asked Medusa.

"Very little. I'm afraid that I've never explored the place. I do know that the city itself managed to survive a full two centuries after the Great Disaster. Then its inhabitants abandoned it for reasons unknown. The nomads shun it. They say the ruins are cursed. Now, only Jackals, wild dogs, vultures and other vermin dwell there," he replied.

"Why don't you just transport us to the ruins with your magic?" Chatha asked.

"That particular spell took a lot out of me. I'll need several hours to recuperate. Besides, there may be other clues along the way. We'd never see them from up there," Merlin said.

As the rescue party continued its trek across the desert, far off in his lair, Ned the Knower was still trying to pinpoint the source of the disturbance. After days of tireless searching, he discovered not one but *several* anomalies. He sat back and massaged his temples to let this data sink in.

Some*one* or some*thing* had punched several holes in the delicate membrane that separated the universe from other dimensions and universes as yet unknown to man. These new portals—and the things on the other side—posed a very real threat to Earth. Unless each portal could be found and sealed, all sorts of terrifying things would come through them.

In short, all Hell would break loose.

He was almost certain that it had something to do with the horrific war between the creatures of the Abyss and those who dwelled beyond it—whatever *they* were. Even Ned had only a vague idea as to what sort of creatures dwelled in those other dimensions beyond the rim. Anything could happen now.

Simply closing the portals wouldn't be enough. Whoever was behind this would simply open more gates. They had to find him before he could do more harm.

Before he could awaken The Beast.

"I'll need help," he decided.

Merlin felt it, too. But he was busy at the moment. Finding his missing friends was far more important to him than fretting over some long-range problems. He'd help Ned deal with that later.

Back in Thule, Mayumi noticed that Zhijima seemed more agitated then she usually felt when Pandaar was in danger. Given the circumstances, that was understandable. Mayumi was also quite worried but she hid her fears under a mask of calmness.

Besides them, the children, Leo and a handful of servants and guards were in the palace right now. Most of the lights were out and the children were asleep in their rooms.

She knew how to calm Zhijima.

After watching her friend pace awhile, she decided to help her out. She poured two glasses of wine and invited Zhijima to join her in the bedroom . . .

They traveled down one long corridor after another without incident for several hours. Everywhere they went, torches in wall sconces sparkled to life to light they path. Arka-Dal watched the shadows carefully, his entire being on alert for any nasty surprise that might come their way.

They soon came to a place where several corridors intersected. Kashi help up a fist and looked around. If anyone was going to spring a trap on them, this would be the perfect place. Seeing nothing, he signaled the others to follow. As soon as the last one entered the intersection, they became surrounded by a dull orange light. The light stretched from floor to ceiling and effectively blocked each corridor.

Pandaar sneered at the light and walked ahead, only to be thrown back onto his behind by a sudden and painful jolt of electricity. He slowly picked himself off the floor and looked around. Almost gingerly, he reached out and touched the wall of light and quickly recoiled in pain.

As he shook his hand, he looked at the others.

"Looks like we've walked straight into a trap," he said. "That light is electrically charged."

The others also attempted to touch the wall only to be forced back by the pain that raced through their arms.

All that is, but Gorinna.

To Gorinna's surprise, her hand easily passed through the strange wall, but the energy it contained made her entire body tingle unpleasantly.

"I think I can get through," she called out.

Arka-Dal walked over and touched the wall, only to have his hand repelled by what felt like a powerful jolt of electricity. He withdrew and shook off the numbness.

"I *can't*. Maybe it doesn't affect you because of your magic. Keep going. Let's see what happens," he said.

She nodded and pushed her entire arm into the wall. When nothing nasty happened, she kept going. Seconds later, she found herself standing outside looking in at the others. She saw Arka-Dal's lips moving but couldn't hear him. That's when she realized that the inside was a vacuum. If she didn't find a way to get them out, they'd be suffocated.

She attempted to use her spells on the wall. Each one simply dissipated in a shower of brightly colored sparks. She leaned against the wall to try and get back inside. This time, the wall held firm. Frustrated, she stepped back to think. In desperation, she called out.

"Merlin where are you when I need you?"

"I'm here—just outside the ruins," came the reply much to her amazement. "Where are *you*?"

"I'm not really sure," she replied. "This place is a labyrinth."

"Focus on my thoughts and follow them to me," Merlin said. "You'll come to us shortly."

"*Us?*" she asked as she began running through the corridors.

"Yes. Medusa, Chatha and Galya are here with me. We've come to rescue you!" Merlin replied.

"That's good because we sure as Hell *need* it!" Gorinna said as she quickened her pace.

Fifteen minutes passed before she felt fresh air wafting down the passageway. She followed the cool sensation all the way to the entrance and almost collapsed in Merlin's arms when she burst from the ruins.

"Thank the gods you're here!" she gasped as he helped her steady herself.

"Open your thoughts. Let me see where the others are," Merlin said.

She nodded and concentrated. He saw Arka-Dal and the others trapped inside a strange wall of light. He broke off contact and nodded.

"We have to act quickly," he said.

Gorinna stood completely still and looked southward.

"We've got company," she said. "I sense riders approaching."

"Friend or foe?" asked Merlin.

"Friend—I hope," she replied.

As James and his party approached the ruins, they spotted the horses. As they drew closer, they also saw five people moving around near the entrance. One was especially large and sported horns much like a bull. James raised his hand to signal a halt then quietly slid off his horse. The others did the same.

"Looks like we aren't the only ones who decided to come here," James said. "Let's proceed with caution until we discover who the others are."

They left the horses where they were and crept toward the ruins on foot. They could see that three of the others were women. The fourth was a tall, thin man in a hooded cloak. James put a finger to his lips and motioned for the others to follow him.

While Merlin and the others stood near the entrance wondering what to do next, Galya stayed back with horses to protect them from would-be predators. As she listened in on their conversation, she heard a footfall behind her. She drew her sword and turned just as James emerged from the shadows.

"You!" they both shouted.

James stopped in his tracks and stared at Galya. She saw his surprise give way to anger. Although helpless without her powers, she stood her ground and attempted to bluff him.

"So, Red Cleric! We meet again after all these years," she almost growled as she took up a defensive stance.

"Bitch! You escaped me before but you'll not be so lucky this time!" James said as he pointed his staff at her.

Before Galya could react, a beam of light crackled from the staff and headed right for her chest. As she closed her eyes expecting the worst, the beam suddenly dissipated inches from its target. When the glare died, James and Galya were both surprised to see a very angry Gorinna standing between them with her arms crossed.

"Harm a single hair on her head and I'll turn you into something *unspeakable*!" Gorinna warned.

"*You're* defending *her?* She's Satan's daughter! She's the most vile and evil thing that walks this Earth!" James said as he readied his staff to strike again.

Gorinna clapped her hands. To James' embarrassment, his staff flew from his hands and landed several yards away. He stared at her in wonder. No one had ever disarmed him before. The Red Witch was even more powerful than he had heard. Going up against her would be like committing suicide.

"Galya is the fourth wife of the Emperor Arka-Dal. She is also my friend," Gorinna said sternly.

"And mine as well," Merlin said from behind him. "Stay your hand, James Colla. Things are not as they appear."

He picked up the staff and returned it to him. James leaned on it and listened while Merlin explained the situation. Afterwards, he shook his head in disbelief. He took a deep breath and looked at Galya.

"You almost killed me the last time," he said.

"And you me," Galya said. "What is past is past. Much has changed of late. My husband, the man I love with all of my being, and our friends are somewhere in these ruins. We have come to find them. Why are you here?"

"The legends say these ruins are haunted. We've come to see by what," James answered.

"He means *he* did. We came with him for the Hell of it," Zorn said as he took in Galya's obvious beauty. "Are you *really* Satan's daughter?"

"That is but one of the names my father is known by," Galya replied. "Even without my powers, I can sense that this place reeks of evil. It almost seems alive somehow."

"I feel it, too," Merlin agreed.

"Where are the others?" asked Medusa.

Gorinna pointed down into the ruins.

"Everyone's down there. The place is quite confusing to navigate, but I can take us to them. They're all trapped in that chamber. I was able to get out of it but I could not get back in nor free them with my spells. I've never seen anything like it before," she said. "When I sensed you were near, I sought you out. We'd better hurry. There's precious little air left inside. We must free them before they are suffocated."

Galya realized that Rolf was staring at her. His amber eyes seemed to be able to see right through her. His gaze made her uncomfortable. Then he smiled at her.

"What did you see?" she asked.

"The real you," he replied.

"Did you like what you saw?" she asked.

"Yes. There is much good and beauty in your heart. It runs deeper than you know," he said.

James looked into her eyes.

"The boy's right," he said after a few seconds.

"We *told* you so," said Gorinna.

"So you did," James said. "I suggest we leave the women up here to guard our horses and to make certain nothing goes in behind us."

"Good idea. We'll build a fire to keep wild animals at bay. But hurry. There isn't much time," Medusa agreed.

Galya pouted but nodded.

Chatha seemed even more irritated by James' suggestion. She was about to say something in protest until Patty offered to stay with them.

With that settled, Merlin turned to Gorinna.

"Take us to them," he said.

They plunged back into the labyrinth. Shazzar walked beside Gorinna and searched the walls and floors for any signs of booby traps. Jun brought up the rear to guard against surprise attacks.

As before, each time they turned down a corridor, torches flickered to life in wall sconces to light their way—and to lead them. It was obvious to everyone that whoever was behind this wanted them to reach Arka-Dal and the others.

But who was behind this?

And why was he playing this strange game?

Arka-Dal himself was wondering the same things as he examined their predicament. He'd been in traps before but this one was a masterpiece.

Still surrounded by the strange wall, he and the others grew more and more uncomfortable. Breathing became harder and they could feel the air being sucked out of the room.

Arka-Dal looked up the corridor and wondered where Gorinna was. Had she made it out alive? If so, what was her plan?

He looked around at the others. Pandaar, Kashi and Perseus were seated cross-legged on the floor. All panted as the air inside the chamber lessened with each passing second. Soon, they wouldn't be able to breathe at all.

"I don't want to die like this," he thought.

He walked around and touched every side of the strange shield. Each time, intense waves of energy surged through his arm and he was forced to draw back in pain. He jumped up to touch the ceiling. The jolt knocked him to his knees. That's when he realized that he could touch the floor without feeling any discomfort.

"The trap doesn't include the floor," he thought as he examined it carefully.

It was solid stone and they had no way of digging through it. There wasn't enough air left in the trap to allow them to give it a try either.

"It's up to Gorinna now," he said to himself.

Patty watched while Galya lit the fire and fanned the flames.

"From where do you know James?" she asked.

"We've had several battles over the years. We have crossed paths many times. The last involved his brother, Byron. I had almost bagged him when James intervened. After a long and nasty fight, we both retreated. I decided Byron's soul wasn't worth dying over and returned to the Lower Planes," Galya answered.

"You nearly bagged Byron?" Patty asked.

Galya nodded.

"It was easy enough, considering his penchant for sexy women," she said.

"Do you know anyone else in our group?" asked Patty as she sat beside her.

"Not directly. Father *did* sign a contract with the elder Yaren concerning his future sons but I have no idea what the details are. Father doesn't bother to tell me such things," Galya said as she used a stick to stir the fire.

Patty stared at the flames.

"So Rolf and Zorn's father made a pact with the Devil? I wonder what was in it? Did it concern either of them?" she thought.

She studied Galya.

She was slender and perfectly proportioned. Her facial features were remarkably pretty and much softer than she imagined they'd be. Her hair was also gorgeous. Even at night, it seemed to sparkle magically.

"No wonder Arka-Dal fell in love with you. You're *beautiful*," she said.

Galya smiled.

"His love brings out the beauty inside of me," she said honestly. "As does your love for the younger Yaren."

Patty laughed.

"I should have known you'd be able read my thoughts," she said.

"I didn't have to. The way you look at him reveals how you feel," Galya said.

"I didn't realize I was so obvious," Patty remarked.

"You are," Galya assured her.

"Love is difficult to hide," Chatha added. "It's far too strong."

Just as he was about to give up, Arka-Dal saw Gorinna and the others race into the room. They stopped short of the barrier. He couldn't hear anything. He watched as Merlin and the one in the red cloak touched the barrier with their hands and quickly pulled back.

"Let's try combining our powers to break down the shield," Merlin suggested.

Gorinna nodded.

James watched as they joined hands and cast a spell designed to shatter the barrier. The spell had no effect on the wall—but those trapped within were now writhing in agony.

"A pain box!" James said. "I haven't seen one of these in years!"

"Indeed. This is very ancient magic. The kind that has long passed from our universe. If we attack the box again, the energy that's released inside will surely kill the others. We'll have to find a way to bypass it," Merlin said thoughtfully as they paced in front of it.

That's when James happened to notice that Arka-Dal was tapping the palm of his hand against the floor.

"That's it! We must go under the box!" he shouted.

"Stand back!" Merlin said.

He stamped his foot hard as he uttered a spell. Almost instantly, the floor began to liquefy. It sunk downward about ten feet then turned and went under the barrier. Seconds later, the stone in the center of the trap eddied downward like water spiraling down a drain. The sudden rush of air jetting into the box revived those trapped within.

"Everyone down into the hole! Now!" shouted the Emperor.

Kashi jumped in first.

Then went Perseus with Pandaar close behind.

Arka-Dal jumped in last.

One-by-one, they emerged from the hole at Merlin's feet and were helped out by Shazzar and Zorn. As soon as Kashi reached safety, Gorinna threw her arms around his neck and kissed him.

Merlin made the introductions of their new friends.

"So you're the famous Red Cleric? I've heard much about you," Arka-Dal said as he shook James' hand.

"And I've heard much about you. If any of it is true, you are quite extraordinary," James said.

"Few men ever live up to others' expectations. What brings you to this forsaken place?" asked Arka-Dal.

"Rumors and legends abound of this place. What brought you here?" James replied.

"That remains to be seen. Whoever it is, he has a sick sense of humor," Arka-Dal said.

"The name of Alzari keeps popping up all over this place," Pandaar said.

"The Mad Poet? What's he have to do with this place?" asked Shazzar.

"I don't know, but there's one way to find out," Arka-Dal said. "Are you with us?"

"Now you've fired up my curiosity. There's no turning back," James assured him. "Before we continue, let's think this out. Someone brought you all here for a specific reason. Someone very powerful and knowledgeable in the use of rather unusual magic. Any idea who that might be?"

"None. But I doubt that you and your friends were part of his original equation. You're here by chance and that may give us an edge," Arka-Dal said. "I also doubt that he planned to invite Merlin to his little party. That might prove to be an even bigger surprise."

"I doubt we're much of a surprise anymore. Anyone *that* powerful is surely watching our every move," Merlin said.

"I almost feel as if someone is *testing* us," Gorinna said.

"Ah, but I *am* testing you!"

The voice seemed to come from everywhere. They stopped and looked around. The voice came again.

"Pass my test and you live. Fail, and you die."

"Where are you? Show yourself!" Arka-Dal demanded.

"All in good time," the voice said.

"That voice—where have I heard that voice?" Gorinna wondered aloud.

"That's what that squirrel always says," Shazzar said.

"*What* squirrel?" asked Pandaar.

"The one that hangs out with the moose in that old cartoon," Shazzar replied.

"What are you babbling about?" Gorinna queried.

"Don't fret over it. It would take too long to explain," Zorn said as he jabbed Shazzar in the ribs with his elbow.

"I'll take the point," Shazzar volunteered.

"I'll go with him," said Kashi.

Arka-Dal nodded and gave them a ten second head start before leading the rest of the group after them. They traveled on for several minutes, up one narrow passage and down another, through archways and half-open doors. Every few yards, a torch flickered to life to light the way ahead. Kashi and Shazzar turned a corner and suddenly found themselves staring into a deep and wide hole in the floor. They signaled to the others to stop.

"That's a fine mess. How in Hell do we get over?" asked Pandaar. "It's too far to jump and I see no way around."

James studied the hole for a few seconds then casually stepped into it. The others watched as, instead of plummeting to his death, the Red Cleric walked to the center of the hole, then turned and smiled.

"It's quite solid," he called out.

"An illusion! That bastard's playing with out minds again," Gorinna said.

Before he stepped across, Zorn stopped and watched as something dark and amorphous slowly emerged from the wall directly behind and above James.

"Duck!" he shouted as he raised his shotgun and fired both barrels.

The shells struck the mass dead-center. It shrieked in agony and melted into the floor like a shadow. Zorn reloaded his weapon as he walked over to James.

"*That* was not an illusion," James said.

"Is that what haunts this place?" asked Shazzar.

"I fear that it is only one of many things that prowl these ruins. Let us continue and be wary of more traps," James replied.

They moved slower now. The corridor widened a few yards ahead. Shazzar raised his hand and put his finger to his lips. They stopped and listened.

"I hear a rumbling sound," Gorinna said.

"It sounds like a wagon moving down a cobblestone street," said Kashi.

Merlin stepped to the front and raised his hands just as the source of the rumbling came into view.

"A chariot!" gasped Arka-Dal.

"With bladed wheels! Another illusion?" asked Pandaar.

Perseus somehow found himself in front of everyone else. He saw the chariot bearing down on him and braced himself for the expected impact. Instead, all that hit him was a wave of small white feathers, most of which collided harmlessly with his upraised shield.

He lowered his shield, spat out a mouthful of feathers, and shrugged.

James and the others laughed.

"That was a good one, Merlin!" James said as he slapped him on the back. "I'll wager that's really pissed off our host, too."

"Before this is ended, I plan on doing more than just piss him off," Merlin said.

They kicked their way through the heap of feathers and continued down the hall. As always, torches sparkled to life and lit the way ahead.

"We're being led," Arka-Dal mused. "But to where?"

They soon entered a large, rectangular chamber. Rolf stopped in the middle of the room and drew his sword.

"Here they come!" he shouted as he swung at empty air.

To everyone's astonishment, blood splattered everywhere and a hideously malformed, half-human thing fell dead at his feet. The others drew their weapons and followed his example. Soon, the entire chamber echoed with yelps of pain, hisses, angry growls and the sounds of frantic combat. Creature after creature hit the floor. Blood spattered on everyone and everything. They swung blindly at the things they could not see. But there were so many of them that most of their swings found their marks

"There's hundreds of them!" yelled Zorn as he fired his shotgun.

The shells struck something directly in front of him and showered him with bits of flesh, shattered bone and thick, sticky blood. Before he could reload, he felt something clawing at him from several directions. He drew his sword and lashed out with the fury of a tornado until the clawing stopped and several of the things lay dead or dying around him in pools of blood.

The wild melee continued for several long minutes with no end in sight. Frustrated, Gorinna raised her hands above her head.

"I've had just about enough of this! Be gone!" she shouted as she clapped as hard as she could.

The chamber filed with light. When it died out, the floor was covered with the charred remains of their eerie attackers.

"Impressive," James commented.

"Thanks," Gorinna said with a smile and a nod of her head.

"What are these things?" asked Pandaar.

"Dead," said Rolf.

"Well put," said James. "Now, let's find our host."

Galya sat by the fire and watched the shadows between the buildings for signs of movement. Besides the intermittent screeches of a distant hyena and the buzzing of the insects, all was quiet. A few feet away, Patty leaned against a wall and dozed. Medusa was next to the fire, curled up in her sleeping bag. On the other side of the camp, Chatha paced near the horses, which seemed unusually edgy. They snorted and scraped the ground with their hooves. The ruins gave Chatha the creeps. The others had gone into the ruin hours ago. She thought they should have returned by now. *If* they were able to.

Someone had gone through a lot of trouble to bring them here. Someone very *powerful.* But who? What was he after?

She was so lost in her thoughts, she failed to notice the panther lurking in the shadows on the crumbling roof above her until it was too late. The animal emitted a growl of warning and sprang at Chatha. She flinched and tried to draw her sword. To her surprise, the big cat hit the ground at her feet and lay still. There was shortsword protruding from its throat.

Chatha breathed a sigh of relief and watched as Galya retrieved her sword and wiped the blood off on the panther's hide. Galya looked at her and smiled. Chatha hugged her gratefully.

"Thank you," she said softly.

The commotion woke Medusa and Patty. Both leapt to their feet with weapons drawn. Then they saw the dead panther. Patty sheathed her sword and sat back down. Medusa ran over and hugged Chatha and Galya.

Galya had fought in countless battles over her long life. In fact, she was still the nominal commander of 30 of the best legions of troops on the Lower Planes. As a result of her experiences, she had become an expert with every known weapon from several planes. Bringing down the panther was child's play for her.

"One of the things I haven't lost is my night vision," she said as they all walked back to fire.

"Lucky for me you didn't," said Chatha.

While the others walked ahead, James engaged Merlin in a quiet conversation to the rear. Merlin saw the look of consternation on James' face and asked him what bothered him.

"It's this whole thing with Galya. Did you not have several run-ins with her and her wicked father?" James asked.

"More than I care to count," Merlin replied.

"Was not Galya among your bitterest enemies?" asked James.

"That she was," he said as recalled some of their nastiest battles. "But that is past now."

"Do you really *trust* her?" James asked.

"I trust her with Arka-Dal's life—as does he," Merlin said. "Their love runs deep and their bond is unbreakable. And their children are treasures."

"I see. What of her father? Have you made peace with him as well?" asked James.

"Let's just say that we have put aside or differences—at least while we are both in Thule. Beyond that, it's business as usual. Only now, we try not to kill each other," Merlin answered with a smile.

"You sound as if you *like* him," James observed.

"In many respects, I do. Besides, he has sworn to protect Thule for as long as a member of Arka-Dal's and Galya's line dwells there. One cannot ask for a more powerful ally than *that*," Merlin said.

"Is the Knower aware of this?" asked James.

"He is," Merlin assured him. "In fact, he finds this whole situation rather ironic—and somewhat amusing."

"It is when you think about it," James said.

"Indeed," said Merlin.

A faint scratching noise that came from the far end of the corridor caused everyone to stop in his tracks. They listened as the scratching grew more pronounced. After a few seconds, it became accompanied by the sounds of heavy breathing. Shazzar and Kashi drew their swords and took up positions on either side of the hall as they waited for the source of the strange sounds to appear. Perseus stood a few feet beyond them with his sword at the ready and his heavy shield raised. Pandaar and Arka-Dal were a few feet behind him.

The scraping/panting grew louder and louder. They saw a huge shadow appear on the wall in front of Kashi and Shazzar. The heavy breathing became loud sniffing as if the owner of the shadow had picked up their scent. A few seconds later, two gigantic canine heads peaked at them from around the corner. Its red eyes focused on Perseus and it opened its hideous mouths to emit a low, threatening growl. The next moment, the entire animal appeared.

Everyone stared in disbelief at the eight-foot tall, powerfully-built two headed canine crouched at the end of the corridor. It barked several times, then charged straight at them. It bowled over both Kashi and Shazzar and made for Perseus. The Greek dug in heels and prepared himself for a hard fight. To his surprise, the creature passed right through him as if it were made of air and suddenly vanished.

"What the fuck happened?" asked Shazzar as he and Kashi helped each other up.

Perseus shrugged and shook his head.

"I don't get it. That thing knocked the stuffing out of us and passed harmlessly through you!" Kashi said.

"I don't understand it either," Perseus said as he looked at James and Merlin.

Both simply shrugged.

"I'm sick of this game. We can't be sure what's real or what's illusory. It's like someone's making up the rules as we go along," Arka-Dal complained.

"This guy's good. That was one of the best tricks I ever saw," Gorinna commented. "I wonder how he did that?"

"You can ask him yourself when we find him," Arka-Dal said. "But where is he?"

"I see him," said Rolf.

"Where?" asked James.

"There," he said as he pointed to a blank wall.

Merlin studied the blank wall a second, then waved his hand.

"An arch!" Arka-Dal said.

"It was hidden by a spell. Our young friend here can see things that most others can't," Merlin said.

"How?" asked Pandaar and Kashi.

"It's a gift," Rolf said smugly.

"From who?" asked Gorinna.

"Dunno," Rolf replied.

They stepped through the arch and into an octagonal chamber with a high, vaulted ceiling. Several torches on the wall flickered to life when they entered. The chamber was empty save for a single, high-backed chair that faced the far wall.

"Ah, Merlinus. We meet again after so many years," came a voice from the chair as it spun around slowly.

Merlin squinted at the seated figure gently stroking the black cat in his lap. The man's face was hidden in the shadows of his hooded cloak while the cat fixed its gaze on Merlin.

"You!" Merlin said with a mixture of surprise and disgust.

"You were expecting maybe Mary Poppins?" quipped the cat.

"I expected to see anyone but *you!*" Merlin said as he stepped closer.

The man smiled as he saw Gorinna and James emerge from behind Merlin.

"I never planned to bring you here, Merlinus," he said. "I only wanted to lure the witch into my trap.

"What do you want with me?" Gorinna demanded.

"You have something that belongs to me," he said softly as the cat stared up at her.

"What could I possibly have that would interest you?" she asked as she circled to the left.

The cat followed her movements and yawned.

"You have a certain tome that I asked you and your friends to retrieve for me. The one you gave me was a fake. A good one, but a fake nonetheless," he said.

"And what if I refuse to hand it over?" she asked.

"In that case, none of you shall leave here alive," the wizard assured her.

"Is that why you brought the others here, too? As bargaining chips in your silly game?" Gorinna asked snippily.

"Precisely," the wizard said smugly.

"Why Alzari?" asked Merlin.

"I chose the Mad Poet's name because I knew it would provide impetus for you to keep searching the ruins. Also, the book the witch stole from me is one of his most important works. I need it to complete my collection," he replied.

"That's impossible! Arka-Dal destroyed the only copies in existence years ago!" Gorinna said.

"Foolish woman. Do you think those were the only copies ever printed? I assure you that several more of Alzari's books yet exist and I won't rest until I have them all," the wizard snapped.

He saw the expressions on their faces and laughed.

"My plan was simple. I brought you and your friends here and herded you into that bubble trap. I knew that you would be able to escape it easily enough because of your magical nature, but the others would remain trapped. Any attempts to rescue them sent thousands of volts of electricity surging through them. At the same time, the air was being drawn from their lungs. I figured that rather than watch them all die, you'd gladly turn the book over to me.

I never imagined that Arka-Dal's wives would round up Merlin and mount a rescue expedition. Nor did I foresee the timely arrival of you, Red Cleric," the old wizard explained.

"I would have figured a way around your trap eventually," Gorinna pointed out smugly.

"Perhaps. But in your near-panic state of mind, the solution might have come to you too late. As death neared, you would have surrendered the book," the wizard said through the cat.

"Not hardly. I burned that damned book myself when she brought it to the palace," Arka-Dal said.

"You *destroyed* it?" the wizard asked incredulously.

"I sure as Hell did," Arka-Dal replied.

"In that case, I shall have to kill all of you in retaliation," the wizard threatened as James circled around to the right.

"Harm them and I swear I will make you suffer like never before," Merlin warned.

"Stay out of this, Merlinus. This is not your concern!" the wizard said.

"Anything that concerns my friends also concerns me," Merlin said as he stood his ground.

"And me, too," James warned as he raised his staff.

"Cross me again, Red Cleric, and I warn you the results will be much different than last we met," the wizard said calmly.

"You know this guy, James?" asked Shazzar.

"Let's just say that we've crossed paths," James said. "You'd better back off. This could get nasty."

Gorinna whispered to Merlin.

"Just how powerful *is* he?" she asked.

"Very," said Merlin.

"As powerful as the three of us combined?" asked James.

"That we are about to discover," Merlin replied. "Prepare yourselves!"

As if on cue, both he and Gorinna hurled potent spells at the wizard. He calmly blocked both simply by raising his hand, then retaliated. Gorinna deflected his attack. The spell struck the ceiling above and behind her and sent a cloud of dust and debris raining down on the others who quickly covered themselves to avoid getting hit. Merlin captured the spell hurled at him in his open hand. He turned to Gorinna and nodded.

Again they attacked simultaneously.

While the wizard fended off their spells, he failed to pay attention to James, who seized the opportunity and hurled his staff straight at his chest. The staff struck him in the breastbone and pinned him to the back of the chair. As the wizard slumped over, the cat hissed and fled the scene in a puff of smoke. Merlin and Gorinna lowered their hands while James retrieved his staff.

They stood and watched as the wizard's body began to bubble like suds in a bathtub.

"Your plan worked," Gorinna said.

"They *usually* do," James said smugly.

The others gathered around and watched the wizard's body as it slowly liquidized. Arka-Dal shook his head.

"Now *that's* disgusting!" he remarked.

"A most fitting end if I do say so myself," Merlin said.

"But what does all of this lunacy have to do with Alzari?" asked Gorinna.

"The only connection between the Mad Poet and this place is in his twisted mind. He believes the books will give him the keys to unlock incredible sources of power. What he plans to do with it is anyone's guess," Merlin said.

"But he's already powerful. You said he draws his magic from a source beyond this universe," she said.

"Yes. And it has almost driven him mad. He desires yet more power and he will do anything he can to obtain it, regardless of the consequences," Merlin said.

By now, all that remained of the wizard was his crumpled clothes floating in a pool of nasty red liquid. The cat was also gone.

"Just as I expected. He's escaped. That son of a bitch is going to be very difficult to kill," Merlin cursed.

"So are *you*!" Arka-Dal said, referring to their early battles.[17]

Merlin laughed and slapped him on the back as they left the room . . .

---

[17] Read: THE AVENGER OF THULE

Once they reached the surface, Galya, Medusa and Chatha raced to Arka-Dal and kissed him with incredible passion. They walked back to the horses. Arka-Dal and the others were surprised to see their horses, saddled and waiting, nearby.

"They showed up just a few minutes ago. It was if they'd been summoned here," Medusa explained.

Arka-Dal stroked the nose of his white charger and smiled.

"Raindancer always knows where to find me. He's just like his father," he said gratefully. "And where he goes, the others follow."

"Will you be coming to Thule with us?" asked Chatha.

James shook his head.

"We have business elsewhere. We'll come to Thule by and by," he said. He turned to Galya and smiled.

She returned it.

"Do I detect a change of heart in you, Red Cleric?" she asked.

He nodded.

"If Arka-Dal loves and trusts you, then I shall also trust you. Our wars are over, Galya. I wish you well," he said as he mounted his horse. "There is one thing you should know before I leave.."

"Yes?" she asked.

"Despite the legends, your powers are *not* gone. They are simply *dormant* and in need of some dire emergency to return them to their full potential. They will return when they are most needed," he said as he turned his horse and rode west.

"And keep an eye on your son! One day, he will be able to give Merlin a good run for his money!" he called back.

"Where are you going, James?" shouted Merlin.

"There are many mysteries yet to solve and so little time to solve them. We'll meet again, Merlin, I promise you," James replied.

Shazzar laughed.

"And we go where James goes! Farewell, my friends and good luck!" he said as he and the others galloped after James.

Galya turned to Merlin.

"Was the Red Cleric right?" she asked.

"Yes," Merlin replied.

"Why didn't you tell me this?" she asked.

"I didn't have to. You already knew this. The answers to all of your questions lie deep within your own heart. You need only to be quiet and *listen,*" he assured her with a knowing smile.

"Tell me, Merlin, just who *is* that wizard?" Gorinna asked.

"A long time ago, we were apprentices together. While I chose the path of light, he opted to travel a much darker road in search of the source of power used by the Elder Gods. His pursuits have twisted his heart and mind and blackened his soul beyond redemption. He is nearly mad," Merlin explained.

"Does he have a name?" asked Galya.

"Not any longer," Merlin replied.

"I've got one for him—son of a bitch," Arka-Dal suggested.

Merlin laughed.

"It's as good a name as any," he said.

"If he bothers us again, his name will be *mud*," Galya vowed.

"Let's go home, people," Arka-Dal said.

As they rode away from the ruins, everyone failed to notice the small black cat watching from his shadowy perch atop a crumbling wall. The cat watched until they were out of his line of vision then slowly faded into nothingness, leaving only his smile behind. After a while, it faded, too . . .

The Devil to Pay

In the 50h year of the reign of Arka-Dal.

The royal palace was alive with the gleeful, raucous sounds of many children at play. From early morning to early evening, the long halls resounded with the sounds of tiny running feet, shouts and joyous laughter. Their wild games usually involved toy swords and shields, toy soldiers, dolls or rubber balls and other new things their mothers brought home from their daily trips through the city markets.

The most boisterous of the bunch was little Hercemes, the adopted son of Arka-Dal and Mayumi. Quick on his feet, strong and imaginative, it was he who came up with the newest ideas for games and adventures. Herc was undoubtedly the leader of the pack and his games often resulted in things being broken. When this occurred, he and the others were usually admonished for being careless and banished to the outdoors. Although the breakages sometimes irritated the women, Arka-Dal wrote them as "children being children" and considered it somewhat amusing. The palace, after all, contained few antiques or rare art objects. Arka-Dal always believed that such things were best kept in museums so that everyone could enjoy them. The bric-a-brac around the palace was easily replaceable.

When his granddaughter, Mut, was around, their play became even more free-spirited. That's when things *really* were at risk of being destroyed.

When the children weren't at play, they at school learning. Leo and Medusa oversaw their basic educational needs, such as writing, reading, logic, lore, history, math and the sciences. Master Koto taught them self-discipline and the martial arts. Their learned respect and manners from their mothers and demonic lore from Galya. They learned to swim in the big pool and survival skills from the men around the palace. Most were even riding their own ponies.

And they traveled everywhere with their parents.

They especially loved the trips to the toy stores and zoos and local sporting events.

Since they were always out in public, the people got to know each of them quite well. And they *loved* them. Most of the Thulians felt that Arka-Dal's children were also their children. The royal family was also their family. They had a particular fondness for Arka-Dal's newest wife, Galya.

Galya's love for Arka-Dal ran deep.

He occupied her every thought. He was the focus of her emotions. Love was new for her. It made her feel light hearted and happy. It made her happier still to know that he felt the same about her.

She'd sacrificed much to be with him.

Her magical powers.

Her immortality.

He was her entire world now.

Her life.

Her father had always told her that love made one weak.

"You're wrong, Father," she told him. "It makes one strong because it makes life worth living. It gives it meaning."

He didn't argue with her.

Galya was happy now and that's all that mattered.

Besides, he actually liked Arka-Dal. And Arka-Dal actually liked him. Thule was the only place on Earth where he was openly welcomed and his daughter was adored. To the people of Thule, she wasn't the hated Devil's daughter. She was the Emperor's fourth wife and that made her an icon. They even made and sold objects with her image on them.

His, too!

They were now part of Thulian pop culture—just like Arka-Dal and the rest of his friends and family. Their images adorned greeting cards, broaches, cameos, pottery, etched mirrors, clothing—you name it.

Thulian women of all ages had also adopted versions of Galya's hairstyle and clothing. A few even sported fake horns on their foreheads. Thanks to Thule's hot climate, women's fashions had always been quite revealing compared to women of other nations. Now that many had decided to emulate Galya, their dresses were even more revealing. In fact, they left little to the imagination. This, of course, made Thulian men very happy.

Among the "in" crowd, dressing like the Devil was considered to be a mark wealth and good taste. Men going out on the town often donned long, silken high-collared capes and dark suits. Some even sported goatees and horns.

The Devil viewed this all with amusement.

"I've become a fashion icon! It's become trendy to dress like me," he observed.

"It's the price of popularity. You'll get used to it," Leo assured him.

Even Thule's universities were affected.

Thanks to the vast volumes of history on the Lower Planes Galya had provided, such studies were now among the most popular courses. Arka-Dal had insisted that Leo provide copies of each set to every university that desired them. Much to the Devil's surprise, several religious academies also requested copies and offered courses on the Lower Planes.

"It's a shame that we can't get similar information on those who dwell in the Abyss," Leo said. "We know virtually nothing at all about them."

"It's better you don't," the Devil advised. "Some things are best kept in the shadows."

"Father is right, Leo," Galya added. "It's best not get too nosy. There are things down there even *we* know nothing about."

But while Arka-Dal's popularity was at an all-time high, certain people who dwelled on the fringes of society weren't all that enamored with his fourth wife, Galya. This was especially true of a young, charismatic priest named Tumlecar who had recently emigrated to Thule from Europe.

Tumlecar was about 40, tall, athletic and disarmingly handsome. It was said that he could talk even a hungry squirrel out its nuts and was reputed to be a real ladies' man.

He was a hard-line fundamentalist, too. To him, every word in the Bible was the word of God himself. There could be no deviations from the way it was written. No deviations from its true meaning. But his interpretation of the Bible was more than a little bit twisted. Some said that he took it far too literally.

This mind set quickly put him at odds with the goings on in Thule.

Galya was the daughter of Satan. To him, she represented all that was dark and evil. She was a devil. A monster with a heart of blackness and an unrepentant seductress. He hated her with a passion and was unwilling to give her the benefit of the doubt like other members of his church had.

The fact that she was married to Arka-Dal rubbed him the wrong way. He was certain that she was stringing him along and that she would soon lead him down the wrong path—and Thule with him. He believed that she had been sent to Thule by her despicable father for the sole purpose of destroying it.

To save Thule, he must first save the Emperor.

That meant Galya had to go.

At first, his fire and brimstone sermons were somewhat popular with the congregation. As long as they turned out to hear him preach, they put money in the offering plate that was passed around the church.

He preached against sinners. He warned against demons. He said there was only one true god and that his word was law.

"Unalterable! His words are etched in stone and woe be to all nonbelievers for they shall burn in the eternal flames of Hell! No man or woman can escape the wrath of the Lord!"

His style was flamboyant and a little nutty. He was also quite a showman. He knew how to bring people in. And come they did each Sunday. Tumlecar provided good theater for them. And hardly anyone took him seriously.

Because of his popularity, Monsignor Bartolomy let him continue. Besides, he wasn't hurting anyone.

But after several weeks, his sermons grew darker. His preaching grew shriller. That's when he started speaking out directly against Galya and her father and their growing evil influences on the Empire. To emphasize this, he added pyrotechnics to wow the parishioners and give them a taste of what he thought Hell was really like. This kept them coming for awhile and enabled him to continue his verbal attacks against Galya. He gradually stepped up his vitriolic rhetoric to the point where he was literally screaming from the pulpit and demanding that she be executed to save the emperor and the Empire from her evil influences.

After that, the people tired of his sermons and verbal attacks against their beloved Emperor and Galya. Church attendance dropped steadily. Fewer and fewer people were in the pews on days when he preached. Several parishioners even complained to Bartolomy and asked that he remove Tumlecar from the order or send him to some remote station so they wouldn't be subjected to his sermons of hatred. Even Leo questioned the wisdom of allowing him to continue preaching in a letter to the monsignor.

Bartolomy had heard enough.

He called Tumlecar on the carpet and demanded that he cease his baseless attacks against Galya and the Emperor. But the headstrong priest stubbornly stuck to his guns and continued to speak out against them.

And the complaints continued to mount.

After several more attempts to rein him in, Bartolomy had no choice but to defrock him.

"There's madness in you," Bartolomy said. "You need to seek help to overcome it lest it get the better of you."

"I thought Thulians had the right of freedom of speech," Tumlecar countered.

"Freedom of speech and religion *are* constitutional rights. Exhorting people to commit murder is *not*. Before things get out of hand, I have decided to remove you from the priesthood. You are hereby banned from all properties owned and operated by the Catholic Church," Bartolomy said.

Word quickly spread to other religious sects in the Empire. Once the leaders learned that Tumlecar had been expelled from the Catholic Church, they also elected to shun him. Undaunted, he and his sidekick, a small, dark-haired man with a quiet demeanor named Delrosario, decided to form a new cult. Naturally, they would be the leaders and they would take their sermons to the streets and public places.

The open-minded Thulians tolerated their almost comical anti-Galya sermons until a band of their followers went on a rampage. They broke into several churches and temples and destroyed every statue and icon they found. This rampage continued until a squad of heavily-armed Thulian policemen subdued them and dragged them before the Emperor for judgment.

Arka-Dal ordered them to pay full restitution for the damages and sentenced each of them to six months hard labor. Most took poison rather than submit to what they believed to be a "gross miscarriage of justice and an affront to God."

The Emperor considered the matter closed but ordered Leo to closely monitor the cult members.

All was peaceful for a few more weeks. Tumlecar and his followers seemed to have gotten the message and they toned down their sermons. Then a band of cult members accosted a group of party goers who were dressed in the latest devilish fashions. A brawl erupted and quickly spread around the neighborhood. It took several squads of police to break up the fights and the cult members who instigated the melees were brought before Arka-Dal the next morning.

This was the last straw.

Disgusted, Arka-Dal banned the cult altogether and ordered them to leave the Empire immediately or face execution for treason. At the time, the cult numbered less than 90 members—even after weeks of vigorous recruitment. Rather than leave the Empire, about half of them decided it was far wiser to leave the cult. They denounced Tumlecar and joined more legitimate sects.

Tumlecar was disgusted but unbowed. He was still certain that his was the only true path and he was determined to save the Empire from itself, even if it meant he had to murder the entire royal family.

Delrosario decided to remain loyal to him and their "divine cause". Besides, he was almost as notorious as Tumlecar and really had nowhere else to go. As he watched their followers pack up their meager belongings, he turned to Tumlecar.

"Where to now?" asked Delrosario.

"We need to fade into the shadows for a while," Tumlecar said. "We need time to regroup and plan a new strategy. We also need to gather more followers. When we are strong enough, we'll return to the cities and challenge the church."

"Again I ask—where to?" Delrosario reiterated.

"There is but one place left to us. The *Cathedral!*" Tumlecar said.

Delrosario's eyes grew to twice their normal size at the mention of the name. After giving it some thought, he nodded. It seemed like the most appropriate place for them, given its long history.

The ancient brownstone structure was built sometime during the First Age by an order of Franciscan monks. They occupied the site for more than a thousand years and their order performed many good deeds for the people around them. Then came the Great Disaster. The monks held out for another decade or so after that then vanished. No one ever discovered what happened to them.

The structure stood empty for several hundred years. Then the dawn of the Second Age ushered in a new era for the venerated building.

The Cathedral became the base of operations for a cult of blue-haired assassins. The cult grew in power and influence until the mere mention of its name sent shivers down the spines of most who heard it. Unfortunately for them, they ran afoul of Gorinna and Kashi and paid a most terrible price. The ancient Cathedral was left standing as a grim reminder to all that assassination cults were not tolerated in Thule.

The once-imposing structure was now a weatherworn ruin. No one went there. No one even cared about it. It was quite far from any major cities or towns and well off any beaten path. Those who knew of it feared it was haunted.

Or cursed.

That's precisely why Tumlecar chose it as his new headquarters. His followers, or "true believers" as he preferred to call them, had the same twisted view of religion he did. They believed that churches and temples should contain no icons or statues, no images of saints and that only priests and members of the inner circle should have access to God's word. Those who failed to see the light were to be brutally chastised as blasphemers.

Or beaten repeatedly until they, too, saw the light.

Tumlecar preached that evil in *any* form needed to be exposed for what it was and destroyed. He urged violence against Satan and his minions and all those who harbor demons and devils in their homes.

Since Galya was the Devil's daughter, Tumlecar and his cult believed that she had to be done away with. It was the only way to save Arka-Dal and the Empire from falling under her evil influence.

If anyone was trying to exert an evil influence on Thule, it most certainly wasn't Galya. Despite Tumlecar's beliefs, she had very little influence on Arka-Dal or anyone else in the palace. In fact, it was *she* who had fallen under Arka-Dal's spell. Their love for each other openly blossomed and the people of Thule liked her and her children the same way they liked Arka-Dal's other wives and children.

Not even her famous father had any influence on Thule.

The *real* evil existed in the twisted minds and hearts of Tumlecar and his sick band of followers.

Tumlecar believed that by killing Galya and her children, the people of Thule would think of him as their savior. They would flock to his side by the millions and give him enough power to take over the Empire and reshape it to fit his idea of a true Christian state.

He would then be God's only true representative on Earth and all would be under His diving law—as interpreted and administered by Tumlecar himself, of course.

He kept these thoughts to himself for now. He didn't want to alienate the few followers he had. There would time for such things later—after Galya was dead and the people were hailing him as a savior.

Even Delrosario didn't know about this.

The younger man was a bit more pragmatic than Tumlecar. He didn't believe in violence or murder. He believed that, if given enough information, the people would understand the truth in their words and eventually come around to their way of thinking. He also knew this would take time.

Perhaps years.

Tumlecar didn't have that kind of patience. Madmen never did.

After several days of hard riding, Tumlecar and his disciples reached the crumbling ruin known as the Cathedral. The building had no doors now and only one of the twelve original stained glass windows remained intact. The interior was littered with debris and charred human remains. Inches of dust and cobwebs covered everything and the walls were cracked and badly scorched.

"This will be our home for a while," he announced as they looked around. "Rest first. We'll start cleaning up tomorrow."

While his followers looked for places to sleep, Tumlecar and Delrosario explored the inner sanctum of the Cathedral. They soon found a large room furnished with an antique desk, bookshelves and several chairs.

"This will be my office," Tumlecar decided as he knocked the dust from the large leather chair and sat down.

The chair creaked noisily. He leaned on the desk and looked up at Delrosario.

"The bitch must be killed," he said of Galya.

"How? She's the Devil's daughter. She has great power," Delrosario pointed out.

"Not any more. According to the legends, when a supernatural being marries a human, she forfeits both her powers and her immortality. Galya is *human* now. That means she can be killed like the rest of us," Tumlecar said.

"Even so, an assassin would never be able to get close enough to her to do the job. There are usually other members of the royal family with her," Delrosario said.

"We'd have to kill her from a distance. We'll need rifles," Tumlecar said.

"Firearms are strictly controlled. They're hard to come by, even on the black market. And they cost a fortune," Delrosario countered.

"Even so, I'd like you to put out some feelers to see if they can be obtained. While you do that, I'll screen our cult members for likely candidates we can turn into assassins," Tumlecar said.

He watched Delrosario leave and shut the door behind him. He was right. Firearms were very difficult to come by. To purchase one legally required a special permit from a royal governor. Of course, the firearms would then be registered. That meant it could easily be traced to whoever bought it.

He didn't want anything traceable.

He would have to try and buy guns on the black market—and *that* would cost him plenty. Also the quality of the weapons could not be guaranteed.

Months passed.

Tumlecar and Delrosario selected their two most fanatical followers to be the assassins. One was a young, dark skinned man from Lagash with a faraway gleam in his eyes. His name was Calloso and even Delrosario had to admit that his religious fervor was far beyond the pale.

The second, Markus, was from Osumel. He had been a mullah in one of the mosques until he was expelled for reasons he kept to himself. He thought of himself as "God's enforcer" and was more than eager to kill Galya to prove his value to the cult.

While Tumlecar waited for news on his rifles, he dispatched both men to Thule to keep a close watch on Galya's everyday habits.

"Follow her wherever she goes. Try to discern some sort of pattern to her activities so you can determine where and when it would be best to strike at her," he instructed.

The two would-be assassins did their jobs well. They spent several weeks tailing Galya, her children and her friends. They discovered that she enjoyed roaming through the markets and malls the same as any woman. She also seemed to be fascinated with museums and zoos. Before long, they were able to discern a sort of regular pattern to Galya's activities.

They also realized that she was quite popular with the people and that many seemed to gather around her wherever she went. That meant it would be next to impossible to get a good shot off at her without being seen. More careful planning was needed to avoid capture.

Tumlecar didn't care if his men were captured or killed as long as they did the job. He figured they'd just become martyrs for his cause. Symbols for his future followers to rally around.

Delrosario wasn't so sure.

"If our men fail—which is likely—they'll be traced back to us. The Emperor's vengeance will be fearsome and swift," he warned. "You must also take into consideration what Galya's *father* might do!"

Tumlecar simply shrugged it off as "God's will".

He was more determined than ever to go through with his plan. He sent out feelers to most of the dealers of black market goods he knew. Weeks passed. Then months. He was about to give up on the idea.

Then one of his feelers bore fruit.

He was told that the merchandise he sought could be had by going to Eshnunna and speaking with a dealer known only as "the Wombat". He was also told to bring money.

Lots of money.

He ordered his followers to give them all their money. He said it was "God's will" and their sacrifice was part of his divine plan. To his surprise, he collected nearly 4,000 Dals—enough, he thought, to purchase the firearms.

He left for Eshnunna the following morning.

While Tumlecar traveled south, news reached Bartolomy that the outlawed cult had set up housekeeping in the Cathedral. He immediately sent word of this to Leo who, in turn, passed it on to Arka-Dal.

The Emperor shrugged it off.

"Bartolomy says he has fewer than 50 followers. That's not enough to be alarmed about. At least they are outside the boundaries of the Empire," he said.

"Even so, I've asked Bartolomy to keep an eye on them—just in case," Leo said. "Tumlecar is a madman. There is no telling what he might dream up."

Arka-Dal nodded.

"If he tries anything, I'll make him feel sorry he was ever born," he assured him. "Right now, there's an important matter of state to tend to. You might want to sit in on this one."

Leo followed him to his private office. As soon as they entered, Joshua, Maltry and a handful of senators from his fledgling empire stood to show respect. Arka-Dal shook Joshua's and Maltry's hands and welcomed the senators warmly. As everyone took their seats around the table, Joshua handed him a scroll. Arka-Dal unrolled it, read it carefully then passed it to Leo.

"Are you sure this is what you want?" he asked.

"I've never been more sure of anything in my life. I've not the temperament to govern. I'm a soldier. My place is in the field at the front of my troops," Joshua said.

"And my place is at his side," added Maltry.

"We held a referendum two months ago. The people have spoken," said the eldest of the senators. "We wish to be included in the Empire of Thule with all of the rights and responsibilities that go with it."

"More than 90 percent of the people voted for inclusion, Sire," said another senator. "That is why we have come to you with this petition. We hope you will accept it and welcome our people into your nation."

"This is all quite proper and legal," Leo declared after he'd read the petition. "All that is needed is the signatures of Joshua and an a representative from each of the new provinces on the Constitution and it's a done deal."

"What about you, Joshua? What do you want from this?" asked Arka-Dal.

"You will need to raise at least three new armies to defend the new provinces. I'd like a commission to command one of them," Joshua said.

"Done. I'll give you the rank of field marshal and pace you in command of the new Northwestern Army. As for you, Maltry, I'll appoint you as his second in command. I know you'll make the people of Thule proud," Arka-Dal decided as he extended his hand.

Satisfied, Joshua and Maltry shook his hand, then saluted. At that point, Leo produced a copy of the Constitution and placed it on the table. One by one, the senators rose and signed the document. Joshua and Maltry signed last. Arka-Dal poured each a tall glass of wine and they toasted the occasion.

"This calls for a celebration! We'll declare tomorrow a national holiday to welcome our three new provinces into the Empire," Arka-Dal said.

Later that night, Arka-Dal studied the new map of the Empire. The addition of Joshua's empire increased the size of Thule by another 875,000 square miles and added another 3.7 million people. Thule now had major ports on both the Black and Caspian Seas. The Northeastern Province of Anatolia afforded Thule a more direct trade route with Byzantium and Egypt and points north. The Northwestern Province extended Thule's borders to the Afghan Frontier and Trollegia gave him control of the most important deep water port on the Caspian.

Joshua was correct when he said that Thule would have to create three new armies to defend these provinces. Arka-Dal realized that he'd also need two new fleets to protect their new harbors.

New communication lines had to set up. New roads had to be built, along with new schools, universities, forts, outposts. The new provinces had to be connected to the rest of the Empire. This would take massive amounts of money and manpower. Luckily, Thule had plenty of both.

The new citizens had to become fluent in the Thulian language. The young me had to serve in the armed forces in accordance with the laws of the Constitution. New territories meant new responsibilities.

He sighed.

"How am I supposed the govern all of that?" he asked aloud.

"With the same wisdom, courage, imagination and sense of justice by which you have always governed," said Merlin as he and Leo entered.

Arka-Dal smiled.

"I never imagined that the Empire would become so vast," he said. "We now have more than 125 million citizens living in more than 2,500 cities, towns and villages. We now control millions of square miles. How did it ever come to this?"

"Manifest destiny," Merlin said smugly. "Thule was always *destined* to control most of the Middle East. The remarkable thing is that you forged this empire without the use of arms or threats. Every Thulian citizen is part of the Empire because he or she *wanted* to be part of it. You should feel proud."

"I'm also humbled. I've been very fortunate to have so many good, able people around me to help run the Empire. Without you and the others, I'm afraid I'd be lost," Arka-Dal said.

"No man is an island unto himself. Effective rulers always surround themselves with good, bright and loyal people. Those who have tried to govern vast empires alone have failed and their empires died with them," Merlin agreed.

"You're a rare type of emperor. You've set personal standards of courage, integrity and honor that few men can match. You always lead from the front and never ask your people to do anything you would not do yourself. And you always put the good of the Empire and its people above your own needs," Leo added.

"Indeed. In fact, more often than not, I've heard people who are faced with tough choices or problems sit back and ask themselves: 'what would Arka-Dal do?' I dare say that most of the men in Thule strive to be just like you."

"And most of the women want to sleep with you," said Mayumi as she walked into the room. "But only a lucky few of us have that pleasure."

"You're embarrassing me! You make me sound like some sort of god!" Arka-Dal protested.

"You're not a god—but you *are* a hero to your people. Think on this: if anyone else throughout history had announced he was marrying the Devil's daughter, the people would have rose up in anger. They might even have toppled the government. But your people admire, adore and trust you so much, they not only welcomed Galya with open arms, they celebrated your union. They don't even mind that you include her infamous father among your closest friends now. Their attitude is and always has been, what's good for you is good for the Empire," Leo pointed out.

"Since you love and trust Galya, the people also love and trust her. If you are happy, they are happy," Mayumi added.

"That's enough of that nonsense. Now to the matter of the new provinces. Leo, I want you make sure their transition into the Empire goes smoothly. I want everyone to be fully aware of their rights and responsibilities as citizens of Thule. I'll send engineers and surveyors out to map every square mile of the provinces. Once that's done, we'll sit down and decide what needs to be done and how quickly," Arka-Dal said, abruptly changing the subject.

"Everything will work out fine—just as it always does. You'll see," Merlin assured him as he poured himself a flagon of wine.

A few days later, Tumlecar was in Eshnunna. It was a little past sunset and the streets were still alive with people going about their daily business. It was raining, too. A light, penetrating rain.

He left the main street and made his way down a dirty, rain-washed alley for several blocks. When he reached Hallat Street, he turned west toward the center of the city and away from the docks. After making several more turns and stopping to ask for directions, he found himself standing at the door of an old tavern with weatherworn siding and dingy windows. The door opened inward. He stepped aside to allow two drunken seamen to leave, then entered.

The place was dimly lit and clouded by smoke from pipes and cigars. From the looks of it, the saloon was a hangout for all sorts of lowlifes and other unsavory types who inhabited Thule's underworld. Tumlecar walked to the bar and waited until the barkeep meandered over. He was tall, bald headed and sported a handlebar mustache. He also had a jagged scar that ran across the bridge of his nose. Along the way he stopped to chat with a short, plump woman of indeterminate age who was one of his regulars. Tumlecar cleared his throat loudly to let him know he was waiting. The barkeep sighed and walked over.

"What'll it be?" he asked gruffly.

"I seek a man known as the Wombat," Tumlecar said.

The barkeep nodded at a small table across the room. A medium sized, dirty looking man was seated at it. In front of him were several empty ale bottles and a flagon. The man seemed to be deep in his cups. Tumlecar nodded and walked across the floor. He stopped at the table. The man glanced up at him and continued drinking.

"Are you the Wombat?" Tumlecar asked.

"Who wants to know?" came the response in a raspy sort of voice.

Tumlecar sat down and leaned close.

"An acquaintance of yours told me that you deal in hard to find items," he said.

"I deal in lots of things. What are *you* lookin' for?" the Wombat asked.

"Firearms. Rifles in particular," Tumlecar said.

Wombat raised an eyebrow.

"Guns are hard to come by. They're strictly controlled and *expensive*," he said.

"Price is no object," Tumlecar assured him. "Can you get them?"

"That depends. How many do ya need?" the Wombat asked.

"Two should do the trick—along with the proper ammunition for each," Tumlecar replied.

"I think I might have something that should suit you just fine. How soon do ya need them?" Wombat asked.

"As soon as possible," Tumlecar replied.

"I can have your merchandise for you in three weeks. Where should I bring them?" Wombat said.

Tumlecar handed him a slip of paper. Wombat read it and nodded.

"This'll cost ya—*big*!" he said as he stuffed the paper into his pocket.

"How big?" Tumlecar asked.

Wombat took out a piece of paper and short pencil. Tumlecar watched as he scribbled down his price. He winced when he saw the figure, but agreed to pay it anyway. It's not like he had a choice. The two men shook hands.

"I'll need half up front and the rest on delivery," Wombat said.

Tumlecar reached into his cloak and took out two small pouches filled with silver Dals. Wombat hefted each sack and stuck them into his pocket.

"We have what's called a 'gentlemen's agreement'," he said with a crooked smile.

"Will this be good merchandise?" Tumlecar asked.

"The Wombat doesn't deal in junk. They'll be as good as you can get anywhere else," he said.

Tumlecar rose and left the tavern. As he made his way back up the alley, he wondered if the Wombat was really trustworthy.

Tumlecar took deliver of his merchandise at a small oasis on the edge of the Western Desert right on schedule. The rifles were a few years old but in good condition. Both were bolt action carbines and came with six clips of ammunition. Tumlecar paid Wombat the balance he owed and bade him farewell. No questions were asked. No explanations were offered. The Wombat didn't care why he wanted the rifles. All he wanted was his payment and Tumlecar gave him that without haggling.

When he reached the Cathedral, he showed the rifles to Delrosario. The younger cleric shook his head.

"I don't like this, Tumlecar. Not one bit. If your men fail, it'll be *our* asses in the sling!" he said.

"Our men won't fail. Have they returned from Thule yet?" Tumlecar asked.

"They arrived this morning," Delrosario said.

"Good. It's time to begin their training. Send them to me," Tumlecar decided.

He gave his assassins instructions on how to load, aim and fire the rifles. Then he had Delrosario set up some targets in the nearby hills and sent his men out to practice. They used up four of the magazines trying to get the hang of the weapons. When it looked like each of them could hit what he was aiming at, Tumlecar handed them the last of the ammunition and ordered them to return to Thule.

"Don't return until you've killed that monster," he said. "Fail me and you'll live to regret it."

They bowed and went to their rooms to pack. Delrosario watched them and shook his head. He knew they weren't ready. He also had a sick feeling deep in his stomach that this was going to go very badly for the cult.

It was a clear and sunny day. At mid-morning, Calloso made his way to the top of a hotel roof on the edge of the Western Plaza. He had a long, leather case with him. When he reached the edge of the roof, he placed the bundle down next to him and looked out upon the plaza.

The shops were already open and the place teemed with shoppers and vendors. After weeks of observation, he knew this was the day that Galya and Gorinna usually came to the plaza. An hour went by. Then two. Calloso almost gave up when he spotted them. He unzipped the case and took out the rifle. He then reached into his pocket, took out the ammo clip and slid it into the stock.

He found a comfortable spot to lean on then aimed the weapon as Galya's chest as she climbed a set of steps that encircled an ornate lion fountain in the middle of the plaza. When he was certain he couldn't miss, he fired.

Unfortunately, he flinched when he pulled the trigger.

The bullet missed Galya and struck an innocent bystander a few feet behind her. The woman screamed, clutched her stomach and tumbled down the steps. Gorinna turned in the direction the shot had come from and raised her hand. Calloso fired again. This time, the bullet bounced harmlessly off the magic shield she had thrown up. Frustrated, he fired twice more with similar results.

Disgusted, he packed his weapon and fled.

Or tried to.

An alert Thulian police officer saw him leap from the roof and hurled his spear. It struck Caloso in the spine a split second before his feet touched the ground. He emitted a groan and fell. He was dead when the officer, Gorinna and Galya reached him.

"Stand back," Gorinna said to gathering crowd.

Everyone backed off and watched as she knelt beside the dead man and placed her right hand on his forehead. Images of a familiar, run-down structure in the middle of nowhere flashed through her mind.

Then came a name.

Tumlecar.

Arka-Dal and Kashi were in the living room talking and drinking ale when Gorinna entered with the rifle nestled in the crook of her arm. She walked over and placed it on the table between them.

"Where'd you find this?" asked Arka-Dal as he eyed the weapon.

"I took it from the man who just tried to kill Galya," she replied as she sat down with them.

"What? Is she alright?" Arka-Dal asked with a start.

"She's fine. So's the poor woman he accidentally shot," Gorinna said.

Kashi picked up the weapon and laughed.

"This is pretty crude. Black Market quality. What about the assassin?" he asked.

"One of the guards killed him when he tried to escape. His body's been taken to the City Morgue. I did, however, manage to pull some images from his mind before they took him," Gorinna said.

"What did you see?" asked Arka-Dal.

"A place I never thought I'd see again. The Cathedral," she replied.

"Isn't that where Tumlecar went with his nutty followers?" Kashi asked.

She nodded.

"Do we go after him?" asked Kashi.

"Not yet. I want more proof that he's behind this," Arka-Dal said.

"Well, he *did* call for Galya's head on a plate and the destruction of all things and people associated with her or her father," Leo said as he walked in with Galya. "I'd say that was proof enough."

"Not good enough. It wouldn't hold up in court. While we wait for him to make another move, I want our best men to guard Galya wherever she goes," Arka-Dal said.

"I'll guard her myself," Kashi volunteered.

"So will I," vowed Gorinna.

"Thanks. I can't ask for better than that," Arka-Dal said.

"If I still had my powers, I wouldn't need bodyguards—*he* would," Galya remarked. "If Father finds out about this, I pity whoever is behind this. He will not be the least bit merciful."

"Neither will *I*," Arka-Dal said. "When I find whoever's behind this, I'll let him live just long enough to regret it."

"Sounds like what you did to the Turks," Leo remarked.

"They butchered helpless woman and children. They got what they *deserved*," Arka-Dal pointed out.

"Father also detests those who harm the weak and helpless. In all of his years, he has never harmed anyone who did not deserve it. He is not like those vile things in the Abyss. He does not kill for pleasure nor eat souls," Galya said.

Arka-Dal smiled.

"The more I learn of your father, the more I like him. We have more in common than I thought," he said.

She laughed.

"Perhaps that's why I love you so much," she said.

Medusa and Mayumi had entered the parlor a few moments earlier. As they giggled at Galya's remarks, Chatha walked in from the garden, where she had been practicing with Master Koto. She ran over to Galya and hugged her.

"I heard what happened. I'm so glad that you're safe," she said. "If it's alright with you, I'd like to be one of your guards."

"I would be honored. Just don't take any unnecessary chances," Galya said as she returned the hug warmly.

"Now you know I can't promise you *that*!" Chatha said.

A few hours later, news reached that palace that an angry mob of local citizens had stormed the morgue, dragged Calloso's corpse out into the street and beat it bloody with sticks and rocks. When they grew tired of this, they carried it outside the city and tossed it into the woods for animals to feast upon. The people were outraged at the assassination attempt and demanded justice.

The episode astonished Galya.

"They did this of their own accord. They did it because they *love* you and to show that such things are not tolerated in Thule," Mayumi explained.

The angry demonstration did not go unnoticed by Delrosario. The people had rallied around Galya. Another such attack might produce the exact opposite of Tumlecar's hoped-for results.

"Any attack on a member of Arka-Dal's family will be looked upon as an attack on *all* the people of Thule. You must abandon this path at once!" he advised.

But Tumlecar would not budge.

"The die is cast. What's done cannot be undone. The people will come around to our way of thinking yet," he assured him.

"You are so blinded by your hatred that you cannot see the handwriting on the wall. This will be our undoing!" Delrosario argued.

"You can leave any time you wish," Tumlecar offered.

"No. I took a vow to stand by you and I will do so to the very end," Delrosario said. "Where's Markus?"

"Somewhere in Thule. He should be ready to strike soon," Tumlecar said. "Like I said, the die is cast."

Delrosario nodded and left the office. As he stepped out into the cold night air, he cursed himself for taking such a stupid vow.

Markus was a better marksman than Calloso—but only slightly better. He attempted to kill Galya three days later while she, Gorinna, Kashi and Chatha were meandering through the shops and boutiques along the waterfront. He shot at her from ground level. He was barely 100 feet away, yet his shot just grazed Galya's right shoulder.

Before Kashi, Gorinna and Chatha could spring into action, Markus found himself running for his life from an incredibly irate mob. They chased him down several avenues and side streets, with more and more people joining the party every step of the way.

Markus tried cutting across one of the plazas only to find himself completely surrounded by hundreds of people brandishing sticks, hoes, rakes, bricks and even swords.

"Death to Satan's daughter!" he shouted shrilly as the mob closed in.

They hurled bottles and bricks at him. He desperately tried to shield himself with his arms.

"She *must* die! She's evil!" he shouted in a last attempt to reason with them.

A hail of bricks, bottles and stones brought him down. He tried to rise to his feet but they beat him with clubs and sticks until he fell to his knees. He curled up in a fetal position to protect himself.

"She's the Devil's daughter!" he screamed.

"She's the Emperor's wife!" several of the people shouted as they beat him to a bloody pulp.

By the time the police arrived to break it up, all that was left of Markus was a pile of broken bones, torn flesh and bloodied clothes.

When Kashi and Gorinna brought the news to Arka-Dal, he became livid.

"That did it! We're going to go to the Cathedral to put an end to this nasty little cult once and for all!" he shouted in a rage.

He calmed down and smiled at Galya. Outside of a small bandage on her shoulder, she seemed none the worse for wear. He hugged her.

"I'm alright. Gorinna mended my wound. It was just a little scratch, really," she assured him.

"How many of these bastards are we dealing with?" he asked.

"According to our scouts, Tumlecar has less than 50 followers," Kashi said.

"I'm about to teach them a lesson they won't soon forget. They tried to kill Galya twice. Now they are about to learn the error of their ways. Take no prisoners. I want them all dead so this never happens again. No one attacks a member of my family and lives to tell about it," Arka-Dal decided.

"If you do that, you may make martyrs of them," Leo warned.

"I doubt that. Their attacks on Galya really pissed our people off. They showed how they feel about that cult when they tore the last assassin to pieces before the police could save him. Our people are intelligent and compassionate. They are not in the habit of turning would-be killers into heroic martyrs. My orders stand. I want this group wiped off the face of the Earth," Arka-Dal said adamantly.

"Why are they trying to kill me? I've done nothing to them that I'm aware of," Galya said.

"Their leader is a sick, twisted monster. He blames you for all of the evils in this world and thinks he can save the Empire by killing you," Leo explained.

"If Father finds them, there will be Hell to pay—literally!" Galya remarked.

Pandaar and Perseus entered the room. Both were dressed for battle. Pandaar smiled at Arka-Dal.

"I heard what went down. Are you going to lead this little party as usual?" he asked.

Arka-Dal nodded.

"I want to personally deal out a fitting punishment to this Tumlecar. In fact, I'd like to use his head for a football," he said.

"Then let's get it on!" Gorinna said as they gathered around her.

She raised her hands above her head and chanted. Seconds later, the entire group was surrounded by a bright golden globe. Galya, Mayumi, Chatha, Medusa and Zhijima watched as they globe lifted off the floor and zoomed out through the open double doors.

"Does your father know about this?" asked Mayumi.

Galya nodded.

"I wonder who will get there first—Aka-san or him?" Mayumi asked.

"Either way, things are about to get real ugly for Tumlecar," Chatha said with a smirk. "I've seen Arka-Dal in action many times. When he's angry, his fury is unmatched."

"And he's *very* angry," Medusa added.

Tumlecar was seated behind his desk going over some scripture when Delrosario entered. He looked up and put down his pen.

"Any news?" he asked.

"Yes—and it's all bad," Delrosario said.

"Let me hear it," Tumlecar said.

"Our second attempt on Galya also failed miserably. Your assassin was run down and torn to pieces by an angry mob before he could escape," Delrosario reported.

"We shall make him a martyr," Tumlecar said calmly.

"He's no martyr. He's a bloody pulp—as will we all be once Arka-Dal finds us," Delrosario said. "I suggest that we fold our tents and get out of here while the getting's good."

"Why should I fear a mere Emperor when God is on our side?" Tumlecar said.

"It is not the Emperor you should fear," came a voice from the shadows.

Tumlecar turned and stared at the tall, dark figure on the other side of the room. He scowled.

"Who *are* you? How did you get in here?" he demanded.

"Those questions will soon be answered," the visitor said flatly.

Tumlecar pushed a button on the side of his desk. Within seconds, his entire office was crowded with his hooded, armed followers.

"Dispose of our uninvited guest," Tumlecar instructed.

The visitor laughed. His laughter seemed to fill every space in the Cathedral. It was eerie. Even bone chilling. Enough to make the cult members shrink in fear.

"Kill him!" Tumlecar shouted.

The visitor laughed as Tumlecar's followers tried to encircle him. This time, his laughter had more than a note of contempt to it.

"This is what I think of your men!" he said as he waved his hand.

Tumlecar watched in awed silence as an assortment of weapons and dark brown robes clattered to the stone floor—including Delrosario who had been standing alongside him. Seconds later, swarms of sickly, bloated maggots and worms emerged from beneath the robes and slithered across the floor.

The man laughed louder.

"So much for your half-witted followers. They are now what they were truly born to be. Now, it's *your* turn," he said as he stepped into the light.

Tumlecar's eyes grew three times their normal size.

"Satan!" he gasped.

"Did you think that you could attack my daughter without drawing my ire? Did you think I would allow such a deed to go unpunished?" the Devil said as he stepped toward him.

Tumlecar reached into his desk drawer and pulled out a pistol. He aimed it at the Devil and fired all six shots. The Devil laughed as the bullets passed harmlessly through him and pinged off a stone column several feet away.

"Fool! No Earthly weapon can harm me," he said.

Tumlecar watched in horror as the pistol turned into a handful of wet, wriggling worms. He shook them off in disgust and took a step back.

"Don't leave. We have unfinished business to conduct," the Devil said as he walked toward him.

"What will you do to me?" he asked.

"I should do to you what I did to your followers. But that's too easy. Too nice. I have a more interesting and fitting fate in mind for you," the Devil replied.

"Like what?" Tumlecar asked.

Just then, the doors flew open and in marched an enraged Arka-Dal at the head of his usual band. The Devil smiled.

"I'm going to give you to *him*," he said.

Arka-Dal glowered at Tumlecar.

"Prepare yourself, mother fucker!" he roared as he stepped toward him and seized him by the front of his robes.

He dragged him from behind the desk and spat in his face to show his utter contempt.

"How dare you try to kill my wife? Just who do you think you are?" he snarled.

He let him go and slapped him hard several times. By the time the last blow landed, Tumlecar's face was bruised in several places and his lips were split and bleeding.

"Kill me then and be done with it!" he said defiantly.

"Death is too good, too easy—and far too quick. I want you to die slowly. Painfully. I want to leave you with something to think about before you meet whatever nasty god spawned you," Arka-Dal said

He kicked Tumlecar on the side of his head and sent him tumbling over the desk. Then he picked him up and punched him as hard as he could. The punch decked him.

"I didn't know you had such a mean streak," the Devil said as he watched Arka-Dal straddle the half-conscious cleric.

"I can be real mean when someone harms those I love and this simpering bastard is about to feel the full measure of my wrath," Arka-Dal said as he drew Excalibur.

He smiled at Tumlecar.

"You're gonna love this!" he said.

Tumlecar screamed as he deftly sliced both of his legs off just above the knees. As the terrified cleric lay wallowing in his own blood, Arka-Dal severed each arm at the elbow. This done, he wiped the blood off his sword on Tumlecar's robes and sheathed it.

He stepped back and smiled at the Devil.

"Care to add any embellishments?" he asked.

The Devil nodded.

He snapped his fingers.

Tumlecar screamed as each of his eyeballs exploded in their sockets and oozed down his cheeks like a sickly sap. Another snap of his fingers transformed his tongue into a swollen, pus-filled penis. A third snap painfully tore off Tumlecar's testicles and implanted them into his now-empty eye sockets. This done, the Devil stepped back to admire his work.

"That should do it," he said.

"Not quite," Gorinna said as she stepped forward and used her magic to stop Tumlecar from bleeding to death. She leaned over him.

"Hear me, asshole. You will live for a few more days. Then you'll either die of thirst or starvation. Maybe the vermin in this place will devour you before that happens. Either way, your death will be slow in coming. Until then, you can lay here in the wreckage of your body and think about this fate you have brought upon yourself," she said.

Tumlecar heard them leave.

He wanted to scream but had no tongue. No one would hear him anyway. All of his followers were dead or turned into maggots and worms.

He was completely powerless.

And truly fucked.

He died less than a day later.

As soon as Arka-Dal reached home, he radioed Jun and told him what had happened. He then ordered him to have his men level the Cathedral.

"Leave not a stone standing. After you've eradicated the place, have your men plant trees in its place so that nature can reclaim it," he directed.

This done, he went into the parlor to join the others. When he sat down in the large chair closest to the fireplace, Galya handed him a drink and sat on the floor at his feet. Her father raised an eyebrow as he'd always considered that an act of supplication. After a while, he smiled. He realized that it was Galya's way of honoring the man she loved.

He decided that she looked positively radiant. She was totally happy now. He never once imagined that he'd see her like this or that she would fall in love with and marry a mortal. For that matter, he never imagined that she'd give him grandchildren!

On the other side of the room, Leo and Kashi were seated at a table, deeply involved in a game of chess. Pandaar was on the sofa next to Perseus. Both had already consumed large volumes of alcohol and looked blissfully tired. In the background, he heard the sounds of the children at play. The household cats—five of them— were curled up on the rug before the fireplace fast asleep.

All except Fred.

He was in his customary place on the back of Arka-Dal's chair. The animal was never more than a few feet away from Arka-Dal, who sometimes referred to him as his "familiar".

The Devil smiled.

Loyalty was a quality that was not limited to humans. Arka-Dal seemed to inspire it amongst his family, his friends, his soldiers and the people of Thule—even amongst his former enemies.

He also noticed that no one in the Empire seemed to be shocked at Tumlecar's fate. Most of the people believed that he and his weird cult simply got what they deserved. A few even voiced opinions that they got off too easy and that Arka-Dal had been too merciful.

"I am truly amazed at the outpouring of affection your people have for my daughter. I am even more amazed at the outrage they displayed when she was attacked. Such things could only happen in Thule," the Devils said.

"You should not be amazed, Father. I told you that the people here are different than the ones in other lands. Thulians are more open-minded. They accept things and people that others will not," Galya said.

"Thulians take genuine pride in the royal family. In fact, they truly love them and most consider them to be members of their own families. Many would not hesitate to lay down their lives for them because they believe that Arka-Dal and the rest of us would lay down our lives for them," Leo explained.

The Devil smiled.

"You have married well, Galya. Better than I or anyone else could have hoped," he said as he gently patter he knee.

"I know, Father," she said as she cast a loving look up at Arka-Dal.

Later that evening, Merlin went in search of Chatha and found her seated by herself on a marble bench near the lily pond. A swan floated on the dark green water and she was tossing bread crusts to it. She laughed as it flapped its wing while it gobbled up the bread as if it was a morsel from a royal feast. Merlin walked over and sat beside her. She smiled without looking at him.

"I see that you're with child again," he said matter-of-factly.

Chatha nodded.

"I thought you said that you saw no more offspring in Arka-Dal's life," she teased.

"Even a wizard can be wrong once in a while," Merlin said. "In seven months, another son's cries will echo through this palace."

Chatha beamed.

"What do you see in *his* future?" she asked.

"I can see nothing. There is a veil over him," Merlin replied.

"Is that good or bad?" she asked.

"Alas, my dear. I cannot tell. Not yet," he said.

He patted her knee to comfort her.

"Don't worry over it. What will be, will be. I'm sure that all will be well," he assured her. "Perhaps after he's arrived, the gods will reveal his future. Maybe then I'll have some news for you."

"How come you never give a direct answer?" she asked.

He laughed.

"I do—but only when such answers are available to me. The future is shrouded by mists. Sometimes, the mist parts long enough for me to see through it. Other times, the vision is blurred or there is nothing at all. Second sight is something that even *I* cannot control," he explained. "But your child will be the product of two good, strong parents. I'm sure his future will be very bright."

Chatha smiled.

"I think I'll name him Theron. It was the name of a great Atlantean king," she said.

"Theron . . . I like it," Arka-Dal said as he walked out of the bushes. "What's it mean?"

"Bright as the Sun," Chatha replied.

Merlin watched as they held each other close and kissed. Then, hand-in-hand, they left and walked back up the path toward the palace. Merlin remained at the pond and smiled as he considered the true meaning of that name.

The Day the Gods Wept

In the 51st year of the reign of Arka-Dal.

Late summer in Thule was a time to sit back and relax. The crops were growing in the fields and the markets were filled with all sorts of goods from every part of the globe. Out beyond the city limits, in the middle of an open meadow where goatherds watch their flocks, stands the ruins of a once beautiful mosque. The ornate minaret, from which First Age imams shouted out the call to prayer, is now a pile of rubble. The rest of the mosque is but a pale skeleton. The mosque has been deserted for centuries now. Only bats and other vermin flutter and scurry amid the ruins. Little did anyone suspect that these long-silent ruins would be the place where Gods cried . . .

It was a warm, humid summer night. Out on the open plain just to the south of Thule, two sweaty goatherds swat at mosquitoes as they follow the trail of one of their errant charges. They discovered the animal had wandered off while doing their hourly head count and decided to chase after it before it got away completely. A missing goat meant their pay would be docked to pay for the animal and neither could afford that.

They followed the trail a couple of miles north and west. They were just about to give up when one of the men spotted the goat a few yards away, chewing on a shrub. They approached it from two sides cautiously and the goat paid them little mind as it continued to eat. They were about to grab it when it bleated and darted off again. The two men cursed at it as they gave chase. The goat led them up one hill and down the next and stopped suddenly just before it came to an ancient, crumbling ruin in the middle of the plain. The men stopped, too.

They'd always known the ruins were there. After all, they'd been there for countless centuries. At one time, it was a grand mosque with a tall, ornate minaret from which the mullahs would issue the daily calls to prayer to the faithful. The minaret had toppled long ago, taking the ceiling of the mosque with it. The ruins had been dark and silent ever since.

Until tonight.

The goatherds stared as balls of white, red and blue light flickered and danced through the ruins. At the same time, a low-lying mist rose from the floor and slowly followed the lights.

One of the men tied a rope around the goat's neck and began to drag it back to the herd. The other man watched the lights for a while longer then, he, too, returned to the camp.

The men told the people of their village what they had seen. Most laughed at them. A few decided to check the ruins out themselves. About 20 villagers converged on the ruins the next evening. They took their places in the grass just outside the walls and waited for something to happen.

It did.

The dancing lights returned.

So did the mist.

The villagers watched as if enchanted. When the lights died out an hour later, they hurried back to the village to tell everyone what they'd seen.

The next morning, the mayor led a search party to the ruins. They scoured the place as best as they could but all they could find was a crudely drawn pentagram with half-molten black candles at each point of the star. There was a dish of some foul-smelling liquid in the center of the pentagram but they found nothing else.

No footprints had disturbed the centuries of dust and sand save their own. And there was no sign of anyone entering or leaving the ruins. Puzzled, the mayor sent a report of the activities to police headquarters in Thule and asked that it be investigated. He was afraid that some weird cult of wanna-be witches was using the ruins for rituals.

Arka-Dal was in the garden watching Chatha practice the one-second katana draw under the demanding glare of his weapon master, Masaichi Koto. Chatha was quick, but not quite quick enough to suit Koto who insisted she do it over and over again. When she appeared to be tiring, Koto drew his katana, whirled around and slashed at her. To his surprise, she deftly blocked the stroke with her own blade, then ducked down and used a leg sweep to knock him off his feet. Koto countered by seizing her wrist and flipping her over him. Chatha managed to hold onto her sword and deliver what would have been a killing stroke as she rose to one knee.

Koto sheathed his weapon, then bowed respectfully. Chatha did the same.

Arka-Dal applauded.

"That was great! I couldn't have done better myself. You're as quick as a cat," he complimented as she picked up her towel and wiped the sweat from her face.

She sat down next to him.

"Father taught me to fight like this. Since I am not as strong as most male warriors, he taught me to compensate by being faster and more flexible. Master Koto's training me to be faster still. He's very good," she said.

"He's the best weapon master I've ever had. I've learned things from him that have saved my ass in battle many times over," Arka-Dal agreed.

"But I have still not showed you everything I know," Koto said as he joined them. "I like to hold back. Save the best things for last."

Arka-Dal laughed.

"We've been at this for three hours now. Take the rest of the day off, Koto-san. You've earned it," he said.

Koto bowed and walked off. Arka-Dal hugged Chatha.

"You're becoming one of the best fighters I've ever seen," he said.

"Thank you. But I sometimes feel so useless around here. All of my life, I was trained to lead soldiers into battle. Although I enjoy my life here with you and the others, I'm growing bored. I need something more to do," she said.

"Well, you *are* the commander of the Atlantean Regiments of the Central Army and I *do* expect you to lead them in battle should the time arise," he reminded her. "Thule is at peace now, so there's no need for you to do that."

"I know. It's just that I want to feel that I'm of use to you in some way. All of your other wives brings something special to the table. I want to provide something special, too," she said.

He leaned over and kissed her gently.

"You *are* special. Don't ever feel otherwise. You are a beautiful and remarkably talented woman. All of my wives are," he assured her.

"And which of us do you feel most passion for?" she asked, putting him on the spot.

"I have passion enough for each of you," he replied diplomatically. "There is nothing that I wouldn't do for any of you."

She hugged him tightly and smiled. He stroked her hair and kissed her forehead.

"Leo tells me that you've developed quite an interest in military engineering. Does that come from your father?" he asked.

"Yes. It does," she said. "He always said that a good general has to know how to find the weakest points in a city's defenses in order to exploit them. Right now, I'm trying to adapt Atlantean with Thulian methods to make them more effective."

"Good idea. I'm always looking for better and faster ways to do things. After you've figured it out, I'll probably have to you teach the new methods to most of our training officers," he said.

"Really?" she asked.

"Really," he said. "See? I told you that weren't useless. None of my wives are."

Chatha smiled.

He was right as usual. Each of them had her own unique talents and abilities. When combined for a common cause, they made a formidable team.

Mayumi was a sensible and wise administrator who ruled the Empire whenever Arka-Dal was away. Medusa was a brilliant archaeologist, historian, civil engineer and she spoke several languages fluently. She could also turn people into statues when angered. Galya's knowledge of the occult and Lower Planes was invaluable and she could summon legions of demonic troops if necessary. She also spoke most known languages and several dead ones.

"And I am the warrior queen!" she thought to herself.

Arka-Dal rose and held out his hand. Chatha beamed and took it as he led her back into the palace.

"Let's bathe together," he suggested.

Gorinna was at the top of the stairs when Arka-Dal and Chatha raced past her and went into their quarters.

She sighed.

Chatha was lucky, she decided. She got to make love with Arka-Dal. His other wives were lucky, too.

Very lucky.

That's when she found herself wishing she were one of them.

Again.

The thoughts kept recurring and were becoming more frequent. Several times she caught herself staring wistfully at Arka-Dal. One time, he even had to snap his fingers in front of her to bring her out of it. That was most embarrassing.

She heard laughter and the sounds of running feet and watched as several of the Dal children rushed out of the palace, brandishing toy weapons and shields.

Children.

She'd always wanted some of her own, but the path she chose in her youth had left her unable to bear any. Even if she could, Merlin warned her such a thing might cost her her magical powers. She might even begin aging like a normal person.

"Maybe it would be worth it—especially if the child was Arka-Dal's," she thought. "Damn! This is becoming an obsession. I need to talk to someone about it before I lose my mind."

She went downstairs and found Kashi and Pandaar. They were seated at one of the tables in the parlor playing cards. She walked over and put her hand on Kashi's shoulder. He looked up and asked her what was bothering her.

Frustrated to the breaking point, Gorinna poured her heart out. She told Kashi all about her almost uncontrollable desires and how she'd always wanted to bear a child. She also admitted that she was finding Arka-Dal more and more difficult to resist.

"My crush as you always called it, is becoming more than a distraction. It's almost as if I'm obsessed with him now. It's all I can do to keep from throwing myself at him and begging him to take me. Please help me find a way to get over this before I lose my mind!" she said.

He sat there and sipped his drink in silence as she bared her soul. Of course, he'd heard it all before.

Many times.

"What do you think?" she asked at long last.

"About what?" he asked.

"Why you—you!" she growled as she hauled off and gave him a right cross to the jaw.

The unexpected blow knocked Kashi off his chair. As he sat on the floor massaging the side of his face, he watched Gorinna storm off in anger.

He laughed.

He'd heard every word.

Again.

Normally, he'd try to comfort her. This time, he decided to let her vent then make light of it. Of course, that decision came with certain consequences, like a hard punch to the jaw. He picked himself up, poured another drink and sat down on the sofa near the fireplace. That's when he heard Pandaar's laughter.

"I forgot you were here," he said.

"That was quite a wallop," Pandaar replied as he poured himself a drink.

"That probably wasn't the smartest thing I've done lately," Kashi said as he rubbed his jaw again.

Pandaar laughed.

"She sounds like she's becoming obsessed with Arka-Dal and about having a kid," he said.

Kashi sipped his drink and nodded.

"Hell, Pandaar. I'm tired of hearing her rant. Of course she wants a child. I do, too. But she went into this with both eyes wide open. She knew what the circumstances would be when she chose this path. We both did," Kashi said.

"She was very young when she made her decision. She probably didn't foresee any of this at that time," Pandaar said.

"Yes I did," Gorinna said as she returned with an icepack which she applied to Kashi's jaw. "I'm sorry I hit you so hard but you *deserved* it."

"I guess I did," Kashi admitted. "I don't know why you keep harping on this. After all, there's nothing anyone can do about it now."

"Have you ever wished that you had not married me?" she asked.

"Never! Not once in all of the years we've been together," Kashi said with an assuring smile. "We make a great team. And we love each other, even if you do have a crush on Arka-Dal."

She sat down on his lap and hugged him.

"Does it bother you?" she asked.

"Not really. In fact, Arka-Dal and I sometimes joke about it. Considering how free-spirited and willful you are, I'm rather amazed that you haven't tried to fulfill your fantasies," Kashi replied.

"What would you do if I did?" she asked.

"The same as I did when you seduced Zhijima. Nothing. I can't and won't tell you what you can do with your body. But in the case of Arka-Dal, I'd probably feel a little jealous," he said.

"Jealous? Why?" she asked.

"He has a way of making most women fall hopelessly in love with him," Kashi answered.

"But I'm *not* like other women," Gorinna said. "You have nothing to worry about, my love. Arka-Dal would never let me seduce him because I'm a married woman. You know his feelings on such things."

Kashi nodded.

"Still, I'd like to *try*," Gorinna said.

"In that case, I advise you take a number and wait in line. There are four other women ahead of you," Kashi joked.

"Five," Pandaar cut in.

"Five?" asked Gorinna.

"Yes. Zhijima would also like to give him a try," Pandaar said. "I overheard her talking about it with Galya. Apparently, she's been fantasizing about it for years."

"Wow! Whatever he has, he should bottle it and sell it," Kashi said. "If you do manage to get him to sleep with you, please return to me after you've finished. I need you much more than he does and far more than I can express in mere words."

"I promised long ago that you and I would be together forever. I will keep that promise, my love," Gorinna assured him.

Gorinna's growing obsession with Arka-Dal wasn't exactly a secret. Aware of what might happen between Arka-Dal and Gorinna, Merlin wracked his brain for ways to head it off. His thoughts returned to an earlier kingdom and the love triangle that eventually brought it all crashing down. When the king learned of his wife's affair with his best warrior, he locked her in a distant tower and banished him to parts unknown. Afterwards, wracked by guilt, his mood swung wildly between fits of uncontrollable rage and wallowing self pity. Then paranoia set in.

The king became a ruthless tyrant after that and the nobles rallied behind the banner of his half-sister Morgana and their illegitimate son. The civil war that ensued was hard-fought and very bloody. In the end, both the king and his bastard lay dead on the field of battle and the kingdom was in ruins.

He sighed.

Neither Arka-Dal nor any of his close friends displayed any such flaws. The things that brought down Camelot would not bring down Thule. There could be no civil war because the throne of Thule could not be inherited. There were no heirs to the throne and no aristocracy to try to usurp it.

There were no titled nobles.

No private armies.

No feudal system.

Power could pass from one emperor to the next only by the will of the people in an open election. It was the one thing that Arka-Dal had insisted upon putting into the Constitution. He had also wanted a 25 year term limit on the emperor, but the Senate insisted that he, at least, rule for his entire life. At Leo's urging, Arka-Dal agreed to accept their mandate. Thule was a new and rising nation. It needed stability and Arka-Dal was the only man who could bring it that.

A few years later, the Senate amended the Constitution by a 96% vote to allow Empress Mayumi to assume the throne if and when Arka-Dal died. She would also rule for the remainder of her life.

It was a very wise decision, Merlin thought.

But who would follow?

Would it be one of Arka-Dal's offspring?

One of his wives?

Or someone totally unconnected with the Dal line?

It was moot for now. After all, he and Gorinna had extended Arka-Dal's life and that of everyone else in his inner circle and family by at least 250-300 years. There was more than enough time to worry about a successor.

He was so lost in his thoughts, he failed to notice Arka-Dal until he sat down next to him.

"You're up to something, Merlin. I can feel it," Arka-Dal said with a smile.

"I was just thinking about the future," Merlin said.

"Immediate or distant?" asked the Emperor.

"That all depends on your point of view. I was wondering who would succeed you after you're gone," Merlin replied.

"It won't matter to me. I'll be dead and in no position to voice my opinion," Arka-Dal said.

"But *I'll* be here. So will your children and grandchildren. It might matter to *them*," Merlin said.

"Maybe. But it's up to the people to elect the next emperor. It's their country after all," Arka-Dal reminded him. "Anyway, it's too far into the future to worry about now. Hell, things can change. Thule might not last that long."

"Oh, Thule will endure far beyond your lifetime and the lifetimes of your children. It is the path it may follow that most concerns me. While this nation has been founded on the ideals of freedom, justice and humanity, future rulers may try to change that," Merlin said. "It has happened before."

"Empires rise and fall. History is littered with their ruins. Thule is no different. Nothing lasts forever," Arka-Dal said. "Will any others of my line become Emperors?"

"The House of Dal will rule for three generations after your death. After that, a new House will rise to power and last until another of your line topples it on the 1,000th anniversary of the founding of Thule. After that, the future is clouded," Merlin said.

"So Thule will last at least 1,000 years? That's a good long run in anyone's book," Arka-Dal said.

"It is less than an eye blink in the grand scheme of things," Merlin countered. "I have lived nearly ten times as long and I have witnessed horrors and wonders that you can't even begin to imagine. But never in all my years have I witnessed anything like what you have created here."

Arka-Dal smiled.

"You give me too much credit, Merlin," he said modestly. "I just try to do what's right for our people."

"And you've done an exceptional job," Galya said as she entered the room.

She sat down on Arka-Dal's lap and kissed him. Merlin smiled and decided they made a perfect match. She looked back at Merlin.

"Don't you think he's exceptional, Merlin?" she asked.

"Indeed he is," Merlin said.

After her conversation with Kashi, Gorinna took a long, hot bath to soothe her mind. Unable to do this, she sought out Arka-Dal to discuss the matter with him. She found him seated behind his desk, going over the usual mound of paperwork that went with ruling the ever—expanding Empire. He put down the stack when she entered and smiled.

"Can I speak with you about something very personal?" she asked as she sat on the edge of the desk.

He stood up and nodded.

"Of course. After all these years, you know you can speak with me about anything you desire," he assured her.

She sat down on the edge of his desk. As she did, she noticed that his gaze went straight to the place between her thighs. She let him look a bit then crossed her legs, pleased that he felt attracted to her.

"What's on your mind?" he asked.

"Hamid told me that you feel attracted to me and that the two of you even joke about it sometimes. Is that true?" she asked.

"Yes on both counts. The jokes are all in good fun. I mean no disrespect," he replied.

"I know. I don't mind it, either. I'm just kind of flattered that you feel that way toward me. What do you usually joke about?" she asked as she uncrossed her legs. She noticed that his gaze went to her thighs again then he quickly made eye contact.

"I tell Kashi that I'd be afraid to make love with you because you might be so good I'd refuse to give you back," he said, aware of the fact she was flirting with him. He always liked her legs. They were smooth, firm and flawless and he always wondered what it would be like to get between her thighs.

Gorinna laughed.

"Is there any truth to your jest?" she asked.

"More than you know," he admitted. "I really *am* afraid of doing anything like that simply because you are so *beautiful, sexy and intelligent.* You might say that I'm afraid of falling under your spell. So much so, that I wouldn't even hazard a kiss."

She almost blushed at his compliments. He'd never opened up like this before.

"I never knew you felt that way," she said softly. "So you meant what you said when that nutcase wizard trapped us in those ruins a few years ago?"

"Every word of it. We've been working so closely with each other for so long, it's impossible *not* to love you," he admitted.

"So you find me sexy?" she asked as she slowly parted her thighs again.

His gaze went right to them. She decided to tempt him further by slowly pulling up her skirt. She saw a bulge appear in his pants and smiled appreciatively.

"I see you do," she said. "If you like me so much, why don't you just take me in your arms and make love to me?"

"Because Kashi and I are like brothers. I don't want to do anything that might jeopardize that relationship. Besides, you're married and that makes you off-limits to me," Arka-Dal added.

"Kashi knew you'd say that. So did I," she said.

"You both know me very well," he replied.

"Well, we *are* family," she said as she slid off his desk. As she did, she hiked up her skirt again. "I want you to know that I will *never* be off-limits to you. I am yours whenever you want me. You need only ask."

He nodded then hugged her. On an impulse, she suddenly kissed him. The sensation was unexpectedly powerful. She pulled back and looked into his eyes.

"You felt that, too, didn't you?" she asked.

"I sure did," he replied.

Instead of making an attempt to follow it up, Gorinna turned and left the room. When she reached the door, she cast a glance back at him. He watched her leave and shook his head to help the shock wear off. That's when he heard Galya's laughter. He turned just as she entered from another door.

"I saw what happened. You look as if you've been struck by lightning," she teased.

"It was unexpected. That nearly stunned me. It was almost as powerful as our first kiss. Remember?" he asked.

She giggled and hugged him tight.

"And every kiss since," she said as she pressed her lips to his.

Gorinna walked downstairs and out into the rose garden. She had to walk and think. Something new had been added to the strange brew that was her life. And it was something quite strong. She was bedeviled by a storm of emotions and she wondered if she should keep resisting them or throw caution to the wind and act on her impulses. If she took the former route, she'd probably go crazy. If she took the latter, all Hell might break loose.

Merlin emerged from a hedge maze just as she approached a pond. He saw her agitation and bade her to sit beside him on one of the marble benches. She then told him what had happened.

"You never should have done that, my dear. Now that you have, I advise you to go no further. We do not want Thule to go the way of Camelot," he warned.

"It won't, Merlin. I promise. Almost everyone here understands the situation. Even the women. They all know that no matter what happens, Arka-Dal will not risk losing Kashi's friendship and Kashi has no desire to lose his. But I tell you this, I've never in my entire life felt anything like that before. It made me weak in the knees," Gorinna said. "This will give Arka-Dal and Kashi something more to jest about."

"You think he'll tell Kashi?" asked Merlin.

"There are no secrets between any of us. There never have been," she replied. "Just this morning, Kashi told me I was free to act as I please as long as I still returned to his bed each evening. He said that he had no control over me and my body was mine to do with as I please as always."

"Remarkable attitude," Merlin mused. "What do you plan on doing?"

"I don't know," she admitted. "I need more time to think about this. Now I understand why Arka-Dal said he was afraid to start anything with me."

Merlin chuckled.

"What about you? Are you also afraid?" he asked.

"More than I can say!" she confessed.

When the other women of the palace found out about the kiss, they teased Gorinna mercilessly. She took it good-naturedly and even teased them back. But it was Mayumi, as always, who put it all into perspective.

"If you hunger for him so strongly, then you should find a way to satisfy that hunger. I have no objections to you and Aka-san having sex with each other—just as long as you don't become his next wife," she said.

"Mayumi's right. It's okay to screw him once in a while, but you can't marry him. He already has enough wives and I'd object to adding you to the already fierce competition I have now," Chatha added.

"It's your pussy. You can share it with whomever you please. Just don't make it a permanent thing or I might have to turn you into a statue!" Medusa joked.

"And don't get pregnant! It'll play Hell with your magical powers!" Galya warned. "If you do manage to bed our husband, make sure you give him back. As good as *you* are in bed, he might want to keep you."

"Then you really don't mind?" Gorinna asked.

"Oh, we *mind*. It's just that we all realize that there's nothing we can do about it," Mayumi said. "Once Aka-san sees what's between your lovely thighs, he will not be able to resist you. I know that *I* cannot."

They all laughed hard at this.

They'd all had sex with each other more than once. Gorinna had seduced every woman in the palace and none of them have been able to resist her since. This was especially true with Pandaar's wife, Zhijima, who had fallen in love with Gorinna.

She wondered how this might affect their relationship. Although she had resisted Gorinna's advances at first, she now looked forward to their lovemaking, especially when it was her turn to be the "man". Would Gorinna still have time for her after she'd been with Arka-Dal?

"You like Arka-Dal a lot. Why don't *you* try to seduce him, too?" asked Gorinna jokingly.

Zhijima blushed and laughed.

"He barely notices me," she replied.

"Well, you *are* kind of small. Maybe if you stood on a chair naked?" Medusa suggested. "I'm sure that once he sees your pretty body, he'll whisk you off to the bedroom."

They laughed.

But Zhijima knew if that ever happened, Pandaar would have trouble dealing with it. He wasn't as open-minded as Kashi was about such things. He already had trouble dealing with her affair with Gorinna, even though he joked about it.

"I think I'll wait and see how Arka-Dal handles *you* first," she said to Gorinna.

Naturally, Arka-Dal told Kashi what had transpired. Kashi laughed and made several crude jokes which the Emperor countered with some of his own. Then, in all seriousness, Kashi slapped him on the back.

"Go for it, my friend! Gorinna wants you and I think you now want her. Just do me one favor," he said.

"What?" Arka-Dal asked.

"Give her back to me when you're finished," Kashi said.

"What if she refuses to come back to you?" asked Pandaar who had been listening to the entire thing.

Kashi shrugged.

"I guess I'd have to find myself another wife," he said.

"You really wouldn't do that. Would you?" asked Pandaar.

"If Gorinna decided to stay with Arka-Dal, what else could I do? You know how strong-willed she is. Once she decides to do something, no one can change her mind. Besides, we've been married over 50 years. I might like a change!" Kashi said half in jest.

"You'd be lost with her and she without you," Arka-Dal said. "I'd better find a way to dissuade her from going any further in order to preserve your marriage."

"Good luck with that one! This is Gorinna we're speaking of, not some run-of-the-mill woman. I'd hate to piss her off. She might decide to turn you into a vole or worse," Kashi said as he drained his glass. "If you want to preserve the peace of this house, I advise you to sleep with her. As agitated as she feels right now, she's no good to anyone, especially me. If you were a true friend, you'd help her relieve her tension."

Arka-Dal couldn't believe his ears.

Was Kashi telling him to have sex with Gorinna?

"Are you sure about this?" he asked.

Kashi nodded as he refilled his glass at the bar.

"I know Gorinna is and that's good enough for me," he said as he rejoined them on the sofa. "I'm afraid that your fate is sealed, my friend. You are doomed to make love with Gorinna and you'll have to suffer all of the consequences that come with it."

"You're crazy!" Arka-Dal said.

"But not crazy enough to go against Gorinna's desires," Kashi said with a grin. "Besides, you'll enjoy it greatly. She's very good. Even the other women say so. Right, Pandaar?"

Pandaar laughed.

"Zhijima has no complaints," he said. "She especially loves it when Gorinna let's her be the "man". In fact, I don't think she can get enough of her."

"If you truly value our friendship, Arka-Dal, then I ask you to make love with my wife for my sake. If you don't, she'll drive me crazy with her constant agitation," Kashi said.

Arka-Dal finished his brandy and nodded.

"You're serious, aren't you?" he asked.

"Very serious," Kashi assured him. "You can screw her as much as you desire. Just don't keep her."

"What if she *wants* me to keep her?" Arka-Dal asked. "That could screw things up royally."

"She does have that effect on people. If you're worried how this might affect our friendship, I assure you that after all we've been through together, nothing in this universe can break the bond that is between us. If Gorinna decides that she would like to become your next wife, so be it. I've had her for more than 50 years so she might want to move on," Kashi replied.

"You know this is insane, don't you?" Arka-Dal asked.

"No more so than many of the other things we've been through in the past. Please do me this one great favor, my friend. Help Gorinna realize her fantasies before she drives me over the edge," Kashi pled.

Arka-Dal finished his drink and stared at Kashi. He knew his friend was dead serious. So was Gorinna. He knew the Red Witch well enough to know that she would keep after him. Since he also found her very attractive, maybe he'd allow her to catch him.

"Since you put it that way, I'll do my best to grant your request. I'll have to think about this for a while first," he said as he rose and headed up to his office to finish some paperwork.

Later that evening, Arka-Dal sat on the balcony perusing the news in the Thule Times. But try as he might, he simply couldn't concentrate on it. His mind kept drifting back to the conversation he'd had with Gorinna and Kashi.

Mayumi walked out and joined him. He smiled as she sat down in front of him. Her presence always lifted his spirits and made him feel that all was right with the world.

"Galya told us what happened. So did Gorinna," Mayumi said.

He folded the paper and placed it on the table.

"I told Kashi about it, too. He didn't seem surprised. In fact, he urged me to let Gorinna seduce me so she could fulfill her fantasies. It was all so weird," he said.

"And are you?" Mayumi asked.

"Not if I can help it. Why do you ask?" he replied.

"Me and the other women have decided that it would be good for you and Gorinna to have sex just as long as she doesn't try to become your next wife," Mayumi said. "In other words, you cannot keep her."

He laughed.

"That's what Kashi said," he replied. "I assure you, my love, that as alluring as Gorinna is and despite how much I've always liked her, I have no plans to have sex with her," he said.

"But I think you should," Mayumi countered.

He raised an eyebrow at this.

"Why?" he asked.

"If you refuse her, she will only become more agitated and frustrated. She might not be able to think straight. If that should happen, Gorinna may not be able to function when an emergency arises," she said.

"So you want me to do it for the good of the Empire? Any other reason?" he asked.

"Hai. If you don't do it, then you will both go through life wondering what it would feel like. I don't want either of you to have any regrets," she answered.

He laughed again.

She scowled.

"And you would regret it," she added.

"You're probably right as usual. What would *you* do in my place?" he asked.

"I would take Gorinna for a long cruise and spend some time at the beach house with her—like you did with Chatha. Make it nice and romantic. Something special so she will never forget it," Mayumi suggested.

"Maybe I'll do that—one day," he said.

"Make it soon, Aka-san. Gorinna is going crazy over this. Please act quickly to ease her discomfort," Mayumi urged as she threw her arms around his neck. "But tonight, I need you to ease mine!"

The next morning, he went for a walk in the rose garden with Gorinna. To her surprise, he reached out and took her hand.

"I've decided to take the yacht downriver to the beach house tomorrow. I was wondering if you'd care to come with me," he offered.

She beamed and hugged his arm tight.

"I'd *love* to come with you. When do we leave?" she accepted.

"After breakfast tomorrow. It'll be just the two of us and there's no hurry to get back," he said.

"None whatsoever," she said with a smile. "I'll bring my sexiest clothes."

"Everything looks sexy on you. It always has," he complimented.

"Has Kashi spoken with you about this?" she asked.

"Him and several other people," he replied.

She giggled.

"Did they have to twist your arm?" she asked.

"No. But they did ease any misgivings I may have had over this. Now that I know that no one's feelings will be hurt by this, we can relax and live out our fantasies," he said.

"And how long have you had such fantasies about me?" she asked.

"For as long as you've had yours about me," he answered.

Gorinna told Kashi of Arka-Dal's offer that very night. He listened quietly and smiled at her.

"Sounds like it will be a nice vacation for the both of you," he said.

"Then you really don't mind my going?" she asked.

"If I said I did, would you still go?" he asked.

"I think so," she admitted. "Are you upset?" she asked.

"No. This is something you both need to get out of your systems. I can't have you moping around here and making my life miserable while you wonder what it might have been like," Kashi said.

"I make you miserable?" she asked.

"Only when you keep harping about this. Other than that, our life together is a pure joy. I only wish to see you happy, my love. If this will make you happy, then I say go for it. Besides, there's nothing I can do to stop you once you've made up your mind," he said.

She laughed.

"You know me too well. Do I hold no surprises or mystery for you anymore?" she teased.

"There is one mystery that's been puzzling me forever," he said.

"And what is that?" she pressed.

"I've always been mystified as to why you chose to spend most of your life with me," he said.

"That's no mystery," she said. "You and I are perfect together. I could not have chosen a better man to spend my life with than you."

He pulled her close and they kissed.

"Come back to me," he whispered.

"Always," she promised.

Galya and Leo were playing chess in the parlor. Galya moved her knight to take Leo's rook only to lose it to his bishop. He could tell her mind wasn't really on the match.

"You seem to be having trouble concentrating tonight," he observed.

"I am. What do you think of this situation with Arka-Dal and Gorinna?" she asked.

Leo leaned back in his chair and clasped his hands over his stomach.

"I'm not sure what to think. We all knew that Gorinna harbored deep and passionate feelings toward Arka-Dal and that he felt something similar for her. Yet I never imagined they would act them out," he said. "What about you? How do *you* feel?"

"A little jealous but happy for them. I love Arka-Dal more than I can say with mere words and I also love Gorinna. If they want to spend some time together, who am I to deny them? I have always lived my life to the fullest. I have no regrets for the things I have done. I don't want them to have any, either," she said.

Leo smiled.

"You sound like Mayumi," he pointed out.

"I take that as a compliment. We all gave Arka-Dal permission to do this but we all told him that he couldn't keep her," she said. "I have had many sex partners throughout my life. Too many to even count. From where I sit, I figure that I have no right to pass moral judgment on anyone."

Leo laughed.

"I suppose you're right," he said.

"If Arka-Dal and Gorinna want to become lovers, so be it. But while he lives, I will remain loyal and loving to him only. After he passes on, who knows? I may never again take on another lover. Arka-Dal is the only man I ever truly loved. He is impossible to replace. Because I love him, I don't mind if he wants to sample Gorinna."

"Merlin wouldn't like this one bit," he said.

"Merlin doesn't like a lot of things," Galya pointed out. "He'll just have to get over it."

And Merlin didn't like it.

When Arka-Dal told him of his plans, the sorcerer almost hit the ceiling.

"Are you quite insane? Gorinna is a married woman. In fact, she's married to one of your very best friends!" he exclaimed.

"That's the odd part. Kashi urged us to do it. If he hadn't given us the go ahead, I doubt I would have considered it. Mayumi and the other women also urged us to do it," Arka-Dal explained.

"Indeed!" Merlin said as he sat down on the balcony rail.

"Kashi said if I was a true friend, I'd help Gorinna fulfill her fantasies so he could get some peace of mind. He said that Gorinna was driving him crazy over it," Arka-Dal added.

Merlin shook his head.

"He's mad! You're all mad!" he said.

"I agree. This entire thing is incredibly bizarre," Arka-Dal said as he sat next to him.

Merlin sighed.

"Gorinna told me many times how she felt toward you. Her feelings are very deep and strong. I sense that yours are, too. I don't want this to get out of hand. I don't want this to become another Camelot," he warned.

"It won't. We're too tightly knit for that," Arka-Dal assured him.

"Even so, this worries me," Merlin said.

"I must admit I'm a little worried myself," Arka-Dal said.

"About what?" asked Merlin.

"I'm worried that I may not be able to live up to Gorinna's expectations. I don't want to disappoint her," Arka-Dal said.

Merlin grinned.

"You haven't yet disappointed any woman that I'm aware of," he said. "I'm sure that you'll more than satisfy Gorinna. But what if she decides she wants to remain with you?"

"I've already discussed that with Kashi. He said he'd understand and there'd be no hard feelings," Arka-Dal replied.

"Incredible!" Merlin exclaimed.

"Indeed," agreed Arka-Dal.

As Arka-Dal packed for the trip, Mayumi noticed that he seemed lost in thought. She asked him what was troubling him.

"I wonder what our people will think when they find out about all this?" he asked.

"Some will smile and joke about it as they always do. Some will gossip as they are wont to do. Nothing will change. You have ruled the Empire well and wisely for more than half a century. As long as you continue to do so, the people will support you. Our people idolize and trust you more than anyone else on Earth. You are one of them. You share their hardships, dreams and ambitions. You protect them. You are like a member of their own families. Whatever makes you happy makes them happy, too," Mayumi said assuringly.

"You always manage to say the right things at the right times to put my mind at rest," he said with a smile.

"And you do the same for me," she said.

The next morning, Kashi and Pandaar escorted Arka-Dal and Gorinna to the royal yacht at the main pier. Gorinna winked and boarded the vessel while Arka-Dal shook hands and said farewell.

"What about the ruins? You want us to check them out?" Pandaar asked.

"Not unless someone goes missing or turns up dead. Tell the City Guards to make regular trips out there. Maybe they'll find something. If not, I'll check it out when I get back," Arka-Dal said.

"And when will *that* be?" asked Kashi.

"Two, perhaps three weeks. I haven't decided yet. Don't worry. I'll bring her back," Arka-Dal said.

"It's not *her* I'm worried about," he said with a laugh. "You might come back on a stretcher when she's done with you. Did you see that tiny bag she carried aboard?"

"It *was* pretty small," Arka-Dal said.

"She told me that she wouldn't need much clothing on this trip. Only the bare essentials," Kashi warned with a wink.

"Wow!" exclaimed Pandaar.

"Exactly!" said Kashi.

Arka-Dal bade them farewell again and boarded the yacht. Gorinna greeted him on deck and waved. Kashi waved back. They watched as the crew untied the yacht and eased it away from the pier.

"Doesn't this bother you?" Pandaar asked.

"Years ago, it certainly would have. Now, it doesn't bother me at all. Gorinna always does as she wishes and I usually go along with it," Kashi replied.

"If that was *my* wife on that yacht now, I'd be pissed," Pandaar said. "Since you're not, I have to say that you're a bigger man than I am."

"I've always known that. It's about time you've realized it, too," Kashi joked. "I'm thirsty. Let's find a tavern."

"Suits me," said Pandaar as they strolled toward the main street.

Back at the palace, Leo and Medusa were going over some ancient texts when she looked up and closed the book.

"What do *you* think of this situation, Leo?" she asked.

He sat back and folded his hands across his belly.

"I think the goings on around here grow stranger by the day. When Arka-Dal and Galya wed, I didn't think I'd live long enough to see anything else surprise me. This thing with Gorinna proved me wrong. What makes it really strange is the fact that everyone concerned—including yourself—*encouraged* them to do this," he said.

"It's not all that strange. In fact, to us, it seemed *inevitable.* They have been very attracted to each other for decades. We just thought it was best for them to get it out of their systems. To Arka-Dal, Gorinna was tempting because he considered her to be forbidden fruit. Perhaps now that she's no longer forbidden, the temptation to sample her won't be as great," Medusa explained.

"What if their attraction grows even stronger?" asked Leo.

She shrugged.

"In that case, we'll just have to learn to share him with yet another woman. I hope he can handle the five of us," she said.

"I bet Merlin doesn't like this at all," Leo remarked.

"That's just too bad. Merlin will have to get over it just as he had to get over Arka-Dal's marriage to Galya. I think what upsets Merlin most is the fact that he didn't foresee that happening. He didn't foresee this thing with Gorinna, either," Medusa said.

"Second sight only works when you try to see into a specific future. The gods do not reveal everything to us," Merlin said as he materialized.

Leo scowled.

"I wish you'd knock once in a while," he commented.

"Why? It's more fun this way," Merlin said as he sat down at the table with them.

"*You* don't reveal all that you see, either," Medusa pointed out. "You always withhold something."

"I do that out of necessity and to keep from alarming anyone needlessly," Merlin said. "Besides, no one's future is carved in stone. There are always several possibilities revealed to me at any given time. The choice of which path to follow lies with those who seek the answers."

"What do you see in Gorinna's future?" asked Medusa.

"Alas, hers is clouded. I do know that she will one day be forced to make a most terrible choice. One that may cripple her emotionally," Merlin said.

Many miles away, an old man in a long gray cloak sits peering into a basin of clear water while a black cat perches on his shoulder. The water swirls with images of people and places, which slowly drift away on the ripples. The images of Arka-Dal and Gorinna intrigued him. He never once imagined they were enamored with each other. This gave him even more ammunition to use against them.

"The Red Witch's actions are causing her to play right into my hands. By the time she realizes she is my pawn, it will be too late," he said.

The cat shook his head in disgust.

"I never knew you were a dirty old man," he said. "Spying on people while they are in the throes of passion! Have you no decency at all?"

"The Red Witch has a wonderfully sexy body," the wizard remarked. "This love affair of theirs will enable me to trap them more easily. All I need do is find a way to use Arka-Dal as the bait. If she thinks he is in danger, she will come to his rescue."

"She looked like she was already coming," the cat quipped sarcastically.

The wizard sneered at him. The two had an odd connection. While he could speak directly to the cat, he was forced to use the cat as a conduit in order to speak to anyone else. It was the price he had to pay for summoning the creature and making it his familiar. If *he* died, the cat could actually restore him to life. If the cat died, it was all over for him as well.

Fortunately for them both, the animal was virtually indestructible. And being a creature created by dark magic, the cat was also immortal. As long as it lived, so would the wizard—although he *did* age but at a much slower rate than normal people. The wizard looked every bit as old as he supposedly was and his body ached and creaked just like any other very old man. This was also part of the trade-off for delving into the more forbidden realms of magical power.

Merlin had warned him against this, but he laughed him off. After that, they went their separate ways. Merlin chose to follow the path of white magic and enlightenment. He followed the darker road.

And it destroyed his soul and twisted his mind.

He craved power for its own sake and cared not how he attained it or who he had to kill to get it. Along the way, he had caused much misery, suffering and calamities.

At one point, many centuries earlier, he attempted to strike a bargain with the Devil to get even more power. But the Devil refused to have anything to do with him. He no longer had a soul, so he had nothing with which to bargain.

"You're a real nasty piece of work, wizard," the Devil said. "Even if you had a soul, I don't think I'd want it."

He wasn't sure if he'd been insulted or complimented. He didn't care. He'd attain the knowledge and power he desired without his help.

He did.

And he became addicted to it.

But now he wondered, in the back of his mind, did he have enough power to take on the Red Witch? Or Merlin? Or both?

If his plan worked, he'd surely slay Gorinna. In that case, he'd bring the wrath of Merlin down upon his head.

"And *that* would be a battle to remember!" he said aloud.

The cat yawned.

"Why bother yourself with all this? The book is destroyed. You can't bring it back," he said.

"It's not about the book anymore. The witch made a fool of me. She must be taught a lesson," the wizard answered.

The cat shook his head.

"So this is about *pride*?" he asked.

"Precisely," the wizard said.

"Beware. Pride goeth before a fall as the old saying goes. I advise you to drop the matter," the cat warned.

"Bah! What sort of man would take advice from a cat?" the wizard shot back.

"The same type who converses with one," the cat shot back.

News of the "affair" traveled quickly throughout the Empire. It even made the gossip column of the Thule Times. Most of the men who read it joked about how "lucky" Arka-Dal was to be nailing one of the most beautiful women in the Empire. Many wished they could take his place. Some of the older women feigned indignation. Most people simply shrugged it off.

After all, it was reported that neither Hamid Kashi nor the royal wives objected to this. If they didn't, why should anyone else?

"Thulians are very open-minded," Leo observed as he put down the morning paper. "Most of the editorials wish them well."

"Arka-Dal and Gorinna are national heroes. When something like this happens, it shows the people that they are human, too. I think it makes the people feel even closer to them," Medusa said.

"People in other countries would feel scandalized by something like this. It might even have led to riots or open revolts. But not our people," Chatha said with a smile.

"Scandals are what one makes them out to be. In the eyes of our people, Arka-Dal can do no wrong. They believe in him and everything he stands for. They know he always acts in their best interest. So if he wants to have an affair, they say more power to him!" Medusa said.

The only one who was actually surprised by this was the Minotaur Jun. The Field Marshall had come to Thule bearing the monthly training reports. He usually gave them to Arka-Dal personally then they sat down to discuss any needs or shortcomings he saw among the troops. Instead, Pandaar accepted the reports and invited Jun to stay for dinner as usual. When he found out where Arka-Dal was and with whom, he was taken aback.

"I had no idea they felt this way toward each other, "he said. "I always thought they were just very good friends."

"After this, they'll be even better friends," Pandaar joked as they sat down to eat.

The yacht made good speed as it sailed downriver. Whenever the vessel sailed, hundreds of local citizens stood on the banks and waved at it. Arka-Dal and Gorinna waved back at them then went below to continue their trip in private.

The royal cabin was well-appointed. It was 40 feet long and 20 wide with mahogany furnishings, large closets, a private shower and toilet and a big, four-posted bed. There were six large, picture windows that could be opened to admit the breezes and a door that led out to a private deck.

The yacht was one of the few real luxuries Arka-Dal allowed himself and was his favorite way to get around the Empire. It was 128 feet long and 40 feet wide and had a shallow draft to enable it to safely navigate the Po River. The yacht also boasted a full galley, dining area, a dozen smaller cabins for guests, the crew's quarters below decks, a large common living room, sun deck and weapons lockers. It could be powered by either steam or sails and was quite maneuverable.

It had no real name but most people referred to it as the Royal Barge. Arka-Dal simply called it the yacht or the boat.

Arka-Dal sat at the table in his cabin and watched as Gorinna unpacked. She stood before the full-length mirror and held up one sheer dress after another as she asked him what he thought.

"What should I wear?" she asked.

"Whatever makes you comfortable," he replied.

"But I want to wear something that really *excites* you," she said as she looked in the mirror again.

"You've been exciting me ever since we first met. Whatever you decide to wear is fine with me—as long as it's very easy to remove," he said softly.

Before she could say another word, he scooped her up in his arms and carried her to the bed . . .

Gorinna woke just before dawn and smiled down at the sleeping Arka-Dal. Their first night together had been everything she'd imagined.

And more.

She felt warm inside now.

Content.

Satisfied.

She rose slowly so as not to wake him and threw on a light robe. Then, as quietly as possible, she opened the cabin door and stepped out onto the deck. She moved to the rail and watched as the sun began to rise.

They had done it.

They had actually made love.

It was magical, too.

Spellbinding.

Awesome.

Three times he had entered her. Each time felt better than the last. Each time, he had filled her with his seed.

His love.

Each time, she had eagerly accepted and gave him her love in return.

A soft breeze wafted through her long, raven locks. As she reached up to push her hair from her face, Arka-Dal walked out and put his arms around her waist. She looked up at him and sighed.

"I feel like a different person," she said. "It's as if I've left my old life behind and started a new one. If this is a dream, I don't want it to end. I want this to last forever."

She turned and slid her tongue into his mouth. They held each other close for a long time, then stopped to breathe.

"We'll be at the beach house in two more days. Once there, we can stay awhile. There's no need to rush back," he said.

"No need at all," she agreed.

They arrived at the beach house, which was really a 15 room manor with three smaller guest cottages not 200 feet from the ocean, late in the evening. When he saw them coming up the stone walk, Kozlori, the caretaker, greeted them at the door.

"Welcome back, Sir and you, too, Gorinna. It's good to see you again. The house is ready. Where's the Empress?" he asked as he peered over the shoulders for her.

"Mayumi did not accompany me this time, Kozlori," Arka-Dal answered as he handed them their bags.

"Shall I prepare the guest suite then?" Kozlori asked.

"No. The master suite will be just fine," Arka-Dal assured him as he grasped Gorinna's hand.

The caretaker smiled then laughed.

"In that case, I'll have my wife bring up fresh flowers and some chilled wine," he said as hurried off.

"Kozlori knows you very well," Gorinna remarked as she and Arka-Dal walked into the parlor.

"He should. He's been my caretaker for nearly 40 years. I imagine he'll be here for 40 more before he decides to retire," Arka-Dal said as he poured them each a drink.

Kozlori had been a soldier in the Northern Army when Arka-Dal first met him. He fought side-by-side with him in three major battles and suffered a career-ending wound in the last. Arka-Dal rewarded him by giving him a full pension and then hired him to be the caretaker of the beach house. Of course, Kozlori's wife, Luka, was also part of the package.

Luka was almost the same age as her husband. She was tall, slender and wore her dark hair very long. She was cheerful, friendly and sometimes outspoken. Arka-Dal always enjoyed her company and appreciated her directness. Luka rarely pulled her punches when giving her opinions.

While Kozlori tended the grounds and saw to the maintenance of the manor and guest houses, Luka cleaned and did the cooking. The couple had three teenaged sons who also helped out. They lived in the manor house when it was empty. When Arka-Dal was there, they moved into the larger of the two guest cottages until he left.

All-in-all, it was a very nice arrangement.

Kozlori's sons were nearly at the age when they would have to serve in the Army of Thule for a few years. Like most boys their ages, they looked forward to it. Kozlori knew they would all serve proudly and well.

Just as he did.

Just like every Thulian soldier.

Midnight.

Two members of the City Guards rode up to the crumbling mosque and dismounted. They were investigating more reports of lights and other activities coming from within the ruins. They drew their swords and entered. After searching for an hour, all they found were the half-molten remains of several black candles arranged in a large circle.

The reports were the same every night.

Each night, several lights were seen moving through the ruins. Most likely the lights came from the candles as they were being carried by whoever was behind this. It was probably part of some sort of ceremony. By the time the guards got out there, the ceremony was over and those conducting it were gone.

It wasn't illegal to hold ceremonies in ruins.

Not as long as no animals or people were sacrificed.

Pandaar decided to keep compiling information until something more unusual occurred. Right now, it all seemed rather harmless. There was no need to be concerned.

Kashi entered and sat down at the desk next to him. Pandaar passed him the reports.

"Looks like nothing's changed," he said after he perused them. "Unless it takes a nasty turn, we've been told to not to do anything until Arka-Dal returns."

"I remember. But it *is* tempting," Pandaar said. "Can I ask you something?"

Kashi shrugged and nodded.

"What will you do if Arka-Dal and Gorinna fall in love with each other?" he asked.

"In case it escaped you, they've been in love for years. There's not a damned thing I or anyone else can do about it either," Kashi said.

"Aren't you even a little bit jealous or upset by this?" Pandaar asked.

"Of course I'm jealous but there's no sense getting upset over it. This would have happened sooner or later. At least this way, it's in the open. Everyone is aware of it and there are no hurt feelings," he replied.

"You amaze me," Pandaar remarked.

Kashi laughed.

"What would *you* do if Zhijima decided she wanted to do the same thing?" he asked.

"What *could* I do?" Pandaar asked.

"Not a damned thing," Kashi assured him.

"Zhijima does want to fuck Arka-Dal. The trouble is, he doesn't seem to really notice her. He treats her like his little sister or something and that really frustrates her," Pandaar said as he leaned back.

"She *is* kind of short. Perhaps is she took off her clothes and stood on a chair?" Kashi joked.

Pandaar laughed.

"Let's go downstairs and have a drink," he suggested.

"Or three," Kashi agreed.

Gorinna propped herself up on her elbow and smiled at Arka-Dal.

"That was wonderful," she said. "Each time we do it, it feels better and better."

"Yes, it does," he agreed as he stroked her hair.

"I don't want this to end—ever!" she said.

"Me neither," he said.

"Then what do we do?" she asked as she lay back down.

"We relax and enjoy every moment of the time we share together. Enjoy each other as much as we can before we return to Thule," he suggested.

Go back, he said. She wasn't sure she wanted to now.

"I love you," she said softly.

"And I love you," he assured her.

He'd been afraid of this but now that they'd both said it, it felt so right. Perhaps they had loved each other for all this time but were too afraid it would tear their world apart if they admitted it. Now, it didn't seem to matter.

"Should we tell the others when we return?" he asked.

"There's no need to. Everyone already knows. That's why they encouraged us to do this. They wanted us to get it out of our systems," she said.

"I don't think it's working," he joked.

"Maybe if we keep doing it, we'll grow tired of it?" she joked.

"Let's find out," he said as he rolled onto her again.

The next morning, Gorinna walked into the dining room and sat down at the smaller table. Luka saw her and hurried over.

"Eating alone this morning?" she asked as she poured Gorinna a glass of juice.

"I let Arka-Dal sleep in today. I guess I sort of wore him out last night," Gorinna replied with a very tired, satisfied grin.

Luka laughed.

"What can I get you this morning?" she asked.

"Eggs, sausages and some fresh fruit and bread would be nice," Gorinna replied.

"No problem. You should be careful while you're here or you'll end up pregnant," Luka warned.

"What do you mean?" Gorinna asked.

"All the women who come here end up pregnant. This is where Mayumi became pregnant with Armet. Next came Medusa. Then Chatha. This is where we had all three of our boys. You'll be next if you're not careful," Luka explained.

"Don't worry about that, Luka. I *can't* become pregnant," Gorinna assured her.

"I wouldn't be too sure about that. There's something special about this place. Something almost *magical,"* Luka said.

Gorinna smiled.

"If it were only true! I wouldn't mind having a child. I've always wanted one," she said wistfully.

"In this house, such wishes have a knack for coming true," Luka said as she scurried to the kitchen to prepare breakfast.

For the next three weeks, they feasted on shellfish and other delicacies. They rode horses through the nearby forests, strolled along the beach at sunset and explored local bazaars.

And they made love.

Lots of love.

The more they did, the stronger their passions grew. For Gorinna, it seemed like they were the only two people left on Earth. Nothing else mattered as long as they were together and everything was possible.

Arka-Dal was gallant and attentive.

Humorous and cheerful.

Loving and charming and caring.

He fed her both physically and emotionally. And she did the same for him. Their long standing friendship had soared to the next level. It had blossomed into love.

It was at this time the wizard became aware of the odd goings-on at the deserted mosque. He realized that a minor cult of some sort was now holding their masses there and that the lights and mists they had accidentally invoked were causing a stir among the locals.

"I can make use of that place," he told the cat.

"And exactly how will you do that?" asked the cat as it stopped licking itself.

"It's a well-known fact that Arka-Dal is fascinated with strange things. If I use my magic to intensify the lights and mists at the mosque, he will surely go there himself to investigate. Once he does, I'll be able to spring my trap," the wizard said confidently.

"So you're going to try and trap him in order to lure the witch to the mosque?" the cat asked.

"Exactly," the wizard replied.

"And when she goes there, then what?" asked the cat.

"That's the part I haven't worked out yet," the wizard admitted. "I'm sure something will come to me."

The cat laughed.

"It better come to you before the witch does or you'll be in for a very bad time," he said.

"You sound like you doubt I can handle her," the wizard observed.

"I do. Gorinna is one of the most powerful magic users who ever lived. She just may surprise you," the cat said. "If I were you, I'd forget about her and go about my business."

"Now you know I can't do that," the wizard said.

"Can't—or *won't*?" the cat asked.

"Both," the wizard replied.

"Okay. It's *your* ass on the line, not mine," the cat said with a yawn.

"I thought familiars were supposed to stay with their masters no matter what," the wizard said.

"First of all, you are *not* my master. Ours is more a symbiotic relationship. Second, I refuse to stick around and take the same punishment you so eagerly want to bring down upon yourself. Besides, I can always bring you back later," the cat replied. "*If I so desire.*"

"You sound as if you're afraid of Gorinna," the wizard said.

"I am. You should be, too. The Red Witch is no joke. You have no idea what she can do, especially when she's angry," the cat warned.

"Bah! I can handle her," the wizard sneered.

"Like you did the last two times?" the cat jabbed. "That last one worked out really well!"

"Don't be so sarcastic!" the wizard snapped.

"I'm a cat. I can be whatever I want to be," the cat said with an air of obvious superiority.

Three weeks later, Arka-Dal and Gorinna bade farewell to Kozlori and his family and boarded the yacht for the trip upriver to Thule. It took another three days to reach the city. During that time, they never left the cabin.

They reached the dock at mid-morning and took a carriage back to the palace. Along the way, Gorinna wondered what she'd say to everyone. For nearly a month, she and Arka-Dal were lovers and she knew they'd have to be ready to field a lot of embarrassing questions and to counter the usual rounds of crude jokes and sly humor.

The first person she met on her return was Zhijima. She was in the parlor watching the children at play. She smiled when she saw Gorinna and hugged her warmly.

"When did you get back?" she asked.

"Just this moment. I had a really wonderful time," Gorinna said.

"I envy you, Gorinna," Zhijima said.

"Why?" she asked.

"You got to make love with Arka-Dal and I didn't. I'd love to get close to him just once in my life," Zhijima said wistfully.

"If you kiss my lips after he and I make love, you might be able to *taste* him," Gorinna suggested.

"Which lips?" asked Zhijima with a wry smile.

"Both sets," Gorinna said. "Would that be close enough for you?"

"It will have to do until I can come up with something else," Zhijima said. "Is he as good as you expected?"

"No. He's far better than I even imagined. You really need to give him a try one day," she teased.

"If I dared to do it, it would be all over the palace. You know how hard it is to keep secrets around here," Zhijima said.

Gorinna laughed and went in search of Kashi.

Zhijima smiled.

Although many considered her to be quite alluring, with her long black hair, deep brown eyes and slender, sexy body, the other women in the palace kept Arka-Dal too busy to notice her. Now that Gorinna had become part of that special circle, Zhijima felt even more left out. To make matters worse, the other women knew of her fantasies and teased her about them.

She also realized that Arka-Dal didn't think of her in a sexual way. To him, she was just like a little sister and he was content to keep it that way.

So was Pandaar.

He didn't like the idea that his wife wanted to have sex with his best friend. He had little desire to share her with anyone. He felt that things inside the palace were weird enough already and didn't want to add to the confusion.

But now that Gorinna had fulfilled her fantasies with Arka-Dal, Zhijima felt even more determined to try and fulfill hers. She was normally a little shy and reserved like Mayumi. To get Arka-Dal's attention, she would have to turn up the heat. She would have to make herself into a seductress.

But, she wondered, would she be able to make herself irresistible to Arka-Dal? That remained to be seen.

One of the servants told Gorinna that Kashi was headed out the door to the garden. She rushed into the entry to intercept him. He heard her familiar footsteps and turned just as he reached the door.

He smiled broadly.

As soon as she saw him, she hurried into his arms.

"It's good to have you home," he whispered.

"It's good to be home," she said.

He held her at arm's length. Her dark eyes literally sparkled and she seemed so radiant.

"You look fantastic, my love. Can I assume that you've had a good time?" he asked.

"I've had a wonderful time," she said as they walked into the garden hand—in—hand.

"Was everything as you expected it to be?" he asked.

She beamed at him. Her smile spoke volumes.

"Are you sure you'll be able to return to the way we were before?" he asked.

"To be honest, Hamid, I may be tempted to drink from this well again," she admitted.

"I see," he said solemnly.

"I won't do it if you tell me not to," she hedged.

"You know that I would never tell you any such thing," he said. "Our relationship has always been an open and honest one. I love and respect you far too much to try and put restrictions on you now. If I order you to stay away from him, it would only make you and him feel miserable. Me, too, because you'd never let me hear the end of it."

"Then an occasional dalliance is permitted?" she teased.

"Of course it is. Tell me, is he as good as he's reputed to be?" Kashi asked.

She laughed.

"No. He's far better than that!" she said.

"Is he as good as me?" Kashi pressed.

"No, my love. No one is *that* good!" she assured him.

She kissed him and hurried inside to unpack. She bumped into Merlin in the entry hall and giggled.

Merlin noticed the happy bounce in her gait and smiled.

"I take it that you've had a good trip?" he asked.

"I had a wonderful trip! A marvelous trip! I feel so alive!" she crowed as she sat down next to him.

"And what are your feelings toward Arka-Dal now?" Merlin asked.

"I love him even more. When I see him, I feel as if I'm dancing on air," she replied.

"I was afraid of this," he muttered.

She elbowed him and laughed.

"Don't be. Everyone here understands the situation. Up until our trip, Kashi was the only man I'd ever been with. We still have something special between us. Nothing can change that, not even my love for Arka-Dal," she said. "If you're worried about this becoming another Camelot, I assure you that your fears are unwarranted. Arka-Dal is *not* Arthur. Kashi is *not* Lancelot and I am *not* Guinevere."

"Can you actually share your love with two men?" he asked.

"Arka-Dal shares his love with several women. I can certainly handle two men. You fret too much," she replied.

"Perhaps I do," Merlin said.

The next morning, Gorinna woke feeling sick and dizzy. With her head reeling, she rose and staggered to the bathroom. Kashi heard her vomiting and walked in to see her leaning over the bowl. She was sweating profusely, too.

"What's wrong?" he asked.

"I don't know. I just feel sick to my stomach. I must be coming down with something," she said weakly.

"That's impossible. You've never been sick a day in your life," Kashi said as he helped her up.

"Nevertheless, I feel rotten. There's a first time for everything you know," she insisted.

"You'd better go and let Leo check you out," Kashi suggested.

Gorinna nodded.

Leo was also the resident physician in the palace. He knew how to diagnose and cure just about everything. Surely he'd be able to handle this.

She dressed and went downstairs to Leo's office. Kashi went to have breakfast with the others. When he explained where Gorinna was, Mayumi and the other wives looked at each other and giggled.

While they ate, Pandaar brought up the subject of the unusual goings on at the ruined tower in the plain a few miles south of the capital.

"The tower was built during the latter part of the First Age. I think it was called a minaret. Leo told me that old Islamic priests used to issue the daily calls to prayer from it. It fell into ruin during a minor quake about 450 years ago and was abandoned.

No one's been there for decades, but we're still getting reports of activity from out there," Pandaar said.

"What sort of activity?" asked Arka-Dal.

"Flickering lights at night. High-pitched wails. You know, the usual things associated with a haunting. The thing is, the tower isn't supposed to be haunted. There have been no unusual happenings out there until recently," Pandaar replied.

"Anything else?" asked Arka-Dal.

"Not really. It sounds like another run-of-the-mill haunting to me," Pandaar said with a shrug.

"Keep sending two of the city guards to check it out—just in case," Arka-Dal decided.

Pandaar nodded.

"I'm what?" she almost shouted.

"Pregnant," Leo repeated.

"I can't be. You know that I'm unable to bear children. There must be some mistake," she insisted. She was unable to wrap her mind around it.

"I've run the test three times and the results were positive each time. You're pregnant, Gorinna. With child," Leo said.

"But Merlin said that I couldn't become pregnant," she said as she looked him in the eyes.

"No. He said that you *shouldn't*. He never said that you *couldn't*," Leo corrected.

She shook her head.

"All these years with Kashi and I've never become pregnant. I always believed it was because of what I am," she said. She was still in a state of denial.

"Perhaps the problem lies with Kashi—not you," Leo suggested. "No matter. You are pregnant now and there's no denying it. How do you feel?"

"Confused. Scared. Happy—I don't really know," she replied.

"Do you think it's Arka-Dal's?" asked Leo.

"I'm *positive* it's his. Oh my! What do I tell Hamid?" she asked.

"The truth as you always have. He deserves nothing less. The bigger question is: how will he react?" Leo said.

"And what of Arka-Dal? How will he take this news?" she asked as she felt herself becoming nervous.

"Like he takes everything around here—in stride. Very little upsets or phases him. He'll probably make jokes about it," Leo said with a smile.

She thought back to what Luka had told her about the beach house. It truly *was* enchanted. Mayumi, Medusa, Chatha and Galya had all become pregnant while there. Now she had, too, even though she was supposedly barren.

Luka was right about the house.

There was no other way to explain it.

Gorinna left Leo's office and went upstairs in search of Kashi. She found him in the living room playing chess with Arka-Dal. She walked over and sat at the table with them. Kashi looked up.

"You seem kind of edgy, my love. Is something bothering you?" he asked.

Gorinna took a deep breath, exhaled slowly and told them everything. When she was finished, Kashi surprised her by offering his hand to Arka-Dal.

"Congratulations!" he said sincerely.

The two men shook hands then took turns hugging Gorinna. She was obviously taken aback by their reactions. Neither man seemed angry or hurt by the news. Both said they were happy for her and even joked about it. Their attitudes put her mind at ease. A long, pleasant chat ensued which covered everything from possible names for the child to rearing it. Arka-Dal then suggested that Gorinna inform Merlin of the circumstances.

"What if I lose my powers because of this?" she asked.

Arka-Dal smiled.

"It doesn't matter. You'll still be who you are and we'll still feel the same toward you. *That* will never change," he assured her.

"But I won't be of any use to you without my magic," she protested.

"That's nonsense. You bring over 50 years of knowledge and experience to the table with you each time you sit down. Nothing is more valuable than that," Arka-Dal said. "Your role will become more of an advisory one, of course. I won't have you risking your life in the field like you do now."

"Like Leo says: knowledge is power. Without it, we are all blind," Kashi chimed in.

Gorinna smiled and hugged each of them, then hurried off to find Merlin. They watched her leave then returned to their match.

Arka-Dal looked at Kashi.

"You're really good with this?" he asked.

Kashi nodded.

"You made Gorinna very happy by giving her that which she yearned for most. If she's happy, I'm happy. Besides, the bond between you and me is too strong to be broken by something like this," he replied. "We are like brothers."

"Better!" Arka-Dal said as they slapped hands.

Naturally, Leo told Medusa about Gorinna's condition. Unable to contain herself, Medusa quickly spread the news to the other women in the palace. They went in search of Gorinna and ran into her in the main hallway. To her surprise, they all hugged her warmly and congratulated her. They even offered to help her raise the child.

"After all, we are *family*. Never forget that you are also part of our family. We love you, Gorinna," Mayumi said.

"Especially now," Medusa added with a wink.

"I don't know if this world is ready for another one of Arka-Dal's offspring. There seems to be too many of them now," Chatha joked.

"The world had better get ready for another is on its way," Galya said. "How many does this make now? Ten? A dozen?"

"I don't know. I have lost count," Mayumi said.

"Do you want a boy or a girl?" asked Medusa.

"Yes," Gorinna said.

After more hugging and laughing, Gorinna felt more relaxed. But she expected the women to be supportive.

It was Merlin who worried her.

How would he react when she told him?

Gorinna spent the next hour searching for Merlin. She found the sorcerer on the roof of the palace watching the sun set.

"I've been looking for you," she said.

"You've found me," Merlin replied obviously. "I sense your predicament."

Gorinna chuckled.

Merlin scowled.

"Is there anything you do not know?" she asked.

"More than you can ever imagine. In your case, I sense the heart beating within your womb. I cautioned you against this. If your child is born, your powers will be forfeited," Merlin said.

"I didn't think this could happen. I believed I was barren, made so by the path I chose to follow. I was quite surprised when I found out," Gorinna said.

"I imagine you were. What will you do?" Merlin asked.

"I don't know. On the one hand, my heart is filled with joy. But my mind is troubled. If I lose my powers, I will be of little use to Arka-Dal or the Empire. This vexes me to no end, Merlin," she replied.

"What did Arka-Dal say?" asked Merlin. "After all, it is *his* child you carry."

"He said the decision was mine to make and that he will stand with me no matter what. He seems happy that I'm bearing his child, even though we are not married and this was not intended."

"And Kashi?" Merlin queried.

"He said that as long as I am happy, he is happy. He also told me that I should feel honored to carry the child of the man he loves and respects above all others," Gorinna said.

Merlin smiled.

"Will you and Kashi raise the child or will Arka-Dal?" he asked.

"We *all* will, just like all the other children in the palace. We're all one big family here," she said with a broad grin.

"You people never cease to amaze me. If this had happened in any other royal household, it would have torn them asunder. It might even have plunged the nation into a bloody civil war to determine the legitimate heir to the throne," Merlin mused.

"I guess we are kind of unusual in that respect. There is no hereditary monarchy in Thule and such things can't happen here. In all of our years together, there hasn't even been one serious disagreement or argument. We seem to be above such things," Gorinna said.

"That's because of the circumstances that have brought you all together. You have stood shoulder-to-shoulder against terrifying opponents and fought countless battles together and you have always looked out for each other. Such bonds cannot be broken by men or gods. And you have always put the good of the Empire and its people above your own wants or needs," Merlin pointed out. "Had Arthur had any of your qualities, I doubt that Camelot would have fallen so quickly."

"Galya said that she is slowly regaining her powers. Perhaps after my child is born, I will, too," Gorinna said hopefully.

"Do not compare yourself with Galya. You are human. She is not. The same laws do not apply to you," Merlin warned.

Then he smiled.

"Still, I think you'll make a wonderful mother," he said with a wink.

"Then you think I should keep the baby?" she asked.

"I think that you decided to do just that the moment you realized you were pregnant," Merlin said. "After the child is born, I'll do whatever I can to help you recover some of your powers, but I fear that will be a long time coming."

"Thank you, Merlin. I knew I could rely on you. Tell me, did you foresee this?" she asked.

He shook his head.

"The gods do not reveal all of their secrets to me. I confess that this one caught me by surprise as it did you," he said.

Gorinna left and headed down to the parlor. She saw Galya seated before the fireplace sipping wine and perusing the Thule Times. She walked over and sat beside her. Galya looked up and smiled.

"You really surprise me, Galya," Gorinna said.

"In what way?" asked Galya.

"Our past encounters have led me to believe that you were spiteful, jealous and vindictive. I half expected you to go crazy when I told you I was pregnant with Arka-Dal's child. Instead, you've taken it very well," Gorinna explained.

"Why shouldn't I? Is this not what you've always wished for? You now carry the child of the man you truly love. To me, that's cause for rejoicing. Aren't you happy?" Galya asked.

"I am. But I'm also worried," Gorinna admitted.

"About losing your powers?" Galya asked.

Gorinna nodded.

"I was, too. After it happened and I saw the faces of Hawk and Melody for the first time, nothing else mattered. All that truly matters is the fact that Arka-Dal and I love each other and we have two beautiful children together. If my powers return, that's great. If not, I won't mind. I'm still elated with the choices I've made. You should be, too," Galya said.

"I am happy," Gorinna said.

"Good. Then I'm also happy for you," Galya assured her.

"You're a good friend, Galya," Gorinna said as they hugged.

"Thank you. So are you," Galya said.

Gorinna smiled and left the room. At that point, Merlin entered. He walked to the bar and poured himself a drink then joined Galya on the couch.

"That was very nice of you," he opined. "It was something I'd expect Mayumi to say."

"Mayumi is my very best friend. I think she has influenced me a lot. I meant everything I said, Merlin. I *am* happy for Gorinna.

Yet I'm a little concerned with how this situation might affect the friendship between Arka-Dal and Kashi," she said.

"I think we have no need to worry about that. Those two have shared far too many harrowing experiences and saved each others' lives time and again. A friendship forged under such circumstances is unbreakable," Merlin assured her.

"Will Gorinna lose her powers?" asked Galya.

Merlin shrugged.

"It has happened to others in the past," he said.

"But Gorinna is *not* like those others," Galya pointed out.

After a hard morning's training session and long, hot bath, Arka-Dal decided to have a drink in the living room and relax. When he arrived, Pandaar and Kashi were playing a game of darts while Gorinna watched from the sofa. She smiled when she saw him. Leo and Medusa entered a few seconds later. Medusa sat beside Gorinna while Leo went to the bar to get himself a drink.

"Any more news of the goings-on at the ruined mosque?" asked Arka-Dal.

"The city guards sent two men out there several times over the last month to check it out," Pandaar said.

"They find anything?" asked Gorinna.

Pandaar shrugged.

"The guards reported some white, hazy, shapeless mass whirling around the ruins. When they went inside, the figure was nowhere to be seen. There was a pentagram painted on the floor where some rubble had been cleared away and a handful of melted, black candles scattered around," Pandaar said.

"Were there any signs of a sacrifice?" asked Gorinna.

"None they could see," Pandaar said. "But some of the locals have reported missing sheep and goats since the activity started."

"This has all of the earmarks of a black cult," Gorinna said. "There may be witches in the ruins."

"Or witch wannabes," Leo said.

"That could be even more dangerous. There's nothing worse than idiots fooling around with things they shouldn't. They might unleash something from the other side, like a demon or a wraith," Gorinna said.

"Interesting. I think I'll ride out there and check it out," Arka-Dal said.

"Want me to go with you?" asked Pandaar.

"No. This sounds like someone's idea of a joke. The ruin is only ten miles south of here. I'll stop by on one of my morning rides. If there is anything supernatural happening, I'll have Gorinna take care of it later," Arka-Dal said. "Besides, this could be fun."

Arka-Dal rode off the next morning with a promise to return before lunch. Lunch came and went. So did dinner.

Arka-Dal had not returned.

He had taken a detour from his usual route to check out the ruins. He arrived around nine a.m.. As he approached from the north, he could see a strange, low-lying mist hugging the floor of the interior. It was pale green and almost sparkled in the sunlight. Instead of moving with the light breeze that wafted through the ruins, the mist inexplicably remained stationary.

Intrigued, he dismounted and peered inside.

The mosque was almost a total loss now. It had no windows or doors left and the ornate ceiling had fallen in ages ago. Only the thickness of the marble and alabaster walls had kept them from toppling, too, and the entire floor was covered with debris. Bats, slumbering while wrapped in their leathery wings, now clung to the sides of the half-fallen columns, waiting for nightfall so they could feed upon the rats and other vermin that now haunted the ruins.

All seemed oblivious to him as he walked through the ruins.

All was eerily quiet.

So quiet, it made the hair on the back of his neck tingle.

That's when he realized that the mist was moving. It converged on him like a noxious cloud and swirled madly around. He felt himself grow dizzy and reached out to the remains of a column for support.

Too late.

He felt himself hitting the floor.

Then all went dark.

After much discussion, Pandaar and Kashi decided to wait until morning, then ride out to the ruins to search for him. They told everyone there was no need to worry as Arka-Dal was very capable of taking care of himself.

But the women *did* worry.

Especially Gorinna.

This was not like Arka-Dal. He always returned when he said he would or managed to send word if he couldn't. There had been no word. She decided that she'd go out and find him the next morning and did her best to allay her fears.

But she couldn't shake them.

That night, she forced herself to sleep. It proved to be fitful at best.

Around two a.m., Gorinna woke suddenly as if startled from a dream. As she sat bolt upright in bed, she disturbed the sleeping Kashi next to her. He rubbed his eyes and stretched as he looked at her.

"What's wrong?" he asked.

"Arka-Dal's in danger," she replied as she rose and dressed in a hurry.

"How do you know?" asked Kashi as he dressed, too.

"He's calling to me. I can hear him inside my head. He needs help," she said as she strapped on her shortsword. "I have to go to him."

"I'll get our horses," Kashi said.

"There's no time!" Gorinna said as she raised her hands above her head.

Instantly, she was encased by a golden ball of light. Kashi watched as it lifted from the floor and sailed out through the open balcony doors.

"Damn it!" he shouted as he finished dressing.

He ran down the hall and pounded on the door to Pandaar's quarters. The still-sleepy warrior opened the door, saw Kashi was dressed for battle and nodded. A few seconds later, both were sprinting toward the stable.

Gorinna arrived at the ruins ten minutes later. She hovered above them for a while as she checked the place out, then slowly settled to the ground and dissipated the bubble. She studied the building for a little while, then cautiously approached it. Everything about this smelled like a trap. Someone *wanted* her here and she had a fairly good idea who that someone was.

"If it is him, I'll stuff that cat up his ass," she said.

The ruin was much larger than she thought. At one time, it had obviously been a major mosque. Although half the minaret had toppled onto the main building many centuries before, what remained was still quite impressive. It no longer had a ceiling, doors or even windows. The large hall where the faithful once bowed in prayer three times each day, was littered with the debris of broken support columns, roof tiles, glass and other detritus. Rough desert shrubs and grasses now sprouted hideously from large cracks in the mosaic floor and the entire place was dusted with a coat of sand.

It looked empty and forlorn now.

As if it were waiting for someone.

"Me?" she wondered as she stepped inside.

The pale moonlight shining through the open roof gave the place an eerie, unearthly atmosphere. Small bats fluttered among the broken columns while rats and other small vermin played amid the rubble beneath her feet. Other than that, there were no signs of life.

As she walked across the rubble strewn floor, she came upon the crude pentagram in a circle and the half-molten black candles the guards had reported. There was a small tin dish in the center. She knelt to examine it and wrinkled her nose at the pungent odor of spoiled chicken blood.

"Someone's childish attempt at fiddling with the occult. I hope the fools didn't open a gate. There's no telling what might come through," she though as she looked around.

That's when she heard the distinct sounds of something heavy shuffling through the rubble. She stood and listened as it came closer and closer. The shuffling was soon accompanied by heavy breathing and snorting sounds.

"I know you're here. Show yourself—if you dare," she called out as she readied a spell.

The sounds stopped as if what was making them was trying to decide what to do. She could see a large outline of a horned head and powerful shoulders just beyond the glare of her light.

A minor demon.

Nothing she couldn't handle.

"I know you, Witch," it said in a deep guttural voice that sounded like many. "I was brought here to prevent your passage."

"Then try and do so!" she challenged.

The demon growled and charged straight at her. She unloosed her spell at the same time. The spell struck the demon head-on. When the glare subsided, only a pile of dust and charred bones remained and the air stunk of brimstone.

"Enough of these games. It's time to find Arka-Dal," she said as she closed her eyes and concentrated.

"Where *are* you?" she asked.

"Below," came the response. "Hurry!"

She began to scour the place for any sign of a door or entrance that would take her beneath the building. She finally located an open arch at the back of the structure with a flight of stairs that led down into the pitch black cellar.

She held out her hand and watched as a bright ball of light formed in her palm.

"That's much better." She said as she began her descent.

When she reached the bottom of the steps she found herself standing in a long corridor that ran from right to left. She stopped and concentrated again.

"I go left," she decided.

Arka-Dal woke to find himself suspended above the floor in a strange, glimmering cube. He had barely enough room to get to his knees. When he did, he saw the reason for his predicament.

"You again?" he asked sarcastically.

"In the flesh," said the wizard.

"Seems to me I've been in a similar trap before.[18] Aren't you afraid of becoming redundant?" Arka-Dal mocked.

"Not really. This time, I've encased you inside a life-draining trap. In little more than an hour, all of your life force will be sucked from your body and your heart will cease to beat," the wizard said smugly.

"When I get out of here, I'm going to kick you so hard that your damned cat will feel it for years to come!" Arka-Dal threatened.

"Ah, but you cannot escape this time. At least not without help," the wizard assured him.

"So I'm the bait?" Arka-Dal asked.

"Again," the wizard said.

"You're pathetic," Arka-Dal said with disgust.

"I may be pathetic, but you'll soon be dead if your rescuer doesn't arrive soon. Since I have no real issues with you, I just might release you after I've exacted vengeance upon the witch," the wizard said.

"If you harm Gorinna, we *will* have issues. I'll tear your fucking head off and shit down your throat!" Arka-Dal threatened.

The wizard grinned.

"You're hardly in a position to make threats. From inside that box, you can do nothing but watch her die," he said.

"Be careful. You might get far more than you expect out of this. She can be something terrifying when she's pissed," Arka-Dal warned.

"We shall see. Regardless, I fear her not. Compared to mine, her powers are so much parlor magic. The witch will be here soon—in answer to your summons," the wizard said.

---

18 See Prime Evil and Other Tales

"I didn't summon anybody," Arka-Dal pointed out.

"No. But *I* did," the wizard assured him.

"What makes you so sure she'll be here?" Arka-Dal asked.

"Simple. I've been observing you from afar for the past few months. The Witch's feelings for you run deep and strong. Because of this, she will certainly rush to your aid," the wizard said. "That's when I'll spring the trap."

"Just who *are* you, anyway?" Arka-Dal asked.

"Like Merlinus, my names are legion. I have had several through the millennia. Far more than even I can recollect," the wizard replied as he stroked the cat.

Arka-Dal scowled at him.

"I've a got few for you that you probably haven't heard yet," he said.

The wizard laughed.

"Just what I would expect to hear from a barbarian. Now, if you'll excuse me, I'll turn on my trap," the wizard said.

Almost immediately, Arka-Dal found himself face-down in the box. He felt so weak, he couldn't move a muscle.

Or speak.

In fact, he had difficulty even breathing.

He felt no pain. He could, however, feel his energy leaving his body little by little. Soon, he'd be a dead, empty shell.

"No doubt about it. I really need Gorinna," he thought.

He also knew she'd be walking into a trap and that there was nothing he could do about it. He also knew that Gorinna probably realized it was a trap and would be on guard against almost anything.

As Gorinna walked along a narrow passageway, several torches in wall sconces suddenly flickered to life the moment she came near them. The familiar effect caused her to smirk disdainfully.

Now she knew who her adversary was.

Now she was even more determined to shove his furry companion up into his nether orifice.

As she turned a corner, two more of the same demons tried to bar her way by emerging from the walls to attack. She dispatched each of them with ease and continued on her way. At the end of passageway, she saw a pointed arch. She slowed down as she approached it and saw that it had a heavy wooden door. She leaned her head against it and listened.

All was silent on the other side.

She looked around. The hallway ended at the door. There were no others. Nowhere else to turn.

"This *has* to be it," she decided.

She also knew it was a trap. Probably a deadly one, too. Whoever was on the other side *expected* her to enter. She decided to take the place by storm. She stepped back, gestured at the door and watched as it fell to pieces with a loud cracking sound.

"Now we'll settle this once and forever!" she said.

Gorinna burst into the room and stopped when she saw the wizened old man garbed in a dark gray hooded cloak. He was seated in a high backed wooden chair, stroking the black cat that lay indifferently on his lap.

"You again!" she growled.

"We meet again, witch. Before you decide to do anything rash, cast your eyes upward," the wizard suggested.

She looked where he said and blanched at the sight of Arka-Dal. He was suspended some twenty feet above the floor, encased in a bright green cube of light. She could hear his labored breathing and dull heartbeat and realized he'd been sealed within a life-draining field. He would be dead in less than a minute if she didn't do something fast.

"Release him this instant or I'll blow you to atoms!" she demanded.

He chuckled.

Or rather, the cat did.

"I brought him here in order to lure you here. We have a score to settle, witch," he said.

"I'll settle *you* alright! Let him go!" she insisted as she mentally prepared one of her more potent spells.

"Something new has been added to the equation. I sense you are with child. How fascinating. I didn't think one of your kind could bear children. This puts an entirely new slant on the matter," the wizard said smugly.

Gorinna slowly circled to his right. The cat followed her with his yellow eyes. At the same time, she kept an eye on Arka-Dal inside the cube.

He was motionless now and barely breathing. She sensed that his heartbeat was getting weaker with each passing second. If she didn't act soon, he would surely die. If she *did* act, the sudden, explosive use of her magic might kill her unborn child. It was a decision she never imagined she'd ever have to make.

The madman wizard had placed them both in an awful spot. And for what? A twisted idea of revenge? Revenge against her for depriving him of that stupid book?

"You're insane!" she almost spat.

He laughed.

Or rather, the cat did.

The high-pitched cackling sound irritated her. It made her angry.

Boiling mad.

"How *dare* he do this to us?" she thought.

"Choose, witch!" he demanded. "Who will live? The Emperor or your unborn child?"

His tone was mocking. That made her even madder.

If she turned and walked away, her unborn child would be safe. But Arka-Dal would certainly die and the Empire would die with him. She knew she'd never be able to live with herself if she did that. Nor could she leave the man she loved to suffer such a horrible fate. And she could not allow the dreams and visions of Thule to die along with him.

She'd always wanted a child. Now that she was carrying one, she was being forced to make the most terrible decision of her entire life.

And was all because of that bastard wizard!

"Pregnant or not, I'm going to finish you once and forever, filth!" she threatened.

The wizard sneered disdainfully.

"Would you risk the life of your unborn child? In order to save him, you will have do battle with me. That will take every last bit of your powers. If you do this, the resultant shock to your system will strain you to the limit. Such and expenditure of energy would surely kill the child that is now within your womb. Are you willing to sacrifice the one thing you've wanted most to save the life of Arka-Dal?" he challenged.

Gorinna looked up at Arka-Dal.

He was barely breathing now and his heartbeat was very slow. He was almost unconscious.

Almost dead.

She felt the child moving inside her belly.

His child.

If she used her magic to destroy the wizard, the resulting shock to her system would surely kill the child. It might also kill her. Yet, she couldn't just walk away. She couldn't let the wizard win.

She knew she couldn't defeat him with simple, low-powered spells. She'd battled him before. She knew that she would have to gamble everything on one powerful spell and pray that it would be enough to destroy him. No matter what, she *had* to save Arka-Dal.

"Choose, Witch! What shall it be? Your child or Arka-Dal?" the wizard demanded.

"I can't let him die!" she said.

With tears welling up in her eyes, she summoned every last bit of power she had inside of her and hurled it at the wizard. Just before the spell struck, he raised his hand and the cat beat a hasty retreat from the room through a solid wall. There was a loud boom and a bright, blinding flash of yellow light.

Gorinna heard herself scream.

Then all went dark.

"I—I'm sorry—my son—," she gasped as she hit the floor.

At that moment, the cube surrounding Arka-Dal vanished. He also hit the floor.

Hard.

The impact knocked the wind back into him. That's when he realized he had been hurt in the fall. He shook the cobwebs from his brain and forced himself to his knees. The pain in his knee was almost excruciating. He stifled a moan and looked at Gorinna. She wasn't moving.

Ignoring his pain, he struggled to his feet and stumbled over to her. He saw that she was barely breathing and there was a pool of blood directly beneath her. Somehow, he managed to scoop her up in his arms and carry outside to his grazing horse. He threw her across the saddle in front of him, seized the reins, and galloped east as fast as his horse could travel.

Kashi and Pandaar met him halfway between the ruins and Thule. Arka-Dal transferred the unconscious Gorinna to Kashi's saddle to give both himself and his horse a break, then all three hurried back to Thule. When they reached the palace two hours later, Mayumi and the other wives met them at the door. Kashi rushed upstairs with Gorinna in his arms while Arka-Dal and Pandaar limped over to the couch and plopped down.

"I'll get Leo!" Medusa said as she rushed down to the archives.

Mayumi poured Arka-Dal a drink. He drained the flagon in one gulp and passed it back to her. She quickly refilled and returned it. She sat down next to him as he drank more slowly. Zhijima walked over with a flagon of ale and handed it to Pandaar. He smiled as he took it from her.

That's when they saw Leo race up the stairs to Kashi's suite with his medical bag in hand and Medusa trailing behind him. Arka-Dal took a deep breath and let it out slowly, then told everyone what had happened.

"How bad is she?" asked Mayumi.

"I don't know. She's bleeding badly. I'm afraid the ride home didn't help her much either," Arka-Dal said. "I've never heard anyone scream like that. It made me feel sick all over."

"The poor thing! It must have been terrible," Galya said sadly. "When I find that bastard wizard, I'll make him pay for this a thousand times over."

Kashi plodded down the stairs and poured himself a drink. He sat down next to Arka-Dal and sighed heavily.

"How is she?" asked Galya.

"We got her cleaned up and made her comfortable. Leo and Medusa are still working on her. Leo said she'll probably be out for days. He doesn't know much else right now," he replied.

"Did she kill that bastard?" Pandaar asked.

Arka-Dal shrugged.

"I don't know. The entire room lit up like the sun. When the light faded, both the wizard and his cat were gone. The only thing I saw was a huge scorch mark where he'd been seated," he said. "She also blew out the entire wall of his lair. That must have been one Helluva spell!"

"Here's to Gorinna!" Kashi said as he raised his flagon.

Arka-Dal and Pandaar clinked theirs against it then they all drank.

"To Gorinna," Arka-Dal repeated.

She woke weeks later in her bed at the palace, surrounded by her friends. The first face she recognized was Kashi's hovering anxiously above her.

"Good morning, my love. It's good to see you open your eyes after so many days," he said as he kissed her hand.

"How long have I been out?" she asked as she tried to sit up. Her head throbbed painfully and she lay back down.

"Three weeks," Leo said. "We almost lost you a couple of times. It's a good thing that your will to live is so strong. How do you feel?"

"Like shit. My entire body aches and I feel as heavy as lead. How did I get home?" she asked.

"Arka-Dal brought you back," Kashi said. "He was in pretty bad shape himself. We met him on his way here."

"Where is he?" she asked.

"Right here," came a voice from the doorway.

She watched him limp in. He was leaning on a cane. She smiled.

"We did it," she said.

"No. *You* did it. You blasted that wizard to atoms but the backlash nearly killed you. I barely got you home in time," he said.

"Thank you," she said. "What happened to your leg?"

"I broke my kneecap when the trap disintegrated and I hit the floor. I didn't realize until a couple of days later," he said. "I'll be fine in another week or two."

She looked up at the others. They shrugged and left the room so she and Arka-Dal could talk in private.

"I lost our baby," she said hoarsely. "I'm so sorry."

"Don't be. You had no choice. If you had shown the slightest sign of weakness, that bastard would have killed you. You did what you had to do. He expected you to back down to save our child. Instead, you attacked him. He wasn't prepared for that. He never expected you to sacrifice our child to save me. You're a very special lady, Gorinna," he said. "Very special."

He reached out and held her hand until she fell back to sleep. He kissed her forehead and gimped out of the room. He saw Kashi seated in a chair in the hallway and put a hand on his shoulder.

Kashi smiled.

"Leo said she'll be up and about soon. There's no permanent physical damage," he said. "How do *you* feel, my friend?"

"Sore as Hell. That bastard nearly had me. I'm glad that Gorinna was there to save my ass—again. You have a real special lady, Hamid," Arka-Dal said.

"I know. I'm really sorry about your child," Kashi said.

"Me too. Perhaps it's better this way. Maybe you two will have a child of your own one day," Arka-Dal suggested.

Maybe. Buy you a drink?" Kashi asked.

"Several!" Arka-Dal replied.

Many miles away, a large black cat sits in the frameless window of a decaying keep high atop a rocky cliff, licking himself in places where his fur had been scorched. A few feet away, a wizened man, garbed in a gray cloak and hood, sits at a wooden table leafing slowly through the yellowed pages of an ancient tome. The wizard's hands and face are swathed in bandages, painful reminders of what happens to those who are foolish enough to raise the ire of the Red Witch.

He now realizes that his wounds are permanent. The witch's powerful spell assured they will never heal, never close. He will always be in pain.

So will his cat.

As he pondered his next move, he failed to notice the sudden and silent appearance of the tall, dark-skinned and horned man in front of him until it was too late. Startled, he raised his hands as if to cast a spell, only to have them go numb and drop back to the table.

The visitor scowled.

The scowl chilled the wizard's blood.

"We have business, you and I," the Devil stated.

"We do? I have no contract with you that I am aware of," the wizard said.

"Our business has nothing to do with a contract. It's far more *personal* than that," the Devil said as he leaned closer and grinned.

"What do you mean?" the wizard demanded.

"This is about Arka-Dal and Gorinna," the Devil said.

"I've had run-ins with them in the past and you did nothing. Why interfere now?" the wizard asked.

"My daughter *asked* me to. She's tired of your attacks on her husband so she asked me to get rid of you—and I shall," the Devil responded. "You attempted to kill my son-in-law. For that, you must pay—*dearly*," the Devil said.

The wizard stared as the meaning of the words sunk in. It was then he realized that he'd made a far bigger mistake than he'd imagined. He also realized that as powerful as he was, not even he could take on the Devil and expect to win. The cat stopped licking and yawned indifferently as cats are wont to do.

"You're on your own this time," the animal said. "You brought this down upon yourself even when I advised against it."

"So you're *deserting* me?" the wizard asked.

The cat responded by yawning and resumed licking itself. The wizard tried to bluff his way through this.

"You don't scare me! After all, what could you possibly do to me?" he asked.

"I can do things to you—unspeakable things— that you've never imagined possible, not in all your many pathetic lives," the Devil said as he seized his robe. "I can put you in a place where the pain will increase exponentially each and every day that you're there until you beg me to kill you to make it stop. I can torment and torture you for eternity or turn you into a pile of vermin that befits your character. But all that would be too easy. Too gentle for the likes of you."

He released him and stood upright.

"You should have taken the advice of your familiar. You should have let things be. But you didn't. For that, you must suffer greatly," he said.

By now, the wizard was visibly shaking. His hands were still stuck to the table, too. That made it impossible to cast spells. He was truly helpless.

"I want you to suffer for all eternity. I want you to have time to think about what you did to Arka-Dal, Gorinna and everyone else you've made miserable down through the ages," the Devil said.

The wizard watched as he raised his left hand and gestured. The blood-curdling scream that followed echoed through the mountains and valleys for days on end before finally fading away . . .

Neither the wizard nor the cat were ever seen again.

Soon after, Galya received the telepathic message from her father that he had located the wizard and dealt with him accordingly.

"He can no longer trouble you nor anyone else. There is no escape from where I've sent him and he probably wishes he were dead right about now. There is nothing left for him but agonizing pain and horrific nightmares," he assured her.

"Thank you, Father," Galya said.

"I'm only sorry that I wasn't able to find him sooner to prevent this from happening. Give my best to Arka-Dal and Gorinna," the Devil said as he broke contact.

"I'm sorry, too," Galya sighed.

Gorinna finally summoned enough strength to rise from her bed a few hours later. She forced herself to bathe and dress then decided to take a walk in the rose garden to get some fresh air and sunshine. Her body still ached a bit from lying in bed for so long but the warmth of the sun soon made her feel like her old self. The pleasant scent of the roses and other blossoms also helped lift her spirits as she meandered along the twisting paths. After a while, she began to feel hungry and decided to head back inside to find something to eat. Instead, she ended up on a bench in front of one of the many lily ponds, pondering the path her life had taken.

Galya spotted Gorinna, staring into the dark green water. She walked over, sat beside her and put her arm around her in a sisterly way and told her what her father had done.

"How do you feel?" Galya asked.

"Hollow," Gorinna replied. "I feel empty inside."

"Will you be alright?" Galya asked.

"I think so. In time. Damn it, Galya! I really *wanted* that child!" Gorinna sobbed.

"I know. If you need anything at all, I'm here for you. We are all here for you. For what it's worth, you made the only decision possible and it's not your fault," Galya said softly.

"Everyone keeps saying that but it doesn't ease the pain I feel inside. That bastard of a wizard put me in a damned awful situation. No matter what the risks, I just *had* to save Arka-Dal. I just didn't think that losing my baby would be so emotionally draining."

"You'll recover with time. So will Arka-Dal," Galya said.

"Arka-Dal?" asked Gorinna as she wiped her tears away.

"Yes. He feels terribly guilty about this whole thing. He thinks it's his fault that you were forced to make that choice," Galya said.

"But it *wasn't*. It was the fault of that fucking wizard and his damned cat! *He* caused all of this. He put us in that spot and no one else. I didn't know Arka-Dal felt that way. Where is he now? I must talk to him," Gorinna said.

"He's in the study," replied Galya.

Gorinna hurried back to the palace as fast as she could. Galya watched her and smiled.

She'd soon be so busy consoling Arka-Dal that she'd forget about her own problems. He would soon be too busy trying to reassure her that his burdens would be lifted.

The more she thought about it, the more Galya smiled.

"The things I do for love," she said.

The Usurper

In the 52nd year of the reign of Arka-Dal

On a cool December morning, Arka-Dal became saddened by a radio message from the kingdom of Pandolia. His long-time friend and ally, Malle Doux and king of Pandolia, had died in his sleep. He had gone to bed early the night before after complaining about chest and stomach pains. As usual, he refused to let his doctors examine him. When the servant went to wake him the next morning, he was as cold as stone.

The news was relayed to Arka-Dal by Malle Doux's chief advisor and head of the Council, Erasmus Bey. He said there would be a state funeral in one week followed by a two week long period of mourning. Afterward, the Council would convene to decide the fate of their nation.

Malle Doux's wife of 55 years had died a year ago. She drowned in a boating accident. There were no heirs to the Pandolian throne and most of the Council members were much older than their late king. Bey was the youngest of the lot and he was 97.

Arka-Dal suggested that the Council come up with two or three different solutions and let the people of Pandolia decide which they liked best via a public vote. Bey agreed to bring the suggestion at the next Council meeting.

Arka-Dal sighed.

Malle Doux had most probably succumbed to his old war wounds. He had always led his troops from the front. As a result, he had suffered several nasty wounds, two of which had nearly killed him. Both times, he had managed to cheat death.

But one can only cheat the Reaper so many times. In the end, he always wins. He always gets what he wants.

Malle Doux had been engaged in a project with King Prium of neighboring Arda, concerning the possibility of uniting the two nations. Prium and Malle Doux had been close friends for decades and the two nations shared open borders and trade with each other. There was no need for guarded borders between friends.

Prium took the news hard.

In fact, he wept.

"Losing Malle is like losing a beloved brother," he remarked. "His death leaves a hole in my soul. May he enjoy a happy Afterlife."

Prium was in his 70s.

Still young by Second Age standards. He would most likely rule Arda for the next 40-50 years. If the Council decided to choose a new king, would he enjoy the same close ties he'd had with Malle Doux?

And did the notion of uniting the two lands die with his friend?

Unification made good sense, both economically and politically. With open borders, the two peoples had nearly blended into one culture. Their languages, dress and cultures were similar and their people frequently intermarried. It was hard to tell an Ardan from a Pandolian now.

Separately, neither nation was an economic powerhouse. If united, their combined merchant fleets, deep water ports and open markets could possibly double or even triple their annual incomes. They could use that money to modernize their harbors and rebuild several roads and bridges.

And their combined armies would be a formidable force for anyone to reckon with. Of course, once the details were hammered out, the final bill would be put before the people of both nations so they could vote on it.

Did it all die with Malle Doux?

Malle Doux's Prime Minister, Axelrod, was 60 years old and walked with slight limp thanks to wound he'd suffered during a battle several years before. A brilliant statesman and orator, he was fluent in eight languages and was a highly respected administrator. Like Malle Doux, Axelrod favored merging with Arda. With the king dead, he was the interim head-of-state until a new one could be chosen sometime after the funeral. He expected everything to go smoothly.

As he sat behind his desk pondering the appropriate funeral arrangement for Mall Doux, the door to his office creaked open. He looked up just as General Osmund Beyaro, commander of the First Army, and four of his officers strode in. All were dressed in battle armor and bearing swords. Axelrod eyed them suspiciously as they stopped in front of his desk.

"Why are you and your men dressed for war? Pandolia is at peace," he queried.

"The death of our king has left Pandolia adrift, like a ship without a rudder. There's a power vacuum at the top that must be filled immediately," Beyaro said.

"A new king will be chosen two weeks after the funeral. The country can wait until then," Axelrod said.

"I say that it cannot! We must have a new ruler immediately. Someone strong. Someone powerful enough and dedicated enough to keep our nation from being taken over by outside forces," the general almost shouted.

"Outside forces? Can I assume you mean the Ardans?" Axelrod asked.

"That's exactly who I mean! They've been wanting to take over Pandolia for years. With Mallc Doux gone, this gives them the chance they desire," Beyaro said.

"Might I remind you that the Ardans are our close friends and allies? In fact, our two nations are on the verge of merging into one," Axelrod said.

"Not while I live! Pandolia will remain free and independent forever. I will not have our culture soiled by closer contact with foreigners! That's why I've decided to seize power and place the country under martial law until this national emergency passes," Beyaro declared.

"So you've decided to make yourself king? Hah! The people will never stand for *that*. Nor will the Senate," Axelrod said.

"They have no choice. After all, *I* command the army and my officers are loyal to me," Beyaro said smugly.

"*You* control but one of the Pandolian armies. The others have taken oaths of loyalty to uphold the laws and constitution of the land. The Second Army is commanded by General Mornay in Jericho. The Third Army by General Waleco in Jerusalem. Both will march against you as soon as they learn of your treason. And I shouldn't have to remind you where Admiral Zedo's loyalties lie!" Axelrod pointed out. "Your little power grab will be short-lived and the nation will be plunged into a civil war. Only a madman would attempt to go through with such a plan."

"The die has been cast. There's nothing you can do to stop me now," Beyaro said confidently.

"*I* don't have to stop you." Axelrod said smugly.

Just then, a perspiring soldier burst into the room and saluted Beyaro.

"Report!" the general ordered.

"Rioting has broken out all over Azum Phala. The moment we put up the posters declaring martial law, all Hell broke loose. Our men are being attacked by mobs in every section of the city. They've even set fire to First Army Headquarters!" the soldier said.

"Use any measures to put down the rioters. Be as harsh as the situations call for. Don't stop until you've subdued the entire city," Beyaro ordered. "We will teach this rabble a lesson they won't soon forget!"

"But those are *our own* people! They are our friends, neighbors and families! We can't use deadly force against them. It will only make things worse!" said one of the officers, a tall, brown haired colonel of the 1st Cavalry.

"The colonel's right. We should lift martial law at once. This isn't working as we planned," said another officer.

"I'm in command now! Do as I say or resign your commissions!" Beyaro snapped.

"I will never raise my sword against my own people. Nor will I command my soldiers to do so," the colonel declared as he tore off his insignia and threw it at Beyaro.

One-by-one, the other officers followed the colonel's example and left the room. Beyaro stared at them incredulously as they shut the door behind them.

Axelrod laughed hysterically.

"Your revolution is dying even before it begins. I suspect that more of your 'loyal officers' will soon do likewise. Most of their troops will probably go with them leaving you only a skeleton force to feed your ambitions," he said mockingly.

Beyaro turned to the messenger.

"Escort Axelrod to his quarters and place a guard on him. Make sure he doesn't get out and that no one gets in to see him until further notice," he ordered.

The soldier saluted and nodded to Axelrod.

"Please come with me, Prime Minister," he said politely.

"Don't worry, lad. This is not your fault," Axelrod assured him. "The next time we meet, General, I expect to see your head up on a pole in front of the palace. Have a nice day."

The rioting soon spread throughout the entire city. Mobs tore down Beyaro's posters and beat any soldier who attempted to stop them to a bloody pulp. As Axelrod had predicted, almost half of the soldiers of the First Army refused to take part in the action, leaving the rest hopelessly outnumbered by an increasingly outraged populace.

News of the attempted takeover quickly reached Jericho and Jerusalem. Both generals quickly mobilized their armies and marched on Azum Phala to put down the rebellion and remove the would-be king from the throne. When word reached Admiral Zedo in the main harbor, he sailed his entire fleet up the coast to blockade the port at Azum Phala and cut off Beyaro's escape route.

King Prium of Arda marched two divisions of his army to the Pandolian border in a show of support for the Pandolian people. He would not enter the country unless bidden to do so, lest his gesture be mistaken for an invasion. As his forces pitched their tents on the open field, a rider from Gen. Waleco galloped into the camp. He saluted when Prium approached and handed him a letter.

Prium smiled.

"Gen. Waleco bids us welcome. He has asked us to rendezvous with his army in Jerusalem and join him on the march to Azum Phala to depose the usurper," he said to his commanders who had gathered nearby. He looked up at the rider.

"Tell Gen. Waleco we will be there in six days," he said. "We will be proud to fight alongside our Pandolian brothers."

The rider saluted and galloped off. Prium turned to his officers.

"Make sure the men are fed and rested. We break camp at sunrise!" he ordered.

Of course this did not go unreported by Arka-Dal's ambassador in Azum Phala. As soon as he received the news, he gathered his usual team in the War Room to discuss the situation.

"Right now, I think the people of Pandolia have the situation in hand. I doubt that Beyaro will be able to withstand an attack from the main armies," Kashi assessed.

"I agree. But the country is on the verge of what could be a bloody civil war, especially if Beyaro decides to hunker down in Azum Phala. The city could hold out for a long time without being resupplied. In the meantime, thousands of people might be killed and all because of Beyaro's blind ambitions," Leo said.

"But that's only if Beyaro's troops decide to fight for him. Our ambassador reported that he has less than a dozen officers still loyal to him and his soldiers are deserting by the dozens," Kashi said.

"Our ambassador has heard rumors that Beyaro has sworn an oath to burn Azum Phala to the ground rather than surrender. He's decided to fight to the bitter end," Leo added.

"Right now, this is purely a Pandolian affair. But we need to do something to get Beyaro's attention. Something that might cause him to change his mind and surrender without a fight. Which of our armies is closest to Pandolia now?" Arka-Dal asked.

"That would be the Northwestern Army. That's Joshua's command," Pandaar replied.

"Good. Have him move four light cavalry regiments to the Pandolian border at once in a show of force. Tell him not to move into the country until I order him to do so. That should get Beyaro's attention," Arka-Dal decided.

While things on the foreign front were well in hand, things on the home front were about to take a surprising turn.

Later that day, Pandaar's wife, Zhijima, decided to go up to their chambers and get a small sewing kit from her closet. As she walked toward the closet, she was distracted by strange moans and grunts coming from her bedroom. She crept to the door and listened. She realized the sounds were being made by two people who were obviously caught up in the throes of sexual passion.

Zhijima pushed the door open and was astonished to see Pandaar romping around on the bed naked with an equally naked palace maid.

"You son of a bitch!" she screamed.

They stopped in mid-stroke and looked at her. Before Pandaar could react, Zhijima picked up one of the heavy ceramic vases and smashed it over the top of his head. As he lay there in a daze surrounded by pieces of the vase, dirt and flowers, Zhijima stormed out and slammed the door behind her.

She was angry.

Hopping mad.

Mad enough to kill somebody.

She paced the hall to try and calm down. The more she thought about it, the more she felt betrayed. She had just caught the man she loved and trusted above all others in *their* bed having sex with another woman.

A maid!

Images of all sorts of nasty and painful things she could do to him flashed through her mind. Most he'd never recover from.

Not fully, anyway.

But that, she decided, would be letting him off easy.

"Two can play at this game," she said.

She'd always harbored a crush on Arka-Dal. Always wondered what it would be like to have sex with him. Up to now, she'd been too shy and too loyal to Pandaar to try to do anything about it. His betrayal changed that.

She decided to go after Arka-Dal.

But how?

She was new at the seduction game, almost innocent by Thulian standards. She'd have to do something to make him notice her. Something bold and dramatic. Something highly risqué and erotic.

She had to make him really *want* her.

As she thought it over, she smiled.

Inside the bedroom, the maid did her best to help Pandaar clean up the mess left by the shattered vase. He went to the bathroom to wash the dirt and blood from his hair and winced when the warm water made contact with the gash on top of his head.

Zhijima had struck him hard. Hard enough to shatter the vase and crack open his skull. Unable to staunch the bleeding, Pandaar went downstairs to get some first aid from Leo and Medusa.

Naturally, they both laughed when he told them what had happened. Medusa told him he got exactly what he deserved then called him something in her native Greek. From the way she said it, Pandaar knew it wasn't a compliment.

After Leo stopped the bleeding, Pandaar headed to the parlor to get himself a good, strong drink. There was no sense in tracking down Zhijima. She didn't want to hear an explanation and he knew she'd never accept an apology. So he simply plopped down on the sofa with a bottle of brandy and a tall glass.

Kashi walked in a few moments later and saw him sitting there with a bandage on his head. He sat down next to him and asked him what happened. The always-honest Pandaar told him everything. Kashi laughed.

"Good thing she didn't get her hands on a battle ax," he said.

"*Tell* me about it!" Pandaar agreed.

"So what are you going to do?" asked Kashi.

"Not a damned thing. I'm just going to let nature run its course," Pandaar said.

"Nature *is* running its course. *Hurricane Zhijima* is now raging through the palace and she's a big one," Kashi said.

With Axelrod and members of the Senate under house arrest, Beyaro felt he was in complete control. Since he was in charge, he decided to take over the late king's office and make it his command center. The office was on the top floor of the palace and had a set of double doors that opened onto a balcony that overlooked the harbor. Malle Doux had spent the better part of most of his days there, buried behind stacks of official documents.

But Malle Doux was dead.

Beyaro was the new king. He smiled as he turned the ornate brass handle and opened the heavy oaken door.

He walked into the office of the late king and sat down in high-backed leather chair. His eyes went to the heavy bookshelves which went from floor to ceiling and covered two walls of the office. There were thousands of books on every subject imaginable. He scowled disdainfully.

He had no use for scholars. He considered them nuisances.

"Books and laws mean nothing now. Only might makes right," he said.

He pulled open the middle drawer of the desk and saw the nickel-plated revolver that had belonged to Malle Doux. The weapon was a gift from Arka-Dal. He picked it up and spun the chamber. The revolver was fully loaded.

"I'll wear it at my coronation ceremony," he thought as he put it back down.

One of his loyal officers entered and saluted. Beyaro returned it.

"Have you put down the riots?" he asked.

"Not yet. Most of the troops are reluctant to use force against our own people. Those who have were badly beaten. A couple of our men have been killed," the officer replied.

"How bad is it?" Beyaro asked.

"It's ugly and getting worse. It looks like everyone in the city is up in arms. The rioters have forced stores to close and they've shut down the city's essential services. Mobs now rule most of the squares," the officer said. "What should we do, sir?"

"I'm not sure. I wasn't expecting this," Beyaro said. "Block all of the main streets that lead to the government offices and the palace and order the men to take harsher measures to quiet things down."

"I'll try, but I doubt it will work. The people are really pissed off. They're calling for your head on a pike," the officer said as he left.

Beyaro shook his head as Axelrod's words echoed in his ears.

When her initial anger had abated somewhat, Zhijima decided that the way to attract Arka-Dal's attention was by using a direct approach. She recalled what her friends had jokingly suggested and smiled. It would amount to an act of desperation on her part. And it would be blatantly obvious. It might even cause Arka-Dal to laugh at her because it would be so completely out of character.

"Oh, well. I've nothing to lose but my dignity," she decided.

She then took a nice warm bath in perfumed water, brushed out her long black hair and tossed on a light, almost sheer pink gown. She knew this was the time of day that Arka-Dal normally spent in the study doing official paperwork and raced down the hall to get there ahead of him.

"Good. He's not here yet," she said as she entered the room.

She pulled his chair away from his desk and listened for his familiar footsteps. Just as he entered, she climbed up onto the chair, faced him, untied her gown and let it slide slowly to her ankles. The sight of her slender nude body stopped him in his tracks. He'd never seen her naked before and he liked what he saw. When he regained his composure, he smiled at her.

"What on Earth are you doing?" he asked as she struck a suggestive pose.

"Several people around here have suggested that the only way I'd get you to notice me is by standing on a chair naked, so I decided to give it a try," she explained.

"Well, you most certainly have my attention," he said. "But why are you doing this?"

She stepped down but made no attempt to dress.

"Isn't it obvious? I *want* you, Arka-Dal. I've *always* wanted you. Now that Gorinna's had you, I want you even more," she said.

"What about Pandaar? How will *he* feel about this?" Arka-Dal asked.

"Who cares about him? Just this morning, I walked into our chambers and caught him the act of screwing one of the servants—on *our* bed, too! Since he won't remain loyal to me, I see no reason to remain loyal to him. Two can play that game," she said angrily.

"That old dog! Which maid was it?"

"The red haired one," Zhijima said.

"Harmanee? Why? She's nowhere near as pretty as *you*. Why would he do that?" Arka-Dal asked.

"Why don't you ask *him*?" she suggested.

"I will—and he'd better have a good reason. That was more than a little disrespectful of him, especially after all these years you've been together," Arka-Dal said as he picked up her gown and handed it to her.

She simply slung it over her shoulder and opened her stance. His eyes went straight to the dark triangle between her thighs.

"If you like what you see, you can have me any time you like. After this morning, I will never be Pandaar's again," she said as she strode out of the room.

Mayumi and Chatha passed her in doorway and laughed when Arka-Dal told them what had happened.

"Pandaar's been boning every maid in the palace over the past few weeks. In fact, Zhijima's complained that he's barely touched her lately and wondered why. We just didn't have the heart to tell her," Chatha said.

"We thought she'd find out herself sooner or later. Aka-san, do you know what's gotten into Pandaar?" asked Mayumi.

He shook his head.

"I had no idea about this until a few minutes ago. He seems to the same to me. You say he's nailed *every* maid in the palace? We have a dozen of them!" he said.

"Hai. He's been most discreet about it until today. Why is he doing this? Does he no longer love Zhijima?" Mayumi asked.

"I don't know—but I *will* find out. I want Zhijima to be there when I question him. She deserves some answers," he said.

Both women nodded.

Arka-Dal wanted to clear the air. He didn't want this to have an adverse affect on his friendship with Pandaar, but he liked Zhijima well enough to try and put things right. When he confronted Pandaar about it, he was his usually blunt self.

"I'll tell you why. I'm *bored*. I've been tapping the same old pussy for the last 50 years and I'm tired of it. I think Zhijima's bored, too. That's why she's been spending more time with Gorinna lately.

When she's not with her, she's looking at you like some lovesick schoolgirl," he said.

He turned to Zhijima.

"I've been a good, loyal husband for most of our lives. It's time for me to try other women. I need some variety in my life," he said.

Zhijima glared at him. Before either he or Arka-Dal could react, she lashed out with all of her strength and punched him right in the nose. The blow took Pandaar by surprise and sent him to the floor. When he tried to get back up, she kicked him in the midsection and punched him twice more. This was followed by a stream of epithets in both Dihhuri and Thulian that were enough to turn the air blue around her.

"I *bore* you? Sex with me is *boring*? You miserable bastard! I'm going to show you just how wrong you are. I'm going to screw Arka-Dal into the mattress every chance I get and I'd be willing to bet that *he* won't find me *boring*!" she screamed.

She turned and stormed off in a huff. When she reached the doorway, she turned and shouted again.

"I want a divorce!"

Arka-Dal helped Pandaar into a chair and handed him a brandy. The battered warrior winced as he smiled.

"That'll leave a mark," Arka-Dal said of the bruise on the side of Pandaar's jaw.

"Yes it will. Damn. She certainly hits hard for a little person. That really hurt. Oh, well. It's all for the best," Pandaar said.

"How do you figure that?" asked Arka-Dal.

"This way, we both get what we want. I get to fuck any woman I feel like fucking and Zhijima is free to fuck you. You do find her attractive, don't you?" he replied.

"I always have. Do you really mean all this?" Arka-Dal asked.

Pandaar nodded.

"Every last word of it. If she wants a divorce, I'll gladly give her one. I just don't feel too comfortable about her having no one to look after her," he said.

"Zhijima doesn't need anyone to look after her. She's pretty smart and a lot tougher than you know. She'll be fine. Besides, she'll still be living here. She'll still have us. She's family. She always will be family," Arka-Dal assured him.

"That's good," Pandaar said.

"Er, why the maids?" Arka-Dal asked.

"They're easy and they're cheap—in more ways than one. A couple of them are real wild in bed, too," he replied.

"Well, the twelve of them should keep you plenty busy for a long time," Arka-Dal said.

"What are you going to do about Zhijima? She's nuts about you, you know. She has been for a long, long time," Pandaar asked.

"I don't know. This is kind of an awkward position for me," Arka-Dal said.

"What's so awkward? She wants you and she won't give up until you want her, too," Pandaar said.

"The awkward part is the way my wives are teasing me about her. They're all betting that I'm about to acquire yet another wife—and more children to go with her," Arka-Dal said.

Pandaar laughed and winced.

"Go for it, I say. You won't regret a second of it," he urged.

"Is she really boring?" Arka-Dal asked.

"She's pretty good, actually. It's just that I've been humping the same piece of ass for decades. You wouldn't understand because you have several women who keep you entertained. And if I know Zhijima, you're about to get another," Pandaar said.

"She's really serious, isn't she?" Arka-Dal asked.

"Oh, yes. She's going to ride you hard and put you away wet, then ride you some more. She's been itching to do this for years now, so there's a lot of lost time to make up for. She's all yours now, my friend. As for me, there are many younger, hotter and more willing females waiting for me out there and I'm going to find them," Pandaar said

Two rooms away, the other women sat and listened to Zhijima rant and rave about Pandaar's betrayal with amusement. They smiled as she paced the floor and called Pandaar every nasty thing she could think of. The amusement came from the fact that the usually quiet and reserved Zhijima not only knew such language but also how to use it.

"I'm giving you all fair warning, ladies," she said after she stopped to calm down. "I intend to have sex with Arka-Dal—lots of sex. In fact, I'm going to fuck his eyeballs out!"

To her surprise, they all laughed hysterically at her bold statement. Medusa laughed so hard that tears rolled down her cheeks.

"What's so funny? I'm serious!" she shouted.

"Of course you are. We all know that," Medusa said. "It's just the way you said it that sounded so funny."

Chatha stood up and touched Zhijima's shoulder.

"Do you really plan to divorce Pandaar?" she asked.

"I sure as Hell will divorce that rat. Then I'm going to marry Arka-Dal!" Zhijima swore.

This statement elicited another chorus of laughter from the women. Their reaction made Zhijima even more determined to go through with her plans.

"I don't know if Aka-san can handle five of us," Mayumi said.

"Six. Don't forget about Gorinna," Chatha corrected.

"If he can satisfy Galya and keep the rest of us happy like he's been doing, I think he can handle one more wife—provided Zhijima doesn't wear him out altogether," Medusa said jokingly.

"Aren't you being a little overly ambitious? What if Arka-Dal doesn't want to marry you?" asked Chatha.

Galya hiked up her skirt and ran her finger over Zhijima's pubic hair.

"I doubt any man could resist this," she stated. "Once he tastes your sweet nectar, he'll be hooked for life. I know that I *am*."

She eased her middle finger up into Zhijima's slit and moved it in and out. Zhijima quivered excitedly but remained well aware that the others were watching.

"You're nice and tight, too. He'll *really* love that!" Galya said.

"Just don't go to the beach house with him," Medusa warned.

"Why not?" asked Zhijima as she quivered even harder.

"You'll end up pregnant. We already have enough children around here," Medusa replied.

"Then one more won't matter," Zhijima said as she backed away from Galya and into the arms of Chatha who was standing behind her.

Chatha slid her hand between Zhijima's thighs and immediately picked up where Galya had left off. Zhijima moaned softly.

"You *want* a child?" Chatha asked.

"Yes. If I do become his next wife, I also expect to bear him a child—or two—just like the rest of you," Zhijima replied.

Heavy and unseasonal rains pounded Pandolia. They muddied the roads and brought the armies of Mornay and Waleco to a standstill while they waited out the storm. The downpour also drove the rioters indoors and provided Beyaro's beleaguered men with a much-needed respite.

As he stood by the window of the office watching the rain pelt the city, Beyaro knew it was a temporary break in the action. As soon as the rain stopped and the roads dried, Mornay and Waleco would resume their advance on the capital.

And the riots would begin again.

But for now, all was quiet. For now, he ruled Pandolia. How long his rule would last was another matter.

A loud knock on the door broke his train of thought. Without waiting for an invitation, Herald Maartens, Thule's ambassador to Pandolia, barged in. Maartens was a retired and decorated army officer. Arka-Dal appointed him to his current post because he read, wrote and spoke Pandolian and his wife, Liima, was a distant cousin of the late Malle Doux.

Maartens also harbored a strong dislike for Beyaro. He'd had several run-ins with the hot-tempered general over the past five years and considered him to be self-absorbed, egotistical and power hungry.

So it was with great pleasure that he marched into Beyaro's office to deliver Arka-Dal's ultimatum. Beyaro listened as Maartens read it verbatim.

"You are hereby put on notice that the Empires of Thule and Egypt have decided to send expeditionary forces to Pandolia as a show of support for the government troops and the people of this nation whom they consider brethren. I strongly advise you to evacuate the throne you wrongfully usurped immediately or suffer the consequences."

Beyaro stared at him.

"What consequences does your Emperor refer to?" he asked.

"In the event you decide to try and hold the throne and trigger and all-out civil war between your pirates and government troops, both Thule and Egypt will enter on the side of the loyalists and *remove* you," Maartens said smugly. "You have just 72 hours to comply with this ultimatum."

"What are your Emperor's terms?" Beyaro asked.

"There are none other than I just stated. The terms of your surrender will be dictated by the Pandolian government," Maartens said. "Taking into consideration the way your thugs have mistreated the citizens of this city, I imagine those terms will be quite harsh."

"You're enjoying this, aren't you?" Beyaro asked.

"Immensely," Maartens assured him.

Beyaro cursed as the ambassador walked out. He turned to the window and thought about his situation carefully.

There was food and water enough for a prolonged siege. Troop strength was barely enough to hold the city. He had six partial regiments and about a dozen loyal officers to command them, but those numbers were decreasing steadily each day. If attacked, they'd be forced to deal with an enemy outside the walls and rioters within the city.

It was a hopeless situation at best.

Kashi and Pandaar went into Arka-Dal's study to give him the news.

"Maartens radioed that the capital was fairly quiet, but only because of the heavy storms they have there now. Beyaro's soldiers are deserting in droves and his officers seem to be demoralized. I doubt things went as well as he planned," Kashi said as they sat down at the desk.

"What of my ultimatum?" Arka-Dal asked.

"It was delivered at 2:00 yesterday. Beyaro hasn't responded yet," Pandaar said. "Arkaneton informed us that the expeditionary force under Horem Heb has been assembled. Once they reach Arda, they'll head for the Pandolian border."

"They're right on time, as usual. When Joshua reaches the border, have him move on to Jericho and await further instructions. Remind him not to take any action unless he comes under attack by rebel forces," Arka-Dal ordered.

Arka-Dal already knew that King Prium had crossed into Pandolia to link forces with government soldiers. By the time they reached Azum Phala, Beyaro's men would be outnumbered at least 25 to 1.

Would he be crazy enough to try and fight against such odds?

The day after the storms abated, Beyaro stood on the balcony overlooking the harbor. After a few minutes, he sighted what appeared to be dozens of sails in the distance. He picked up his telescope and aimed it at the mouth of the harbor. He watched in dismay as several warships of various sizes stopped at the entrance and dropped anchor.

Admiral Zedo had arrived.

He had 28 ships in all and he positioned his fleet so that it completely blocked the harbor. Nothing could get in or out.

Beyaro also knew that roads were now dry enough for the two loyalist armies to renew their marches on Azum Phala and some 8,000

Thulian horsemen were moving toward the northeastern border. With an Egyptian force headed for Ilium and Prium's army camped on the southern border, he knew he was trapped.

And outnumbered.

"The noose tightens," he thought. "It will soon be around my neck. I could try and hold Azum Phala but at what cost? I'd still lose. Still end up dead. This turned into a bum deal really fast."

Within the hour, a messenger from Zedo arrived with a letter demanding Beyaro's surrender. Beyaro laughed.

"Tell your admiral to go fuck himself," he said.

Zedo's reply an hour later was also to the point. He had his men fire a small rocket at the palace. It hissed over the outer wall and exploded in the courtyard not ten feet from the front doors.

Beyaro cursed as he watched his men scramble for cover.

Zedo's ships were out of range of his rockets and he had no ships of his own with which to take the fight to him.

Moments later, a second rocket struck the façade and blew the balcony to atoms. The blast also took out the double doors and half the room beyond them and showered the soldiers below with rubble and shattered glass. A third rocket followed swiftly and landed in almost the same spot. This one shook the palace so violently, it shattered every window in the building.

Beyaro remained unmoved.

Two days later, a dispatch rider from General Waleco arrived bearing a letter also demanding Beyaro's immediate and unconditional surrender. Beyaro sent him back with the same reply he'd given to Zedo.

When a third messenger from General Mornay arrived six hours with a similar demand, Beyaro snarled and kicked him out. At the same time, he decided it might be wise to pay Axelrod a visit.

Arka-Dal's ambassador informed him of these events on a daily basis. He knew that riots had again broken out all over the city. This time, the mobs were better organized and coordinated their efforts in order to exhaust Beyaro's troops. There were ten riots the first day. Fifteen the next and 25 the following day. All erupted in different parts of the city at different times and forced Beyaro's soldiers to rush back and forth to try and quell them.

By the fifth day, Beyaro's men were too exhausted to even try to quell the riots. They stopped responding to them and mobs of angry citizens soon took over the streets.

Arka-Dal pondered the fate of Pandolia. While the rebels held the capital (barely!), their bold takeover had the rest of the country up in arms. Pandolians loved their freedom.

Enough to fight for it.

And they *would* as long as they knew they had the support of two thirds of the army and the entire Pandolian navy. Beyaro's men were essentially bottled up within Azum Phala. Once the two remaining armies encircled the city, that's exactly where they'd stay.

He heard the door open. He looked up and smiled as his four wives entered and gathered around his desk.

"How do you feel about us, my love?" asked Galya.

"Yes. Tell us the truth," Chatha prodded.

They seemed a little miffed over something. And he was fairly sure what it was.

"I love you all dearly and passionately," Arka-Dal said.

"What about Zhijima? Do you also love her?" asked Mayumi.

"Yes—but more in the way I would love my little sister," he replied.

"Be careful, my love. Your 'little sister' seeks to have an incestuous relationship with you," Galya warned.

"She won't give up, either," Mayumi said.

"Then what do you all advise me to do?" he asked.

"She wants you to fuck her, so fuck her. That way, you'll both be happy. Just don't marry her. You already have enough wives around here," Chatha said.

"Chatha's right. Our bed can't possibly hold another body, not even one as tiny as hers," Medusa said.

"I think you *should* marry her," Galya said to everyone's surprise. "That way, your offspring will be legitimate. There will be no questioning their birthrights. No speculation or nasty rumors and no questions for future historians. Besides, that's what she wants. You will, too, once you've been with her awhile."

"I think you're all crazy," Arka-Dal said. "I'm going to take a nice hot bath and try to clear this from my mind."

Zhijima watched him enter the bathroom and waited a few minutes to give him time to get into the water and relax. As he sat there soaking and letting the tension leave his muscles, Zhijima walked over, scooped up a handful of water and playfully threw it at him. He opened his eyes to see her wonderful nude body slide into the tub in front of him. Before he could do or say anything, she put her arms around his neck and stuck her tongue into his mouth.

Caught up in the moment, he ran his hands all over her body and kissed her back.

Their kiss lingered and lingered. The longer it lasted, the more passionate it became and the more he explored and caressed her lean, sexy body. Zhijima felt his hardness between her thighs. With one deft move, she opened her legs and impaled herself on him. He gasped at her tightness. He pulled her closer and they began to make love. Good, hard, passionate love.

They spent a lot of time in the tub that morning.

A lot of time making love.

Zhijima was good, too. Far better than he ever suspected she'd be. Far more passionate. Far more energetic and flexible, too.

"Do you find me boring, too?" she teased in mid-stroke.

"I can think of many words to describe this moment but 'boring' isn't one of them," he replied as he pulled her close and fired his seed into her. "In fact, you are a wonderful lover!"

"And I'm yours, now and forever! I love you, Arka-Dal! I love you!" she cried.

When they finally climbed out of the tub, they made love on one of the padded benches. This time, he began by eating her. The more he ate her, the more he liked it and the more passionate her cries became. Zhijima tasted like fine honey mixed with a little bit of salt. The flavor reminded him much of Mayumi. This made her even more interesting. More irresistible.

While she was still in the throes of her orgasm, he entered her again. This time, they did it nice and easy.

Later that evening, Arka-Dal's other wives sought Zhijima out. They found her seated on a bench near one of the lily ponds in the garden. She had a dreamy, satisfied look in her eyes.

"You did it, didn't you? You had sex with Arka-Dal," Galya said.

Zhijima smiled and nodded.

"It was exquisite, too," she sighed. "Better than I ever hoped it would be."

"So are you two in love now?" asked Chatha. "Or are you just lovers?"

"Right now, I think we're just lovers. Although I love him more than ever, he remains oddly silent on the matter. I think he's afraid to admit anything for now," Zhijima replied.

"He is not sure if he wants another wife around here," Mayumi pointed out. "The four of us keep him very busy."

"Five—if you count Gorinna," Chatha reminded her.

"Now what?" asked Medusa. "Are you still going to try and get him to marry you?"

"Of course I am. I don't want to be his *mistress.* I want to be his wife. I want to bear him a child or two," Zhijima assured her. "But I won't force him to do it. I want him to say he loves me. I want *him* to propose to me."

"Now that you've got his attention, you'll have to spend a lot more time with him. That won't be easy around here. Especially with *us* around," Chatha pointed out.

"I, for one, will not stay out of your way. After all, he *is* my husband and I need him as much as you do," Galya said.

"I won't make it easy for you either," Medusa added. "If you want him, you're really going to have to work for him."

"I agree with them," Mayumi said. "I will not make it too easy for you to catch my husband on the rebound. You will just have to 'steal' moments with him like you did this morning. If Aka-san really wants to spend some private time with you, he will request it. When that happens, I will grant his request."

"But what if he never does?" asked Zhijima.

"Tough!" said Galya.

Then everyone laughed. Zhijima wondered if they were having fun at her expense or if they actually meant what they said.

Later that morning, Zhijima went down into the royal archives and found Leo at his desk slumped over a large, ancient book. He looked up and smiled at her. Medusa, who was busy filing some papers, suppressed a giggle but kept working.

"I want to divorce Pandaar. Can you help arrange it?" Zhijima asked.

"I've already drawn up the necessary documents. Pandaar requested them yesterday. In fact, he's already signed them," Leo said as he took a folder out of his desk drawer and handed it to her.

Zhijima fumed as she leafed through it.

"That dirty son-of-bitch! He beat me to it," she almost growled.

"Everything is official and legal. As soon as you sign the documents, you'll no longer be man and wife. He's also relinquished his honorary title as king of the Dihhuris. He said he didn't deserve it anymore," Leo explained.

"He's certainly right about that. Where do I sign?" Zhijima asked.

"Right beneath his signature on the last page," Leo instructed.

She took a pen from his desk, leaned over and signed where he'd indicated. Then she handed the papers back to him and smiled.

"You are officially a free woman," Leo announced.

Zhijima smiled and left the archives. Medusa watched her walk up the stairs and laughed.

"Looks like you just got a new rival," Leo observed.

"Not really. We'll run interference between her and Arka-Dal for a week or two then give them whatever alone time they need to work things out. We all love Zhijima. She's sort of our little sister. We just want to have some fun with her," Medusa explained.

"Then you really won't mind if she becomes Arka-Dal's fifth wife?" Leo asked.

Medusa shook her head.

"Of course not. In fact, Galya said she thought they'd make a good match. The rest of us think so, too," she said.

Leo laughed.

"I must say I think you're all extraordinary women. You rarely disagree about anything and you never seem to mind sharing him amongst yourselves," he said.

"We all love each other, Leo. We love Zhijima, too. After what Pandaar's done to her, we feel she deserves some happiness. And if she can achieve that by marrying Arka-Dal, more power to her!" Medusa said.

"What would you have done if you had caught Arka-Dal with another woman you didn't approve of?" Leo asked.

"I'd beat him to a pulp. Then I'd forgive him," Medusa replied.

Pandaar took a large bottle of brandy and two glasses from the bar and went in search of Kashi. He found him on the balcony that was situated above the entryway, smoking his pipe and looking up at the stars. Pandaar sat down at the table with him, poured out two drinks and handed him one.

"I thought you'd like to help me celebrate," he said.

"What's the occasion?" asked Kashi.

"Today I became a free man. A bachelor," he said as he held up his glass.

Kashi clinked his against it and drank. As soon as he set it down, Pandaar refilled it.

"Zhijima signed the divorce papers this morning. Now I'm free to chase all of the tail I feel like chasing and I don't have to hide it from her," Pandaar continued.

They clinked and drank again.

"Well, it's what you wanted. I hope you'll both be happy," Kashi said.

"I know *I* will. It might bother me for awhile to see her every day, but I'll get over it. What's going on with you and Gorinna?" Pandaar asked.

"We sleep together each night. The fire still burns bright within us. I doubt that will ever change. I know one thing: I won't grow *bored* with her," Kashi said as he needled his friend.

"But she still screws Arka-Dal when she wants. Doesn't it bother you?" Pandaar asked as he refilled their glasses.

"Not really. It's *her* body. She can share it with whomever she pleases. She told me I could sleep with other women if I desire, but I told her that I wouldn't. No one else interests me like she does," Kashi said. "How will *you* feel if Zhijima weds Arka-Dal?"

"I'll give them both my sincerest blessings and carry on with my life. I hope they do marry. I want her to be happy. Hell, I hope they have a couple of kids!"

"That's quite magnanimous of you," Kashi said.

"*I* think so," Pandaar agreed.

Kashi looked at bruise next to Pandaar's nose and smiled.

"It's healing nicely," he observed.

"Better than my ribs. She broke two of them when she kicked me," Pandaar said.

"You're lucky she didn't knife you. She was really pissed," Kashi said. "I've never heard anyone called what she called you. On top of that, you said she was boring. Now she's going to go out of her way to prove you wrong."

Pandaar refilled their glasses again.

"I deserved everything she did to me. I'm probably exactly what she said I am, too," he said.

"And more," Kashi said. "How long before Zhijima campaigns to get Arka-Dal to marry her?"

"Shit. She's already started. One of the maids told me they were fucking like jackrabbits in the bath this morning," Pandaar replied.

He poured another round of brandy then hefted the bottle.

"It's empty. Don't worry. There's plenty more where this came from," he said as he headed down to the bar.

Hours later, Gorinna found both of them passed out on the balcony with three empty bottles on the table between them. She shook her head at the pathetic sight. She knew that Kashi would most likely wake up with a nasty hangover. He really didn't drink all that much because he didn't like the way he felt the morning after.

"I can't let him suffer," she decided as she rubbed his temples and intoned a healing spell. "He'll be fine tomorrow."

She looked at Pandaar and decided to have a little fun. She reached down and rubbed his temples, too. Only this time the spell served to magnify the effects of the hangover ten times over. Pandaar would wake with the very worst hangover of his entire life.

"That's for doing what you did to Zhijima," she said as she walked away.

Arka-Dal entered the dining room the next morning room and saw Pandaar at the table massaging his temples. His eyes were bright red and he looked as if he'd been through Hell. He sat down across from him and smiled.

"You look like death warmed over," he said.

"I feel much worse than I look. My head is pounding like surf against rocks and I've been puking my guts out all morning. I asked Zhijima to help like she always did but she just snarled at me and told me to ask one the maids to help me. Then she yelled at me again. That made my head ache even more."

"Did you ask Leo for a remedy?" Arka-Dal suggested.

"Yes. He whipped up some concoction that looked like coal tar and smelled like an open sewer. I couldn't bring myself to drink it," Pandaar replied.

Gorinna entered and laughed at him. Then she leaned close and shouted in his ear.

"How the Hell are you this morning? Enjoying your hangover? I know I am!"

Pandaar covered his ears and groaned. She laughed again and sat down.

"Am I right to suspect that you had something to do with the magnitude of my hangover?" Pandaar asked.

"It wouldn't surprise me if I did," she said coyly.

"This is a bad one. Every little sound is amplified a thousand fold. This morning I even cursed one of the cats for stomping around," Pandaar complained.

Arka-Dal laughed, too.

"My but you're a sympathetic pair!" he said sarcastically.

Later that afternoon, Pandaar entered the study and found Arka-Dal seated at his desk. To his surprise, Zhijima was there, too. She sat on the edge of the desk wearing a dress that left very little to the imagination.

He smiled at her.

She looked away in disgust.

"I just got a radio message from Joshua. He left the main base with his cavalry at dawn this morning. He expects to be at the Pandolian border within four days," he reported.

"Good. Radio King Prium with the news. Assure him that we not enter Pandolia unless the government requests it. We still consider this to be an internal matter," Arka-Dal said.

"Do you think it will become a full-scale civil war?" Pandaar asked.

"Let's hope not. A civil war would devastate the country and leave Azum Phala in ruins. In that event, we'd be forced to intervene. That would make us an occupying force and the Pandolians might not go for that," Arka-Dal replied.

"I wouldn't worry too much about that. I'm sure the government forces are strong enough and capable enough to take care of everything with a minimum of bloodshed. After all, they outnumber the rebels and have the support of all of the people," Zhijima said.

Pandaar raised an eyebrow.

This was the first time in decades that Zhijima had offered an opinion on an important matter. She also seemed to have a good grasp of the matter. She saw the expression on his face and smirked as if to say: "See? I *do* have a brain!"

"Good point. But we'd best prepare for the worst. If we are forced to go in, we'll act in concert with the Pandolian army and *only* as a reserve force. We will not fight unless we're directly attacked," Arka-Dal said.

"What about the Ardans?" Pandaar asked.

"They have much more at stake in this mess than we do. Their entire economy is closely bound to Pandolia's and their peoples have been intermarrying for decades. If Pandolia goes south, Prium might fear that Arda will follow. Prium's already reached Jerusalem. I expect him to march north," Arka-Dal said.

"The Egyptian Army is already at sea in transport ships. Arkaneton advised us they should reach Ilium the day after tomorrow. A second force under Tutmose should leave Alexandria at the end of this week," Pandaar said.

"Good. The Egyptians will follow our lead. We're providing a show of force in support of the Pandolian government. A *strong* one, too. Let's hope it will be enough to force the rebels to surrender," Arka-Dal said.

Pandaar nodded and left the room.

Zhijima chuckled.

"I seem to have surprised him with my comments. He looked dumbfounded," she said.

"Pandaar's forgotten how truly intelligent you are. Over the years, you allowed him to take you for granted and relegated yourself to the quiet wife role. You barely said anything about important matters but you've always been a big help to me behind the scenes. He doesn't know how valuable you really are," Arka-Dal said with a smile.

"Oh, well. That's *his* loss and *your* gain—unless you think I'm too hot to handle," she said.

"You're hot alright, but I can handle you," he said as he slid his hand up her thigh.

Horem Heb's force disembarked at Ilium a day ahead of schedule. He quickly organized his units and marched them north to the Pandolian border. He would wait until Tutmose arrived before entering the country.

When Joshua and his cavalry reached Pandolia, they rode straight for Jericho where the mayor and people gave the Thulians a warm welcome. As ordered, Joshua radioed Arka-Dal that he'd arrived and would remain in Jericho until ordered to move.

All this time, Zedo's warships fired three rockets per day at the palace. Most of the façade was now scorched, the windows were shattered and half the east wing lay in ruins. There were also several large craters and scorch marks on the wide lawn in front of the palace.

And Beyaro's soldiers kept deserting him.

He was now down to less than one regiment and had only four officers still loyal to him—and even they were grumbling about surrender. Their situation was now untenable. In desperation, he decided to try one last thing.

On the 24th day of his "rise to power", Beyaro went to Axelrod's home and discovered that the soldiers assigned to guard him had also deserted. He found the Prime Minister in the library eating an apple and drinking wine. He scowled at Beyaro but bade him to sit and talk. He soon realized that the rebel leader had come to discuss surrender terms. He also knew there was no need to negotiate.

"Terms? You'll get the same terms as any traitor. You'll be drawn and quartered in the city square and your head will be put on a pole in front of the palace gates. The officers who have remained at your side through your attempted rebellion will be tried and executed. Your soldiers will each be given 100 lashes with a bullwhip and dishonorably discharged from the army. They will also be permanently exiled from Pandolia along with their immediate families.

Those are the only terms you deserve, traitor!" he said.

Properly chastised, Beyaro left Axelrod's house and returned to the palace.

He was over a barrel now. Within days, Azum Phala would be completely surrounded. As coups go, this one was a real disaster. He had gambled everything on the loyalty of his soldiers and lost. It went just as Axelrod said it would. The freedom loving Pandolians would *not* stomach a dictatorship.

"Nothing ventured . . ." he said to himself.

When he reached his office, he learned that the Egyptians, at the request of General Waleco, had entered Pandolia and occupied Jerusalem. The Thulian army was now in Jericho and the Ardans were marching north to help besiege the capital. It was a well-coordinated operation led by five seasoned commanders.

He knew that the Egyptians and Thulians were there only as reserves, but the Ardans intended to join the battle. He also knew that his men could never hold out very long against such forces.

He *could* gamble everything on a single roll of the dice and march out to meet one of the armies before it reached the city. But he doubted his men would actually fight.

"It is time to put an end to this farce," he said.

He opened the desk drawer, picked up Malle Doux's revolver, stuck the barrel into his mouth and pulled the trigger. The shot echoed through the halls of the palace and caught the attention of his guards. They raced into the office to find Beyaro lying face-down on his desk in a poll of blood. The back of his skull was gone and bits of brain, bone and blood were splattered over the back of the chair, desk and the wall behind him.

They immediately rushed into the street to spread the news.

Had any of them lingered a few moments, they might have witness the sudden appearance of tall, handsome, goateed man dressed in black. He looked down at Beyaro's corpse and laughed.

"Another contract fulfilled to the letter. You got *exactly* what you desired, General. You got to rule Pandolia for the rest of your life. Unfortunately, you did not specify exactly how much longer you wanted to live. You left that part blank. Left it up to me to decide. I hope you enjoyed your brief rule," he said as he slowly vanished.

Maartens reported the news immediately to Pandaar who relayed it to Arka-Dal.

"Beyaro took the coward's way out. He shot himself with Malle Doux's revolver," Pandaar said.

Arka-Dal nodded.

"That seems strangely appropriate. It's as if Malle Doux himself killed him. What about his army?" he asked.

"They all surrendered without a fight. Axelrod had them all sent to a prison camp to await trial. I doubt they'll be treated with kid gloves," Pandaar said.

"Nor should they. They followed their general all through his attempted coup. Now they must suffer the consequences for their misplaced loyalty," Arka-Dal said.

"What would you do in this case?" asked Pandaar.

"Same as you. I'd execute the entire lot of them and be done with it. Rebellions should be crushed without mercy, unless the cause is to remove a tyrant or oust a foreign occupier. Remember, *we* were rebels ourselves once.[19] Had we lost, we would have been shown no mercy either," Arka-Dal said.

"True," Pandaar agreed.

Now that the Pandolian crisis was over, Arka-Dal issued orders to Joshua to bring his troops home. This done, he decided to go for his morning ride to think over the situation in the palace.

Zhijima had become impossible to ignore or resist. Each time they were alone, they made love. Each time, it was different. She loved to experiment with new positions and new ways to arouse him. They also spoke with each other more than ever. He found the pretty

---

19 Read THE AVENGER OF THULE

Dihhuri queen to be bright, funny and able to converse on a wide range of subjects. They had connected on both the intellectual and physical levels and that connection was becoming stronger.

After four hours, he headed back to the palace. By then, he'd already made up his mind about her.

When he arrived, he was greeted at the door by all four of his wives. From the expressions on their faces, he realized there was trouble.

"What's wrong?" he asked.

"Zhijima!" they all said at once.

"She's been clinging to you like cheap, wet underwear ever since this started," Medusa said.

"You have to do something about her," added Galya.

"What do you mean?" he asked as they surrounded him and walked with him into the parlor.

"She's crazy about you. So crazy, she's making us crazy, too," Chatha said.

"Hai. She walks around humming the wedding song all day. We cannot get her to stop." Mayumi said.

"Not unless we beat her," Medusa added.

"Even *that* might not stop her. Can you do something with her before she drives us all nuts?" asked Galya.

"What do you *want* me to do?" he asked.

"Marry her already!" Chatha said.

"Hai. Please marry her. At least it would make her stop that crazy humming. Maybe then we'll get some quiet around here," Mayumi agreed.

"You might as well marry her, my love. If you don't, we'll have to kill her to shut her up and we don't want to kill her," Galya said.

"Not *yet*, anyway," Chatha added. "After a few more days of that damned humming, I might consider it."

"Me, too. Please marry her. You know you want to anyway," Medusa urged.

"Stop putting it off. Propose to her already. Then marry her quickly and take her away for a month," Mayumi urged.

"Or three!" said Chatha.

"If you don't hurry and do this, we cannot be held responsible for any actions we might take to get her to cease that humming!" Galya warned.

"The only time she is quiet is when she is with *you*, Aka-san," Mayumi said.

"That's because her mouth is full," Chatha said.

They all laughed hard at her comment. Arka-Dal laughed, too, then shook his head as he poured himself a drink.

"Since you all insist upon it, I *will* ask her to marry me. Are you certain you want me to do this?" he asked.

They all looked at each other and nodded.

"Can you handle *five* wives?" Medusa asked.

"I'm sure he can. After all, he's been doing just fine so far. Haven't you?" said Chatha

"After you marry her, we'll help you work out a schedule to make sure you don't neglect any of us. You would not want to hurt our feelings, would you, Aka-san?" Mayumi teased.

"Remember, you're the *head* of state and we all want an equal share of it," Medusa joked.

That earned a collective groan from the other women. Arka-Dal watched as they trooped off into a side parlor. He finished his drink, poured another and headed to his office.

Zhijima was waiting in the side parlor. When the women entered, they beamed at her.

"It's done," Galya announced. "We teamed up on him and told him to marry you before we kill you."

"Now you must do *your* part and turn up the heat in your relationship by a few notches. That shouldn't be too difficult," Medusa said.

"Not for a slut like you," Chatha teased.

Zhijima thanked each of them with a warm hug and scurried off to Arka-Dal's office. Galya laughed.

"You know we're crazy for doing this," she said.

"Totally insane," Medusa agreed.

"It's a good think we all love Zhijima," Mayumi said.

"Yes, it is," said Chatha.

That same evening, Arka-Dal and Zhijima walked in the garden hand-in-hand, gazing up at the vast tapestry of stars in the night sky. He pulled her close and gently stroked her long, silken hair.

"I love you," he said softly.

"I know. I love you, too," she replied.

"So, you want to get married?" he asked.

"Sure. When?" she agreed.

"When would you like to?" he asked.

"Yesterday—but I'll settle for as soon as possible," she replied.

He laughed.

They kissed and walked back to the palace to tell everyone what they already knew. Pandaar was the first to congratulate them.

"You two are a perfect match. You think alike and Zhijima has many of Mayumi's finer qualities," he said.

"And I don't *bore* him in bed. Do I?" she needled.

"Not in bed or anywhere else for that matter," he assured her.

"I hope you can handle the five of us. If you devote too much of your time to Zhijima, I may have to kill her," Mayumi warned.

"Not if *I* kill her first," Chatha said as she hugged Zhijima warmly. "Welcome to the nest, dear."

"Thank you. Thank you all. I'd like a simple wedding. Something low-key," Zhijima suggested.

"You know better than that. We never do anything low-key around here. Especially weddings," Medusa said.

"You helped to plan ours, now we'll plan yours. Don't worry about a thing. It'll be perfect," Galya promised.

Zhijima looked up at Arka-Dal.

"Can we honeymoon at the beach house?" she asked.

Later that evening, Zhijima entered the parlor and scowled when she saw Pandaar waiting for her. She walked over to the sofa and sat down. Pandaar sat down beside her.

"What do *you* want?" she demanded.

The iciness on her voice made him shiver inside. He took a deep breath.

"This isn't easy for me. I've never apologized before," he said.

"Oh? And *what* are you apologizing for? Are you sorry you cheated on me with all those other women?" she asked.

"No. I'm not sorry for that at all. That was a lot of fun. I'm sorry for the way you had to find out. I'm sorry that I didn't have the nerve to tell you how I felt sooner. I didn't want to hurt your feelings," he said.

She stared at him.

"Well, you blew that, didn't you?" she asked.

"I sure as Hell did," he admitted.

"If you'd had any respect for me at all, you would have told me the truth. Instead, I had to catch you in bed with that trollop. I had to find out the hard way. It *crushed* me, Pandaar. It really broke my heart and made me angry. So angry, I wanted to kill you on the spot!" she said.

"Then you *insulted* me in front of Arka-Dal by saying I'm boring. *I'm boring?* Listen, asshole, if *you're* so damned hot in bed, why would I have turned to Gorinna for excitement? Did you ever think of *that*?"

She got up and virtually snarled at him. He attempted to get up but she shoved him back down.

"I'm not finished with you yet!" she shouted.

He sat quietly and looked at the floor while she continued her tongue lashing.

"Now you want to *apologize,* but not for cheating on me. You're sorry because I *caught* you doing it? You say you didn't want to hurt me? Well, it's too fucking late for *that*! I don't want your damned apology and I'll never forgive you for this for as long as I live. You lose an all counts, because I have a *real* man now. One who loves and respects me. *He* won't betray me like you did and he does not find me boring in the least," she said.

When he looked up at her, she made as if to strike him. Pandaar flinched. Zhijima laughed and walked away.

He heard laughter behind and turned to see both Leo and Gorinna standing a few feet away.

"That didn't turn out quite like I planned," he said sheepishly. "I know what I really *wanted* to say. The words just came out wrong."

"She'll get over in another 25-30 years," Leo advised.

"Or the moment she gives birth to their first child," said Gorinna. "Arka-Dal's child. You certainly have a way with women. You're a regular silver-tongued devil."

"A real Prince Charming," Leo said. "Lucky for you that it takes but little to charm the pants off the maids around here. If you had to rely on your ability to charm women, you'd have the hairiest palms in the Empire by now."

"Thanks. I feel *much* better now," Pandaar said sarcastically.

"Don't mention it," said Leo.

"I won't," Pandaar promised.

"But *I* will," Gorinna said.

"Thanks, Hangover Lady. I knew I could count on you," Pandaar joked. "I guess it's better this way. Zhijima is happy now. Arka-Dal will take good care of her and give her the love and respect she needs. She'll be good for him, too. In the end, that's all that really matters."

Leo feigned surprise.

"That almost sounded *noble and selfless*. I can tell that you're quite sincere, too. You've surprised me, Pandaar."

"Me, too," said Gorinna. "Maybe you're not that big of a rat after all."

When Merlin returned to the palace later that evening, Gorinna filled him in on the latest news. He sat and stared at her for a few moments, then shook his head.

"Do you think Pandaar agreed to divorce Zhijima because he really *was* bored with her? Or was he weary of seeing her pine for Arka-Dal and decided to clear the way for them?" he asked.

"A little of both, I suspect," Gorinna said. "For the last three months, he's been screwing every maid in the palace. The shit really hit the fan when Zhijima caught him at it. You should have seen the beating she gave him!"

"I'm sorry I missed it. And you say Arka-Dal's wives *approve* of the wedding?" Merlin asked.

"They sure do. In fact, they conspired to bring them together. They even got *me* involved in their little plot," Gorinna said.

"Naturally, Arka-Dal saw through this," Merlin conjectured.

Gorinna nodded.

"Since he actually does love Zhijima, he went along with it. Mayumi and Galya were the ringleaders. They're both very fond of Zhijima. So are Chatha and Medusa. They think its best for everyone that Zhijima becomes part of the family," she explained.

"And just how do *you* feel about all this?" Merlin asked.

She smiled.

"I'm okay with it, Merlin. I think I'm also a little bit jealous of Zhijima. Arka-Dal and I still make love when we can, but those times don't come as often as I wish they did. Lucky for me I still have Hamid. He keeps me grounded," she said.

"I think you've all gone mad around here," Merlin said.

Just then, Zhijima came in from the rose garden. She beamed when she saw Merlin then practically skipped over and hugged him.

"Has Gorinna told you the good news?" she asked.

"She has. Are you sure you know what you're doing?" he replied.

"No—but that's what makes it so much fun! I'll tell the others you're here," she said as she skipped off humming.

"Was she humming the wedding song?" Merlin asked.

Gorinna nodded.

"Incredible. Has the press gotten wind of this yet?" he asked.

"Not yet. A couple of weeks ago, the divorce made a big splash in the gossip section and the editorials raked Pandaar over the coals for treating his 'poor, loyal and beautiful wife' so badly. One commentator even suggested that Zhijima should find a real man, one who will treat her with love and respect. She went so far as to hint she should marry Arka-Dal," Gorinna said.

Merlin laughed.

"In that case, the press will *really* love this turn of events," he said.

And they did.

The very next morning, Pandaar was seated on a couch in one of the side parlors, trying to repair one of his favorite scabbards when Zhijima stormed in brandishing a copy of the Thule Times. She stopped in front of him and almost snarled.

He looked up and saw the anger in her eyes.

"Care to explain *this*?" she demanded as she showed him the headline on the front page.

"EMPEROR TO WED PANDAAR'S 'BORING' EX"

He winced.

"I'm waiting!" she said.

"Well, I, um, that is—" he stammered.

"Go on," she insisted.

"The reported asked me why I divorced you, so I told him," he admitted.

"You told the reporter I was *boring*?! Why you miserable fucking worm!" she shouted as she rolled up the paper and proceeded to beat him with it.

At the same time, she called him every nasty thing she could think of. Pandaar attempted to ward off the blows but she always managed to hit him in an unprotected spot. The din attracted the attention of Gorinna, Medusa and Galya who were chatting in the next room. They rushed in and tried to restrain Zhijima but the feisty little queen still managed to deal out a few more good shots.

"What's wrong? Why are you beating Pandaar?" asked Galya as she tried to pull her away.

"This!" Zhijima said as she unrolled the newspaper.

Galya read it and showed it to the others. They all glared angrily at Pandaar. Galya rerolled the paper and started beating Pandaar herself. She, too, called him every name she could think of. When she was tired, she passed the paper to Gorinna who continued the beating, then handed it off to Medusa. After she had vented her anger in the same manner, she handed what remained of the paper back to Zhijima, who hurled it at Pandaar and stormed out of the room. The other women followed.

Pandaar picked himself up off the floor and straightened out his clothes. He shook his head and whistled.

"Wow! That old saying about a woman scorned was right on target!" he commented.

"It sure as Hell is," Arka-Dal said as he entered the room.

"How long were you standing there?" asked Pandaar.

"Long enough. I didn't know Zhijima had such a violent temper," Arka-Dal said as they left the room and headed over to the bar.

"Me neither. Maybe you should rethink your wedding plans," Pandaar suggested.

"I think I'll just be careful not to piss her off. I saw the article. You deserved that one," Arka-Dal said. "I was on my way to talk with you about it when I saw them attack you. It was quite a show, especially when the others took turns to beat you, too."

"Glad you enjoyed it. I suppose it *was* kind of comical. Good thing it was only a newspaper," Pandaar said with a smile. "How come your wives don't beat up on you?"

"I guess I don't make a habit of pissing them off too much. Women are wired differently from us. You can never be sure what will set them off. Mostly I think their brains are short-circuited in some way," Arka-Dal said.

"Even Mayumi?" Pandaar asked.

"She's the exception. She's very level-headed and thoughtful, but sometimes her logic can be rather bizarre. I've just learned to try and see things from her perspective and she from mine. Also, I never hide anything from my wives," Arka-Dal said.

"You've always discussed everything with them. Why?" Pandaar asked.

"It's better that way. Mayumi runs Thule when I'm away and the other women help her. It's important that they all know everything that's going on. Zhijima helps, too," Arka-Dal said.

"She does? I've never noticed," Pandaar said.

"I know. You've always treated her condescendingly, like an ordinary woman. I assure you that Zhijima is anything but ordinary. She trains with Master Koto and Mayumi and has become an expert shot with a bow. She reads everything she can get her hands on and she's been studying military tactics and logistics with Chatha. Like I said, she's no ordinary woman," Arka-Dal explained.

"If she was, you wouldn't dream of marrying her," Pandaar said.

"That's right," Arka-Dal admitted.

"It's a good thing she didn't have that bow when she caught with the maid or I'd have second asshole right now. I still have a bruise on the top of my head where she hit me with that vase. I *know* how good she is with a bow. She gave me a demonstration about a month ago."

He then went on to tell him what transpired on the practice field behind the palace on cool morning.

He'd set up the target on one end of the field, turned and marked off 50 paces. While he was doing this, he failed to notice that Zhijima had stepped out of the palace with a bow and a quiver filled with arrows.

He went to a small stand where he kept his throwing axes and hefted one as he eyed the target. Then he reared back and hurled at as hard as he could. To his surprise, it was knocked spiraling to the ground in mid-flight by an arrow. He turned and smiled at Zhijima. He watched her nock another arrow and draw back the string. He seized the second ax and let it fly toward the target only to see it knocked off its course by Zhijima's second shot.

She laughed and went back inside.

He walked over to retrieve his axes and was amazed to see that both her arrows had struck each ax right in the center of its blade.

Arka-Dal laughed.

"She's very accurate with throwing knives, too," he warned. "Master Koto's been working with her for months. Just yesterday he told me she was pretty good with a katana *and* unarmed combat—as you found out."

"The *hard* way, too," Pandaar agreed. "I guess I should have paid more attention to her over the years."

"A *lot* more," Arka-Dal said. "*I* have, even though she thinks I didn't. The more I got to know her, the more she surprised and impressed me. That's why I told Koto and Leo to teach her anything and everything she wanted. She's become an expert in civil law and even fills in at trials for Mayumi once in a while."

"You sound as if you've a lot of confidence in Zhijima," Pandaar said.

"I do. She had good judgment and intuition. I value her opinions. That's why I've asked her to sit in on most of our important meetings over the years. She's good, Pandaar. Very good," Arka-Dal praised.

When they reached the main parlor, all six women were already there talking up a storm. They became completely silent the moment they saw Pandaar and walked out. Only Mayumi stayed. She smiled at Arka-Dal when he sat next to her and giggled at Pandaar.

"Why didn't you leave with them?" he asked. "Aren't you mad at me, too?"

"Of course I am, but I also think that you have been punished enough," she said. Then she turned to Arka-Dal. "Aka-san, you received a letter from Axelrod in Pandolia this morning. He wrote that he and King Prium of Arda are planning to merge their two countries. He wants to know if you have any objections to this."

"None at all. The blending together of their economic and military power will strengthen them considerably. I think it's a great idea," he replied. "I'll write Axelrod and Prium tonight."

"A have already written the letters. You only need to sign them," she said.

He smiled and kissed her.

"Thank you. I can always count on you to take care of such things for me," he said. "I don't know what I'd do without you."

"I'm glad it ended without bloodshed. It would have been disastrous if Pandolia became embroiled in a civil war," Pandaar said.

"There wasn't much chance of that happening. The rebels never had the support of the people or the military. When Prium crossed the border to join forces with Pandolian government troops, the rebel army disintegrated. The arrival of the Egyptian force and our regiments was the final straw," Arka-Dal explained. "Beyaro had little choice but to take his own life."

"I see what you mean," Pandaar said. "Even if the fools had decided to fight, the Pandolian army would have made short work of them. This way, a lot of unnecessary bloodshed and the destruction of Azum Phala was avoided."

Arka-Dal nodded.

He returned to his office and signed the letters Mayumi had written. He then placed them in envelopes and affixed his official to the flap. He felt two arms slide around his neck and looked up to see Zhijima. He smiled at her as she swung around and sat on his lap. She was barely dressed.

"I have a fire between my thighs. I need you to put it out," she said.

"I'll do my best," he said as he picked her up and carried her over to a nearby sofa.

Later that evening, Merlin arrived at the palace. As he walked into the parlor, he saw Pandaar seated on the couch with one of the palace maids on his lap. Both were quite tipsy. Pandaar smiled up at him.

"I see you're really upset over your divorce," Merlin said sarcastically.

"I am—but I've learned to hide my sorrows," Pandaar replied. "In fact, I plan to hide them between this young lady's thighs—repeatedly."

The maid giggled as he groped her. Merlin shook his head and left in disgust. He decided to head up to the roof to think things out. He was surprised to find Arka-Dal standing there gazing up at the stars. He had a drink in one hand and a bottle in the other. He turned when he heard Merlin approach.

"You seem to be in a rather thoughtful mood this evening. What troubles you, my boy?" Merlin asked.

"Nothing important. I was just thinking that I have too many women in my life. Too many wives now," Arka-Dal said with a smile. "I love them all dearly but they are hard to keep up with. Now that Gorinna's part of mix, it's even more difficult."

"As kings go, the number of wives you have puts you in the lower range. As I recall, King Solomon of ancient Judea had more than 1,000. You only have seven. That makes you a piker by comparison," Merlin joked.

Arka-Dal laughed.

"Under most circumstances, royal wives can be a conniving, jealous and even murderous bunch. Many atrocious murders and assassinations were carried out in order to put their children in line to inherit the throne. That can't happen here. The throne of Thule cannot be inherited so there is no line of succession to scheme over. And your wives are highly unusual—they actually love each other. They rarely argue about anything. You should consider it a blessing," Merlin said.

"I do, Merlin," Arka-Dal assured him.

The wedding took place a week later. It was a grand affair with a band, belly dancers, fireworks and several long tables of food, drinks and snacks. Arka-Dal's other wives decided on a springtime motif, with bright colors and tons of flowers, multi-colored streamers and matching drapes.

Zhijima opted for a long, lacy, cloud white gown which signified a new beginning. Mayumi presented with a bouquet of red, pink and yellow roses. Arka-Dal was dressed in the traditional Thulian marriage tunic and trousers with knee-high black boots and a large gold medallion signifying his royal status.

Mayumi, Galya, Chatha and Medusa escorted Zhijima down the aisle to the foot of the dais where Arka-Dal and Leo waited. As officials and other guests from all over the Empire and nearby nations watched, Leo performed the official ritual and pronounced them husband and wife. Then the highest ranking clerics from the major religions of Thule stepped forward to bless the union.

As soon as the last blessing ended, Galya signaled for the fireworks to go off and the entire city broke into a wild celebration. The reception lasted for several hours, with the last of the guests taking their leave of the happy couple just a little after midnight. Arka-Dal and Zhijima decided to head up to the bedroom.

As they passed through the parlor, they saw Pandaar seated in front of the fireplace with a large drink in his hand. They walked over. Arka-Dal placed a hand on his friend's shoulder. Pandaar looked up and smiled.

"It was a nice wedding. I'm really happy for you both. May your life together be long and filled with love and joy," he said softly.

Zhijima pulled a rose from her bouquet and gave it to him. She leaned over and kissed him on the cheek.

"Thank you," she said.

He nodded and shook both their hands. They watched as he rose from the couch and left the parlor, the rose in one hand, a drink in the other.

"That's enough of *that*," Zhijima said as she took Arka-Dal's hand. "This is *our* night!"